DOROTHY L. SAYERS

THE COMPLETE STORIES

HARPER

NEW YORK · LONDON · TORONTO · SYDNEY

FIRST BOURBON STREET BOOKS EDITION PUBLISHED 2013. REPRINTED IN HARPER PAPERBACKS 2020.

Library of Congress Cataloging-in-Publication Data is available upon request.

ISBN 978-0-06-227549-3

HB 12.01.2022

CONTENTS

Montague Egg Stories

Other Stories

INTRODUCTION

by James Sandoe

Lord Peter's first recorded utterance is "Oh, damn!" as he remembers his forgetfulness and asks a cab driver to go back to 110 Piccadilly for the Brocklebury sale catalogue, since he had hoped to pick up a book or two. But there is his mother on the telephone asking him to see what can be done for luckless little Mr. Thipps, who is embarrassed by an unknown dead man in his bathtub "with nothing on but a pair of pince-nez." *Whose Body?*, subtitled *The Singular Adventure of the Man with the Golden Pince-nez* (1923), began the succession.

In this first chronicle we had a good deal: Peter himself; Freddy Arbuthnot, mild and engaging; the splendid Dowager Duchess, Peter's extremely apposite mother; the quietly splendid Bunter (obviously related to Jeeves); Parker of the Yard, who was later to become Peter's brother-in-law; that formidable defender, Sir Impey Biggs; the sedulous Sugg (Miss Sayers's Inspector Lestrade, whom she invented to discard); and who else that delighted us after that?

Miss Sayers herself reread *Whose Body?* without much admiration,[*] a judgment characteristically severe and (characteristically?) lofty. We need not agree.

[*] "Gaudy Night" in *Titles to Fame*, edited by Denys Kilham Roberts (London, 1937).

Clouds of Witness (1926) followed and set Lord Peter the problem of his amiable if foolish brother, the Duke of Denver (married to a shrew, Helen) accused of murder and tried before the House of Lords, a rare but remarkable occasion. A number of old friends persist happily and we have a fuller chance to meet others including that correct solicitor Mr. Murbles. There is even a glimpse of Denver's son, Peter's young nephew, identified as Pickled Gherkins. Much later, as an Oxford undergraduate, he will fall (understandably) in love with Harriet Vane. Lord Peter flies across the Atlantic to make his climactic appearance before the assembled Lords. It was at that date no casual event.

There followed *The Dawson Pedigree* (*Unnatural Death*, 1927), one of Miss Sayers's cunningest puzzles but just as memorable for introducing us to the breathless Miss Climpson, one of the most energetically emphatic correspondents in history.

Miss Climpson is not recruited for the singular excitements comprising *The Unpleasantness at the Bellona Club* (1928), that exceedingly staid military fellowship so startled on Armistice Day by the demise of General Fentiman, but Mr. Murbles is present, correct and concerned as always. And it is here that we have one of our glimpses of the pleasing Marjorie Phelps, who is Lord Peter's entree to Chelsea, "a pleasant-looking young woman with curly hair and a blue overall heavily smudged with clay" whose statuette of Peter amuses him decidedly.

The dozen adventures comprising *Lord Peter Views the Body* (1928) followed; and as they are before you in this volume, you may make such additions to these reminiscing notes as they seem to stimulate. I find them as delightful as ever.

Strong Poison (1930) is rich on many scores. We meet again the reporters Salcombe Hardy and Waffles Newton, Sir Impey, Marjorie Phelps, Lady Mary Wimsey (not yet married to Parker), the chilly Duchess, and the pleasant if opaque Duke of Denver together with Freddy Arbuthnot, engaged now to Rachel Levy (see *Whose Body?*). We also meet Harriet Vane, who at the beginning of the novel is on trial, charged with the murder (by arsenic) of her trying lover, Philip Boyes. Peter is fiercely (nay, frantically) sure that she is innocent, and what follows proves that he is right. But he is also in love with the lady, who has no taste for his pity and refuses him without dashing his hopes entirely.

In the same year was published a much too-little-known novel, *The Documents in the Case,* which Miss Sayers wrote in collaboration with Robert Eustace, a physician and mystery writer who had earlier been one of Conan Doyle's fellow contributors to *The Strand Magazine.* It is for about half of its course an epistolary tale of considerable teasing charm but a tale of detection that does not involve Lord Peter (for all that Sir James Lubbock is invoked) and hence a sort of stepchild in the succession, however regrettably.

Miss Sayers never quite explained why, having boxed Lord Peter up in this understandable passion for the poised Harriet, she postponed dealing with it. There is no hint of Harriet in *The Five Red Herrings* (published in the United States first as *Suspicious Characters,* 1931), a sort of apogee among tales of timetable detection involving alibis of the kind Freeman Wills Crofts had been occupying himself with for years. I find it a dry tale in remembrance but reread it each time with pleasure in its human engagements, which oil the mathematics of train schedules. Its setting is Scotland and it is brightly and vigorously peopled for all that its schematics seem to dominate.

Harriet Vane returned to the scene and to Peter's fierce concern in *Have His Carcase* (1932), a monumentally if not very fruitfully long novel which was as much about the wooing of Harriet as about the corpse that Harriet discovered on a coastal rock between Lesston Hoe and Wilvercombe. At the end of this slightly tiresome stretch of self-indulgence we are as sure of Lord Peter's interest in Harriet as before but still hanging romantically on a cliff.

Miss Sayers was to keep us there for two novels more, because this second involvement of Lord Peter and Harriet is nowhere invoked in the two tales that follow. The first of them was *Murder Must Advertise* (1933), in which Miss Sayers played pretty games with a world (publicity) that she knew as a paid practitioner. A lot of old friends and acquaintances are there (Lady Mary is now married to Parker and Freddy to Rachel) and there are such new acquaintances as young Ginger, whose "catapult" (we should call it a slingshot) is vital to the action.

The other interloper between our glimpses of Lord Peter's prolonged wooing was "changes rung on an old theme in two short touches and two full peals," a tale that is many readers' favorite, *The Nine Tailors* (1934). Fenchurch St. Paul in the fen country is Miss Sayers's setting, and its criminal concerns are, of course, ingeniously wound in the ancient art of change-ring-ing. It is a long, complex, very rich tale with astonishingly lit-tle dependence on the stock company which Miss Sayers had by that time evoked. Sugg is mentioned in passing (as retired) and Parker is briefly apparent, but our concern is much more with the villagers and their gentle clergyman, a scholarly soul, Rector Venables.

I see that I have overlooked that second collection of short stories, *Hangman's Holiday* (1933), in which we have a few more short stories about Lord Peter, the first appearances of that shrewd old character, Mr. Montague Egg, "travelling rep-resentative of Plummet & Rose, Wines and Spirits, Picca-dilly." He has a keen remembrance of the apothegms contained in the *Salesman's Handbook* and an even sharper regard for the vagaries of human nature. The alert reader of those few tales concerning Lord Peter will find references to Freddy Arbuth-not, Parker, the Soviet Club, Peter's nephew, Gherkins (Vis-count St. George, to the correct), and other friends and acquaintances.

Nowadays we can move readily from *Strong Poison* to *Have His Carcase* to *Gaudy Night* and then to *Busman's Honeymoon*. But Miss Sayers's first readers had a very long wait before coming to the singular excitements of *Gaudy Night* (1935), which never in its considerable length ever finds need to dis-cover excitement in a corpse. There is ample engagement without a body.

It is pre-eminently an Oxford novel and, in spite of Miss Sayers's disclaimers, a Somerville novel, set amongst the tight academic and nonacademic concerns of the college. Here Peter returns to his active pursuit of Harriet (who, in the last line, succumbs in suitable Latin), but it is all delightful if unsentimental nostalgia.*

The last of the Lord Peter novels was *Busman's Honeymoon, A Love Story with Detective Interruptions* (1937), which began life as a play written by Miss Sayers and Muriel St. Claire Byrne and was later translated into a film starring Robert Montgomery as Lord Peter, Constance Cummings as Lady Harriet, and Sir Seymour Hicks as Bunter. Miss Sayers, always precise, describes it fairly, and through its course she invokes all sorts of old friends from the splendidly garrulous Dowager Duchess to "Mrs. Merdle,"† the ninth Daimler of that name.

So far as Lord Peter is involved there is very little more to record. He is twice apparent in the collection of stories called *In the Teeth of the Evidence* (1939), a volume involving Mr. Montague Egg again, and a number of those detective and crime stories which dot the other volumes, often happily. But a good many readers have never met the ultimate tales about Lord Peter, which have not until now been gathered among her own tales. "Striding Folly" is welcome but less memorable than "The Haunted Policeman," which begins as Peter views his firstborn with incredulity. The adventure that follows is trivial, if agreeable: the event is some sort of climax.

There are glimpses of the Wimseys through the earlier war years in Miss Sayers's contributions of "The Wimsey Papers" to the English newspaper *The Spectator*. And there was at least one projected Lord Peter novel, *Thrones, Dominations,* which was never published, probably never written.

Meantime, the remarkable Miss Sayers (Mrs. Atherton Fleming) had had a number of other interests, all of them literate, many of them scholarly, and none of them worth the omis-

---

*Readers with proper curiosity will be interested at the glimpses of Dorothy L. Sayers in Vera Brittain's *Testament of Youth* (1933).
†The name may come from Dickens. See *Little Dorrit*.

sion or neglect they are bound to receive here. She began publication as a poet and, more specifically, as a Christian poet (see *Op. 1:* Oxford, 1916), and translated the fragments of *Tristan in Brittany* from the Anglo-Norman poet Thomas (1929 in publication, although the translation must have been done much earlier).

Her critical study of Wilkie Collins never got itself written, unfortunately (although her bibliography graces the *Cambridge Bibliography of English Literature*). She wrote some lively verse plays, including variations on the Faust theme (*The Devil to Pay,* 1939).

The crown of her creativity and of her scholarship came, certainly, with her translation of Dante's *Divine Comedy* (Penguin commissioned it; Hell appeared in 1949, Purgatory in 1955, and Paradise, completed by her friend Barbara Reynolds, after her death and in 1962). The concern with Dante is further expressed in at least two other volumes, *Introductory Papers on Dante* (1954) and *Further Papers on Dante* (1957).

Our purpose here has been for the most part to recall just that part of Dorothy L. Sayers's much more varied career than concerns Lord Peter Wimsey. These affectionate notes have suggested some of her other (and, to her, more important) concerns. The curious reader may discover notes toward a bibliography (*Bulletin of Bibliography,* May/August 1944) sadly incomplete but symptomatic.

Meantime, what you have here are all of the stories about Lord Peter, a lively assembly which suggests the Sayers sense of responsibility toward a "medium" (the tale of detection) which she wrote with skill and reviewed with acuity. She wrote ingeniously, wittily, and cleanly (in spite of the *longueurs* of *The Five Red Herrings* and *Have His Carcase; Gaudy Night* is long but I detect no fat on its frame), and with as deep a responsibility to the tale of detection as she brought to the tale of salvation while translating Dante.

DOROTHY L. SAYERS
THE COMPLETE STORIES

LORD PETER WIMSEY
STORIES

THE ABOMINABLE HISTORY OF THE
MAN WITH COPPER FINGERS

The Egotists' Club is one of the most genial places in London. It is a place to which you may go when you want to tell that odd dream you had last night, or to announce what a good dentist you have discovered. You can write letters there if you like, and have the temperament of a Jane Austen, for there is no silence room, and it would be a breach of club manners to appear busy or absorbed when another member addresses you. You must not mention golf or fish, however, and, if the Hon. Freddy Arbuthnot's motion is carried at the next committee meeting (and opinion so far appears very favourable), you will not be allowed to mention wireless either. As Lord Peter Wimsey said when the matter was mooted the other day in the smoking-room, those are things you can talk about anywhere. Otherwise the club is not specially exclusive. Nobody is ineligible *per se*, except strong, silent men. Nominees are, however, required to pass certain tests, whose nature is sufficiently indicated by the fact that a certain distinguished explorer came to grief through accepting, and smoking, a powerful Trichinopoly cigar as an accompaniment to a '63 port. On the other hand, dear old Sir Roger Bunt (the coster millionaire who won the £20,000 ballot offered by the *Sunday Shriek*, and used it to found his immense catering business in the Midlands) was highly commended and unanimously elected after declaring frankly that beer and a pipe were all he really cared for in that way. As Lord Peter said again: "Nobody minds coarseness but one must draw the line at cruelty."

On this particular evening, Masterman (the cubist poet) had brought a guest with him, a man named Varden. Varden had started life as a professional athlete, but a strained heart had obliged him to cut short a brilliant career, and turn his handsome face and remarkably beautiful body to account in the service of the cinema screen. He had come to London from Los Angeles to stimulate publicity for his great new film, *Marathon*, and turned out to be quite a pleasant, unspoiled person — greatly to the relief of the club, since Masterman's guests were apt to be something of a toss-up.

There were only eight men, including Varden, in the brown room that evening. This, with its panelled walls, shaded lamps, and heavy blue curtains, was perhaps the cosiest and pleasantest of the small smoking-rooms, of which the club possessed half a dozen or so. The conversation had begun quite casually by Armstrong's relating a curious little incident which he had witnessed that afternoon at Temple Station, and Bayes had gone on to say that that was nothing to the really very odd thing which had happened to him, personally, in a thick fog one night in the Euston Road.

Masterman said that the more secluded London squares teemed with subjects for a writer, and instanced his own singular encounter with a weeping woman and a dead monkey, and then Judson took up the tale and narrated how, in a lonely suburb, late at night, he had come upon the dead body of a woman stretched on the pavement with a knife in her side and a policeman standing motionless near by. He had asked if he could do anything, but the policeman had only said, "I wouldn't interfere if I was you, sir; she deserved what she got." Judson said he had not been able to get the incident out of his mind, and then Pettifer told them of a queer case in his own medical practice, when a totally unknown man had led him to a house in Bloomsbury where there was a woman suffering from strychnine poisoning. This man had helped him in the most intelligent manner all night, and, when the patient was out of danger, had walked straight out of the house and never reappeared; the odd thing being that, when he (Pettifer) questioned the woman, she answered in great surprise that she had never seen the man in her life and had taken him to be Pettifer's assistant.

"That reminds me," said Varden, "of something still stranger that happened to me once in New York—I've never been able to make out whether it was a madman or a practical joke, or whether I really had a very narrow shave."

This sounded promising, and the guest was urged to go on with his story.

"Well, it really started ages ago," said the actor, "seven years it must have been—just before America came into the war. I was twenty-five at the time, and had been in the film business a little over two years. There was a man called Eric P. Loder, pretty well known in New York at that period, who would have been a very fine sculptor if he hadn't had more money than was good for him, or so I understood from the people who go in for that sort of thing. He used to exhibit a good deal and had a lot of one-man shows of his stuff to which the highbrow people went—he did a good many bronzes, I believe. Perhaps you know about him, Masterman?"

"I've never seen any of his things," said the poet, "but I remember some photographs in *The Art of Tomorrow*. Clever, but rather overripe. Didn't he go in for a lot of that chryselephantine stuff? Just to show he could afford to pay for the materials, I suppose."

"Yes, that sounds very like him."

"Of course—and he did a very slick and very ugly realistic group called Lucina, and had the impudence to have it cast in solid gold and stood in his front hall."

"Oh, that thing! Yes—simply beastly I thought it, but then I never could see anything artistic in the idea. Realism, I suppose you'd call it. I like a picture or a statue to make you feel good, or what's it there for? Still, there was something very attractive about Loder."

"How did you come across him?"

"Oh, yes. Well, he saw me in that little picture of mine, *Apollo Comes to New York* — perhaps you remember it. It was my first star part. About a statue that's brought to life — one of the old gods, you know — and how he gets on in a modern city. Dear old Reubenssohn produced it. Now, there was a man who could put a thing through with consummate artistry. You couldn't find an atom of offence from beginning to end, it was all so tasteful, though in the first part one didn't have anything to wear except a sort of scarf — taken from the classical statue, you know."

"The Belvedere?"

"I dare say. Well, Loder wrote to me, and said as a sculptor he was interested in me, because I was a good shape and so on, and would I come and pay him a visit in New York when I was free. So I found out about Loder, and decided it would be good publicity, and when my contract was up, and I had a bit of time to fill in, I went up east and called on him. He was very decent to me, and asked me to stay a few weeks with him while I was looking around.

"He had a magnificent great house about five miles out of the city, crammed full of pictures and antiques and so on. He was somewhere between thirty-five and forty, I should think, dark and smooth, and very quick and lively in his movements. He talked very well; seemed to have been everywhere and have seen everything and not to have any too good an opinion of anybody. You could sit and listen to him for hours; he'd got anecdotes about everybody, from the Pope to old Phineas E. Groot of the Chicago Ring. The only kind of story I didn't care about hearing from him was the improper sort. Not that I don't enjoy an after-dinner story — no, sir, I wouldn't like you to think I was a prig — but he'd tell it with his eye upon you as if he suspected you of having something to do with it. I've known women do that and I've seen men do it to women and seen the women squirm, but he was the only man that's ever given *me* that feeling. Still, apart from that, Loder was the most fascinating fellow I've ever known. And, as I say, his house surely was beautiful, and he kept a first-class table.

"He liked to have everything of the best. There was his mistress, Maria Morano. I don't think I've ever seen anything to touch her, and when you work for the screen you're apt to have a pretty exacting standard of female beauty. She was one of those big, slow, beautifully moving creatures, very placid, with a slow, wide smile. We don't grow them in the States. She'd come from the South—had been a cabaret dancer he said, and she didn't contradict him. He was very proud of her, and she seemed to be devoted to him in her own fashion. He'd show her off in the studio with nothing on but a fig-leaf or so—stand her up beside one of the figures he was always doing of her, and compare them point by point. There was literally only one half inch of her, it seemed, that wasn't absolutely perfect from the sculptor's point of view—the second toe of her left foot was shorter than the big toe. He used to correct it, of course, in the statues. She'd listen to it all with a good-natured smile, sort of vaguely flattered, you know. Though I think the poor girl sometimes got tired of being gloated over that way. She'd sometimes hunt me out and confide to me that what she had always hoped for was to run a restaurant of her own, with a cabaret show and a great many cooks with white aprons, and lots of polished electric cookers. 'And then I would marry,' she'd say, 'and have four sons and one daughter,' and she told me all the names she had chosen for the family. I thought it was rather pathetic. Loder came in at the end of one of these conversations. He had a sort of a grin on, so I dare say he'd overheard. I don't suppose he attached much importance to it, which shows that he never really understood the girl. I don't think he ever imagined any woman would chuck up the sort of life he'd accustomed her to, and if he was a bit possessive in his manner, at least he never gave her a rival. For all his talk and his ugly statues, she'd got him, and she knew it.

"I stayed there getting on for a month altogether, having a thundering good time. On two occasions Loder had an art spasm, and shut himself up in his studio to work and wouldn't let anybody in for several days on end. He was rather given to that sort of stunt, and when it was over we would have a party, and all Loder's friends and hangers-on would come to have a look at the work of art. He was doing a figure of some nymph or goddess, I fancy, to be cast in silver, and Maria used to go along and sit for him. Apart from those times, he went about everywhere, and we saw all there was to be seen.

"I was fairly annoyed, I admit, when it came to an end. War was declared, and I'd made up my mind to join up when that happened. My heart put me out of the running for trench service, but I counted on getting some sort of a job, with perseverance, so I packed up and went off.

"I wouldn't have believed Loder would have been so genuinely sorry to say good-bye to me. He said over and over again that we'd meet again soon. However, I did get a job with the hospital people, and was sent over to Europe, and it wasn't till 1920 that I saw Loder again.

"He'd written to me before, but I'd had two big pictures to make in '19 and it couldn't be done. However, in '20 I found myself back in New York, doing publicity for *The Passion Streak*, and got a note from Loder begging me to stay with him, and saying he wanted me to sit for him. Well, that was advertisement that he'd pay for himself, you know, so I agreed. I had accepted an engagement to go out with Mystofilms Ltd. in *Jake of Dead Man's Bush*—the dwarfmen picture, you know, taken on the spot among the Australian bushmen. I wired them that I would join them at Sydney the third week in April, and took my bags out to Loder's.

"Loder greeted me very cordially, though I thought he looked older than when I last saw him. He had certainly grown more nervous in his manner. He was—how shall I describe it?—more *intense*—more real, in a way. He brought out his pet cynicisms as if he thoroughly meant them, and more and more with that air of getting at you personally. I used to think his disbelief in everything was a kind of artistic pose, but I began to feel I had done him an injustice. He was really unhappy, I could see that quite well, and soon I discovered the reason. As we were driving out in the car I asked after Maria.

" 'She left me,' he said.

"Well, now, you know, that really surprised me. Honestly, I hadn't thought the girl had that much initiative. 'Why,' I said, 'has she gone and set up in that restaurant of her own she wanted so much?'

" 'Oh! she talked to you about restaurants, did she?' said Loder. 'I suppose you are one of the men that women tell things to. No. She made a fool of herself. She's gone.'

"I didn't quite know what to say. He was so obviously hurt in his vanity, you know, as well as in his feelings. I muttered the usual things, and added that it must be a great loss to his work as well as in other ways. He said it was.

"I asked him when it had happened and whether he'd finished the nymph he was working on before I left. He said, 'Oh, yes,' he'd finished that and done another — something pretty original, which I should like.

"Well, we got to the house and dined, and Loder told me he was going to Europe shortly, a few days after I left myself, in fact. The nymph stood in the dining-room, in a special niche let into the wall. It really was a beautiful thing, not so showy as most of Loder's work, and a wonderful likeness of Maria. Loder put me opposite it, so that I could see it during dinner, and, really, I could hardly take my eyes off it. He seemed very proud of it, and kept on telling me over and over again how glad he was that I liked it. It struck me that he was falling into a trick of repeating himself.

"We went into the smoking-room after dinner. He'd had it rearranged, and the first thing that caught one's eye was a big settee drawn before the fire. It stood about a couple of feet from the ground, and consisted of a base made like a Roman couch, with cushions and a highish back, all made of oak with a silver inlay, and on top of this, forming the actual seat one sat on, if you follow me, there was a great silver figure of a nude woman, fully life-size, lying with her head back and her arms extended along the sides of the couch. A few big loose cushions made it possible to use the thing as an actual settee, though I must say it never was really comfortable to sit on respectably. As a stage prop for registering dissipation it would have been excellent, but to see Loder sprawling over it by his own fireside gave me a kind of shock. He seemed very much attached to it, though.

" 'I told you,' he said, 'that it was something original.'

"Then I looked more closely at it, and saw that the figure actually was Maria's, though the face was rather sketchily done, if you understand what I mean. I suppose he thought a bolder treatment more suited to a piece of furniture.

"But I did begin to think Loder a trifle degenerate when I saw that couch. And in the fortnight that followed I grew more and more uncomfortable with him. That personal manner of his grew more marked every day, and sometimes, while I was giving him sittings, he would sit there and tell one of the most beastly things, with his eyes fixed on one in the nastiest way, just to see how one would take it. Upon my word, though he certainly did me uncommonly well, I began to feel I'd be more at ease among the bushmen.

"Well, now I come to the odd thing."

Everybody sat up and listened a little more eagerly.

"It was the evening before I had to leave New York," went on Varden. "I was sitting—"

Here somebody opened the door of the brown room, to be greeted by a warning sign from Bayles. The intruder sank obscurely into a large chair and mixed himself a whisky with extreme care not to disturb the speaker.

"I was sitting in the smoking-room," continued Varden, "waiting for Loder to come in. I had the house to myself, for Loder had given the servants leave to go to some show or lecture or other, and he himself was getting his things together for his European trip and had had to keep an appointment with his man of business. I must have been very nearly asleep, because it was dusk when I came to with a start and saw a young man quite close to me.

"He wasn't at all like a housebreaker, and still less like a ghost. He was, I might almost say, exceptionally ordinary-looking. He was dressed in a grey English suit, with a fawn overcoat on his arm, and his soft hat and stick in his hand. He had sleek, pale hair, and one of those rather stupid faces, with a long nose and a monocle. I stared at him, for I knew the front door was locked, but before I could get my wits together he spoke. He had a curious, hesitating, husky voice and a strong English accent. He said, surprisingly:

" 'Are you Mr. Varden?'

" 'You have the advantage of me,' I said.

"He said, 'Please excuse my butting in; I know it looks like bad manners, but you'd better clear out of this place very quickly, don't you know.'

" 'What the hell do you mean?' I said.

"He said, 'I don't mean it in any impertinent way, but you must realize that Loder's never forgiven you, and I'm afraid he means to make you into a hatstand or an electric-light fitting, or something of that sort.'

"My God! I can tell you I felt queer. It was such a quiet voice, and his manners were perfect, yet the words were quite meaningless! I remembered that madmen are supposed to be extra strong, and edged towards the bell—and then it came over me with rather a chill that I was alone in the house.

" 'How did you get in here?' I asked, putting a bold face on it.

" 'I'm afraid I picked the lock,' he said, as casually as though he were apologizing for not having a card about him. 'I couldn't be sure Loder hadn't come back. But I do really think you had better get out as quickly as possible.'

" 'See here,' I said, 'who are you and what the hell are you driving at? What do you mean about Loder never forgiving me? Forgiving me for what?'

" 'Why,' he said, 'about—you *will* pardon me prancing in on your private affairs, won't you— about Maria Morano.'

" '*What* about her, in the devil's name?' I cried. 'What do you know about her, anyway? She went off while I was at the war. What's it to do with me?'

" 'Oh!' said the very odd young man, 'I beg your pardon. Perhaps I have been relying too much on Loder's judgement. Damned foolish; but the possibility of his being mistaken did not occur to me. He fancies you were Maria Morano's lover when you were here last time.'

" 'Maria's lover?' I said. 'Preposterous! She went off with her man, whoever he was. He must know she didn't go with me.'

" 'Maria never left the house,' said the young man, 'and if you don't get out of it this moment, I won't answer for *your* ever leaving, either.'

" 'In God's name,' I cried, exasperated, 'what do you mean?'

"The man turned and threw the blue cushions off the foot of the silver couch.

" 'Have you ever examined the toes of this?' he asked.

" 'Not particularly,' I said, more and more astonished. 'Why should I?'

" 'Did you ever know Loder make any figure of her but this with that short toe on the left foot?' he went on.

"Well, I did take a look at it then, and saw it was as he said—the left foot had a short second toe.

" 'So it is,' I said, 'but, after all, why not?'

" 'Why not, indeed?' said the young man. 'Wouldn't you like to see why, of all the figures Loder made of Maria Morano, this is the only one that has the feet of the living woman?'

"He picked up the poker.

" 'Look!' he said.

"With a lot more strength than I should have expected from him, he brought the head of the poker down with a heavy crack on the silver couch. It struck one of the arms of the figure neatly at the elbow-joint, smashing a jagged hole in the silver. He wrenched at the arm and brought it away. It was hollow, and, as I am alive, I tell you there was a long, dry arm-bone inside it!"

Varden paused, and put away a good mouthful of whisky.

"Well?" cried several breathless voices.

"Well," said Varden, "I'm not ashamed to say I went out of that house like an old buck-rabbit that hears the man with the gun. There was a car standing just outside, and the driver opened the door. I tumbled in, and then it came over me that the whole thing might be a trap, and I tumbled out again and ran till I reached the trolley-cars. But I found my bags at the station next day, duly registered for Vancouver.

"When I pulled myself together I did rather wonder what Loder was thinking about my disappearance, but I could no more have gone back into that horrible house than I could have taken poison. I left for Vancouver next morning, and from that day to this I never saw either of those men again. I've still not the faintest idea who the fair man was, or what became of him, but I heard in a roundabout way that Loder was dead—in some kind of an accident, I fancy."

There was a pause. Then:

"It's a damned good story, Mr. Varden," said Armstrong—he was a dabbler in various kinds of handiwork, and was, indeed, chiefly responsible for Mr. Arbuthnot's motion to ban wireless—"but are you suggesting there was a complete skeleton inside that silver casting? Do you mean Loder put it into the core of the mould when the casting was done? It would be awfully difficult and dangerous—the slightest accident would have put him at the mercy of his workmen. And that statue must have been considerably over life-size to allow of the skeleton being well covered."

"Mr. Varden has unintentionally misled you, Armstrong," said a quiet, husky voice suddenly from the shadow behind Varden's chair. "The figure was not silver, but electro-plated on a copper base deposited direct on the body. The lady was Sheffield-plated, in fact. I fancy the soft parts of her must have been digested away with pepsin, or some preparation of the kind, after the process was complete, but I can't be positive about that."

"Hullo, Wimsey," said Armstrong, "was that you came in just now? And why this confident pronouncement?"

The effect of Wimsey's voice on Varden had been extraordinary. He had leapt to his feet, and turned the lamp so as to light up Wimsey's face.

"Good evening, Mr. Varden," said Lord Peter. "I'm delighted to meet you again and to apologize for my unceremonious behaviour on the occasion of our last encounter."

Varden took the proffered hand, but was speechless.

"D'you mean to say, you mad mystery-monger, that *you* were Varden's Great Unknown?" demanded Bayes. "Ah, well," he added rudely, "we might have guessed it from his vivid description."

"Well, since you're here," said Smith-Hartington, the *Morning Yell* man, "I think you ought to come across with the rest of the story."

"Was it just a joke?" asked Judson.

"Of course not," interrupted Pettifer, before Lord Peter had time to reply. "Why should it be? Wimsey's seen enough queer things not to have to waste his time inventing them."

"That's true enough," said Bayes. "Comes of having deductive powers and all that sort of thing, and always sticking one's nose into things that are better not investigated."

"That's all very well, Bayes," said his lordship, "but if I hadn't just mentioned the matter to Mr. Varden that evening, where would he be?"

"Ah, where? That's exactly what we want to know," demanded Smith-Hartington. "Come on, Wimsey, no shirking; we must have the tale."

"And the whole tale," added Pettifer.

"And nothing but the tale," said Armstrong, dexterously whisking away the whisky-bottle and the cigars from under Lord Peter's nose. "Get on with it, old son. Not a smoke do you smoke and not a sup do you sip till Burd Ellen is set free."

"Brute!" said his lordship plaintively. "As a matter of fact," he went on, with a change of tone, "it's not really a story I want to get about. It might land me in a very unpleasant sort of position — manslaughter probably, and murder possibly."

"Gosh!" said Bayes.

"That's all right," said Armstrong, "nobody's going to talk. We can't afford to lose you from the club, you know. Smith-Hartington will have to control his passion for copy, that's all."

Pledges of discretion having been given all round, Lord Peter settled himself back and began his tale.

"The curious case of Eric P. Loder affords one more instance of the strange manner in which some power beyond our puny human wills arranges the affairs of men. Call it Providence — call it Destiny —"

"We'll call it off," said Bayes; "you can leave out that part."

Lord Peter groaned and began again.

"Well, the first thing that made me feel a bit inquisitive about Loder was a casual remark by a man at the Emigration Office in New York, where I happened to go about that silly affair of Mrs. Bilt's. He said, 'What on earth is Eric Loder going to do in Australia? I should have thought Europe was more in his line.'

" 'Australia?' I said, 'you're wandering, dear old thing. He told me the other day he was off to Italy in three weeks' time.'

" 'Italy, nothing,' he said, 'he was all over our place today, asking about how you got to Sydney and what were the necessary formalities, and so on.'

" 'Oh,' I said, 'I suppose he's going by the Pacific route, and calling at Sydney on his way.' But I wondered why he hadn't said so when I'd met him the day before. He had distinctly talked about sailing for Europe and doing Paris before he went on to Rome.

"I felt so darned inquisitive that I went and called on Loder two nights later.

"He seemed quite pleased to see me, and was full of his forthcoming trip. I asked him again about his route, and he told me quite distinctly he was going via Paris.

"Well, that was that, and it wasn't really any of my business, and we chatted about other things. He told me that Mr. Varden was coming to stay with him before he went, and that he hoped to get him to pose for a figure before he left. He said he'd never seen a man so perfectly formed. 'I meant to get him to do it before,' he said, 'but war broke out, and he went and joined the army before I had time to start.'

"He was lolling on that beastly couch of his at the time, and, happening to look round at him, I caught such a nasty sort of glitter in his eye that it gave me quite a turn. He was stroking the figure over the neck and grinning at it.

" 'None of your efforts in Sheffield-plate, I hope,' said I.

" 'Well,' he said, 'I thought of making a kind of companion to this, *The Sleeping Athlete*, you know, or something of that sort.'

" 'You'd much better cast it,' I said. 'Why did you put the stuff on so thick? It destroys the fine detail.'

"That annoyed him. He never liked to hear any objection made to that work of art.

" 'This was experimental,' he said. 'I mean the next to be a real masterpiece. You'll see.'

"We'd got to about that point when the butler came in to ask should he make up a bed for me, as it was such a bad night. We hadn't noticed the weather particularly, though it had looked a bit threatening when I started from New York. However, we now looked out, and saw that it was coming down in sheets and torrents. It wouldn't have mattered, only that I'd only brought a little open racing car and no overcoat, and certainly the prospect of five miles in that downpour wasn't altogether attractive. Loder urged me to stay, and I said I would.

"I was feeling a bit fagged, so I went to bed right off. Loder said he wanted to do a bit of work in the studio first, and I saw him depart along the corridor.

"You won't allow me to mention Providence, so I'll only say it was a very remarkable thing that I should have woken up at two in the morning to find myself lying in a pool of water. The man had stuck a hot-water bottle into the bed, because it hadn't been used just lately, and the beastly thing had gone and unstoppered itself. I lay awake for ten minutes in the deeps of damp misery before I had sufficient strength of mind to investigate. Then I found it was hopeless—sheets, blankets, mattress, all soaked. I looked at the armchair, and then I had a brilliant idea. I remembered there was a lovely great divan in the studio, with a big skin rug and a pile of cushions. Why not finish the night there? I took the little electric torch which always goes about with me, and started off.

"The studio was empty, so I supposed Loder had finished and trotted off to roost. The divan was there, all right, with a screen drawn partly across it, so I rolled myself up under the rug and prepared to snooze off.

"I was just getting beautifully sleepy again when I heard footsteps, not in the passage, but apparently on the other side of the room. I was surprised, because I didn't know there was any way out in that direction. I lay low, and presently I saw a streak of light appear from the cupboard where Loder kept his tools and things. The streak widened, and Loder emerged, carrying an electric torch. He closed the cupboard door very gently after him, and padded across the studio. He stopped before the easel and uncovered it; I could see him through a crack in the screen. He stood for some minutes gazing at a sketch on the easel, and then gave one of the nastiest gurgly laughs I've ever had the pleasure of hearing. If I'd ever seriously thought of announcing my unauthorized presence, I abandoned all idea of it then. Presently he covered the easel again, and went out by the door at which I had come in.

"I waited till I was sure he had gone, and then got up—uncommonly quietly, I may say. I tiptoed over to the easel to see what the fascinating work of art was. I saw at once it was the design for the figure of *The Sleeping Athlete*, and as I looked at it I felt a sort of horrid conviction stealing over me. It was an idea which seemed to begin in my stomach, and work its way up to the roots of my hair.

"My family say I'm too inquisitive. I can only say that wild horses wouldn't have kept me from investigating that cupboard. With the feeling that something absolutely vile might hop out at me—I was a bit wrought up, and it was a rotten time of night—I put a heroic hand on the door knob.

"To my astonishment, the thing wasn't even locked. It opened at once, to show a range of perfectly innocent and orderly shelves, which couldn't possibly have held Loder.

"My blood was up, you know, by this time, so I hunted round for the spring-lock which I knew must exist, and found it without much difficulty. The back of the cupboard swung noiselessly inwards, and I found myself at the top of a narrow flight of stairs.

"I had the sense to stop and see that the door could be opened from the inside before I went any farther, and I also selected a good stout pestle which I found on the shelves as a weapon in case of accident. Then I closed the door and tripped with elf-like lightness down that jolly old staircase.

"There was another door at the bottom, but it didn't take me long to fathom the secret of that. Feeling frightfully excited, I threw it boldly open, with the pestle ready for action.

"However, the room seemed to be empty. My torch caught the gleam of something liquid, and then I found the wall-switch.

"I saw a biggish square room, fitted up as a workshop. On the right-hand wall was a big switchboard, with a bench beneath it. From the middle of the ceiling hung a great flood-light, illuminating a glass vat, fully seven feet long by about three wide. I turned on the floodlight, and looked down into the vat. It was filled with a dark brown liquid which I recognized as the usual compound of cyanide and copper-sulphate which they use for copper-plating.

"The rods hung over it with their hooks all empty, but there was a packing-case half-opened at one side of the room, and, pulling the covering aside, I could see rows of copper anodes—enough of them to put a plating over a quarter of an inch on a life-size figure. There was a smaller case, still nailed up, which from its weight and appearance I guessed to contain the silver for the rest of the process. There was something else I was looking for, and I soon found it—a considerable quantity of prepared graphite and a big jar of varnish.

"Of course, there was no evidence, really, of anything being on the cross. There was no reason why Loder shouldn't make a plaster cast and Sheffield-plate it if he had a fancy for that kind of thing. But then I found something that couldn't have come there legitimately.

"On the bench was an oval slab of copper about an inch and a half long—Loder's night's work, I guessed. It was an electrotype of the American Consular seal, the thing they stamp on your passport photograph to keep you from hiking it off and substituting the picture of your friend Mr. Jiggs, who would like to get out of the country because he is so popular with Scotland Yard.

"I sat down on Loder's stool, and worked out that pretty little plot in all its details. I could see it all turned on three things. First of all, I must find out if Varden was purposing to make tracks shortly for Australia, because, if he wasn't, it threw all my beautiful theories out. And, secondly, it would help matters greatly if he happened to have dark hair like Loder's, as he has, you see— near enough, anyway, to fit the description on a passport. I'd only seen him in that Apollo Belvedere thing, with a fair wig on. But I knew if I hung about I should see him presently when he came to stay with Loder. And, thirdly, of course, I had to discover if Loder was likely to have any grounds for a grudge against Varden.

"Well, I figured out I'd stayed down in that room about as long as was healthy. Loder might come back at any moment, and I didn't forget that a vatful of copper-sulphate and cyanide of potassium would be a highly handy means of getting rid of a too-inquisitive guest. And I can't say I had any great fancy for figuring as part of Loder's domestic furniture. I've always hated things made in the shape of things—volumes of Dickens that turn out to be a biscuit-tin, and dodges like that; and, though I take no overwhelming interest in my own funeral, I should like it to be in good taste. I went so far as to wipe away any finger-marks I might have left behind me, and then I went back to the studio and rearranged that divan. I didn't feel Loder would care to think I'd been down there.

"There was just one other thing I felt inquisitive about. I tiptoed back through the hall and into the smoking-room. The silver couch glimmered in the light of the torch. I felt I disliked it fifty times more than ever before. However, I pulled myself together and took a careful look at the feet of the figure. I'd heard all about that second toe of Maria Morano's.

"I passed the rest of the night in the armchair after all.

"What with Mrs. Bilt's job and one thing and another, and the inquiries I had to make, I had to put off my interference in Loder's little game till rather late. I found out that Varden had been staying with Loder a few months before the beautiful Maria Morano had vanished. I'm afraid I was rather stupid about that, Mr. Varden. I thought perhaps there *had* been something."

"Don't apologize," said Varden, with a little laugh. "Cinema actors are notoriously immoral."

"Why rub it in?" said Wimsey, a trifle hurt. "I apologize. Anyway, it came to the same thing as far as Loder was concerned. Then there was one bit of evidence I had to get to be absolutely certain. Electro-plating—especially such a ticklish job as the one I had in mind—wasn't a job that could be finished in a night; on the other hand, it seemed necessary that Mr. Varden should be seen alive in New York up to the day he was scheduled to depart. It was also clear that Loder meant to be able to prove that a Mr. Varden had left New York all right, according to plan, and had actually arrived in Sydney. Accordingly, a false Mr. Varden was to depart with Varden's papers and Varden's passport, furnished with a new photograph duly stamped with the Consular stamp, and to disappear quietly at Sydney and be retransformed into Mr. Eric Loder, travelling with a perfectly regular passport of his own. Well, then, in that case, obviously a cablegram would have to be sent off to Mystofilms Ltd., warning them to expect Varden by a later boat than he had arranged. I handed over this part of the job to my man, Bunter, who is uncommonly capable. The devoted fellow shadowed Loder faithfully for getting on for three weeks, and at length, the very day before Mr. Varden was due to depart, the cablegram was sent from an office in Broadway, where by a happy providence (once more) they supply extremely hard pencils."

"By Jove!" cried Varden, "I remember now being told something about a cablegram when I got out, but I never connected it with Loder. I thought it was just some stupidity of the Western Electric people."

"Quite so. Well, as soon as I'd got that, I popped along to Loder's with a picklock in one pocket and an automatic in the other. The good Bunter went with me, and, if I didn't return by a certain time, had orders to telephone for the police. So you see everything was pretty well covered. Bunter was the chauffeur who was waiting for you, Mr. Varden, but you turned suspicions — I don't blame you altogether — so all we could do was to forward your luggage along to the train.

"On the way out we met the Loder servants *en route* for New York in a car, which showed us that we were on the right track, and also that I was going to have a fairly simple job of it.

"You've heard all about my interviews with Mr. Varden. I really don't think I could improve upon his account. When I'd seen him and his traps safely off the premises, I made for the studio. It was empty, so I opened the secret door, and, as I expected, saw a line of light under the workshop door at the far end of the passage."

"So Loder was there all the time?"

"Of course he was. I took my little pop-gun tight in my fist and opened the door very gently. Loder was standing between the tank and the switchboard, very busy indeed — so busy he didn't hear me come in. His hands were black with graphite, a big heap of which was spread on a sheet on the floor, and he was engaged with a long, springy coil of copper wire, running to the output of the transformer. The big packing-case had been opened, and all the hooks were occupied.

" 'Loder!' I said.

"He turned on me with a face like nothing human. 'Wimsey!' he shouted, 'what the hell are you doing here?'

" 'I have come,' I said, 'to tell you that I know how the apple gets into the dumpling.' And I showed him the automatic.

"He gave a great yell and dashed at the switchboard, turning out the light, so that I could not see to aim. I heard him leap at me — and then there came in the darkness a crash and a splash — and a shriek such as I never heard — not in five years of war — and never want to hear again.

"I groped forward for the switchboard. Of course, I turned on everything before I could lay my hand on the light, but I got it at last — a great white glare from the floodlight over the vat.

"He lay there, still twitching faintly. Cyanide, you see, is about the swiftest and painfullest thing out. Before I could move to do anything, I knew he was dead — poisoned and drowned and dead. The coil of wire that had tripped him had gone into the vat with him. Without thinking, I touched it, and got a shock that pretty well staggered me. Then I realized that I must have turned on the current when I was hunting for the light. I looked into the vat again. As he fell, his dying hands had clutched at the wire. The coils were tight round his fingers, and the current was methodically depositing a film of copper all over his hands, which were blackened with the graphite.

"I had just sense enough to realize that Loder was dead, and that it might be a nasty sort of look-out for me if the thing came out, for I'd certainly gone along to threaten him with a pistol.

"I searched about till I found some solder and an iron. Then I went upstairs and called in Bunter, who had done his ten miles in record time. We went into the smoking-room and soldered the arm of that cursed figure into place again, as well as we could, and then we took everything back into the workshop. We cleaned off every finger-print and removed every trace of our presence. We left the light and the switchboard as they were, and returned to New York by an extremely round-about route. The only thing we brought away with us was the facsimile of the Consular seal, and that we threw into the river.

"Loder was found by the butler next morning. We read in the papers how he had fallen into the vat when engaged on some experiments in electro-plating. The ghastly fact was commented upon that the dead man's hands were thickly cop-pered over. They couldn't get it off without irreverent vio-lence, so he was buried like that.

"That's all. Please, Armstrong, may I have my whisky-and-soda now?"

"What happened to the couch?" inquired Smith-Hartington presently.

"I bought it at the sale of Loder's things," said Wimsey, "and got hold of a dear old Catholic priest I knew, to whom I told the whole story under strict vow of secrecy. He was a very sensible and feeling old bird; so one moonlight night Bunter and I carried the thing out in the car to his own little church, some miles out of the city, and gave it Christian burial in a corner of the graveyard. It seemed the best thing to do."

THE ENTERTAINING EPISODE OF
THE ARTICLE IN QUESTION

The unprofessional detective career of Lord Peter Wimsey was regulated (though the word has no particular propriety in this connexion) by a persistent and undignified inquisitiveness. The habit of asking silly questions—natural, though irritating, in the immature male—remained with him long after his immaculate man, Bunter, had become attached to his service to shave the bristles from his chin and see to the due purchase and housing of Napoleon brandies and Villar y Villar cigars. At the age of thirty-two his sister Mary christened him Elephant's Child. It was his idiotic inquiries (before his brother, the Duke of Denver, who grew scarlet with mortification) as to what the Woolsack was really stuffed with that led the then Lord Chancellor idly to investigate the article in question, and to discover, tucked deep within its recesses, that famous diamond necklace of the Marchioness of Writtle which had disappeared on the day Parliament was opened and been safely secreted by one of the cleaners. It was by a continual and personal badgering of the Chief Engineer at 2LO on the question of "What is Oscillation and How is it Done?" that his lordship incidentally unmasked the great Ploffsky gang of Anarchist conspirators, who were accustomed to converse in code by a methodical system of howls, superimposed (to the great annoyance of listeners in British and European stations) upon the London wavelength and duly relayed by 5XX over a radius of some five or six hundred miles. He annoyed persons of more leisure than decorum by suddenly taking into his head to descend to the Underground by way of the stairs, though the only exciting things he ever actually found there were the bloodstained boots of the Sloane Square murderer; on the other hand, when the drains were taken up at Glegg's Folly, it was by hanging about and hindering the plumbers at their job that he accidentally made the discovery which hanged that detestable poisoner, William Girdlestone Chitty.

Accordingly, it was with no surprise at all that the reliable Bunter, one April morning, received the announcement of an abrupt change of plan.

They had arrived at the Gare Saint-Lazare in good time to register the luggage. Their three months' trip to Italy had been purely for enjoyment, and had been followed by a pleasant fortnight in Paris. They were now intending to pay a short visit to the Duc de Sainte-Croix in Rouen on their way back to England. Lord Peter paced the Salle des Pas Perdus for some time, buying an illustrated paper or two and eyeing the crowd. He bent an appreciative eye on a slim, shingled creature with the face of a Paris *gamin*, but was forced to admit to himself that her ankles were a trifle on the thick side; he assisted an elderly lady who was explaining to the bookstall clerk that she wanted a map of Paris and not a *carte postale*, consumed a quick cognac at one of the little green tables at the far end, and then decided he had better go down and see how Bunter was getting on.

In half an hour Bunter and his porter had worked themselves up to the second place in the enormous queue — for, as usual, one of the weighing-machines was out of order. In front of them stood an agitated little group — the young woman Lord Peter had noticed in the Salle des Pas Perdus, a sallow-faced man of about thirty, their porter, and the registration official, who was peering eagerly through his little *guichet*.

"*Mais je te répète que je ne les ai pas,*" said the sallow man heatedly. "*Voyons, voyons. C'est bien toi qui les as pris, n'est-ce pas? Eh bien, alors, comment veux-tu que je les aie, moi?*"

"*Mais non, mais non, je te les ai bien donnés là-haut, avant d'aller chercher les journaux.*"

"*Je t'assure que non. Enfin, c'est évident! J'ai cherché partout, que diable! Tu ne m'as rien donné, du tout, du tout.*"

"*Mais puisque je t'ai dit d'aller faire enregistrer les bagages! Ne faut-il pas que je t'aie bien remis les billets? Me prends-tu pour un imbécile? Va! On n'est pas dépourvu de sens! Mais regarde l'heure! Le train part à 11 h. 20 m. Cherche un peu, au moins.*"

"*Mais puisque j'ai cherché partout—le gilet, rien! Le jacquet rien, rien! Le pardessus—rien! rien! rien! C'est toi—*"

Here the porter, urged by the frantic cries and stamping of the queue, and the repeated insults of Lord Peter's porter, flung himself into the discussion.

"*P't-être qu' m'sieur a bouté les billets dans son pantalon,*" he suggested.

"*Triple idiot!*" snapped the traveller, "*je vous le demande—est-ce qu'on a jamais entendu parler de mettre des billets dans son pantalon? Jamais—*"

The French porter is a Republican, and, moreover, extremely ill-paid. The large tolerance of his English colleague is not for him.

"*Ah!*" said he, dropping two heavy bags and looking round for moral support. "*Vous dites? En voilà du joli! Allons, mon p'tit, ce n'est pas parce qu'on porte un faux-col qu'on a le droit d'insulter les gens.*"

The discussion might have become a full-blown row, had not the young man suddenly discovered the missing tickets—incidentally, they were in his trousers-pocket after all—and continued the registration of his luggage, to the undisguised satisfaction of the crowd.

"Bunter," said his lordship, who had turned his back on the group and was lighting a cigarette, "I am going to change the tickets. We shall go straight on to London. Have you got that snapshot affair of yours with you?"

"Yes, my lord."

"The one you can work from your pocket without anyone noticing?"

"Yes, my lord."

"Get me a picture of those two."

"Yes, my lord."

"I will see to the luggage. Wire to the Duc that I am unexpectedly called home."

"Very good, my lord."

Lord Peter did not allude to the matter again till Bunter was putting his trousers in the press in their cabin on board the *Normania*. Beyond ascertaining that the young man and woman who had aroused his curiosity were on the boat as second-class passengers, he had sedulously avoided contact with them.

"Did you get that photograph?"

"I hope so, my lord. As your lordship knows, the aim from the breast-pocket tends to be unreliable. I have made three attempts, and trust that one at least may prove to be not unsuccessful."

"How soon can you develop them?"

"At once, if your lordship pleases. I have all the materials in my suitcase."

"What fun!" said Lord Peter, eagerly tying himself into a pair of mauve silk pyjamas. "May I hold the bottles and things?"

Mr. Bunter poured three ounces of water into an eight-ounce measure, and handed his master a glass rod and a minute packet.

"If your lordship would be so good as to stir the contents of the white packet slowly into the water," he said, bolting the door, "and, when dissolved, add the contents of the blue packet."

"Just like a Seidlitz powder," said his lordship happily. "Does it fizz?"

"Not much, my lord," replied the expert, shaking a quantity of hypo crystals into the hand-basin.

"That's a pity," said Lord Peter. "I say, Bunter, it's no end of a bore to dissolve."

"Yes, my lord," returned Bunter sedately. "I have always found that part of the process exceptionally tedious, my lord."

Lord Peter jabbed viciously with the glass rod.

"Just you wait," he said, in a vindictive tone, "till we get to Waterloo."

Three days later Lord Peter Wimsey sat in his book-lined sitting-room at 110A Piccadilly. The tall bunches of daffodils on the table smiled in the spring sunshine, and nodded to the breeze which danced in from the open window. The door opened, and his lordship glanced up from a handsome edition of the *Contes de la Fontaine*, whose handsome hand-coloured Fragonard plates he was examining with the aid of a lens.

"Morning, Bunter. Anything doing?"

"I have ascertained, my lord, that the young person in question has entered the service of the elder Duchess of Medway. Her name is Célestine Berger."

"You are less accurate than usual, Bunter. Nobody off the stage is called Célestine. You should say 'under the name of Célestine Berger.' And the man?"

"He is domiciled at this address in Guilford Street, Bloomsbury, my lord."

"Excellent, My Bunter. Now give me *Who's Who*. Was it a very tiresome job?"

"Not exceptionally so, my lord."

"One of these days I suppose I shall give you something to do which you *will* jib at," said his lordship, "and you will leave me and I shall cut my throat. Thanks. Run away and play. I shall lunch at the club."

The book which Bunter had handed his employer indeed bore the words *Who's Who* engrossed upon its cover, but it was to be found in no public library and in no bookseller's shop. It was a bulky manuscript, closely filled, in part with the small print-like handwriting of Mr. Bunter, in part with Lord Peter's neat and altogether illegible hand. It contained biographies of the most unexpected people, and the most unexpected facts about the most obvious people. Lord Peter turned to a very long entry under the name of the Dowager Duchess of Medway. It appeared to make satisfactory reading, for after a time he smiled, closed the book, and went to the telephone.

"Yes—this is the Duchess of Medway. Who is it?"

The deep, harsh old voice pleased Lord Peter. He could see the imperious face and upright figure of what had been the most famous beauty in the London of the sixties.

"It's Peter Wimsey, duchess."

"Indeed, and how do you do, young man? Back from your Continental jaunting?"

"Just home—and longing to lay my devotion at the feet of the most fascinating lady in England."

"God bless my soul, child, what do you want?" demanded the duchess. "Boys like you don't flatter an old woman for nothing."

"I want to tell you my sins, duchess."

"You should have lived in the great days," said the voice appreciatively. "Your talents are wasted on the young fry."

"That is why I want to talk to you, duchess."

"Well, my dear, if you've committed any sins worth hearing I shall enjoy your visit."

"You are as exquisite in kindness as in charm. I am coming this afternoon."

"I will be at home to you and to no one else. There."

"Dear lady, I kiss your hands," said Lord Peter, and he heard a deep chuckle as the duchess rang off.

"You may say what you like, duchess," said Lord Peter from his reverential position on the fender-stool, "but you are the youngest grandmother in London, not excepting my own mother."

"Dear Honoria is the merest child," said the duchess. "I have twenty years more experience of life, and have arrived at the age when we boast of them. I have every intention of being a great-grandmother before I die. Sylvia is being married in a fortnight's time, to that stupid son of Attenbury's."

"Abcock?"

"Yes. He keeps the worst hunters I ever saw, and doesn't know still champagne from sauterne. But Sylvia is stupid, too, poor child, so I dare say they will get on charmingly. In my day one had to have either brains or beauty to get on—preferably both. Nowadays nothing seems to be required but a total lack of figure. But all the sense went out of society with the House of Lords' veto. I except you, Peter. You have talents. It is a pity you do not employ them in politics."

"Dear lady, God forbid."

"Perhaps you are right, as things are. There were giants in my day. Dear Dizzy. I remember so well, when his wife died, how hard we all tried to get him—Medway had died the year before—but he was wrapped up in that stupid Bradford woman, who had never even read a line of one of his books, and couldn't have understood 'em if she had. And now we have Abcock standing for Midhurst, and married to Sylvia!"

"You haven't invited me to the wedding, duchess dear. I'm so hurt," sighed his lordship.

"Bless you, child, *I* didn't send out the invitations, but I suppose your brother and that tiresome wife of his will be there. You must come, of course, if you want to. I had no idea you had a passion for weddings."

"Hadn't you?" said Peter. "I have a passion for this one. I want to see Lady Sylvia wearing white satin and the family lace and diamonds, and to sentimentalize over the days when my fox-terrier bit the stuffing out of her doll."

"Very well, my dear, you shall. Come early and give me your support. As for the diamonds, if it weren't a family tradition, Sylvia shouldn't wear them. She has the impudence to complain of them."

"I thought they were some of the finest in existence."

"So they are. But she says the settings are ugly and old-fashioned, and she doesn't like diamonds, and they won't go with her dress. Such nonsense. Whoever heard of a girl not liking diamonds? She wants to be something romantic and moonshiny in pearls. I have no patience with her."

"I'll promise to admire them," said Peter — "use the privilege of early acquaintance and tell her she's an ass and so on. I'd love to have a view of them. When do they come out of cold storage?"

"Mr. Whitehead will bring them up from the Bank the night before," said the duchess, "and they'll go into the safe in my room. Come round at twelve o'clock and you shall have a private view of them."

"That would be delightful. Mind they don't disappear in the night, won't you?"

"Oh, my dear, the house is going to be over-run with policemen. Such a nuisance. I suppose it can't be helped."

"Oh, I think it's a good thing," said Peter. "I have rather an unwholesome weakness for policemen."

On the morning of the wedding-day, Lord Peter emerged from Bunter's hands a marvel of sleek brilliance. His primrose-coloured hair was so exquisite a work of art that to eclipse it with his glossy hat was like shutting up the sun in a shrine of polished jet; his spats, light trousers, and exquisitely polished shoes formed a tone-symphony in monochrome. It was only by the most impassioned pleading that he persuaded his tyrant to allow him to place two small photographs and a thin, foreign letter in his breast-pocket. Mr. Bunter, likewise immaculately attired, stepped into the taxi after him. At noon precisely they were deposited beneath the striped awning which adorned the door of the Duchess of Medway's house in Park Lane. Bunter promptly disappeared in the direction of the back entrance, while his lordship mounted the steps and asked to see the dowager.

The majority of the guests had not yet arrived, but the house was full of agitated people, flitting hither and thither, with flowers and prayer-books, while a clatter of dishes and cutlery from the dining-room proclaimed the laying of a sumptuous breakfast. Lord Peter was shown into the morning-room while the footman went to announce him, and here he found a very close friend and devoted colleague, Detective-Inspector Parker, mounting guard in plain clothes over a costly collection of white elephants. Lord Peter greeted him with an affectionate hand-grip.

"All serene so far?" he inquired.

"Perfectly O.K."

"You got my note?"

"Sure thing. I've got three of our men shadowing your friend in Guilford Street. The girl is very much in evidence here. Does the old lady's wig and that sort of thing. Bit of a coming-on disposition, isn't she?"

"You surprise me," said Lord Peter. "No"—as his friend grinned sardonically—"you really do. Not seriously? That would throw all my calculations out."

"Oh, no! Saucy with her eyes and her tongue, that's all."

"Do her job well?"

"I've heard no complaints. What put you on to this?"

"Pure accident. Of course I may be quite mistaken."

"Did you receive any information from Paris?"

"I wish you wouldn't use that phrase," said Lord Peter peevishly. "It's so of the Yard—yardy. One of these days it'll give you away."

"Sorry," said Parker. "Second nature, I suppose."

"Those are the things to beware of," returned his lordship, with an earnestness that seemed a little out of place. "One can keep guard on everything but just those second-nature tricks." He moved across to the window, which overlooked the trades-men's entrance. "Hullo!" he said, "here's our bird."

Parker joined him, and saw the neat, shingled head of the French girl from the Gare Saint-Lazare, topped by a neat black bandeau and bow. A man with a basket full of white nar-cissi had rung the bell, and appeared to be trying to make a sale. Parker gently opened the window, and they heard Céles-tine say with a marked French accent, "No, nossing today, sank you." The man insisted in the monotonous whine of his type, thrusting a big bunch of the white flowers upon her, but she pushed them back into the basket with an angry exclamation and flirted away, tossing her head and slapping the door smartly to. The man moved off muttering. As he did so a thin, unhealthy-looking lounger in a check cap detached himself from a lamp-post opposite and mouched along the street after him, at the same time casting a glance up at the window. Mr. Parker looked at Lord Peter, nodded, and made a slight sign with his hand. At once the man in the check cap removed his cigarette from his mouth, extinguished it, and, tucking the stub behind his ear, moved off without a second glance.

"Very interesting," said Lord Peter, when both were out of sight. "Hark!"

There was a sound of running feet overhead—a cry—and a general commotion. The two men dashed to the door as the bride, rushing frantically downstairs with her bevy of brides-maids after her, proclaimed in a hysterical shriek: "The diamonds! They're stolen! They're gone!"

Instantly the house was in an uproar. The servants and the caterer's men crowded into the hall; the bride's father burst out from his room in a magnificent white waistcoat and no coat; the Duchess of Medway descended upon Mr. Parker, demanding that something should be done; while the butler, who never to the day of his death got over the disgrace, ran out of the pantry with a corkscrew in one hand and a priceless bottle of crusted port in the other, which he shook with all the vehemence of a town-crier ringing a bell. The only dignified entry was made by the dowager duchess, who came down like a ship in sail, dragging Célestine with her, and admonishing her not to be so silly.

"Be quiet, girl," said the dowager. "Anyone would think you were going to be murdered."

"Allow me, your grace," said Mr. Bunter, appearing suddenly from nowhere in his usual unperturbed manner, and taking the agitated Célestine firmly by the arm. "Young woman, calm yourself."

"But what is to be *done?*" cried the bride's mother. "How did it happen?"

It was at this moment that Detective-Inspector Parker took the floor. It was the most impressive and dramatic moment in his whole career. His magnificent calm rebuked the clamorous nobility surrounding him.

"Your grace," he said, "there is no cause for alarm. Our measures have been taken. We have the criminals and the gems, thanks to Lord Peter Wimsey, from whom we received inf—"

"Charles!" said Lord Peter in an awful voice.

"Warning of the attempt. One of our men is just bringing in the male criminal at the front door, taken red-handed with your grace's diamonds in his possession." (All gazed round, and perceived indeed the check-capped lounger and a uniformed constable entering with the flower-seller between them.) "The female criminal, who picked the lock of your grace's safe, is—here! No, you don't," he added, as Célestine, amid a torrent of apache language which nobody, fortunately, had French enough to understand, attempted to whip out a revolver from the bosom of her demure black dress. "Célestine Berger," he continued, pocketing the weapon, "I arrest you in the name of the law, and I warn you that anything you say will be taken down and used as evidence against you."

"Heaven help us," said Lord Peter; "the roof would fly off the court. And you've got the name wrong, Charles. Ladies and gentlemen, allow me to introduce you to Jacques Lerouge, known as Sans-culotte—the youngest and cleverest thief, safe-breaker, and female impersonator that ever occupied a dossier in the Palais de Justice."

There was a gasp. Jacques Sans-culotte gave vent to a low oath and cocked a *gamin* grimace at Peter.

"*C'est parfait*," said he; "*toutes mes félicitations, milord*, what you call a fair cop, *hein?* And now I know him," he added, grinning at Bunter, "the so-patient Englishman who stand behind us in the queue at Saint-Lazare. But tell me, please, how you know me, that I may correct it *next time*."

"I have mentioned to you before, Charles," said Lord Peter, "the unwisdom of falling into habits of speech. They give you away. Now, in France, every male child is brought up to use masculine adjectives about himself. He says: *Que je suis beau!* But a little girl has it rammed home to her that she is female; she must say: *Que je suis belle!* It must make it beastly hard to be a female impersonator. When I am at a station and I hear an excited young woman say to her companion, *"Me prends-tu pour un imbécile"*—the masculine article arouses curiosity. And that's that!" he concluded briskly. "The rest was merely a matter of getting Bunter to take a photograph and communicating with our friends of the Sûreté and Scotland Yard."

Jacques Sans-culotte bowed again.

"Once more I congratulate milord. He is the only Englishman I have ever met who is capable of appreciating our beautiful language. I will pay great attention in future to the article in question."

With an awful look, the Dowager Duchess of Medway advanced upon Lord Peter.

"Peter," she said, "do you mean to say you *knew* about this, and that for the last three weeks you have allowed me to be dressed and undressed and put to bed by a *young man?*"

His lordship had the grace to blush.

"Duchess," he said humbly, "on my honour I didn't know absolutely for certain till this morning. And the police were so anxious to have these people caught red-handed. What can I do to show my penitence? Shall I cut the privileged beast in pieces?"

The grim old mouth relaxed a little.

"After all," said the dowager duchess, with the delightful consciousness that she was going to shock her daughter-in-law, "there are very few women of my age who could make the same boast. It seems that we die as we have lived, my dear."

For indeed the Dowager Duchess of Medway had been notable in her day.

THE FASCINATING PROBLEM OF
UNCLE MELEAGER'S WILL

You look a little worried, Bunter," said his lordship kindly to his manservant. "Is there anything I can do?"

The valet's face brightened as he released his employer's grey trousers from the press.

"Perhaps your lordship could be so good as to think," he said hopefully, "of a word in seven letters with S in the middle, meaning two."

"Also," suggested Lord Peter thoughtlessly.

"I beg your lordship's pardon. T-w-o. And seven letters."

"Nonsense!" said Lord Peter. "How about that bath?"

"It should be just about ready, my lord."

Lord Peter Wimsey swung his mauve silk legs lightly over the edge of the bed and stretched appreciatively. It was a beautiful June that year. Through the open door he saw the delicate coils of steam wreathing across a shaft of yellow sunlight. Every step he took into the bathroom was a conscious act of enjoyment. In a husky light tenor he carolled a few bars of *"Maman, dites-moi."* Then a thought struck him, and he turned back.

"Bunter!"

"My lord?"

"No bacon this morning. Quite the wrong smell."

"I was thinking of buttered eggs, my lord."

"Excellent. Like primroses. The Beaconsfield touch," said his lordship approvingly.

His song died into a rapturous crooning as he settled into the verbena-scented water. His eyes roamed vaguely over the pale blue-and-white tiles of the bathroom walls.

Mr. Bunter had retired to the kitchen to put the coffee on the stove when the bell rang. Surprised, he hastened back to the bedroom. It was empty. With increased surprise, he realized that it must have been the bathroom bell. The words "heart-attack" formed swiftly in his mind, to be displaced by the still more alarming thought, "No soap." He opened the door almost nervously.

"Did you ring, my lord?" he demanded of Lord Peter's head, alone visible.

"Yes," said his lordship abruptly. "Ambsace."

"I beg your lordship's pardon?"

"Ambsace. Word of seven letters. Meaning two. With S in the middle. Two aces. Ambsace."

Bunter's expression became beatified.

"Undoubtedly correct," he said, pulling a small sheet of paper from his pocket, and entering the word upon it in pencil. "I am extremely obliged to your lordship. In that case the 'indifferent cook in six letters ending with *red*' must be Alfred."

Lord Peter waved a dismissive hand.

On re-entering his bedroom, Lord Peter was astonished to see his sister Mary seated in his own particular chair and consuming his buttered eggs. He greeted her with a friendly acerbity, demanding why she should look him up at that unearthly hour.

"I'm riding with Freddy Arbuthnot," said her ladyship, "as you might see by my legs, if you were really as big a Sherlock as you make out."

"Riding," replied her brother, "I had already deduced, though I admit that Freddy's name was not writ large, to my before-breakfast eye, upon the knees of your breeches. But why this visit?"

"Well, because you were on the way," said Lady Mary, "and I'm booked up all day and I want you to come and dine at the Soviet Club with me tonight."

"Good God, Mary, why? You know I hate the place. Cooking's beastly, the men don't shave, and the conversation gets my goat. Besides, last time I went there, your friend Goyles plugged me in the shoulder. I thought you'd chucked the Soviet Club."

"It isn't me. It's Hannah Marryat."

"What, the intense young woman with the badly bobbed hair and the brogues?"

"Well, she's never been able to afford a good hairdresser. That's just what I want your help about."

"My dear child, I can't cut her hair for her. Bunter might. He can do most things."

"Silly. No. But she's got—that is, she used to have—an uncle, the very rich, curmudgeony sort, you know, who never gave anyone a penny. Well, he's dead, and they can't find his will."

"Perhaps he didn't make one."

"Oh, yes, he did. He wrote and told her so. But the nasty old thing hid it, and it can't be found."

"Is the will in her favour?"

"Yes."

"Who's the next-of-kin?"

"She and her mother are the only members of the family left."

"Well, then, she's only got to sit tight and she'll get the goods."

"No—because the horrid old man left two wills, and, if she can't find the latest one, they'll prove the first one. He explained that to her carefully."

"Oh, I see. H'm. By the way, I thought the young woman was a Socialist."

"Oh, she is. Terrifically so. One really can't help admiring her. She has done some wonderful work —"

"Yes, I dare say. But in that case I don't see why she need be so keen on getting uncle's dollars."

Mary began to chuckle.

"Ah! But that's where Uncle Meleager —"

"Uncle *what?*"

"Meleager. That's his name. Meleager Finch."

"Oh!"

"Yes — well, that's where he's been so clever. Unless she finds the new will, the old will comes into force and hands over every penny of the money to the funds of the Primrose League."

Lord Peter gave a little yelp of joy.

"Good for Uncle Meleager! But, look here, Polly, I'm a Tory, if anything. I'm certainly not a Red. Why should I help to snatch the good gold from the Primrose Leaguers and hand it over to the Third International? Uncle Meleager's a sport. I take to Uncle Meleager."

"Oh, but Peter, I really don't think she'll do that with it. Not at present, anyway. They're awfully poor, and her mother ought to have some frightfully difficult operation or something, and go and live abroad, so it really is ever so important they should get the money. And perhaps Hannah wouldn't be quite so Red if she'd ever had a bean of her own. Besides, you could make it a condition of helping her that she should go and get properly shingled at Bresil's."

"You are a very cynically-minded person," said his lordship. "However, it would be fun to have a go at Uncle M. Was he obliging enough to give any clues for finding the will?"

"He wrote a funny sort of letter, which we can't make head or tail of. Come to the club tonight and she'll show it to you."

"Right-ho! Seven o'clock do? And we could go on and see a show afterwards. Do you mind clearing out now? I'm going to get dressed."

•　•　•

Amid a deafening babble of voices in a low-pitched cellar, the Soviet Club meets and dines. Ethics and sociology, the latest vortices of the Whirligig school of verse, combine with the smoke of countless cigarettes to produce an inspissated atmosphere, through which flat, angular mural paintings dimly lower upon the revellers. There is painfully little room for the elbows, or indeed for any part of one's body. Lord Peter—his feet curled under his chair to avoid the stray kicks of the heavy brogues opposite him—was acutely conscious of an unbecoming attitude and an overheated feeling about the head. He found it difficult to get any response from Hannah Marryat. Under her heavy, ill-cut fringe her dark eyes gloomed somberly at him. At the same time he received a strong impression of something enormously vital. He had a sudden fancy that if she were set free from self-defensiveness and the importance of being earnest, she would exhibit unexpected powers of enjoyment. He was interested, but oppressed. Mary, to his great relief, suggested that they should have their coffee upstairs.

They found a quiet corner with comfortable chairs.

"Well, now," said Mary encouragingly.

"Of course you understand," said Miss Marryat mournfully, "that if it were not for the monstrous injustice of Uncle Meleager's other will, and mother being so ill, I shouldn't take any steps. But when there is £250,000, and the prospect of doing real good with it—"

"Naturally," said Lord Peter, "it isn't the money you care about, as the dear old bromide says, it's the principle of the thing. Right you are! Now supposin' we have a look at Uncle Meleager's letter."

Miss Marryat rummaged in a very large handbag and passed the paper over.

This was Uncle Meleager's letter, dated from Siena twelve months previously.

MY DEAR HANNAH, When I die—which I propose to do at my convenience and not at that of my family—you will at last discover my monetary worth. It is, of course, considerably less than you had hoped, and quite fails, I assure you, adequately to represent my actual worth in the eyes of the discerning. I made my will yesterday, leaving the entire sum, such as it is, to the Primrose League—a body quite as fatuous as any other in our preposterous state, but which has the advantage of being peculiarly obnoxious to yourself. This will will be found in the safe in the library.

I am not, however, unmindful of the fact that your mother is my sister, and you and she my only surviving relatives. I shall accordingly amuse myself by drawing up today a second will, superseding the other and leaving the money to you.

I have always held that woman is a frivolous animal. A woman who pretends to be serious is wasting her time and spoiling her appearance. I consider that you have wasted your time to a really shocking extent. Accordingly, I intend to conceal this will, and that in such a manner that you will certainly never find it unless by the exercise of a sustained frivolity.

I hope you will contrive to be frivolous enough to become the heiress of your affectionate

UNCLE MELEAGER

"Couldn't we use that letter as proof of the testator's intention, and fight the will?" asked Mary anxiously.

" 'Fraid not," said Lord Peter. "You see, there's no evidence here that the will was ever actually drawn up. Though I suppose we could find the witnesses."

"We've tried," said Miss Marryat, "but, as you see, Uncle Meleager was travelling abroad at the time, and he probably got some obscure people in some obscure Italian town to witness it for him. We advertised, but got no answer."

"H'm. Uncle Meleager doesn't seem to have left things to chance. And, anyhow, wills are queer things, and so are the probate and divorce wallahs. Obviously the thing to do is to find the other will. Did the clues he speaks of turn up among his papers?"

"We hunted through everything. And, of course, we had the whole house searched from top to bottom for the will. But it was quite useless."

"You've not destroyed anything, of course. Who were the executors of the Primrose League will?"

"Mother and Mr. Sands, Uncle Meleager's solicitor. The will left mother a silver teapot for her trouble."

"I like Uncle Meleager more and more. Anyhow, he did the sporting thing. I'm beginnin' to enjoy this case like anything. Where did Uncle Meleager hang out?"

"It's an old house down at Dorking. It's rather quaint. Somebody had a fancy to build a little Roman villa sort of thing there, with a veranda behind, with columns and a pond in the front hall, and statues. It's very decent there just now, though it's awfully cold in the winter, with all those stone floors and stone stairs and the sky light over the hall! Mother said perhaps you would be very kind and come down and have a look at it."

"I'd simply love to. Can we start tomorrow? I promise you we'll be frivolous enough to please even Uncle Meleager, if you'll do your bit, Miss Marryat. Won't we, Mary?"

"Rather! And, I say, hadn't we better be moving if we're going to the Pallambra?"

"I never go to music halls," said Miss Marryat ungraciously.

"Oh, but you must come tonight," said his lordship persuasively. "It's so frivolous. Just think how it would please Uncle Meleager."

Accordingly, the next day found the party, including the indispensable Mr. Bunter, assembled at Uncle Meleager's house. Pending the settlement of the will question, there had seemed every reason why Mr. Finch's executrix and next-of-kin should live in the house, thus providing every facility for what Lord Peter called the "Treasures hunt." After being introduced to Mrs. Marryat, who was an invalid and remained in her room, Lady Mary and her brother were shown over the house by Miss Marryat, who explained to them how carefully the search had been conducted. Every paper had been examined, every book in the library scrutinized page by page, the walls and chimneys tapped for hiding-places, the boards taken up, and so forth, but with no result.

"Y'know," said his lordship, "I'm sure you've been going the wrong way to work. My idea is, old Uncle Meleager was a man of his word. If he said frivolous, he meant really frivolous. Something beastly silly. I wonder what it was."

He was still wondering when he went up to dress. Bunter was putting studs in his shirt. Lord Peter gazed thoughtfully at him, and then inquired:

"Are any of Mr. Finch's old staff still here?"

"Yes, my lord. The cook and the housekeeper. Wonderful old gentleman they say he was, too. Eighty-three, but as up to date as you please. Had his wireless in his bedroom, and enjoyed the Savoy bands every night of his life. Followed his politics, and was always ready with the details of the latest big law-cases. If a young lady came to see him, he'd like to see she had her hair shingled and the latest style in fashions. They say he took up crosswords as soon as they came in, and was remarkably quick at solving them, my lord, and inventing them. Took a ten-pound prize in the *Daily Yell* for one, and was wonderfully pleased to get it, they say, my lord, rich as he was."

"Indeed."

"Yes, my lord. He was a great man for acrostics before that, I understood them to say, but, when crosswords came in, he threw away his acrostics and said he liked the new game better. Wonderfully adaptable, if I may say so, he seems to have been for an old gentleman."

"Was he, by Jove?" said his lordship absently, and then, with sudden energy:

"Bunter, I'd like to double your salary, but I suppose you'd take it as an insult."

The conversation bore fruit at dinner.

"What," inquired his lordship, "happened to Uncle Meleager's crosswords?"

"Crosswords?" said Hannah Marryat, knitting her heavy brows. "Oh, those puzzle things! Poor old man, he went mad over them. He had every newspaper sent him, and in his last illness he'd be trying to fill the wretched things in. It was worse than his acrostics and his jig-saw puzzles. Poor old creature, he must have been senile, I'm afraid. Of course, we looked through them, but there wasn't anything there. We put them all in the attic."

"The attic for me," said Lord Peter.

"And for me," said Mary. "I don't believe there was anything senile about Uncle Meleager."

The evening was warm, and they had dined in the little viridarium at the back of the house, with its tall vases and hanging baskets of flowers and little marble statues.

"Is there an attic here?" said Peter. "It seems such a—well, such an un-Attic thing to have in a house like this."

"It's just a horrid poky little hole over the porch," said Miss Marryat, rising and leading the way. "Don't tumble into the pond, will you? It's a great nuisance having it there, especially at night. I always tell them to leave a light on."

Lord Peter glanced into the miniature impluvium, with its tiling of red, white, and black marble.

"That's not a very classic design," he observed.

"No. Uncle Meleager used to complain about it and say he must have it altered. There was a proper one once, I believe, but it got damaged, and the man before Uncle Meleager had it replaced by some local idiot. He built three bay windows out of the dining-room at the same time, which made it very much lighter and pleasanter, of course, but it looks awful. Now, this tiling is all right; uncle put that in himself."

She pointed to a mosaic dog at the threshold with the motto "Cave canem," and Lord Peter recognized it as a copy of a Pompeian original.

A narrow stair brought them to the "attic," where the Wimseys flung themselves with enthusiasm upon a huge heap of dusty old newspapers and manuscripts. The latter seemed the likelier field, so they started with them. They consisted of a quantity of crosswords in manuscript—presumably the children of Uncle Meleager's own brain. The square, the list of definitions, and the solution were in every case neatly pinned together. Some (early efforts, no doubt) were childishly simple, but others were difficult, with allusive or punning clues; some of the ordinary newspaper type, others in the form of rhymed distichs. They scrutinized the solutions closely, and searched the definitions for acrostics or hidden words, unsuccessfully for a long time.

"This one's a funny one," said Mary, "nothing seems to fit. Oh! it's two pinned together. No, it isn't—yes, it is—it's only been pinned up wrong. Peter, have you seen the puzzle belonging to these clues anywhere?"

"What one's that?"

"Well, it's numbered rather funnily, with Roman and Arabic numerals, and it starts off with a thing that hasn't got any numbers at all:

" *'Truth, poor girl, was nobody's daughter;*
She took off her clothes and jumped into the water.' "

"Frivolous old wretch!" said Miss Marryat.

"Friv—here, gimme that!" cried Lord Peter. "Look here, I say, Miss Marryat, you oughtn't to have overlooked this."

"I thought it just belonged to that other square."

"Not it. It's different. I believe it's our thing. Listen:

" *'Your expectation to be rich*
Here will reach its highest pitch.'

That's one for you, Miss Marryat. Mary, hunt about. We *must* find the square that belongs to this."

But, though they turned everything upside-down, they could find no square with Roman and Arabic numerals.

"Hang it all!" said Peter, "it must be made to fit one of these others. Look! I know what he's done. He's just taken a fifteen-letter square, and numbered it with Roman figures one way and Arabic the other. I bet it fits into that one it was pinned up with."

But the one it was pinned up with turned out to have only thirteen squares.

"Dash it all," said his lordship, "we'll have to carry the whole lot down, and work away at it till we find the one it *does* fit."

He snatched up a great bundle of newspapers, and led the way out. The others followed, each with an armful. The search had taken some time, and the atrium was in semi-darkness.

"Where shall I take them?" asked Lord Peter, calling back over his shoulder.

"Hi!" cried Mary; and, "Look where you're going!" cried her friend.

They were too late. A splash and a flounder proclaimed that Lord Peter had walked, like Johnny Head-in-Air, over the edge of the impluvium, papers and all.

"You ass!" said Mary.

His lordship scrambled out, spluttering, and Hannah Marryat suddenly burst out into the first laugh Peter had ever heard her give.

> *"Truth, they say, was nobody's daughter;*
> *She took off her clothes and fell into the water,"*

she proclaimed.

"Well, I couldn't take my clothes off with you here, could I?" grumbled Lord Peter. "We'll have to fish out the papers. I'm afraid they've got a bit damp."

Miss Marryat turned on the lights, and they started to clear the basin.

"Truth, poor girl—" began Lord Peter, and suddenly with a little shriek, began to dance on the marble edge of the impluvium.

"One, two, three, four, five, six—"

"Quite, quite demented," said Mary. "How shall I break it to mother?"

"Thirteen, fourteen, *fifteen!*" cried his lordship, and sat down, suddenly and damply, exhausted by his own excitement.

"Feeling better?" asked his sister acidly.

"I'm well. I'm all right. Everything's all right. I *love* Uncle Meleager. Fifteen squares each way. Look at it. *Look* at it. The truth's in the water. Didn't he say so? Oh, frabjous day! Calloo! callay! I chortle. Mary, what became of those definitions?"

"They're in your pocket, all damp," said Mary.

Lord Peter snatched them out hurriedly.

"It's all right, they haven't run," he said. "Oh, *darling* Uncle Meleager. Can you drain the impluvium, Miss Marryat, and find a bit of charcoal. Then I'll get some dry clothes on and we'll get down to it. Don't you see? *There's* your missing crossword square—on the floor of the impluvium!"

It took, however, some time to get the basin emptied, and it was not till the next morning that the party, armed with sticks of charcoal, squatted down in the empty impluvium to fill in Uncle Meleager's crossword on the marble tiles. Their first difficulty was to decide whether the red squares counted as stops or had to be filled in, but after a few definitions had been solved, the construction of the puzzle grew apace. The investigators grew steadily hotter and more quickly covered with charcoal, while the attentive Mr. Bunter hurried to and fro between the atrium and the library, and the dictionaries piled upon the edge of the impluvium.

Here was Uncle Meleager's crossword square:

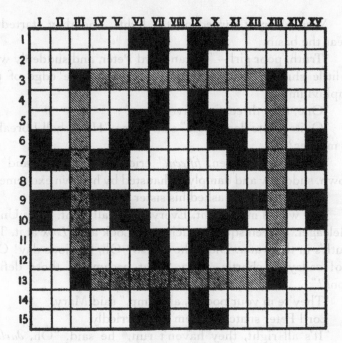

Truth, poor girl, was nobody's daughter;
She took off her clothes and jumped into the water.

ACROSS

I.1   Foolish or wise, yet one remains alone,
'Twixt Strength and Justice on a heavenly
throne.

XI.1   O to what ears the chink of gold was sweet;
The greed for treasure brought him but
defeat.

"That's a hint to us," said Lord Peter.

I.2   One drop of vinegar to two of oil
Dresses this curly head sprung from the soil.

X.2   Nothing itself, it needs but little more
To be that nothingness the Preacher saw.

I.3   Dusty though my fellows be,
        We are a kingly company.

IV.3   Have your own will, though here, I hold,
        The new is *not* a patch upon the old.

XIV.3   Any loud cry would do as well,
        Or so the poet's verses tell.

I.4   This is the most unkindest cut of all,
        Except your skill be mathematical.

X.4   Little and hid from mortal sight.
        I darkly work to make all light.

I.5   The need for this (like that it's cut off short)
        The building of a tower to humans taught.

XI.5   "More than mind discloses and more than
        men believe"
        (A definition by a man whom Pussyfoot doth
        grieve).

II.6   Backward observe her turn her way,
        The way of wisdom, wise men say.

VII.6   Grew long ago by river's edge
        Where grows today the common sedge.

XII.6   One of three by which, they say,
        You'll know the Cornishmen alway.

VI.7   Blow upon blow; five more the vanquished
        Roman shows
        And if the foot slip one, on crippled feet one goes.

I.8   By this Jew's work the whole we find,
        In a glass clearly, darkly in the mind.

IX.8   Little by little see it grow
        Till cut off short by hammer-blow.

VI.9   Watch him go, heel and toe,
        Across the wide Karroo!

II.10   In expectation to be rich
        Here you reach the highest pitch.

VII.10   Of this, concerning nothing, much —
        Too often do we hear of such!

XII.10   O'er land and sea, passing on deadly wings,
        Pain to the strong, to weaklings death it brings.

I.11	Requests like these, however long they be, Stop just too soon for common courtesy.
XI.11	Caesar, the living dead salute thee here, Facing for thy delight tooth, claw, and spear.
I.12	One word had served, but he in ranting vein "Lend me your ears" must mouth o'er Caesar slain.
X.12	Helical circumvolution Adumbrates correct solution.
I.13	One that works for Irish men Both by word and deed and pen.

"That's an easy one," said Miss Marryat.

IV.13	Seven out of twelve this number makes complete As the sun journeys on from seat to seat.
XIV.13	My brothers play with planets; Cicero, Master of words, my master is below.
I.14	Free of her jesses let the falcon fly, With sight undimmed into the azure sky.
X.14	And so you dine with Borgia? Let me lend You this as a precaution, my poor friend.
I.15	Friendship carried to excess Got him in a horrid mess.
XI.15	Smooth and elastic and, I guess, The dearest treasure you possess.

DOWN

1.I	If step by step the Steppes you wander through Many of those in this, of these in those you'll view.

"Bunter," said Lord Peter, "bring me a whisky-and-soda!"

11.I	If me without my head you do, Then generously my head renew,

	Or put it to my hinder end — Your cheer it shall nor mar nor mend.
1.II	Quietly, quietly, 'twixt edge and edge, Do this unto the thin end of the wedge.
10.II	"Something that hath a reference to my state?" Just as you like, it shall be written straight.
1.III	When all is read, then give the world its due, And never need the world read this of you.

"That's a comfort," said Lady Mary. "It shows we're on the right lines."

4.III	Sing *Nunc Dimittis* and *Magnificat* — But look a little farther back than that.
14.III	Here in brief epitome Attribute of royalty.
1.IV	Lo! at a glance The Spanish gipsy and her dance.
10.IV	Bring me skin and a needle or a stick — A needle does it slowly, a stick does it quick.
1.V	It was a brazen business when King Phalaris made these for men.
11.V	This king (of whom not much is known) By Heaven's mercy was o'erthrown.
2.VI	"Bid ὃν καὶ μὴ ὃν farewell?" Nay, in this The sterner Roman stands by that which is.
7.VI	This the termination is Of many minds' activities.
12.VI	I mingle on Norwegian shore, With ebbing water's backward roar.
6.VII	I stand a ladder to renown, Set 'twixt the stars and Milan town.
1.VIII	Highest and lowliest both to me lay claim, The little hyssop and the king of fame.

"That makes that point about the squares clear," said Mary. "I think it's even more significant," said her brother.

9.VIII This sensible old man refused to tread
The path to Hades in a youngster's stead.

6.IX Long since, at Nature's call, they let it drop,
Thoughtlessly thoughtful for our next year's
crop.

2.X To smallest words great speakers greatness
give;
Here Rome propounded her alternative.

7.X We heap up many with toil and trouble,
And find that the whole of our gain is a bubble.

12.X Add it among the hidden things —
A fishy tale to light it brings.

1.XI "Lions," said a Gallic critic, "are not these."
Benevolent souls — they'd make your heart's
blood freeze.

11.XI An epithet for husky fellows,
That stand, all robed in greens and yellows.

1.XII Whole without holes behold me here,
My meaning should be wholly clear.

10.XII Running all around, never setting foot to floor,
If there isn't one in this room, there may be
one next door.

1.XIII Ye gods! think also of that goddess' name
Whose might two hours on end the mob pro-
claim.

4.XIII The Priest uplifts his voice on high,
The choristers make their reply.

14.XIII When you've guessed it, with one voice
You'll say it was a golden choice.

1.XIV Shall learning die amid a war's alarms?
I, at my birth, was clasped in iron arms.

10.XIV At sunset see the labourer now
Loose all his oxen from the plough.

1.XV Without a miracle it cannot be —
At this point, Solver, bid him pray for thee!

11.XV Two thousand years ago and more
(Just as we do today),

> The Romans saw these distant lights —
> But, oh! how hard the way!

The most remarkable part of the search — or so Lord Peter thought — was its effect on Miss Marryat. At first she hovered disconsolately on the margin, aching with wounded dignity, yet ashamed to dissociate herself from people who were toiling so hard and so cheerfully in her cause.

"I think that's so-and-so," Mary would say hopefully.

And her brother would reply enthusiastically, "Holed it in one, old lady. Good for you! We've got it this time, Miss Marryat" — and explain it.

And Hannah Marryat would say with a snort:

"That's just the childish kind of joke Uncle Meleager *would* make."

Gradually, however, the fascination of seeing the squares fit together caught her, and, when the first word appeared which showed that the searchers were definitely on the right track, she lay down flat on the floor and peered over Lord Peter's shoulder as he grovelled below, writing letters in charcoal, rubbing them out with his handkerchief and mopping his heated face, till the Moor of Venice had nothing on him in the matter of blackness. Once, half scornfully, half timidly, she made a suggestion; twice, she made a suggestion; the third time she had an inspiration. The next minute she was down in the mêlée, crawling over the tiles, flushed and excited, wiping important letters out with her knees as fast as Peter could write them in, poring over the pages of Roget, her eyes gleaming under her tumbled black fringe.

Hurried meals of cold meat and tea sustained the exhausted party, and towards sunset Peter, with a shout of triumph, added the last letter to the square.

They crawled out and looked at it.

"All the words can't be clues," said Mary. "I think it must be just those four."

"Yes, undoubtedly. It's quite clear. We've only got to look it up. Where's a Bible?"

Miss Marryat hunted it out from the pile of reference books. "But that isn't the name of a Bible book," she said. "It's those things they have at evening service."

"That's all you know," said Lord Peter. "I was brought up religious, I was. It's Vulgate, that's what that is. You're quite right, of course, but, as Uncle Meleager says, we must 'look a little farther back than that.' Here you are. Now, then."

"But it doesn't say what chapter."

"So it doesn't. I mean, nor it does."

"And, anyhow, all the chapters are too short."

"Damn! Oh! Here, suppose we just count right on from the beginning—one, two, three—"

"Seventeen in chapter one, eighteen, nineteen—this must be it."

Two fair heads and one dark one peered excitedly at the small print, Bunter hovering decorously on the outskirts.

O my dove, that art in the clefts of the rock, in the covert of the steep place.

"Oh, dear!" said Mary, disappointed, "that does sound rather hopeless. Are you sure you've counted right? It might mean *anything.*"

Lord Peter scratched his head.

"This is a bit of a blow," he said. "I don't like Uncle Meleager half as much as I did. Old beast!"

"After all our work!" moaned Mary.

"It must be right," cried Miss Marryat. "Perhaps there's some kind of anagram in it. We can't give up now!"

"Bravo!" said Lord Peter. "That's the spirit. 'Fraid we're in for another outburst of frivolity, Miss Marryat."

"Well, it's been great fun," said Hannah Marryat.

"If you will excuse me," began the deferential voice of Bunter.

"I'd forgotten you, Bunter," said his lordship. "Of course you can put us right—you always can. Where have we gone wrong?"

"I was about to observe, my lord, that the words you mention do not appear to agree with my recollection of the passage in question. In my mother's Bible, my lord, it ran, I fancy, somewhat differently."

Lord Peter closed the volume and looked at the back of it.

"Naturally," he said, "you are right again, of course. This is a Revised Version. It's your fault, Miss Marryat. You *would* have a Revised Version. But can we imagine Uncle Meleager with one? No. Bring me Uncle Meleager's Bible."

"Come and look in the library," cried Miss Marryat, snatching him by the hand and running. "Don't be so dreadfully calm."

On the centre of the library table lay a huge and venerable Bible — reverend in age and tooled leather binding. Lord Peter's hands caressed it, for a noble old book was like a song to his soul. Sobered by its beauty, they turned the yellow pages over:

In the clefts of the rocks, in the secret places of the stairs.

"Miss Marryat," said his lordship, "if your Uncle's will is not concealed in the staircase, then — well, all I can say is, he's played a rotten trick on us," he concluded lamely.

"Shall we try the main staircase, or the little one up to the porch?"

"Oh, the main one, I think. I hope it won't mean pulling it down. No. Somebody would have noticed if Uncle Meleager had done anything drastic in that way. It's probably quite a simple hiding-place. Wait a minute. Let's ask the housekeeper."

Mrs. Meakers was called, and perfectly remembered that about nine months previously Mr. Finch had pointed out to her a "kind of a crack like" on the under surface of the staircase, and had had a man in to fill it up. Certainly, she could point out the exact place. There was the mark of the plaster filling quite clear.

"Hurray!" cried Lord Peter. "Bunter — a chisel or something. Uncle Meleager, Uncle Meleager, we've *got* you! Miss Marryat, I think yours should be the hand to strike the blow.

It's your staircase, you know—at least, if we find the will, so if any destruction has to be done it's up to you."

Breathless they stood round, while with a few blows the new plaster flaked off, disclosing a wide chink in the stonework. Hannah Marryat flung down hammer and chisel and groped in the gap.

"There's something," she gasped. "Lift me up; I can't reach. Oh, it is! it is! it *is* it!" And she withdrew her hand, grasping a long, sealed envelope, bearing the superscription:

POSITIVELY THE **LAST** WILL AND TESTAMENT OF MELEAGER FINCH

Miss Marryat gave a yodel of joy and flung her arms round Lord Peter's neck.

Mary executed a joy-dance. "I'll tell the world," she proclaimed.

"Come and tell mother!" cried Miss Marryat.

Mr. Bunter interposed.

"Your lordship will excuse me," he said firmly, "but your lordship's face is all over charcoal."

"Black but comely," said Lord Peter, "but I submit to your reproof. How clever we've all been. How topping everything is. How rich you are going to be. How late it is and how hungry I am. Yes, Bunter, I will wash my face. Is there anything else I can do for anybody while I feel in the mood?"

"If your lordship would be so kind," said Mr. Bunter, producing a small paper from his pocket, "I should be grateful if you could favour me with a South African quadruped in six letters, beginning with Q."

NOTE: The solution of the crossword will be found on page 287.

THE FANTASTIC HORROR OF THE
CAT IN THE BAG

The Great North Road wound away like a flat, steel-grey ribbon. Up it, with the sun and wind behind them, two black specks moved swiftly. To the yokel in charge of the hay-wagon they were only two of "they dratted motor-cyclists," as they barked and zoomed past him in a rapid succession. A little farther on, a family man, driving delicately with a two-seater side-car, grinned as the sharp rattle of the o.h.v. Norton was succeeded by the feline shriek of an angry Scott Flying-Squirrel. He, too, in bachelor days, had taken a side in that perennial feud. He sighed regretfully as he watched the racing machines dwindle away northwards.

At that abominable and unexpected S-bend across the bridge above Hatfield, the Norton man, in the pride of his heart, turned to wave a defiant hand at his pursuer. In that second, the enormous bulk of a loaded charabanc loomed down upon him from the bridgehead. He wrenched himself away from it in a fierce wobble, and the Scott, cornering melodramatically, with left and right foot-rests alternately skimming the tarmac, gained a few triumphant yards. The Norton leapt forward with wide-open throttle. A party of children, seized with sudden panic, rushed helter-skelter across the road. The Scott lurched through them in drunken swerves. The road was clear, and the chase settled down once more.

It is not known why motorists, who sing the joys of the open road, spend so much petrol every week-end grinding their way to Southend and Brighton and Margate, in the stench of each other's exhausts, one hand on the horn and one foot on the brake, their eyes starting from their orbits in the nerve-racking search for cops, corners, blind turnings, and cross-road suicides. They ride in a baffled fury, hating each other. They arrive with shattered nerves and fight for parking places. They return, blinded by the headlights of fresh arrivals, whom they hate even worse than they hate each other. And all the time the Great North Road winds away like a long, flat, steel-grey ribbon—a surface like a racetrack, without traps, without hedges, without side-roads, and without traffic. True, it leads to nowhere in particular; but, after all, one pub is very much like another.

The tarmac reeled away, mile after mile. The sharp turn to the right at Baldrock, the involute intricacies of Biggleswade, with its multiplication of sign-posts, gave temporary check, but brought the pursuer no nearer. Through Tempsford at full speed, with bellowing horn and exhaust, then, screaming like a hurricane past the R.A.C. post where the road forks in from Bedford. The Norton rider again glanced back; the Scott rider again sounded his horn ferociously. Flat as a chessboard, dyke and field revolved about the horizon.

The constable at Eaton Socon was by no means an anti-motor fiend. In fact, he had just alighted from his pushbike to pass the time of day with the A.A. man on point duty at the cross-roads. But he was just and God-fearing. The sight of two maniacs careering at seventy miles an hour into his protectorate was more than he could be expected to countenance—the more, that the local magistrate happened to be passing at that very moment in a pony-trap. He advanced to the middle of the road, spreading his arms in a majestic manner. The Norton rider looked, saw the road beyond complicated by the pony-trap and a traction-engine, and resigned himself to the inevitable. He flung the throttle-lever back, stamped on his squealing brakes, and skidded to a standstill. The Scott, having had notice, came up mincingly, with a voice like a pleased kitten.

"Now, then," said the constable, in a tone of reproof, "ain't you got no more sense than to come drivin' into the town at a 'undred mile an hour? This ain't Brooklands, you know. I never see anything like it. 'Ave to take your names and numbers, if *you* please. You'll bear witness, Mr. Nadgett, as they was doin' over eighty."

The A.A. man, after a swift glance over the two sets of handlebars to assure himself that the black sheep were not of his flock, said, with an air of impartial accuracy, "About sixty-six and a half, I should say, if you was to ask me in court."

"Look here, you blighter," said the Scott man indignantly to the Norton man, "why the hell couldn't you stop when you heard me hoot? I've been chasing you with your beastly bag nearly thirty miles. Why can't you look after your own rotten luggage?"

He indicated a small, stout bag, tied with string to his own carrier.

"That?" said the Norton man, with scorn. "What do you mean? It's not mine. Never saw it in my life."

This bare-faced denial threatened to render the Scott rider speechless.

"Of all the —" he gasped. "Why, you crimson idiot, I saw it fall off, just the other side of Hatfield. I yelled and blew like fury. I suppose that overhead gear of yours makes so much noise, you can't hear anything else. I take the trouble to pick the thing up, and go after you, and all you do is to race off like a lunatic and run me into a cop. Fat lot of thanks one gets for trying to be decent to fools on the road."

"That ain't neither here nor there," said the policeman. "Your licence, please, sir."

"Here you are," said the Scott man, ferociously flapping out his pocket-book. "My name's Walters, and it's the last time I'll try to do anybody a good turn, you can lay your shirt."

"Walters," said the constable, entering the particulars laboriously in his note-book, "and Simpkins. You'll 'ave your summonses in doo course. It'll be for about a week 'ence, on Monday or thereabouts, I shouldn't wonder."

"Another forty bob gone west," growled Mr. Simpkins, toying with his throttle. "Oh, well, can't be helped, I suppose."

"Forty bob?" snorted the constable. "What do *you* think? Furious driving to the common danger, that's wot it is. You'll be lucky to get off with five quid apiece."

"Oh, blast!" said the other, stamping furiously on the kick-starter. The engine roared into life, but Mr. Walters dexterously swung his machine across the Norton's path.

"Oh, no, you don't," he said viciously. "You jolly well take your bleeding bag, and no nonsense. I tell you, I *saw* it fall off."

"Now, no language," began the constable, when he suddenly became aware that the A.A. man was staring in a very odd manner at the bag and making signs to him.

" 'Ullo," he demanded, "wot's the matter with the — bleedin' bag, did you say? 'Ere, I'd like to 'ave a look at that 'ere bag, sir, if you don't mind."

"It's nothing to do with me," said Mr. Walters, handing it over. "I saw it fall off and —" His voice died away in his throat, and his eyes became fixed upon one corner of the bag, where something damp and horrible was seeping darkly through.

"Did you notice this 'ere corner when you picked it up?" asked the constable. He prodded it gingerly and looked at his fingers.

"I don't know — no — not particularly," stammered Walters. "I didn't notice anything. I — I expect it burst when it hit the road."

The constable probed the split seam in silence, and then turned hurriedly round to wave away a couple of young women who had stopped to stare. The A.A. man peered curiously, and then started back with a sensation of sickness.

"Ow, Gawd!" he gasped. "It's curly — it's a woman's."

"It's not me," screamed Simpkins. "I swear to heaven it's not mine. This man's trying to put it across me."

"Me?" gasped Walters. "Me? Why, you filthy, murdering brute, I tell you I saw it fall off your carrier. No wonder you blinded off when you saw me coming. Arrest him, constable. Take him away to prison—"

"Hullo, officer!" said a voice behind them. "What's all the excitement? You haven't seen a motor-cyclist go by with a little bag on his carrier, I suppose?"

A big open car with an unnaturally long bonnet had slipped up to them, silent as an owl. The whole agitated party with one accord turned upon the driver.

"Would this be it, sir?"

The motorist pushed off his goggles, disclosing a long, narrow nose and a pair of rather cynical-looking grey eyes.

"It looks rather—" he began; and then, catching sight of the horrid relic protruding from one corner, "In God's name," he inquired, "what's that?"

"That's what we'd like to know, sir," said the constable grimly.

"H'm," said the motorist, "I seem to have chosen an uncommonly suitable moment for inquirin' after my bag. Tactless. To say now that it is not my bag is simple, though in no way convincing As a matter of fact, it is not mine, and I may say that, if it had been, I should not have been at any pains to pursue it."

The constable scratched his head.

"Both these gentlemen—" he began.

The two cyclists burst into simultaneous and heated disclaimers. By this time a small crowd had collected, which the A.A. scout helpfully tried to shoo away.

"You'll all 'ave to come with me to the station," said the harassed constable. "Can't stand 'ere 'oldin' up the traffic. No tricks, now. You wheel them bikes, and I'll come in the car with you, sir."

"But supposing I was to let her rip and kidnap you," said the motorist, with a grin. "Where'd you be? Here," he added, turning to the A.A. man, "can you handle this outfit?"

"You bet," said the scout, his eye running lovingly over the long sweep of the exhaust and the rakish lines of the car.

"Right. Hop in. Now, officer, you can toddle along with the other suspects and keep an eye on them. Wonderful head I've got for detail. By the way, that foot-brake's on the fierce side. Don't bully it, or you'll surprise yourself."

The lock of the bag was forced at the police-station in the midst of an excitement unparalleled in the calm annals of Eaton Socon, and the dreadful contents laid reverently upon a table. Beyond a quantity of cheese-cloth in which they had been wrapped, there was nothing to supply any clue to the mystery.

"Now," said the superintendent, "what do you gentlemen know about this?"

"Nothing whatever," said Mr. Simpkins, with a ghastly countenance, "except that this man tried to palm it off on me."

"I saw it fall off this man's carrier just the other side of Hatfield," repeated Mr. Walters firmly, "and I rode after him for thirty miles trying to stop him. That's all I know about it, and I wish to God I'd never touched the beastly thing."

"Nor do I know anything about it personally," said the car-owner, "but I fancy I know what it is."

"What's that?" asked the superintendent sharply.

"I rather imagine it's the head of the Finsbury Park murder—though, mind you, that's only a guess."

"That's just what I've been thinking myself," agreed the superintendent, glancing at a daily paper which lay on his desk, its headlines lurid with the details of that very horrid crime, "and, if so, you are to be congratulated, constable, on a very important capture."

"Thank you, sir," said the gratified officer, saluting.

"Now I'd better take all your statements," said the superintendent. "No, no; I'll hear the constable first. Yes, Briggs?"

The constable, the A.A. man, and the two motor-cyclists having given their versions of the story, the superintendent turned to the motorist.

"And what have you got to say about it?" he inquired. "First of all, your name and address."

The other produced a card, which the superintendent copied out and returned to him respectfully.

"A bag of mine, containing some valuable jewellery, was stolen from my car yesterday, in Piccadilly," began the motorist. "It is very much like this, but has a cipher lock. I made inquiries through Scotland Yard, and was informed today that a bag of precisely similar appearance had been cloak-roomed yesterday afternoon at Paddington, main line. I hurried round there, and was told by the clerk that just before the police warning came through the bag had been claimed by a man in motor-cycling kit. A porter said he saw the man leave the station, and a loiterer observed him riding off on a motor-bicycle. That was about an hour before. It seemed pretty hopeless, as, of course, nobody had noticed even the make of the bike, let alone the number. Fortunately, however, there was a smart little girl. The smart little girl had been dawdling round outside the station, and had heard a motor-cyclist ask a taxi-driver the quickest route to Finchley. I left the police hunting for the taxi-driver, and started off, and in Finchley I found an intelligent boy-scout. He had seen a motor-cyclist with a bag on the carrier, and had waved and shouted to him that the strap was loose. The cyclist had got off and tightened the strap, and gone straight on up the road towards Chipping Barnet. The boy hadn't been near enough to identify the machine—the only thing he knew for certain was that it wasn't a Douglas, his brother having one of that sort. At Barnet I got an odd little story of a man in a motor-coat who had staggered into a pub with a ghastly white face and drunk two double brandies and gone out and ridden off furiously. Number?—of course not. The barmaid told me. *She* didn't notice the number. After that it was a tale of furious driving all along the road. After Hatfield, I got the story of a road-race. And here we are."

"It seems to me, my lord," said the superintendent, "that the furious driving can't have been all on one side."

"I admit it," said the other, "though I do plead in extenuation that I spared the women and children and hit up the miles in the wide, open spaces. The point at the moment is—"

"Well, my lord," said the superintendent, "I've got your

story, and, if it's all right, it can be verified by inquiry at Paddington and Finchley and so on. Now, as for these two gentlemen—"

"It's perfectly obvious," broke in Mr. Walters, "the bag dropped off this man's carrier, and, when he saw me coming after him with it, he thought it was a good opportunity to saddle me with the cursed thing. Nothing could be clearer."

"It's a lie," said Mr. Simpkins. "Here's this fellow has got hold of the bag—I don't say how, but I can guess—and he has the bright idea of shoving the blame on me. It's easy enough to *say* a thing's fallen off a man's carrier. Where's the proof? Where's the strap? If his story's true, you'd find the broken strap on my bus. The bag *was* on *his* machine—tied on, tight."

"Yes, with string," retorted the other. "If I'd gone and murdered someone and run off with their head, do you think I'd be such an ass as to tie it on with a bit of two-penny twine? The strap's worked loose and fallen off on the road somewhere; that's what happened to that."

"Well, look here," said the man addressed as "my lord," "I've got an idea for what it's worth. Suppose, superintendent, you turn out as many of your men as you think adequate to keep an eye on three desperate criminals, and we all tool down to Hatfield together. I can take two in my bus at a pinch, and no doubt you have a police car. If this thing *did* fall off the carrier, somebody beside Mr. Walters may have seen it fall."

"They didn't," said Mr. Simpkins.

"There wasn't a soul," said Mr. Walters, "but how do *you* know there wasn't, eh? I thought you didn't know anything about it."

"I mean, it didn't fall off, so nobody *could* have seen it," gasped the other.

"Well, my lord," said the superintendent, "I'm inclined to accept your suggestion, as it gives us a chance of inquiring into your story at the same time. Mind you, I'm not saying I doubt it, you being who you are. I've read about some of your detective work, my lord, and very smart I considered it. But, still, it wouldn't be my duty not to get corroborative evidence if possible."

"Good egg! Quite right," said his lordship. "Forward the light brigade. We can do it easily in — that is to say, at the legal rate of progress it needn't take us much over an hour and a half."

About three-quarters of an hour later, the racing car and the police car loped quietly side by side into Hatfield. Henceforward, the four-seater, in which Walters and Simpkins sat glaring at each other, took the lead, and presently Walters waved his hand and both cars came to a stop.

"It was just about here, as near as I can remember, that it fell off," he said. "Of course, there's no trace of it now."

"You're quite sure as there wasn't a strap fell off with it?" suggested the superintendent, "because, you see, there must 'a' been something holding it on."

"Of course there wasn't a strap," said Simpkins, white with passion. "You haven't any business to ask him leading questions like that."

"Wait a minute," said Walters slowly. "No, there was no strap. But I've got a sort of recollection of seeing something on the road about a quarter of a mile farther up."

"It's a lie!" screamed Simpkins. "He's inventing it."

"Just about where we passed that man with the side-car a minute or two ago," said his lordship. "I told you we ought to have stopped and asked if we could help him, superintendent. Courtesy of the road, you know, and all that."

"He couldn't have told us anything," said the superintendent. "He'd probably only just stopped."

"I'm not so sure," said the other. "Didn't you notice what he was doing? Oh, dear, dear, where were your eyes? Hullo! here he comes."

He sprang out into the road and waved to the rider, who, seeing four policemen, thought it better to pull up.

"Excuse me," said his lordship. "Thought we'd just like to stop you and ask if you were all right, and all that sort of thing, you know. Wanted to stop in passing, throttle jammed open, couldn't shut the confounded thing. Little trouble, what?"

"Oh, yes, perfectly all right, thanks, except that I would be glad if you could spare a gallon of petrol. Tank came adrift. Beastly nuisance. Had a bit of a struggle. Happily, Providence placed a broken strap in my way and I've fixed it. Split a bit, though, where that bolt came off. Lucky not to have an explosion, but there's a special cherub for motor-cyclists."

"Strap, eh?" said the superintendent. "Afraid I'll have to trouble you to let me have a look at that."

"What?" said the other. "And just as I've got the damned thing fixed? What the —? All right, dear, all right" —to his passenger. "Is it something serious, officer?"

"Afraid so, sir. Sorry to trouble you."

"Hi!" yelled one of the policemen, neatly fielding Mr. Simpkins as he was taking a dive over the back of the car. "No use doin' that. You're for it, my lad."

"No doubt about it," said the superintendent trimphantly, snatching at the strap which the side-car rider held out to him. "Here's his name on it, 'J. SIMPKINS,' written on in ink as large as life. Very much obliged to *you*, sir, I'm sure. You've helped us effect a very important capture."

"No! *Who* is it?" cried the girl in the side-car. "How frightfully thrilling! Is it a murder?"

"Look in your paper tomorrow, miss," said the superintendent, "and you may see something. Here, Briggs, better put the handcuffs on him."

"And how about my tank?" said the man mournfully. "It's all right for you to be excited, Babs, but you'll have to get out and help push."

"Oh, no," said his lordship. "Here's a strap. A *much* nicer strap. A really superior strap. And petrol. *And* a pocket-flask. Everything a young man ought to have. And, when you're in town, mind you both look me up. Lord Peter Wimsey, 110A Piccadilly. Delighted to see you any time. Chin, chin!"

"Cheerio!" said the other, wiping his lips and much mollified. "Only too charmed to be of use. Remember it in my favour, officer, next time you catch me speeding."

"Very fortunate we spotted him," said the superintendent complacently, as they continued their way into Hatfield. "Quite providential, as you might say."

"I'll come across with it," said the wretched Simpkins, sitting handcuffed in the Hatfield police-station. "I swear to God I know nothing whatever about it—about the murder, I mean. There's a man I know who has a jewellery business in Birmingham. I don't know him very well. In fact, I only met him at Southend last Easter, and we got pally. His name's Owen— Thomas Owen. He wrote me yesterday and said he'd accidentally left a bag in the cloakroom at Paddington and asked if I'd take it out—he enclosed the ticket—and bring it up next time I came that way. I'm in transport service, you see—you've got my card—and I'm always up and down the country. As it happened, I was just going up in that direction with this Norton, so I fetched the thing out at lunch-time and started off with it. I didn't notice the date on the cloakroom ticket. I know there wasn't anything to pay on it, so it can't have been there long. Well, it all went just as you said up to Finchley, and there that boy told me my strap was loose and I went to tighten it up. And then I noticed that the corner of the bag was split, and it was damp—and—well, I saw what you saw. That sort of turned me over, and I lost my head. The only thing I could think of was to get rid of it, quick. I remembered there were a lot of lonely stretches on the Great North Road, so I cut the strap nearly through—that was when I stopped for that drink at Barnet—and then, when I thought there wasn't anybody in sight, I just reached back and gave it a tug, and it went—strap and all; I hadn't put it through the slots. It fell off, just like a great weight dropping off my mind. I suppose Walters must have just come round into sight as it fell. I had to slow down a mile or two farther on for some sheep going into a field, and then I heard him hooting at me—and—oh, my God!"

He groaned, and buried his head in his hands.

"I see," said the Eaton Socon superintendent. "Well, that's your statement. Now, about this Thomas Owen—"

"Oh," cried Lord Peter Wimsey, "never mind Thomas Owen. He's not the man you want. You can't suppose that a bloke who'd committed a murder would want a fellow tailin' after him to Birmingham with the head. It stands to reason that was intended to stay in Paddington cloakroom till the ingenious perpetrator had skipped, or till it was unrecognizable, or both. Which, by the way, is where we'll find those family heirlooms of mine, which your engaging friend Mr. Owen lifted out of my car. Now, Mr. Simpkins, just pull yourself together and tell us who was standing next to you at the cloakroom when you took out that bag. Try hard to remember, because this jolly little island is no place for him, and he'll be taking the next boat while we stand talking."

"I can't remember," moaned Simpkins. "I didn't notice. My head's all in a whirl."

"Never mind. Go back. Think quietly. Make a picture of yourself getting off your machine—leaning it up against something—"

"No, I put it on the stand."

"Good! That's the way. Now, think—you're taking the cloakroom ticket out of your pocket and going up—trying to attract the man's attention."

"I couldn't at first. There was an old lady trying to cloakroom a canary, and a very bustling man in a hurry with some golf-clubs. He was quite rude to a quiet little man with a—by Jove! yes, a hand-bag like that one. Yes, that's it. The timid man had had it on the counter quite a long time, and the big man pushed him aside. I don't know what happened, quite, because mine was handed out to me just then. The big man pushed his luggage in front of both of us and I had to reach over it—and I suppose—yes, I must have taken the wrong one. Good God! Do you mean to say that that timid little insignificant-looking man was a murderer?"

"Lots of 'em like that," put in the Hatfield superintendent. "But what was he like—come!"

"He was only about five foot five, and he wore a soft hat and a long, dust-coloured coat. He was very ordinary, with rather weak, prominent eyes, I think, but I'm not sure I should know him again. Oh, wait a minute! I do remember one thing. He had an odd scar—crescent-shaped—under his left eye."

"That settles it," said Lord Peter. "I thought as much. Did you recognize the—the face when we took it out, superintendent? No? I did. It was Dahlia Dallmeyer, the actress, who is supposed to have sailed for America last week. And the short man with the crescent-shaped scar is her husband, Philip Storey. Sordid tale and all that. She ruined him, treated him like dirt, and was unfaithful to him, but it looks as though he had had the last word in the argument. And now, I imagine, the Law will have the last word with him. Get busy on the wires, superintendent, and you might ring up the Paddington people and tell 'em to let me have my bag, before Mr. Thomas Owen tumbles to it that there's been a slight mistake."

"Well, anyhow," said Mr. Walters, extending a magnanimous hand to the abashed Mr. Simpkins, "it was a top-hole race—well worth a summons. We must have a return match one of these days."

Early the following morning a little, insignificant-looking man stepped aboard the trans-Atlantic liner *Volucria*. At the head of the gangway two men blundered into him. The younger of the two, who carried a small bag, was turning to apologize, when a light of recognition flashed across his face.

"Why, if it isn't Mr. Storey!" he exclaimed loudly. "Where are you off to? I haven't seen you for an age."

"I'm afraid," said Philip Storey, "I haven't the pleasure—"

"Cut it out," said the other, laughing. "I'd know that scar of yours anywhere. Going out to the States?"

"Well, yes," said the other, seeing that his acquaintance's boisterous manner was attracting attention. "I beg your pardon. It's Lord Peter Wimsey, isn't it? Yes, I'm joining the wife out there."

"And how is she?" inquired Wimsey, steering the way into the bar and sitting down at a table. "Left this week didn't she? I saw it in the papers."

"Yes. She's just cabled me to join her. We're—er—taking a holiday in—er—the lakes. Very pleasant there in summer."

"Cabled you, did she? And so here we are on the same boat. Odd how things turn out, what? I only got my sailing orders at the last minute. Chasing criminals—my hobby, you know."

"Oh, really?" Mr. Storey licked his lips.

"Yes. This is Detective-Inspector Parker of Scotland Yard—great pal of mine. Yes. Very unpleasant matter, annoying and all that. Bag that ought to have been reposin' peacefully at Paddington Station turns up at Eaton Socon. No business there, what?"

He smacked the bag on the table so violently that the lock sprang open.

Storey leapt to his feet with a shriek, flinging his arms across the opening of the bag as though to hide its contents.

"How did you get that?" he screamed. "Eaton Socon? It— I never—"

"It's mine," said Wimsey quietly, as the wretched man sank back, realizing that he had betrayed himself. "Some jewellery of my mother's. What did you think it was?"

Detective Parker touched his charge gently on the shoulder.

"You needn't answer that," he said. "I arrest you, Philip Storey, for the murder of your wife. Anything that you say may be used against you."

THE UNPRINCIPLED AFFAIR OF THE PRACTICAL JOKER

The *Zambesi*, they said, was expected to dock at six in the morning. Mrs. Ruyslaender booked a bedroom at the Magnifical, with despair in her heart. A bare nine hours and she would be greeting her husband. After that would begin the sickening period of waiting—it might be days, it might be weeks, possibly even months—for the inevitable discovery.

The reception-clerk twirled the register towards her. Mechanically, as she signed it, she glanced at the preceding entry:

"Lord Peter Wimsey and valet—London—Suite 24."

Mrs. Ruyslaender's heart seemed to stop for a second. Was it possible that, even now, God had left a loophole? She expected little from Him—all her life he had shown Himself a sufficiently stern creditor. It was fantastic to base the frailest hope on this signature of a man she had never even seen.

Yet the name remained in her mind while she dined in her own room. She dismissed her maid presently, and sat for a long time looking at her own haggard reflection in the mirror. Twice she rose and went to the door—then turned back, calling herself a fool. The third time she turned the handle quickly and hurried down the corridor, without giving herself time to think.

A large golden arrow at the corner directed her to Suite 24. It was eleven o'clock, and nobody was within view. Mrs. Ruyslaender gave a sharp knock on Lord Peter Wimsey's door and stood back, waiting, with the sort of desperate relief one experiences after hearing a dangerous letter thump the bottom of the pillar-box. Whatever the adventure, she was committed to it.

The manservant was of the imperturbable sort. He neither invited nor rejected, but stood respectfully upon the threshold.

"Lord Peter Wimsey?" murmured Mrs. Ruyslaender.

"Yes, madam."

"Could I speak to him for a moment?"

"His lordship has just retired, madam. If you will step in, I will inquire."

Mrs. Ruyslaender followed him into one of those palatial sitting-rooms which the Magnifical provides for the wealthy pilgrim.

"Will you take a seat, madam?"

The man stepped noiselessly to the bedroom door and passed, shutting it behind him. The lock, however, failed to catch, and Mrs. Ruyslaender caught the conversation.

"Pardon me, my lord, a lady has called. She mentioned no appointment, so I considered it better to acquaint your lordship."

"Excellent discretion," said a voice. It had a slow, sarcastic intonation, which brought a painful flush to Mrs. Ruyslaender's cheek. "I never make appointments. Do I know the lady?"

"No, my lord. But—hem—I know her by sight, my lord. It is Mrs. Ruyslaender."

"Oh, the diamond merchant's wife. Well, find out tactfully what it's all about, and, unless it's urgent, ask her to call tomorrow."

The valet's remark was inaudible, but the reply was:

"Don't be coarse, Bunter."

The valet returned.

"His lordship desires me to ask you, madam, in what way he can be of service to you?"

"Will you say to him that I have heard of him in connexion with the Attenbury diamond case, and am anxious to ask his advice."

"Certainly, madam. May I suggest that, as his lordship is greatly fatigued, he would be better able to assist you after he has slept."

"If tomorrow would have done, I would not have thought of disturbing him tonight. Tell him, I am aware of the trouble I am giving—"

"Excuse me one moment, madam."

This time the door shut properly. After a short interval Bunter returned to say, "His lordship will be with you immediately, madam," and to place a decanter of wine and a box of Sobranies beside her.

Mrs. Ruyslaender lit a cigarette, but had barely sampled its flavour when she was aware of a soft step beside her. Looking round, she perceived a young man, attired in a mauve dressing-gown of great splendour, from beneath the hem of which peeped coyly a pair of primrose silk pyjamas.

"You must think it very strange of me, thrusting myself on you at this hour," she said, with a nervous laugh.

Lord Peter put his head on one side.

"Don't know the answer to that," he said. "If I say, 'Not at all,' it sounds abandoned. If I say, 'Yes, very,' it's rude. Supposin' we give it a miss, what? and you tell me what I can do for you."

Mrs. Ruyslaender hesitated. Lord Peter was not what she had expected. She noted the sleek, straw-coloured hair, brushed flat back from a rather sloping forehead, the ugly, lean, arched nose, and the faintly foolish smile, and her heart sank within her.

"I—I'm afraid it's ridiculous of me to suppose you can help me," she began.

"Always my unfortunate appearance," moaned Lord

Peter, with such alarming acumen as to double her discomfort. "Would it invite confidence more, d'you suppose, if I dyed my hair black an' grew a Newgate fringe? It's very tryin', you can't think, always to look as if one's name was Algy."

"I only meant," said Mrs. Ruyslaender, "that I don't think *anybody* could possibly help. But I saw your name in the hotel book, and it seemed just a chance."

Lord Peter filled the glasses and sat down.

"Carry on," he said cheerfully; "it sounds interestin'."

Mrs. Ruyslaender took the plunge.

"My husband," she explained, "is Henry Ruyslaender, the diamond merchant. We came over from Kimberley ten years ago, and settled in England. He spends several months in Africa every year on business, and I am expecting him back on the *Zambesi* tomorrow morning. Now, this is the trouble. Last year he gave me a magnificent diamond necklace of a hundred and fifteen stones—"

"The Light of Africa—I know," said Wimsey.

She looked a little surprised, but assented. "The necklace has been stolen from me, and I can't hope to conceal the loss from him. No duplicate would deceive him for an instant."

She paused, and Lord Peter prompted gently:

"You have come to me, I presume, because it is not to be a police matter. Will you tell me quite frankly why?"

"The police would be useless. I know who took it."

"Yes?"

"There is a man we both know slightly—a man called Paul Melville."

Lord Peter's eyes narrowed. "M'm, yes, I fancy I've seen him about the clubs. New Army, but transferred himself into the Regulars. Dark. Showy. Bit of an ampelopsis, what?"

"Ampelopsis?"

"Suburban plant that climbs by suction. *You* know—first year, tender little shoots—second year, fine show—next year, all over the shop. Now tell me I am rude."

Mrs. Ruyslaender giggled. "Now you mention it, he is *exactly* like an ampelopsis. What a relief to be able to think of him as that . . . Well, he is some sort of distant relation of my husband's. He called one evening when I was alone. We talked about jewels, and I brought down my jewel-box and showed him the Light of Africa. He knows a good deal about stones. I was in and out of the room two or three times, but didn't think to lock up the box. After he left, I was putting the things away, and I opened the jeweller's case the diamonds were in—and they had gone!"

"H'm—pretty barefaced. Look here, Mrs. Ruyslaender, you agree he's an ampelopsis, but you won't call in the police. Honestly, now—forgive me; you're askin' my advice, you know—is he worth botherin' about?"

"It's not that," said the woman in a low tone. "Oh, no! But he took something else as well. He took—a portrait—a small painting set with diamonds."

"Oh!"

"Yes. It was in a secret drawer in the jewel-box. I can't imagine how he knew it was there, but the box was an old casket, belonging to my husband's family, and I fancy he must have known about the drawer and—well, thought that investigation might prove profitable. Anyway, the evening the diamonds went the portrait went too, and he knows I daren't try to get the necklace back because they'd both be found together."

"Was there something more than just the portrait, then? A portrait in itself isn't necessarily hopeless of explanation. It was given you to take care of, say."

"The names were on it—and—and an inscription which nothing, *nothing* could ever explain away. A—a passage from Petronius."

"Oh, dear!" said Lord Peter, "dear me, yes. Rather a lively author."

"I was married very young," said Mrs. Ruyslaender, "and my husband and I have never got on well. Then one year, when he was in Africa, it all happened. We were wonderful— and shameless. It came to an end. I was bitter. I wish I had not been. He left me, you see, and I couldn't forgive it. I prayed day and night for revenge. Only now—I don't want it to be through me!"

"Wait a moment," said Wimsey, "you mean that, if the diamonds are found and the portrait is found too, all this story is bound to come out."

"My husband would get a divorce. He would never forgive me—or him. It is not so much that I mind paying the price myself, but—"

She clenched her hands.

"I have cursed him again and again, and the clever girl who married him. She played her card so well. This would ruin them both."

"But if *you* were the instrument of vengeance," said Wimsey gently, "you would hate yourself. And it would be terrible to you because he would hate you. A woman like you couldn't stoop to get your own back. I see that. If God makes a thunderbolt, how awful and satisfying—if you help to make a beastly row, what a rotten business it would be."

"You seem to understand," said Mrs. Ruyslaender. "How unusual."

"I understand perfectly. Though let me tell you," said Wimsey, with a wry little twist of the lips, "that it's sheer foolishness for a woman to have a sense of honour in such matters. It only gives her excruciating pain, and nobody expects it, anyway. Look here, don't let's get all worked up. You certainly shan't have your vengeance thrust upon you by an ampelopsis. Why should you? Nasty fellow. We'll have him up—root, branch, and little suckers. Don't worry. Let's see. My business here will only take a day. Then I've got to get to know Melville—say a week. Then I've got to get the doings—say another week, provided he hasn't sold them yet, which isn't likely. Can you hold your husband off 'em for a fortnight, d'you think?"

"Oh, yes. I'll say they're in the country, or being cleaned, or something. But do you really think you can—?"

"I'll have a jolly good try, anyhow, Mrs. Ruyslaender. Is the fellow hard up, to start stealing diamonds?"

"I fancy he has got into debt over horses lately. And possibly poker."

"Oh! Poker player, is he? That makes an excellent excuse for gettin' to know him. Well, cheer up—we'll get the goods, even if we have to buy 'em. But we won't, if we can help it. Bunter!"

"My lord?" The valet appeared from the inner room.

"Just go an' give the 'All Clear,' will you?"

Mr. Bunter accordingly stepped into the passage, and, having seen an old gentleman safely away to the bathroom and a young lady in a pink kimono pop her head out of an adjacent door and hurriedly pop it back on beholding him, blew his nose with a loud, trumpeting sound.

"Good night," said Mrs. Ruyslaender, "and thank you."

She slipped back to her room unobserved.

"Whatever has induced you, my dear boy," said Colonel Marchbanks, "to take up with that very objectionable fellow Melville?"

"Diamonds," said Lord Peter. "Do you find him so, really?"

"Perfectly dreadful man," said the Hon. Frederick Arbuthnot. "Hearts. What did you want to go and get him a room here for? This used to be quite a decent club."

"Two clubs?" said Sir Impey Biggs, who had been ordering a whisky, and had only caught the last word.

"No, no, one heart."

"I beg your pardon. Well, partner, how about spades? Perfectly good suit."

"Pass," said the Colonel. "I don't know what the Army's coming to nowadays."

"No trumps," said Wimsey. "It's all right, children. Trust your Uncle Pete. Come on, Freddy, how many of those hearts are you going to shout for?"

"None, the Colonel havin' let me down so 'orrid," said the Hon. Freddy.

"Cautious blighter. All content? Righty-ho! Bring out your dead, partner. Oh, very pretty indeed. We'll make it a

slam this time. I'm rather glad to hear that expression of opinion from you, Colonel, because I particularly want you and
Biggy to hang on this evening and take a hand with Melville
and me."

"What happens to me?" inquired the Hon. Freddy.

"You have an engagement and go home early, dear old
thing. I've specially invited friend Melville to meet the
redoubtable Colonel Marchbanks and our greatest criminal
lawyer. Which hand am I supposed to be playin' this from?
Oh, yes. Come on, Colonel—you've got to hike that old king
out some time, why not now?"

"It's a plot," said Mr. Arbuthnot, with an exaggerated
expression of mystery. "Carry on, don't mind me."

"I take it you have your own reasons for cultivating the
man," said Sir Impey.

"The rest are mine, I fancy. Well, yes, I have. You and the
Colonel would really do me a favour by letting Melville cut in
tonight."

"If you wish it," growled the Colonel, "but I hope the
impudent young beggar won't presume on the acquaintance."

"I'll see to that," said his lordship. "Your cards, Freddy.
Who had the ace of hearts? Oh! I had it myself, of course.
Our honours . . . Hullo! Evenin', Melville."

The ampelopsis was rather a good-looking creature in his
own way. Tall and bronzed, with a fine row of very persuasive
teeth. He greeted Wimsey and Arbuthnot heartily, the Colonel
with a shade too much familiarity, and expressed himself
delighted to be introduced to Sir Impey Biggs.

"You're just in time to hold Freddy's hand," said Wimsey;
"he's got a date. Not his little paddy-paw, I don't mean—but
the dam' rotten hand he generally gets dealt him. Joke."

"Oh, well," said the obedient Freddy, rising, "I s'pose I'd
better make a noise like a hoop and roll away. Night, night,
everybody."

Melville took his place, and the game continued with vary-
ing fortunes for two hours, at the end of which time Colonel

Marchbanks, who had suffered much under his partner's eloquent theory of the game, was beginning to wilt visibly.

Wimsey yawned.

"Gettin' a bit bored, Colonel? Wish they'd invent somethin' to liven this game up a bit."

"Oh, bridge is a one-horse show, anyway," said Melville.
"Why not have a little flutter at poker, Colonel? Do you all the
good in the world. What d'you say, Biggs?"

Sir Impey turned on Wimsey a thoughtful eye, accustomed to the sizing-up of witnesses. Then he replied:

"I'm quite willing, if the others are."

"Damn good idea," said Lord Peter. "Come now, Colonel,
be a sport. You'll find the chips in that drawer, I think. I
always lose money at poker, but what's the odds so long as
you're happy. Let's have a new pack."

"Any limit?"

"What do *you* say, Colonel?"

The Colonel proposed a twenty-shilling limit. Melville,
with a grimace, amended this to one-tenth of the pool. The
amendment was carried and the cards cut, the deal falling to
the Colonel.

Contrary to his own prophecy, Wimsey began by winning
considerably, and grew so garrulously imbecile in the process
that even the experienced Melville began to wonder whether
this indescribable fatuity was the cloak of ignorance or the
mask of the hardened poker-player. Soon, however, he was
reassured. The luck came over to his side, and he found himself winning hands down, steadily from Sir Impey and the
Colonel, who played cautiously and took little risk — heavily
from Wimsey, who appeared reckless and slightly drunk, and
was staking foolishly on quite impossible cards.

"I never knew such luck as yours, Melville," said Sir
Impey, when that young man had scooped in the proceeds
from a handsome straight-flush.

"My turn tonight, yours tomorrow," said Melville, pushing the cards across to Biggs, whose deal it was.

Colonel Marchbanks required one card. Wimsey laughed vacantly and demanded an entirely fresh hand; Biggs asked for three; and Melville, after a pause for consideration, took one.

It seemed as though everybody had something respectable this time—though Wimsey was not to be depended upon, frequently going the limit upon a pair of jacks in order, as he expressed it, to keep the pot a-boiling. He became peculiarly obstinate now, throwing his chips in with a flushed face, in spite of Melville's confident air.

The Colonel got out, and after a short time Biggs followed his example. Melville held on till the pool mounted to something under a hundred pounds, when Wimsey suddenly turned restive and demanded to see him.

"Four kings," said Melville.

"Blast you!" said Lord Peter, laying down four queens. "No holdin' this feller tonight, is there? Here, take the ruddy cards, Melville, and give somebody else a look in, will you."

He shuffled them as he spoke, and handed them over. Melville dealt, satisfied the demands of the other three players, and was in the act of taking three new cards for himself, when Wimsey gave a sudden exclamation, and shot a swift hand across the table.

"Hullo! Melville," he said, in a chill tone which bore no resemblance to his ordinary speech, "what exactly does this mean?"

He lifted Melville's left arm clear of the table and, with a sharp gesture, shook it. From the sleeve something fluttered to the table and glided away to the floor. Colonel Marchbanks picked it up, and in a dreadful silence laid the joker on the table.

"Good God!" said Sir Impey.

"You young blackguard!" gasped the Colonel, recovering speech.

"What the hell do you mean by this?" gasped Melville, with a face like chalk. "How dare you! This is a trick—a plant—" A horrible fury gripped him. "You dare to say that I have been cheating. You liar! You filthy sharper. You put it there. I tell you, gentlemen," he cried, looking desperately round the table, "he must have put it there."

"Come, come," said Colonel Marchbanks, "no good carryin' on that way, Melville. Dear me, no good at all. Only makes matters worse. We all saw it, you know. Dear, dear, I don't know what the Army's coming to."

"Do you mean you believe it?" shrieked Melville. "For God's sake, Wimsey, is this a joke or what? Biggs—you've got a head on your shoulders—are you going to believe this half-drunk fool and this doddering old idiot who ought to be in his grave?"

"That language won't do you any good, Melville," said Sir Impey. "I'm afraid we all saw it clearly enough."

"I've been suspectin' this some time, y'know," said Wimsey. "That's why I asked you two to stay tonight. We don't want to make a public row, but—"

"Gentlemen," said Melville more soberly, "I swear to you that I am absolutely innocent of this ghastly thing. Can't you believe me?"

"I can believe the evidence of my own eyes, sir," said the Colonel, with some heat.

"For the good of the club," said Wimsey, "this couldn't go on, but—also for the good of the club—I think we should all prefer the matter to be quietly arranged. In the face of what Sir Impey and the Colonel can witness, Melville, I'm afraid your protestations are not likely to be credited."

Melville looked from the soldier's face to that of the great criminal lawyer.

"I don't know what your game is," he said sullenly to Wimsey, "but I can see you've laid a trap and pulled it off all right."

"I think, gentlemen," said Wimsey, "that if I might have a word in private with Melville in his own room, I could get the thing settled satisfactorily, without undue fuss."

"He'll have to resign his commission," growled the Colonel.

"I'll put it to him in that light," said Peter. "May we go to your room for a minute, Melville?"

With a lowering brow, the young soldier led the way. Once alone with Wimsey, he turned furiously on him.

"What do you want? What do you mean by making this monstrous charge? I'll take action for libel!"

"Do," said Wimsey coolly, "if you think anybody is likely to believe your story."

He lit a cigarette, and smiled lazily at the angry young man.

"Well, what's the meaning of it, anyway?"

"The meaning," said Wimsey, "is simply that you, an officer and a member of this club, have been caught red-handed cheating at cards while playing for money, the witnesses being Sir Impey Biggs, Colonel Marchbanks, and myself. Now, I suggest to you, Captain Mellville, that your best plan is to let me take charge of Mrs. Ruyslaender's diamond necklace and portrait, and then just to trickle away quiet-like from these halls of dazzlin' light—without any questions asked."

Melville leapt to his feet.

"My God!" he cried. "I can see it now. It's blackmail."

"You may certainly call it blackmail, and theft too," said Lord Peter, with a shrug. "But why use ugly names? I hold five aces, you see. Better chuck in your hand."

"Suppose I say I never heard of the diamonds?"

"It's a bit late now, isn't it?" said Wimsey flatly. "But in that case, I'm beastly sorry and all that, of course, but we shall have to make tonight's business public."

"Damn you!" muttered Melville, "you sneering devil."

He showed all his white teeth, half springing, with crouched shoulders. Wimsey waited quietly, his hands in his pockets.

The rush did not come. With a furious gesture, Melville pulled out his keys and unlocked his dressing-case.

"Take them," he growled, flinging a small parcel on the table; "you've got me. Take 'em and go to hell."

"Eventually—why not now?" murmured his lordship. "Thanks frightfully. Man of peace myself, you know—hate unpleasantness and all that." He scrutinized his booty carefully, running the stones expertly between his fingers. Over

the portrait he pursed up his lips. "Yes," he murmured, "that
would have made a row." He replaced the wrapping and
slipped the parcel into his pocket.

"Well, good night, Melville—and thanks for a pleasant
game."

"I say, Biggs," said Wimsey, when he had returned to the
card-room. "You've had a lot of experience. What tactics
d'you think one's justified in usin' with a blackmailer?"

"Ah!" said the K.C. "There you've put your finger on Society's sore place, where the Law is helpless. Speaking as a man,
I'd say nothing could be too bad for the brute. It's a crime cru-
eller and infinitely worse in its results than murder. As a
lawyer, I can only say that I have consistently refused to
defend a blackmailer or to prosecute any poor devil who does
away with his tormentor."

"H'm," replied Wimsey. "What do you say, Colonel?"

"A man like that's a filthy pest," said the little warrior
stoutly. "Shootin's too good for him. I knew a man—close personal friend, in fact—hounded to death—blew his brains
out—one of the best. Don't like to talk about it."

"I want to show you something," said Wimsey.

He picked up the pack which still lay scattered on the
table, and shuffled it together.

"Catch hold of these, Colonel, and lay 'em out face downwards. That's right. First of all you cut 'em at the twentieth
card—you'll see the seven of diamonds at the bottom. Correct? Now I'll call 'em. Ten of hearts, ace of spades, three of
clubs, five of clubs, king of diamonds, nine, jack, two of hearts.
Right? I could pick 'em all out, you see, except the ace of
hearts, and that's here."

He leaned forward and produced it dexterously from Sir
Impey's breast-pocket.

"I learnt it from a man who shared my dug-out near
Ypres," he said. "You needn't mention tonight's business, you
two. There are crimes which the Law cannot reach."

THE UNDIGNIFIED MELODRAMA
OF THE BONE OF CONTENTION

I am afraid you have brought shocking weather with you, Lord Peter," said Mrs. Frobisher-Pym, with playful reproof. "If it goes on like this they will have a bad day for the funeral."

Lord Peter Wimsey glanced out of the morning-room window to the soaked green lawn and the shrubbery, where the rain streamed down remorselessly over the laurel leaves, stiff and shiny like mackintoshes.

"Nasty exposed business, standing round at funerals," he agreed.

"Yes, I always think it's such a shame for the old people. In a tiny village like this it's about the only pleasure they get during the winter. It makes something for them to talk about for weeks."

"Is it anybody's funeral in particular?"

"My dear Wimsey," said his host, "it is plain that you, coming from your little village of London, are quite out of the swim. There has never been a funeral like it in Little Doddering before. It's an event."

"Really?"

"Oh, dear, yes. You may possibly remember old Burdock?"

"Burdock? Let me see. Isn't he a sort of local squire, or something?"

"He was," corrected Mr. Frobisher-Pym. "He's dead—died in New York about three weeks ago, and they're sending him over to be buried. The Burdocks have lived in the big house for hundreds of years, and they're all buried in the churchyard, except, of course, the one who was killed in the war. Burdock's secretary cabled the news of his death across, and said the body was following as soon as the embalmers had finished with it. The boat gets in to Southampton this morning, I believe. At any rate, the body will arrive here by the 6:30 from Town."

"Are you going down to meet it, Tom?"

"No, my dear. I don't think that is called for. There will be a grand turn-out of the village, of course. Joliffe's people are having the time of their lives; they borrowed an extra pair of horses from young Mortimer for the occasion. I only hope they don't kick over the traces and upset the hearse. Mortimer's horseflesh is generally on the spirited side."

"But, Tom, we must show some respect to the Burdocks."

"We're attending the funeral tomorrow, and that's quite enough. We must do that, I suppose, out of consideration for the family, though, as far as the old man himself goes, respect is the very last thing anybody would think of paying him."

"Oh, Tom, he's dead."

"And quite time too. No, Agatha, it's no use pretending that old Burdock was anything but a spiteful, bad-tempered, dirty-living old blackguard that the world's well rid of. The last scandal he stirred up made the place too hot to hold him. He had to leave the country and go to the States, and, even so, if he hadn't had the money to pay the people off, he'd probably have been put in gaol. That's why I'm so annoyed with Hancock. I don't mind his calling himself a priest, though clergyman was always good enough for dear old Weeks—who, after all, was a canon—and I don't mind his vestments. He can wrap himself up in a Union Jack if he likes—it doesn't worry *me*. But when it comes to having old Burdock put on trestles in the south aisle, with candles round him, and Hubbard from the 'Red Cow' and Duggins's boy praying over him half the night, I think it's time to draw the line. The people don't like it, you know—at least, the older generation don't. It's all right for the young ones, I dare say; they must have their amusement; but it gives offence to a lot of the farmers. After all, they knew Burdock a bit too well. Simpson—he's people's warden, you know—came up quite in distress to speak to me about it last night. You couldn't have a sounder man than Simpson. I said I would speak to Hancock. I did speak to him this morning, as a matter of fact, but you might as well talk to the west door of the church."

"Mr. Hancock is one of those young men who fancy they know everything," said his wife. "A sensible man would have listened to you, Tom. You're a magistrate and have lived here all your life, and it stands to reason you know considerably more about the parish than he does."

"He took up the ridiculous position," said Mr. Frobisher-Pym, "that the more sinful the old man had been the more he needed praying for. I said, 'I think it would need more praying than you or I could do to help old Burdock out of the place he's in now.' Ha, ha! So he said, 'I agree with you, Mr. Frobisher-Pym; that is why I am having eight watchers to pray all through the night for him.' I admit he had me there."

"Eight people?" exclaimed Mrs. Frobisher-Pym.

"Not all at once, I understand; in relays, two at a time. 'Well,' I said, 'I think you ought to consider that you will be giving a handle to the Nonconformists.' Of course, he couldn't deny that."

Wimsey helped himself to marmalade. Nonconformists, it seemed, were always searching for handles. Though what kind—whether door-handles, tea-pot handles, pump-handles, or starting-handles—was never explained, nor what the handles were to be used for when found. However, having been brought up in the odour of the Establishment, he was familiar with this odd dissenting peculiarity, and merely said:

"Pity to be extreme in a small parish like this. Disturbs the

ideas of the simple fathers of the hamlet and the village blacksmith, with his daughter singin' in the choir and the Old Hundredth and all the rest of it. Don't Burdock's family have
anything to say to it? There are some sons, aren't there?"

"Only the two, now. Aldine was the one that was killed, of
course, and Martin is somewhere abroad. He went off after
that row with his father, and I don't think he has been back in
England since."

"What was the row about?"

"Oh, that was a disgraceful business. Martin got a girl into
trouble—a film actress or a typist or somebody of that sort—
and insisted on marrying her."

"Oh?"

"Yes, so dreadful of him," said the lady, taking up the tale,
"when he was practically engaged to the Delaprime girl—the
one with glasses, you know. It made a terrible scandal. Some
horribly vulgar people came down and pushed their way into
the house and insisted on seeing old Mr. Burdock. I will say
for him he stood up to them—he wasn't the sort of person you
could intimidate. He told them the girl had only herself to
blame, and they could sue Martin if they liked—*he* wouldn't
be blackmailed on his son's account. The butler was listening
at the door, naturally, and told the whole village about it. And
then Martin Burdock came home and had a quarrel with his
father you could have heard for miles. He said that the whole
thing was a lie, and that he meant to marry the girl, anyway. I
cannot understand how anybody could marry into a blackmailing family like that."

"My dear," said Mr. Frobisher-Pym gently, "I don't think
you're being quite fair to Martin, or his wife's parents, either.
From what Martin told me, they were quite decent people,
only not his class, of course, and they came in a well-meaning
way to find out what Martin's 'intentions' were. You would
want to do the same yourself, if it were a daughter of ours. Old
Burdock, naturally, thought they meant blackmail. He was the
kind of man who thinks everything can be paid for; and he
considered a son of his had a perfect right to seduce a young

woman who worked for a living. I don't say Martin was altogether in the right—"

"Martin is a chip off the old block, I'm afraid," retorted the
lady. "He married the girl, anyway, and why should he do
that, unless he had to?"

"Well, they've never had any children, you know," said
Mr. Frobisher-Pym.

"That's as may be. I've no doubt the girl was in league with
her parents. And you know the Martin Burdocks have lived in
Paris ever since."

"That's true," admitted her husband. "It was an unfortunate affair altogether. They've had some difficulty in tracing
Martin's address, too, but no doubt he'll be coming back
shortly. He is engaged in producing some film play, they tell
me, so possibly he can't get away in time for the funeral."

"If he had any natural feeling, he would not let a film play
stand in his way," said Mrs. Frobisher-Pym.

"My dear, there are such things as contracts, with very
heavy monetary penalties for breaking them. And I don't suppose Martin could afford to lose a big sum of money. It's not
likely that his father will have left him anything."

"Martin is the younger son, then?" asked Wimsey, politely
showing more interest than he felt in the rather well-worn plot
of this village melodrama.

"No, he is the eldest of the lot. The house is entailed, of
course, and so is the estate, such as it is. But there's no money
in the land. Old Burdock made his fortune in rubber shares
during the boom, and the money will go as he leaves it—wherever that may be, for they haven't found any will yet. He's
probably left it all to Haviland."

"The younger son?"

"Yes. He's something in the City—a director of a company—connected with silk stockings, I believe. Nobody has
seen very much of him. He came down as soon as he heard of
his father's death. He's staying with the Hancocks. The big
house has been shut up since old Burdock went to the States
four years ago. I suppose Haviland thought it wasn't worth-

while opening it up till they knew what Martin was going to do about it. That's why the body is being taken to the church."

"Much less trouble, certainly," said Wimsey.

"Oh, yes—though, mind you, I think Haviland ought to take a more neighbourly view of it. Considering the position the Burdocks have always held in the place, the people had a right to expect a proper reception after the funeral. It's usual. But these business people think less of tradition than we do down here. And, naturally, since the Hancocks are putting Haviland up, he can't raise much objection to the candles and the prayers and things."

"Perhaps not," said Mrs. Frobisher-Pym, "but it would have been more suitable if Haviland had come to us, rather than to the Hancocks, whom he doesn't even know."

"My dear, you forget that very unpleasant dispute I had with Haviland Burdock about shooting over my land. After the correspondence that passed between us, last time he was down here, I could scarcely offer him hospitality. His father took a perfectly proper view of it, I will say that for him, but Haviland was exceedingly discourteous to me, and things were said which I could not possibly overlook. However, we mustn't bore you, Lord Peter, with our local small-talk. If you've finished your breakfast, what do you say to a walk around the place? It's a pity it's raining so hard—and you don't see the garden at its best this time of year, of course— but I've got some cocker span'els you might like to have a look at."

Lord Peter expressed eager anxiety to see the spaniels, and in a few minutes' time found himself squelching down the gravel path which led to the kennels.

"Nothing like a healthy country life," said Mr. Frobisher-Pym. "I always think London is so depressing in the winter. Nothing to do with oneself. All right to run up for a day or two and see a theatre now and again, but how you people stick it week in and week out beats me. I must speak to Plunkett about this archway," he added. "It's getting out of trim."

He broke off a dangling branch of ivy as he spoke. The

plant shuddered revengefully, tipping a small shower of water down Wimsey's neck.

The cocker spaniel and her family occupied a comfortable and airy stall in the stable buildings. A youngish man in breeches and leggings emerged to greet the visitors, and produced the little bundles of puppy-hood for their inspection. Wimsey sat down on an upturned bucket and examined them gravely one by one. The bitch, after cautiously reviewing his boots and grumbling a little, decided that he was trustworthy and slobbered genially over his knees.

"Let me see," said Mr. Frobisher-Pym, "how old are they?"

"Thirteen days, sir."

"Is she feeding them all right?"

"Fine, sir. She's having some of the malt food. Seems to suit her very well, sir."

"Ah, yes. Plunkett was a little doubtful about it, but I heard it spoken very well of. Plunkett doesn't care for experiments, and, in a general way, I agree with him. Where is Plunkett, by the way?"

"He's not very well this morning, sir."

"Sorry to hear that, Merridew. The rheumatics again?"

"No, sir. From what Mrs. Plunkett tells me, he's had a bit of a shock."

"A shock? What sort of a shock? Nothing wrong with Alf or Elsie, I hope?"

"No, sir. The fact is — I understand he's seen something, sir."

"What do you mean, seen something?"

"Well, sir — something in the nature of a warning, from what he says."

"A warning? Good heavens, Merridew, he mustn't get those sort of ideas in his head. I'm surprised at Plunkett; I always thought he was a very level-headed man. What sort of warning did he say it was?"

"I couldn't say, sir."

"Surely he mentioned what he thought he'd seen."

Merridew's face took on a slightly obstinate look.

"I can't say, I'm sure, sir."

"This will never do. I must go and see Plunkett. Is he at the cottage?"

"Yes, sir."

"We'll go down there at once. You don't mind, do you, Wimsey? I can't allow Plunkett to make himself ill. If he's had a shock he'd better see a doctor. Well, carry on, Merridew, and be sure you keep her warm and comfortable. The damp is apt to come up through these brick floors. I'm thinking of having the whole place re-set with concrete, but it takes money, of course. I can't imagine," he went on, as he led the way past the greenhouse towards a trim cottage set in its own square of kitchen-garden, "what can have happened to have upset Plunkett. I hope it's nothing serious. He's getting elderly, of course, but he ought to be above believing in warnings. You wouldn't believe the extraordinary ideas these people get hold of. Fact is, I expect he's been round at the Weary Traveller, and caught sight of somebody's washing hung out on the way home."

"Not washing," corrected Wimsey mechanically. He had a deductive turn of mind which exposed the folly of the suggestion even while irritably admitting that the matter was of no importance. "It poured with rain last night, and, besides, it's Thursday. But Tuesday and Wednesday were fine, so the drying would have all been done then. No washing."

"Well, well—something else then—a post, or old Mrs. Giddens's white donkey. Plunkett does occasionally take a drop too much, I'm sorry to say, but he's a very good kennel-man, so one overlooks it. They're superstitious round about these parts, and they can tell some queer tales if once you get into their confidence. You'd be surprised how far off the main track we are as regards civilization. Why, not here, but at Abbotts Bolton, fifteen miles off, it's as much as one's life's worth to shoot a hare. Witches, you know, and that sort of thing."

"I shouldn't be a bit surprised. They'll still tell you about werewolves in some parts of Germany."

"Yes, I dare say. Well, here we are." Mr. Frobisher-Pym

rapped loudly with his walking-stick on the door of the cottage and turned the handle without waiting for permission.

"You there, Mrs. Plunkett? May we come in? Ah! good morning. Hope we're not disturbing you, but Merridew told me Plunkett was not so well. This is Lord Peter Wimsey—a very old friend of mine; that is to say, I'm a very old friend of *his*; ha, ha!"

"Good morning, sir; good morning, your lordship. I'm sure Plunkett will be very pleased to see you. Please step in. Plunkett, here's Mr. Pym to see you."

The elderly man who sat crouching over the fire turned a mournful face towards them, and half rose, touching his forehead.

"Well, now, Plunkett, what's the trouble?" inquired Mr. Frobisher-Pym, with the hearty bedside manner adopted by country gentlefolk visiting their dependants. "Sorry not to see you out and about. Touch of the old complaint, eh?"

"No, sir; no, sir. Thank you, sir. I'm well enough in myself. But I've had a warning, and I'm not long for this world."

"Not long for this world? Oh, nonsense, Plunkett. You mustn't talk like that. A touch of indigestion, that's what you've got, I expect. Gives one the blues, I know. I'm sure I often feel like nothing on earth when I've got one of my bilious attacks. Try a dose of castor-oil, or a good old-fashioned blue pill and black draught. Nothing like it. Then you won't talk about warnings and dying."

"No medicine won't do no good to *my* complaint, sir. Nobody as see what I've seed ever got the better of it. But as you and the gentleman are here, sir, I'm wondering if you'll do me a favour."

"Of course, Plunkett, anything you like. What is it?"

"Why, just to draw up my will, sir. Old Parson, he used to do it. But I don't fancy this new young man, with his candles and bits of things. It don't seem as if he'd make it good and legal, sir, and I wouldn't like it if there was any dispute after I was gone. So as there ain't much time left me, I'd be grateful if you'd put it down clear for me in pen and ink that I wants my little bit all to go to Sarah here, and after her to Alf and Elsie, divided up equal."

"Of course I'll do that for you, Plunkett, any time you like. But it's all nonsense to be talking about wills. Bless my soul, I shouldn't be surprised if you were to see us all underground."

"No, sir. I've been a hale and hearty man, I'm not denying. But I've been called, sir, and I've got to go. It must come to all of us, I know that. But it's a fearful thing to see the death-coach come for one, and know that the dead are in it, that cannot rest in the grave."

"Come now, Plunkett, you don't mean to tell me you believe in that old foolishness about the death-coach. I thought you were an educated man. What would Alf say if he heard you talking such nonsense?"

"Ah, sir, young people don't know everything, and there's many more things in God's creation than what you'll find in the printed books."

"Oh, well," said Mr. Frobisher-Pym, finding this opening irresistible, "we know there are more things in heaven and earth, Horatio, than are dreamt of in your philosophy. Quite so. But that doesn't apply nowadays," he added contradictorily. "There are no ghosts in the twentieth century. Just you think the matter out quietly, and you'll find you've made a mistake. There's probably some quite simple explanation. Dear me! I remember Mrs. Frobisher-Pym waking up one night and having a terrible fright, because she thought somebody'd been and hanged himself on our bedroom door. Such a silly idea, because I was safe in bed beside her—snoring, *she* said, ha, ha!—and, if anybody was feeling like hanging himself, he wouldn't come into our bedroom to do it. Well, she clutched my arm in a great state of mind, and when I went to see what had alarmed her, what do you think it was? My trousers, which I'd hung up by the braces, with the socks still in the legs! My word! and didn't I get a wigging for not having put my things away tidy!"

Mr. Frobisher-Pym laughed, and Mrs. Plunkett said dutifully, "There now!" Her husband shook his head.

"That may be, sir, but I see the death-coach last night with my own eyes. Just striking midnight it was, by the church clock, and I see it come up the lane by the old priory wall."

"And what were you doing out of bed at midnight, eh?"

"Well, sir, I'd been round to my sister's, that's got her boy home on leaf of his ship."

"And you'd been drinking his health, I dare say, Plunkett," Mr. Frobisher-Pym wagged an admonitory forefinger.

"No, sir, I don't deny I'd had a glass or two of ale, but not to fuddle me. My wife can tell you I was sober enough when I got home."

"That's right, sir. Plunkett hadn't taken too much last night, that I'll swear to."

"Well, what was it you saw, Plunkett?"

"I see the death-coach, same as I'm telling you, sir. It come up the lane, all ghostly white, sir, and never making no more sound than the dead—which it were, sir."

"A wagon or something going through to Lymptree or Herriotting."

"No, sir—'tweren't a wagon. I counted the horses—four white horses, and they went by with never a sound of hoof or bridle. And that weren't—"

"Four horses! Come, Plunkett, you must have been seeing double. There's nobody about here would be driving four horses, unless it was Mr. Mortimer from Abbotts Bolton, and he wouldn't be taking his horseflesh out at midnight."

"Four horses they was, sir. I see them plain. And it weren't Mr. Mortimer, neither, for he drives a drag, and this were a big, heavy coach, with no lights on it, but shinin' all of itself, with a colour like moonshine."

"Oh, nonsense, man! You couldn't see the moon last night. It was pitch-dark."

"No, sir, but the coach shone all moony-like, all the same."

"And no lights? I wonder what the police would say to that."

"No mortal police could stop that coach," said Plunkett

contemptuously, "nor no mortal man could abide the sight on it. I tell you, sir, that ain't the worst of it. The horses —"

"Was it going slowly?"

"No, sir. It were going at a gallop, only the hoofs didn't touch the ground. There weren't no sound, and I see the black road and the white hoofs half a foot off of it. And the horses had no heads."

"No heads?"

"No, sir."

Mr. Frobisher-Pym laughed.

"Come, come, Plunkett, you don't expect us to swallow that. No heads? How could even a ghost drive horses with no heads? How about the reins, eh?"

"You may laugh, sir, but we know that with God all things are possible. Four white horses they was. I see them clearly, but there was neither head nor neck beyond the collar, sir. I see the reins shining like silver, and they ran up to the rings of the hames, and they didn't go no further. If I was to drop down dead this minute, sir, that's what I see."

"Was there a driver to this wonderful turn-out?"

"Yes, sir, there was a driver."

"Headless too, I suppose?"

"Yes, sir, headless too. At least, I couldn't see nothing of him beyond his coat, which had them old-fashioned capes at the shoulders."

"Well, I must say, Plunkett, you're very circumstantial. How far off was this — er — apparition when you saw it?"

"I was passing by the War Memorial, sir, when I see it come up the lane. It wouldn't be above twenty or thirty yards from where I stood. It went by at a gallop, and turned off to the left round the churchyard wall."

"Well, well, it sounds odd, certainly, but it was a dark night, and at that distance your eyes may have deceived you. Now, if you'll take my advice you'll think no more about it."

"Ah, sir, it's all very well saying that, but everybody knows the man who sees the death-coach of the Burdocks is doomed to die within the week. There's no use rebelling against it, sir; it is so. And if you'll be so good as to oblige me over that matter of a will, I'd die happier for knowing as Sarah and the children was sure of their bit of money."

Mr. Frobisher-Pym obliged over the will, though much against the grain, exhorting and scolding as he wrote. Wimsey added his own signature as one of the witnesses, and contributed his own bit of comfort.

"I shouldn't worry too much about the coach, if I were you," he said. "Depend upon it, if it's the Burdock coach it'll just have come for the soul of the old squire. It couldn't be expected to go to New York for him, don't you see? It's just gettin' ready for the funeral tomorrow."

"That's likely enough," agreed Plunkett. "Often and often it's been seen in these parts when one of the Burdocks was taken. But it's terrible unlucky to see it."

The thought of the funeral seemed, however, to cheer him a little. The visitors again begged him not to think about it, and took their departure.

"Isn't it wonderful," said Mr. Frobisher-Pym, "what imagination will do with these people? And they're obstinate. You could argue with them till you were black in the face."

"Yes. I say, let's go down to the church and have a look at the place. I'd like to know how much he could really have seen from where he was standing."

The parish church of Little Doddering stands, like so many country churches, at some distance from the houses. The main road from Herriotting, Abbotts Bolton, and Frimpton runs past the west gate of the churchyard—a wide God's acre, crowded with ancient stones. On the south side is a narrow and gloomy lane, heavily overhung with old elm trees, dividing the church from the still more ancient ruins of Doddering Priory. On the main road, a little beyond the point where Old Priory Lane enters, stands the War Memorial, and from here the road runs straight on into Little Doddering. Round the remaining two sides of the churchyard winds another lane, known to the village simply as the Back Lane.

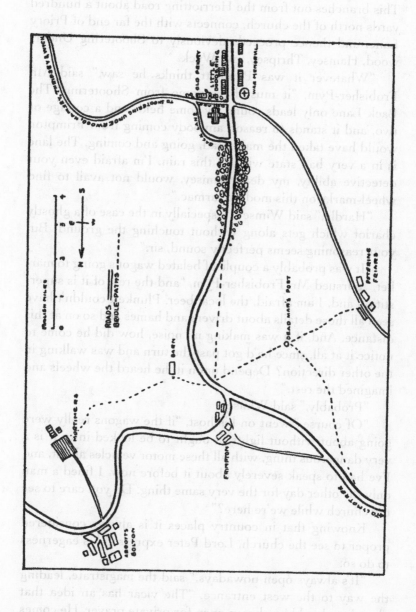

This branches out from the Herriotting road about a hundred yards north of the church, connects with the far end of Priory Lane, and thence proceeds deviously to Shootering Underwood, Hamsey, Thripsey, and Wyck.

"Whatever it was Plunkett thinks he saw," said Mr. Frobisher-Pym, "it must have come from Shootering. The Back Lane only leads round by some fields and a cottage or two, and it stands to reason anybody coming from Frimpton would have taken the main road, going and coming. The lane is in a very bad state with all this rain. I'm afraid even your detective ability, my dear Wimsey, would not avail to find wheel-marks on this modern tarmac."

"Hardly," said Wimsey, "especially in the case of a ghostly chariot which gets along without touching the ground. But your reasoning seems perfectly sound, sir."

"It was probably a couple of belated wagons going to market," pursued Mr. Frobisher-Pym, "and the rest of it is superstition and, I am afraid, the local beer. Plunkett couldn't have seen all those details about drivers and hames and so on at this distance. And, if it was making no noise, how did he come to notice it at all, since he'd got past the turn and was walking in the other direction? Depend upon it, he heard the wheels and imagined the rest."

"Probably," said Wimsey.

"Of course," went on his host, "if the wagons really were going about without lights, it ought to be looked into. It is a very dangerous thing, with all these motor vehicles about, and I've had to speak severely about it before now. I fined a man only the other day for the very same thing. Do you care to see the church while we're here?"

Knowing that in country places it is always considered proper to see the church, Lord Peter expressed his eagerness to do so.

"It's always open nowadays," said the magistrate, leading the way to the west entrance. "The vicar has an idea that churches should be always open for private prayer. He comes from a town living, of course. Round about here the people are always out on the land, and you can't expect them to come into church in their working clothes and muddy boots. They wouldn't think it respectful, and they've other things to do. Besides, I said to him, consider the opportunity it gives for undesirable conduct. But he's a young man, and he'll have to learn by experience."

He pushed the door open. A curious, stuffy waft of stale incense, damp, and stoves rushed out at them as they entered—a kind of concentrated extract of Church of England. The two altars, bright with flowers and gilding, and showing as garish splashes among the heavy shadows and oppressive architecture of the little Norman building, sounded the same note of contradiction; it was the warm and human that seemed exotic and unfamiliar; the cold and unwelcoming that seemed native to the place and people.

"This Lady-chapel, as Hancock calls it, in the south aisle, is new, of course," said Mr. Frobisher-Pym. "It aroused a good deal of opposition, but the Bishop is lenient with the High Church party—too lenient, some people think—but, after all, what does it matter? I'm sure I can say my prayers just as well with two communion-tables as with one. And, I will say for Hancock, he is very good with the young men and girls. In these days of motor-cycles, it's something to get them interested in religion at all. Those trestles in the chapel are for old Burdock's coffin, I suppose. Ah! Here is the vicar."

A thin man in a cassock emerged from a door beside the high altar and came down towards them, carrying a tall, oaken candlestick in his hand. He greeted them with a slightly professional smile of welcome. Wimsey diagnosed him promptly as earnest, nervous, and not highly intellectual.

"The candlesticks have only just come," he observed after the usual introductions had been made. "I was afraid they would not be here in time. However, all is now well."

He set the candlestick beside the coffin-trestles, and proceeded to decorate its brass spike with a long candle of unbleached wax, which he took from a parcel in a neighbouring pew.

Mr. Frobisher-Pym said nothing. Wimsey felt it incumbent on him to express his interest, and did so.

"It is very gratifying," said Mr. Hancock, thus encouraged, "to see the people beginning to take a real interest in their church. I have really had very little difficulty in finding watchers for tonight. We are having eight watchers, two by two, from ten o'clock this evening—till which time I shall be myself on duty—till six in the morning, when I come in to say Mass. The men will carry on till two o'clock, then my wife and daughter will relieve them, and Mr. Hubbard and young Rawlinson have kindly consented to take the hours from four till six."

"What Rawlinson is that?" demanded Mr. Frobisher-Pym.

"Mr. Graham's clerk from Herriotting. It is true he is not a member of the parish, but he was born here, and was good enough to wish to take his turn in watching. He is coming over on his motor-cycle. After all, Mr. Graham has had charge of Burdock's family affairs for very many years, and no doubt they wished to show their respect in some way."

"Well, I only hope he'll be awake enough to do his work in the morning, after gadding about all night," said Mr. Frobisher-Pym gruffly. "As for Hubbard, that's his own lookout, though I must say it seems an odd occupation for a publican. Still, if he's pleased and you're pleased, there's no more to be said about it."

"You've got a very beautiful old church here, Mr. Hancock," said Wimsey, seeing that controversy seemed imminent.

"Very beautiful indeed," said the vicar. "Have you noticed that apse? It is rare for a village church to possess such a perfect Norman apse. Perhaps you would like to come and look at it." He genuflected as they passed a hanging lamp which burned before a niche. "You see, we are permitted Reservation. The Bishop—" He prattled cheerfully as they wandered up the chancel, digressing from time to time to draw attention to the handsome miserere seats ("Of course, this was the original Priory Church"), and a beautifully carved piscina and aumbry ("It is rare to find them so well preserved"). Wimsey assisted him to carry down the remaining candles from the vestry, and, when these had been put in position, joined Mr. Frobisher-Pym at the door.

"I think you said you were dining with the Lumsdens tonight," said the magistrate, as they sat smoking after lunch. "How are you going? Will you have the car?"

"I'd rather you'd lend me one of the saddle horses," said Wimsey. "I get few opportunities of riding in town."

"Certainly, my dear boy, certainly. Only I'm afraid you'll have rather a wet ride. Take Polly Flinders; it will do her good to get some exercise. You are quite sure you would prefer it? Have you got your kit with you?"

"Yes—I brought an old pair of bags down with me, and, with this raincoat, I shan't come to any harm. They won't expect me to dress. How far is it to Frimpton, by the way?"

"Nine miles by the main road, and tarmac all the way, I'm afraid, but there's a good wide piece of grass each side. And, of course, you can cut off a mile or so by going across the common. What time will you want to start?"

"Oh, about seven o'clock, I should think. And, I say, sir— will Mrs. Frobisher-Pym think it very rude if I'm rather late back? Old Lumsden and I went through the war together, and if we get yarning over old times we may go on into the small hours. I don't want to feel I'm treating your house like a hotel, but—"

"Of course not, of course not! That's absolutely all right. My wife won't mind in the very least. We want you to enjoy your visit and do exactly what you like. I'll give you the key, and I'll remember not to put the chain up. Perhaps you wouldn't mind doing that yourself when you come in?"

"Rather not. And how about the mare?"

"I'll tell Merridew to look out for you; he sleeps over the stables. I only wish it were going to be a better night for you. I'm afraid the glass is going back. Yes. Dear, dear! It's a bad lookout for tomorrow. By the way, you'll probably pass the funeral procession at the church. It should be along by about then, if the train is punctual."

The train, presumably, was punctual, for as Lord Peter cantered up to the west gate of the church he saw a hearse of great funereal pomp drawn up before it, surrounded by a little crowd of people. Two mourning coaches were in attendance; the driver of the second seemed to be having some difficulty with the horses, and Wimsey rightly inferred that this was the pair which had been borrowed from Mr. Mortimer. Restraining Polly Flinders as best he might, he sidled into a respectful position on the edge of the crowd, and watched the coffin taken from the hearse and carried through the gate, where it was met by Mr. Hancock, in full pontificals, attended by a thurifer and two torch-bearers. The effect was a little marred by the rain, which had extinguished the candles, but the village seemed to look upon it as an excellent show nevertheless. A massive man, dressed with great correctness in a black frock coat and tall hat, and accompanied by a woman in handsome mourning and furs, was sympathetically commented on. This was Haviland Burdock of silk-stocking fame, the younger son of the deceased. A vast number of white wreaths were then handed out, and greeted with murmurs of admiration and approval. The choir struck up a hymn, rather raggedly, and the procession filed away into the church. Polly Flinders shook her head vigorously, and Wimsey, taking this as a signal to be gone, replaced his hat and ambled gently away towards Frimpton.

He followed the main road for about four miles, winding up through finely wooded country to the edge of Frimpton Common. Here the road made a wide sweep, skirting the common and curving gently down into Frimpton village. Wimsey hesitated for a moment, considering that it was growing dark and that both the way and the animal he rode were strange to him. There seemed, however, to be a well-defined bridle-path across the common, and eventually he decided to take it. Polly Flinders seemed to know it well enough, and cantered along without hesitation. A ride of about a mile and a half brought them without adventure into the main road again. Here a fork in the road presented itself confusingly; an electric torch, how-

ever, and a signpost solved the problem; after which ten minutes' ride brought the traveller to his goal.

Major Lumsden was a large, cheerful man—none the less
cheerful for having lost a leg in the war. He had a large, cheerful wife, a large, cheerful house, and a large, cheerful family.
Wimsey soon found himself seated before a fire as large and
cheerful as the rest of the establishment, exchanging gossip
with his hosts over a whisky-and-soda. He described the Burdock funeral with irreverent gusto, and went on to tell the
story of the phantom coach. Major Lumsden laughed.

"It's a quaint part of the country," he said. "The policeman
is just as bad as the rest of them. Do you remember, dear, the
time I had to go out and lay a ghost, down at Pogson's farm?"

"I do, indeed," said his wife emphatically. "The maids had
a wonderful time. Trivett—that's our local constable—came
rushing in here and fainted in the kitchen, and they all sat
round howling and sustaining him with our best brandy, while
Dan went down and investigated."

"Did you find the ghost?"

"Well, not the ghost, exactly, but we found a pair of boots
and half a pork-pie in the empty house, so we put it all down
to a tramp. Still, I must say odd things do happen about here.
There were those fires on the common last year. They were
never explained."

"Gipsies, Dan."

"Maybe; but nobody ever saw them, and the fires would
start in the most unexpected way, sometimes in the pouring
rain; and, before you could get near one, it would be out, and
only a sodden wet black mark left behind it. And there's
another bit of the common that animals don't like—near what
they call the Dead Man's Post. My dogs won't go near it.
Funny brutes. I've never seen anything there, but even in broad
daylight they don't seem to fancy it. The common's not got a
good reputation. It used to be a great place for highwaymen."

"Is the Burdock coach anything to do with highwaymen?"

"No. I fancy it was some rakehelly dead-and-gone Burdock. Belonged to the Hell-fire Club or something. The usual

sort of story. All the people round here believe in it, of course. It's rather a good thing. Keeps the servants indoors at night. Well, let's go and have some grub, shall we?"

"Do you remember," said Major Lumsden, "that damned old mill, and the three elms by the pig-sty?"

"Good Lord, yes! You very obligingly blew them out of the landscape for us, I remember. They made us a damned sight too conspicuous."

"We rather missed them when they were gone."

"Thank heaven you didn't miss them when they were there. I'll tell you what you did miss, though."

"What's that?"

"The old sow."

"By Jove, yes. Do you remember old Piper fetching her in?"

"I'll say I do. That reminds me. You knew Bunthorne . . ."

"I'll say good night," said Mrs. Lumsden, "and leave you people to it."

"Do you remember," said Lord Peter Wimsey, "that awkward moment when Popham went off his rocker?"

"No. I'd been sent back with a batch of prisoners. I heard about it, though. I never knew what became of him."

"I got him sent home. He's married now and living in Lincolnshire."

"Is he? Well, he couldn't help himself, I suppose. He was only a kid. What's happened to Philpotts?"

"Oh, Philpotts . . ."

"Where's your glass, old man?"

"Oh, rot, old man. The night is still young . . ."

"Really? Well, but look here, why not stay the night? My wife will be delighted. I can fix you up in no time."

"No, thanks most awfully. I must be rolling off home. I said I'd be back; and I'm booked to put the chain on the door."

"As you like, of course, but it's still raining. Not a good night for a ride on an open horse."

"I'll bring a saloon next time. We shan't hurt. Rain's good for the complexion—makes the roses grow. Don't wake your man up. I can saddle her myself."

"My dear man, it's no trouble."

"No, really, old man."

"Well, I'll come along and lend you a hand."

A gust of rain and wind blew in through the hall door as they struggled out into the night. It was past one in the morning and pitch-dark. Major Lumsden again pressed Wimsey to stay.

"No, thanks, really. The old lady's feelings might be hurt. It's not so bad, really—wet, but not cold. Come up, Polly, stand over, old lady."

He put the saddle on and girthed it, while Lumsden held the lantern. The mare, fed and rested, came delicately dancing out of the warm loose-box, head well stretched forward, and nostrils snuffing at the rain.

"Well, so long, old lad. Come back and look us up again. It's been great."

"Rather! By Jove, yes. Best respects to madame. Is the gate open?"

"Yes."

"Well, cheerio!"

"Cheerio!"

Polly Flinders, with her nose turned homewards, settled down to make short work of the nine miles of high-road. Once outside the gates, the night seemed lighter, though the rain poured heavily. Somewhere buried behind the thronging clouds there was a moon, which now and again showed as a pale stain on the sky, a paler reflection on the black road. Wimsey, with a mind full of memories and a skin full of whisky, hummed to himself as he rode.

As he passed the fork, he hesitated for a moment. Should he take the path over the common or stick to the road? On consideration, he decided to give the common a miss—not because of its sinister reputation, but because of ruts and rabbit-holes. He shook the reins, bestowed a word of encouragement on his mount, and continued by the road, having the common on his right hand, and, on the left, fields bounded by high hedges, which gave some shelter from the driving rain.

He had topped the rise, and passed the spot where the bridle-path again joined the high-road, when a slight start and stumble drew his attention unpleasantly to Polly Flinders.

"Hold up, mare," he said disapprovingly.

Polly shook her head, moved forward, tried to pick up her easy pace again. "Hullo!" said Wimsey, alarmed. He pulled her to a standstill.

"Lame in the near fore," he said, dismounting. "If you've been and gone and strained anything, my girl, four miles from home, father *will* be pleased." It occurred to him for the first time how curiously lonely the road was. He had not seen a single car. They might have been in the wilds of Africa.

He ran an exploratory hand down the near foreleg. The mare stood quietly enough, without shrinking or wincing. Wimsey was puzzled.

"If these had been the good old days," he said, "I'd have thought she'd picked up a stone. But what—"

He lifted the mare's foot, and explored it carefully with fingers and pocket-torch. His diagnosis had been right, after all. A steel nut, evidently dropped from a passing car, had wedged itself firmly between the shoe and the frog. He grunted and felt for his knife. Happily, it was one of that excellent old-fashioned kind which included, besides blades and corkscrews, an ingenious apparatus for removing foreign bodies from horses' feet.

The mare nuzzled him gently as he stooped over his task. It was a little awkward getting to work; he had to wedge the torch under his arm, so as to leave one hand free for the tool and the other to hold the hoof. He was swearing gently at these difficulties when, happening to glance down the road ahead, he fancied he caught the gleam of something moving. It was not easy to see, for at this point the tall trees stood up on both sides of the road, which dipped abruptly from the edge of the common. It was not a car; the light was too faint. A wagon, probably, with a dim lantern. Yet it seemed to move fast. He puzzled of a moment, then bent to work again.

The nut resisted his efforts, and the mare, touched in a tender spot, pulled away, trying to get her foot down. He soothed her with his voice and patted her neck. The torch slipped from his arm. He cursed it impatiently, set down the hoof, and picked up the torch from the edge of the grass, into which it had rolled. As he straightened himself again, he looked along the road and saw.

Up from under the dripping dark of the trees it came, shining with a thin, moony radiance. There was no clatter of hoofs, no rumble of wheels, no ringing of bit or bridle. He saw the white, sleek, shining shoulders with the collar that lay on each, like a faint fiery ring, enclosing nothing. He saw the gleaming reins, their cut ends slipping back and forward unsupported through the ring of the hames. The feet, that never touched earth, ran swiftly—four times four noiseless hoofs, bearing the pale bodies by like smoke. The driver leaned forward, brandishing his whip. He was faceless and headless, but his whole attitude bespoke desperate haste. The coach was barely visible through the driving rain, but Wimsey saw the dimly spinning wheels and a faint whiteness, still and stiff, at the window. It went past at a gallop—headless driver and headless horse and silent coach. Its passing left a stir, a sound that was less a sound than a vibration—and the wind roared suddenly after it, with a great sheer of water blown up out of the south.

"Good God!" said Wimsey. And then: "How many whiskies did we have?"

He turned and looked back along the road, straining his eyes. Then suddenly he remembered the mare, and, without troubling further about the torch, picked up her foot and went to work by touch. The nut gave no more trouble, but dropped out into his hand almost immediately. Polly Flinders sighed gratefully and blew into his ear.

Wimsey led her forward a few steps. She put her feet

down firmly and strongly. The nut, removed without delay, had left no tenderness. Wimsey mounted, let her go—then pulled her head round suddenly.

"I'm going to see," he said resolutely. "Come up, mare! We won't let any headless horses get the better of *us*. Perfectly indecent, goin' about without heads. Get on, old lady. Over the common with you. We'll catch 'em at the crossroads."

Without the slightest consideration for his host or his host's property, he put the mare to the bridle-path again, and urged her into a gallop.

At first he thought he could make out a pale, fluttering whiteness, moving away ahead of him on the road. Presently, as high-road and bridle-path diverged, he lost it altogether. But he knew there was no side-road. Bar any accident to his mount, he was bound to catch it before it came to the fork. Polly Flinders, answering easily to the touch of his heel, skimmed over the rough track with the indifference born of familiarity. In less than ten minutes her feet rang out again on the tarmac. He pulled her up, faced round in the direction of Little Doddering, and stared down the road. He could see nothing yet. Either he was well ahead of the coach, or it had already passed at unbelievable speed, or else—

He waited. Nothing. The violent rain had ceased, and the moon was struggling out again. The road appeared completely deserted. He glanced over his shoulder. A small beam of light near the ground moved, turned, flashed green, and red, and white again, and came towards him. Presently he made out that it was a policeman wheeling a bicycle.

"A bad night, sir," said the man civilly, but with a faint note of inquiry in his voice.

"Rotten," said Wimsey.

"Just had to mend a puncture, to make it all the pleasanter," added the policeman.

Wimsey expressed sympathy. "Have you been here long?" he added.

"Best part o' twenty minutes."

"Did you see anything pass along this way from Little Doddering?"

"Ain't been nothing along while I've been here. What sort of thing did you mean, sir?"

"I thought I saw—" Wimsey hesitated. He did not care about the idea of making a fool of himself. "A carriage with four horses," he said hesitatingly. "It passed me on this road not a quarter of an hour ago—down at the other end of the common. I—I came back to see. It seemed unusual—" He became aware that his story sounded very lame.

The policeman spoke rather sharply and rapidly.

"There ain't been nothing past here."

"You're sure?"

"Yes, sir; and, if you don't mind me sayin' so, you'd best be getting home. It's a lonesome bit o' road."

"Yes, isn't it?" said Wimsey. "Well, good night, sergeant."

He turned the mare's head back along the Little Doddering road, going very quietly. He saw nothing, heard nothing, and passed nothing. The night was brighter now, and, as he rode back, he verified the entire absence of side-roads. Whatever the thing was which he had seen, it had vanished somewhere along the edge of the common; it had not gone by the main road, nor by any other.

Wimsey came down rather late for breakfast in the morning, to find his hosts in a state of some excitement.

"The most extraordinary thing has happened," said Mrs. Frobisher-Pym.

"Outrageous!" added her husband. "I warned Hancock—he can't say I didn't warn him. Still, however much one may disapprove of his goings-on, there is no excuse whatever for such abominable conduct. Once let me get hold of the beggars, whoever they are—"

"What's up?" said Wimsey, helping himself to broiled kidneys at the sideboard.

"A most scandalous thing," said Mrs. Frobisher-Pym. "The vicar came up to Tom at once—I hope we didn't disturb you, by the way, with all the excitement. It appears that when Mr. Hancock got to the church this morning at six o'clock to take the early service—"

"No, no, my dear, you've got it wrong. Let *me* tell it. When Joe Grinch—that's the sexton, you know, and he has to get there first to ring the bell—when he arrived, he found the south door wide open and nobody in the chapel, where they should have been, beside the coffin. He was very much perplexed, of course, but he supposed that Hubbard and young Rawlinson had got sick of it and gone off home. So he went on to the vestry to get the vestments and things ready, and to his amazement he heard women's voices, calling out to him from inside. He was so astonished, didn't know where he was, but he went on and unlocked the door—"

"With his own key?" put in Wimsey.

"The key was in the door. As a rule it's kept hanging up on a nail under a curtain near the organ, but it was in the lock— where it ought not to have been. And inside the vestry he found Mrs. Hancock and her daughter, nearly dead with fright and annoyance."

"Great Scott!"

"Yes, indeed. They had a most extraordinary story to tell. They'd taken over at two o'clock from the other pair of watchers, and had knelt down by the coffin in the Lady-chapel, according to plan, to say the proper sort of prayers, whatever they are. They'd been there, to the best of their calculation, about ten minutes, when they heard a noise up by the High Altar, as though somebody was creeping stealthily about. Miss Hancock is a very plucky girl, and she got up and walked up the aisle in the dark, with Mrs. Hancock following on behind because, as she said, she didn't want to be left alone. When they'd got as far as the rood-screen, Miss Hancock called out aloud, 'Who's there?' At that they heard a sort of rustling sound, and a noise like something being knocked over. Miss Hancock most courageously snatched up one of the church-warden's staffs, which was clipped on to the choir-stalls, and ran forward, thinking, she says, that somebody was trying to steal the ornaments off the altar. There's a very fine fifteenth-century cross—"

"Never mind the cross, Tom. That hasn't been taken, at any rate."

"No, it hasn't, but she thought it might be. Anyhow, just as she got up to the sanctuary steps, with Mrs. Hancock coming close after her and begging her to be careful, somebody seemed to rush out of the choir-stalls, and caught her by the arms and frog's-marched her—that's her expression—into the vestry. And before she could get breath even to shriek, Mrs. Hancock was pushed in beside her, and the door locked on them."

"By Jove! You do have exciting times in your village."

"Well," said Mr. Frobisher-Pym, "of course they were dreadfully frightened, because they didn't know but what these wretches would come back and murder them, and, in any case, they thought the church was being robbed. But the vestry windows are very narrow and barred, and they couldn't do anything except wait. They tried to listen, but they couldn't hear much. Their only hope was that the four-o'clock watchers might early and catch the thieves at work. But they waited and they waited, and they heard four strike, and five, and nobody came."

"What had happened to what's-his-name and Rawlinson then?"

"They couldn't make out, and nor could Grinch. However, they had a good look round the church, and nothing seemed to be taken or disturbed in any way. Just then the vicar came along, and they told him all about it. He was very much shocked, naturally, and his first thought—when he found the ornaments were safe and the poor-box all right—was that some Kensitite people had been stealing the wafers from the what d'you call it."

"The tabernacle," suggested Wimsey.

"Yes, that's his name for it. That worried him very much, and he unlocked it and had a look, but the wafers were all there all right, and, as there's only one key, and that was on his own watch-chain, it wasn't a case of anyone substituting unconsecrated wafers for consecrated ones, or any practical joke of that kind. So he sent Mrs. and Miss Hancock home, and had a look round the church outside, and the first thing he saw, lying in the bushes near the south door, was young Rawlinson's motor-cycle."

"Oho!"

"So his next idea was to hunt for Rawlinson and Hubbard. However, he didn't have to look far. He'd got round the church as far as the furnace-house on the north side, when he heard a terrific hullabaloo going on, and people shouting and thumping on the door. So he called Grinch, and they looked in through the little window, and there, if you please, were Hubbard and young Rawlinson, bawling and going on and using the most shocking language. It seems they were set on in exactly the same way, only before they got inside the church. Rawlinson had been passing the evening with Hubbard, I understand, and they had a bit of a sleep downstairs in the back bar, to avoid disturbing the house early—or so they say, though I dare say if the truth was known they were having drinks; and if that's Hancock's idea of a suitable preparation for going to church and saying prayers, all I can say is, it isn't mine. Anyway, they started off just before four, Hubbard going down on the carrier of Rawlinson's bicycle. They had to get off at the south gate, which was pushed to, and while Rawlinson was wheeling the machine up the path two or three men—they couldn't see exactly—jumped out from the trees. There was a bit of a scuffle, but what with the bicycle, and its being so unexpected, they couldn't put up a very good fight, and the men dropped blankets over their heads, or something. I don't know all the details. At any rate, they were bundled into the furnace-house and left there. They may be there still, for all I know, if they haven't found the key. There should be a spare key, but I don't know what's become of it. They sent up for it this morning, but I haven't seen it about for a long time."

"It wasn't left in the lock this time, then?"

"No, it wasn't. They've had to send for the locksmith. I'm

going down now to see what's to be done about it. Like to come, if you're ready?"

Wimsey said he would. Anything in the nature of a problem always fascinated him.

"You were back pretty late, by the way," said Mr. Frobisher-Pym jovially, as they left the house. "Yarning over old times, I suppose."

"We were, indeed," said Wimsey.

"Hope the old girl carried you all right. Lonely bit of road, isn't it? I don't suppose you saw anybody worse than yourself, as the saying goes?"

"Only a policeman," said Wimsey thoughtfully. He had not yet quite decided about the phantom coach. No doubt Plunkett would be relieved to know that he was not the only person to whom the "warning" had come. But, then, had it really been the phantom coach, or merely a delusion, begotten by whisky upon reminiscence? Wimsey, in the cold light of day, was none too certain.

On arriving at the church, the magistrate and his guest found quite a little crowd collected, conspicuous among whom were the vicar, in cassock and biretta, gesticulating freely, and the local policeman, his tunic buttoned awry and his dignity much impaired by the small fry of the village, who clustered round his legs. He had just finished taking down the statements of the two men who had been released from the stoke-hole. The younger of these, a fresh-faced, impudent-looking fellow of twenty-five or so, was in the act of starting up his motor-cycle. He greeted Mr. Frobisher-Pym pleasantly. "Afraid they've made us look a bit small, sir. You'll excuse me, won't you? I'll have to be getting back to Herriotting. Mr. Graham won't be any too pleased if I'm late for the office. I think some of the bright lads have been having a joke with us." He grinned as he pushed the throttle-lever over and departed in a smother of unnecessary smoke that made Mr. Frobisher-Pym sneeze. His fellow-victim, a large, fat man, who looked the sporting publican that he was, grinned shamefacedly at the magistrate.

"Well, Hubbard," said the latter, "I hoped you've enjoyed your experience. I must say I'm surprised at a man of your size letting himself be shut up in a coal-hole like a naughty urchin."

"Yes, sir, I was surprised myself at the time," retorted the publican, good-humouredly enough. "When that there blanket came down on my head, I was the most surprised man in this here country. I gave 'em a hack or two on the shins, though, to remember me by," he added, with a reminiscent chuckle.

"How many of them were there?" asked Wimsey.

"Three or four, I should say, sir. But not 'avin' seen 'em, I can only tell from 'earin' 'em talk. There was two laid 'old of me, I'm pretty sure, and young Rawlinson thinks there was only one 'ad 'old of 'im, but 'e was a wonderful strong 'un."

"We must leave no stone unturned to find out who these people were," said the vicar excitedly. "Ah, Mrs. Frobisher-Pym, come and see what they have done in the church. It is as I thought—an anti-Catholic protest. We must be most thankful that they have done no more than they have."

He led the way in. Someone had lit two or three hanging lamps in the gloomy little chancel. By their light Wimsey was able to see that the neck of the eagle lectern was decorated with an enormous red-white-and-blue bow, and bore a large placard—obviously pinched from the local newspaper offices—"VATICAN BANS IMMODEST DRESS." In each of the choir-stalls a teddy-bear sat, lumpishly amiable, apparently absorbed in reading the choir-books upside-down, while on the ledge before them copies of the *Pink 'Un* were obtrusively displayed. In the pulpit, a waggish hand had set up a pantomime ass's head, elegantly arrayed in a nightgown, and crowned with a handsome nimbus, cut from gold paper.

"Disgraceful, isn't it?" said the vicar.

"Well, Hancock," replied Mr. Frobisher-Pym. "I must say I think you have brought it upon yourself—though I quite agree, of course, that this sort of thing cannot possibly be allowed, and the offenders must be discovered and severely punished. But you must see that many of your practices appear to these people to be papistical nonsense at best, and while that is no excuse . . ."

His reprimanding voice barked on.

". . . what I really can only look upon as this sacrilegious business with old Burdock — a man whose life . . ."

The policeman had by this time shoved away the attendant villagers and was standing beside Lord Peter at the entrance of the rood-screen.

"Was that you was out on the road this morning, sir? Ah! I thought I reckernized your voice. Did you get home all right, sir? Didn't meet nothing?"

There seemed to be a shade more than idle questioning in the tone of his voice. Wimsey turned quickly.

"No, I met nothing — more. Who is it drives a coach with four white horses about this village of a night, sergeant?"

"Not sergeant, sir — I ain't due for promotion yet awhile. Well, sir, as to white horses, I don't altogether like to say. Mr. Mortimer over at Abbotts Bolton has some nice greys, and he's the biggest horse-breeder about these parts — but, well, there, sir, he wouldn't be driving out in all that rain, sir, would he?"

"It doesn't seem a sensible thing to do, certainly."

"No, sir. And" — the constable leaned close to Wimsey and spoke into his ear — "and Mr. Mortimer is a man that's got a head on his shoulders — *and, what's more, so have his horses.*"

"Why," said Wimsey, a little startled by the aptness of this remark, "did you ever know a horse that hadn't?"

"No, sir," said the policeman, with emphasis. "I never knew no *livin'* horse that hadn't. But that's neether here nor there, as the sayin' goes. But as to this church business, that's just a bit of a lark got up among the boys, that's what that is. They don't mean no harm, you know, sir; they likes to be up to their tricks. It's all very well for the vicar to talk, sir, but this ain't no Kensitites nor anything of that, as you can see with half an eye. Just a bit of fun, that's all it is."

"I'd come to the same conclusion myself," said Wimsey, interested, "but I'd rather like to know what makes you think so."

"Lord bless you, sir, ain't it plain as the nose on your face? If it had a-bin these Kensitites, wouldn't they have gone for the crosses and the images and the lights and—that there?" He extended a horny finger in the direction of the tabernacle. "No, sir, these lads what did this ain't laid a finger on the things what you might call sacred images—and they ain't done no harm neether to the communion-table. So I says as it ain't a case of con*trov*versy, but more a bit of fun, like. And they've treated Mr. Burdock's corpse respectful, sir, you see, too. That shows they wasn't meaning anything wrong at heart, don't you see?"

"I agree absolutely," said Wimsey. "In fact, they've taken particular care not to touch anything that a church-man holds really sacred. How long have you been on this job, officer?"

"Three years, sir, come February."

"Ever had any idea of going to town or taking up the detective side of the business?"

"Well, sir—I have—but it isn't just ask and have, as you might say."

Wimsey took a card from his note-case.

"If you ever think seriously about it," he said, "give this card to Chief Inspector Parker, and have a chat with him. Tell him I think you haven't got opportunities enough down here. He's a great friend of mind, and he'll give you a good chance, I know."

"I've heard of you, my lord," said the constable, gratified, "and I'm sure it's very kind of your lordship. Well, I suppose I'd best be getting along now. You leave it to me, Mr. Frobisher-Pym, sir; we'll soon get at the bottom of this here."

"I hope you do," said the magistrate. "Meanwhile, Mr. Hancock, I trust you will realize the inadvisability of leaving the church doors open at night. Well, come along, Wimsey; we'll leave them to get the church straight for the funeral. What have you found there?"

"Nothing," said Wimsey, who had been peering at the floor of the Lady-chapel. "I was afraid you'd got the worm in here, but I see it's only sawdust." He dusted his fingers as he spoke, and followed Mr. Frobisher-Pym out of the building.

When you are staying in a village, you are expected to take part in the interests and amusements of the community. Accordingly, Lord Peter duly attended the funeral of Squire Burdock, and beheld the coffin safely committed to the ground, in a drizzle, certainly, but not without the attendance of a large and reverent congregation. After this ceremony, he was formally introduced to Mr. and Mrs. Haviland Burdock, and was able to confirm his previous impression that the lady was well, not to say too well, dressed, as might be expected from one whose wardrobe was based upon silk stockings. She was a handsome woman, in a large, bold style, and the hand that clasped Wimsey's was quite painfully encrusted with diamonds. Haviland was disposed to be friendly—and, indeed, silk manufacturers have no reason to be otherwise to rich men of noble birth. He seemed to be aware of Wimsey's reputation as an antiquarian and book-collector, and extended a hearty invitation to him to come and see the old house.

"My brother Martin is still abroad," he said, "but I'm sure he would be delighted to have you come and look at the place. I'm told there are some very fine old books in the library. We shall be staying here till Monday—if Mrs. Hancock will be good enough to have us. Suppose you come along tomorrow afternoon."

Wimsey said he would be delighted.

Mrs. Hancock interposed and said, wouldn't Lord Peter come to tea at the vicarage first.

Wimsey said it was very good of her.

"Then that's settled," said Mrs. Burdock. "You and Mr. Pym come to tea, and then we'll all go over the house together. I've hardly seen it myself yet."

"It's very well worth seeing," said Mr. Frobisher-Pym. "Fine old place, but takes some money to keep up. Has nothing been seen of the will yet, Mr. Burdock?"

"Nothing whatever," said Haviland. "It's curious, because Mr. Graham—the solicitor, you know, Lord Peter—certainly drew one up, just after poor Martin's unfortunate difference with our father. He remembers it perfectly."

"Can't he remember what's in it?"

"He could, of course, but he doesn't think it etiquette to say. He's one of the crusted old type. Poor Martin always called him an old scoundrel—but then, of course, he never approved of Martin, so Martin was not altogether unprejudiced. Besides, as Mr. Graham says, all that was some years ago, and it's quite possible that the governor destroyed the will later, or made a new one in America."

" 'Poor Martin' doesn't seem to have been popular hereabouts," said Wimsey to Mr. Frobisher-Pym, as they parted from the Burdocks and turned homewards.

"N-no," said the magistrate. "Not with Graham, anyway. Personally, I rather liked the lad, though he was a bit harum-scarum. I dare say he's sobered up with time—and marriage. It's odd that they can't find the will. But, if it was made at the time of the rumpus, it's bound to be in Haviland's favour."

"I think Haviland thinks so," said Wimsey. "His manner seemed to convey a chastened satisfaction. I expect the discreet Graham made it fairly clear that the advantage was not with the unspeakable Martin."

The following morning turned out fine, and Wimsey, who was supposed to be enjoying a rest-and-fresh-air cure in Little Doddering, petitioned for a further loan of Polly Flinders. His host consented with pleasure, and only regretted that he could not accompany his guest, being booked to attend a Board of Guardians' meeting in connexion with the workhouse.

"But you could go up and get a good blow on the common," he suggested. "Why not go round by Petering Friars, turn off across the common till you get to Dead Man's Post, and come back by the Frimpton road? It makes a very pleasant round—about nineteen miles. You'll be back in nice time for lunch if you take it easy."

Wimsey fell in with the plan—the more readily that it exactly coincided with his own inward purpose. He had a reason for wishing to ride over the Frimpton road by daylight.

"You'll be careful about Dead Man's Post," said Mrs. Frobisher-Pym a little anxiously. "The horses have a way of shying at it. I don't know why. People say, of course—"

"All nonsense," said her husband. "The villagers dislike the place and that makes the horses nervous. It's remarkable how a rider's feelings communicate themselves to his mount. *I've* never had any trouble at Dead Man's Post."

It was a quiet and pretty road, even on a November day, that led to Petering Friars. Jogging down the winding Essex lanes in the wintry sunshine, Wimsey felt soothed and happy. A good burst across the common raised his spirits to exhilaration pitch. He had entirely forgotten Dead Man's Post and its uncanny reputation, when a violent start and swerve, so sudden that it nearly unseated him, recalled him to what he was doing. With some difficulty, he controlled Polly Flinders, and brought her to a standstill.

He was at the highest point of the common, following a bridle-path which was bordered on each side by gorse and dead bracken. A little way ahead of him another bridle-path seemed to run into it, and at the junction of the two was something which he had vaguely imagined to be a decayed sign-post. Certainly it was short and thick for a sign-post, and had no arms. It appeared, however, to bear some sort of inscription on the face that was turned towards him.

He soothed the mare, and urged her gently towards the post. She took a few hesitating steps, and plunged sideways, snorting and shivering.

"Queer!" said Wimsey. "If this is my state of mind communicating itself to my mount, I'd better see a doctor. My nerves must be in a rotten state. Come up, old lady! What's the matter with you!"

Polly Flinders, apologetic but determined, refused to budge. He urged her gently with his heel. She sidled away, with ears laid back, and he saw the white of a protesting eye.

He slipped from the saddle, and, putting his hand through the bridle, endeavoured to lead her forward. After a little persuasion, the mare followed him, with stretched neck and treading as though on egg-shells. After a dozen hesitating paces, she stopped again, trembling in all her limbs. He put his hand on her neck and found it wet with sweat.

"Damn it all!" said Wimsey. "Look here, I'm jolly well going to read what's on that post. If you won't come, will you stand still?"

He dropped the bridle. The mare stood quietly with hanging head. He left her and went forward, glancing back from time to time to see that she showed no disposition to bolt. She stood quietly enough, however, only shifting her feet uneasily.

Wimsey walked up to the post. It was a stout pillar of ancient oak, newly painted white. The inscription, too, had been recently blacked in. It read:

ON THIS SPOT
GEORGE WINTER
WAS FOULLY MURTHERED
IN DEFENSE OF
HIS MASTER'S GOODS
BY BLACK RALPH
OF HERRIOTTING
WHO WAS AFTERWARD
HANGED IN CHAINS
ON THE PLACE OF HIS CRIME
9 NOVEMBER 1674

FEAR JUSTICE

"And very nice, too," said Wimsey. "Dead Man's Post without a doubt. Polly Flinders seems to share the local feeling about the place. Well, Polly, if them's your sentiments, I won't do violence to them. But may I ask why, if you're so sensitive about a mere post, you should swallow a death-coach and four headless horses with such hardened equanimity?"

The mare took the shoulder of his jacket gently between her lips and mumbled at it.

"Just so," said Wimsey. "I perfectly understand. You would if you could, but you really can't. But those horses, Polly—did they bring with them no brimstone blast from the nethermost pit? Can it be that they really exuded nothing but an honest and familiar smell of stables?"

He mounted, and, turning Polly's head to the right, guided her in a circle, so as to give Dead Man's Post a wide berth before striking the path again.

"The supernatural explanation is, I think, excluded. Not on *a priori* grounds, which would be unsound, but on the evidence of Polly's senses. There remain the alternatives of whisky and jiggery-pokery. Further investigation seems called for."

He continued to muse as the mare moved quietly forward.

"Supposing I wanted, for some reason, to scare the neighbourhood with the apparition of a coach and headless horses, I should choose a dark, rainy night. Good! It was that kind of night. Now, if I took black horses and painted their bodies white—poor devils! what a state they'd be in. No. How do they do these Maskelyne-and-Devant stunts where they cut off people's heads? White horses, of course—and black felt clothing over their heads. Right! And luminous paint on the harness, with a touch here and there on their bodies, to make good contrast and ensure that the whole show wasn't invisible. No difficulty about that. But they must go silently. Well, why not? Four stout black cloth bags filled with bran, drawn well up and tied round the fetlocks would make any horse go quietly enough, especially if there was a bit of a wind going. Rags round the bridle-rings to prevent clinking, and round the ends of the traces to keep from squeaking. Give 'em a coachman in a white coat and a black mask, hitch 'em to a rubber-tyred fly, picked out with phosphorus and well-oiled at the joints—and I swear I'd make something quite ghostly enough to startle a rather well-irrigated gentleman on a lonely road at half past two in the morning."

He was pleased with this thought, and tapped his boot cheerfully with his whip.

"But damn it all! They never passed me again. Where did they go to? A coach-and-horses can't vanish into thin air, you know. There must be a side-road after all—or else, Polly Flinders, you've been pulling my leg all the time."

The bridle-path eventually debouched upon the highway at the now familiar fork where Wimsey had met the policeman. As he slowly ambled homewards, his lordship scanned the left-hand hedgerow, looking for the lane which surely must exist. But nothing rewarded his search. Enclosed fields with padlocked gates presented the only breaks in the hedge, till he again found himself looking down the avenue of trees up which the death-coach had come galloping two nights before.

"Damn!" said Wimsey.

It occurred to him for the first time that the coach might perhaps have turned round and gone back through Little Doddering. Certainly it had been seen by Little Doddering Church on Wednesday. But on that occasion, also, it had galloped off in the direction of Frimpton. In fact, thinking it over, Wimsey concluded that it had approached from Frimpton, gone round the church—widdershins, naturally—by the Back Lane, and returned by the high-road whence it came. But in that case—

"Turn again, Whittington," said Wimsey, and Polly Flinders rotated obediently in the road. "Through one of those fields it went, or I'm a Dutchman."

He pulled Polly into a slow walk, and passed along the strip of grass at the right-hand side, staring at the ground as though he were an Aberdonian who had lost a sixpence.

The first gate led into a ploughed field, harrowed smooth and sown with autumn wheat. It was clear that no wheeled thing had been across it for many weeks. The second gate looked more promising. It gave upon fallow ground, and the entrance was seamed with innumerable wheel-ruts. On further examination, however, it was clear that this was the one and only gate. It seemed unlikely that the mysterious coach should have been taken into a field from which there was no way out. Wimsey decided to seek farther.

The third gate was in bad repair. It sagged heavily from its hinges; the hasp was gone, and gate and post had been secured with elaborate twists of wire. Wimsey dismounted and examined these, convincing himself that their rusty surface had not been recently disturbed.

There remained only two more gates before he came to the cross-roads. One led into plough again, where the dark ridge-and-furrow showed no sign of disturbance, but at sight of the last gate Wimsey's heart gave a leap.

There was plough-land here also, but round the edge of the field ran a wide, beaten path, rutted and water-logged. The gate was not locked, but opened simply with a spring catch. Wimsey examined the approach. Among the wide ruts made by farm-wagons was the track of four narrow wheels — the unmistakable prints of rubber tyres. He pushed the gate open and passed through.

The path skirted two sides of the plough; then came another gate and another field, containing a long barrow of mangold wurzels and a couple of barns. At the sound of Polly's hoofs, a man emerged from the nearest barn, with a paint-brush in his hand, and stood watching Wimsey's approach.

"Morning!" said the latter genially.

"Morning, sir."

"Fine day after the rain."

"Yes, it is, sir."

"I hope I'm not trespassing?"

"Where was you wanting to go, sir?"

"I thought, as a matter of fact — hullo!"

"Anything wrong, sir?"

Wimsey shifted in the saddle.

"I fancy this girth's slipped a bit. It's a new one." (This was a fact.) "Better have a look."

The man advanced to investigate, but Wimsey had dismounted and was tugging at the strap, with his head under the mare's belly.

"Yes, it wants taking up a trifle. Oh! Thanks most awfully. Is this a short cut to Abbotts Bolton, by the way?"

"Not to the village, sir, though you can get through this way. It comes out by Mr. Mortimer's stables."

"Ah, yes. This his land?"

"No, sir, it's Mr. Topham's land, but Mr. Mortimer rents this field and the next for fodder."

"Oh, yes." Wimsey peered across the hedge. "Lucerne, I suppose. Or clover."

"Clover, sir. And the mangolds is for the cattle."

"Oh—Mr. Mortimer keeps cattle as well as horses?"

"Yes, sir."

"Very jolly. Have a gasper?" Wimsey had sidled across to the barn in his interest, and was gazing absently into its dark interior. It contained a number of farm implements and a black fly of antique construction, which seemed to be undergoing renovation with black varnish. Wimsey pulled some vestas from his pocket. The box was apparently damp, for, after one or two vain attempts he abandoned it, and struck a match on the wall of the barn. The flame, lighting up the ancient fly, showed it to be incongruously fitted with rubber tyres.

"Very fine stud, Mr. Mortimer's, I understand," said Wimsey carelessly.

"Yes, sir, very fine indeed."

"I suppose he hasn't any greys, by any chance. My mother—queenly woman, Victorian ideas, and all that—is rather keen on greys. Sports a carriage and pay-ah, don't you know."

"Yes, sir? Well, Mr. Mortimer would be able to suit the lady, I think, sir. He has several greys."

"No? has he though? I must really go over and see him. Is it far?"

"Matter of five or six mile by the fields, sir."

Wimsey looked at his watch.

"Oh, dear! I'm really afraid it's too far for this morning. I absolutely promised to get back to lunch. I must come over another day. Thanks *so* much. Is that girth right now? Oh, really, I'm immensely obliged. Get yourself a drink, won't you—and tell Mr. Mortimer not to sell his greys till I've seen them. Well, *good* morning, and many thanks."

He set Polly Flinders on the homeward path and trotted gently away. Not till he was out of sight of the barn did he pull up and, stooping from the saddle, thoughtfully examine his boots. They were liberally plastered with bran.

"I must have picked it up in the barn," said Wimsey. "Curious, if true. Why should Mr. Mortimer be lashing the stuffing out of the greys in an old fly at dead of night—and with muffled hoofs and no heads to boot? It's not a kind thing to do. It frightened Plunkett very much. It made me think I was drunk—a thought I hate to think. Ought I to tell the police? Are Mr. Mortimer's jokes any business of mine? What do *you* think, Polly?"

The mare, hearing her name, energetically shook her head.

"You think not? Perhaps you are right. Let us say that Mr. Mortimer did it for a wager. Who am I to interfere with his amusements? All the same," added his lordship, "I'm glad to know it wasn't Lumsden's whisky."

"This is the library," said Haviland, ushering in his guests. "A fine room—and a fine collection of books, I'm told, though literature isn't much in my line. It wasn't much in the governor's line, either, I'm afraid. The place wants doing up, as you see. I don't know whether Martin will take it in hand. It's a job that'll cost money, of course."

Wimsey shivered a little as he gazed round—more from sympathy than from cold, though a white November fog lay curled against the tall windows and filtered damply through the frames.

A long, mouldering room, in the frigid neo-classical style, the library was melancholy enough in the sunless grey afternoon, even without the signs of neglect which wrung the book-collector's heart. The walls, panelled to half their height with bookcases, ran up in plaster to the moulded ceiling. Damp had blotched them into grotesque shapes, and here and there were ugly cracks and squamous patches, from which the plaster had fallen in yellowish flakes. A wet chill seemed to ooze from the books, from the calf bindings peeling and perishing, from the stains of greenish mildew which spread horridly from volume to volume. The curious musty odour of decayed leather and damp paper added to the general cheerlessness of the atmosphere.

"Oh, dear, dear!" said Wimsey, peering dismally into this sepulchre of forgotten learning. With his shoulders hunched like the neck-feathers of a chilly bird, with his long nose and half-shut eyes, he resembled a dilapidated heron, brooding over the stagnation of a wintry pool.

"What a freezing-cold place!" exclaimed Mrs. Hancock. "You really ought to scold Mrs. Lovall, Mr. Burdock. When she was put in here as caretaker, I said to my husband—didn't I, Philip?—that your father had chosen the laziest woman in Little Doddering. She ought to have kept up big fires here, *at least* twice a week! It's really shameful, the way she has let things go."

"Yes, isn't it?" agreed Haviland.

Wimsey said nothing. He was nosing along the shelves, every now and then taking a volume down and glancing at it.

"It was always rather a depressing room," went on Haviland. "I remember, when I was a kid, it used to overawe me rather. Martin and I used to browse about among the books, you know, but I think we were always afraid that something or somebody would stalk out upon us from the dark corners. What's that you've got there, Lord Peter? Oh, *Foxe's Book of Martyrs*. Dear me! How those pictures did terrify me in the old days! And there was a *Pilgrim's Progress*, with a most alarming picture of Apollyon straddling over the whole breadth of the way, which gave me many nightmares. Let me see. It used to live over in this bay, I think. Yes, here it is. How it does bring all back, to be sure! Is it valuable, by the way?"

"No, not really. But this first edition of Burton is worth money; badly spotted, though—you'd better send it to be cleaned. And this is an extremely fine Boccaccio; take care of it."

"John Boccace — *The Dance of Machabree*. It's a good title, anyhow. Is that the same Boccaccio that wrote the naughty stories?"

"Yes," said Wimsey, a little shortly. He resented this attitude towards Boccaccio.

"Never read them," said Haviland, with a wink at his wife, "but I've seen 'em in the windows of those surgical shops — so I suppose they're naughty, eh? The vicar's looking shocked."

"Oh, not at all," said Mr. Hancock, with a conscientious assumption of broad-mindedness. "*Et ego in Arcadia* — that is to say, one doesn't enter the Church without undergoing a classical education, and making the acquaintance of much more worldly authors even than Boccaccio. Those woodcuts are very fine, to my uninstructed eye."

"Very fine indeed," said Wimsey.

"There's another old book I remember, with jolly pictures," said Haviland. "A chronicle of some sort — what's 'is name — place in Germany — *you* know — where that hangman came from. They published his diary the other day. I read it, but it wasn't really exciting; not half as gruesome as old Harrison Ainsworth. What's the name of the place?"

"Nuremberg?" suggested Wimsey.

"That's it, of course — the *Nuremberg Chronicle*. I wonder if that's still in its old place. It was over here by the window, if I remember rightly."

He led the way to the end of one of the bays, which ran up close against a window. Here the damp seemed to have done its worst. A pane of glass was broken, and rain had blown in.

"Now where has it gone to? A big book, it was, with a stamped leather binding. I'd like to see the old *Chronicle* again. I haven't set eyes on it for donkey's years."

His glance roamed vaguely over the shelves. Wimsey, with the book-lover's instinct, was the first to spot the *Chronicle*, wedged at the extreme end of the shelf against the outer wall. He hitched his finger into the top edge of the spine, but finding that the rotting leather was ready to crumble at a touch, he dislodged a neighbouring book and drew the *Chronicle* gently out, using his whole hand.

"Here he is—in pretty bad condition, I'm afraid. Hullo!"

As he drew the book away from the wall, a piece of folded parchment came away with it, and fell at his feet. He stooped and picked it up.

"I say, Burdock—isn't this what you've been looking for?"

Haviland Burdock, who had been rooting about on one of the lower shelves, straightened himself quickly, his face red from stooping.

"By Jove!" he said, turning first redder and then pale with excitement. "Look at this, Winnie. It's the governor's will. What an extraordinary thing! Whoever would have thought of looking for it here, of all places?"

"Is it really the will?" cried Mrs. Hancock.

"No doubt about it, I should say," observed Wimsey coolly. "Last Will and Testament of Simon Burdock." He stood, turning the grimy document over and over in his hands, looking from the endorsement to the plain side of the folded parchment.

"Well, well!" said Mr. Hancock. "How strange! It seems almost providential that you should have taken that book down."

"What does the will say?" demanded Mrs. Burdock, in some excitement.

"I beg your pardon," said Wimsey, handing it over to her. "Yes, as you say, Mr. Hancock, it does almost seem as if I was meant to find it." He glanced down again at the *Chronicle*, mournfully tracing with his finger the outline of a damp stain which had rotted the cover and spread to the inner pages, almost obliterating the colophon.

Haviland Burdock meanwhile had spread the will out on the nearest table. His wife leaned over his shoulder. The Hancocks, barely controlling their curiosity, stood near, awaiting the result. Wimsey, with an elaborate pretence of non-interference in this family matter, examined the wall against which the *Chronicle* had stood, feeling its moist surface and

examining the damp-stains. They had assumed the appearance of a grinning face. He compared them with the corresponding mark on the book, and shook his head desolately
over the damage.

Mr. Frobisher-Pym, who had wandered away some time
before and was absorbed in an ancient book of Farriery,
now approached, and enquired what the excitement was
about.

"Listen to this!" cried Haviland. His voice was quiet, but a
suppressed triumph throbbed in it and glittered from his eyes.

" 'I bequeath everything of which I die possessed'—there's
a lot of enumeration of properties here, which doesn't matter—'to my eldest son, Martin'—"

Mr. Frobisher-Pym whistled.

"Listen! 'To my eldest son Martin, for so long as my body
shall remain above ground. But so soon as I am buried, I
direct that the whole of this property shall revert to my
younger son Haviland absolutely'—"

"Good God!" said Mr. Frobisher-Pym.

"There's a lot more," said Haviland, "but that's the gist of it."

"Let me see," said the magistrate.

He took the will from Haviland, and read it through with
a frowning face.

"That's right," he said. "No possible doubt about it. Martin
has had his property and lost it again. How very curious. Up
till yesterday everything belonged to him, though nobody
knew it. Now it is all yours, Burdock. This certainly is the
strangest will I ever saw. Just fancy that. Martin the heir, up
to the time of the funeral. And now—well, Burdock, I must
congratulate you."

"Thank you," said Haviland. "It is very unexpected." He
laughed unsteadily.

"But what a queer idea!" cried Mrs. Burdock. "Suppose
Martin had been at home. It almost seems a mercy that he
wasn't, doesn't it? I mean, it would all have been so awkward.
What would have happened if he had tried to stop the funeral,
for instance?"

"Yes," said Mrs. Hancock. "Could he have done anything? Who decides about funerals?"

"The executors, as a rule," said Mr. Frobisher-Pym.

"Who are the executors in this case?" enquired Wimsey.

"I don't know. Let me see." Mr. Frobisher-Pym examined the document again. "Ah, yes! Here we are. 'I appoint my two sons, Martin and Haviland, joint executors of this my will.' What an extraordinary arrangement."

"I call it a wicked, un-Christian arrangement," cried Mrs. Hancock. "It might have caused dreadful mischief if the will hadn't been—quite providentially—lost!"

"Hush, my dear!" said her husband.

"I'm afraid," said Haviland grimly, "that that was my father's idea. It's no use my pretending he wasn't spiteful; he was, and I believe he hated both Martin and me like poison."

"Don't say that," pleaded the vicar.

"I do say it. He made our lives a burden to us, and he obviously wanted to go on making them a burden after he was dead. If he'd seen us cutting each other's throats, he'd only have been too pleased. Come, vicar, it's no use pretending. He hated our mother and was jealous of us. Everybody knows that. It probably pleased his unpleasant sense of humour to think of us squabbling over his body. Fortunately, he overreached himself when he hid the will here. He's buried now, and the problem settles itself."

"Are you quite sure of that?" said Wimsey.

"Why, of course," said the magistrate. "The property goes to Mr. Haviland Burdock as soon as his father's body is underground. Well, his father was buried yesterday."

"But are you sure of *that?*" repeated Wimsey. He looked from one to the other quizzically, his long lips curling into something like a grin.

"Sure of that?" exclaimed the vicar. "My dear Lord Peter, you were present at the funeral. You saw him buried yourself."

"I saw his coffin buried," said Wimsey mildly. "That the body was in it is merely an unverified inference."

"I think," said Mr. Frobisher-Pym, "this is rather an

unseemly kind of jest. There is no reason to imagine that the body was not in the coffin."

"I saw it in the coffin," said Haviland, "and so did my wife."

"And so did I," said the vicar. "I was present when it was transferred from the temporary shell in which it crossed over from the States to a permanent lead-and-oak coffin provided by Joliffe. And, if further witnesses are necessary, you can easily get Joliffe himself and his men, who put the body in and screwed it down."

"Just so," said Wimsey. "I'm not denying that the body was in the coffin when the coffin was placed in the chapel. I only doubt whether it was there when it was put in the ground."

"That is a most unheard-of suggestion to make, Lord Peter," said Mr. Frobisher-Pym, with severity. "May I ask if you have anything to go upon? And, if the body is not in the grave, perhaps you wouldn't mind telling us where you imagine it to be?"

"Not at all," said Wimsey. He perched himself on the edge of the table and sat, swinging his legs and looking down at his own hands, as he ticked his points off on his fingers.

"I think," he said, "that this story begins with young Rawlinson. He is a clerk in the office of Mr. Graham, who drew up this will, and I fancy he knows something about its conditions. So, of course, does Mr. Graham, but I don't somehow suspect *him* of being mixed up in this. From what I can hear, he is not a man to take sides—or not Mr. Martin's side, at any rate.

"When the news of Mr. Burdock's death was cabled over from the States, I think young Rawlinson remembered the terms of the will, and considered that Mr. Martin—being abroad and all that—would be rather at a disadvantage. Rawlinson must be rather attached to your brother, by the way—"

"Martin always had a way of picking up good-for-nothing youths and wasting his time with them," agreed Haviland sulkily.

The vicar seemed to feel that this statement needed some

amendment, and murmured that he had always heard how good Martin was with the village lads.

"Quite so," said Wimsey. "Well, I think young Rawlinson wanted to give Martin an equal chance of securing the legacy, don't you see. He didn't like to say anything about the will—which might or might not turn up—and possibly he thought that even if it did turn up there might be difficulties. Well, anyway, he decided that the best thing to do was to steal the body and keep it above ground till Martin came home to see to things himself."

"This is an extraordinary accusation," began Mr. Frobisher-Pym.

"I dare say I'm mistaken," said Wimsey, "but it's just my idea. It makes a damn good story, anyhow—you see! Well, then, young Rawlinson saw that this was too big a job to carry out alone, so he looked round for somebody to help him. And he pitched on Mr. Mortimer."

"Mortimer?"

"I don't know Mr. Mortimer personally, but he seems to be a sportin' sort of customer from what I can hear, with certain facilities which everybody hasn't got. Young Rawlinson and Mortimer put their heads together and worked out a plan of action. Of course, Mr. Hancock, you helped them enormously, with this lying-in-state idea of yours. Without that, I don't know if they could have worked it."

Mr. Hancock made an embarrassed clucking sound.

"The idea was this. Mortimer was to provide an antique fly and four white horses, made up with luminous paint and black cloth to represent the Burdock death-coach. The advantage of that idea was that nobody would feel inclined to inspect the turn-out too closely if they saw it hangin' round the churchyard at unearthly hours. Meanwhile, young Rawlinson had to get himself accepted as a watcher for the chapel, and to find a sporting companion to watch with him and take a hand in the game. He fixed things up with the publican-fellow, and spun a tale for Mr. Hancock, so as to get the vigil from four to six. Didn't it strike you as odd, Mr. Hancock, that he should be so keen to come all the way from Herriotting?"

"I am accustomed to find keenness in my congregation," said Mr. Hancock stiffly.

"Yes, but Rawlinson didn't belong to your congregation. Anyway it was all worked out, and there was a dress rehearsal on the Wednesday night, which frightened your man Plunkett into fits, sir."

"If I thought this was true—" said Mr. Frobisher-Pym.

"On Thursday night," pursued Wimsey, "the conspirators were ready, hidden in the chancel at two in the morning. They waited till Mrs. and Miss Hancock had taken their places, and then made a row to attract their attention. When the ladies courageously advanced to find out what was up, they popped out and bundled 'em into the vestry."

"Good gracious!" said Mrs. Hancock.

"That was when the death-coach affair was timed to drive up to the south door. It came round the Back Lane, I fancy, though I can't be sure. Then Mortimer and the other two took the embalmed body out of the coffin and filled its place up with bags of sawdust. I know it was sawdust, because I found the remains of it on the Lady-chapel floor in the morning. They put the body in the fly, and Mortimer drove off with it. They passed me on the Herriotting Road at half past two, so they can't have wasted much time over the job. Mortimer may have been alone, or possibly he had someone with him to see to the body while he himself did the headless coachman business in a black mask. I'm not certain about that. They drove through the last gate before you come to the fork at Frimpton, and went across the fields to Mortimer's barn. They left the fly there—I know that, because I saw it, and I saw the bran they used to muffle the horses' hoofs, too. I expect they took it on from there in a car, and fetched the horses up next day—but that's a detail. I don't know, either, where they took the body to, but I expect, if you went and asked Mortimer about it, he would be able to assure you that it was still above ground."

Wimsey paused. Mr. Frobisher-Pym and the Hancocks were looking only puzzled and angry, but Haviland's face was green. Mrs. Haviland showed a red, painted spot on each cheek, and her mouth was haggard. Wimsey picked up the *Nuremberg Chronicle* and caressed its covers thoughtfully as he went on.

"Meanwhile, of course, young Rawlinson and his companion were doing the camouflage in the church, to give the idea of a Protestant outrage. Having fixed everything up neat and pretty, all they had to do was to lock themselves up in the furnace-house and chuck the key through the window. You'll probably find it there, Mr. Hancock, if you care to look. Didn't you think that story of an assault by two or three men was a bit thin? Hubbard is a hefty great fellow, and Rawlinson's a sturdy lad—and yet, on their own showing, they were bundled into a coal-hole like helpless infants, without a scratch on either of 'em. Look for the men in buckram, my dear sir, look for the men in buckram!"

"Look here, Wimsey, are you sure you're not romancing?" said Mr. Frobisher-Pym. "One would need some very clear proof before—"

"Certainly," said Wimsey. "Get a Home Office order. Open the grave. You'll soon see whether it's true or whether it's just my diseased imagination."

"I think this whole conversation is disgusting," cried Mrs. Burdock. "Don't listen to it, Haviland. Anything more heartless on the day after father's funeral than sitting here and inventing such a revolting story I simply can't imagine. It is not worth paying a moment's attention to. You will certainly not permit your father's body to be disturbed. It's horrible. It's a desecration."

"It is very unpleasant indeed," said Mr. Frobisher-Pym gravely, "but if Lord Peter is seriously putting forward this astonishing theory, which I can scarcely credit—"

Wimsey shrugged his shoulders.

"—then I feel bound to remind you, Mr. Burdock, that

your brother, when he returns, may insist on having the matter investigated."

"But he can't, can he?" said Mrs. Burdock.

"Of course he can, Winnie," snapped her husband savagely. "He's an executor. He has as much right to have the governor dug up as I have to forbid it. Don't be a fool."

"If Martin had any decency, he would forbid it, too," said Mrs. Burdock.

"Oh, well!" said Mrs. Hancock, "shocking as it may seem, there's the money to be considered. Mr. Martin might think it a duty to his wife, and his family, if he should ever have any—"

"The whole thing is preposterous," said Haviland decidedly. "I don't believe a word of it. If I did, naturally I should be the first person to take action in the matter—not only in justice to Martin, but on my own account. But if you ask me to believe that a responsible man like Mortimer would purloin a corpse and desecrate a church—the thing only has to be put into plain words to show how absurd and unthinkable it is. I suppose Lord Peter Wimsey, who consorts, as I understand, with criminals and police officers, finds the idea conceivable. I can only say that I do not. I am sorry that his mind should have become so blunted to all decent feeling. That's all. Good afternoon."

Mr. Frobisher-Pym jumped up.

"Come, come, Burdock, don't take that attitude. I am sure Lord Peter intended no discourtesy. I must say I think he's all wrong, but, 'pon my soul, things have been so disturbed in the village these last few days, I'm not surprised anybody should think there was something behind it. Now, let's forget about it—and hadn't we better be moving out of this terribly cold room? It's nearly dinner-time. Bless me, what will Agatha think of us?"

Wimsey held out his hand to Burdock, who took it reluctantly.

"I'm sorry," said Wimsey. "I suffer from hypertrophy of

the imagination, y'know. Over-stimulation of the thyroid probably. Don't mind me. I apologize, and all that."

"I don't think, Lord Peter," said Mrs. Burdock acidly, "you ought to exercise your imagination at the expense of good taste."

Wimsey followed her from the room in some confusion. Indeed, he was so disturbed that he carried away the *Nuremberg Chronicle* beneath his arm, which was an odd thing for him to do under the circumstances.

"I am gravely distressed," said Mr. Hancock.

He had come over, after Sunday evening service, to call upon the Frobisher-Pyms. He sat upright on his chair, his thin face flushed with anxiety.

"I could never have believed such a thing of Hubbard. It has been a grievous shock to me. It is not only the great wickedness of stealing a dead body from the very precincts of the church, though that is grave enough. It is the sad hypocrisy of his behaviour—the mockery of sacred things— the making use of the holy services of his religion to further worldly ends. He actually attended the funeral, Mr. Frobisher-Pym, and exhibited every sign of grief and respect. Even now he hardly seems to realize the sinfulness of his conduct. I feel it very much, as a priest and as a pastor—very much indeed."

"Oh, well, Hancock," said Mr. Frobisher-Pym, "you must make allowances, you know. Hubbard's not a bad fellow, but you can't expect refinement of feeling from a man of his class. The point is, what are we to do about it? Mr. Burdock must be told, of course. It's a most awkward situation. Dear me! Hubbard confessed the whole conspiracy, you say? How did he come to do that?"

"I taxed him with it," said the parson. "When I came to think over Lord Peter Wimsey's remarks, I was troubled in my mind. It seemed to me—I cannot say why—that there might be some truth in the story, wild as it appeared. I was so worried about it that I swept the floor of the Lady-chapel myself last night, and I found quite a quantity of sawdust among the sweepings. That led me to search for the key of the furnace-house, and I discovered it in some bushes at a little distance—in fact, within a stone's throw—of the furnace-house window. I sought guidance in prayer—and from my wife, whose judgement I greatly respect—and I made up my mind to speak to Hubbard after Mass. It was a great relief to me that he did not present himself at Early Celebration. Feeling as I did, I should have had scruples."

"Just so, just so," said the magistrate, a little impatiently. "Well, you taxed him with it, and he confessed?"

"He did. I am sorry to say he showed no remorse at all. He even laughed. It was a most painful interview."

"I am sure it must have been," said Mrs. Frobisher-Pym sympathetically.

"We must go and see Mr. Burdock," said the magistrate, rising. "Whatever old Burdock may or may not have intended by that iniquitous will of his, it's quite evident that Hubbard and Mortimer and Rawlinson were entirely in the wrong. Upon my word, I've no idea whether it's an indictable offence to steal a body. I must look it up. But I should say it was. If there is any property in a corpse, it must belong to the family or the executors. And in any case, it's sacrilege, to say nothing of the scandal in the parish. I must say, Hancock, it won't do us any good in the eyes of the Nonconformists. However, no doubt you realize that. Well, it's an unpleasant job, and the sooner we tackle it the better. I'll run over to the vicarage with you and help you to break it to the Burdocks. How about you, Wimsey? You were right, after all, and I think Burdock owes you an apology."

"Oh, I'll keep out of it," said Wimsey. "I shan't be exactly *persona grata*, don't you know. It's going to mean a deuce of a big financial loss to the Haviland Burdocks."

"So it is. Most unpleasant. Well, perhaps you're right. Come along, vicar."

Wimsey and his hostess sat discussing the matter by the fire for half an hour or so, when Mr. Frobisher-Pym suddenly put his head in and said:

"I say, Wimsey—we're all going over to Mortimer's. I wish you'd come and drive the car. Merridew always has the day off on Sunday, and I don't care about driving at night, particularly in this fog."

"Right you are," said Wimsey. He ran upstairs, and came down in a few moments wearing a heavy leather flying-coat, and with a parcel under his arm. He greeted the Burdocks briefly, climbed into the driving-seat, and was soon steering cautiously through the mist along the Herriotting Road.

He smiled a little grimly to himself as they came up under the trees to the spot where the phantom coach had passed him. As they passed the gate through which the ingenious apparition had vanished, he indulged himself by pointing it out, and was rewarded by hearing a snarl from Haviland. At the well-remembered fork, he took the right-hand turning into Frimpton and drove steadily for six miles or so, till a warning shout from Mr. Frobisher-Pym summoned him to look out for the turning up to Mortimer's.

Mr. Mortimer's house, with its extensive stabling and farm buildings, stood about two miles back from the main road. In the darkness Wimsey could see little of it; but he noticed that the ground-floor windows were all lit up, and, when the door opened to the magistrate's imperative ring, a loud burst of laughter from the interior gave evidence that Mr. Mortimer was not taking his misdoings too seriously.

"Is Mr. Mortimer at home?" demanded Mr. Frobisher-Pym, in the tone of a man not to be trifled with.

"Yes, sir. Will you come in, please?"

They stepped into a large, old-fashioned hall, brilliantly lit, and made cosy with a heavy oak screen across the door. As Wimsey advanced, blinking, from the darkness, he saw a large, thick-set man, with a ruddy face, advancing with hand outstretched in welcome.

"Frobisher-Pym! By Jove! how decent of you to come over! We've got some old friends of yours here. Oh!" (in a slightly altered tone) "Burdock! Well, well—"

"Damn you!" said Haviland Burdock, thrusting furiously

past the magistrate, who was trying to hold him back. "Damn you, you swine! Chuck this bloody farce. What have you done with the body?"

"The body, eh?" said Mr. Mortimer, retreating in some confusion.

"Yes, curse you! Your friend Hubbard's split. It's no good denying it. What the devil do you mean by it? You've got the body here somewhere. Where is it? Hand it over!"

He strode threateningly round the screen into the lamp-light. A tall, thin man rose up unexpectedly from the depths of an armchair and confronted him.

"Hold hard, old man!"

"Good God!" said Haviland, stepping heavily back on Wimsey's toes. "Martin!"

"Sure," said the other. "Here I am. Come back like a bad half-penny. How are you?"

"So *you're* at the bottom of this!" stormed Haviland. "I might have known it. You damned, dirty hound! I suppose you think it's decent to drag your father out of his coffin and tote him about the country like a circus. It's degrading. It's disgusting. It's abominable. You must be perfectly dead to all decent feeling. You don't deny it, I suppose?"

"I say, Burdock!" expostulated Mortimer.

"Shut up, curse you!" said Haviland. "I'll deal with you in a minute. Now, look here, Martin, I'm not going to stand any more of this disgraceful behaviour. You'll give up that body, and—"

"Just a moment, just a moment," said Martin. He stood, smiling a little, his hands thrust into the pockets of his dinner-jacket. "This *éclaircissement* seems to be rather public. Who are all these people? Oh, it's the vicar. I see. I'm afraid we owe you a little explanation, vicar. And, er—"

"This is Lord Peter Wimsey," put in Mr. Frobisher-Pym, "who discovered your—I'm afraid, Burdock, I must agree with your brother in calling it your disgraceful plot."

"Oh, Lord!" said Martin. "I say, Mortimer, you didn't know you were up against Lord Peter Wimsey, did you? No wonder the cat got out of the bag. The man's known to be a perfect Sherlock. However, I seem to have got home at the crucial moment, so there's no harm done. Diana, this is Lord Peter Wimsey—my wife."

A young and pretty woman in a black evening dress greeted Wimsey with a shy smile, and turned deprecatingly to her brother-in-law.

"Haviland, we want to explain—"

He paid no attention to her.

"Now then, Martin, the game's up."

"I think it is, Haviland. But why make all this racket?"

"Racket! I like that. You take your own father's body out of its coffin—"

"No, no, Haviland. I knew nothing about it. I swear that. I only got the news of his death a few days ago. We were right out in the wilds, filming a show in the Pyrenees, and I came straight back as soon as I could get away. Mortimer here, with Rawlinson and Hubbard, staged the whole show by themselves. I never heard a word about it till yesterday morning in Paris, when I found his letter waiting at my old digs. Honestly, Haviland, I had nothing to do with it. Why should I? I didn't need to."

"What do you mean?"

"Well, if I'd been here, I should only have had to speak to stop the funeral altogether. Why on earth should I have gone to the trouble of stealing the body? Quite apart from the irreverence and all that. As it is, when Mortimer told me about it, I must say I was a bit revolted at the idea, though I appreciated the kindness and the trouble they'd been to on my account. I think Mr. Hancock has most cause for wrath, really. But Mortimer has been as careful as possible, sir—really he has. He has placed the old governor quite reverently and decently in what used to be the chapel, and put flowers round him and so on. You will be quite satisfied, I'm sure."

"Yes, yes," said Mortimer. "No disrespect intended, don't you know. Come and see him."

"This is dreadful," said the vicar helplessly.

"They had to do the best they could, don't you see, in my absence," said Martin. "As soon as I can, I'll make proper arrangement for a suitable tomb—above ground, of course. Or possibly cremation would fit the case."

"What!" gasped Haviland. "Do you mean to say you imagine I'm going to let my father stay unburied, simply because of your disgusting greed about money?"

"My dear chap, do you think I'm going to let you put him underground, simply to enable you to grab my property?"

"I'm the executor of his will, and I say he shall be buried, whether you like it or not!"

"And *I'm* an executor too—and I say he shan't be buried. He can be kept absolutely decently above ground, and he shall be."

"But hear me," said the vicar, distracted between these two disagreeable and angry young men.

"I'll see what Graham says about you," bawled Haviland.

"Oh, yes—the honest lawyer, Graham," sneered Martin. *"He* knew what was in the will, didn't he? I suppose he didn't mention it to *you* by any chance?"

"He did not," retorted Haviland. "He knew too well the sort of skunk *you* were to say anything about it. Not content with disgracing us with your miserable, blackmailing marriage—"

"Mr. Burdock, Mr. Burdock—"

"Take care, Haviland!"

"You have no more decency—"

"Stop it!"

"Than to steal your father's body and my money so that you and your damned wife can carry on your loose-living, beastly ways with a parcel of film-actors and chorus-girls—"

"Now then, Haviland. Keep your tongue off my wife and my friends. How about your own? Somebody told me Winnie'd been going the pace pretty well—next door to bankruptcy, aren't you, with the gees and the tables and God knows what! No wonder you want to do your brother out of his money. I never thought much of you, Haviland, but by God—"

"One moment!"

Mr. Frobisher-Pym at last succeeded in asserting himself, partly through the habit of authority, and partly because the brothers had shouted themselves breathless.

"One moment, Martin. I will call you so, because I have known you a long time, and your father too. I understand your anger at the things Haviland has said. They were unpardonable, as I am sure he will realize when he comes to his right mind. But you must remember that he has been greatly shocked and upset—as we all have been—by this very painful business. And it is not fair to say that Haviland has tried to 'do you out' of anything. He knew nothing about this iniquitous will, and he naturally saw to it that the funeral arrangements were carried out in the usual way. You must settle the future amicably between you, just as you would have done had the will not been accidentally mislaid. Now, Martin—and Haviland too—think it over. My dear boys, this scene is simply appalling. It really must not happen. Surely the estate can be divided up in a friendly manner between you. It is horrible that an old man's body should be a bone of contention between his own sons, just over a matter of money."

"I'm sorry," said Martin. "I forgot myself. You're quite right, sir. Look here, Haviland, forget it. I'll let you have half the money—"

"Half the money! But it's all mine. *You'll* let me have half? How damned generous! My own money!"

"No, old man. It's mine at the moment. The governor's not buried yet, you know. That's right, isn't it, Mr. Frobisher-Pym?"

"Yes; the money is yours, legally, at this moment. You must see that, Haviland. But your brother offers you half, and—"

"Half! I'm damned if I'll take half. The man's tried to swindle me out of it. I'll send for the police, and have him put in gaol for robbing the Church. You see if I don't. Give me the telephone."

"Excuse me," said Wimsey. "I don't want to butt in on your family affairs any more than I have already, but I really don't advise you to send for the police."

"*You* don't, eh? What the hell's it got to do with you?"

"Well," said Wimsey deprecatingly, "if this will business comes into court, I shall probably have to give evidence, because I was the bird who found the thing, don't you see?"

"Well, then?"

"Well, then. They might ask how long the will was supposed to have been where I found it."

Haviland appeared to swallow something which obstructed his speech.

"What about it, curse you!"

"Yes. Well, you see, it's rather odd when you come to think of it. I mean, your late father must have hidden that will in the bookcase before he went abroad. That was—how long ago? Three years? Five years?"

"About four years."

"Quite. And since then your bright caretaker has let the damp get into the library, hasn't she? No fires, and the window getting broken, and so on. Ruinous to the books. Very distressin' to anybody like myself, you know. Yes. Well, supposin' they asked that question about the will—and you said it had been there in the damp for four years. Wouldn't they think it a bit funny if I told 'em that there was a big stain like a grinning face on the end of the bookshelf, and a big, damp, grinning face on the jolly old *Nuremberg Chronicle* to correspond with it, and no stain on the will which had been sittin' for four years between the two?"

Mrs. Haviland screamed suddenly. "Haviland! You fool! You utter fool!"

"Shut up!"

Haviland snapped round at his wife with a cry of rage, and she collapsed into a chair, with her hand snatched to her mouth.

"Thank you, Winnie," said Martin. "No, Haviland—don't trouble to explain. Winnie's given the show away. So you knew—you *knew* about the will, and you deliberately hid it away and let the funeral go on. I'm immensely obliged to you—nearly as obliged as I am to the discreet Graham. Is it fraud or conspiracy or what, to conceal wills? Mr. Frobisher-Pym will know."

"Dear, dear!" said the magistrate. "Are you certain of your facts, Wimsey?"

"Positive," said Wimsey, producing the *Nuremberg Chronicle* from under his arm. "Here's the stain—you can see it yourself. Forgive me for having borrowed your property, Mr. Burdock. I was rather afraid Mr. Haviland might think this little discrepancy over in the still watches of the night, and decide to sell the *Chronicle*, or give it away, or even think it looked better without its back pages and cover. Allow me to return it to you, Mr. Martin—intact. You will perhaps excuse my saying that I don't very much admire any of the roles in this melodrama. It throws, as Mr. Pecksniff would say, a sad light on human nature. But I resent extremely the way in which I was wangled up to that bookshelf and made to be the bright little independent witness who found the will. I may be an ass, Mr. Haviland Burdock, but I'm not a bloody ass. Good night. I will wait in the car till you are all ready."

Wimsey stalked out with some dignity.

Presently he was followed by the vicar and by Mr. Frobisher-Pym.

"Mortimer's taking Haviland and his wife to the station," said the magistrate. "They're going back to town at once. You can send their traps off in the morning, Hancock. We'd better make ourselves scarce."

Wimsey pressed the self-starter.

As he did so, a man ran hastily down the steps and came up to him. It was Martin.

"I say," he muttered. "You've done me a good turn—more than I deserve, I'm afraid. You must think I'm a damned swine. But I'll see the old man decently put away, and I'll share with Haviland. You mustn't judge him too hardly, either. That wife of his is an awful woman. Run him over head and ears in debt. Bust up his business. I'll see it's all squared up. See? Don't want you to think us too awful."

"Oh, right-ho!" said Wimsey.

He slipped in the clutch, and faded away into the wet, white fog.

THE VINDICTIVE STORY OF THE
FOOTSTEPS THAT RAN

Mr. Bunter withdrew his head from beneath the focusing cloth.

"I fancy that will be quite adequate, sir," he said deferentially, "unless there are any further patients, if I may call them so, which you would wish put on record."

"Not today," replied the doctor. He took the last stricken rat gently from the table, and replaced it in its cage with an air of satisfaction. "Perhaps on Wednesday, if Lord Peter can kindly spare your services once again—"

"What's that?" murmured his lordship, withdrawing his long nose from the investigation of a number of unattractive-looking glass jars. "Nice old dog," he added vaguely. "Wags his tail when you mention his name, what? Are these monkey-glands, Hartman, or a south-west elevation of Cleopatra's duodenum?"

"You don't know anything, do you?" said the young physician, laughing. "No use playing your bally-fool-with-an-eyeglass tricks on me, Wimsey. I'm up to them. I was saying to Bunter that I'd be no end grateful if you'd let him turn up again three days hence to register the progress of the specimens—always supposing they do progress, that is."

"Why ask, dear old thing?" said his lordship. "Always a

pleasure to assist a fellow-sleuth, don't you know. Trackin' down murderers—all in the same way of business and all that. All finished? Good egg! By the way, if you don't have that cage mended you'll lose one of your patients—Number 5. The last wire but one is workin' loose—assisted by the intelligent occupant. Jolly little beasts, aren't they? No need of dentists—wish I was a rat—wire much better for the nerves than that fizzlin' drill."

Dr. Hartman uttered a little exclamation.

"How in the world did you notice that, Wimsey? I didn't think you'd even looked at the cage."

"Built noticin'—improved by practice," said Lord Peter quietly. "Anythin' wrong leaves a kind of impression on the eye; brain trots along afterwards with the warnin'. I saw that when we came in. Only just grasped it. Can't say my mind was glued on the matter. Shows the victim's improvin', anyhow. All serene, Bunter?"

"Everything perfectly satisfactory, I trust, my lord," replied the manservant. He had packed up his camera and plates, and was quietly restoring order in the little laboratory, whose fittings—compact as those of an ocean liner—had been disarranged for the experiment.

"Well," said the doctor, "I am enormously obliged to you, Lord Peter, and to Bunter too. I am hoping for a great result from these experiments, and you cannot imagine how valuable an assistance it will be to me to have a really good series of photographs. I can't afford this sort of thing—yet," he added, his rather haggard young face wistful as he looked at the great camera, "and I can't do the work at the hospital. There's no time; I've got to be here. A struggling G.P. can't afford to let his practice go, even in Bloomsbury. There are times when even a half-crown visit makes all the difference between making both ends meet and having an ugly hiatus."

"As Mr. Micawber said," replied Wimsey, " 'Income twenty pounds, expenditure nineteen, nineteen, six—result: happiness; expenditure twenty pounds, ought, six—result: misery.' Don't prostrate yourself in gratitude, old bean;

nothin' Bunter loves like messin' round with pyro and hypo-sulphite. Keeps his hand in. All kinds of practice welcome. Finger-prints and process plates spell seventh what-you-may-call-it of bliss, but focal-plane work on scurvy-ridden rodents (good phrase!) acceptable if no crime forthcoming. Crimes have been rather short lately. Been eatin' our heads off, haven't we, Bunter? Don't know what's come over London. I've taken to prying into my neighbour's affairs to keep from goin' stale. Frightened the postman into a fit the other day by askin' him how his young lady at Croydon was. He's a married man, livin' in Great Ormond Street."

"How did you know?"

"Well, I didn't really. But he lives just opposite to a friend of mine—Inspector Parker; and his wife—not Parker's, he's unmarried; the postman's, I mean—asked Parker the other day whether the flyin' shows at Croydon went on all night. Parker, bein' flummoxed, said 'No,' without thinkin'. Bit of a giveaway, what? Thought I'd give the poor devil a word in season, don't you know. Uncommonly thoughtless of Parker."

The doctor laughed. "You'll stay to lunch, won't you?" he said. "Only cold meat and salad, I'm afraid. My woman won't come Sundays. Have to answer my own door. Deuced unprofessional, I'm afraid, but it can't be helped."

"Pleasure," said Wimsey, as they emerged from the laboratory and entered the dark little flat by the back door. "Did you build this place on?"

"No," said Hartman; "the last tenant did that. He was an artist. That's why I took the place. It comes in very useful, ramshackle as it is, though this glass roof is a bit sweltering on a hot day like this. Still, I had to have something on the ground floor, cheap, and it'll do till times get better."

"Till your vitamin experiments make you famous, eh?" said Peter cheerfully. "You're goin' to be the comin' man, you know. Feel it in my bones. Uncommonly neat little kitchen you've got, anyhow."

"It does," said the doctor. "The lab makes it a bit gloomy, but the woman's only here in the daytime."

He led the way into a narrow little dining-room, where the table was laid for a cold lunch. The one window at the end farthest from the kitchen looked out into Great James Street. The room was little more than a passage, and full of doors—the kitchen door, a door in the adjacent wall leading into the entrance-hall, and a third on the opposite side, through which his visitor caught a glimpse of a moderate-sized consulting-room.

Lord Peter Wimsey and his host sat down to table, and the doctor expressed a hope that Mr. Bunter would sit down with them. That correct person, however, deprecated any such suggestion.

"If I might venture to indicate my own preference, sir," he said, "it would be to wait upon you and his lordship in the usual manner."

"It's no use," said Wimsey. "Bunter likes me to know my place. Terrorizin' sort of man, Bunter. Can't call my soul my own. Carry on, Bunter; we wouldn't presume for the world."

Mr. Bunter handed the salad, and poured out the water with a grave decency appropriate to a crusted old tawny port.

It was a Sunday afternoon in that halcyon summer of 1921. The sordid little street was almost empty. The ice-cream man alone seemed thriving and active. He leaned luxuriously on the green post at the corner, in the intervals of driving a busy trade. Bloomsbury's swarm of able-bodied and able-voiced infants was still; presumably within-doors, eating steamy Sunday dinners inappropriate to the tropical weather. The only disturbing sounds came from the flat above, where heavy footsteps passed rapidly to and fro.

"Who's the merry-and-bright bloke above?" inquired Lord Peter presently. "Not an early riser, I take it. Not that anybody is on a Sunday mornin'. Why an inscrutable Providence ever inflicted such a ghastly day on people livin' in town I can't imagine. I ought to be in the country, but I've got to meet a friend at Victoria this afternoon. Such a day to choose... Who's the lady? Wife or accomplished friend? Gather she takes a properly submissive view of woman's duties in the home, either way. That's the bedroom overhead, I take it."

Hartman looked at Lord Peter in some surprise.

" 'Scuse my beastly inquisitiveness, old thing," said Wimsey. "Bad habit. Not my business."

"How did you — ?"

"Guesswork," said Lord Peter, with disarming frankness. "I heard the squawk of an iron bedstead on the ceiling and a heavy fellow get out with a bump, but it may quite well be a couch or something. Anyway, he's been potterin' about in his stocking feet over these few feet of floor for the last half-hour, while the woman has been clatterin' to and fro, in and out of the kitchen and away into the sittin'-room, with her high heels on, ever since we've been here. Hence deduction as to domestic habits of the first-floor tenants."

"I thought," said the doctor, with an aggrieved expression, "you'd been listening to my valuable exposition of the beneficial effects of Vitamin B, and Lind's treatment of scurvy with fresh lemons in 1755."

"I was listenin'," agreed Lord Peter hastily, "but I heard the footsteps as well. Fellow's toddled into the kitchen — only wanted the matches, though; he's gone off into the sittin'-room and left her to carry on the good work. What was I sayin'? Oh, yes! You see, as I was sayin' before, one hears a thing or sees it without knowin' or thinkin' about it. Then afterwards one starts meditatin', and it all comes back, and one sorts out one's impressions. Like those plates of Bunter's. Picture's all there, l —, la —, what's the word I want, Bunter?"

"Latent, my lord."

"That's it. My right-hand man, Bunter; couldn't do a thing without him. The picture's latent till you put the developer on. Same with the brain. No mystery. Little grey books all my respected grandmother! Little grey matter's all you want to remember things with. As a matter of curiosity, was I right about those people above?"

"Perfectly. The man's a gas-company's inspector. A bit surly, but devoted (after his own fashion) to his wife. I mean, he doesn't mind hulking in bed on a Sunday morning and letting her do the chores, but he spends all the money he can spare on giving her pretty hats and fur coats and what not. They've only been married about six months. I was called in to her when she had a touch of flu in the spring, and he was almost off his head with anxiety. She's a lovely little woman, I must say — Italian. He picked her up in some eating-place in Soho, I believe. Glorious dark hair and eyes: Venus sort of figure; proper contours in all the right places; good skin — all that sort of thing. She was a bit of a draw to that restaurant while she was there, I fancy. Lively. She had an old admirer round here one day — awkward little Italian fellow, with a knife — active as a monkey. Might have been unpleasant, but I happened to be on the spot, and her husband came along. People are always laying one another out in these streets. Good for business, of course, but one gets tired of tying up broken heads and slits in the jugular. Still, I suppose the girl can't help being attractive, though I don't say she's what you might call stand-offish in her manner. She's sincerely fond of Brotherton, I think, though — that's his name."

Wimsey nodded inattentively. "I suppose life is a bit monotonous here," he said.

"Professionally, yes. Births and drunks and wife-beatings are pretty common. And all the usual ailments, of course. Just at present I'm living on infant diarrhoea chiefly — bound to, this hot weather, you know. With the autumn, flu and bronchitis set in. I may get an occasional pneumonia. Legs, of course, and varicose veins — God!" cried the doctor explosively, "if only I could get away, and do my experiments!"

"Ah!" said Peter, "where's that eccentric old millionaire with a mysterious disease, who always figures in the novels? A lightning diagnosis — a miraculous cure — 'God bless you, doctor; here are five thousand pounds' — Harley Street —"

"That sort doesn't live in Bloomsbury," said the doctor.

"It must be fascinatin', diagnosin' things," said Peter thoughtfully. "How d'you do it? I mean, is there a regular set of symptoms for each disease, like callin' a club to show you want your partner to go no trumps? You don't just say: 'This fellow's got a pimple on his nose, therefore he has fatty degeneration of the heart—' "

"I hope not," said the doctor drily.

"Or is it more like getting' a clue to a crime?" went on Peter. "You see somethin'—a room, or a body, say, all knocked about anyhow, and there's a damn sight of symptoms of somethin' wrong, and you've got just to pick out the ones which tell the story?"

"That's more like it," said Dr. Hartman. "Some symptoms are significant in themselves—like the condition of the gums in scurvy, let us say—others in conjunction with—"

He broke off, and both sprang to their feet as a shrill scream sounded suddenly from the flat above, followed by a heavy thud. A man's voice cried out lamentably; feet ran violently to and fro; then, as the doctor and his guests stood frozen in consternation, came the man himself— falling down the stairs in his haste, hammering at Hartman's door.

"Help! Help! Let me in! My wife! He's murdered her!"

They ran hastily to the door and let him in. He was a big, fair man, in his shirt-sleeves and stockings. His hair stood up, and his face was set in bewildered misery.

"She is dead—dead. He was her lover," he groaned. "Come and look—take her away—Doctor! I have lost my wife! My Maddalena—" He paused, looked wildly for a moment, and then said hoarsely, "Someone's been in—somehow—stabbed her—murdered her. I'll have the law on him, doctor. Come quickly—she was cooking the chicken for my dinner—Ah-h-h!"

He gave a long, hysterical shriek, which ended in a hiccupping laugh. The doctor took him roughly by the arm and shook him. "Pull yourself together, Mr. Brotherton," he said sharply. "Perhaps she is only hurt. Stand out of the way!"

"Only hurt?" said the man, sitting heavily down on the nearest chair. "No—no—she is dead—little Maddalena—Oh, my God!"

Dr. Hartman snatched a roll of bandages and a few surgical appliances from the consulting-room, and he ran upstairs, followed closely by Lord Peter. Bunter remained for a few moments to combat hysterics with cold water. Then he stepped across to the dining-room window and shouted.

"Well, wot is it?" cried a voice from the street.

"Would you be so kind as to step in here a minute, officer?" said Mr. Bunter. "There's been murder done."

When Brotherton and Bunter arrived upstairs with the constable, they found Dr. Hartman and Lord Peter in the little kitchen. The doctor was kneeling beside the woman's body. At their entrance he looked up, and shook his head.

"Death instantaneous," he said. "Clean through the heart. Poor child. She cannot have suffered at all. Oh, constable, it is very fortunate you are here. Murder appears to have been done—though I'm afraid the man has escaped. Probably Mr. Brotherton can give us some help. He was in the flat at the time."

The man had sunk down on a chair, and was gazing at the body with a face from which all meaning seemed to have been struck out. The policeman produced a notebook.

"Now, sir," he said, "don't let's waste any time. Sooner we can get to work the more likely we are to catch our man. Now, you was 'ere at the time, was you?"

Brotherton stared a moment, then, making a violent effort, he answered steadily:

"I was in the sitting-room, smoking and reading the paper. My—*she*—was getting the dinner ready in here. I heard her give a scream, and I rushed in and found her lying on the floor. She didn't have time to say anything. When I found she was dead, I rushed to the window, and saw the fellow scrambling away over the glass roof there. I yelled at him, but he disappeared. Then I ran down—"

" 'Arf a mo'," said the policeman. "Now, see 'ere, sir, didn't you think to go after 'im at once?"

"My first thought was for her," said the man. "I thought

maybe she wasn't dead. I tried to bring her round—" His speech ended in a groan.

"You say he came in through the window," said the policeman.

"I beg your pardon, officer," interrupted Lord Peter, who had been apparently making a mental inventory of the contents of the kitchen. "Mr. Brotherton suggested that the man went *out* through the window. It's better to be accurate."

"It's the same thing," said the doctor. "It's the only way he could have come in. These flats are all alike. The staircase door leads into the sitting-room, and Mr. Brotherton was there, so the man couldn't have come that way."

"And," said Peter, "he didn't get in through the bedroom window, or we should have seen him. We were in the room below. Unless, indeed, he let himself down from the roof. Was the door between the bedroom and the sitting-room open?" he asked suddenly, turning to Brotherton.

The man hesitated a moment. "Yes," he said finally. "Yes, I'm sure it was."

"Could you have seen the man if he had come through the bedroom window?"

"I couldn't have helped seeing him."

"Come, come, sir," said the policeman, with some irritation, "better let *me* ask the questions. Stands to reason the fellow wouldn't get in through the bedroom window in full view of the street."

"How clever of you to think of that," said Wimsey. "Of course not. Never occurred to me. Then it must have been this window, as you say."

"And what's more, here's his marks on the windowsill," said the constable triumphantly, pointing to some blurred traces among the London soot. "That's right. Down he goes by that drain-pipe, over the glass roof down there—what's that the roof of?"

"My laboratory," said the doctor. "Heavens! to think that while we were there at dinner this murdering villain—"

"Quite so, sir," agreed the constable. "Well, he'd get away over the wall into the court be'ind. 'E'll 'ave been seen there, no fear; you needn't anticipate much trouble in layin' 'ands on 'im, sir. I'll go round there in 'arf a tick. Now then, sir"—turning to Brotherton—" 'ave you any idea wot this party might have looked like?"

Brotherton lifted a wild face, and the doctor interposed.

"I think you ought to know, constable," he said, "that there was—well, not a murderous attack, but what might have been one, made on this woman before—about eight weeks ago—by a man named Marincetti—an Italian waiter—with a knife."

"Ah!" The policeman licked his pencil eagerly. "Do you know this party as 'as been mentioned?" he inquired of Brotherton.

"That's the man," said Brotherton, with concentrated fury. "Coming here after my wife—God curse him! I wish to God I had him dead here beside her!"

"Quite so," said the policeman. "Now, sir"—to the doctor—" 'ave you got the weapon wot the crime was committed with?"

"No," said Hartman, "there was no weapon in the body when I arrived."

"Did *you* take it out?" pursued the constable, to Brotherton.

"No," said Brotherton, "he took it with him."

"Took it with 'im," the constable entered the fact in his notes. "Phew! Wonderful 'ot it is in 'ere, ain't it, sir?" he added, mopping his brow.

"It's the gas-oven, I think," said Peter mildly. "Uncommon hot thing, a gas-oven, in the middle of July. D'you mind if I turn it out? There's the chicken inside, but I don't suppose you want—"

Brotherton groaned, and the constable said: "Quite right, sir. A man wouldn't 'ardly fancy 'is dinner after a thing like this. Thank you, sir. Well, now, doctor, wot kind of weapon do you take this to 'ave been?"

"It was a long, narrow weapon—something like an Italian stiletto, I imagine," said the doctor, "about six inches long. It

was thrust in with great force under the fifth rib, and I should
say it had pierced the heart centrally. As you see, there has
been practically no bleeding. Such a wound would cause
instant death. Was she lying just as she is now when you first
saw her, Mr. Brotherton?"

"On her back, just as she is," replied the husband.

"Well, that seems clear enough," said the policeman. "This
'ere Marinetti, or wotever 'is name is, 'as a grudge against the
poor young lady —"

"I believe he was an admirer," put in the doctor.

"Quite so," agreed the constable. "Of course, these foreigners are like that — even the decentest of 'em. Stabbin' and
such-like seems to come nateral to them, as you might say.
Well, this 'ere Marinetti climbs in 'ere, sees the poor young
lady standin' 'ere by the table all alone, gettin' the dinner
ready; 'e comes in be'ind, catches 'er round the waist, stabs
'er — easy job, you see; no corsets nor nothink — she shrieks
out, 'e pulls 'is stiletty out of 'er an' makes tracks. Well, now
we've got to find 'im, and by your leave, sir, I'll be gettin'
along. We'll 'ave 'im by the 'eels before long, sir, don't you
worry. I'll 'ave to put a man in charge 'ere, sir, to keep folks
out, but that needn't worry you. Good mornin', gentlemen."

"May we move the poor girl now?" asked the doctor.

"Certainly. Like me to 'elp you, sir?"

"No. Don't lose any time. We can manage." Dr. Hartman
turned to Peter as the constable clattered downstairs. "Will
you help me, Lord Peter?"

"Bunter's better at that sort of thing," said Wimsey, with a
hard mouth.

The doctor looked at him in some surprise, but said nothing, and he and Bunter carried the still form away. Brotherton
did not follow them. He sat in a grief-stricken heap, with his
head buried in his hands. Lord Peter walked about the little
kitchen, turning over the various knives and kitchen utensils,
peering into the sink bucket, and apparently taking an inventory of the bread, butter, condiments, vegetables, and so forth
which lay about in preparation for the Sunday meal. There

were potatoes in the sink, half peeled, a pathetic witness to the quiet domestic life which had been so horribly interrupted. The colander was filled with green peas. Lord Peter turned these things over with an inquisitive finger, gazed into the smooth surface of a bowl of dripping as though it were a divining-crystal, ran his hands several times right through a bowl of flour—then drew his pipe from his pocket and filled it slowly.

The doctor returned, and put his hand on Brotherton's shoulder.

"Come," he said gently, "we have laid her in the other bedroom. She looks very peaceful. You must remember that, except for that moment of terror when she saw the knife, she suffered nothing. It is terrible for you, but you must try not to give way. The police—"

"The police can't bring her back to life," said the man savagely. "She's dead. Leave me alone, curse you! Leave me alone, I say!"

He stood up, with a violent gesture.

"You must not sit here," said Hartman firmly. "I will give you something to take, and you must try to keep calm. Then we will leave you, but if you don't control yourself—"

After some further persuasion, Brotherton allowed himself to be led away.

"Bunter," said Lord Peter, as the kitchen door closed behind them, "do you know why I am doubtful about the success of those rat experiments?"

"Meaning Dr. Hartman's, my lord?"

"Yes. Dr. Hartman has a theory. In any investigations, my Bunter, it is most damnably dangerous to have a theory."

"I have heard you say so, my lord."

"Confound you—you know it as well as I do! What is wrong with the doctor's theories, Bunter?"

"You wish me to reply, my lord, that he only sees the facts which fit in with the theory."

"Thought-reader!" exclaimed Lord Peter bitterly.

"And that he supplies them to the police, my lord."

"Hush!" said Peter, as the doctor returned.

• • •

"I have got him to lie down," said Dr. Hartman, "and I think the best thing we can do is to leave him to himself."

"D'you know," said Wimsey, "I don't cotton to that idea, somehow."

"Why? Do you think he's likely to destroy himself?"

"That's as good a reason to give as any other, I suppose," said Wimsey, "when you haven't got any reason which can be put into words. But my advice is, don't leave him for a moment."

"But why? Frequently, with a deep grief like this, the presence of other people is merely an irritant. He begged me to leave him."

"Then for God's sake go back to him," said Peter.

"Really, Lord Peter," said the doctor, "I think I ought to know what is best for my patient."

"Doctor," said Wimsey, "this is not a question of your patient. A crime has been committed."

"But there is no mystery."

"There are twenty mysteries. For one thing, when was the window-cleaner here last?"

"The window-cleaner?"

"Who shall fathom the ebony-black enigma of the window-cleaner?" pursued Peter lightly, putting a match to his pipe. "You are quietly in your bath, in a state of more or less innocent nature, when an intrusive head appears at the window, like the ghost of Hamilton Tighe, and a gruff voice, suspended between earth and heaven, says 'Good morning, sir.' Where do window-cleaners go between visits? Do they hibernate, like busy bees? Do they — ?"

"Really, Lord Peter," said the doctor, "don't you think you're going a bit beyond the limit?"

"Sorry you feel like that," said Peter, "but I really want to know about the window-cleaner. Look how clear these panes are."

"He came yesterday, if you want to know," said Dr. Hartman, rather stiffly.

"You are sure?"

"He did mine at the same time."

"I thought as much," said Lord Peter. "In the words of
the song:

I thought as much,
It was a little — window-cleaner.

In that case," he added, "it is absolutely imperative that Brotherton should not be left alone for a moment. Bunter! Confound it all, where's that fellow got to?"

The door into the bedroom opened.

"My lord?" Mr. Bunter unobtrusively appeared, as he had
unobtrusively stolen out to keep an unobtrusive eye upon the
patient.

"Good," said Wimsey. "Stay where you are." His lack-
adaisical manner had gone, and he looked at the doctor as
four years previously he might have looked at a refractory
subaltern.

"Dr. Hartman," he said, "something is wrong. Cast your
mind back. We were talking about symptoms. Then came the
scream. Then came the sound of feet running. *Which direction
did they run in?*"

"I'm sure I don't know."

"Don't you? Symptomatic, though, doctor. They have
been troubling me all the time, subconsciously. Now I know
why. They ran *from the kitchen.*"

"Well?"

"Well! And now the window-cleaner —"

"What about him?"

"Could you swear that it wasn't the window-cleaner who
made those marks on the sill?"

"And the man Brotherton saw —?"

"Have we examined your laboratory roof for his footsteps?"

"But the weapon? Wimsey, this is madness! Someone
took the weapon."

"I know. But did you think the edge of the wound was clean enough to have been made by a smooth stiletto? It looked ragged to me."

"Wimsey, what are you driving at?"

"There's a clue here in the flat—and I'm damned if I can remember it. I've seen it—I know I've seen it. It'll come to me presently. Meanwhile, don't let Brotherton—"

"What?"

"Do whatever it is he's going to do."

"But what is it?"

"If I could tell you that I could show you the clue. Why couldn't he make up his mind whether the bedroom door was open or shut? Very good story, but not quite thought out. Anyhow—I say, doctor, make some excuse, and strip him, and bring me his clothes. And send Bunter to me."

The doctor stared at him, puzzled. Then he made a gesture of acquiescence and passed into the bedroom. Lord Peter followed him, casting a ruminating glance at Brotherton as he went. Once in the sitting-room, Lord Peter sat down on a red velvet armchair, fixed his eyes on a gilt-framed oleograph, and became wrapped in contemplation.

Presently Bunter came in, with his arms full of clothing. Wimsey took it, and began to search it, methodically enough, but listlessly. Suddenly he dropped the garments, and turned to the manservant.

"No," he said, "this is a precaution, Bunter mine, but I'm on the wrong track. It wasn't here I saw—whatever I did see. It was in the kitchen. Now, what was it?"

"I could not say, my lord, but I entertain a conviction that I was also, in a manner of speaking, conscious—not consciously conscious, my lord, if you understand me, but still conscious of an incongruity."

"Hurray!" said Wimsey suddenly. "Cheer-oh! for the subconscious what's-his-name! Now let's remember the kitchen. I cleared out of it because I was gettin' obfuscated. Now then. Begin at the door. Fryin'-pans and saucepans on the wall. Gas-stove—oven goin'—chicken inside. Rack of wooden spoons

on the wall, gas-lighter, pan-lifter. Stop me when I'm gettin'
hot. Mantelpiece. Spice-boxes and stuff. Anything wrong with
them? No. Dresser. Plates. Knives and forks—all clean; flour
dredger—milk-jug—sieve on the wall—nutmeg-grater. Three-
tier steamer. Looked inside—no grisly secrets in the steamer."

"Did you look in all the dresser drawers, my lord?"

"No. That could be done. But the point is, I *did* notice
somethin'. What did I notice? That's the point. Never mind.
On with the dance—let joy be unconfined! Knife-board.
Knife-powder. Kitchen table. Did you speak?"

"No," said Bunter, who had moved from his attitude of
wooden deference.

"Table stirs a chord. Very good. On table. Choppin'-
board. Remains of ham and herb stuffin'. Packet of suet.
Another sieve. Several plates. Butter in a glass dish. Bowl of
drippin'—"

"Ah!"

"Drippin'—! Yes, there was—"

"Something unsatisfactory, my lord—"

"About the drippin'! Oh, my head! what's that they say in
Dear Brutus, Bunter? 'Hold on to the workbox.' That's right.
Hold on to the drippin'. Beastly slimy stuff to hold on to—
Wait!"

There was a pause.

"When I was a kid," said Wimsey, "I used to love to go
down into the kitchen and talk to old cookie. Good old soul
she was, too. I can see her now, gettin' chicken ready, with me
danglin' my legs on the table. *She* used to pluck an' draw 'em
herself. I revelled in it. Little beasts boys are, ain't they,
Bunter? Pluck it, draw it, wash it, stuff it, tuck its little tail
through its little what-you-may-call-it, truss it, grease the
dish—Bunter?"

"My lord!"

"Hold on to the—"

"The bowl, my lord—"

"The bowl—visualize it—what was wrong?"

"It was full, my lord!"

"Got it—got it—*got* it! The bowl was full—smooth surface. Golly! I knew there was something queer about it. Now why shouldn't it be full? Hold on to the—"

"The bird was in the oven."

"Without dripping!"

"Very careless cookery, my lord."

"The bird—in the oven—no dripping. Bunter! Suppose it was never put in till after she was dead? Thrust in hurriedly by someone who had something to hide—horrible!"

"But with what object, my lord?"

"Yes, why? That's the point. One more mental association with the bird. It's just coming. Wait a moment. Pluck, draw, wash, stuff, tuck up, truss—By God!"

"My lord?"

"Come on, Bunter. Thank Heaven we turned off the gas!"

He dashed through the bedroom, disregarding the doctor and the patient, who sat up with a smothered shriek. He flung open the oven door and snatched out the baking-tin. The skin of the bird had just begun to discolour. With a little gasp of triumph, Wimsey caught the iron ring that protruded from the wing, and jerked out—the six-inch spiral skewer.

The doctor was struggling with the excited Brotherton in the door-way. Wimsey caught the man as he broke away, and shook him into the corner with a ju-jitsu twist.

"Here is the weapon," he said.

"Prove it, blast you!" said Brotherton savagely.

"I will," said Wimsey. "Bunter, call in the policeman whom you will find at the door. Doctor, we shall need your microscope."

In the laboratory the doctor bent over the microscope. A thin layer of blood from the skewer had been spread upon the slide.

"Well?" said Wimsey impatiently.

"It's all right," said Hartman. "The roasting didn't get anywhere near the middle. My God, Wimsey, yes, you're right—

round corpuscles, diameter 1/3621—mammalian blood—probably human—"

"Her blood," said Wimsey.

"It was very clever, Bunter," said Lord Peter, as the taxi trundled along on the way to his flat in Piccadilly. "If that fowl had gone on roasting a bit longer the blood-corpuscles might easily have been destroyed beyond all hope of recognition. It all goes to show that the unpremeditated crime is usually the safest."

"And what does your lordship take the man's motive to have been?"

"In my youth," said Wimsey meditatively, "they used to make me read the Bible. Trouble was, the only books I ever took to naturally were the ones they weren't over and above keen on. But I got to know the Song of Songs pretty well by heart. Look it up, Bunter; at your age it won't hurt you; it talks sense about jealousy."

"I have perused the work in question, your lordship," replied Mr. Bunter, with a sallow blush. "It says, if I remember rightly: *Jealousy is cruel as the grave.*"

THE BIBULOUS BUSINESS OF A
MATTER OF TASTE

"**H**alte-là! . . . *Attention!* . . . *F—e!*"

The young man in the grey suit pushed his way through the protesting porters and leapt nimbly for the footboard of the guard's van as the Paris-Évreux express steamed out of the Invalides. The guard, with an eye to a tip, fielded him adroitly from among the detaining hands.

"It is happy for monsieur that he is so agile," he remarked. "Monsieur is in a hurry?"

"Somewhat. Thank you. I can get through by the corridor?"

"But certainly. The *premières* are two coaches away, beyond the luggage-van."

The young man rewarded his rescuer, and made his way forward, mopping his face. As he passed the piled-up luggage, something caught his eye, and he stopped to investigate. It was a suitcase, nearly new, of expensive-looking leather, labelled conspicuously:

LORD PETER WIMSEY,
Hôtel Saumon d'Or,
Verneuil-sur-Eure

and bore witness to its itinerary thus:

London   Paris
(Waterloo)   (Gare Saint-Lazare)
via Southhampton-Havre.

Paris — Verneuil
(Ch. de Fer de l'Ouest)

The young man whistled, and sat down on a trunk to think it out.

Somewhere there had been a leakage, and they were on his trail. Nor did they care who knew it. There were hundreds of people in London and Paris who would know the name of Wimsey, not counting the police of both countries. In addition to belonging to one of the oldest ducal families in England, Lord Peter had made himself conspicuous by his meddling with crime detection. A label like this was a gratuitous advertisement.

But the amazing thing was that the pursuers were not troubling to hide themselves from the pursued. That argued very great confidence. That he should have got into the guard's van was, of course, an accident, but, even so, he might have seen it on the platform, or anywhere.

An accident? It occurred to him — not for the first time, but definitely now, and without doubt — that it was indeed an accident for them that he was here. The series of maddening delays that had held him up between London and the Invalides presented itself to him with an air of pre-arrangement. The preposterous accusation, for instance, of the woman who had accosted him in Piccadilly, and the slow process of extricating himself at Marlborough Street. It was easy to hold a man up on some trumped-up charge till an important plan had matured. Then there was the lavatory door at Waterloo, which had so ludicrously locked itself upon him. Being athletic, he had climbed over the partition, to find the attendant mysteriously absent. And, in Paris, was it by chance that he had had a deaf taxi-driver, who mistook the direction "Quai d'Orléans" for "Gare de Lyon," and drove a mile and a half in the wrong direction before the shouts of his fare attracted his attention? They were clever, the pursuers, and circumspect. They had accurate information; they would delay him, but without taking any overt step; they knew that, if only they could keep time on their side, they needed no other ally.

Did they know he was on the train? If not, he still kept the advantage, for they would travel in a false security, thinking him to be left, raging and helpless, in the Invalides. He decided to make a cautious reconnaissance.

The first step was to change his grey suit for another of inconspicuous navy-blue cloth, which he had in his small black bag. This he did in the privacy of the toilet, substituting for his grey soft hat a large travelling-cap, which pulled well down over his eyes.

There was little difficulty in locating the man he was in search of. He found him seated in the inner corner of a first-class compartment, facing the engine, so that the watcher could approach unseen from behind. On the rack was a handsome dressing-case, with the initials P. D. B. W. The young man was familiar with Wimsey's narrow, beaky face, flat yellow hair, and insolent drooped eyelids. He smiled a little grimly.

"He is confident," he thought, "and has regrettably made the mistake of underrating the enemy. Good! This is where I retire into a *seconde* and keep my eyes open. The next act of this melodrama will take place, I fancy, at Dreux."

It is a rule on the Chemin de Fer de l'Ouest that all Paris-Évreux trains, whether of Grande Vitesse or what Lord Peter Wimsey preferred to call Grande Paresse, shall halt for an interminable period at Dreux. The young man (now in navy-blue) watched his quarry safely into the refreshment-room, and slipped unobtrusively out of the station. In a quarter of an hour he was back—this time in a heavy motoring-coat, helmet, and goggles, at the wheel of a powerful hired Peugeot.

Coming quietly on to the platform, he took up his station behind the wall of the *lampisterie*, whence he could keep an eye on the train and the buffet door. After fifteen minutes his patience was rewarded by the sight of his man again boarding the express, dressing-case in hand. The porters slammed the doors, crying: "Next stop Verneuil!" The engine panted and groaned; the long train of grey-green carriages clanked slowly away. The motorist drew a breath of satisfaction, and, hurrying past the barrier, started up the car. He knew that he had a good eighty miles an hour under his bonnet, and there is no speed-limit in France.

Mon Souci, the seat of that eccentric and eremitical genius the Comte de Rueil, is situated three kilometres from Verneuil. It is a sorrowful and decayed *château*, desolate at the termination of its neglected avenue of pines. The mournful state of a nobility without an allegiance surrounds it. The stone nymphs droop greenly over their dry and mouldering fountains. An occasional peasant creaks with a single wagon-load of wood along the ill-forested glades. It has the atmosphere of sunset at all hours of the day. The woodwork is dry and gaping for lack of paint. Through the *jalousies* one sees the prim *salon*, with its beautiful and faded furniture. Even the last of its ill-dressed, ill-favoured women has withered away from Mon Souci, with her inbred, exaggerated features and her long white gloves. But at the rear of the *château* a chimney smokes incessantly. It is the furnace of the laboratory, the only living and modern thing among the old and dying; the only place tended and loved, petted and spoiled, heir to the long solicitude which counts of a more light-hearted day had given to stable and kennel, portrait-gallery and ballroom. And below, in the cool cellar, lie row upon row the dusty bottles, each an enchanted glass coffin in which the Sleeping Beauty of the vine grows ever more ravishing in sleep.

As the Peugeot came to a standstill in the courtyard, the driver observed with considerable surprise that he was not the count's only visitor. An immense super-Renault, like a *merveilleuse* of the Directoire, all bonnet and no body, had been drawn so ostentatiously across the entrance as to embarrass the approach of any newcomer. Its glittering panels were embellished with a coat of arms, and the count's elderly servant was at that moment staggering beneath the weight of two large and elaborate suit-cases bearing in silver letters that could be read a mile away the legend: LORD PETER WIMSEY.

The Peugeot driver gazed with astonishment at this display, and grinned sardonically. "Lord Peter seems rather ubiquitous in this country," he observed to himself. Then, taking pen and paper from his bag, he busied himself with a little letter-writing. By the time that the suit-cases had been carried in, and the Renault had purred its smooth way to the outbuildings, the document was complete and enclosed in an envelope addressed to the Comte de Rueil. "The hoist with his own petard touch," said the young man, and stepping up to the door, presented the envelope to the manservant.

"I am the bearer of a letter of introduction to monsieur le comte," he said. "Will you have the obligingness to present it to him? My name is Bredon — Death Bredon."

The man bowed, and begged him to enter.

"If monsieur will have the goodness to seat himself in the hall for a few moments. Monsieur le comte is engaged with another gentleman, but I will lose no time in making monsieur's arrival known."

The young man sat down and waited. The windows of the hall looked out upon the entrance, and it was not long before the *château*'s sleep was disturbed by the hooting of yet another motor-horn. A station taxi-cab came noisily up the avenue. The man from the first-class carriage and the luggage labelled P. D. B. W. were deposited upon the doorstep. Lord Peter Wimsey dismissed the driver and rang the bell.

"Now," said Mr. Bredon, "the fun is going to begin." He effaced himself as far as possible in the shadow of a tall *armoire normande*.

"Good evening," said the newcomer to the manservant, in

admirable French, "I am Lord Peter Wimsey. I arrive upon the invitation of monsieur le comte de Rueil. Monsieur le comte is at liberty?"

"Milord Peter Wimsey? Pardon, monsieur, but I do not understand. Milord de Wimsey is already arrived and is with monsieur le comte at this moment."

"You surprise me," said the other, with complete imperturbability, "for certainly no one but myself has any right to that name. It seems as though some person more ingenious than honest has had the bright idea of impersonating me."

The servant was clearly at a loss.

"Perhaps," he suggested, "monsieur can show his *papiers d'identité.*"

"Although it is somewhat unusual to produce one's credentials on the doorstep when paying a private visit," replied his lordship, with unaltered good humour, "I have not the slightest objection. Here is my passport, here is a *permis de séjour* granted to me in Paris, here my visiting-card, and here a quantity of correspondence addressed to me at the Hôtel Meurice, Paris, at my flat in Piccadilly, London, at the Marlborough Club, London, and at my brother's house at King's Denver. Is that sufficiently in order?"

The servant perused the documents carefully, appearing particularly impressed by the *permis de séjour.*

"It appears there is some mistake," he murmured dubiously; "if monsieur will follow me, I will acquaint monsieur le comte."

They disappeared through the folding doors at the back of the hall and Bredon was left alone.

"Quite a little boom in Richmonds today," he observed, "each of us more unscrupulous than the last. The occasion calls for a refined subtlety of method."

After what he judged to be a hectic ten minutes in the count's library, the servant reappeared, searching for him.

"Monsieur le comte's compliments, and would monsieur step this way?"

Bredon entered the room with a jaunty step. He had created for himself the mastery of this situation. The count, a thin, elderly man, his fingers deeply stained with chemicals, sat, with a perturbed expression, at his desk. In two armchairs sat the two Wimseys. Bredon noted that, while the Wimsey he had seen in the train (whom he mentally named Peter I) retained his unruffled smile, Peter II (he of the Renault) had the flushed and indignant air of an Englishman affronted. The two men were superficially alike, both fair, lean, and long-nosed, with the nondescript, inelastic face which predominates in any assembly of well-bred Anglo-Saxons.

"Mr. Bredon," said the count, "I am charmed to have the pleasure of making your acquaintance, and regret that I must at once call upon you for a service as singular as it is important. You have presented to me a letter of introduction from your cousin, Lord Peter Wimsey. Will you now be good enough to inform me which of these gentlemen he is?"

Bredon let his glance pass slowly from the one claimant to the other, meditating what answer would best serve his own ends. One, at any rate, of the men in this room was a formidable intellect, trained in the detection of imposture.

"Well?" said Peter II. "Are you going to acknowledge me, Bredon?"

Peter I extracted a cigarette from a silver case. "Your confederate does not seem very well up in his part," he remarked, with a quiet smile at Peter II.

"Monsieur le comte," said Bredon, "I regret extremely that I cannot assist you in the matter. My acquaintance with my cousin, like your own, has been made and maintained entirely through correspondence on a subject of common interest. My profession," he added, "has made me unpopular with my family."

There was a very slight sigh of relief somewhere. The false Wimsey—whichever he was—had gained a respite. Bredon smiled.

"An excellent move, Mr. Bredon," said Peter I, "but it will hardly explain—Allow me." He took the letter from the count's hesitating hand. "It will hardly explain the fact that the ink of this letter of recommendation, dated three weeks ago, is even now scarcely dry—though I congratulate you on the very plausible imitation of my handwriting."

"If *you* can forge my handwriting," said Peter II, "so can this Mr. Bredon." He read the letter aloud over his double's shoulder.

" 'Monsieur le comte—I have the honour to present to you my friend and cousin, Mr. Death Bredon, who, I understand, is to be travelling in your part of France next month. He is very anxious to view your interesting library. Although a journalist by profession, he really knows something about books.' I am delighted to learn for the first time that I have such a cousin. An interviewer's trick, I fancy, monsieur le comte. Fleet Street appears well informed about our family names. Possibly it is equally well informed about the object of my visit to Mon Souci?"

"If," said Bredon boldly, "you refer to the acquisition of the de Rueil formula for poison gas for the British Government, I can answer for my own knowledge, though possibly the rest of Fleet Street is less completely enlightened." He weighed his words carefully now, warned by his slip. The sharp eyes and detective ability of Peter I alarmed him far more than the caustic tongue of Peter II.

The count uttered an exclamation of dismay.

"Gentlemen," he said, "one thing is obvious—that there has been somewhere a disastrous leakage of information. Which of you is the Lord Peter Wimsey to whom I should entrust the formula I do not know. Both of you are supplied with papers of identity; both appear completely instructed in this matter; both of your handwritings correspond with the letters I have previously received from Lord Peter, and both of you have offered me the sum agreed upon in Bank of England notes. In addition, this third gentleman arrives endowed with an equal facility in handwritings, an introductory letter surrounded by most suspicious circumstances, and a degree of acquaintance with this whole matter which alarms me. I can see but one solution. All of you must remain here at the *château* while I send to England for some elucidation of this mystery. To the genuine Lord Peter I offer my apologies, and assure him that I will endeavour to make his stay as agreeable as possible. Will this satisfy you? It will? I am delighted to hear it. My servants will show you to your bedrooms, and dinner will be at half past seven."

"It is delightful to think," said Mr. Bredon, as he finished his glass and passed it before his nostrils with the air of a connoisseur, "that whichever of these gentlemen has the right to the name which he assumes is assured tonight of a truly Olympian satisfaction." His impudence had returned to him, and he challenged the company with an air. "Your cellars, monsieur le comte, are as well known among men endowed with a palate as your talents among men of science. No eloquence could say more."

The two Lord Peters murmured assent.

"I am the more pleased by your commendation," said the count, "that it suggests to me a little test which, with your kind cooperation, will, I think, assist us very much in determining which of you gentlemen is Lord Peter Wimsey and which his talented impersonator. Is it not matter of common notoriety that Lord Peter has a palate for wine almost unequalled in Europe?"

"You flatter me, monsieur le comte," said Peter II modestly.

"I wouldn't like to say unequalled," said Peter I, chiming in like a well-trained duet; "let's call it fair to middling. Less liable to misconstruction and all that."

"Your lordship does yourself an injustice," said Bredon, addressing both men with impartial deference. "The bet which you won from Mr. Frederick Arbuthnot at the Egotists' Club when he challenged you to name the vintage years of seventeen wines blindfold, received its due prominence in the *Evening Wire*."

"I was in extra form that night," said Peter I.

"A fluke," laughed Peter II.

"The test I propose, gentlemen, is on similar lines," pursued the count, "though somewhat less strenuous. There are six courses ordered for dinner tonight. With each we shall drink a different wine, which my butler shall bring me with the label concealed. You shall each in turn give me your opinion upon the vintage. By this means we shall perhaps arrive at something, since the most brilliant forger—of whom I gather I have at least two at my table tonight—can scarcely forge a palate for wine. If too hazardous a mixture of wines should produce a temporary incommodity in the morning, you will, I feel sure, suffer it gladly for this once in the cause of truth."

The two Wimseys bowed.

"*In vino veritas,*" said Mr. Bredon, with a laugh. He at least was well seasoned, and foresaw opportunities for himself.

"Accident, and my butler, having placed you at my right hand, monsieur," went on the count, addressing Peter I, "I will ask you to begin by pronouncing, as accurately as may be, upon the wine which you have just drunk."

"That is scarcely a searching ordeal," said the other, with a smile. "I can say definitely that it is a very pleasant and well-matured Chablis Moutonne; and, since ten years is an excellent age for a Chablis—a real Chablis—I should vote for 1916, which was perhaps the best of the war vintages in that district."

"Have you anything to add to that opinion, monsieur?" inquired the count, deferentially, of Peter II.

"I wouldn't like to be dogmatic to a year or so," said that gentleman critically, "but if I must commit myself, don't you know, I should say 1915—decidedly 1915."

The count bowed, and turned to Bredon.

"Perhaps you, too, monsieur, would be interested to give an opinion," he suggested, with the exquisite courtesy always shown to the plain man in the society of experts.

"I'd rather not set a standard which I might not be able to live up to," replied Bredon, a little maliciously. "I know that it is 1915, for I happened to see the label."

Peter II looked a little disconcerted.

"We will arrange matters better in future," said the count. "Pardon me." He stepped apart for a few moments' conference with the butler, who presently advanced to remove the oysters and bring in the soup.

The next candidate for attention arrived swathed to the lip in damask.

"It is your turn to speak first, monsieur," said the count to Peter II. "Permit me to offer you an olive to cleanse the palate. No haste, I beg. Even for the most excellent political ends, good wine must not be used with disrespect."

The rebuke was not unnecessary, for, after a preliminary sip, Peter II had taken a deep draught of the heady white richness. Under Peter I's quizzical eye he wilted quite visibly.

"It is—it is Sauterne," he began, and stopped. Then, gathering encouragement from Bredon's smile, he said, with more aplomb, "Château Yquem, 1911—ah! the queen of white wines, sir, as what's-his-name says." He drained his glass defiantly.

The count's face was a study as he slowly detached his fascinated gaze from Peter II to fix it on Peter I.

"If I had to be impersonated by somebody," murmured the latter gently, "it would have been more flattering to have had it undertaken by a person to whom all white wines were *not* alike. Well, now, sir, this admirable vintage is, of course, a Montrachet of—let me see"—he rolled the wine delicately upon his tongue—"of 1911. And a very attractive wine it is, though, with all due deference to yourself, monsieur le comte, I feel that it is perhaps slightly too sweet to occupy its present place in the menu. True, with this excellent *consommé marmite*, a sweetish wine is not altogether out of place, but, in my own humble opinion, it would have shown to better advantage with the *confitures*."

"There, now," said Bredon innocently, "it just shows how one may be misled. Had not I had the advantage of Lord Peter's expert opinion—for certainly nobody who could mistake Montrachet for Sauterne has any claim to the name of Wimsey—I should have pronounced this to be, not the Montrachet-Aîné, but the Chevalier-Montrachet of the same year, which is a trifle sweeter. But no doubt, as your lordship says, drinking it with the soup has caused it to appear sweeter to me than it actually is."

The count looked sharply at him, but made no comment.

"Have another olive," said Peter I kindly. "You can't judge wine if your mind is on other flavours."

"Thanks frightfully," said Bredon. "And that reminds me —" He launched into a rather pointless story about olives, which lasted out the soup and bridged the interval to the entrance of an exquisitely cooked sole.

The count's eye followed the pale amber wine rather thoughtfully as it trilled into the glasses. Bredon raised his in the approved manner to his nostrils, and his face flushed a little. With the first sip he turned excitedly to his host.

"Good God, sir —" he began.

The lifted hand cautioned him to silence.

Peter I sipped, inhaled, sipped again, and his brows clouded. Peter II had by this time apparently abandoned his pretensions. He drank thirstily, with a beaming smile and a lessening hold upon reality.

"*Eh bien, monsieur?*" inquired the count gently.

"This," said Peter I, "is certainly hock, and the noblest hock I have ever tasted, but I must admit that for the moment I cannot precisely place it."

"No?" said Bredon. His voice was like bean-honey now, sweet and harsh together. "Nor the other gentleman? And yet I fancy I could place it within a couple of miles, though it is a wine I had hardly looked to find in a French cellar at this time. It is hock, as your lordship says, and at that it is Johannisberger. Not the plebeian cousin, but the *echter* Schloss Johannisberger from the castle vineyard itself. Your lordship must have missed it (to your great loss) during the war years. My father laid some down the year before he died, but it appears that the ducal cellars at Denver were less well furnished."

"I must set about remedying the omission," said the remaining Peter, with determination.

The *poulet* was served to the accompaniment of an argument over the Lafitte, his lordship placing it at 1878, Bredon maintaining it to be a relic of the glorious 'seventy-fives, slightly overmatured, but both agreeing as to its great age and noble pedigree.

As to the Clos-Vougeôt, on the other hand, there was complete agreement; after a tentative suggestion of 1915, it was pronounced finally by Peter I to belong to the equally admirable though slightly lighter 1911 crop. The *pré-salé* was removed amid general applause, and the dessert was brought in.

"Is it necessary," asked Peter I, with a slight smile in the direction of Peter II—now happily murmuring, "Damn good wine, damn good dinner, damn good show"—"is it necessary to prolong this farce any further?"

"Your lordship will not, surely, refuse to proceed with the discussion?" cried the count.

"The point is sufficiently made, I fancy."

"But no one will surely ever refuse to discuss wine," said Bredon, "least of all your lordship, who is so great an authority."

"Not on this," said the other. "Frankly, it is a wine I do not care about. It is sweet and coarse, qualities that would damn any wine in the eyes—the mouth, rather—of a connoisseur. Did your excellent father have this laid down also, Mr. Bredon?"

Bredon shook his head.

"No," he said, "no. Genuine Imperial Tokay is beyond the opportunities of Grub Street, I fear. Though I agree with you that it is horribly overrated—with all due deference to yourself, monsieur le comte."

"In that case," said the count, "we will pass at once to the liqueur. I admit that I had thought of puzzling these gentlemen with the local product, but, since one competitor seems to have scratched, it shall be brandy—the only fitting close to a good wine-list."

In a slightly embarrassing silence the huge, round-bellied balloon glasses were set upon the table, and the few precious drops poured gently into each and set lightly swinging to release the bouquet.

"This," said Peter I, charmed again into amiability, "is, indeed, a wonderful old French brandy. Half a century old, I suppose."

"Your lordship's praise lacks warmth," replied Bredon. "This is *the* brandy — the brandy of brandies — the superb — the incomparable — the true Napoleon. It should be honoured like the emperor it is."

He rose to his feet, his napkin in his hand.

"Sir," said the count, turning to him, "I have on my right a most admirable judge of wine, but you are unique." He motioned to Pierre, who solemnly brought forward the empty bottles, unswathed now, from the humble Chablis to the stately Napoleon, with the imperial seal blown in the glass. "Every time you have been correct as to the growth and year. There cannot be six men in the world with such a palate as yours, and I thought that but one of them was an Englishman. Will you not favour us, this time, with your real name?"

"It doesn't matter what his name is," said Peter I. He rose. "Put up your hands, all of you. Count, the formula!"

Bredon's hands came up with a jerk, still clutching the napkin. The white folds spurted flame as his shot struck the other's revolver cleanly between trigger and barrel, exploding the charge, to the extreme detriment of the glass chandelier. Peter I stood shaking his paralysed hand and cursing.

Bredon kept him covered while he cocked a wary eye at Peter II, who, his rosy visions scattered by the report, seemed struggling back to aggressiveness.

"Since the entertainment appears to be taking a lively turn," observed Bredon, "perhaps you would be so good, count, as to search these gentlemen for further firearms. Thank you. Now, why should we not all sit down again and pass the bottle round?"

"You — *you* are —" growled Peter I.

"Oh, my name is Bredon all right," said the young man cheerfully. "I loathe aliases. Like another fellow's clothes, you know — never seem quite to fit. Peter Death Bredon Wimsey — a bit lengthy and all that, but handy when taken in instalments. I've got a passport and all those things, too, but I didn't offer them, as their reputation here seems a little blown upon, so to speak. As regards the formula, I think I'd better give you my personal cheque for it—all sorts of people seem able to go about flourishing Bank of England notes. Personally, I think all this secret diplomacy work is a mistake, but that's the War Office's pigeon. I suppose we all brought similar credentials. Yes, I thought so. Some bright person seems to have sold himself very successfully in two places at once. But you two must have been having a lively time, each thinking the other was me."

"My lord," said the count heavily, "these two men are, or were, Englishmen, I suppose. I do not care to know what governments have purchased their treachery. But where they stand, I, alas! stand too. To our venal and corrupt Republic I, as a Royalist, acknowledge no allegiance. But it is in my heart that I have agreed to sell my country to England because of my poverty. Go back to your War Office and say I will not give you the formula. If war should come between our countries—which may God avert—I will be found on the side of France. That, my lord, is my last word."

Wimsey bowed.

"Sir," said he, "it appears that my mission has, after all, failed. I am glad of it. This trafficking in destruction is a dirty kind of business after all. Let us shut the door upon these two, who are neither flesh nor fowl, and finish the brandy in the library."

THE LEARNED ADVENTURE
OF THE DRAGON'S HEAD

Uncle Peter!"

"Half a jiff, Gherkins. No, I don't think I'll take a Catullus, Mr. Ffolliott. After all, thirteen guineas is a bit steep without either the title or the last folio, what? But you might send me round the Vitruvius and the Satyricon when they come in; I'd like to have a look at them, anyhow. Well, old man, what is it?"

"Do come and look at these pictures, Uncle Peter. I'm sure it's an awfully old book."

Lord Peter Wimsey sighed as he picked his way out of Mr. Ffolliott's dark back shop, strewn with the flotsam and jetsam of many libraries. An unexpected outbreak of measles at Mr. Bultridge's excellent preparatory school, coinciding with the absence of the Duke and Duchess of Denver on the Continent, had saddled his lordship with his ten-year-old nephew, Viscount St. George, more commonly known as Young Jerry, Jerrykins, or Pickled Gherkins. Lord Peter was not one of those born uncles who delight old nurses by their fascinating "way with" children. He succeeded, however, in earning tolerance on honourable terms by treating the young with the same scrupulous politeness which he extended to their elders. He therefore prepared to receive Gherkins's discovery with respect, though a child's taste was not to be trusted, and the book might quite well be some horror of woolly mezzotints or an inferior modern reprint adorned with leprous electros. Nothing much better was really to be expected from the "cheap shelf" exposed to the dust of the street.

"Uncle! there's such a funny man here, with a great long nose and ears and a tail and dogs' heads all over his body. *Monstrum hoc Cracoviae*—that's a monster, isn't it? I should jolly well think it was. What's *Cracoviae*, Uncle Peter?"

"Oh," said Lord Peter, greatly relieved, "the Cracow monster?" A portrait of that distressing infant certainly argued a respectable antiquity. "Let's have a look. Quite right, it's a very old book—Munster's *Cosmographia Universalis*. I'm glad you know good stuff when you see it, Gherkins. What's the *Cosmographia* doing out here, Mr. Ffolliott, at five bob?"

"Well, my lord," said the bookseller, who had followed his customers to the door, "it's in a very bad state, you see; covers loose and nearly all the doublepage maps missing. It came in a few weeks ago—dumped in with a collection we bought from a gentleman in Norfolk—you'll find his name in it—Dr. Conyers of Yelsall Manor. Of course, we might keep it and try to make up a complete copy when we get another example. But it's rather out of our line, as you know, classical authors being our specialty. So we just put it out to go for what it would fetch in the *status quo*, as you might say."

"Oh, look!" broke in Gherkins. "Here's a picture of a man being chopped up in little bits. What does it say about it?"

"I thought you could read Latin."

"Well, but it's all full of sort of pothooks. What do they mean?"

"They're just contractions," said Lord Peter patiently. " '*Solent quoque hujus insulae cultores*'—It is the custom of the dwellers in this island, when they see their parents stricken in years and of no further use, to take them down into the market-place and sell them to the cannibals, who kill them and eat them for food. This they do also with younger persons when they fall into any desperate sickness."

"Ha, ha!" said Mr. Ffolliott. "Rather sharp practice on the

poor cannibals. They never got anything but tough old joints or diseased meat, eh?"

"The inhabitants seem to have had thoroughly advanced notions of business," agreed his lordship.

The viscount was enthralled.

"I *do* like this book," he said; "could I buy it out of my pocket-money, please?"

"Another problem for uncles," thought Lord Peter, rapidly ransacking his recollections of the *Cosmographia* to determine whether any of its illustrations were indelicate; for he knew the duchess to be straitlaced. On consideration, he could only remember one that was dubious, and there was a sporting chance that the duchess might fail to light upon it.

"Well," he said judicially, "in your place, Gherkins, I should be inclined to buy it. It's in a bad state, as Mr. Ffolliott has honourably told you—otherwise, of course, it would be exceedingly valuable; but, apart from the lost pages, it's a very nice clean copy, and certainly worth five shillings to you, if you think of starting a collection."

Till that moment, the viscount had obviously been more impressed by the cannibals than by the state of the margins, but the idea of figuring next term at Mr. Bultridge's as a collector of rare editions had undeniable charm.

"None of the other fellows collect books," he said; "they collect stamps, mostly. I think stamps are rather ordinary, don't you, Uncle Peter? I was rather thinking of giving up stamps. Mr. Porter, who takes us for history, has got a lot of books like yours, and he is a splendid man at footer."

Rightly interpreting this reference to Mr. Porter, Lord Peter gave it as his opinion that book-collecting could be a perfectly manly pursuit. Girls, he said, practically never took it up, because it meant so much learning about dates and type-faces and other technicalities which called for a masculine brain.

"Besides," he added, "it's a very interesting book in itself, you know. Well worth dipping into."

"I'll take it, please," said the viscount, blushing a little at transacting so important and expensive a piece of business; for the duchess did not encourage lavish spending by little boys, and was strict in the matter of allowances.

Mr. Ffolliott bowed, and took the *Cosmographia* away to wrap it up.

"Are you all right for cash?" inquired Lord Peter discreetly. "Or can I be of temporary assistance?"

"No, thank you, uncle; I've got Aunt Mary's half-crown and four shillings of my pocket-money, because, you see, with the measles happening, we didn't have our dormitory spread, and I was saving up for that."

The business being settled in this gentlemanly manner, and the budding bibliophile taking personal and immediate charge of the stout, square volume, a taxi was chartered which, in due course of traffic delays, brought the *Cosmographia* to 110A Piccadilly.

"And who, Bunter, is Mr. Wilberforce Pope?"

"I do not think we know the gentleman, my lord. He is asking to see your lordship for a few minutes on business."

"He probably wants me to find a lost dog for his maiden aunt. What it is to have acquired a reputation as a sleuth! Show him in. Gherkins, if this good gentleman's business turns out to be private, you'd better retire into the dining-room."

"Yes, Uncle Peter," said the viscount dutifully. He was extended on his stomach on the library hearthrug, laboriously picking his way through the more exciting-looking bits of the *Cosmographia*, with the aid of Messrs. Lewis & Short, whose monumental compilation he had hitherto looked upon as a barbarous invention for the annoyance of upper forms.

Mr. Wilberforce Pope turned out to be a rather plump, fair gentleman in the late thirties, with a prematurely bald forehead, horn-rimmed spectacles, and an engaging manner.

"You will excuse my intrusion, won't you?" he began. "I'm sure you must think me a terrible nuisance. But I wormed your name and address out of Mr. Ffolliott. Not his fault,

really. You won't blame him, will you? I positively badgered
the poor man. Sat down on his doorstep and refused to go,
though the boy was putting up the shutters. I'm afraid you
will think me very silly when you know what it's all about. But
you really mustn't hold poor Mr. Ffolliott responsible, now,
will you?"

"Not at all," said his lordship. "I mean, I'm charmed and
all that sort of thing. Something I can do for you about books?
You're a collector, perhaps? Will you have a drink or anything?"

"Well, no," said Mr. Pope, with a faint giggle. "No, not
exactly a collector. Thank you very much, just a spot—no,
no, literally a spot. Thank you; no"—he glanced round the
bookshelves, with their rows of rich old leather bindings—
"certainly not a collector. But I happen to be, er, interested—
sentimentally interested—in a purchase you made yesterday.
Really, such a very small matter. You will think it foolish.
But I am told you are the present owner of a copy of Munster's *Cosmographia,* which used to belong to my uncle, Dr.
Conyers."

Gherkins looked up suddenly, seeing that the conversation had a personal interest for him.

"Well, that's not quite correct," said Wimsey. "I was there
at the time, but the actual purchaser is my nephew. Gerald,
Mr. Pope is interested in your *Cosmographia.* My nephew, Lord
St. George."

"How do you do, young man," said Mr. Pope affably. "I
see that the collecting spirit runs in the family. A great Latin
scholar, too, I expect, eh? Ready to decline *jusjurandum* with
the best of us? Ha, ha! And what are you going to do when
you grow up? Be Lord Chancellor, eh? Now, I bet you think
you'd rather be an engine-driver, what, what?"

"No, thank you," said the viscount, with aloofness.

"What, not an engine-driver? Well, now, I want you to be
a real business man this time. Put through a book deal, you
know. Your uncle will see I offer you a fair price, what? Ha,
ha! Now, you see, that picture-book of yours has a great value

for me that it wouldn't have for anybody else. When *I* was a little boy of your age it was one of my very greatest joys. I used to have it to look at on Sundays. Ah, dear! the happy hours I used to spend with those quaint old engravings, and the funny old maps with the ships and salamanders and *'Hic dracones'*—you know what *that* means, I dare say. What does it mean?"

"Here are dragons," said the viscount, unwillingly but still politely.

"Quite right. I *knew* you were a scholar."

"It's a very attractive book," said Lord Peter. "My nephew was quite entranced by the famous Cracow monster."

"Ah yes—a glorious monster, isn't it?" agreed Mr. Pope, with enthusiasm. "Many's the time I've fancied myself as Sir Lancelot or somebody on a white war horse, charging that monster, lance in rest, with the captive princess cheering me on. Ah! childhood! You're living the happiest days of your life, young man. You won't believe me, but you are."

"Now what is it exactly you want my nephew to do?" inquired Lord Peter a little sharply.

"Quite right, quite right. Well now, you know, my uncle, Dr. Conyers, sold his library a few months ago. I was abroad at the time, and it was only yesterday, when I went down to Yelsall on a visit, that I learnt the dear old book had gone with the rest. I can't tell you how distressed I was. I know it's not valuable—a great many pages missing and all that—but I can't bear to think of its being gone. So, purely from sentimental reasons, as I said, I hurried off to Ffolliott's to see if I could get it back. I was quite upset to find I was too late, and gave poor Mr. Ffolliott no peace till he told me the name of the purchaser. Now, you see, Lord St. George, I'm here to make you an offer for the book. Come, now, double what you gave for it. That's a good offer, isn't it, Lord Peter? Ha, ha! And you will be doing me a very great kindness as well."

Viscount St. George looked rather distressed, and turned appealingly to his uncle.

"Well, Gerald," said Lord Peter, "it's your affair, you know. What do you say?"

The viscount stood first on one leg and then on the other. The career of a book collector evidently had its problems, like other careers.

"If you please, Uncle Peter," he said, with embarrassment, "may I whisper?"

"It's not usually considered the thing to whisper, Gherkins, but you could ask Mr. Pope for time to consider his offer. Or you could say you would prefer to consult me first. That would be quite in order."

"Then, if you don't mind, Mr. Pope, I should like to consult my uncle first."

"Certainly, certainly; ha, ha!" said Mr. Pope. "Very prudent to consult a collector of greater experience, what? Ah! the younger generation, eh, Lord Peter? Regular little business men already."

"Excuse us, then, for one moment," said Lord Peter, and drew his nephew into the dining-room.

"I say, Uncle Peter," said the collector breathlessly, when the door was shut, "*need* I give him my book? I don't think he's a very nice man. I *hate* people who ask you to decline nouns for them."

"Certainly you needn't, Gherkins, if you don't want to. The book is yours, and you've a right to it."

"What would *you* do, uncle?"

Before replying, Lord Peter, in the most surprising manner, tiptoed gently to the door which communicated with the library and flung it suddenly open, in time to catch Mr. Pope kneeling on the hearthrug intently turning over the pages of the coveted volume, which lay as the owner had left it. He started to his feet in a flurried manner as the door opened.

"Do help yourself, Mr. Pope, won't you?" cried Lord Peter hospitably, and closed the door again.

"What is it, Uncle Peter?"

"If you want my advice, Gherkins, I should be rather careful how you had any dealings with Mr. Pope. I don't think he's telling the truth. He called those wood-cuts engravings—though, of course, that may be just his ignorance. But I can't believe that he spent all his childhood's Sunday afternoons studying those maps and picking out the dragons in them, because, as you may have noticed for yourself, old Munster put very few dragons into his maps. They're mostly just plain maps—a bit queer to our ideas of geography, but perfectly straightforward. That was why I brought in the Cracow monster, and, you see, he thought it was some sort of dragon."

"Oh, I say, uncle! So you said that on purpose!"

"If Mr. Pope wants the *Cosmographia*, it's for some reason he doesn't want to tell us about. And, that being so, I wouldn't be in too big a hurry to sell, if the book were mine. See?"

"Do you mean there's something frightfully valuable about the book, which we don't know?"

"Possibly."

"How exciting! It's just like a story in the *Boys' Friend Library*. What am I to say to him, uncle?"

"Well, in your place I wouldn't be dramatic or anything. I'd just say you've considered the matter, and you've taken a fancy to the book and have decided not to sell. You thank him for his offer, of course."

"Yes—er, won't you say it for me, uncle?"

"I think it would look better if you did it yourself."

"Yes, perhaps it would. Will he be very cross?"

"Possibly," said Lord Peter, "but if he is, he won't let on. Ready?"

The consulting committee accordingly returned to the library. Mr. Pope had prudently retired from the hearthrug and was examining a distant bookcase.

"Thank you very much for your offer, Mr. Pope," said the viscount, striding stoutly up to him, "but I have considered it, and I have taken a-a-a fancy for the book and decided not to sell."

"Sorry and all that," put in Lord Peter, "but my nephew's adamant about it. No, it isn't the price; he wants the book. Wish I could oblige you, but it isn't in my hands. Won't you take something else before you go? Really? Ring the bell, Gherkins. My man will see you to the lift. Good evening."

When the visitor had gone, Lord Peter returned and thoughtfully picked up the book.

"We were awful idiots to leave him with it, Gherkins, even for a moment. Luckily, there's no harm done."

"You don't think he found out anything while we were away, do you, uncle?" gasped Gherkins, open-eyed.

"I'm sure he didn't."

"Why?"

"He offered me fifty pounds for it on the way to the door. Gave the game away. H'm! Bunter."

"My lord?"

"Put this book in the safe and bring me back the keys. And you'd better set all the burglar alarms when you lock up."

"Oo-er!" said Viscount St. George.

On the third morning after the visit of Mr. Wilberforce Pope, the viscount was seated at a very late breakfast in his uncle's flat, after the most glorious and soul-satisfying night that ever boy experienced. He was almost too excited to eat the kidneys and bacon placed before him by Bunter, whose usual impeccable manner was not in the least impaired by a rapidly swelling and blackening eye.

It was about two in the morning that Gherkins—who had not slept very well, owing to too lavish and grown-up a dinner and theatre the evening before—became aware of a stealthy sound somewhere in the direction of the fire-escape. He had got out of bed and crept very softly into Lord Peter's room and woken him up. He had said: "Uncle Peter, I'm sure there's burglars on the fire-escape." And Uncle Peter, instead of saying, "Nonsense, Gherkins, hurry up and get back to bed," had sat up and listened and said: "By Jove, Gherkins, I believe you're right." And had sent Gherkins to call Bunter. And on his return, Gherkins, who had always regarded his uncle as a very top-hatted sort of person, actually saw him take from his handkerchief-drawer an undeniable automatic pistol.

It was at this point that Lord Peter was apotheosed from the state of Quite Decent Uncle to that of Glorified Uncle. He said:

"Look here, Gherkins, we don't know how many of these blighters there'll be, so you must be jolly smart and do anything I say sharp, on the word of command—even if I have to say 'Scoot.' Promise?"

Gherkins promised, with his heart thumping, and they sat waiting in the dark, till suddenly a little electric bell rang sharply just over the head of Lord Peter's bed and a green light shone out.

"The library window," said his lordship, promptly silencing the bell by turning a switch. "If they heard, they may think better of it. We'll give them a few minutes."

They gave them five minutes, and then crept very quietly down the passage.

"Go round by the dining-room, Bunter," said his lordship; "they may bolt that way."

With infinite precaution, he unlocked and opened the library door, and Gherkins noticed how silently the locks moved.

A circle of light from an electric torch was moving slowly along the bookshelves. The burglars had obviously heard nothing of the counter-attack. Indeed, they seemed to have troubles enough of their own to keep their attention occupied. As his eyes grew accustomed to the dim light, Gherkins made out that one man was standing holding the torch, while the other took down and examined the books. It was fascinating to watch his apparently disembodied hands move along the shelves in the torch-light.

The men muttered discontentedly. Obviously the job was proving a harder one than they had bargained for. The habit of ancient authors of abbreviating the titles on the backs of their volumes, or leaving them completely untitled, made things extremely awkward. From time to time the man with the torch extended his hand into the light. It held a piece of paper, which they anxiously compared with the title-page of a book. Then the volume was replaced and the tedious search went on.

Suddenly some slight noise — Gherkins was sure *he* did not make it; it may have been Bunter in the dining-room — seemed to catch the ear of the kneeling man.

"Wot's that?" he gasped, and his startled face swung round into view.

"Hands up!" said Lord Peter, and switched the light on.

The second man made one leap for the dining-room door, where a smash and an oath proclaimed that he had encountered Bunter. The kneeling man shot his hands up like a marionette.

"Gherkins," said Lord Peter, "do you think you can go across to that gentleman by the bookcase and relieve him of the article which is so inelegantly distending the right-hand pocket of his coat? Wait a minute. Don't on any account get between him and my pistol, and mind you take the thing out *very* carefully. There's no hurry. That's splendid. Just point it at the floor while you bring it across, would you? Thanks. Bunter has managed for himself, I see. Now run into my bedroom, and in the bottom of my wardrobe you will find a bundle of stout cord. Oh! I beg your pardon; yes, put your hands down by all means. It must be very tiring exercise."

The arms of the intruders being secured behind their backs with a neatness which Gherkins felt to be worthy of the best traditions of Sexton Blake, Lord Peter motioned his captives to sit down and despatched Bunter for whisky-and-soda.

"Before we send for the police," said Lord Peter, "you would do me a great personal favour by telling me what you were looking for, and who sent you. Ah! thanks, Bunter. As our guests are not at liberty to use their hands, perhaps you would be kind enough to assist them to a drink. Now then, say when."

"Well, you're a gentleman, guv'nor," said the First Burglar, wiping his mouth politely on his shoulder, the back of his hand not being available. "If we'd a known wot a job this wos goin' ter be, blow me if we'd a touched it. The bloke said, ses 'e, 'It's takin' candy from a baby,' 'e ses. 'The gentleman's a reg'lar softie,' 'e ses, 'one o' these 'ere sersiety toffs wiv a maggot fer old books,' that's wot 'e ses, 'an' ef yer can find this 'ere old book fer me,' 'e ses, 'there's a pony fer yer.' Well! Sech a job! 'E didn't mention as 'ow there'd be five 'undred fousand bleedin' ole books all as alike as a regiment o' bleedin' dragoons. Nor as 'ow yer kept a nice little machine-gun like that 'andy by the bedside, *nor* yet as 'ow yer was so bleedin' good at tyin' knots in a bit o' string. No—'e didn't think ter mention them things."

"Deuced unsporting of him," said his lordship. "Do you happen to know the gentleman's name?"

"No—that was another o' them things wot 'e didn't mention. 'E's a stout, fair party, wiv 'orn rims to 'is goggles and a bald 'ead. One o' these 'ere philanthropists, I reckon. A friend o' mine, wot got inter trouble onct, got work froo 'im, and the gentleman comes round and ses to 'im, 'e ses, 'Could yer find me a couple o' lads ter do a little job?' 'e ses, an' my friend finkin' no 'arm, you see, guv'nor, but wot it might be a bit of a joke like, 'e gets 'old of my pal an' me, an' we meets the gentleman in a pub dahn Whitechapel way. W'ich we was ter meet 'im there again Friday night, us 'avin' allowed that time fer ter git 'old of the book."

"The book being, if I may hazard a guess, the *Cosmographia Universalis*?"

"Sumfink like that, guv'nor. I got its jaw-breakin' name wrote down on a bit o' paper, wot my pal 'ad in 'is 'and. Wot did yer do wiv that 'ere bit o' paper, Bill?"

"Well, look here," said Lord Peter, "I'm afraid I must send for the police, but I think it likely, if you give us your assistance to get hold of your gentleman, whose name I strongly suspect to be Wilberforce Pope, that you will get off pretty easily. Telephone the police, Bunter, and then go and put something on that eye of yours. Gherkins, we'll give these gentlemen another drink, and then I think perhaps you'd better hop back to bed; the fun's over. No? Well, put a good thick coat on, there's a good fellow, because what your mother will say to me if you catch a cold I don't like to think."

So the police had come and taken the burglars away, and

now Detective-Inspector Parker, of Scotland Yard, a great personal friend of Lord Peter's, sat toying with a cup of coffee and listening to the story.

"But what's the matter with the jolly old book, anyhow, to make it so popular?" he demanded.

"I don't know," replied Wimsey; "but after Mr. Pope's little visit the other day I got kind of intrigued about it and had a look through it. I've got a hunch it may turn out rather valuable, after all. Unsuspected beauties and all that sort of thing. If only Mr. Pope had been a trifle more accurate in his facts, he might have got away with something to which I feel pretty sure he isn't entitled. Anyway, when I'd seen—what I saw, I wrote off to Dr. Conyers of Yelsall Manor, the late owner—"

"Conyers, the cancer man?"

"Yes. He's done some pretty important research in his time, I fancy. Getting on now, though; about seventy-eight, I fancy. I hope he's more honest than his nephew, with one foot in the grave like that. Anyway, I wrote (with Gherkins's permission, naturally) to say we had the book and had been specially interested by something we found there, and would he be so obliging as to tell us something of its history. I also—"

"But what did you find in it?"

"I don't think we'll tell him yet, Gherkins, shall we? I like to keep policemen guessing. As I was saying, when you so rudely interrupted me, I also asked him whether he knew anything about his good nephew's offer to buy it back. His answer has just arrived. He says he knows of nothing specially interesting about the book. It has been in the library untold years, and the tearing out of the maps must have been done a long time ago by some family vandal. He can't think why his nephew should be so keen on it, as he certainly never pored over it as a boy. In fact, the old man declares the engaging Wilberforce has never even set foot in Yelsall Manor to his knowledge. So much for the fire-breathing monsters and the pleasant Sunday afternoons."

"Naughty Wilberforce!"

"M'm. Yes. So, after last night's little dust-up, I wired the old boy we were tooling down to Yelsall to have a heart-to-heart talk with him about his picture-book and his nephew."

"Are you taking the book down with you?" asked Parker. "I can give you a police escort for it if you like."

"That's not a bad idea," said Wimsey. "We don't know where the insinuating Mr. Pope may be hanging out, and I wouldn't put it past him to make another attempt."

"Better be on the safe side," said Parker. "I can't come myself, but I'll send down a couple of men with you."

"Good egg," said Lord Peter. "Call up your myrmidons. We'll get a car round at once. You're coming, Gherkins, I suppose? God knows what your mother would say. Don't ever be an uncle, Charles; it's frightfully difficult to be fair to all parties."

Yelsall Manor was one of those large, decaying country mansions which speak eloquently of times more spacious than our own. The original late Tudor construction had been masked by the addition of a wide frontage in the Italian manner, with a kind of classical portico surmounted by a pediment and approached by a semi-circular flight of steps. The grounds had originally been laid out in that formal manner in which grove nods to grove and each half duly reflects the other. A late owner, however, had burst out into the more eccentric sort of landscape gardening which is associated with the name of Capability Brown. A Chinese pagoda, somewhat resembling Sir William Chambers's erection in Kew Gardens, but smaller, rose out of a grove of laurustinus towards the eastern extremity of the house, while at the rear appeared a large artificial lake, dotted with numerous islands, on which odd little temples, grottos, tea-houses, and bridges peeped out from among clumps of shrubs, once ornamental, but now sadly overgrown. A boat-house, with wide eaves like the designs on a willow-pattern plate, stood at one corner, its landing-stage fallen into decay and wreathed with melancholy weeds.

"My disreputable old ancestor, Cuthbert Conyers, settled down here when he retired from the sea in 1732," said Dr.

Conyers, smiling faintly. "His elder brother died childless, so the black sheep returned to the fold with the determination to become respectable and found a family. I fear he did not succeed altogether. There were very queer tales as to where his money came from. He is said to have been a pirate, and to have sailed with the notorious Captain Blackbeard. In the village, to this day, he is remembered and spoken of as Cut-throat Conyers. It used to make the old man very angry, and there is an unpleasant story of his slicing the ears off a groom who had been heard to call him 'Old Cut-throat.' He was not an uncultivated person, though. It was he who did the landscape-gardening round at the back, and he built the pagoda for his telescope. He was reputed to study the Black Art, and there were certainly a number of astrological works in the library with his name on the fly-leaf, but probably the telescope was only a remembrance of his seafaring days.

"Anyhow, towards the end of his life he became more and more odd and morose. He quarrelled with his family, and turned his younger son out of doors with his wife and children. An unpleasant old fellow.

"On his deathbed he was attended by the parson — a good earnest, God-fearing sort of man, who must have put up with a deal of insult in carrying out what he firmly believed to be the sacred duty of reconciling the old man to this shamefully treated son. Eventually, 'Old Cut-throat' relented so far as to make a will, leaving to the younger son 'My treasure which I have buried in Munster.' The parson represented to him that it was useless to bequeath a treasure unless he also bequeathed the information where to find it, but the horrid old pirate only chuckled spitefully, and said that, as he had been at the pains to collect the treasure, his son might well be at the pains of looking for it. Further than that he would not go, and so he died, and I dare say went to a very bad place.

"Since then the family has died out, and I am the sole representative of the Conyerses, and heir to the treasure, whatever and wherever it is, for it was never discovered. I do not suppose it was very honestly come by, but, since it would be useless now to try and find the original owners, I imagine I have a better right to it than anybody living.

"You may think it very unseemly, Lord Peter, that an old, lonely man like myself should be greedy for a hoard of pirate's gold. But my whole life has been devoted to studying the disease of cancer, and I believe myself to be very close to a solution of one part at least of the terrible problem. Research costs money, and my limited means are very nearly exhausted. The property is mortgaged up to the hilt, and I do most urgently desire to complete my experiments before I die, and to leave a sufficient sum to found a clinic where the work can be carried on.

"During the last year I have made very great efforts to solve the mystery of 'Old Cut-throat's' treasure. I have been able to leave much of my experimental work in the most capable hands of my assistant, Dr. Forbes, while I pursued my researches with the very slender clue I had to go upon. It was the more expensive and difficult that Cuthbert had left no indication in his will whether Münster in Germany or Munster in Ireland was the hiding-place of the treasure. My journeys and my search in other places cost money and brought me no further on my quest. I returned, disheartened, in August, and found myself obliged to sell my library, in order to defray my expenses and obtain a little money with which to struggle on with my sadly delayed experiments."

"Ah!" said Lord Peter. "I begin to see light."

The old physician looked at him inquiringly. They had finished tea, and were seated around the great fireplace in the study. Lord Peter's interested questions about the beautiful, dilapidated old house and estate had led the conversation naturally to Dr. Conyers's family, shelving for the time the problem of the *Cosmographia*, which lay on a table beside them.

"Everything you say fits into the puzzle," went on Wimsey, "and I think there's not the smallest doubt what Mr. Wilberforce Pope was after, though how he knew that you had the *Cosmographia* here I couldn't say."

"When I disposed of the library, I sent him a catalogue,"

said Dr. Conyers. "As a relative, I thought he ought to have the right to buy anything he fancied. I can't think why he didn't secure the book then, instead of behaving in this most shocking fashion."

Lord Peter hooted with laughter.

"Why, because he never tumbled to it till afterwards," he said. "And oh, dear, how wild he must have been! I forgive him everything. Although," he added, "I don't want to raise your hopes too high, sir, for, even when we've solved old Cuthbert's riddle, I don't know that we're very much nearer to the treasure."

"To the *treasure?*"

"Well, now, sir. I want you first to look at this page, where there's a name scrawled in the margin. Our ancestors had an untidy way of signing their possessions higgledy-piggledy in margins instead of in a decent, Christian way in the fly-leaf. This is a handwriting of somewhere about Charles I's reign: 'Jac: Coniers.' I take it that goes to prove that the book was in the possession of your family at any rate as early as the first half of the seventeenth century, and has remained there ever since. Right, now we turn to page 1099, where we find a description of the discoveries of Christopher Columbus. It's headed, you see, by a kind of map, with some of Mr. Pope's monsters swimming about in it, and apparently representing the Canaries, or, as they used to be called, the Fortunate Isles. It doesn't look much more accurate than old maps usually are, but I take it the big island on the right is meant for Lanzarote, and the two nearest to it may be Teneriffe and Gran Canaria."

"But what's that writing in the middle?"

"That's just the point. The writing is later than 'Jac: Coniers's' signature; I should put it about 1700—but, of course, it may have been written a good deal later still. I mean, a man who was elderly in 1730 would still use the style of writing he adopted as a young man, especially if, like your ancestor the pirate, he had spent the early part of his life in outdoor pursuits and hadn't done much writing."

"Do you mean to say, Uncle Peter," broke in the viscount excitedly, "that that's 'Old Cut-throat's' writing?"

"I'd be ready to lay a sporting bet it is. Look here, sir, you've been scouring round Münster in Germany and Munster in Ireland — but how about good old Sebastian Munster here in the library at home?"

"God bless my soul! Is it possible?"

"It's pretty nearly certain, sir. Here's what he says, written, you see, round the head of that sort of sea-dragon:

Hic in capite draconis ardet perpetuo Sol.
Here the sun shines perpetually upon the Dragon's Head.

Rather doggy Latin — sea-dog Latin, you might say, in fact."

"I'm afraid," said Dr. Conyers, "I must be very stupid, but I can't see where that leads us."

"No: 'Old Cut-throat' was rather clever. No doubt he thought that, if anybody read it, they'd think it was just an allusion to where it says, further down, that 'the islands were called *Fortunatae* because of the wonderful temperature of the air and the clemency of the skies.' But the cunning old astrologer up in his pagoda had a meaning of his own. Here's a little book published in 1678 — Middleton's *Practical Astrology* — just the sort of popular handbook an amateur like 'Old Cut-throat' would use. Here you are: 'If in your figure you find Jupiter or Venus or *Dragon's Head*, you may be confident there is Treasure in the place supposed. . . . If you find *Sol* to be the significator of the hidden Treasure, you may conclude there is Gold, or some jewels.' You know, sir, I think we may conclude it."

"Dear me!" said Dr. Conyers. "I believe, indeed, you must be right. And I am ashamed to think that if anybody had suggested to me that it could ever be profitable to me to learn the terms of astrology, I should have replied in my vanity that my time was too valuable to waste on such foolishness. I am deeply indebted to you."

THE DRAGON'S HEAD

Liber V.   1099
DE NOVIS INSVLIS,
quomodo, quando, & per quem
illæ inuentæ sint.

Hristophorus Columbus natione Genuensis, cùm diu in insula regis Hispan-
rum deuersatus fuisset, animum induxit, ut hactenus inaccessas orbis partes p
aorarer Petnt rnionterea à rege irkubzo sug nondceslts fururu sibi & tracilsii.

"Yes," said Gherkins, "but where *is* the treasure, uncle?"

"That's just it," said Lord Peter. "The map is very vague;
there is no latitude or longitude given; and the directions, such
as they are, seem not even to refer to any spot on the islands,
but to some place in the middle of the sea. Besides, it is nearly
two hundred years since the treasure was hidden, and it may
already have been found by somebody or other."

Dr. Conyers stood up.

"I am an old man," he said, "but I still have some strength.
If I can by any means get together the money for an expedition, I will not rest till I have made every possible effort to find
the treasure and to endow my clinic."

"Then, sir, I hope you'll let me give a hand to the good
work," said Lord Peter.

Dr. Conyers had invited his guests to stay the night, and,
after the excited viscount had been packed off to bed, Wimsey

and the old man sat late, consulting maps and diligently reading Munster's chapter "De Novis Insulis," in the hope of discovering some further clue. At length, however, they separated, and Lord Peter went upstairs, the book under his arm. He was restless, however, and, instead of going to bed, sat for a long time at his window, which looked out upon the lake. The moon, a few days past the full, was riding high among small, windy clouds, and picked out the sharp eaves of the Chinese tea-houses and the straggling tops of the unpruned shrubs. "Old Cut-throat" and his landscape gardening! Wimsey could have fancied that the old pirate was sitting now beside his telescope in the preposterous pagoda, chuckling over his riddling testament and counting the craters of the moon. "If *Luna,* there is silver." The water of the lake was silver enough; there was a great smooth path across it, broken by the sinister wedge of the boat-house, the black shadows of the islands, and, almost in the middle of the lake, a decayed fountain, a writhing Celestial dragon-shape, spiny-backed and ridiculous.

Wimsey rubbed his eyes. There was something strangely familiar about the lake; from moment to moment it assumed the queer unreality of a place which one recognizes without having ever known it. It was like one's first sight of the Leaning Tower of Pisa—too like its picture to be quite believable. Surely, thought Wimsey, he knew that elongated island on the right, shaped rather like a winged monster, with its two little clumps of buildings. And the island to the left of it, like the British Isles, but warped out of shape. And the third island, between the others, and nearer. The three formed a triangle, with the Chinese fountain in the centre, the moon shining steadily upon its dragon head. *Hic in capite draconis ardet perpetuo —*

Lord Peter sprang up with a loud exclamation, and flung open the door into the dressing-room. A small figure wrapped in an eiderdown hurriedly uncoiled itself from the window-seat.

"I'm sorry, Uncle Peter," said Gherkins. "I was so *dreadfully* wide awake, it wasn't any good staying in bed."

"Come here," said Lord Peter, "and tell me if I'm mad or dreaming. Look out of the window and compare it with the map—Old Cut-throat's 'New Islands.' He made 'em, Gherkins; he put 'em here. Aren't they laid out just like the Canaries? Those three islands in a triangle, and the fourth down here in the corner? And the boat-house where the big ship is in the picture? And the dragon fountain where the dragon's head is? Well, my son, that's where your hidden treasure's gone to. Get your things on, Gherkins, and damn the time when all good little boys should be in bed! We're going for a row on the lake, if there's a tub in that boat-house that'll float."

"Oh, Uncle Peter! This is a *real* adventure!"

"All right," said Wimsey. "Fifteen men on the dead man's chest, and all that! Yo-ho-ho, and a bottle of Johnnie Walker! Pirate expedition fitted out in dead of night to seek hidden treasure and explore the Fortunate Isles! Come on, crew!"

Lord Peter hitched the leaky dinghy to the dragon's knobbly tail and climbed out carefully, for the base of the fountain was green and weedy.

"I'm afraid it's your job to sit there and bail, Gherkins," he said. "All the best captains bag the really interesting jobs for themselves. We'd better start with the head. If the old blighter said head, he probably meant it." He passed an arm affectionately round the creature's neck for support, while he methodically pressed and pulled the various knobs and bumps of its anatomy. "It seems beastly solid, but I'm sure there's a spring somewhere. You won't forget to bail, will you? I'd simply hate to turn round and find the boat gone. Pirate chief marooned on island and all that. Well, it isn't its back hair, anyhow. We'll try its eyes. I say, Gherkins, I'm sure I felt something move, only it's frightfully stiff. We might have thought to bring some oil. Never mind; it's dogged as does it. It's coming. It's coming. Booh! Pah!"

A fierce effort thrust the rusted knob inwards, releasing a huge spout of water into his face from the dragon's gaping throat. The fountain, dry for many years, soared rejoicingly heavenwards, drenching the treasure-hunters, and making rainbows in the moonlight.

"I suppose this is 'Old Cut-throat's' idea of humour," grumbled Wimsey, retreating cautiously round the dragon's neck. "And now I can't turn it off again. Well, dash it all, let's try the other eye."

He pressed for a few moments in vain. Then, with a grinding clang, the bronze wings of the monster clapped down to its sides, revealing a deep square hole, and the fountain ceased to play.

"Gherkins!" said Lord Peter, "we've done it. (But don't neglect bailing on that account!) There's a box here. And it's beastly heavy. No; all right, I can manage. Gimme the boat-hook. Now I do hope the old sinner really did have a treasure. What a bore if it's only one of his little jokes. Never mind— hold the boat steady. There. Always remember, Gherkins, that you can make quite an effective crane with a boat-hook and a stout pair of braces. Got it? That's right. Now for home and beauty . . . Hullo! what's all that?"

As he paddled the boat round, it was evident that something was happening down by the boat-house. Lights were moving about, and a sound of voices came across the lake.

"They think we're burglars, Gherkins. Always misunderstood. Give way, my hearties—

"*A-roving, a-roving, since roving's been my ru-i-in,*
I'll go no more a-roving with you, fair maid."

"Is that you, my lord?" said a man's voice as they drew in to the boat-house.

"Why, it's our faithful sleuths!" cried his lordship. "What's the excitement?"

"We found this fellow sneaking round the boat-house," said the man from Scotland Yard. "He says he's the old gentleman's nephew. Do you know him, my lord?"

"I rather fancy I do," said Wimsey. "Mr. Pope, I think.

Good evening. Were you looking for anything? Not a treasure, by any chance? Because we've just found one. Oh! don't
say that. *Maxima reverentia,* you know. Lord St. George is of
tender years. And, by the way, thank you so much for sending
your delightful friends to call on me last night. Oh, yes,
Thompson, I'll charge him all right. You there, doctor? Splendid. Now, if anybody's got a spanner or anything handy, we'll
have a look at Great-grandpapa Cuthbert. And if he turns out
to be old iron, Mr. Pope, you'll have had an uncommonly good
joke for your money."

An iron bar was produced from the boat-house and thrust
under the hasp of the chest. It creaked and burst. Dr. Conyers
knelt down tremulously and threw open the lid.

There was a little pause.

"The drinks are on you, Mr. Pope," said Lord Peter. "I
think, doctor, it ought to be a jolly good hospital when it's finished."

THE PISCATORIAL FARCE OF THE
STOLEN STOMACH

"**W**hat in the world," said
Lord Peter Wimsey, "is that?"

Thomas Macpherson disengaged the tall jar from its final
swathings of paper and straw and set it tenderly upright
beside the coffee-pot.

"That," he said, "is Great-Uncle Joseph's legacy."

"And who is Great-Uncle Joseph?"

"He was my mother's uncle. Name of Ferguson. Eccentric
old boy. I was rather a favourite of his."

"It looks like it. Was that all he left you?"

"Imph'm. He said a good digestion was the most precious
thing a man could have."

"Well, he was right there. Is this his? Was it a good one?"

"Good enough. He lived to be ninety-five, and never had a
day's illness."

Wimsey looked at the jar with increased respect.

"What did he die of?"

"Chucked himself out of a sixth-storey window. He had a
stroke, and the doctors told him—or he guessed for himself—
that it was the beginning of the end. He left a letter. Said he
had never been ill in his life and wasn't going to begin now.

They brought in temporary insanity, of course, but I think he was thoroughly sensible."

"I should say so. What was he when he was functioning?"

"He used to be in business—something to do with ship-building, I believe, but he retired long ago. He was what the papers call a recluse. Lived all by himself in a little top flat in Glasgow, and saw nobody. Used to go off by himself for days at a time, nobody knew where or why. I used to look him up about once a year and take him a bottle of whisky."

"Had he any money?"

"Nobody knew. He ought to have had—he was a rich man when he retired. But, when we came to look into it, it turned out he only had a balance of about five hundred pounds in the Glasgow Bank. Apparently he drew out almost everything he had about twenty years ago. There were one or two big bank failures round about that time, and they thought he must have got the wind up. But what he did with it, goodness only knows."

"Kept it in an old stocking, I expect."

"I should think Cousin Robert devoutly hopes so."

"Cousin Robert?"

"He's the residuary legatee. Distant connexion of mine, and the only remaining Ferguson. He was awfully wild when he found he'd only got five hundred. He's rather a bright lad, is Robert, and a few thousands would have come in handy."

"I see. Well, how about a bit of brekker? You might stick Great-Uncle Joseph out of the way somewhere. I don't care about the looks of him."

"I thought you were rather partial to anatomical specimens."

"So I am, but not on the breakfast-table. 'A place for everything and everything in its place,' as my grandmother used to say. Besides, it would give Maggie a shock if she saw it."

Macpherson laughed, and transferred the jar to a cupboard.

"Maggie's shock-proof. I brought a few odd bones and things with me, by way of a holiday task. I'm getting near my final, you know. She'll just think this is another of them. Ring the bell, old man, would you? We'll see what the trout's like."

The door opened to admit the housekeeper, with a dish of grilled trout and a plate of fried scones.

"These look good, Maggie," said Wimsey, drawing his chair up and sniffing appreciatively.

"Aye, sir, they're gude, but they're awfu' wee fish."

"Don't grumble at them," said Macpherson. "They're the sole result of a day's purgatory upon Loch Whyneon. What with the sun fit to roast you and an east wind, I'm pretty well flayed alive. I very nearly didn't shave at all this morning." He passed a reminiscent hand over his red and excoriated face. "Ugh! It's a stiff pull up the hill, and the boat was going wallop, wallop all the time, like being in the Bay of Biscay."

"Damnable, I should think. But there's a change coming. The glass is going back. We'll be having some rain before we're many days older."

"Time, too," said Macpherson. "The burns are nearly dry, and there's not much water in the Fleet." He glanced out of the window to where the little river ran tinkling and skinkling over the stones at the bottom of the garden. "If only we get a few days' rain now, there'll be some grand fishing."

"It *would* come just as I've got to go, naturally," remarked Wimsey.

"Yes; can't you stay a bit longer? I want to have a try for some sea-trout."

"Sorry, old man, can't be done. I must be in town on Wednesday. Never mind. I've had a fine time in the fresh air and got in some good rounds of golf."

"You must come up another time. I'm here for a month — getting my strength up for the exams and all that. If you can't get away before I go, we'll put it off till August and have a shot at the grouse. The cottage is always at your service, you know, Wimsey."

"Many thanks. I may get my business over quicker than I think, and, if I do, I'll turn up here again. When did you say your great-uncle died?"

Macpherson stared at him.

"Some time in April, as far as I can remember. Why?"

"Oh, nothing—I just wondered. You were a favourite of his, didn't you say?"

"In a sense. I think the old boy liked my remembering him from time to time. Old people are pleased by little attentions, you know."

"M'm. Well, it's a queer world. What did you say his name was?"

"Ferguson—Joseph Alexander Ferguson, to be exact. You seem extraordinarily interested in Great-Uncle Joseph."

"I thought, while I was about it, I might look up a man I know in the ship-building line, and see if he knows anything about where the money went to."

"If you can do that, Cousin Robert will give you a medal. But, if you really want to exercise your detective powers on the problem, you'd better have a hunt through the flat in Glasgow."

"Yes—what is the address, by the way?"

Macpherson told him the address.

"I'll make a note of it, and, if anything occurs to me, I'll communicate with Cousin Robert. Where does he hang out?"

"Oh, he's in London, in a solicitor's office. Crosbie & Plump, somewhere in Bloomsbury. Robert was studying for the Scottish Bar, you know, but he made rather a mess of things, so they pushed him off among the Sassenachs. His father died a couple of years ago—he was a Writer to the Signet in Edinburgh—and I fancy Robert has rather gone to the bow-wows since then. Got among a cheerful crowd down there, don't you know, and wasted his substance somewhat."

"Terrible! Scotsmen shouldn't be allowed to leave home. What are you going to do with Great-Uncle?"

"Oh, I don't know. Keep him for a bit, I think. I liked the old fellow, and I don't want to throw him away. He'll look rather well in my consulting-room, don't you think, when I'm qualified and set up my brass plate. I'll say he was presented by a grateful patient on whom I performed a marvellous operation."

"That's a good idea. Stomach-grafting. Miracle of surgery never before attempted. He'll bring sufferers to your door in flocks."

"Good old Great-Uncle—he may be worth a fortune to me after all."

"So he may. I don't suppose you've got such a thing as a photograph of him, have you?"

"A photograph?" Macpherson stared again. "Great-Uncle seems to be becoming a passion with you. I don't suppose the old man had a photograph taken these thirty years. There was one done then—when he retired from business. I expect Robert's got that."

"Och aye," said Wimsey, in the language of the country.

Wimsey left Scotland that evening, and drove down through the night towards London, thinking hard as he went. He handled the wheel mechanically, swerving now and again to avoid the green eyes of rabbits as they bolted from the roadside to squat fascinated in the glare of his head-lamps. He was accustomed to say that his brain worked better when his immediate attention was occupied by the incidents of the road.

Monday morning found him in town with his business finished and his thinking done. A consultation with his shipbuilding friend had put him in possession of some facts about Great-Uncle Joseph's money, together with a copy of Great-Uncle Joseph's photograph, supplied by the London representative of the Glasgow firm to which he had belonged. It appeared that old Ferguson had been a man of mark in his day. The portrait showed a fine, dour old face, long-lipped and high in the cheek-bones—one of those faces which alter little in a lifetime. Wimsey looked at the photograph with satisfaction as he slipped it into his pocket and made a bee-line for Somerset House.

Here he wandered timidly about the wills department, till

a uniformed official took pity on him and inquired what he wanted.

"Oh, thank you," said Wimsey effusively, "thank you so much. Always feel nervous in these places. All these big desks and things, don't you know, so awe-inspiring and business-like. Yes, I just wanted to have a squint at a will. I'm told you can see anybody's will for a shilling. Is that really so?"

"Yes, sir, certainly. Anybody's will in particular, sir?"

"Oh, yes, of course—how silly of me. Yes. Curious, isn't it, that when you're dead any stranger can come and snoop round your private affairs—see how much you cut up for and who your lady friends were, and all that. Yes. Not at all nice. Horrid lack of privacy, what?"

The attendant laughed.

"I expect it's all one when you're dead, sir."

"That's awfully true. Yes, naturally, you're dead by then and it doesn't matter. May be a bit trying for your relations, of course, to learn what a bad boy you've been. Great fun annoyin' one's relations. Always do it myself. Now, what were we sayin'? Ah! yes—the will. (I'm always so absentminded.) Whose will, you said? Well, it's an old Scots gentleman called Joseph Ferguson that died at Glasgow—you know Glasgow, where the accent's so strong that even Scotsmen faint when they hear it—in April, this last April as ever was. If it's not troubling you too much, may I have a bob's-worth of Joseph Alexander Ferguson?"

The attendant assured him that he might, adding the caution that he must memorize the contents of the will and not on any account take notes. Thus warned, Wimsey was conducted into a retired corner, where in a short time the will was placed before him.

It was a commendably brief document, written in holograph, and was dated the previous January. After the usual preamble and the bequest of a few small sums and articles of personal ornament to friends, it proceeded somewhat as follows:

And I direct that, after my death, the alimentary organs be removed entire with their contents from my body, commencing with the oesophagus and ending with the anal canal, and that they be properly secured at both ends with a suitable ligature, and be enclosed in a proper preservative medium in a glass vessel and given to my great-nephew Thomas Macpherson of the Stone Cottage, Gatehouse-of-the-Fleet, in Kirkcudbrightshire, now studying medicine in Aberdeen. And I bequeath him these my alimentary organs with their contents for his study and edification, they having served me for ninety-five years without failure or defect, because I wish him to understand that no riches in the world are comparable to the riches of a good digestion. And I desire of him that he will, in the exercise of his medical profession, use his best endeavours to preserve to his patients the blessing of good digestion unimpaired, not needlessly filling their stomachs with drugs out of concern for his own pocket, but exhorting them to a sober and temperate life agreeably to the design of Almighty Providence.

After this remarkable passage, the document went on to make Robert Ferguson residuary legatee without particular specification of any property, and to appoint a firm of lawyers in Glasgow executors of the will.

Wimsey considered the bequest for some time. From the phraseology he concluded that old Mr. Ferguson had drawn up his own will without legal aid, and he was glad of it, for its wording thus afforded a valuable clue to the testator's mood and intention. He mentally noted three points: the "alimentary organs with their contents" were mentioned twice over, with a certain emphasis; they were to be ligatured top and bottom; and the legacy was accompanied by the expression of a wish that the legatee should not allow his financial necessities to interfere with the conscientious exercise of his professional duties. Wimsey chuckled. He felt he rather liked Great-Uncle Joseph.

He got up, collected his hat, gloves and stick, and advanced with the will in his hand to return it to the attendant. The latter was engaged in conversation with a young man, who seemed to be expostulating about something.

"I'm sorry, sir," said the attendant, "but I don't suppose the other gentleman will be very long. Ah!" He turned and saw Wimsey. "Here is the gentleman."

The young man, whose reddish hair, long nose, and slightly sodden eyes gave him the appearance of a dissipated fox, greeted Wimsey with a disagreeable stare.

"What's up? Want me?" asked his lordship airily.

"Yes, sir. Very curious thing, sir; here's a gentleman inquiring for that very same document as you've been studying, sir. I've been in this department fifteen years, and I don't know as I ever remember such a thing happening before."

"No," said Wimsey, "I don't suppose there's much of a run on any of your lines as a rule."

"It's a very curious thing indeed," said the stranger, with marked displeasure in his voice.

"Member of the family?" suggested Wimsey.

"I *am* a member of the family," said the foxy-faced man. "May I ask whether *you* have any connexion with us?"

"By all means," replied Wimsey graciously.

"I don't believe it. I don't know you."

"No, no—I meant you might ask, by all means."

The young man positively showed his teeth.

"Do you mind telling me who you are, anyhow, and why you're so damned inquisitive about my great-uncle's will?"

Wimsey extracted a card from his case and presented it with a smile. Mr. Robert Ferguson changed colour.

"If you would like a reference as to my respectability," went on Wimsey affably, "Mr. Thomas Macpherson will, I am sure, be happy to tell you about me. I am inquisitive," said his lordship—"a student of humanity. Your cousin mentioned to me the curious clause relating to your esteemed great-uncle's—er—stomach and appurtenances. Curious clauses are a passion with me. I came to look it up and add it to my collection of curious wills. I am engaged in writing a book on the subject — *Clauses and Consequences.* My publishers tell me it should enjoy a ready sale. I regret that my random jottings should have encroached upon your doubtless far more serious studies. I wish you a very good morning."

As he beamed his way out, Wimsey, who had quick ears, heard the attendant informing the indignant Mr. Ferguson that he was "a very funny gentleman — not quite all there, sir." It seemed that his criminological fame had not penetrated to the quiet recesses of Somerset House. "But," said Wimsey to himself, "I am sadly afraid that Cousin Robert has been given food for thought."

Under the spur of this alarming idea, Wimsey wasted no time, but took a taxi down to Hatton Garden, to call upon a friend of his. This gentleman, rather curly in the nose and fleshy about the eyelids, nevertheless came under Mr. Chesterton's definition of a nice Jew, for his name was neither Montagu nor McDonald, but Nathan Abrahams, and he greeted Lord Peter with a hospitality amounting to enthusiasm.

"So pleased to see you. Sit down and have a drink. You have come at last to select the diamonds for the future Lady Peter, eh?"

"Not yet," said Wimsey.

"No? That's too bad. You should make haste and settle down. It is time you became a family man. Years ago we arranged I should have the privilege of decking the bride for the happy day. That is a promise, you know. I think of it when the fine stones pass through my hands. I say, 'That would be the very thing for my friend Lord Peter.' But I hear nothing, and I sell them to stupid Americans who think only of the price and not of the beauty."

"Time enough to think of the diamonds when I've found the lady."

Mr. Abrahams threw up his hands.

"Oh, yes! And then everything will be done in a hurry! 'Quick, Mr. Abrahams! I have fallen in love yesterday and I

am being married tomorrow.' But it may take months—
years—to find and match perfect stones. It can't be done
between today and tomorrow. Your bride will be married in
something ready-made from the jeweller's."

"If three days are enough to choose a wife," said Wimsey,
laughing, "one day should surely be enough for a necklace."

"That is the way with Christians," replied the diamond-
merchant resignedly. "You are so casual. You do not think of
the future. Three days to choose a wife! No wonder the
divorce-courts are busy. My son Moses is being married next
week. It has been arranged in the family these ten years.
Rachel Goldstein, it is. A good girl, and her father is in a very
good position. We are all very pleased, I can tell you. Moses is
a good son, a very good son, and I am taking him into partner-
ship."

"I congratulate you," said Wimsey heartily. "I hope they
will be very happy."

"Thank you, Lord Peter. They will be happy, I am sure.
Rachel is a sweet girl and very fond of children. And she is
pretty, too. Prettiness is not everything, but it is an advantage
for a young man in these days. It is easier for him to behave
well to a pretty wife."

"True," said Wimsey. "I will bear it in mind when my time
comes. To the health of the happy pair, and may you soon be
an ancestor. Talking of ancestors, I've got an old bird here that
you may be able to tell me something about."

"Ah, yes! Always delighted to help you in any way, Lord
Peter."

"This photograph was taken some thirty years ago, but
you may possibly recognize it."

Mr. Abrahams put on a pair of horn-rimmed spectacles,
and examined the portrait of Great-Uncle Joseph with serious
attention.

"Oh, yes, I know him quite well. What do you want to know
about him, eh?" He shot a swift and cautious glance at Wimsey.

"Nothing to his disadvantage. He's dead, anyhow. I thought
it just possible he had been buying precious stones lately."

"It is not exactly business to give information about a customer," said Mr. Abrahams.

"I'll tell you what I want it for," said Wimsey. He lightly sketched the career of Great-Uncle Joseph, and went on: "You see, I looked at it this way. When a man gets a distrust of banks, what does he do with his money? He puts it into property of some kind. It may be land, it may be houses—but that means rent, and more money to put into banks. He is more likely to keep it in gold or notes, or to be put into precious stones. Gold and notes are comparatively bulky; stones are small. Circumstances in this case led me to think he might have chosen stones. Unless we can discover what he did with the money, there will be a great loss to his heirs."

"I see. Well, if it is as you say, there is no harm in telling you. I know you to be an honourable man, and I will break my rule for you. This gentleman, Mr. Wallace—"

"Wallace, did he call himself?"

"That was not his name? They are funny, these secretive old gentlemen. But that is nothing unusual. Often, when they buy stones, they are afraid of being robbed, so they give another name. Yes, yes. Well, this Mr. Wallace used to come to see me from time to time, and I had instructions to find diamonds for him. He was looking for twelve big stones, all matching perfectly and of superb quality. It took a long time to find them, you know."

"Of course."

"Yes. I supplied him with seven altogether, over a period of twenty years or so. And other dealers supplied him also. He is well known in this street. I found the last one for him—let me see—in last December, I think. A beautiful stone—beautiful! He paid seven thousand pounds for it."

"Some stone. If they were all as good as that, the collection must be worth something."

"Worth anything. It is difficult to tell how much. As you know, the twelve stones, all matched together, would be worth far more than the sum of the twelve separate prices paid for the individual diamonds."

"Naturally they would. Do you mind telling me how he was accustomed to pay for them?"

"In Bank of England notes—always—cash on the nail. He insisted on discount for cash," added Mr. Abrahams, with a chuckle.

"He was a Scotsman," replied Wimsey. "Well, that's clear enough. He had a safe-deposit somewhere, no doubt. And, having collected the stones, he made his will. That's clear as daylight, too."

"But what has become of the stones?" inquired Mr. Abrahams, with professional anxiety.

"I think I know that too," said Wimsey. "I'm enormously obliged to you, and so, I fancy, will his heir be."

"If they should come into the market again—" suggested Mr. Abrahams.

"I'll see you have the handling of them," said Wimsey promptly.

"That is kind of you," said Mr. Abrahams. "Business is business. Always delighted to oblige you. Beautiful stones—beautiful. If you thought of being the purchaser, I would charge you a special commission, as my friend."

"Thank you," said Wimsey, "but as yet I have no occasion for diamonds, you know."

"Pity, pity," said Mr. Abrahams. "Well, very glad to have been of service to you. You are not interested in rubies? No? Because I have something very pretty here."

He thrust his hand casually into a pocket, and brought out a little pool of crimson fire like a miniature sunset.

"Look nice in a ring, now, wouldn't it?" said Mr. Abrahams. "An engagement ring, eh?"

Wimsey laughed, and made his escape.

He was strongly tempted to return to Scotland and attend personally to the matter of Great-Uncle Joseph, but the thought of an important book sale next day deterred him. There was a manuscript of Catullus which he was passionately anxious to secure, and he never entrusted his interests to dealers. He contented himself with sending a wire to Thomas Macpherson:

Advise opening up Greatuncle Joseph immediately.

The girl at the post-office repeated the message aloud and rather doubtfully. "Quite right," said Wimsey, and dismissed the affair from his mind.

He had great fun at the sale next day. He found a ring of dealers in possession, happily engaged in conducting a knock-out. Having lain low for an hour in a retired position behind a large piece of statuary, he emerged, just as the hammer was falling upon the Catullus for a price representing the tenth part of its value, with an overbid so large, prompt, and sonorous that the ring gasped with a sense of outrage. Skrymes—a dealer who had sworn an eternal enmity to Wimsey on account of a previous little encounter over a Justinian—pulled himself together and offered a fifty-pound advance. Wimsey promptly doubled his bid. Skrymes overbid him fifty again. Wimsey instantly jumped another hundred, in the tone of a man prepared to go on till Doomsday. Skrymes scowled and was silent. Somebody raised it fifty more; Wimsey made it guineas and the hammer fell. Encouraged by this success, Wimsey, feeling that his hand was in, romped happily into the bidding for the next lot, a *Hypnerotomachia* which he already possessed, and for which he felt no desire whatever. Skrymes, annoyed by his defeat, set his teeth, determining that, if Wimsey was in the bidding mood, he should pay through the nose for his rashness. Wimsey, entering into the spirit of the thing, skied the bidding with enthusiasm. The dealers, knowing his reputation as a collector, and fancying that there must be some special excellence about the book that they had failed to observe, joined in whole-heartedly, and the fun became fast and furious. Eventually they all dropped out again, leaving Skrymes and Wimsey in together. At which point Wimsey, observing a note of hesitation in the dealer's voice, neatly extricated himself and left Mr. Skrymes with the baby. After this disaster, the ring became sulky and demoralized and refused to bid at all, and a timid little outsider, suddenly flinging himself into the

arena, became the owner of a fine fourteenth-century missal at
bargain price. Crimson with excitement and surprise, he paid
for his purchase and ran out of the room like a rabbit, hugging
the missal as though he expected to have it snatched from him.
Wimsey thereupon set himself seriously to acquire a few fine
early printed books, and, having accomplished this, retired,
covered with laurels and hatred.

After this delightful and satisfying day, he felt vaguely
hurt at receiving no ecstatic telegram from Macpherson. He
refused to imagine that his deductions had been wrong, and
supposed rather that the rapture of Macpherson would come
the next day by post. However, at eleven next morning the
telegram arrived. It said:

> Just got your wire what does it mean greatuncle
> stolen last night burglar escaped please write fully.

Wimsey committed himself to a brief comment in language usually confined to soldiery. Robert had undoubtedly
got Great-Uncle Joseph, and, even if they could trace the burglary to him, the legacy was by this time gone for ever. He had
never felt so furiously helpless. He even cursed the Catullus,
which had kept him from going north and dealing with the
matter personally.

While he was meditating what to do, a second telegram
was brought in. It ran:

> Greatuncle's bottle found broken in fleet dropped by
> burglar in flight contents gone what next.

Wimsey pondered this.

"Of course," he said, "if the thief simply emptied the bottle
and put Great-Uncle in his pocket, we're done. Or if he's simply emptied Great-Uncle and put the contents in his pocket,
we're done. But 'dropped in flight' sounds rather as though
Great-Uncle had gone overboard lock, stock, and barrel. Why

can't the fool of a Scotsman put a few more details into his wires? It'd only cost him a penny or two. I suppose I'd better go up myself. Meanwhile a little healthy occupation won't hurt him."

He took a telegraph form from the desk and despatched a further message:

Was greatuncle in bottle when dropped if so drag river if not pursue burglar probably Robert Ferguson spare no pains starting for Scotland tonight hope arrive early tomorrow urgent important put your back into it will explain.

The night express decanted Lord Peter Wimsey at Dumfries early the following morning, and a hired car deposited him at the Stone Cottage in time for breakfast. The door was opened to him by Maggie, who greeted him with hearty cordiality:

"Come awa' in, sir. All's ready for ye, and Mr. Macpherson will be back in a few minutes, I'm thinkin'. Ye'll be tired with your long journey, and hungry, maybe? Aye. Will ye tak' a bit parritch to your eggs and bacon? There's nae troot the day, though yesterday was a gran' day for the fush. Mr. Macpherson has been up and doun, up and doun the river wi' my Jock, lookin' for ane of his specimens, as he ca's them, that was dropped by the thief that cam' in. I dinna ken what the thing may be—my Jock says it's like a calf's pluck to look at, by what Mr. Macpherson tells him."

"Dear me!" said Wimsey. "And how did the burglary happen, Maggie?"

"Indeed, sir, it was a vera' remarkable circumstance. Mr. Macpherson was awa' all day Monday and Tuesday, up at the big loch by the viaduct, fishin'. There was a big rain Saturday and Sunday, ye may remember, and Mr. Macpherson says, 'There'll be grand fishin' the morn, Jock,' says he. 'We'll go up to the viaduct if it stops rainin' and we'll spend the nicht at the keeper's lodge.' So on Monday it stoppit rainin' and was a grand warm, soft day, so aff they went together. There was a telegram come for him Tuesday mornin', and I set it up on the mantelpiece, where he'd see it when he cam' in, but it's been in my mind since that maybe that telegram had something to do wi' the burglary."

"I wouldn't say but you might be right, Maggie," replied Wimsey gravely.

"Aye, sir, that wadna surprise me." Maggie set down a generous dish of eggs and bacon before the guest and took up her tale again.

"Well, I was sittin' in my kitchen the Tuesday nicht, waitin' for Mr. Macpherson and Jock to come hame, and sair I pitied them, the puir souls, for the rain was peltin' down again, and the nicht was sae dark I was afraid they micht ha' tummelt into a bog-pool. Weel, I was listenin' for the sound o' the door-sneck when I heard something movin' in the front room. The door wasna lockit, ye ken, because Mr. Macpherson was expectit back. So I up from my chair and I thocht they had mebbe came in and I not heard them. I waited a meenute to set the kettle on the fire, and then I heard a crackin' sound. So I cam' out and I called, 'Is't you, Mr. Macpherson?' And there was nae answer, only anither big crackin' noise, so I ran forrit, and a man cam' quickly oot o' the front room, brushin' past me an puttin' me aside wi' his hand, so, and oot o' the front door like a flash o' lightnin'. So, wi' that, I let oot a skelloch, an' Jock's voice answered me fra' the gairden gate. 'Och!' I says, 'Jock! here's a burglar been i' the hoose!' An' I heerd him runnin' across the gairden, doun tae the river, tramplin' doun a' the young kail and the stra'berry beds, the blackguard!"

Wimsey expressed his sympathy.

"Aye, that was a bad business. An' the next thing, there was Mr. Macpherson and Jock helter-skelter after him. If Davie Murray's cattle had broken in, they couldna ha' done mair deevastation. An' then there was a big splashin' an' crashin', an', after a bit, back comes Mr. Macpherson an' he says, 'He's jumpit intil the Fleet,' he says, 'an' he's awa'. What has he taken?' he says. 'I dinna ken,' says I, 'for it all happened sae quickly I couldna see onything.' 'Come awa' ben,' says he, 'an' we'll see what's missin'.' So we lookit high and low, an' all we could find was the cupboard door in the front room broken open, and naething taken but this bottle wi' the specimen."

"Aha!" said Wimsey.

"Ah! an' they baith went oot tegither wi' lichts, but naething could they see of the thief. Sae Mr. Macpherson comes back, and 'I'm gaun to ma bed,' says he, 'for I'm that tired I can dae nae mair the nicht,' says he. 'Oh!' I said, 'I daurna gae tae bed; I'm frichtened.' An' Jock said, 'Hoots, wumman, dinna fash yersel'. There'll be nae mair burglars the nicht, wi' the fricht we've gied 'em.' So we lockit up a' the doors an' windies an' gaed to oor beds, but I couldna sleep a wink."

"Very natural," said Wimsey.

"It wasna till the next mornin'," said Maggie, "that Mr. Macpherson opened yon telegram. Eh! but he was in a taking. An' then the telegrams startit. Back an' forrit, back an' forrit atween the hoose an' the post-office. An' then they found the bits o' the bottle that the specimen was in, stuck between twa stanes i' the river. And aff goes Mr. Macpherson an' Jock wi' their waders on an' a couple o' gaffs, huntin' in a' the pools an' under the stanes to find the specimen. An' they're still at it."

At this point three heavy thumps sounded on the ceiling.

"Gude save us!" ejaculated Maggie, "I was forgettin' the puir gentleman."

"What gentleman?" enquired Wimsey.

"Him that was feshed oot o' the Fleet," replied Maggie. "Excuse me just a moment, sir."

She fled swiftly upstairs. Wimsey poured himself out a third cup of coffee and lit a pipe.

Presently a thought occurred to him. He finished the coffee—not being a man to deprive himself of his pleasures—and walked quietly upstairs in Maggie's wake. Facing him stood a bedroom door, half open—the room which he had occupied during his stay at the cottage. He pushed it open. In the bed lay a red-headed gentleman, whose long, foxy countenance was in no way beautified by a white bandage, tilted rakishly across the left temple. A breakfast-tray stood on a table by the bed. Wimsey stepped forward with extended hand.

"Good morning, Mr. Ferguson," said he. "This is an unexpected pleasure."

"Good morning," said Mr. Ferguson snappishly.

"I had no idea, when we last met," pursued Wimsey, advancing to the bed and sitting down upon it, "that you were thinking of visiting my friend Macpherson."

"Get off my leg," growled the invalid. "I've broken my kneecap."

"What a nuisance! Frightfully painful, isn't it? And they say it takes years to get right—if it ever does get right. Is it what they call a Potts fracture? I don't know who Potts was, but it sounds impressive. How did you get it? Fishing?"

"Yes. A slip in that damned river."

"Beastly. Sort of thing that might happen to anybody. A keen fisher, Mr. Ferguson?"

"So-so."

"So am I, when I get the opportunity. What kind of fly do you fancy for this part of the country? I rather like a Greenaway's Gadget myself. Ever tried it?"

"No," said Mr. Ferguson briefly.

"Some people find a Pink Sisket better, so they tell me. Do you use one? Have you got your fly-book here?"

"Yes—no," said Mr. Ferguson. "I dropped it."

"Pity. But do give me your opinion of the Pink Sisket."

"Not so bad," said Mr. Ferguson. "I've sometimes caught trout with it."

"You surprise me," said Wimsey, not unnaturally, since he had invented the Pink Sisket on the spur of the moment, and had hardly expected his improvisation to pass muster. "Well, I suppose this unlucky accident has put a stop to your sport for the season. Damned bad luck. Otherwise, you might have helped us to have a go at the Patriarch."

"What's that? A trout?"

"Yes—a frightfully wily old fish. Lurks about in the Fleet. You never know where to find him. Any moment he may turn up in some pool or other. I'm going out with Mac to try for him today. He's a jewel of a fellow. We've nicknamed him Great-Uncle Joseph. Hi! don't joggle about like that—you'll hurt that knee of yours. Is there anything I can get for you?"

He grinned amiably, and turned to answer a shout from the stairs.

"Hullo! Wimsey! is that you?"

"It is. How's sport?"

Macpherson came up the stairs four steps at a time, and met Wimsey on the landing as he emerged from the bedroom.

"I say, d'you know who that is? It's Robert."

"I know. I saw him in town. Never mind him. Have you found Great-Uncle?"

"No, we haven't. What's all this mystery about? And what's Robert doing here? What did you mean by saying he was the burglar? And why is Great-Uncle Joseph so important?"

"One thing at a time. Let's find the old boy first. What have you been doing?"

"Well, when I got your extraordinary messages I thought, of course, you were off your rocker." (Wimsey groaned with impatience.) "But then I considered what a funny thing it was that somebody should have thought Great-Uncle worth stealing, and thought there might be some sense in what you said, after all." ("Dashed good of you," said Wimsey.) "So I went out and poked about a bit, you know. Not that I think there's the faintest chance of finding anything, with the river coming down like this. Well, I hadn't got very far—by the way, I took Jock with me. I'm sure he thinks I'm mad, too. Not that he says anything; these people here never commit themselves—"

"Confound Jock! Get on with it."

"Oh—well, before we'd got very far, we saw a fellow wading about in the river with a rod and a creel. I didn't pay much attention, because, you see, I was wondering what you—Yes.

Well! Jock noticed him and said to me, 'Yon's a queer kind of fisherman, I'm thinkin'.' So I had a look, and there he was, staggering about among the stones with his fly floating away down the stream in front of him; and he was peering into all the pools he came to, and poking about with a gaff. So I hailed him, and he turned round, and then he put the gaff away in a bit of a hurry and started to reel in his line. He made an awful mess of it," added Macpherson appreciatively.

"I can believe it," said Wimsey. "A man who admits to catching trout with a Pink Sisket would make a mess of anything."

"A pink what?"

"Never mind. I only meant that Robert was no fisher. Get on."

"Well, he got the line hooked round something, and he was pulling and hauling, you know, and splashing about, and then it came out all of a sudden, and he waved it all over the place and got my hat. That made me pretty wild, and I made after him, and he looked round again, and I yelled out, 'Good God, it's Robert!' And he dropped his rod and took to his heels. And of course he slipped on the stones and came down an awful crack. We rushed forward and scooped him up and brought him home. He's got a nasty bang on the head and a fractured patella. Very interesting. I should have liked to have a shot at setting it myself, but it wouldn't do, you know, so I sent for Strachan. He's a good man."

"You've had extraordinary luck about this business so far," said Wimsey. "Now the only thing left is to find Great-Uncle. How far down have you got?"

"Not very far. You see, what with getting Robert home and setting his knee and so on, we couldn't do much yesterday."

"Damn Robert! Great-Uncle may be away out to sea by this time. Let's get down to it."

He took up a gaff from the umbrella-stand ("Robert's," interjected Macpherson), and led the way out. The little river was foaming down in a brown spate, rattling stones and small boulders along in its passage. Every hole, every eddy might be a lurking-place for Great-Uncle Joseph. Wimsey peered irresolutely here and there — then turned suddenly to Jock.

"Where's the nearest spit of land where things usually get washed up?" he demanded.

"Eh, well! there's the Battery Pool, about a mile doon the river. Ye'll whiles find things washed up there. Aye. Imph'm. There's a pool and a bit sand, where the river mak's a bend. Ye'll mebbe find it there, I'm thinkin'. Mebbe no. I couldna say."

"Let's have a look, anyway."

Macpherson, to whom the prospect of searching the stream in detail appeared rather a dreary one, brightened a little at this.

"That's a good idea. If we take the car down to just above Gatehouse, we've only got two fields to cross."

The car was still at the door; the hired driver was enjoying the hospitality of the cottage. They pried him loose from Maggie's scones and slipped down the road to Gatehouse.

"Those gulls seem rather active about something," said Wimsey, as they crossed the second field. The white wings swooped backwards and forwards in narrowing circles over the yellow shoal. Raucous cries rose on the wind. Wimsey pointed silently with his hand. A long, unseemly object, like a drab purse, lay on the shore. The gulls, indignant, rose higher, squawking at the intruders. Wimsey ran forward, stooped, rose again with the long bag dangling from his fingers.

"Great-Uncle Joseph, I presume," he said, and raised his hat with old-fashioned courtesy.

"The gulls have had a wee peck at it here and there," said Jock. "It'll be tough for them. Aye. They havena done so vera much with it."

"Aren't you going to open it?" said Macpherson impatiently.

"Not here," said Wimsey. "We might lose something." He dropped it into Jock's creel. "We'll take it home first and show it to Robert."

Robert greeted them with ill-disguised irritation.

"We've been fishing," said Wimsey cheerfully. "Look at our bonny wee fush." He weighed the catch in his hand. "What's inside this wee fush, Mr. Ferguson?"

"I haven't the faintest idea," said Robert.

"Then why did you go fishing for it?" asked Wimsey pleasantly. "Have you got a surgical knife there, Mac?"

"Yes—here. Hurry up."

"I'll leave it to you. Be careful. I should begin with the stomach."

Macpherson laid Great-Uncle Joseph on the table, and slit him open with a practised hand.

"Gude be gracious to us!" cried Maggie, peering over his shoulder. "What'll that be?"

Wimsey inserted a delicate finger and thumb into the cavities of Uncle Joseph. "One—two—three—" The stones glittered like fire as he laid them on the table. "Seven—eight—nine. That seems to be all. Try a little farther down, Mac."

Speechless with astonishment, Mr. Macpherson dissected his legacy.

"Ten—eleven," said Wimsey. "I'm afraid the sea-gulls have got number twelve. I'm sorry, Mac."

"But how did they get there?" demanded Robert foolishly.

"Simple as shelling peas. Great-Uncle Joseph makes his will, swallows his diamonds—"

"He must ha' been a grand man for a pill," said Maggie, with respect.

" —and jumps out of the window. It was as clear as crystal to anybody who read the will. He told you, Mac, that the stomach was given you to study."

Robert Ferguson gave a deep groan.

"I knew there was something in it," he said. "That's why I went to look up the will. And when I saw *you* there, I knew I was right. (Curse this leg of mine!) But I never imagined for a moment—"

His eyes appraised the diamonds greedily.

"And what will the value of these same stones be?" inquired Jock.

"About seven thousand pounds apiece, taken separately. More than that, taken together."

"The old man was mad," said Robert angrily. "I shall dispute the will."

"I think not," said Wimsey. "There's such an offence as entering and stealing, you know."

"My God!" said Macpherson, handling the diamonds like a man in a dream. "My God!"

"Seven thousan' pund," said Jock. "Did I unnerstan' ye richtly to say that one o' they gulls is gaun aboot noo wi' seven thousan' punds' worth o' diamonds in his wame? Ech! it's just awfu' to think of. Guid day to you, sirs. I'll be gaun round to Jimmy McTaggart to ask will he send me the loan o' a gun."

THE UNSOLVED PUZZLE OF THE
MAN WITH NO FACE

And what would *you* say, sir," said the stout man, "to this here business of the bloke what's been found down on the beach at East Felpham?"

The rush of travellers after the Bank Holiday had caused an overflow of third-class passengers into the firsts, and the stout man was anxious to seem at ease in his surroundings. The youngish gentleman whom he addressed had obviously paid full fare for a seclusion which he was fated to forgo. He took the matter amiably enough, however, and replied in a courteous tone:

"I'm afraid I haven't read more than the headlines. Murdered, I suppose, wasn't he?"

"It's murder, right enough," said the stout man, with relish. "Cut about he was, something shocking."

"More like as if a wild beast had done it," chimed in the thin, elderly man opposite. "No face at all he hadn't got, by what my paper says. It'll be one of these maniacs, I shouldn't be surprised, what goes about killing children."

"I wish you wouldn't talk about such things," said his wife, with a shudder. "I lays awake at nights thinking what might 'appen to Lizzie's girls, till my head feels regular in a fever, and I has such a sinking in my inside I has to get up and eat biscuits. They didn't ought to put such dreadful things in the papers."

"It's better they should, ma'am," said the stout man, "then we're warned, so to speak, and can take our measures accordingly. Now, from what I can make out, this unfortunate gentleman had gone bathing all by himself in a lonely spot. Now, quite apart from cramps, as is a thing that might 'appen to the best of us, that's a very foolish thing to do."

"Just what I'm always telling my husband," said the young wife. The young husband frowned and fidgeted. "Well, dear, it really isn't safe, and you with your heart not strong —" Her hand sought his under the newspaper. He drew away, self-consciously, saying, "That'll do, Kitty."

"The way I look at it is this," pursued the stout man. "Here we've been and had a war, what has left 'undreds o' men in what you might call a state of unstable ekilibrium. They've seen all their friends blown up or shot to pieces. They've been through five years of 'orrors and bloodshed, and it's given 'em what you might call a twist in the mind towards 'orrors. They may seem to forget it and go along as peaceable as anybody to all outward appearance, but it's all artificial, if you get my meaning. Then, one day something 'appens to upset them — they 'as words with the wife, or the weather's extra hot, as it is today — and something goes pop inside their brains and makes raving monsters of them. It's all in the books. I do a good bit of reading myself of an evening, being a bachelor without encumbrances."

"That's all very true," said a prim little man, looking up from his magazine, "very true indeed — too true. But do you think it applies in the present case? I've studied the literature of crime a good deal — I may say I make it my hobby — and it's my opinion there's more in this than meets the eye. If you will compare this murder with some of the most mysterious crimes of late years — crimes which, mind you, have never been solved, and, in my opinion, never will be — what do you find?" He paused and looked round. "You will find many features in common with this case. But especially you will find that the face—and the face only, mark you—has been disfigured, as though to prevent recognition. As though to blot out the victim's personality from the world. And you will find that, in spite of the most thorough investigation, the criminal is never discovered. Now what does all that point to? To organization. Organization. To an immensely powerful influence at work behind the scenes. In this very magazine that I'm reading now"—he tapped the page impressively—"there's an account—not a faked-up story, but an account extracted from the annals of the police—of the organization of one of these secret societies, which mark down men against whom they bear a grudge, and destroy them. And, when they do this, they disfigure their faces with the mark of the Secret Society, and they cover up the track of the assassin so completely—having money and resources at their disposal—that nobody is ever able to get at them."

"I've read of such things, of course," admitted the stout man, "but I thought as they mostly belonged to the medeevial days. They had a thing like that in Italy once. What did they call it now? A Gomorrah, was it? Are there any Gomorrahs nowadays?"

"You spoke a true word, sir, when you said Italy," replied the prim man. "The Italian mind is made for intrigue. There's the Fascisti. That's come to the surface now, of course, but it started by being a secret society. And, if you were to look below the surface, you would be amazed at the way in which that country is honeycombed with hidden organizations of all sorts. Don't you agree with me, sir?" he added, addressing the first-class passenger.

"Ah!" said the stout man, "no doubt this gentleman has been in Italy and knows all about it. Should you say this murder was the work of a Gomorrah, sir?"

"I hope not, I'm sure," said the first-class passenger. "I mean, it rather destroys the interest, don't you think? I like a nice, quiet, domestic murder myself, with the millionaire found dead in the library. The minute I open a detective story and find a Camorra in it, my interest seems to dry up and turn to dust and ashes—a sort of Sodom and Camorra, as you might say."

"I agree with you there," said the young husband, "from what you might call the artistic standpoint. But in this particular case I think there may be something to be said for this gentleman's point of view."

"Well," admitted the first-class passenger, "not having read the details—"

"The details are clear enough," said the prim man. "This poor creature was found lying dead on the beach at East Felpham early this morning, with his face cut about in the most dreadful manner. He had nothing on him but his bathing-dress—"

"Stop a minute. Who was he, to begin with?"

"They haven't identified him yet. His clothes had been taken—"

"That looks more like robbery, doesn't it?" suggested Kitty.

"If it was just robbery," retorted the prim man, "why should his face have been cut up in that way? No—the clothes were taken away, as I said, to prevent identification. That's what these societies always try to do."

"Was he stabbed?" demanded the first-class passenger.

"No," said the stout man. "He wasn't. He was strangled."

"Not a characteristically Italian method of killing," observed the first-class passenger.

"No more it is," said the stout man. The prim man seemed a little disconcerted.

"And if he went down there to bathe," said the thin, elderly man, "how did he get there? Surely somebody must have missed him before now, if he was staying at Felpham. It's a busy spot for visitors in the holiday season."

"No," said the stout man, "not East Felpham. You're thinking of West Felpham, where the yacht-club is. East Felpham is one of the loneliest spots on the coast. There's no house near except a little pub all by itself at the end of a long road, and after that you have to go through three fields to get to the sea. There's no real road, only a cart-track, but you can take a car through. I've been there."

"He came in a car," said the prim man. "They found the track of the wheels. But it had been driven away again."

"It looks as though the two men had come there together," suggested Kitty.

"I think they did," said the prim man. "The victim was probably gagged and bound and taken along in the car to the place, and then he was taken out and strangled and—"

"But why should they have troubled to put on his bathing-dress?" said the first-class passenger.

"Because," said the prim man, "as I said, they didn't want to leave any clothes to reveal his identity."

"Quite; but why not leave him naked? A bathing-dress seems to indicate an almost excessive regard for decorum, under the circumstances."

"Yes, yes," said the stout man impatiently, "but you 'aven't read the paper carefully. The two men couldn't have come there in company, and for why? There was only one set of footprints found, and they belonged to the murdered man."

He looked round triumphantly.

"Only one set of footprints, eh?" said the first-class passenger quickly. "This looks interesting. Are you sure?"

"It says so in the paper. A single set of footprints, it says, made by bare feet, which by a careful comparison 'ave been shown to be those of the murdered man, lead from the position occupied by the car to the place where the body was found. What do you make of that?"

"Why," said the first-class passenger, "that tells one quite a lot, don't you know. It gives one a sort of bird's eye view of the place, and it tells one the time of the murder, besides castin' quite a good bit of light on the character and circumstances of the murderer—or murderers."

"How do you make that out, sir?" demanded the elderly man.

"Well, to begin with—though I've never been near the

place, there is obviously a sandy beach from which one can bathe."

"That's right," said the stout man.

"There is also, I fancy, in the neighbourhood, a spur of rock running out into the sea, quite possibly with a handy diving-pool. It must run out pretty far; at any rate, one can bathe there before it is high water on the beach."

"I don't know how you know that, sir, but it's a fact. There's rocks and a bathing-pool, exactly as you describe, about a hundred yards farther along. Many's the time I've had a dip off the end of them."

"And the rocks run right back inland, where they are covered with short grass."

"That's right."

"The murder took place shortly before high tide, I fancy, and the body lay just about at high-tide mark."

"Why so?"

"Well, you say there were footsteps leading right up to the body. That means that the water hadn't been up beyond the body. But there were no other marks. Therefore the murderer's footprints must have been washed away by the tide. The only explanation is that the two men were standing together just below the tide-mark. The murderer came up out of the sea. He attacked the other man — maybe he forced him back a little on his own tracks — and there he killed him. Then the water came up and washed out any marks the murderer may have left. One can imagine him squatting there, wondering if the sea was going to come up high enough."

"Ow!" said Kitty, "you make me creep all over."

"Now, as to these marks on the face," pursued the first-class passenger. "The murderer, according to the idea I get of the thing, was already in the sea when the victim came along. You see the idea?"

"I get you," said the stout man. "You think as he went in off them rocks that we was speaking of, and came up through the water, and that's why there weren't no footprints."

"Exactly. And since the water is deep round those rocks, as you say, he was presumably in a bathing-dress too."

"Looks like it."

"Quite so. Well, now—what was the face-slashing done with? People don't usually take knives out with them when they go for a morning dip."

"That's a puzzle," said the stout man.

"Not altogether. Let's say, either the murderer had a knife with him or he had not. If he had—"

"If he had," put in the prim man eagerly, "he must have laid wait for the deceased on purpose. And, to my mind, that bears out my idea of a deep and cunning plot."

"Yes. But, if he was waiting there with the knife, why didn't he stab the man and have done with it? Why strangle him, when he had a perfectly good weapon there to hand? No—I think he came unprovided, and, when he saw his enemy there, he made for him with his hands in the characteristic British way."

"But the slashing?"

"Well, I think that when he had got his man down, dead before him, he was filled with a pretty grim sort of fury and wanted to do more damage. He caught up something that was lying near him on the sand—it might be a bit of old iron, or even one of those sharp shells you sometimes see about, or a bit of glass—and he went for him with that in a desperate rage of jealousy or hatred."

"Dreadful, dreadful!" said the elderly woman.

"Of course, one can only guess in the dark, not having seen the wounds. It's quite possible that the murderer dropped his knife in the struggle and had to do the actual killing with his hands, picking the knife up afterwards. If the wounds were clean knife-wounds, that is probably what happened, and the murder was premeditated. But if they were rough, jagged gashes, made by an impromptu weapon, then I should say it was a chance encounter, and that the murderer was either mad or—"

"Or?"

"Or had suddenly come upon somebody whom he hated very much."

"What do you think happened afterwards?"

"That's pretty clear. The murderer, having waited, as I said, to see that all his footprints were cleaned up by the tide, waded or swam back to the rock where he had left his clothes, taking the weapon with him. The sea would wash away any blood from his bathing-dress or body. He then climbed out upon the rocks, walked, with bare feet, so as to leave no tracks on any seaweed or anything, to the short grass of the shore, dressed, went along to the murdered man's car, and drove it away."

"Why did he do that?"

"Yes, why? He may have wanted to get somewhere in a hurry. Or he may have been afraid that if the murdered man were identified too soon it would cast suspicion on him. Or it may have been a mixture of motives. The point is, where did he come from? How did he come to be bathing at that remote spot, early in the morning? He didn't get there by car, or there would be a second car to be accounted for. He may have been camping near the spot; but it would have taken him a long time to strike camp and pack all his belongings into the car, and he might have been seen. I am rather inclined to think he had bicycled there, and that he hoisted the bicycle into the back of the car and took it away with him."

"But, in that case, why take the car?"

"Because he had been down at East Felpham longer than he expected, and he was afraid of being late. Either he had to get back to breakfast at some house where his absence would be noticed, or else he lived some distance off, and had only just time enough for the journey home. I think, though, he had to be back to breakfast."

"Why?"

"Because, if it was merely a question of making up time on the road, all he had to do was to put himself and his bicycle on the train for part of the way. No; I fancy he was staying in a smallish hotel somewhere. Not a large hotel, because there nobody would notice whether he came in or not. And not, I think, in lodgings, or somebody would have mentioned before now that they had had a lodger who went bathing at East Felpham. Either he lives in the neighbourhood, in which case he should be easy to trace, or was staying with friends who have an interest in concealing his movements. Or else—which I think is more likely—he was in a smallish hotel, where he would be missed from the breakfast-table, but where his favourite bathing-place was not a matter of common knowledge."

"That seems feasible," said the stout man.

"In any case," went on the first-class passenger, "he must have been staying within easy bicycling distance of East Felpham, so it shouldn't be too hard to trace him. And then there is the car."

"Yes. Where is the car, on your theory?" demanded the prim man, who obviously still had hankerings after the Camorra theory.

"In a garage, waiting to be called for," said the first-class passenger promptly.

"Where?" persisted the prim man.

"Oh! somewhere on the other side of wherever it was the murderer was staying. If you have a particular reason for not wanting it to be known that you were in a certain place at a specified time, it's not a bad idea to come back from the opposite direction. I rather think I should look for the car at West Felpham, and the hotel in the nearest town on the main road beyond where the two roads to East and West Felpham join. When you've found the car, you've found the name of the victim, naturally. As for the murderer, you will have to look for an active man, a good swimmer and ardent bicyclist—probably not very well off, since he cannot afford to have a car—who has been taking a holiday in the neighbourhood of the Felphams, and who has a good reason for disliking the victim, whoever he may be."

"Well, I never," said the elderly woman admiringly. "How beautiful you do put it all together. Like Sherlock Holmes, I do declare."

"It's a very pretty theory," said the prim man, "but, all the same, you'll find it's a secret society. Mark my words. Dear me! We're just running in. Only twenty minutes late. I call that very good for holiday-time. Will you excuse me? My bag is just under your feet."

There was an eighth person in the compartment, who had remained throughout the conversation apparently buried in a newspaper. As the passengers decanted themselves upon the platform, this man touched the first-class passenger upon the arm.

"Excuse me, sir," he said. "That was a very interesting suggestion of yours. My name is Winterbottom, and I am investigating this case. Do you mind giving me your name? I might wish to communicate with you later on."

"Certainly," said the first-class passenger. "Always delighted to have a finger in any pie, don't you know. Here is my card. Look me up any time you like."

Detective-Inspector Winterbottom took the card and read the name:

LORD PETER WIMSEY
110A PICCADILLY

The *Evening Views* vendor outside Piccadilly Tube Station arranged his placard with some care. It looked very well, he thought.

MAN WITH
NO FACE
IDENTIFIED

It was, in his opinion, considerably more striking than that displayed by a rival organ, which announced, unimaginatively:

BEACH MURDER
VICTIM
IDENTIFIED

A youngish gentleman in a grey suit who emerged at that moment from the Criterion Bar appeared to think so too, for he exchanged a copper for the *Evening Views,* and at once plunged into its perusal with such concentrated interest that he bumped into a hurried man outside the station and had to apologize.

The *Evening Views,* grateful to murderer and victim alike for providing so useful a sensation in the dead days after the Bank Holiday, had torn Messrs. Negretti & Zambra's rocketing thermometrical statistics from the "banner" position which they had occupied in the lunch edition, and substituted:

FACELESS VICTIM OF BEACH OUTRAGE
IDENTIFIED

MURDER OF PROMINENT
PUBLICITY ARTIST

POLICE CLUES

The body of a middle-aged man who was discovered, attired only in a bathing-costume and with his face horribly disfigured by some jagged instrument, on the beach at East Felpham last Monday morning has been identified as that of Mr. Coreggio Plant, studio manager of Messrs. Crichton Ltd, the well-known publicity experts of Holborn.

Mr. Plant, who was forty-five years of age and a bachelor, was spending his annual holiday in making a motoring tour along the West Coast. He had no companion with him and had left no address for the forwarding of letters, so that, without the smart work of Detective-Inspector Winterbottom of the Westshire police, his disappearance might not in the ordinary way have been noticed until he became due to return to his place of business in three weeks' time. The murderer had no doubt counted on this, and had removed the motor-car, containing the belongings of his victim, in the hope of covering up all traces of this dastardly outrage so as to gain time for escape.

A rigorous search for the missing car, however, eventuated in its discovery in a garage at West Felpham, where it had been left for decarbonization and repairs to the magneto. Mr. Spiller, the garage proprietor, himself saw the man who left the car, and has furnished a description of him to the police. He is said to be a small, dark man of foreign appearance. The police hold a clue to his identity, and an arrest is confidently expected in the near future.

Mr. Plant was for fifteen years in the employment of Messrs. Crichton, being appointed Studio Manager in the latter years of the war. He was greatly liked by all his colleagues, and his skill in the lay-out and designing of advertisements did much to justify the truth of Messrs. Crichton's well-known slogan: "Crichton's for Admirable Advertising."

The funeral of the victim will take place tomorrow at Golders Green Cemetery.

(Pictures on Back Page.)

Lord Peter Wimsey turned to the back page. The portrait of the victim did not detain him long; it was one of those characterless studio photographs which establish nothing except that the sitter has a tolerable set of features. He noted that Mr. Plant had been thin rather than fat, commercial in appearance rather than artistic, and that the photographer had chosen to show him serious rather than smiling. A picture of East Felpham beach, marked with a cross where the body was found, seemed to arouse in him rather more than a casual interest. He studied it intently for some time, making little surprised noises. There was no obvious reason why he should have been surprised, for the photograph bore out in every detail the deductions he had made in the train. There was the curved line of sand, with a long spur of rock stretching out behind it into deep water, and running back till it mingled with the short, dry turf. Nevertheless, he looked at it for several minutes with close attention, before folding the newspaper and hailing a taxi; and when he was in the taxi he unfolded the paper and looked at it again.

"Your lordship having been kind enough," said Inspector Winterbottom, emptying his glass rather too rapidly for true connoisseurship, "to suggest I should look you up in Town, I made bold to give you a call in passing. Thank you, I won't say no. Well, as you've seen in the papers by now, we found that car all right."

Wimsey expressed his gratification at this result.

"And very much obliged I was to your lordship for the hint," went on the inspector generously, "not but what I wouldn't say but I should have come to the same conclusion myself, given a little more time. And, what's more, we're on the track of the man."

"I see he's supposed to be foreign-looking. Don't say he's going to turn out to be a Camorrist after all!"

"No, my lord." The inspector winked. "Our friend in the corner had got his magazine stories a bit on the brain, if you ask me. And *you* were a bit out too, my lord, with your bicyclist idea."

"Was I? That's a blow."

"Well, my lord, these here theories *sound* all right, but half the time they're too fine-spun altogether. Go for the facts—that's our motto in the Force—facts and motive, and you won't go far wrong."

"Oh! you've discovered the motive, then?"

The inspector winked again.

"There's not many motives for doing a man in," said he. "Women or money—or women *and* money—it mostly comes down to one or the other. This fellow Plant went in for being a bit of a lad, you see. He kept a little cottage down Felpham way, with a nice little skirt to furnish it and keep the love-nest warm for him—see?"

"Oh! I thought he was doing a motor-tour."

"Motor-tour your foot!" said the inspector, with more energy than politeness. "That's what the old [epithet] told 'em at the office. Handy reason, don't you see, for leaving no address behind him. No, no. There was a lady in it all right. I've seen her. A very taking piece too, if you like 'em skinny, which I don't. I prefer 'em better upholstered myself."

"That chair is really more comfortable with a cushion," put in Wimsey, with anxious solicitude. "Allow me."

"Thanks, my lord, thanks. I'm doing very well. It seems that his woman—by the way, we're speaking in confidence, you understand. I don't want this to go further till I've got my man under lock and key."

Wimsey promised discretion.

"That's all right, my lord, that's all right. I know I can rely on you. Well, the long and the short is, this young woman had another fancy man—a sort of an Italiano, whom she'd chucked for Plant, and this same dago got wind of the business and came down to East Felpham on the Sunday night, looking for her. He's one of these professional partners in a Palais de Danse up Cricklewood way, and that's where the girl comes from, too. I suppose she thought Plant was a cut above him. Anyway, down he comes, and busts in upon them Sunday night when they were having a bit of supper—and that's when the row started."

"Didn't you know about this cottage and the goings-on there?"

"Well, you know, there's such a lot of these week-enders nowadays. We can't keep tabs on all of them, so long as they behave themselves and don't make a disturbance. The woman's been there—so they tell me—since last June, with him coming down Saturday to Monday; but it's a lonely spot, and the constable didn't take much notice. He came in the evenings, so there wasn't anybody much to recognize him, except the old girl who did the slops and things, and she's half-blind. And of course, when they found him, he hadn't any face to recognize. It'd be thought he'd just gone off in the ordinary way. I dare say the dago fellow reckoned on that. As I was saying, there was a big row, and the dago was kicked out. He must have lain wait for Plant down by the bathing-place, and done him in."

"By strangling?"

"Well, he *was* strangled."

"Was his face cut up with a knife, then?"

"Well, no — I don't think it was a knife. More like a broken bottle, I should say, if you ask me. There's plenty of them come in with the tide."

"But then we're brought back to our old problem. If this Italian was lying in wait to murder Plant, why didn't he take a weapon with him, instead of trusting to the chance of his hands and a broken bottle?"

The inspector shook his head.

"Flighty," he said. "All these foreigners are flighty. No headpiece. But there's our man and there's our motive, plain as a pikestaff. You don't want more."

"And where is the Italian fellow now?"

"Run away. That's pretty good proof of guilt in itself. But we'll have him before long. That's what I've come to Town about. He can't get out of the country. I've had an all-stations call sent out to stop him. The dance-hall people were able to supply us with a photo and a good description. I'm expecting a report in now any minute. In fact, I'd best be getting along. Thank you very much for your hospitality, my lord."

"The pleasure is mine," said Wimsey, ringing the bell to have the visitor shown out. "I have enjoyed our little chat immensely."

Sauntering into the Falstaff at twelve o'clock the following morning, Wimsey, as he had expected, found Salcombe Hardy supporting his rather plump contours against the bar. The reporter greeted his arrival with a heartiness amounting almost to enthusiasm, and called for two large Scotches immediately. When the usual skirmish as to who should pay had been honourably settled by the prompt disposal of the drinks and the standing of two more, Wimsey pulled from his pocket the copy of last night's *Evening Views*.

"I wish you'd ask the people over at your place to get hold of a decent print of this for me," he said, indicating the picture of East Felpham beach.

Salcombe Hardy gazed limpid inquiry at him from eyes like drowned violets.

"See here, you old sleuth," he said, "does this mean you've got a theory about the thing? I'm wanting a story badly. Must keep up the excitement, you know. The police don't seem to have got any further since last night."

"No; I'm interested in this from another point of view altogether. I did have a theory—of sorts—but it seems it's all wrong. Bally old Homer nodding, I suppose. But I'd like a copy of the thing."

"I'll get Warren to get you one when we come back. I'm just taking him down with me to Crichton's. We're going to have a look at a picture. I say, I wish you'd come too. Tell me what to say about the damned thing."

"Good God! I don't know anything about commercial art."

" 'Tisn't commercial art. It's supposed to be a portrait of this blighter Plant. Done by one of the chaps in his studio or something. Kid who told me about it says it's clever. I don't know. Don't suppose she knows, either. You go in for being artistic, don't you?"

"I wish you wouldn't use such filthy expressions, Sally. Artistic! Who is this girl?"

"Typist in the copy department."

"Oh, Sally!"

"Nothing of that sort. I've never met her. Name's Gladys Twitterton. I'm sure that's beastly enough to put anybody off. Rang us up last night and told us there was a bloke there who'd done old Plant in oils and was it any use to us? Drummer thought it might be worth looking into. Make a change from that everlasting syndicated photograph."

"I see. If you haven't got an exclusive story, an exclusive picture's better than nothing. The girl seems to have her wits about her. Friend of the artist's?"

"No—said he'd probably be frightfully annoyed at her having told me. But I can wangle that. Only I wish you'd come and have a look at it. Tell me whether I ought to say it's an unknown masterpiece or merely a striking likeness."

"How the devil can I say if it's a striking likeness of a bloke I've never seen?"

"I'll say it's that, in any case. But I want to know if it's well painted."

"Curse it, Sally, what's it matter whether it is or not? I've got other things to do. Who's the artist, by the way? Anybody one's ever heard of?"

"Dunno. I've got the name here somewhere." Sally rooted in his hip-pocket and produced a mass of dirty correspondence, its angles blunted by constant attrition. "Some comic name like Buggle or Snagtooth—wait a bit—here it is. Crowder. Thomas Crowder. I knew it was something out of the way."

"Singularly like Buggle or Snagtooth. All right, Sally. I'll make a martyr of myself. Lead me to it."

"We'll have another quick one. Here's Warren. This is Lord Peter Wimsey. This is on me."

"On me," corrected the photographer, a jaded young man with a disillusioned manner. "Three large White Labels, please. Well, here's all the best. Are you fit, Sally? Because we'd better make tracks. I've got to be up at Golders Green by two for the funeral."

Mr. Crowder of Crichton's appeared to have had the news broken to him already by Miss Twitterton, for he received the embassy in a spirit of gloomy acquiescence.

"The directors won't like it," he said, "but they've had to put up with such a lot that I suppose one irregularity more or less won't give 'em apoplexy." He had a small, anxious, yellow face like a monkey. Wimsey put him down as being in his late thirties. He noticed his fine, capable hands, one of which was disfigured by a strip of sticking-plaster.

"Damaged yourself?" said Wimsey pleasantly, as they made their way upstairs to the studio. "Mustn't make a practice of that, what? An artist's hands are his livelihood — except, of course, for Armless Wonders and people of that kind! Awkward job, painting with your toes."

"Oh, it's nothing much," said Crowder, "but it's best to keep the paint out of surface scratches. There's such a thing as lead-poisoning. Well, here's this dud portrait, such as it is. I don't mind telling you that it didn't please the sitter. In fact he wouldn't have it at any price."

"Not flattering enough?" asked Hardy.

"As you say." The painter pulled out a four by three canvas from its hiding-place behind a stack of poster cartoons, and heaved it up on to the easel.

"Oh!" said Hardy, a little surprised. Not that there was any reason for surprise as far as the painting itself was concerned. It was a straight-forward handling enough, the skill and originality of the brushwork being of the kind that interests the painter without shocking the ignorant.

"Oh!" said Hardy. "Was he really like that?"

He moved closer to the canvas, peering into it as he might have peered into the face of the living man, hoping to get something out of him. Under this microscopic scrutiny, the portrait, as is the way of portraits, dislimned, and became no more than a conglomeration of painted spots and streaks. He made the discovery that, to the painter's eye, the human face is full of green and purple patches.

He moved back again, and altered the form of his question:
"So that's what he was like, was he?"

He pulled out the photograph of Plant from his pocket, and compared it with the portrait. The portrait seemed to sneer at his surprise.

"Of course, they touch these things up at these fashionable photographers," he said. "Anyway, that's not my business.

This thing will make a jolly good eye-catcher, don't you think so, Wimsey? Wonder if they'd give us a two-column spread on the front page? Well, Warren, you'd better get down to it."

The photographer, bleakly unmoved by artistic or journalistic considerations, took silent charge of the canvas, mentally resolving it into a question of panchromatic plates and coloured screens. Crowder gave him a hand in shifting the easel into a better light. Two or three people from other departments, passing through the studio on their lawful occasions, stopped and lingered in the neighbourhood of the disturbance, as though it were a street accident. A melancholy, grey-haired man, temporary head of the studio, vice Coreggio Plant, deceased, took Crowder aside, with a muttered apology, to give him some instructions about adapting a whole quad to an eleven-inch treble. Hardy turned to Lord Peter.

"It's damned ugly," he said. "Is it good?"

"Brilliant," said Wimsey. "You can go all out. Say what you like about it."

"Oh, splendid! Could we discover one of our neglected British masters?"

"Yes; why not? You'll probably make the man the fashion and ruin him as an artist, but that's his pigeon."

"But, I say—do you think it's a good likeness? He's made him look a most sinister sort of fellow. After all, Plant thought it was so bad he wouldn't have it."

"The more fool he. Ever heard of the portrait of a certain statesman that was so revealing of his inner emptiness that he hurriedly bought it up and hid it to prevent people like you from getting hold of it?"

Crowder came back.

"I say," said Wimsey, "whom does that picture belong to? You? Or the heirs of the deceased, or what?"

"I suppose it's back on my hands," said the painter. "Plant—well, he more or less commissioned it, you see, but—"

"How more or less?"

"Well, he kept on hinting, don't you know, that he would like me to do him, and, as he was my boss, I thought I'd better.

No price actually mentioned. When he saw it, he didn't like it, and told me to alter it."

"But you didn't."

"Oh—well, I put it aside and said I'd see what I could do with it. I thought he'd perhaps forget about it."

"I see. Then presumably it's yours to dispose of."

"I should think so. Why?"

"You have a very individual technique, haven't you?" pursued Wimsey. "Do you exhibit much?"

"Here and there. I've never had a show in London."

"I fancy I once saw a couple of small seascapes of yours somewhere. Manchester, was it? or Liverpool? I wasn't sure of your name, but I recognized the technique immediately."

"I dare say. I did send a few things to Manchester about two years ago."

"Yes—I felt sure I couldn't be mistaken. I want to buy the portrait. Here's my card, by the way. I'm not a journalist; I collect things."

Crowder looked from the card to Wimsey and from Wimsey to the card, a little reluctantly.

"If you want to exhibit it, of course," said Lord Peter, "I should be delighted to leave it with you as long as you liked."

"Oh, it's not that," said Crowder. "The fact is, I'm not altogether keen on the thing. I should like to—that is to say, it's not really finished."

"My dear man, it's a bally masterpiece."

"Oh, the painting's all right. But it's not altogether satisfactory as a likeness."

"What the devil does the likeness matter? I don't know what the late Plant looked like and I don't care. As I look at the thing it's a damn fine bit of brush-work, and if you tinker about with it you'll spoil it. You know that as well as I do. What's biting you? It isn't the price, is it? You know I shan't boggle about that. I can afford my modest pleasures, even in these thin and piping times. You don't want me to have it? Come now—what's the real reason?"

"There's no reason at all why you shouldn't have it if you

really want it, I suppose," said the painter, still a little sullenly. "If it's really the painting that interests you."

"What do you suppose it is? The notoriety? I can have all I want of *that* commodity, you know, for the asking—or even without asking. Well, anyhow, think it over, and when you've decided, send me a line and name your price."

Crowder nodded without speaking, and the photographer having by this time finished his job, the party took their leave.

As they left the building, they became involved in the stream of Crichton's staff going out to lunch. A girl, who seemed to have been loitering in a semi-intentional way in the lower hall, caught them as the lift descended.

"Are you the *Evening Views* people? Did you get your picture all right?"

"Miss Twitterton?" said Hardy interrogatively. "Yes, rather—thank you so much for giving us the tip. You'll see it on the front page this evening."

"Oh! that's splendid! I'm frightfully thrilled. It has made an excitement here—all this business. Do they know anything yet about who murdered Mr. Plant? Or am I being horribly indiscreet?"

"We're expecting news of an arrest any minute now," said Hardy. "As a matter of fact, I shall have to buzz back to the office as fast as I can, to sit with one ear glued to the telephone. You will excuse me, won't you? And, look here—will you let me come round another day, when things aren't so busy, and take you out to lunch?"

"Of course. I should love to," Miss Twitterton giggled. "I do so want to hear about all the murder cases."

"Then here's the man to tell you about them, Miss Twitterton," said Hardy, with mischief in his eye. "Allow me to introduce Lord Peter Wimsey."

Miss Twitterton offered her hand in an ecstasy of excitement which almost robbed her of speech.

"How do you do?" said Wimsey. "As this blighter is in such a hurry to get back to his gossip-shop, what do you say to having a spot of lunch with me?"

"Well, really—" began Miss Twitterton.

"He's all right," said Hardy; "he won't lure you into any gilded dens of infamy. If you look at him, you will see he has a kind, innocent face."

"I'm sure I never thought of such a thing," said Miss Twitterton. "But you know—really—I've only got my old things on. It's no good wearing anything decent in this dusty old place."

"Oh, nonsense!" said Wimsey. "You couldn't possibly look nicer. It isn't the frock that matters—it's the person who wears it. *That's* all right, then. See you later, Sally! Taxi! Where shall we go? What time do you have to be back, by the way?"

"Two o'clock," said Miss Twitterton regretfully.

"Then we'll make the Savoy do," said Wimsey; "it's reasonably handy."

Miss Twitterton hopped into the waiting taxi with a little squeak of agitation.

"Did you see Mr. Crichton?" she said. "He went by just as we were talking. However, I dare say he doesn't really know me by sight. I hope not—or he'll think I'm getting too grand to need a salary." She rooted in her hand-bag. "I'm sure my face is getting all shiny with excitement. What a silly taxi. It hasn't got a mirror—and I've bust mine."

Wimsey solemnly produced a small looking-glass from his pocket.

"How wonderfully competent of you!" exclaimed Miss Twitterton. "I'm afraid, Lord Peter, you are used to taking girls about."

"Moderately so," said Wimsey. He did not think it necessary to mention that the last time he had used that mirror it had been to examine the back teeth of a murdered man.

"Of course," said Miss Twitterton, "they had to say he was popular with his colleagues. Haven't you noticed that murdered people are always well dressed and popular?"

"They have to be," said Wimsey. "It makes it more mysterious and pathetic. Just as girls who disappear are always bright and home-loving and have no men friends."

"Silly, isn't it?" said Miss Twitterton, with her mouth full of roast duck and green peas. "I should think everybody was only too glad to get rid of Plant—nasty, rude creature. So mean, too, always taking credit for other people's work. All those poor things in the studio, with all the spirit squashed out of them. I always say, Lord Peter, you can tell if a head of a department's fitted for his job by noticing the atmosphere of the place as you go into it. Take the copy-room, now. We're all as cheerful and friendly as you like, though I must say the language that goes on there is something awful, but these writing fellows are like that, and they don't mean anything by it. But then, Mr. Ormerod is a real gentleman—that's our copy-chief, you know—and he makes them all take an interest in the work, for all they grumble about the cheese-bills and the department-store bilge they have to turn out. But it's quite different in the studio. A sort of dead-and-alive feeling about it, if you understand what I mean. We girls notice things like that more than some of the high-up people think. Of course, I'm very sensitive to these feelings—almost psychic, I've been told."

Lord Peter said there was nobody like a woman for sizing up character at a glance. Women, he thought, were remarkably intuitive.

"That's a fact," said Miss Twitterton. "I've often said, if I could have a few frank words with Mr. Crichton, I could tell him a thing or two. There are wheels within wheels beneath the surface of a place like this that these brass-hats have no idea of."

Lord Peter said he felt sure of it.

"The way Mr. Plant treated people he thought were beneath him," went on Miss Twitterton, "I'm sure it was enough to make your blood boil. I'm sure, if Mr. Ormerod sent me with a message to him, I was glad to get out of the room again. Humiliating, it was, the way he'd speak to you. I don't care if he's dead or not; being dead doesn't make a person's past behaviour any better, Lord Peter. It wasn't so much the rude things he said. There's Mr. Birkett, for example; *he's* rude enough, but nobody minds him. He's just like a big, blundering puppy—rather a lamb, really. It was Mr. Plant's nasty sneering way we all hated so. And he was always running people down."

"How about this portrait?" asked Wimsey. "Was it like him at all?"

"It was a lot too like him," said Miss Twitterton emphatically. "That's why he hated it so. He didn't like Crowder, either. But, of course, he knew he could paint, and he made him do it, because he thought he'd be getting a valuable thing cheap. And Crowder couldn't very well refuse, or Plant would have got him sacked."

"I shouldn't have thought that would have mattered much to a man of Crowder's ability."

"Poor Mr. Crowder! I don't think he's ever had much luck. Good artists don't always seem able to sell their pictures. And I know he wanted to get married—otherwise he'd never have taken up this commercial work. He's told me a good bit about himself. I don't know why—but I'm one of the people men seem to tell things to."

Lord Peter filled Miss Twitterton's glass.

"Oh, please! No, really! Not a drop more! I'm talking a lot too much as it is. I don't know what Mr. Ormerod will say when I go in to take his letters. I shall be writing down all kinds of funny things. Ooh! I really must be getting back. Just look at the time!"

"It's not really late. Have a black coffee—just as a corrective." Wimsey smiled. "You haven't been talking at all too much. I've enjoyed your picture of office life enormously. You have a very vivid way of putting things, you know. I see now why Mr. Plant was not altogether a popular character."

"Not in the office, anyway—whatever he may have been elsewhere," said Miss Twitterton darkly.

"Oh?"

"Oh! he was a one," said Miss Twitterton. "He certainly was a one. Some friends of mine met him one evening up in the West End, and they came back with some nice stories. It was quite a joke in the office—old Plant and his rosebuds, you know. Mr. Cowley—he's *the* Cowley, you know, who rides in the motorcycle races—he always said he knew what to think of Mr. Plant and his motor-tours. That time Mr. Plant pretended he'd gone touring in Wales, Mr. Cowley was asking him about the roads, and he didn't know a thing about them. Because Mr. Cowley really had been touring there, and he knew quite well Mr. Plant hadn't been where he said he had; and, as a matter of fact, Mr. Cowley knew he'd been staying the whole time in a hotel at Aberystwyth, in very attractive company."

Miss Twitterton finished her coffee and slapped the cup down defiantly.

"And now I really *must* run away, or I shall be most dreadfully late. And thank you ever so much."

"Hullo!" said Inspector Winterbottom, "you've bought that portrait, then?"

"Yes," said Wimsey. "It's a fine bit of work." He gazed thoughtfully at the canvas. "Sit down, inspector; I want to tell you a story."

"And I want to tell *you* a story," replied the inspector.

"Let's have yours first," said Wimsey, with an air of flattering eagerness.

"No, no, my lord. You take precedence. Go ahead."

He snuggled down with a chuckle into his arm-chair.

"Well!" said Wimsey. "Mine's a sort of a fairy-story. And, mind you, I haven't verified it."

"Go ahead, my lord, go ahead."

"Once upon a time—" said Wimsey, sighing.

"That's the good old-fashioned way to begin a fairy-story," said Inspector Winterbottom.

"Once upon a time," repeated Wimsey, "there was a painter. He was a good painter, but the bad fairy of Financial Success had not been asked to his christening—what?"

"That's often the way with painters," agreed the inspector.

"So he had to take up a job as a commercial artist, because

nobody would buy his pictures, and, like so many people in fairy-tales, he wanted to marry a goose-girl."

"There's many people want to do the same," said the inspector.

"The head of his department," went on Wimsey, "was a man with a mean, sneering soul. He wasn't even really good at his job, but he had been pushed into authority during the war, when better men went to the Front. Mind you, I'm rather sorry for the man. He suffered from an inferiority complex" — the inspector snorted — "and he thought the only way to keep his end up was to keep other people's end down. So he became a little tin tyrant and a bully. He took all the credit for the work of the men under his charge, and he sneered and harassed them till they got inferiority complexes even worse than his own."

"I've known that sort," said the inspector, "and the marvel to me is how they get away with it."

"Just so," said Wimsey. "Well, I dare say this man would have gone on getting away with it all right, if he hadn't thought of getting this painter to paint his portrait."

"Damn silly thing to do," said the inspector. "It was only making the painter-fellow conceited with himself."

"True. But, you see, this tin tyrant person had a fascinating female in tow, and he wanted the portrait for the lady. He thought that, by making the painter do it, he would get a good portrait at starvation price. But unhappily he'd forgotten that, however much an artist will put up with in the ordinary way, he is bound to be sincere with his art. That's the one thing a genuine artist won't muck about with."

"I dare say," said the inspector. "I don't know much about artists."

"Well, you can take it from me. So the painter painted the portrait as he saw it, and he put the man's whole creeping, sneering, paltry soul on the canvas for everybody to see."

Inspector Winterbottom stared at the portrait, and the portrait sneered back at him.

"It's not what you'd call a flattering picture, certainly," he admitted.

"Now, when a painter paints a portrait of anybody," went on Wimsey, "that person's face is never the same to him again. It's like—what shall I say? Well, it's like the way a gunner, say, looks at a landscape where he happens to be posted. He doesn't see it as a landscape. He doesn't see it as a thing of magic beauty, full of sweeping lines and lovely colour. He sees it as so much cover, so many landmarks to aim by, so many gun-emplacements. And when the war is over and he goes back to it, he will still see it as cover and landmarks and gun-emplacements. It isn't a landscape any more. It's a war map."

"I know that," said Inspector Winterbottom. "I was a gunner myself."

"A painter gets just the same feeling of deadly familiarity with every line of a face he's once painted," pursued Wimsey. "And if it's a face he hates, he hates it with a new and more irritable hatred. It's like a defective barrel-organ, everlastingly grinding out the same old maddening tune, and making the same damned awful wrong note every time the barrel goes round."

"Lord! how you can talk!" ejaculated the inspector.

"That was the way the painter felt about this man's hateful face. All day and every day he had to see it. He couldn't get away because he was tied to his job, you see."

"He ought to have cut loose," said the inspector. "It's no good going on like that, trying to work with uncongenial people."

"Well, anyway, he said to himself, he could escape for a bit during his holidays. There was a beautiful little quiet spot he knew on the West Coast, where nobody ever came. He'd been there before and painted it. Oh! by the way, that reminds me—I've got another picture to show you."

He went to a bureau and extracted a small panel in oils from a drawer.

"I saw that two years ago at a show in Manchester, and I happened to remember the name of the dealer who bought it."

Inspector Winterbottom gaped at the panel.

"But that's East Felpham!" he exclaimed.

"Yes. It's only signed T. C., but the technique is rather unmistakable, don't you think?"

The inspector knew little about technique, but initials he understood. He looked from the portrait to the panel and back at Lord Peter.

"The painter—"

"Crowder?"

"If it's all the same to you, I'd rather go on calling him the painter. He packed up his traps on his push-bike carrier, and took his tormented nerves down to this beloved and secret spot for a quiet week-end. He stayed at a quiet little hotel in the neighbourhood, and each morning he cycled off to this lovely little beach to bathe. He never told anybody at the hotel where he went, because it was *his* place, and he didn't want other people to find it out."

Inspector Winterbottom set the panel down on the table, and helped himself to whisky.

"One morning—it happened to be the Monday morning"—Wimsey's voice became slower and more reluctant—"he went down as usual. The tide was not yet fully in, but he ran out over the rocks to where he knew there was a deep bathing-pool. He plunged in and swam about, and let the small noise of his jangling troubles be swallowed up in the innumerable laughter of the sea."

"Eh?"

"Κυμάτων ἀνήριθμον γέλασμα—quotation from the classics. Some people say it means the dimpled surface of the waves in the sunlight—but how could Prometheus, bound upon his rock, have seen it? Surely it was the chuckle of the incoming tide among the stones that came up to his ears on the lonely peak where the vulture fretted at his heart. I remember arguing about it with old Philpotts in class, and getting rapped over the knuckles for contradicting him. I didn't know at the time that he was engaged in producing a translation on his own account, or doubtless I should have contradicted him more rudely and been told to take my trousers down. Dear old Philpotts!"

"I don't know anything about that," said the inspector.

"I beg your pardon. Shocking way I have of wandering. The painter—well! he swam round the end of the rocks, for the tide was nearly in by that time; and, as he came up from the sea, he saw a man standing on the beach—that beloved beach, remember, which he thought was his own sacred haven of peace. He came wading towards it, cursing the Bank Holiday rabble who must needs swarm about everywhere with their cigarette-packets and their kodaks and their gramophones—and then he saw that it was a face he knew. He knew every hated line in it, on that clear sunny morning. And, early as it was, the heat was coming up over the sea like a haze."

"It was a hot week-end," said the inspector.

"And then the man hailed him, in his smug, mincing voice. 'Hullo!' he said, 'you here? How did you find my little bathing-place?' And that was too much for the painter. He felt as if his last sanctuary had been invaded. He leapt at the lean throat—it's rather a stringy one, you may notice, with a prominent Adam's apple—an irritating throat. The water chuckled round their feet as they swayed to and fro. He felt his thumbs sink into the flesh he had painted. He saw, and laughed to see, the hateful familiarity of the features change and swell into an unrecognizable purple. He watched the sunken eyes bulge out and the thin mouth distort itself as the blackened tongue thrust through it—I am not unnerving you, I hope?"

The inspector laughed.

"Not a bit. It's wonderful, the way you describe things. You ought to write a book."

"I sing but as the throstle sings,
Amid the branches dwelling,"

replied his lordship negligently, and went on without further comment.

"The painter throttled him. He flung him back on the

sand. He looked at him, and his heart crowed within him. He stretched out his hand, and found a broken bottle, with a good jagged edge. He went to work with a will, stamping and tearing away every trace of the face he knew and loathed. He blotted it out and destroyed it utterly.

"He sat beside the thing he had made. He began to be frightened. They had staggered back beyond the edge of the water, and there were the marks of his feet on the sand. He had blood on his face and on his bathing-suit, and he had cut his hand with the bottle. But the blessed sea was still coming in. He watched it pass over the bloodstains and the footprints and wipe the story of his madness away. He remembered that this man had gone from his place, leaving no address behind him. He went back, step by step, into the water, and, as it came up to his breast, he saw the red stains smoke away like a faint mist in the brown-blueness of the tide. He went—wading and swimming and plunging his face and arms deep in the water, looking back from time to time to see what he had left behind him. I think that when he got back to the point and drew himself out, clean and cool, upon the rocks, he remembered that he ought to have taken the body back with him and let the tide carry it away, but it was too late. He was clean, and he could not bear to go back for the thing. Besides, he was late, and they would wonder at the hotel if he was not back in time for breakfast. He ran lightly over the bare rocks and the grass that showed no footprint. He dressed himself, taking care to leave no trace of his presence. He took the car, which would have told a story. He put his bicycle in the back seat, under the rugs, and he went—but you know as well as I do where he went."

Lord Peter got up with an impatient movement, and went over to the picture, rubbing his thumb meditatively over the texture of the painting.

"You may say, if he hated the face so much, why didn't he destroy the picture? He couldn't. It was the best thing he'd ever done. He took a hundred guineas for it. It was cheap at a hundred guineas. But then—I think he was afraid to refuse me. My name is rather well known. It was a sort of blackmail, I suppose. But I wanted that picture."

Inspector Winterbottom laughed again.

"Did you take any steps, my lord, to find out if Crowder has really been staying at East Felpham?"

"No." Wimsey swung round abruptly. "I have taken no steps at all. That's your business. I have told you the story, and, on my soul, I'd rather have stood by and said nothing."

"You needn't worry." The inspector laughed for the third time. "It's a good story, my lord, and you told it well. But you're right when you say it's a fairy-story. We've found this Italian fellow— Francesco, he called himself, and he's the man all right."

"How do you know? Has he confessed?"

"Practically. He's dead. Killed himself. He left a letter to the woman, begging her forgiveness, and saying that when he saw her with Plant he felt murder come into his heart. 'I have revenged myself,' he says, 'on him who dared to love you.' I suppose he got the wind up when he saw we were after him— I wish these newspapers wouldn't be always putting these criminals on their guard—so he did away with himself to cheat the gallows. I may say it's been a disappointment to me."

"It must have been," said Wimsey. "Very unsatisfactory, of course. But I'm glad my story turned out to be only a fairy-tale after all. You're not going?"

"Got to get back to my duty," said the inspector, heaving himself to his feet. "Very pleased to have met you, my lord. And I mean what I say—you ought to take to literature."

Wimsey remained after he had gone, still looking at the portrait.

" 'What is Truth?' said jesting Pilate. No wonder, since it is so completely unbelievable. . . . I could prove it . . . if I liked . . . but the man had a villainous face, and there are few good painters in the world."

THE ADVENTUROUS EXPLOIT OF THE CAVE OF ALI BABA

In the front room of a grim and narrow house in Lambeth a man sat eating kippers and glancing through the *Morning Post*. He was smallish and spare, with brown hair rather too regularly waved and a strong, brown beard, cut to a point. His double-breasted suit of navy-blue and his socks, tie, and handkerchief, all scrupulously matched, were a trifle more point-device than the best taste approves, and his boots were slightly too bright a brown. He did not look a gentleman, not even a gentleman's gentleman, yet there was something about his appearance which suggested that he was accustomed to the manner of life in good families. The breakfast-table, which he had set with his own hands, was arrayed with the attention to detail which is exacted of good-class servants. His action, as he walked over to a little side-table and carved himself a plate of ham, was the action of a superior butler; yet he was not old enough to be a retired butler; a footman, perhaps, who had come into a legacy.

He finished the ham with good appetite, and, as he sipped his coffee, read through attentively a paragraph which he had already noticed and put aside for consideration:

LORD PETER WIMSEY'S WILL
BEQUEST TO VALET
£10,000 TO CHARITIES

The will of Lord Peter Wimsey, who was killed last December while shooting big game in Tanganyika, was proved yesterday at £500,000. A sum of £10,000 was left to various charities, including [here followed a list of bequests]. To his valet, Mervyn Bunter, was left an annuity of £500 and the lease of the testator's flat in Piccadilly. [Then followed a number of personal bequests.] The remainder of the estate, including the valuable collection of books and pictures at 110A Piccadilly, was left to the testator's mother, the Dowager Duchess of Denver.

Lord Peter Wimsey was thirty-seven at the time of his death. He was the younger brother of the present Duke of Denver, who is the wealthiest peer in the United Kingdom. Lord Peter was distinguished as a criminologist and took an active part in the solution of several famous mysteries. He was a well-known book collector and man-about-town.

The man gave a sigh of relief.

"No doubt about that," he said aloud. "People don't give their money away if they're going to come back again. The blighter's dead and buried right enough. I'm free."

He finished his coffee, cleared the table, and washed up the crockery, took his bowler hat from the hall-stand, and went out.

A bus took him to Bermondsey. He alighted, and plunged into a network of gloomy streets, arriving after a quarter of an hour's walk at a seedy-looking public-house in a low quarter. He entered and called for a double whisky.

The house had only just opened, but a number of customers, who had apparently been waiting on the doorstep for this desirable event, were already clustered about the bar. The man who might have been a footman reached for his glass, and in doing so jostled the elbow of a flash person in a check suit and regrettable tie.

"Here!" expostulated the flash person, "what d'yer mean by it? We don't want your sort here. Get out!"

He emphasized his remarks with a few highly coloured words, and a violent push in the chest.

"Bar's free to everybody, isn't it?" said the other, returning the shove with interest.

"Now then!" said the barmaid, "none o' that. The gentleman didn't do it intentional, Mr. Jukes."

"Didn't he?" said Mr. Jukes. "Well, I *did*."

"And you ought to be ashamed of yourself," retorted the young lady, with a toss of the head. "I'll have no quarrelling in my bar—not this time in the morning."

"It was quite an accident," said the man from Lambeth. "I'm not one to make a disturbance, having always been used to the best houses. But if any gentleman *wants* to make trouble—"

"All right, all right," said Mr. Jukes, more pacifically. "I'm not keen to give you a new face. Not but what any alteration wouldn't be for the better. Mind your manners another time, that's all. What'll you have?"

"No, no," protested the other, "this one must be on me. Sorry I pushed you. I didn't mean it. But I didn't like to be taken up so short."

"Say no more about it," said Mr. Jukes generously. "I'm standing this. Another double whisky, miss, and one of the usual. Come over here where there isn't so much of a crowd, or you'll be getting yourself into trouble again."

He led the way to a small table in the corner of the room.

"That's all right," said Mr. Jukes. "Very nicely done. I don't think there's any danger here, but you can't be too careful. Now, what about it, Rogers? Have you made up your mind to come in with us?"

"Yes," said Rogers, with a glance over his shoulder, "yes, I have. That is, mind you, if everything seems all right. I'm not looking for trouble, and I don't want to get let in for any dangerous games. I don't mind giving you information, but it's understood as I take no active part in whatever goes on. Is that straight?"

"You wouldn't be allowed to take an active part if you wanted to," said Mr. Jukes. "Why, you poor fish. Number One wouldn't have anybody but experts on his jobs. All you have to do is to let us know where the stuff is and how to get it. The Society does the rest. It's some organization, I can tell you. You won't even know who's doing it, or how it's done. You won't know anybody, and nobody will know you—except Number One, of course. He knows everybody."

"And you," said Rogers.

"And me, of course. But I shall be transferred to another district. We shan't meet again after today, except at the general meetings, and then we shall all be masked."

"Go on!" said Rogers incredulously.

"Fact. You'll be taken to Number One—he'll see you, but you won't see him. Then, if he thinks you're any good, you'll be put on the roll, and after that you'll be told where to make your reports to. There is a divisional meeting called once a fortnight, and every three months there's a general meeting and share-out. Each member is called up by number and has his whack handed over to him. That's all."

"Well, but suppose two members are put on the same job together?"

"If it's a daylight job, they'll be so disguised their mothers wouldn't know 'em. But it's mostly night work."

"I see. But, look here—what's to prevent somebody following me home and giving me away to the police?"

"Nothing, of course. Only I wouldn't advise him to try it, that's all. The last man who had that bright idea was fished out of the river down Rotherhithe way, before he had time to get his precious report in. Number One knows everybody, you see."

"Oh!—and who is this Number One?"

"There's lots of people would give a good bit to know that."

"Does nobody know?"

"Nobody. He's a fair marvel, is Number One. He's a gentleman, I can tell you that, and a pretty high-up one, from his ways. *And* he's got eyes all round his head. *And* he's got an arm as long as from here to Australia. *But* nobody knows anything about him, unless it's Number Two, and I'm not even sure about her."

"There are women in it, then?"

"You can bet your boots there are. You can't do a job without 'em nowadays. But that needn't worry you. The women are safe enough. They don't want to come to a sticky end, no more than you and me."

"But, look here, Jukes—how about the money? It's a big risk to take. Is it worth it?"

"Worth it?" Jukes leant across the little marble-topped table and whispered.

"Coo!" gasped Rogers. "And how much of that would I get, now?"

"You'd share and share alike with the rest, whether you'd been in that particular job or not. There's fifty members and you'd get one-fiftieth, same as Number One and same as me."

"Really? No kidding?"

"See that wet, see that dry!" Jukes laughed. "Say, can you beat it? There's never been anything like it. It's the biggest thing ever been known. He's a great man, is Number One."

"And do you pull off many jobs?"

"Many? Listen. You remember the Carruthers necklace, and the Gorleston Bank robbery? And the Faversham burglary? And the big Rubens that disappeared from the National Gallery? And the Frensham pearls? All done by the Society. And never one of them cleared up."

Rogers licked his lips.

"But now, look here," he said cautiously. "Supposing I was a spy, as you might say, and supposing I was to go straight off and tell the police about what you've been saying?"

"Ah!" said Jukes, "suppose you did, eh? Well, supposing something nasty didn't happen to you on the way there — which I wouldn't answer for, mind —"

"Do you mean to say you've got me watched?"

"You can bet your sweet life we have. Yes. Well, *supposing* nothing happened on the way there, and you was to bring the slops to this pub, looking for yours truly —"

"Yes?"

"You wouldn't find me, that's all. I should have gone to Number Five."

"Who's Number Five?"

"Ah! I don't know. But he's the man that makes you a new face while you wait. Plastic surgery, they call it. And new finger-prints. New everything. We go in for up-to-date methods in our show."

Rogers whistled.

"Well, how about it?" asked Jukes, eyeing his acquaintance over the rim of his tumbler.

"Look here — you've told me a lot of things. Shall I be safe if I say 'no'?"

"Oh, yes — if you behave yourself and don't make trouble for us."

"H'm, I see. And if I say 'yes'?"

"Then you'll be a rich man in less than no time, with money in your pocket to live like a gentleman. And nothing to do for it, except to tell us what you know about the houses you've been to when you were in service. It's money for jam if you act straight by the Society."

Rogers was silent, thinking it over.

"I'll do it!" he said at last.

"Good for you. Miss! The same again, please. Here's to it, Rogers! I knew you were one of the right sort the minute I set eyes on you. Here's to money for jam, and take care of Number One! Talking of Number One, you'd better come round and see him tonight. No time like the present."

"Right you are. Where'll I come to? Here?"

"Nix. No more of this little pub for us. It's a pity because it's nice and comfortable, but it can't be helped. Now, what you've got to do is this. At ten o'clock tonight exactly, you walk north across Lambeth Bridge" (Rogers winced at this intimation that his abode was known), "and you'll see a yellow taxi standing there, with the driver doing something to his engine. You'll say to him, 'Is your bus fit to go?' and he'll say, 'Depends where you want to go to.' And you'll say, 'Take me to Number One, London.' There's a shop called that, by the way, but he won't take you there. You won't know where he *is* taking you, because the taxi-windows will be covered up, but you mustn't mind that. It's the rule for the first visit. Afterwards, when you're regularly one of us, you'll be told the name of the place. And when you get there, do as you're told and speak the truth, because, if you don't, Number One will deal with you. See?"

"I see."

"Are you game? You're not afraid?"

"Of course I'm not afraid."

"Good man! Well, we'd better be moving now. And I'll say good-bye, because we shan't see each other again. Good-bye—and good luck!"

"Good-bye."

They passed through the swing-doors, and out into the mean and dirty street.

The two years subsequent to the enrolment of the ex-footman Rogers in a crook society were marked by a number of startling and successful raids on the houses of distinguished people. There was the theft of the great diamond tiara from the Dowager Duchess of Denver; the burglary at the flat formerly occupied by the late Lord Peter Wimsey, resulting in the disappearance of £7,000 worth of silver and gold plate; the burglary at the country mansion of Theodore Winthrop, the millionaire—which, incidentally, exposed that thriving gentleman as a confirmed Society blackmailer and caused a reverberating scandal in Mayfair; and the snatching of the famous eight-string necklace of pearls from the Marchioness of Dinglewood during the singing of the Jewel Song in *Faust* at Covent Garden. It is true that the pearls turned out to be imitation, the original string having been pawned by the noble lady under circumstances highly painful to the Marquis, but the coup was nevertheless a sensational one.

On a Saturday afternoon in January, Rogers was sitting in his room in Lambeth, when a slight noise at the front door caught his ear. He sprang up almost before it had ceased, dashed through the small hallway, and flung the door open. The street was deserted. Nevertheless, as he turned back to the sitting-room, he saw an envelope lying on the hat-stand. It was addressed briefly to "Number Twenty-one." Accustomed by this time to the somewhat dramatic methods used by the Society to deliver its correspondence, he merely shrugged his shoulders, and opened the note.

It was written in cipher, and, when transcribed, ran thus:

Number Twenty-one, An Extraordinary General Meeting will be held tonight at the house of Number One at 11:30. You will be absent at your peril. The word is FINALITY.

Rogers stood for a little time considering this. Then he made his way to a room at the back of the house, in which there was a tall safe, built into the wall. He manipulated the combination and walked into the safe, which ran back for some distance, forming, indeed, a small strong-room. He pulled out a drawer marked "Correspondence," and added the paper he had just received to the contents.

After a few moments he emerged, re-set the lock to a new combination, and returned to the sitting-room.

"Finality," he said. "Yes — I think so." He stretched out his hand to the telephone — then appeared to alter his mind.

He went upstairs to an attic, and thence climbed into a loft close under the roof. Crawling among the rafters, he made his way into the farthest corner; then carefully pressed a knot on the timber-work. A concealed trap-door swung open. He crept through it, and found himself in the corresponding loft of the next house. A soft cooing noise greeted him as he entered. Under the skylight stood three cages, each containing a carrier pigeon.

He glanced cautiously out of the skylight, which looked out upon a high blank wall at the back of some factory or other. There was nobody in the dim little courtyard, and no window within sight. He drew his head in again, and, taking a small fragment of thin paper from his pocket-book, wrote a few letters and numbers upon it. Going to the nearest cage, he took out the pigeon and attached the message to its wing. Then he carefully set the bird on the window-ledge. It hesitated a moment, shifted its pink feet a few times, lifted its wings, and was gone. He saw it tower up into the already darkening sky over the factory roof and vanish into the distance.

He glanced at his watch and returned downstairs. An hour later he released the second pigeon, and in another hour the third. Then he sat down to wait.

At half past nine he went up to the attic again. It was dark, but a few frosty stars were shining, and a cold air blew through the open window. Something pale gleamed faintly on the floor. He picked it up—it was warm and feathery. The answer had come.

He ruffled the soft plumes and found the paper. Before reading it, he fed the pigeon and put it into one of the cages. As he was about to fasten the door, he checked himself.

"If anything happens to me," he said, "there's no need for you to starve to death, my child."

He pushed the window a little wider open and went downstairs again. The paper in his hand bore only the two letters "O.K." It seemed to have been written hurriedly, for there was a long smear of ink in the upper left-hand corner. He noted this with a smile, put the paper in the fire, and, going out into the kitchen, prepared and ate a hearty meal of eggs and corned beef from a new tin. He ate it without bread, though there was a loaf on the shelf near at hand, and washed it down with water from the tap, which he let run for some time before venturing to drink it. Even then he carefully wiped the tap, both inside and outside, before drinking.

When he had finished, he took a revolver from a locked drawer, inspecting the mechanism with attention to see that it was in working order, and loaded it with new cartridges from an unbroken packet. Then he sat down to wait again.

At a quarter before eleven, he rose and went out into the street. He walked briskly, keeping well away from the wall, till he came out into a well-lighted thoroughfare. Here he took a bus, securing the corner seat next the conductor, from which he could see everybody who got on and off. A succession of buses eventually brought him to a respectable residential quarter of Hampstead. Here he alighted and, still keeping well away from the walls, made his way up to the Heath.

The night was moonless, but not altogether black, and, as he crossed a deserted part of the Heath, he observed one or two other dark forms closing in upon him from various directions. He paused in the shelter of a large tree, and adjusted to his face a black velvet mask, which covered him from brow to chin. At its base the number 21 was clearly embroidered in white thread.

At length a slight dip in the ground disclosed one of those agreeable villas which stand, somewhat isolated, among the rural surroundings of the Heath. One of the windows was lighted. As he made his way to the door, other dark figures, masked like himself, pressed forward and surrounded him. He counted six of them.

The foremost man knocked on the door of the solitary house. After a moment, it was opened slightly. The man advanced his head to the opening; there was a murmur, and the door opened wide. The man stepped in, and the door was shut.

When three of the men had entered, Rogers found himself to be the next in turn. He knocked, three times loudly, then twice faintly. The door opened to the extent of two or three inches, and an ear was presented to the chink. Rogers whispered, "Finality." The ear was withdrawn, the door opened, and he passed in.

Without any further word of greeting, Number Twenty-one passed into a small room on the left, which was furnished like an office, with a desk, a safe, and a couple of chairs. At the desk sat a massive man in evening dress, with a ledger before him. The new arrival shut the door carefully after him; it clicked to, on a spring lock. Advancing to the desk, he announced, "Number Twenty-one, sir," and stood respectfully waiting. The big man looked up, showing the number 1 startlingly white on his velvet mask. His eyes, of a curious hard blue, scanned Rogers attentively. At a sign from him, Rogers removed his mask. Having verified his identity with care, the President said, "Very well, Number Twenty-one," and made an entry in the ledger. The voice was hard and metallic, like his eyes. The close scrutiny from behind the immovable black mask seemed to make Rogers uneasy; he shifted his feet, and his eyes fell. Number One made a sign of dismissal, and Rogers, with a faint sigh as though of relief, replaced his mask and left the room. As he came out, the next comer passed in in his place.

The room in which the Society met was a large one, made by knocking the two largest of the first-floor rooms into one. It was furnished in the standardized taste of twentieth-century suburbia and brilliantly lighted. A gramophone in one corner blared out a jazz tune, to which about ten couples of masked men and women were dancing, some in evening dress and others in tweeds and jumpers.

In one corner of the room was an American bar. Rogers went up and asked the masked man in charge for a double whisky. He consumed it slowly, leaning on the bar. The room filled. Presently somebody moved across to the gramophone and stopped it. He looked round. Number One had appeared on the threshold. A tall woman in black stood beside him. The mask, embroidered with a white 2, covered hair and face completely; only her fine bearing and her white arms and bosom and the dark eyes shining through the eye-slits proclaimed her a woman of power and physical attraction.

"Ladies and gentlemen." Number One was standing at the upper end of the room. The woman sat beside him; her eyes were cast down and betrayed nothing, but her hands were clenched on the arms of the chair and her whole figure seemed tensely aware.

"Ladies and gentlemen. Our numbers are two short tonight." The masks moved; eyes were turned, seeking and counting. "I need not inform you of the disastrous failure of our plan for securing the plans of the Court-Windlesham helicopter. Our courageous and devoted comrades, Number Fifteen and Number Forty-eight, were betrayed and taken by the police."

An uneasy murmur rose among the company.

"It may have occurred to some of you that even the well-known steadfastness of these comrades might give way under examination. There is no cause for alarm. The usual orders have been issued, and I have this evening received the report that their tongues have been effectually silenced. You will, I am sure, be glad to know that these two brave men have been spared the ordeal of so great a temptation to dishonour, and that they will not be called upon to face a public trial and the rigours of a long imprisonment."

A hiss of intaken breath moved across the assembled members like the wind over a barley-field.

"Their dependants will be discreetly compensated in the usual manner. I call upon Numbers Twelve and Thirty-four to undertake this agreeable task. They will attend me in my office for their instructions after the meeting. Will the numbers I have named kindly signify that they are able and willing to perform this duty?"

Two hands were raised in salute. The President continued, looking at his watch:

"Ladies and gentlemen, please take your partners for the next dance."

The gramophone struck up again. Rogers turned to a girl near him in a red dress. She nodded, and they slipped into the movement of a fox-trot. The couples gyrated solemnly and in silence. Their shadows were flung against the blinds as they turned and stepped to and fro.

"What has happened?" breathed the girl in a whisper, scarcely moving her lips. "I'm frightened, aren't you? I feel as if something awful was going to happen."

"It does take one a bit short, the President's way of doing things," agreed Rogers, "but it's safer like that."

"Those poor men —"

A dancer, turning and following on their heels, touched Rogers on the shoulder.

"No talking, please," he said. His eyes gleamed sternly; he twirled his partner into the middle of the crowd and was gone. The girl shuddered.

The gramophone stopped. There was a burst of clapping. The dancers again clustered before the President's seat.

"Ladies and gentlemen. You may wonder why this extraordinary meeting has been called. The reason is a serious one. The failure of our recent attempt was no accident. The police were not on the premises that night by chance. We have a traitor among us."

Partners who had been standing close together fell distrustfully apart. Each member seemed to shrink, as a snail shrinks from the touch of a finger.

"You will remember the disappointing outcome of the Dinglewood affair," went on the President, in his harsh voice. "You may recall other smaller matters which have not turned out satisfactorily. All these troubles have been traced to their origin. I am happy to say that our minds can now be easy. The offender has been discovered and will be removed. There will be no more mistakes. The misguided member who introduced the traitor to our Society will be placed in a position where his lack of caution will have no further ill-effects. There is no cause for alarm."

Every eye roved about the company, searching for the traitor and his unfortunate sponsor. Somewhere beneath the black masks a face must have turned white; somewhere under the stifling velvet there must have been a brow sweating, not with the heat of the dance. But the masks hid everything.

"Ladies and gentlemen, please take your partners for the next dance."

The gramophone struck into an old and half-forgotten tune: "There ain't nobody loves me." The girl in red was claimed by a tall mask in evening dress. A hand laid on Rogers's arm made him start. A small, plump woman in a green jumper slipped a cold hand into his. The dance went on.

When it stopped, amid the usual applause, everyone stood, detached, stiffened in expectation. The President's voice was raised again.

"Ladies and gentlemen, please behave naturally. This is a dance, not a public meeting."

Rogers led his partner to a chair and fetched her an ice. As he stooped over her, he noticed the hurried rise and fall of her bosom.

"Ladies and gentlemen." The endless interval was over. "You will no doubt wish to be immediately relieved from suspense. I will name the persons involved. Number Thirty-seven!"

A man sprang up with a fearful, strangled cry.

"Silence!"

The wretch choked and gasped.

"I never—I swear I never—I'm innocent."

"Silence. You have failed in discretion. You will be dealt with. If you have anything to say in defence of your folly, I will hear it later. Sit down."

Number Thirty-seven sank down upon a chair. He pushed his handkerchief under the mask to wipe his face. Two tall men closed in upon him. The rest fell back, feeling the recoil of humanity from one stricken by mortal disease.

The gramophone struck up.

"Ladies and gentlemen, I will now name the traitor. Number Twenty-one, stand forward."

Rogers stepped forward. The concentrated fear and loathing of forty-eight pairs of eyes burned upon him. The miserable Jukes set up a fresh wail.

"Oh, my God! Oh, my God!"

"Silence! Number Twenty-one, take off your mask."

The traitor pulled the thick covering from his face. The intense hatred of the eyes devoured him.

"Number Thirty-seven, this man was introduced here by you, under the name of Joseph Rogers, formerly second footman in the service of the Duke of Denver, dismissed for pilfering. Did you take steps to verify that statement?"

"I did—I did! As God's my witness, it was all straight. I had him identified by two of the servants. I made inquiries. The tale was straight—I'll swear it was."

The President consulted a paper before him, then he looked at his watch again.

"Ladies and gentlemen, please take your partners . . ."

Number Twenty-one, his arms twisted behind him and bound, and his wrists handcuffed, stood motionless, while the dance of doom circled about him. The clapping, as it ended, sounded like the clapping of the men and women who sat, thirsty-lipped, beneath the guillotine.

"Number Twenty-one, your name has been given as Joseph Rogers, footman, dismissed for theft. Is that your real name?"

"No."

"What is your name?"

"Peter Death Bredon Wimsey."

"We thought you were dead."

"Naturally. You were intended to think so."

"What has become of the genuine Joseph Rogers?"

"He died abroad. I took his place. I may say that no real blame attaches to your people for not having realized who I was. I not only took Rogers's place; I *was* Rogers. Even when

I was alone, I walked like Rogers, I sat like Rogers, I read Rogers's books, and wore Rogers's clothes. In the end, I almost thought Rogers's thoughts. The only way to keep up a successful impersonation is never to relax."

"I see. The robbery of your own flat was arranged?"

"Obviously."

"The robbery of the Dowager Duchess, your mother, was connived at by you?"

"It was. It was a very ugly tiara—no real loss to anybody with decent taste. May I smoke, by the way?"

"You may not. Ladies and gentlemen . . ."

The dance was like the mechanical jigging of puppets. Limbs jerked, feet faltered. The prisoner watched with an air of critical detachment.

"Numbers Fifteen, Twenty-two, and Forty-nine. You have watched the prisoner. Has he made any attempts to communicate with anybody?"

"None." Number Twenty-two was the spokesman. "His letters and parcels have been opened, his telephone tapped, and his movements followed. His water-pipes have been under observation for Morse signals."

"You are sure of what you say?"

"Absolutely."

"Prisoner, have you been alone in this adventure? Speak the truth, or things will be made somewhat more unpleasant for you than they might otherwise be."

"I have been alone. I have taken no unnecessary risks."

"It may be so. It will, however, be as well that steps should be taken to silence the man at Scotland Yard—what is his name?—Parker. Also the prisoner's manservant, Mervyn Bunter, and possibly also his mother and sister. The brother is a stupid oaf, and not, I think, likely to have been taken into the prisoner's confidence. A precautionary watch will, I think, meet the necessities of his case."

The prisoner appeared, for the first time, to be moved.

"Sir, I assure you that my mother and sister know nothing which could possibly bring danger on the Society."

"You should have thought of their situation earlier. Ladies and gentlemen, please take —"

"No — !" Flesh and blood could endure the mockery no longer.

"No! Finish with him. Get it over. Break up the meeting. It's dangerous. The police —"

"Silence!"

The President glanced round at the crowd. It had a dangerous look about it. He gave way.

"Very well. Take the prisoner away and silence him. He will receive Number Four treatment. And be sure you explain it to him carefully first."

"Ah!"

The eyes expressed a wolfish satisfaction. Strong hands gripped Wimsey's arms.

"One moment — for God's sake let me die decently."

"You should have thought this over earlier. Take him away. Ladies and gentlemen, be satisfied — he will not die quickly."

"Stop! Wait!" cried Wimsey desperately. "I have something to say. I don't ask for life — only for a quick death. I-I have something to sell."

"To sell?"

"Yes."

"We make no bargains with traitors."

"No — but listen! Do you think I have not thought of this? I am not so mad. I have left a letter."

"Ah! now it is coming. A letter. To whom?"

"To the police. If I do not return tomorrow —"

"Well?"

"The letter will be opened."

"Sir," broke in Number Fifteen. "This is bluff. The prisoner has not sent any letter. He has been strictly watched for many months."

"Ah! but listen. I left the letter before I came to Lambeth."

"Then it can contain no information of value."

"Oh, but it does."

"What?"

"The combination of my safe."

"Indeed? Has this man's safe been searched?"

"Yes, sir."

"What did it contain?"

"No information of importance, sir. An outline of our organization—the name of this house—nothing that cannot be altered and covered before morning."

Wimsey smiled.

"Did you investigate the inner compartment of the safe?"

There was a pause.

"You hear what he says," snapped the President sharply. "Did you find this inner compartment?"

"There was no inner compartment, sir. He is trying to bluff."

"I hate to contradict you," said Wimsey, with an effort at his ordinary pleasant tone, "but I really think you must have overlooked the inner compartment."

"Well," said the President, "and what do you say is in this inner compartment, if it does exist?"

"The names of every member of this Society, with their addresses, photographs, and finger-prints."

"What?"

The eyes round him now were ugly with fear. Wimsey kept his face steadily turned towards the President.

"How do you say you have contrived to get this information?"

"Well, I have been doing a little detective work on my own, you know."

"But you have been watched."

"True. The finger-prints of my watchers adorn the first page of the collection."

"This statement can be proved?"

"Certainly. I will prove it. The name of Number Fifty, for example—"

"Stop!"

A fierce muttering arose. The President silenced it with a gesture.

"If you mention names here, you will certainly have no hope of mercy. There is a fifth treatment—kept specially for people who mention names. Bring the prisoner to my office. Keep the dance going."

The President took an automatic from his hip-pocket and faced his tightly fettered prisoner across the desk.

"Now speak!" he said.

"I should put that thing away, if I were you," said Wimsey contemptuously. "It would be a much pleasanter form of death than treatment Number Five, and I might be tempted to ask for it."

"Ingenious," said the President, "but a little too ingenious. Now, be quick; tell me what you know."

"Will you spare me if I tell you?"

"I make no promises. Be quick."

Wimsey shrugged his bound and aching shoulders.

"Certainly. I will tell you what I know. Stop me when you have heard enough."

He leaned forward and spoke low. Overhead the noise of the gramophone and the shuffling of feet bore witness that the dance was going on. Stray passers-by crossing the Heath noted that the people in the lonely house were making a night of it again.

"Well," said Wimsey, "am I to go on?"

From beneath the mask the President's voice sounded as though he were grimly smiling.

"My lord," he said, "your story fills me with regret that you are not, in fact, a member of our Society. Wit, courage, and industry are valuable to an association like ours. I fear I cannot persuade you? No—I supposed not."

He touched a bell on his desk.

"Ask the members kindly to proceed to the supper-room," he said to the mask who entered.

The "supper-room" was on the ground-floor, shuttered and curtained. Down its centre ran a long, bare table, with chairs set about it.

"A Barmecide feast, I see," said Wimsey pleasantly. It was the first time he had seen this room. At the far end, a trap-door in the floor gaped ominously.

The President took the head of the table.

"Ladies and gentlemen," he began, as usual—and the foolish courtesy had never sounded so sinister—"I will not conceal from you the seriousness of the situation. The prisoner has recited to me more than twenty names and addresses which were thought to be unknown, except to their owners and to me. There has been great carelessness"—his voice rang harshly—"which will have to be looked into. Finger-prints have been obtained—he has shown me the photographs of some of them. How our investigators came to overlook the inner door of this safe is a matter which calls for inquiry."

"Don't blame them," put in Wimsey. "It was meant to be overlooked, you know. I made it like that on purpose."

The President went on, without seeming to notice the interruption.

"The prisoner informs me that the book with the names and addresses is to be found in this inner compartment, together with certain letters and papers stolen from the houses of members, and numerous objects bearing authentic finger-prints. I believe him to be telling the truth. He offers the combination of the safe in exchange for a quick death. I think the offer should be accepted. What is your opinion, ladies and gentlemen?"

"The combination is known already," said Number Twenty-two.

"Imbecile! This man has told us, and has proved to me, that he is Lord Peter Wimsey. Do you think he will have forgotten to alter the combination? And then there is the secret of the inner door. If he disappears tonight and the police enter his house—"

"I say," said a woman's rich voice, "that the promise

should be given and the information used — and quickly. Time is getting short."

A murmur of agreement went round the table.

"You hear," said the President, addressing Wimsey. "The Society offers you the privilege of a quick death in return for the combination of the safe and the secret of the inner door."

"I have your word for it?"

"You have."

"Thank you. And my mother and sister?"

"If you in your turn will give us your word — you are a man of honour — that these women know nothing that could harm us, they shall be spared."

"Thank you, sir. You may rest assured, upon my honour, that they know nothing. I should not think of burdening any woman with such dangerous secrets — particularly those who are dear to me."

"Very well. It is agreed — yes?"

The murmur of assent was given, though with less readiness than before.

"Then I am willing to give you the information you want. The word of the combination is UNRELIABILITY."

"And the inner door?"

"In anticipation of the visit of the police, the inner door — which might have presented difficulties — is open."

"Good! You understand that if the police interfere with our messenger — "

"That would not help me, would it?"

"It is a risk," said the President thoughtfully, "but a risk which I think we must take. Carry the prisoner down to the cellar. He can amuse himself by contemplating apparatus Number Five. In the meantime, Numbers Twelve and Forty-six — "

"No, no!"

A sullen mutter of dissent arose and swelled threateningly.

"No," said a tall man with a voice like treacle. "No — why should any members be put in possession of this evidence? We have found one traitor among us tonight and more than one

fool. How are we to know that Numbers Twelve and Forty-six
are not fools and traitors also?"

The two men turned savagely upon the speaker, but a
girl's voice struck into the discussion, high and agitated.

"Hear, hear! That's right, I say. How about us? We ain't
going to have our names read by somebody we don't know
nothing about. I've had enough of this. They might sell the 'ole
lot of us to the narks."

"I agree," said another member. "Nobody ought to be
trusted, nobody at all."

The President shrugged his shoulders.

"Then what, ladies and gentlemen, do you suggest?"

There was a pause. Then the same girl shrilled out again:

"I say Mr. President oughter go himself. He's the only one
as knows all the names. It won't be no cop to him. Why should
we take all the risk and trouble and him sit at home and collar
the money? Let him go himself, that's what I say."

A long rustle of approbation went round the table.

"I second that motion," said a stout man who wore a
bunch of gold seals at his fob. Wimsey smiled as he looked at
the seals; it was that trifling vanity which had led him directly
to the name and address of the stout man, and he felt a certain
affection for the trinkets on that account.

The President looked round.

"It is the wish of the meeting, then, that I should go?" he
said, in an ominous voice.

Forty-five hands were raised in approbation. Only the
woman known as Number Two remained motionless and
silent, her strong white hands clenched on the arm of the
chair.

The President rolled his eyes slowly round the threatening
ring till they rested upon her.

"Am I to take it that this vote is unanimous?" he enquired.

The woman raised her head.

"Don't go," she gasped faintly.

"You hear," said the President, in a faintly derisive tone.
"This lady says, don't go."

"I submit that what Number Two says is neither here nor there," said the man with the treacly voice. "Our own ladies might not like us to be going, if they were in madam's privileged position." His voice was an insult.

"Hear, hear!" cried another man. "This is a democratic society, this is. We don't want no privileged classes."

"Very well," said the President. "You hear, Number Two. The feeling of the meeting is against you. Have you any reasons to put forward in favour of your opinion?"

"A hundred. The President is the head and soul of our Society. If anything should happen to him—where should we be? You"—she swept the company magnificently with her eyes—"you have all blundered. We have your carelessness to thank for all this. Do you think we should be safe for five minutes if the President were not here to repair your follies?"

"Something in that," said a man who had not hitherto spoken.

"Pardon my suggesting," said Wimsey maliciously, "that, as the lady appears to be in a position peculiarly favourable for the reception of the President's confidences, the contents of my modest volume will probably be no news to her. Why should not Number Two go herself?"

"Because I say she must not," said the President sternly, checking the quick reply that rose to his companion's lips. "If it is the will of the meeting, I will go. Give me the key of the house."

One of the men extracted it from Wimsey's jacket-pocket and handed it over.

"Is the house watched?" he demanded of Wimsey.

"No."

"That is the truth?"

"It is the truth."

The President turned at the door.

"If I have not returned in two hours' time," he said, "act for the best to save yourselves, and do what you like with the prisoner. Number Two will give orders in my absence."

He left the room. Number Two rose from her seat with a gesture of command.

"Ladies and gentlemen. Supper is now considered over. Start the dancing again."

Down in the cellar the time passed slowly, in the contemplation of apparatus Number Five. The miserable Jukes, alternately wailing and raving, at length shrieked himself into exhaustion. The four members guarding the prisoners whispered together from time to time.

"An hour and a half since the President left," said one.

Wimsey glanced up. Then he returned to his examination of the room. There were many curious things in it, which he wanted to memorize.

Presently the trap-door was flung open. "Bring him up!" cried a voice. Wimsey rose immediately, and his face was rather pale.

The members of the gang were again seated round the table. Number Two occupied the President's chair, and her eyes fastened on Wimsey's face with a tigerish fury, but when she spoke it was with a self-control which roused his admiration.

"The President has been two hours gone," she said. "What has happened to him? Traitor twice over — what has happened to him?"

"How should I know?" said Wimsey. "Perhaps he has looked after Number One and gone while the going was good!"

She sprang up with a little cry of rage, and came close to him.

"Beast! liar!" she said, and struck him on the mouth. "You know he would never do that. He is faithful to his friends. What have you done with him? Speak — or I will make you speak. You two, there — bring the irons. He *shall* speak!"

"I can only form a guess, madame," replied Wimsey, "and I shall not guess any the better for being stimulated with hot irons, like Pantaloon at the circus. Calm yourself, and I will tell you what I think. I think — indeed, I greatly fear — that

Monsieur le Président in his hurry to examine the interesting exhibits in my safe may, quite inadvertently, no doubt, have let the door of the inner compartment close behind him. In which case —"

He raised his eyebrows, his shoulders being too sore for shrugging, and gazed at her with a limpid and innocent regret.

"What do you mean?"

Wimsey glanced round the circle.

"I think," he said, "I had better begin from the beginning by explaining to you the mechanism of my safe. It is rather a nice safe," he added plaintively. "I invented the idea myself — not the principle of its working, of course; that is a matter for scientists — but just the idea of the thing.

"The combination I gave you is perfectly correct as far as it goes. It is a three-alphabet thirteen-letter lock by Bunn & Fishett — a very good one of its kind. It opens the outer door, leading into the ordinary strong-room, where I keep my cash and my Froth Blower's cuff-links and all that. But there is an inner compartment with two doors, which open in quite a different manner. The outermost of these two inner doors is merely a thin steel skin, painted to look like the back of the safe and fitting closely, so as not to betray any join. It lies in the same plane as the wall of the room, you understand, so that if you were to measure the outside and the inside of the safe you would discover no discrepancy. It opens outwards with an ordinary key, and, as I truly assured the President, it was left open when I quitted my flat."

"Do you think," said the woman sneeringly, "that the President is so simple as to be caught in a so obvious trap? He will have wedged open that inner door, undoubtedly."

"Undoubtedly, madame. But the sole purpose of that outer inner door, if I may so express myself, is to appear to be the only inner door. But hidden behind the hinge of that door is another door, a sliding panel, set so closely in the thickness of the wall that you would hardly see it unless you knew it was there. This door was also left open. Our revered Number One had nothing to do but to walk straight through into the inner compartment of the safe, which, by the way, is built into the chimney of the old basement kitchen, which runs up the house at that point. I hope I make myself clear?"

"Yes, yes—get on. Make your story short."

Wimsey bowed, and, speaking with even greater delibera- tion than ever, resumed:

"Now, this interesting list of the Society's activities, which I have had the honour of compiling, is written in a very large book—bigger, even, than Monsieur le Président's ledger which he uses downstairs. (I trust, by the way, madame, that you have borne in mind the necessity of putting that ledger in a safe place. Apart from the risk of investigation by some offi- cious policeman, it would be inadvisable that any junior mem- ber of the Society should get hold of it. The feeling of the meeting would, I fancy, be opposed to such an occurrence.)"

"It is secure," she answered hastily. "*Mon dieu!* get on with your story."

"Thank you—you have relieved my mind. Very good. This big book lies on a steel shelf at the back of the inner compart- ment. Just a moment. I have not described this inner compart- ment to you. It is six feet high, three feet wide, and three feet deep. One can stand up in it quite comfortably, unless one is very tall. It suits me nicely—as you may see, I am not more than five feet eight and a half. The President has the advan- tage of me in height; he might be a little cramped, but there would be room for him to squat if he grew tired of standing. By the way, I don't know if you know it, but you have tied me up rather tightly."

"I would have you tied till your bones were locked together. Beat him, you! He is trying to gain time."

"If you beat me," said Wimsey, "I'm damned if I'll speak at all. Control yourself, madame; it does not do to move hastily when your king is in check."

"Get on!" she cried again, stamping with rage.

"Where was I? Ah! The inner compartment. As I say, it is a little snug—the more so that it is not ventilated in any way. Did I mention that the book lay on a steel shelf?"

"You did."

"Yes. The steel shelf is balanced on a very delicate concealed spring. When the weight of the book—a heavy one, as I said—is lifted, the shelf rises almost imperceptibly. In rising it makes an electrical contact. Imagine to yourself, madame; our revered President steps in—propping the false door open behind him—he sees the book—quickly he snatches it up. To make sure that it is the right one, he opens it—he studies the pages. He looks about for the other objects I have mentioned, which bear the marks of finger-prints. And silently, but very, very quickly—you can imagine it, can you not?—the secret panel, released by the rising of the shelf, leaps across like a panther behind him. Rather a trite simile, but apt, don't you think?"

"My God! oh, my God!" Her hand went up as though to tear the choking mask from her face. "You—you devil—devil! What is the word that opens the inner door? Quick! I will have it torn out of you—the word!"

"It is not a hard word to remember, madame—though it has been forgotten before now. Do you recollect, when you were a child, being told the tale of 'Ali Baba and the Forty Thieves'? When I had that door made, my mind reverted, with rather a pretty touch of sentimentality, in my opinion, to the happy hours of my childhood. The words that open the door are—'Open Sesame.'"

"Ah! How long can a man live in this devil's trap of yours?"

"Oh," said Wimsey cheerfully, "I should think he might hold out a few hours if he kept cool and didn't use up the available oxygen by shouting and hammering. If we went there at once, I dare say we should find him fairly all right."

"I shall go myself. Take this man and—do your worst with him. Don't finish him till I come back. I want to see him die!"

"One moment," said Wimsey, unmoved by this amiable wish. "I think you had better take me with you."

"Why—why?"

"Because, you see, I'm the only person who can open the door."

"But you have given me the word. Was that a lie?"

"No—the word's all right. But, you see, it's one of these new-style electric doors. In fact, it's really the very latest thing in doors. I'm rather proud of it. It opens to the words 'Open Sesame' all right—*but to my voice only.*"

"Your voice? I will choke your voice with my own hands. What do you mean—your voice only?"

"Just what I say. Don't clutch my throat like that, or you may alter my voice so that the door won't recognize it. That's better. It's apt to be rather pernickety about voices. It got stuck up for a week once, when I had a cold and could only implore it in a hoarse whisper. Even in the ordinary way, I sometimes have to try several times before I hit on the exact right intonation."

She turned and appealed to a short, thick-set man standing beside her.

"Is this true? Is it possible?"

"Perfectly, ma'am, I'm afraid," said the man civilly. From his voice Wimsey took him to be a superior workman of some kind—probably an engineer.

"Is it an electrical device? Do you understand it?"

"Yes, ma'am. It will have a microphone arrangement somewhere which converts the sound into a series of vibrations controlling an electric needle. When the needle has traced the correct pattern, the circuit is completed and the door opens. The same thing can be done by light vibrations equally easily."

"Couldn't you open it with tools?"

"In time, yes, ma'am. But only by smashing the mechanism, which is probably well protected."

"You may take that for granted," interjected Wimsey reassuringly.

She put her hands to her head.

"I'm afraid we're done in," said the engineer, with a kind of respect in his tone for a good job of work.

"No—wait! Somebody must know—the workmen who made this thing?"

"In Germany," said Wimsey briefly.

"Or—yes, yes, I have it—a gramophone. This—this—

he—shall be made to say the word for us. Quick—how can it be done?"

"Not possible, ma'am. Where would we get the apparatus at half past three on a Sunday morning? The poor gentleman would be dead long before—"

There was a silence, during which the sounds of the wakening day came through the shuttered windows. A motor-horn sounded distantly.

"I give in," she said. "We must let him go. Take the ropes off him. You will free him, won't you?" she went on, turning piteously to Wimsey. "Devil as you are, you are not such a devil as that! You will go straight back and save him!"

"Let him go, nothing!" broke in one of the men. "He doesn't go to peach to the police, my lady, don't you think it. The President's done in, that's all, and we'd all better make tracks while we can. It's all up, boys. Chuck this fellow down the cellar and fasten him in, so he can't make a row and wake the place up. I'm going to destroy the ledgers. You can see it done if you don't trust me. And you, Thirty, you know where the switch is. Give us a quarter of an hour to clear, and then you can blow the place to glory."

"No! You can't go—you can't leave him to die—your President—your leader—my—I won't let it happen. Set this devil free. Help me, one of you, with the ropes—"

"None of that, now," said the man who had spoken before. He caught her by the wrists, and she twisted, shrieking, in his arms, biting and struggling to get free.

"Think, think," said the man with the treacly voice. "It's getting on to morning. It'll be light in an hour or two. The police may be here any minute."

"The police!" She seemed to control herself by a violent effort. "Yes, yes, you are right. We must not imperil the safety of all for the sake of one man. *He* himself would not wish it. That is so. We will put this carrion in the cellar where it cannot harm us, and depart, every one to his own place, while there is time."

"And the other prisoner?"

"He? Poor fool—he can do no harm. He knows nothing. Let him go," she answered contemptuously.

In a few minutes' time Wimsey found himself bundled unceremoniously into the depths of the cellar. He was a little puzzled. That they should refuse to let him go, even at the price of Number One's life, he could understand. He had taken the risk with his eyes open. But that they should leave him as a witness against them seemed incredible.

The men who had taken him down strapped his ankles together and departed, switching the lights out as they went.

"Hi! Kamerad!" said Wimsey. "It's a bit lonely sitting here. You might leave the light on."

"It's all right, my friend," was the reply. "You will not be in the dark long. They have set the time-fuse."

The other man laughed with rich enjoyment, and they went out together. So that was it. He was to be blown up with the house. In that case the President would certainly be dead before he was extricated. This worried Wimsey; he would rather have been able to bring the big crook to justice. After all, Scotland Yard had been waiting six years to break up this gang.

He waited, straining his ears. It seemed to him that he heard footsteps over his head. The gang had all crept out by this time. . . .

There was certainly a creak. The trap-door had opened; he felt, rather than heard, somebody creeping into the cellar.

"Hush!" said a voice in his ear. Soft hands passed over his face, and went fumbling about his body. There came the cold touch of steel on his wrists. The ropes slackened and dropped off. A key clicked in the handcuffs. The strap about his ankles was unbuckled.

"Quick! Quick! they have set the time-switch. The house is mined. Follow me as fast as you can. I stole back—I said I had left my jewellery. It was true. I left it on purpose. *He* must be saved—only you can do it. Make haste!"

Wimsey, staggering with pain, as the blood rushed back into his bound and numbed arms, crawled after her into the room above. A moment, and she had flung back the shutters and thrown the window open.

"Now go! Release him! You promise?"

"I promise. And I warn you, madame, that this house is surrounded. When my safe-door closed it gave a signal which sent my servant to Scotland Yard. Your friends are all taken—"

"'Ah! But you go—never mind me—quick! The time is almost up.'

"Come away from this!"

He caught her by the arm, and they went running and stumbling across the little garden. An electric torch shone suddenly in the bushes.

"That you, Parker?" cried Wimsey. "Get your fellows away. Quick! the house is going up in a minute."

The garden seemed suddenly full of shouting, hurrying men. Wimsey, floundering in the darkness, was brought up violently against the wall. He made a leap at the coping, caught it, and hoisted himself up. His hands groped for the woman; he swung her up beside him. They jumped; everyone was jumping; the woman caught her foot and fell with a gasping cry. Wimsey tried to stop himself, tripped over a stone, and came down headlong. Then, with a flash and a roar, the night went up in fire.

Wimsey picked himself painfully out from among the débris of the garden wall. A faint moaning near him proclaimed that his companion was still alive. A lantern was turned suddenly upon them.

"Here you are!" said a cheerful voice. "Are you all right, old thing? Good Lord! what a hairy monster!"

"All right," said Wimsey. "Only a bit winded. Is the lady safe? H'm—arm broken, apparently—otherwise sound. What's happened?"

"About half a dozen of 'em got blown up; the rest we've bagged." Wimsey became aware of a circle of dark forms in the wintry dawn. "Good Lord, what a day! What a come-back for a public character! You old stinker—to let us go on for two years thinking you were dead! I bought a bit of black for an arm-band. I did, really. Did anybody know, besides Bunter?"

"Only my mother and sister. I put it in a secret trust—you

know, the thing you send to executors and people. We shall have an awful time with the lawyers, I'm afraid, proving I'm me. Hullo! Is that friend Sugg?"

"Yes, my lord," said Inspector Sugg, grinning and nearly weeping with excitement. "Damned glad to see your lordship again. Fine piece of work, your lordship. They're all wanting to shake hands with you, sir."

"Oh, Lord! I wish I could get washed and shaved first. Awfully glad to see you all again, after two years' exile in Lambeth. Been a good little show, hasn't it?"

"Is he safe?"

Wimsey started at the agonized cry.

"Good Lord!" he cried. "I forgot the gentleman in the safe. Here, fetch a car, quickly. I've got the great big top Moriarty of the whole bunch quietly asphyxiating at home. Here — hop in, and put the lady in too. I promised we'd get back and save him — though" (he finished the sentence in Parker's ear) "there may be murder charges too, and I wouldn't give much for his chance at the Old Bailey. Whack her up. He can't last much longer shut up there. He's the bloke you've been wanting, the man at the back of the Morrison case and the Hope-Wilmington case, and hundreds of others."

The cold morning had turned the streets grey when they drew up before the door of the house in Lambeth. Wimsey took the woman by the arm and helped her out. The mask was off now, and showed her face, haggard and desperate, and white with fear and pain.

"Russian, eh?" whispered Parker in Wimsey's ear.

"Something of the sort. Damn! the front door's blown shut, and the blighter's got the key with him in the safe. Hop through the window, will you?"

Parker bundled obligingly in, and in a few seconds threw open the door to them. The house seemed very still. Wimsey led the way to the back room, where the strong-room stood. The outer door and the second door stood propped open with chairs. The inner door faced them like a blank green wall.

"Only hope he hasn't upset the adjustment with thumping

at it," muttered Wimsey. The anxious hand on his arm clutched feverishly. He pulled himself together, forcing his tone to one of cheerful commonplace.

"Come on, old thing," he said, addressing himself conversationally to the door. "Show us your paces. Open Sesame, confound you. Open Sesame!"

The green door slid suddenly away into the wall. The woman sprang forward and caught in her arms the humped and senseless thing that rolled out from the safe. Its clothes were torn to ribbons and its battered hands dripped blood.

"It's all right," said Wimsey, "it's all right! He'll live—to stand his trial."

*The Solution
of the Crossword Puzzle in
"Uncle Meleager's Will"*

```
      I  II III IV  V  VI VII VIII IX  X  XI XII XIII XIV XV
 1    V  I  R  G  O  .  S  .  .  .  M  I  D  A  S
 2    E  N  D  I  V  E  .  C  .  V  A  N  I  T  A
 3    R  S  .  T  E  S  T  A  M  E  N  T  .  H  I
 4    S  E  C  A  N  T  .  R  .  L  E  A  V  E  N
 5    T  R  A  N  S  .  .  L  .  S  C  E  N  T  .
 6    .  T  .  A  .  .  S  E  G  .  .  T  R  E  .
 7    .  .  T  .  .  .  I  C  T  U  S  .  S  .  .
 8    S  P  I  N  O  Z  A  .  A  U  C  T  I  O  N
 9    .  .  I  .  .  .  E  L  A  N  D  .  .  .  .
10    .  A  L  T  .  .  A  D  O  .  .  F  L  U  .
11    P  L  E  A  S  .  M  .  .  .  A  R  E  N  A
12    L  I  S  T  E  N  .  E  .  T  W  I  S  T  S
13    A  E  .  T  H  I  R  T  Y  O  N  E  .  E  T
14    U  N  H  O  O  D  .  U  .  B  E  Z  O  A  R
15    D  A  M  O  N  .  .  .  .  .  D  E  R  M  A
```

Notes to the Solution

I.1   VIRGO: The sign of the zodiac between LEO (strength) and LIBRA (justice). Allusion to parable of The Ten Virgins.

I.3   R.S.: Royal Society, whose "Fellows" are addicted to studies usually considered dry-as-dust.

IV.3   TESTAMENT (or will); search is to be directed to the Old Testament. Ref. to parable of New Cloth and Old Garment.

XIV.3 HI: He would answer to Hi!
                     Or to any loud cry.
                                The Hunting of the Snark

I.5   TRANS: Abbreviation of Translation; ref. to building of Babel.

XI.5   SCENT: Even the scent of roses
                  Is not what they supposes,
                  But more than mind discloses
                  And more than men believe.
                  G. K. Chesterton: *The Song of Quoodle*

VI.7   ICTUS: Blow; add v (five) and you get VICTUS (vanquished); the ictus is the stress in a foot of verse; if the stress be misplaced the line goes lamely.

I.8   SPINOZA: He wrote on the properties of optical glasses; also on metaphysics.

IV.13 THIRTY-ONE: Seven (months) out of the twelve of the sun's course through the heavens have thirty-one days.

XIV.13 ET: Conjunction. In astrology an aspect of the heavenly bodies. That Cicero was the master of this word indicates that it is a Latin one.

X.14   BEZOAR: The bezoar stone was supposed to be a prophylactic against poison.

11.I   PLAUD: If you would laud, then plaud (var. of applaud); Plaud-it also means "cheer."

10.II   ALIENA: *As You Like It,* II, 1, 130.

1.III   R.D.: "Refer to Drawer."

4.III   CANTICLES: The *Magnificat* and *Nunc Dimittis* are known as the Canticles, but the Book of Canticles (the Vulgate name for the Song of Songs, in which the solution is found) occurs earlier in the Bible.

2.VI   EST: ὄν καὶ μὴ ὄν = *est* and *non est* —the problem of being and not-being. Ref. Marlowe: *Doctor Faustus* I, 1.

12.X   TOB: Add IT to get Tobit; the tale of Tobit and the Fish is in the Apocrypha (the book of hidden things).

1.XI   MANES: *"Un lion est une mâchoire et non pas une crinière:"* Émile Faguet: *Lit. du XVIIe siècle.* Manes: benevolent spirits of the dead.

1.XV   SAINT: Evidence of miraculous power is required for canonization.

THE IMAGE IN THE MIRROR

The little man with the cow-lick seemed so absorbed in the book that Wimsey had not the heart to claim his property, but, drawing up the other armchair and placing his drink within easy reach, did his best to entertain himself with the Dunlop Book, which graced, as usual, one of the tables in the lounge.

The little man read on, his elbows squared upon the arms of his chair, his ruffled red head bent anxiously over the text. He breathed heavily, and when he came to the turn of the page, he set the thick volume down on his knee and used both hands for his task. Not what is called "a great reader," Wimsey decided.

When he reached the end of the story, he turned laboriously back, and read one passage over again with attention. Then he laid the book, still open, upon the table, and in so doing caught Wimsey's eye.

"I beg your pardon, sir," he said in his rather thin Cockney voice, "is this your book?"

"It doesn't matter at all," said Wimsey graciously, "I know it by heart. I only brought it along with me because it's handy for reading a few pages when you're stuck in a place like this for the night. You can always take it up and find something entertaining."

"This chap Wells," pursued the red-haired man, "he's what you'd call a very clever writer, isn't he? It's wonderful how he makes it all so real, and yet some of the things he says, you wouldn't hardly think they could be really possible. Take this story now; would you say, sir, a thing like that could actually happen to a person, as it might be you—or me?"

Wimsey twisted his head round so as to get a view of the page.

The Plattner Experiment," he said, "that's the one about the schoolmaster who was blown into the fourth dimension and came back with his right and left sides reversed. Well, no, I don't suppose such a thing would really occur in real life, though of course it's very fascinating to play with the idea of a fourth dimension."

"Well—" He paused and looked up shyly at Wimsey. "I don't rightly understand about this fourth dimension. I didn't know there was such a place, but he makes it all very clear no doubt to them that know science. But this right-and-left business, now, I know that's a fact. By experience, if you'll believe me."

Wimsey extended his cigarette-case. The little man made an instinctive motion towards it with his left hand and then seemed to check himself and stretched his right across.

"There, you see. I'm always left-handed when I don't think about it. Same as this Plattner. I fight against it, but it doesn't seem any use. But I wouldn't mind that—it's a small thing and plenty of people are left-handed and think nothing of it. No. It's the dretful anxiety of not knowing what I mayn't be doing when I'm in this fourth dimension or whatever it is."

He sighed deeply.

"I'm worried, that's what I am, worried to death."

"Suppose you tell me about it," said Wimsey.

"I don't like telling people about it, because they might think I had a slate loose. But it's fairly getting on my nerves.

Every morning when I wake up I wonder what I've been doing in the night and whether it's the day of the month it ought to be. I can't get any peace till I see the morning paper, and even then I can't be sure. . . .

"Well, I'll tell you, if you won't take it as a bore or a liberty. It all began —" He broke off and glanced nervously about the room. "There's nobody to see. If you wouldn't mind, sir, putting your hand just here a minute —"

He unbuttoned his rather regrettable double-breasted waist-coat, and laid a hand on the part of his anatomy usually considered to indicate the site of the heart.

"By all means," said Wimsey, doing as he was requested.

"Do you feel anything?"

"I don't know that I do," said Wimsey. "What ought I to feel? A swelling or anything? If you mean your pulse, the wrist is a better place."

"Oh, you can feel it *there*, all right," said the little man. "Just try the other side of the chest, sir."

Wimsey obediently moved his hand across.

"I seem to detect a little flutter," he said after a pause.

"You do? Well, you wouldn't expect to find it that side and not the other, would you? Well, that's where it is. I've got my heart on the right side, that's what I wanted you to feel for yourself."

"Did it get displaced in an illness?" asked Wimsey sympathetically.

"In a manner of speaking. But that's not all. My liver's got round the wrong side, too, and my organs. I've had a doctor see it, and he told me I was all reversed. I've got my appendix on my left side — that is, I had till they took it away. If we was private, now, I could show you the scar. It was a great surprise to the surgeon when they told him about me. He said afterwards it made it quite awkward for him, coming left-handed to the operation, as you might say."

"It's unusual, certainly," said Wimsey, "but I believe such cases do occur sometimes."

"Not the way it occurred to me. It happened in an air-raid."

"In an air-raid?" said Wimsey, aghast.

"Yes—and if that was all it had done to me I'd put up with it and be thankful. Eighteen I was then, and I'd just been called up. Previous to that I'd been working in the packing department at Crichton's—you've heard of them, I expect—Crichton's for Admirable Advertising, with offices in Holborn. My mother was living in Brixton, and I'd come up to town on leave from the training-camp. I'd been seeing one or two of my old pals, and I thought I'd finish the evening by going to see a film at the Stoll. It was after supper—I had just time to get in to the last house, so I cut across from Leicester Square through Covent Garden Market. Well, I was getting along when wallop! A bomb came down it seemed to me right under my feet, and everything went black for a bit."

"That was the raid that blew up Oldham's, I suppose."

"Yes, it was January 28th, 1918. Well, as I say, everything went right out. Next thing as I knew, I was walking in some place in broad daylight, with green grass all round me, and trees, and water to the side of me, and knowing no more about how I got there than the man in the moon."

"Good Lord!" said Wimsey. "And was it the fourth dimension, do you think?"

"Well, no, it wasn't. It was Hyde Park, as I come to see when I had my wits about me. I was along the bank of the Serpentine and there was a seat with some women sitting on it, and children playing about."

"Had the explosion damaged you?"

"Nothing to see or feel, except that I had a big bruise on one hip and shoulder as if I'd been chucked up against something. I was fairly staggered. The air-raid had gone right out of my mind, don't you see, and I couldn't imagine how I came there, and why I wasn't at Crichton's. I looked at my watch, but that had stopped. I was feeling hungry. I felt in my pocket and found some money there, but it wasn't as much as I should have had—not by a long way. But I felt I must have a bit of something, so I got out of the Park by the Marble Arch gate, and went into a Lyons. I ordered two poached on toast and a pot of tea, and while I was waiting I took up a paper that somebody had left on the seat. Well, that finished me. The last thing I remembered was starting off to see that film on the 28th—and here was the date on the paper—January 30th! I'd lost a whole day and two nights somewhere!"

"Shock," suggested Wimsey. The little man took the suggestion and put his own meaning on it.

"Shock? I should think it was. I was scared out of my life. The girl who brought my eggs must have thought I was barmy. I asked her what day of the week it was, and she said 'Friday.' There wasn't any mistake.

"Well, I don't want to make this bit too long, because that's not the end by a long chalk. I got my meal down somehow, and went to see a doctor. He asked me what I remembered doing last, and I told him about the film, and he asked whether I was out in the air-raid. Well, then it came back to me, and I remembered the bomb falling, but nothing more. He said I'd had a nervous shock and lost my memory a bit, and that it often happened and I wasn't to worry. And then he said he'd look me over to see if I'd got hurt at all. So he started in with his stethoscope, and all of a sudden he said to me:

" 'Why, you keep your heart on the wrong side, my lad!'

" 'Do I?' said I. 'That's the first I've heard of it.'

"Well, he looked me over pretty thoroughly, and then he told me what I've told you, that I was all reversed inside, and he asked a lot of questions about my family. I told him I was an only child and my father was dead—killed by a motor-lorry, he was, when I was a kid of ten—and I lived with my mother in Brixton and all that. And he said I was an unusual case, but there was nothing to worry about. Bar being wrong side round I was sound as a bell, and he told me to go home and take things quietly for a day or two.

"Well, I did, and I felt all right, and I thought that was the end of it, though I'd overstayed my leave and had a bit of a job explaining myself to the R.T.O. It wasn't till several months afterwards the draft was called up, and I went along for my farewell leave. I was having a cup of coffee in the Mirror Hall at the Strand Corner House—you know it, down the steps?"

Wimsey nodded.

"All the big looking-glasses all round. I happened to look into the one near me, and I saw a young lady smiling at me as if she knew me. I saw her reflection, that is, if you understand me. Well, I couldn't make it out, for I had never seen her before, and I didn't take any notice, thinking she'd mistook me for somebody else. Besides, though I wasn't so very old then, I thought I knew her sort, and my mother had always brought me up strict. I looked away and went on with my coffee, and all of a sudden a voice said quite close to me:

" 'Hullo, Ginger—aren't you going to say good evening?'

"I looked up and there she was. Pretty, too, if she hadn't been painted up so much.

" 'I'm afraid,' I said, rather stiff, 'you have the advantage of me, miss.'

" 'Oh, Ginger,' says she, 'Mr. Duckworthy, and after Wednesday night!' A kind of mocking way she had of speaking.

"I hadn't thought so much of her calling me Ginger, because that's what any girl would say to a fellow with my sort of hair, but when she got my name off so pat, I tell you it did give me a turn.

" 'You seem to think we're acquainted, miss,' said I.

" 'Well, I should rather say so, shouldn't you?' said she.

"There! I needn't go into it all. From what she said I found out she thought she'd met me one night and taken me home with her. And what frightened me most of all, she said it had happened on the night of the big raid.

" 'It *was* you,' she said, staring into my face a little puzzled-like. 'Of course it was you. I knew you in a minute when I saw your face in the glass.'

"Of course, I couldn't say that it hadn't been. I knew no more of what I'd been and done that night than the babe unborn. But it upset me cruelly, because I was an innocent sort of lad in those days and hadn't ever gone with girls, and it seemed to me if I'd done a thing like that I ought know about it. It seemed to me I'd been doing wrong and not getting full value for my money either.

"I made some excuse to get rid of her, and I wondered what else I'd been doing. She couldn't tell me farther than the morning of the 29th, and it worried me a bit wondering if I'd done any other queer things."

"It must have," said Wimsey, and put his finger on the bell. When the waiter arrived, he ordered drinks for two and disposed himself to listen to the rest of Mr. Duckworthy's adventures.

"I didn't think much about it, though," went on the little man; "we went abroad, and I saw my first corpse and dodged my first shell and had my first dose of the trenches, and I hadn't much time for what they call introspection.

"The next queer thing that happened was in the C.C.S. at Ypres. I'd got a blighty one near Caudry in September during the advance from Cambrai—half buried, I was, in a mine explosion and laid out unconscious near twenty-four hours it must have been. When I came to, I was wandering about somewhere behind the lines with a nasty hole in my shoulder. Somebody had bandaged it up for me, but I hadn't any recollection of that. I walked a long way, not knowing where I was, till at last I fetched up in an aid-post. They fixed me up and sent me down the line to a base hospital. I was pretty feverish, and the next thing I knew, I was in bed, with a nurse looking after me. The bloke in the next bed to mine was asleep. I got talking to a chap in the next bed beyond him, and he told me where I was, when all of a sudden the other man woke up and says:

" 'My God,' he says, 'you dirty ginger-haired swine, it's you, is it? What have you done with them vallables?'

"I tell you, I was struck all of a heap. Never seen the man in my life. But he went on at me and made such a row, the nurse came running in to see what was up. All the men were sitting up in bed listening—you never saw anything like it.

"The upshot was, as soon as I could understand what this fellow was driving at, that he'd been sharing a shell-hole with a chap that he said was me, and that this chap and he had talked together a bit and then, when he was weak and helpless, the chap had looted his money and watch and revolver and what not and gone off with them. A nasty, dirty trick, and I couldn't blame him for making a row about it, if true. But I said and stood to it, it wasn't me, but some other fellow of the same name. He said he recognized me — said he and this other chap had been together a whole day, and he knew every feature in his face and couldn't be mistaken. However, it seemed this bloke had said he belonged to the Blankshires, and I was able to show my papers and prove I belonged to the Buffs, and eventually the bloke apologized and said he must have made a mistake. He died, anyhow, a few days after, and we all agreed he must have been wandering a bit. The two divisions were fighting side by side in that dust-up and it was possible for them to get mixed up. I tried afterwards to find out whether by any chance I had a double in the Blankshires, but they sent me back home, and before I was fit again the Armistice was signed, and I didn't take any more trouble.

"I went back to my old job after the war, and things seemed to settle down a bit. I got engaged when I was twenty-one to a regular good girl, and I thought everything in the garden was lovely. And then, one day — up it all went! My mother was dead then, and I was living by myself in lodgings. Well, one day I got a letter from my intended, saying that she had seen me down at Southend on the Sunday, and that was enough for her. All was over between us.

'Now, it was unfortunate that I'd had to put off seeing her that week-end, owing to an attack of influenza. It's a cruel thing to be ill all alone in lodgings, and nobody to look after you. You might die there all on your own and nobody the wiser. Just an unfurnished room I had, you see, and no attendance, and not a soul came near me, though I was pretty bad. But my young lady she said as she had seen me down at Southend with another young woman, and she would take no excuse. Of course, I said, what was *she* doing down at Southend without me, anyhow, and that tore it. She sent me back the ring, and the episode, as they say, was closed.

"But the thing that troubled me was, I was getting that shaky in my mind, how did I know I hadn't been to Southend without knowing it? I thought I'd been half sick and half asleep in my lodgings, but it was misty-like to me. And knowing the things I had done other times—well, there! I hadn't any clear recollection one way or another, except fever-dreams. I had a vague recollection of wandering and walking somewhere for hours together. Delirious, I thought I was, but it might have been sleep-walking for all I knew. I hadn't a leg to stand on by way of evidence. I felt it very hard, losing my intended like that, but I could have got over that if it hadn't been for the fear of myself and my brain giving way or something.

"You may think this is all foolishness and I was just being mixed up with some other fellow of the same name that happened to be very like me. But now I'll tell you something.

"Terrible dreams I got to having about that time. There was one thing as always haunted me—a thing that had frightened me as a little chap. My mother, though she was a good, strict woman, liked to go to a cinema now and again. Of course, in those days they weren't like what they are now, and I expect we should think those old pictures pretty crude if we was to see them, but we thought a lot of them at that time. When I was about seven or eight I should think, she took me with her to see a thing—I remember the name now—*The Student of Prague*, it was called. I've forgotten the story, but it was a costume piece, about a young fellow at the university who sold himself to the devil, and one day his reflection came stalking out of the mirror on its own, and went about committing dreatful crimes, so that everybody thought it was him. At least, I think it was that, but I forget the details, it's so long ago. But what I shan't forget in a hurry is the fright it gave me to see that dretful figure come out of the mirror. It was that ghastly to see it, I cried and yelled, and after a time mother

had to take me out. For months and years after that I used to
dream of it. I'd dream I was looking in a great long glass, same
as the student in the picture, and after a bit I'd see my reflection smiling at me and I'd walk up to the mirror holding out
my left hand, it might be, and seeing myself walking to meet
me with its right hand out. And just as it came up to me, it
would suddenly—that was the awful moment—turn its back
on me and walk away into the mirror again, grinning over its
shoulder, and suddenly I'd know that *it* was the real person
and *I* was only the reflection, and I'd make a dash after it into
the mirror, and then everything would go grey and misty
round me and with the horror of it I'd wake up all of a perspi-
ration."

"Uncommonly disagreeable," said Wimsey. "That legend
of the *Doppelgänger*, it's one of the oldest and the most wide-
spread and never fails to terrify me. When *I* was a kid, my
nurse had a trick that frightened me. If we'd been out, and she
was asked if we'd met anybody, she used to say, 'Oh, no—we
saw nobody nicer than ourselves.' I used to toddle after her in
terror of coming round a corner and seeing a horrid and similar pair pouncing out at us. Of course I'd have rather died than
tell a soul how the thing terrified me. Rum little beasts, kids."

The little man nodded thoughtfully.

"Well," he went on, "about that time the nightmare came
back. At first it was only at intervals, you know, but it grew on
me. At last it started coming every night. I hadn't hardly
closed my eyes before there was the long mirror and the thing
coming grinning along, always with its hand out as if it meant
to catch hold of me and pull me through the glass. Sometimes
I'd wake up with the shock, but sometimes the dream went on,
and I'd be stumbling for hours through a queer sort of
world—all mist and half-lights, and the walls would be all
crooked like they are in that picture of *Dr. Caligari*. Lunatic,
that's what it was. Many's the time I've sat up all night for fear
of going to sleep. I didn't know, you see. I used to lock the
bedroom door and hide the key for fear—you see, I didn't

know what I might be doing. But then I read in a book that sleep-walkers can remember the places where they've hidden things when they were awake. So that was no use."

"Why didn't you get someone to share the room with you?"

"Well, I did." He hesitated. "I got a woman—she was a good kid. The dream went away then. I had blessed peace for three years. I was fond of that girl. Damned fond of her. Then she died."

He gulped down the last of his whisky and blinked.

"Influenza, it was. Pneumonia. It kind of broke me up. Pretty she was, too. . . .

"After that, I was alone again. I felt bad about it. I couldn't—I didn't like—but the dreams came back. Worse. I dreamed about doing things—well! That doesn't matter now.

"And one day it came in broad daylight . . .

"I was going along Holborn at lunch-time. I was still at Crichton's. Head of the packing department I was then, and doing pretty well. It was a wet beast of a day, I remember—dark and drizzling. I wanted a hair-cut. There's a barber's shop on the south side, about half-way along—one of those places where you go down a passage and there's a door at the end with a mirror and the name written across it in gold letters. You know what I mean.

"I went in there. There was a light in the passage, so I could see quite plainly. As I got up to the mirror I could see my reflection coming to meet me, and all of a sudden the awful dream-feeling came over me. I told myself it was all nonsense and put my hand out to the door-handle—my left hand, because the handle was that side and I was still apt to be left-handed when I didn't think about it.

"The reflection, of course, put out its right hand—that was all right, of course—and I saw my own figure in my old squash hat and burberry—but the face—oh, my God! It was grinning at me—and then just like in the dream, it suddenly turned its back and walked away from me, looking over its shoulder—

"I had my hand on the door, and it opened, and I felt myself stumbling and falling over the threshold.

"After that, I don't remember anything more. I woke up in my own bed and there was a doctor with me. He told me I had fainted in the street, and they'd found some letters on me with my address and taken me home.

"I told the doctor all about it, and he said I was in a highly nervous condition and ought to find a change of work and get out in the open air more.

"They were very decent to me at Crichton's. They put me on to inspecting their outdoor publicity. You know. One goes round from town to town inspecting the hoardings and seeing what posters are damaged or badly placed and reporting on them. They gave me a Morgan to run about in. I'm on that job now.

"The dreams are better. But I still have them. Only a few nights ago it came to me. One of the worst I've ever had. Fighting and strangling in a black, misty place. I'd tracked the devil—my other self—and got him down. I can feel my fingers on his throat now—killing myself.

"That was in London. I'm always worse in London. Then I came up here . . .

"You see why that book interested me. The fourth dimension . . . it's not a thing I ever heard of, but this man Wells seems to know all about it. You're educated now. Dare say you've been to college and all that. What do you think about it, eh?"

"I should think, you know," said Wimsey, "it was more likely your doctor was right. Nerves and all that."

"Yes, but that doesn't account for me having got twisted round the way I am, now, does it? Legends, you talked of. Well, there's some people think those medeeval johnnies knew quite a lot. I don't say I believe in devils and all that. But maybe some of them may have been afflicted, same as me. It stands to reason they wouldn't talk such a lot about it if they hadn't felt it, if you see what I mean. But what I'd like to know is, can't I get back any way? I tell you, it's a weight on my mind. I never know, you see."

"I shouldn't worry too much, if I were you," said Wimsey.

"I'd stick to the fresh-air life. And I'd get married. Then you'd have a check on your movements, don't you see. And the dreams might go again."

"Yes. Yes. I've thought of that. But—did you read about that man the other day? Strangled his wife in his sleep, that's what he did. Now, supposing I—that would be a terrible thing to happen to a man, wouldn't it? Those dreams . . ."

He shook his head and stared thoughtfully into the fire. Wimsey, after a short interval of silence, got up and went out into the bar. The landlady and the waiter and the barmaid were there, their heads close together over the evening paper. They were talking animatedly, but stopped abruptly at the sound of Wimsey's footsteps.

Ten minutes later, Wimsey returned to the lounge. The little man had gone. Taking up his motoring-coat, which he had flung on a chair, Wimsey went upstairs to his bedroom. He undressed slowly and thoughtfully, put on his pyjamas and dressing-gown, and then, pulling a copy of the *Evening News* from his motoring-coat pocket, he studied a front-page item attentively for some time. Presently he appeared to come to some decision, for he got up and opened his door cautiously. The passage was empty and dark. Wimsey switched on a torch and walked quietly along, watching the floor. Opposite one of the doors he stopped, contemplating a pair of shoes which stood waiting to be cleaned. Then he softly tried the door. It was locked. He tapped cautiously.

A red head emerged.

"May I come in a moment?" said Wimsey, in a whisper.

The little man stepped back, and Wimsey followed him in.

"What's up?" said Mr. Duckworthy.

"I want to talk to you," said Wimsey. "Get back into bed, because it may take some time."

The little man looked at him, scared, but did as he was told. Wimsey gathered the folds of his dressing-gown closely about him, screwed his monocle more firmly into his eye, and sat down on the edge of the bed. He looked at Mr. Duckworthy a few minutes without speaking, and then said:

"Look here. You've told me a queerish story tonight. For some reason I believe you. Possibly it only shows what a silly ass I am, but I was born like that, so it's past praying for. Nice, trusting nature and so on. Have you seen the paper this evening?"

He pushed the *Evening News* into Mr. Duckworthy's hand and bent the monocle on him more glassily than ever.

On the front page was a photograph. Underneath was a panel in bold type, boxed for greater emphasis:

> The police at Scotland Yard are anxious to get into touch with the original of this photograph, which was found in the handbag of Miss Jessie Haynes, whose dead body was found strangled on Barnes Common last Thursday morning. The photograph bears on the back the words "J. H. with love from R. D." Anybody recognizing the photograph is asked to communicate immediately with Scotland Yard or any police station.

Mr. Duckworthy looked, and grew so white that Wimsey thought he was going to faint.

"Well?" said Wimsey.

"Oh, God, sir! Oh, God! It's come at last." He whimpered and pushed the paper away, shuddering. "I've always known something of this would happen. But as sure as I'm born I knew nothing about it."

"It's you all right, I suppose?"

"The photograph's me all right. Though how it came there I *don't* know. I haven't had one taken for donkey's years, on my oath I haven't—except once in a staff group at Crichton's. But I tell you, sir, honest-to-God, there's times when I don't know what I'm doing, and that's a fact."

Wimsey examined the portrait feature by feature.

"Your nose, now—it has a slight twist—if you'll excuse my referring to it—to the right, and so it has in the photograph. The left eyelid droops a little. That's correct, too. The forehead here seems to have a distinct bulge on the left side—unless that's an accident in the printing."

"No!" Mr. Duckworthy swept his tousled cowlick aside. "It's very conspicuous—unsightly, I always think, so I wear the hair over it."

With the ginger lock pushed back, his resemblance to the photograph was more startling than before.

"My mouth's crooked, too."

"So it is. Slants up to the left. Very attractive, a one-sided smile, I always think—on a face of your type, that is. I have known such things to look positively sinister."

Mr. Duckworthy smiled a faint, crooked smile.

"Do you know this girl, Jessie Haynes?"

"Not in my right senses, I don't, sir. Never heard of her—except, of course, that I read about the murder in the papers. Strangled—oh, my God!" He pushed his hands out in front of him and stared woefully at them.

"What can I do? If I was to get away—"

"You can't. They've recognized you down in the bar. The police will probably be here in a few minutes. No"—as Duckworthy made an attempt to get out of bed—"don't do that. It's no good, and it would only get you into worse trouble. Keep quiet and answer one or two questions. First of all, do you know who I am? No, how should you? My name's Wimsey—Lord Peter Wimsey—"

"The detective?"

"If you like to call it that. Now, listen. Where was it you lived at Brixton?"

The little man gave the address.

"Your mother's dead. Any other relatives?"

"There was an aunt. She came from somewhere in Surrey, I think. Aunt Susan, I used to call her. I haven't seen her since I was a kid."

"Married?"

"Yes—oh, yes—Mrs. Susan Brown."

"Right. Were you left-handed as a child?"

"Well, yes, I was, at first. But mother broke me of it."

"And the tendency came back after the air-raid. And were you ever ill as a child? To have the doctor, I mean?"

"I had measles once, when I was about four."

"Remember the doctor's name?"

"They took me to the hospital."

"Oh, of course. Do you remember the name of the barber in Holborn?"

This question came so unexpectedly as to stagger the wits of Mr. Duckworthy, but after a while he said he thought it was Biggs or Briggs.

Wimsey sat thoughtfully for a moment, and then said:

"I think that's all. Except—oh, yes! What is your Christian name?"

"Robert."

"And you assure me that, so far as you know, you had no hand in this business?"

"That," said the little man, "that I swear to. As far as I know, you know. Oh, my Lord! If only it was possible to prove an alibi! That's my only chance. But I'm so afraid, you see, that I *may* have done it. Do you think—do you think they would hang me for that?"

"Not if you could prove you knew nothing about it," said Wimsey. He did not add that, even so, his acquaintance might probably pass the rest of his life at Broadmoor.

"And you know," said Mr. Duckworthy, "if I'm to go about all my life killing people without knowing it, it would be much better that they should hang me and done with it. It's a terrible thing to think of."

"Yes, but you may not have done it, you know."

"I hope not, I'm sure," said Mr. Duckworthy. "I say—what's that?"

"The police, I fancy," said Wimsey lightly. He stood up as a knock came at the door, and said heartily, "Come in!"

The landlord, who entered first, seemed rather taken aback by Wimsey's presence.

"Come right in," said Wimsey hospitably. "Come in, sergeant; come in, officer. What can we do for you?"

"Don't," said the landlord, "don't make a row if you can help it."

The police sergeant paid no attention to either of them, but stalked across to the bed and confronted the shrinking Mr. Duckworthy.

"It's the man all right," said he. "Now, Mr. Duckworthy, you'll excuse this late visit, but as you may have seen by the papers, we've been looking for a person answering your description, and there's no time like the present. We want—"

"I didn't do it," cried Mr. Duckworthy wildly. "I know nothing about it—"

The officer pulled out his note-book and wrote: "He said before any question was asked him, 'I didn't do it.' "

"You seem to know all about it," said the sergeant.

"Of course he does," said Wimsey; "we've been having a little informal chat about it."

"You have, have you? And who might you be—sir?" The last word appeared to be screwed out of the sergeant forcibly by the action of the monocle.

"I'm so sorry," said Wimsey, "I haven't a card on me at the moment. I am Lord Peter Wimsey."

"Oh, indeed," said the sergeant. "And may I ask, my lord, what you know about this here?"

"You may, and I may answer if I like, you know. I know nothing at all about the murder. About Mr. Duckworthy I know what he has told me and no more. I dare say he will tell you, too, if you ask him nicely. But no third degree, you know, sergeant. No Savidgery."

Baulked by this painful reminder, the sergeant said, in a voice of annoyance:

"It's my duty to ask him what he knows about this."

"I quite agree," said Wimsey. "As a good citizen, it's his duty to answer you. But it's a gloomy time of night, don't you think? Why not wait till the morning? Mr. Duckworthy won't run away."

"I'm not so sure of that."

"Oh, but I am. I will undertake to produce him whenever

you want him. Won't that do? You're not charging him with anything, I suppose?"

"Not yet," said the sergeant.

"Splendid. Then it's all quite friendly and pleasant, isn't it? How about a drink?"

The sergeant refused this kindly offer with some gruffness in his manner.

"On the wagon?" inquired Wimsey sympathetically. "Bad luck. Kidneys? Or liver, eh?"

The sergeant made no reply.

"Well, we are charmed to have had the pleasure of seeing you," pursued Wimsey. "You'll look us up in the morning, won't you? I've got to get back to town fairly early, but I'll drop in at the police-station on my way. You will find Mr. Duckworthy in the lounge, here. It will be more comfortable for you than at your place. Must you be going? Well, good night, all."

Later, Wimsey returned to Mr. Duckworthy, after seeing the police off the premises.

"Listen," he said, "I'm going up to town to do what I can. I'll send you up a solicitor first thing in the morning. Tell him what you've told me, and tell the police what he tells you to tell them and no more. Remember, they can't force you to say anything or to go down to the police-station unless they charge you. If they do charge you, go quietly and say nothing. And whatever you do, don't run away, because if you do, you're done for."

Wimsey arrived in town the following afternoon, and walked down Holborn, looking for a barber's shop. He found it without much difficulty. It lay, as Mr. Duckworthy had described it, at the end of a narrow passage, and it had a long mirror in the door, with the name Briggs scrawled across it in gold letters. Wimsey stared at his own reflection distastefully.

"Check number one," said he, mechanically setting his tie to rights. "Have I been led up the garden? Or is it a case of fourth dimensional mystery? 'The animals went in four by four, *vive la compagnie!* The camel he got stuck in the door.' There is something intensely unpleasant about making a camel of one's self. It goes for days without a drink and its table-manners are objectionable. But there is no doubt that this door is made of looking-glass. Was it always so, I wonder? On, Wimsey, on. I cannot bear to be shaved again. Perhaps a hair-cut might be managed."

He pushed the door open, keeping a stern eye on his reflection to see that it played him no trick.

Of his conversation with the barber, which was lively and varied, only one passage is deserving of record.

"It's some time since I was in here," said Wimsey. "Keep it short behind the ears. Been re-decorated, haven't you?"

"Yes, sir. Looks quite smart, doesn't it?"

"The mirror on the outside of the door—that's new, too, isn't it?"

"Oh, no, sir. That's been there ever since we took over."

"Has it! Then it's longer ago than I thought. Was it there three years ago?"

"Oh, yes, sir. Ten years Mr. Briggs has been here, sir."

"And the mirror too?"

"Oh, yes, sir."

"Then it's my memory that's wrong. Senile decay setting in. 'All, all are gone, the old familiar landmarks.' No, thanks, if I go grey I'll go grey decently. I don't want any hair-tonics today, thank you. No, nor even an electric comb. I've had shocks enough."

It worried him, though. So much so that when he emerged, he walked back a few yards along the street, and was suddenly struck by seeing the glass door of a tea-shop. It also lay at the end of a dark passage and had a gold name written across it. The name was "The Bridget Tea-shop," but the door was of plain glass. Wimsey looked at it for a few moments and then went in. He did not approach the tea-tables, but accosted the cashier, who sat at a little glass desk inside the door.

Here he went straight to the point and asked whether the

young lady remembered the circumstance of a man's having fainted in the doorway some years previously.

The cashier could not say; she had only been there three months, but she thought one of the waitresses might remember. The waitress was produced, and after some consideration, thought she did recollect something of the sort. Wimsey thanked her, said he was a journalist—which seemed to be accepted as an excuse for eccentric questions—parted with half a crown, and withdrew.

His next visit was to Carmelite House. Wimsey had friends in every newspaper office in Fleet Street, and made his way without difficulty to the room where photographs are filed for reference. The original of the "R. D." portrait was produced for his inspection.

"One of yours?" he asked.

"Oh, no. Sent out by Scotland Yard. Why? Anything wrong with it?"

"Nothing. I wanted the name of the original photographer, that's all."

"Oh! Well, you'll have to ask them there. Nothing more I can do for you?"

"Nothing, thanks."

Scotland Yard was easy. Chief-Inspector Parker was Wimsey's closest friend. An inquiry of him soon furnished the photographer's name, which was inscribed at the foot of the print. Wimsey voyaged off at once in search of the establishment, where his name readily secured an interview with the proprietor.

As he had expected, Scotland Yard had been there before him. All information at the disposal of the firm had already been given. It amounted to very little. The photograph had been taken a couple of years previously, and nothing particular was remembered about the sitter. It was a small establishment, doing a rapid business in cheap portraits, and with no pretensions to artistic refinements.

Wimsey asked to see the original negative, which, after some search, was produced.

Wimsey looked it over, laid it down, and pulled from his pocket the copy of the *Evening News* in which the print had appeared.

"Look at this," he said.

The proprietor looked, then looked back at the negative.

"Well, I'm dashed," he said. "That's funny."

"It was done in the enlarging lantern, I take it," said Wimsey.

"Yes. It must have been put in the wrong way round. Now, fancy that happening. You know, sir, we often have to work against time, and I suppose—but it's very careless. I shall have to inquire into it."

"Get me a print of it right way round," said Wimsey.

"Yes, sir, certainly, sir. At once."

"And send one to Scotland Yard."

"Yes, sir. Queer it should have been just this particular one, isn't it, sir? I wonder the party didn't notice. But we generally take three or four positions, and he might not remember, you know."

"You'd better see if you've got any other positions and let me have them too."

"I've done that already, sir, but there are none. No doubt this one was selected and the others destroyed. We don't keep all the rejected negatives, you know, sir. We haven't the space to file them. But I'll get three prints off at once."

"Do," said Wimsey. "The sooner the better. Quick-dry them. And don't do any work on the prints."

"No, sir. You shall have them in an hour or two, sir. But it's astonishing to me that the party didn't complain."

"It's not astonishing," said Wimsey. "He probably thought it the best likeness of the lot. And so it would be—to him. Don't you see—that's the only view he could ever take of his own face. That photograph, with the left and right sides reversed, is the face he sees in the mirror every day—the only face he can really recognize as his. 'Wad the gods the giftie gie us,' and all that."

"Well, that's quite true, sir. And I'm much obliged to you for pointing the mistake out."

Wimsey reiterated the need for haste, and departed. A brief visit to Somerset House followed; after which he called it a day and went home.

Inquiry in Brixton, in and about the address mentioned by Mr. Duckworthy, eventually put Wimsey on to the track of persons who had known him and his mother. An aged lady who had kept a small green-grocery in the same street for the last forty years remembered all about them. She had the encyclopaedic memory of the almost illiterate, and was positive as to the date of their arrival.

"Thirty-two years ago, if we lives another month," she said. "Michaelmas it was they come. She was a nice-looking young woman, too, and my daughter, as was expecting her first, took a lot of interest in the sweet little boy."

"The boy was not born here?"

"Why, no, sir. Born somewheres on the south side, he was, but I remember she never rightly said where—only that it was round about the New Cut. She was one of the quiet sort and kep' herself to herself. Never one to talk, she wasn't. Why even to my daughter, as might 'ave good reason for bein' interested, she wouldn't say much about 'ow she got through 'er bad time. Chlorryform she said she 'ad, I know, and she disremembered about it, but it's my belief it 'ad gone 'ard with 'er and she didn't care to think overmuch about it. 'Er 'usband—a nice man 'e was, too—'e says to me, 'Don't remind 'er of it, Mrs. 'Arbottle, don't remind 'er of it.' Whether she was frightened or whether she was 'urt by it I don't know, but she didn't 'ave no more children. 'Lor!' I says to 'er time and again, 'you'll get used to it, my dear, when you've 'ad nine of 'em same as me,' and she smiled, but she never 'ad no more, none the more for that."

"I suppose it does take some getting used to," said Wimsey, "but nine of them don't seem to have hurt *you*, Mrs. Harbottle, if I may say so. You look extremely flourishing."

"I keeps my 'ealth, sir, I am glad to say, though stouter than I used to be. Nine of them does 'ave a kind of spreading action on the figure. You wouldn't believe it, sir, to look at me now, as I 'ad a eighteen-inch waist when I was a girl. Many's the time me pore mother broke the laces on me, with 'er knee in me back and me 'oldin' on to the bedpost."

"One must suffer to be beautiful," said Wimsey politely. "How old was the baby, then, when Mrs. Duckworthy came to live in Brixton?"

"Three weeks old, 'e was, sir — a darling dear — and a lot of 'air on 'is 'ead. Black 'air it was then, but it turned into the brightest red you ever see — like them carrots there. It wasn't so pretty as 'is ma's, though much the same colour. He didn't favour 'er in the face, neither, nor yet 'is dad. She said 'e took after some of 'er side of the family."

"Did you ever see any of the rest of the family?"

"Only 'er sister, Mrs. Susan Brown. A big, stern, 'ard-faced woman she was — not like 'er sister. Lived at Evesham she did, as well I remembers, for I was getting my grass from there at the time. I never sees a bunch o' grass now but what I think of Mrs. Susan Brown. Stiff, she was, with a small 'ead, very like a stick o' grass."

Wimsey thanked Mrs. Harbottle in a suitable manner and took the next train to Evesham. He was beginning to wonder where the chase might lead him, but discovered, much to his relief, that Mrs. Susan Brown was well known in the town, being a pillar of the Methodist Chapel and a person well respected.

She was upright still, with smooth, dark hair parted in the middle and drawn tightly back — a woman broad in the base and narrow in the shoulder — not, indeed, unlike the stick of asparagus to which Mrs. Harbottle had compared her. She received Wimsey with stern civility, but disclaimed all knowledge of her nephew's movements. The hint that he was in a position of some embarrassment, and even danger, did not appear to surprise her.

"There was bad blood in him," she said. "My sister Hetty was softer by half than she ought to have been."

"Ah!" said Wimsey. "Well, we can't all be people of strong character, though it must be a source of great satisfaction to those that are. I don't want to be a trouble to you, madam, and I know I'm given to twaddling rather, being a trifle on the soft side myself—so I'll get to the point. I see by the register at Somerset House that your nephew, Robert Duckworthy, was born in Southwark, the son of Alfred and Hester Duckworthy. Wonderful system they have there. But of course—being only human—it breaks down now and again—doesn't it?"

She folded her wrinkled hands over one another on the edge of the table, and he saw a kind of shadow flicker over her sharp dark eyes.

"If I'm not bothering you too much—in what name was the other registered?"

The hands trembled a little, but she said steadily:

"I do not understand you."

"I'm frightfully sorry. Never was good at explaining myself. There were twin boys born, weren't there? Under what name did they register the other? I'm so sorry to be a nuisance, but it's really rather important."

"What makes you suppose that there were twins?"

"Oh, I don't suppose it. I wouldn't have bothered you for a supposition. I know there was a twin brother. What became—at least, I do know more or less what became of him—"

"It died," she said hurriedly.

"I hate to seem contradictory," said Wimsey. "Most unattractive behaviour. But it didn't die, you know. In fact, it's alive now. It's only the name I want to know, you know."

"And why should I tell you anything, young man?"

"Because," said Wimsey, "if you will pardon the mention of anything so disagreeable to a refined taste, there's been a murder committed and your nephew Robert is suspected. As a matter of fact, I happen to know that the murder was done by the brother. That's why I want to get hold of him, don't you see. It would be such a relief to my mind — I am naturally nice-minded — if you would help me to find him. Because, if not, I shall have to go to the police, and then you might be subpoena'd as a witness, and I shouldn't like — I really shouldn't like — to see you in the witness-box at a murder trial. So much unpleasant publicity, don't you know. Whereas, if we can lay hands on the brother quickly, you and Robert need never come into it at all."

Mrs. Brown sat in grim thought for a few minutes.

"Very well," she said, "I will tell you."

"Of course," said Wimsey to Chief-Inspector Parker a few days later, "the whole thing was quite obvious when one had heard about the reversal of friend Duckworthy's interior economy."

"No doubt, no doubt," said Parker. "Nothing could be simpler. But all the same, you are aching to tell me how you deduced it and I am willing to be instructed. Are all twins wrong-sided? And are all wrong-sided people twins?"

"Yes. No. Or rather, no, yes. Dissimilar twins and some kinds of similar twins may both be quite normal. But the kind of similar twins that result from the splitting of a single cell *may* come out as looking-glass twins. It depends on the line of fission in the original cell. You can do it artificially with tadpoles and a bit of horsehair."

"I will make a note to do it at once," said Parker gravely.

"In fact, I've read somewhere that a person with a reversed inside practically always turns out to be one of a pair of similar twins. So you see, while poor old R. D. was burbling on about *The Student of Prague* and the fourth dimension, I was expecting the twin-brother.

"Apparently what happened was this. There were three sisters of the name of Dart — Susan, Hester, and Emily. Susan married a man called Brown; Hester married a man called Duckworthy; Emily was unmarried. By one of those cheery little ironies of which life is so full, the only sister who had a baby, or who was apparently capable of having babies, was the unmarried Emily. By way of compensation, she overdid it and had twins.

"When this catastrophe was about to occur, Emily (deserted, of course, by the father) confided in her sisters, the parents being dead. Susan was a tartar—besides, she had married above her station and was climbing steadily on a ladder of good works. She delivered herself of a few texts and washed her hands of the business. Hester was a kind-hearted soul. She offered to adopt the infant, when produced, and bring it up as her own. Well, the baby came, and, as I said before, it was twins.

"That was a bit too much for Duckworthy. He had agreed to one baby, but twins were more than he had bargained for. Hester was allowed to pick her twin, and, being a kindly soul, she picked the weaklier-looking one, which was our Robert—the mirror-image twin. Emily had to keep the other and, as soon as she was strong enough, decamped with him to Australia, after which she was no more heard of.

"Emily's twin was registered in her own name of Dart and baptized Richard. Robert and Richard were two pretty men. Robert was registered as Hester Duckworthy's own child—there were no tiresome rules in those days requiring notification of births by doctors and midwives, and so one could do as one liked about these matters. The Duckworthys, complete with baby, moved to Brixton, where Robert was looked upon as being a perfectly genuine little Duckworthy.

"Apparently Emily died in Australia, and Richard, then a boy of fifteen, worked his passage home to London. He does not seem to have been a nice little boy. Two years afterwards, his path crossed that of Brother Robert and produced the episode of the air-raid night.

"Hester may have known about the wrong-sidedness of Robert, or she may not. Anyway, he wasn't told. I imagine that the shock of the explosion caused him to revert more strongly to his natural left-handed tendency. It also seems to have induced a new tendency to amnesia under similar shock-conditions. The whole thing preyed on his mind, and he became more and more vague and somnambulant.

"I rather think that Richard may have discovered the existence of his double and turned it to account. That explains the central incident of the mirror. I think Robert must have mistaken the glass door of the tea-shop for the door of the barber's shop. It really was Richard who came to meet him, and who retired again so hurriedly for fear of being seen and noted. Circumstances played into his hands, of course—but these meetings do take place, and the fact that they were both wearing soft hats and burberrys is not astonishing on a dark, wet day.

"And then there is the photograph. No doubt the original mistake was the photographer's, but I shouldn't be surprised if Richard welcomed it and chose that particular print on that account. Though that would mean, of course, that he knew about the wrong-sidedness of Robert. I don't know how he could have done that, but he may have had opportunities for inquiry. It was known in the Army, and rumours may have got round. But I won't press that point.

"There's one rather queer thing, and that is that Robert should have had that dream about strangling, on the very night, as far as one could make out, that Richard was engaged in doing away with Jessie Haynes. They say that similar twins are always in close sympathy with one another—that each knows what the other is thinking about, for instance, and contracts the same illness on the same day and all that. Richard was the stronger twin of the two, and perhaps he dominated Robert more than Robert did him. I'm sure I don't know. Dare say it's all bosh. The point is that you've found him all right."

"Yes. Once we'd got the clue there was no difficulty."

"Well, let's toddle round to the Cri and have one."

Wimsey got up and set his tie to rights before the glass.

"All the same," he said, "there's something queer about mirrors. Uncanny, a bit, don't you think so?"

THE INCREDIBLE ELOPEMENT OF
LORD PETER WIMSEY

That house, señor?" said the landlord of the little *posada*. "That is the house of the American physician, whose wife, may the blessed saints preserve us, is bewitched." He crossed himself, and so did his wife and daughter.

"Bewitched, is she?" said Langley sympathetically. He was a professor of ethnology, and this was not his first visit to the Pyrenees. He had, however, never before penetrated to any place quite so remote as this tiny hamlet, clinging, like a rock-plant, high up the scarred granite shoulders of the mountain. He scented material here for his book on Basque folk-lore. With tact, he might persuade the old man to tell his story.

"And in what manner," he asked, "is the lady bespelled?"

"Who knows?" replied the landlord, shrugging his shoulders. " 'The man that asked questions on Friday was buried on Saturday.' Will your honour consent to take his supper?"

Langley took the hint. To press the question would be to encounter obstinate silence. Later, when they knew him better, perhaps—

His dinner was served to him at the family table—the oily, pepper-flavoured stew to which he was so well accus-

tomed, and the harsh red wine of the country. His hosts chattered to him freely enough in that strange Basque language
which has no fellow in the world, and is said by some to be
the very speech of our first fathers in Paradise. They spoke of
the bad winter, and young Esteban Arramandy, so strong
and swift at the pelota, who had been lamed by a falling rock
and now halted on two sticks; of three valuable goats carried
off by a bear; of the torrential rains that, after a dry summer,
had scoured the bare ribs of the mountains. It was raining
now, and the wind was howling unpleasantly. This did not
trouble Langley; he knew and loved this haunted and impen-
etrable country at all times and seasons. Sitting in that rude
peasant inn, he thought of the oak-panelled hall of his Cambridge college and smiled, and his eyes gleamed happily
behind his scholarly pince-nez. He was a young man, in spite
of his professorship and the string of letters after his name.
To his university colleagues it seemed strange that this man,
so trim, so prim, so early old, should spend his vacations eating garlic, and scrambling on mule-back along precipitous
mountain-tracks. You would never think it, they said, to look
at him.

There was a knock at the door.

"That is Martha," said the wife.

She drew back the latch, letting in a rush of wind and rain
which made the candle gutter. A small, aged woman was
blown in out of the night, her grey hair straggling in wisps
from beneath her shawl.

"Come in, Martha, and rest yourself. It is a bad night. The
parcel is ready—oh, yes. Dominique brought it from the town
this morning. You must take a cup of wine or milk before you
go back."

The old woman thanked her and sat down, panting.

"And how goes all at the house? The doctor is well?"

"He is well."

"And *she?*"

The daughter put the question in a whisper, and the landlord shook his head at her with a frown.

"As always at this time of the year. It is but a month now to the Day of the Dead. Jesu-Maria! it is a grievous affliction for the poor gentleman, but he is patient, patient."

"He is a good man," said Dominique, "and a skilful doctor, but an evil like that is beyond his power to cure. You are not afraid, Martha?"

"Why should I be afraid? The Evil One cannot harm *me*. I have no beauty, no wits, no strength for him to envy. And the Holy Relic will protect me."

Her wrinkled fingers touched something in the bosom of her dress.

"You come from the house yonder?" asked Langley.

She eyed him suspiciously.

"The señor is not of our country?"

"The gentleman is a guest, Martha," said the landlord hurriedly. "A learned English gentleman. He knows our country and speaks our language as you hear. He is a great traveller, like the American doctor, your master."

"What is your master's name?" asked Langley. It occurred to him that an American doctor who had buried himself in this remote corner of Europe must have something unusual about him. Perhaps he also was an ethnologist. If so, they might find something in common.

"He is called Wetherall." She pronounced the name several times before he was sure of it.

"Wetherall? Not Standish Wetherall?"

He was filled with extraordinary excitement.

The landlord came to his assistance.

"This parcel is for him," he said. "No doubt the name will be written there."

It was a small package, neatly sealed, bearing the label of a firm of London chemists and addressed to "Standish Wetherall Esq., M.D."

"Good heavens!" exclaimed Langley. "But this is strange. Almost a miracle. I know this man. I knew his wife, too—"

He stopped. Again the company made the sign of the cross.

"Tell me," he said in great agitation, and forgetting his caution, "you say his wife is bewitched—afflicted—how is this? Is she the same woman I know? Describe her. She was tall, beautiful, with gold hair and blue eyes like the Madonna. Is this she?"

There was a silence. The old woman shook her head and muttered something inaudible, but the daughter whispered:

"True—it is true. Once we saw her thus, as the gentleman says—"

"Be quiet," said her father.

"Sir," said Martha, "we are in the hand of God."

She rose, and wrapped her shawl about her.

"One moment," said Langley. He pulled out his notebook and scribbled a few lines. "Will you take this letter to your master the doctor? It is to say that I am here, his friend whom he once knew, and to ask if I may come and visit him. That is all."

"You would not go to that house, excellence?" whispered the old man fearfully.

"If he will not have me, maybe he will come to me here." He added a word or two and drew a piece of money from his pocket. "You will carry my note for me?"

"Willingly, willingly. But the señor will be careful? Perhaps, though a foreigner, you are of the Faith?"

"I am a Christian," said Langley.

This seemed to satisfy her. She took the letter and the money, and secured them, together with the parcel, in a remote pocket. Then she walked to the door, strongly and rapidly for all her bent shoulders and appearance of great age.

Langley remained lost in thought. Nothing could have astonished him more than to meet the name of Standish Wetherall in this place. He had thought that episode finished and done with over three years ago. Of all people! The brilliant surgeon in the prime of his life and reputation, and Alice Wetherall, that delicate piece of golden womanhood—exiled in this forlorn corner of the world! His heart beat a little faster at the thought of seeing her again. Three years ago, he had decided that it would be wiser if he did not see too much of that porcelain loveliness. That folly was past now — but still he could not visualize her except against the background of the great white house in Riverside Drive, with the peacocks and the swimming-pool and the gilded tower with the roof-garden. Wetherall was a rich man, the son of old Hiram Wetherall the automobile magnate. What was Wetherall doing here?

He tried to remember. Hiram Wetherall, he knew, was dead, and all the money belonged to Standish, for there were no other children. There had been trouble when the only son had married a girl without parents or history. He had brought her from "somewhere out west." There had been some story of his having found her, years before, as a neglected orphan, and saved her from something or cured her of something and paid for her education, when he was still scarcely more than a student. Then, when he was a man over forty and she a girl of seventeen, he had brought her home and married her.

And now he had left his house and his money and one of the finest specialist practices in New York to come to live in the Basque country — in a spot so out of the way that men still believed in Black Magic, and could barely splutter more than a few words of bastard French or Spanish — a spot that was uncivilized even by comparison with the primitive civilization surrounding it. Langley began to be sorry that he had written to Wetherall. It might be resented.

The landlord and his wife had gone out to see to their cattle. The daughter sat close to the fire, mending a garment. She did not look at him, but he had the feeling that she would be glad to speak.

"Tell me, child," he said gently, "what is the trouble which afflicts these people who may be friends of mine?"

"Oh!" She glanced up quickly and leaned across to him, her arms stretched out over the sewing in her lap. "Sir, be advised. Do not go up there. No one will stay in that house at this time of the year, except Tomaso, who has not all his wits, and old Martha, who is — "

"What?"

"A saint—or something else," she said hurriedly.

"Child," said Langley again, "this lady when I knew—"

"I will tell you," she said, "but my father must not know. The good doctor brought her here three years ago last June, and then she was as you say. She was beautiful. She laughed and talked in her own speech—for she knew no Spanish or Basque. But on the Night of the Dead—"

She crossed herself.

"All-Hallows Eve," said Langley softly.

"Indeed, I do not know what happened. But she fell into the power of the darkness. She changed. There were terrible cries—I cannot tell. But little by little she became what she is now. Nobody sees her but Martha and she will not talk. But the people say it is not a woman at all that lives there now."

"Mad?" said Langley.

"It is not madness. It is—enchantment. Listen. Two years since on Easter Day—is that my father?"

"No, no."

"The sun had shone and the wind came up from the valley. We heard the blessed church bells all day long. That night there came a knock at the door. My father opened and one stood there like Our Blessed Lady herself, very pale like the image in the church and with a blue cloak over her head. She spoke, but we could not tell what she said. She wept and wrung her hands and pointed down the valley path, and my father went to the stable and saddled the mule. I thought of the flight from bad King Herod. But then—the American doctor came. He had run fast and was out of breath. And she shrieked at sight of him."

A great wave of indignation swept over Langley. If the man was brutal to his wife, something must be done quickly. The girl hurried on.

"He said—Jesu-Maria—he said that his wife was bewitched. At Easter-tide the power of the Evil One was broken and she would try to flee. But as soon as the Holy Season was over, the spell would fall on her again, and therefore it was not safe to let her go. My parents were afraid to have touched the evil thing. They brought out the Holy Water and sprinkled the mule, but the wickedness had entered into the poor beast and she kicked my father so that he was lame for a month. The American took his wife away with him and we never saw her again. Even old Martha does not always see her. But every year the power waxes and wanes—heaviest at Hallow-tide and lifted again at Easter. Do not go to that house, señor, if you value your soul! Hush! they are coming back."

Langley would have liked to ask more, but his host glanced quickly and suspiciously at the girl. Taking up his candle, Langley went to bed. He dreamed of wolves, long, lean, and black, running on the scent of blood.

Next day brought an answer to his letter:

DEAR LANGLEY, Yes, this is myself, and of course I remember you well. Only too delighted to have you come and cheer our exile. You will find Alice somewhat changed, I fear, but I will explain our misfortunes when we meet. Our household is limited, owing to some kind of superstitious avoidance of the afflicted, but if you will come along about half past seven, we can give you a meal of sorts. Martha will show you the way.

CORDIALLY,
STANDISH WETHERALL

The doctor's house was small and old, stuck halfway up the mountain-side on a kind of ledge in the rock-wall. A stream, unseen but clamorous, fell echoing down close at hand. Langley followed his guide into a dim, square room with a great hearth at one end and, drawn close before the fire, an armchair with wide, sheltering ears. Martha, muttering some sort of apology, hobbled away and left him standing there in the half-light. The flames of the wood fire, leaping and falling, made here a gleam and there a gleam, and, as his eyes grew familiar with the room, he saw that in the centre was a table laid for a meal, and that there were pictures on the walls. One of these struck a familiar note. He went close to it and recognized a portrait of Alice Wetherall that he had last seen in New York. It was painted by Sargent in his happiest mood, and the lovely wildflower face seemed to lean down to him with the sparkling smile of life.

A log suddenly broke and fell in the hearth, flaring. As though the little noise and light had disturbed something, he heard, or thought he heard, a movement from the big chair before the fire. He stepped forward, and then stopped. There was nothing to be seen, but a noise had begun; a kind of low, animal muttering, extremely disagreeable to listen to. It was not made by a dog or a cat, he felt sure. It was a sucking, slobbering sound that affected him in a curiously sickening way. It ended in a series of little grunts or squeals, and then there was silence.

Langley stepped backwards towards the door. He was positive that something was in the room with him that he did not care about meeting. An absurd impulse seized him to run away. He was prevented by the arrival of Martha, carrying a big, old-fashioned lamp, and behind her, Wetherall, who greeted him cheerfully.

The familiar American accents dispelled the atmosphere of discomfort that had been gathering about Langley. He held out a cordial hand.

"Fancy meeting *you* here," said he.

"The world is very small," replied Wetherall. "I am afraid that is a hardy bromide, but I certainly am pleased to see you," he added, with some emphasis.

The old woman had put the lamp on the table, and now asked if she should bring in the dinner. Wetherall replied in the affirmative, using a mixture of Spanish and Basque which she seemed to understand well enough.

"I didn't know you were a Basque scholar," said Langley.

"Oh, one picks it up. These people speak nothing else. But of course Basque is your specialty, isn't it?"

"Oh, yes."

"I dare say they have told you some queer things about us. But we'll go into that later. I've managed to make the place reasonably comfortable, though. I could do with a few more modern conveniences. However, it suits us."

Langley took the opportunity to mumble some sort of inquiry about Mrs. Wetherall.

"Alice? Ah, yes, I forgot—you have not seen her yet." Wetherall looked hard at him with a kind of half-smile. "I should have warned you. You were—rather an admirer of my wife in the old days."

"Like everyone else," said Langley.

"No doubt. Nothing specially surprising about it, was there? Here comes dinner. Put it down, Martha, and we will ring when we are ready."

The old woman set down a dish upon the table, which was handsomely furnished with glass and silver, and went out. Wetherall moved over to the fireplace, stepping sideways and keeping his eyes oddly fixed on Langley. Then he addressed the armchair.

"Alice! Get up, my dear, and welcome an old admirer of yours. Come along. You will both enjoy it. Get up."

Something shuffled and whimpered among the cushions. Wetherall stooped, with an air of almost exaggerated courtesy, and lifted it to its feet. A moment, and it faced Langley in the lamplight.

It was dressed in a rich gown of gold satin and lace, that hung rucked and crumpled upon the thick and slouching body. The face was white and puffy, the eyes vacant, the mouth drooled open, with little trickles of saliva running from the loose corners. A dry fringe of rusty hair clung to the half-bald scalp, like the dead wisps on the head of a mummy.

"Come, my love," said Wetherall. "Say how do you do to Mr. Langley."

The creature blinked and mouthed out some inhuman sounds. Wetherall put his hand under its forearm, and it slowly extended a lifeless paw.

"There, she recognized you all right. I thought she would. Shake hands with him, my dear."

With a sensation of nausea, Langley took the inert hand. It was clammy and coarse to the touch and made no attempt to return his pressure. He let it go; it pawed vaguely in the air for a moment and then dropped.

"I was afraid you might be upset," said Wetherall, watching him. "I have grown used to it, of course, and it doesn't affect me as it would an outsider. Not that you are an outsider—anything but that—eh? Premature senility is the lay name for it, I suppose. Shocking, of course, if you haven't met it before. You needn't mind, by the way, what you say. She understands nothing."

"How did it happen?"

"I don't quite know. Came on gradually. I took the best advice, naturally, but there was nothing to be done. So we came here. I didn't care about facing things at home where everybody knew us. And I didn't like the idea of a sanatorium. Alice is my wife, you know—sickness or health, for better, for worse, and all that. Come along; dinner's getting cold."

He advanced to the table, leading his wife, whose dim eyes seemed to brighten a little at the sight of food.

"Sit down, my dear, and eat your nice dinner. (She understands that, you see.) You'll excuse her table-manners, won't you? They're not pretty, but you'll get used to them."

He tied a napkin round the neck of the creature and placed food before her in a deep bowl. She snatched at it hungrily, slavering and gobbling as she scooped it up in her fingers and smeared face and hands with the gravy.

Wetherall drew out a chair for his guest opposite to where his wife sat. The sight of her held Langley with a kind of disgusted fascination.

The food—a sort of salmis—was deliciously cooked, but Langley had no appetite. The whole thing was an outrage, to the pitiful woman and to himself. Her seat was directly beneath the Sargent portrait, and his eyes went helplessly from the one to the other.

"Yes," said Wetherall, following his glance. "There is a difference, isn't there?" He himself was eating heartily and apparently enjoying his dinner. "Nature plays sad tricks upon us."

"Is it always like this?"

"No; this is one of her bad days. At times she will be almost human. Of course these people here don't know what to think of it all. They have their own explanation of a very simple medical phenomenon."

"Is there any hope of recovery?"

"I'm afraid not—not of a permanent cure. You are not eating anything."

"I—well, Wetherall, this has been a shock to me."

"Of course. Try a glass of burgundy. I ought not to have asked you to come, but the idea of talking to an educated fellow-creature once again tempted me, I must confess."

"It must be terrible for you."

"I have become resigned. Ah, naughty, naughty!" The idiot had flung half the contents of her bowl upon the table. Wetherall patiently remedied the disaster, and went on:

"I can bear it better here, in this wild place where everything seems possible and nothing unnatural. My people are all dead, so there was nothing to prevent me from doing as I liked about it."

"No. What about your property in the States?"

"Oh, I run over from time to time to keep an eye on things. In fact, I am due to sail next month. I'm glad you caught me. Nobody over there knows how we're fixed, of course. They just know we're living in Europe."

"Did you consult no American doctor?"

"No. We were in Paris when the first symptoms declared themselves. That was shortly after that visit you paid to us." A flash of some emotion to which Langley could not put a name made the doctor's eyes for a moment sinister. "The best men on this side confirmed my own diagnosis. So we came here."

He rang for Martha, who removed the salmis and put on a kind of sweet pudding.

"Martha is my right hand," observed Wetherall. "I don't know what we shall do without her. When I am away, she looks after Alice like a mother. Not that there's much one can do for her, except to keep her fed and warm and clean—and the last is something of a task."

There was a note in his voice which jarred on Langley. Wetherall noticed his recoil and said:

"I won't disguise from you that it gets on my nerves sometimes. But it can't be helped. Tell me about yourself. What have you been doing lately?"

Langley replied with as much vivacity as he could assume, and they talked of indifferent subjects till the deplorable being which had once been Alice Wetherall began to mumble and whine fretfully and scramble down from her chair.

"She's cold," said Wetherall. "Go back to the fire, my dear."

He propelled her briskly towards the hearth, and she sank back into the armchair, crouching and complaining and thrusting out her hands towards the blaze. Wetherall brought out brandy and a box of cigars.

"I contrive just to keep in touch with the world, you see," he said. "They send me these from London. And I get the latest medical journals and reports. I'm writing a book, you know, on my own subject; so I don't vegetate. I can experiment, too—plenty of room for a laboratory, and no Vivisection Acts to bother me. It's a good country to work in. Are you staying here long?"

"I think not very."

"Oh! If you had thought of stopping on, I would have offered you the use of this house while I was away. You would find it more comfortable than the *posada*, and I should have no qualms, you know, about leaving you alone in the place with my wife—under the peculiar circumstances."

He stressed the last words and laughed. Langley hardly knew what to say.

"Really, Wetherall —"

"Though, in the old days, *you* might have liked the prospect more and *I* might have liked it less. There was a time, I think, Langley, when you would have jumped at the idea of living alone with — *my wife*."

Langley jumped up.

"What the devil are you insinuating, Wetherall?"

"Nothing, nothing. I was just thinking of the afternoon when you and she wandered away at a picnic and got lost. You remember? Yes, I thought you would."

"This is monstrous," retorted Langley. "How dare you say such things — with that poor soul sitting there — ?"

"Yes, poor soul. You're a poor thing to look at now, aren't you, my kitten?"

He turned suddenly to the woman. Something in his abrupt gesture seemed to frighten her, and she shrank away from him.

"You devil!" cried Langley. "She's afraid of you. What have you been doing to her? How did she get into this state? I *will* know!"

"Gently," said Wetherall. "I can allow for your natural agitation at finding her like this, but I can't have you coming between me and *my wife*. What a faithful fellow you are, Langley. I believe you still want her — just as you did before when you thought I was dumb and blind. Come now, have you got designs on *my wife*, Langley? Would you like to kiss her, caress her, take her to bed with you — my beautiful wife?"

A scarlet fury blinded Langley. He dashed an inexpert fist at the mocking face. Wetherall gripped his arm, but he broke away. Panic seized him. He fled stumbling against the furniture and rushed out. As he went he heard Wetherall very softly laughing.

The train to Paris was crowded. Langley, scrambling in at the last moment, found himself condemned to the corridor. He sat down on a suitcase and tried to think. He had not been able to collect his thoughts on his wild flight. Even now, he was not quite sure what he had fled from. He buried his head in his hands.

"Excuse me," said a polite voice.

Langley looked up. A fair man in a grey suit was looking down at him through a monocle.

"Fearfully sorry to disturb you," went on the fair man. "I'm just tryin' to barge back to my jolly old kennel. Ghastly crowd, isn't it? Don't know when I've disliked my fellow-creatures more. I say, you don't look frightfully fit. Wouldn't you be better on something more comfortable?"

Langley explained that he had not been able to get a seat. The fair man eyed his haggard and unshaven countenance for a moment and then said:

"Well, look here, why not come and lay yourself down in my bin for a bit? Have you had any grub? No? That's a mistake. Toddle along with me and we'll get hold of a spot of soup and so on. You'll excuse my mentioning it, but you look as if you'd been backing a system that's come unstuck, or something. Not my business, of course, but do have something to eat."

Langley was too faint and sick to protest. He stumbled obediently along the corridor till he was pushed into a first-class sleeper, where a rigidly correct manservant was laying out a pair of mauve silk pyjamas and a set of silver-mounted brushes.

"This gentleman's feeling rotten, Bunter," said the man with the monocle, "so I've brought him in to rest his aching head upon thy breast. Get hold of the commissariat and tell 'em to buzz a plate of soup along and a bottle of something drinkable."

"Very good, my lord."

Langley dropped, exhausted, on the bed, but when the food appeared he ate and drank greedily. He could not remember when he had last made a meal.

"I say," he said, "I wanted that. It's awfully decent of you. I'm sorry to appear so stupid. I've had a bit of a shock."

"Tell me all," said the stranger pleasantly.

The man did not look particularly intelligent, but he seemed friendly and, above all, normal. Langley wondered how the story would sound.

"I'm an absolute stranger to you," he began.

"And I to you," said the fair man. "The chief use of strangers is to tell things to. Don't you agree?"

"I'd like—" said Langley. "The fact is, I've run away from something. It's queer—it's—but what's the use of bothering you with it?"

The fair man sat down beside him and laid a slim hand on his arm.

"Just a moment," he said. "Don't tell me anything if you'd rather not. But my name is Wimsey—Lord Peter Wimsey— and I am interested in queer things."

It was the middle of November when the strange man came to the village. Thin, pale, and silent, with his great black hood flapping about his face, he was surrounded with an atmosphere of mystery from the start. He settled down, not at the inn, but in a dilapidated cottage high up in the mountains, and he brought with him five mule-loads of mysterious baggage and a servant. The servant was almost as uncanny as the master; he was a Spaniard and spoke Basque well enough to act as an interpreter for his employer when necessary; but his words were few, his aspect gloomy and stern, and such brief information as he vouchsafed, disquieting in the extreme. His master, he said, was a wise man; he spent all his time reading books; he ate no flesh; he was of no known country; he spoke the language of the Apostles and had talked with blessed Lazarus after his return from the grave; and when he sat alone in his chamber by night, the angels of God came and conversed with him in celestial harmonies.

This was terrifying news. The few dozen villagers avoided the little cottage, especially at night-time; and when the pale stranger was seen coming down the mountain path, folded in his black robe and bearing one of his magic tomes beneath his arm, the women pushed their children within doors, and made the sign of the cross.

Nevertheless, it was a child that first made the personal acquaintance of the magician. The small son of the Widow

Etcheverry, a child of bold and inquisitive disposition, went
one evening adventuring into the unhallowed neighbourhood.
He was missing for two hours, during which his mother, in a
frenzy of anxiety, had called the neighbours about her and
summoned the priest, who had unhappily been called away on
business to the town. Suddenly, however, the child reappeared, well and cheerful, with a strange story to tell.

He had crept up close to the magician's house (the bold,
wicked child, did ever you hear the like?) and climbed into a
tree to spy upon the stranger (Jesu-Maria!). And he saw a
light in the window, and strange shapes moving about and
shadows going to and fro within the room. And then there
came a strain of music so ravishing it drew the very heart out
of his body, as though all the stars were singing together. (Oh,
my precious treasure! The wizard has stolen the heart out of
him, alas! alas!) Then the cottage door opened and the wizard
came out and with him a great company of familiar spirits.
One of them had wings like a seraph and talked in an
unknown tongue, and another was like a wee man, no higher
than your knee, with a black face and a white beard, and he
sat on the wizard's shoulder and whispered in his ear. And the
heavenly music played louder and louder. And the wizard had
a pale flame all about his head, like the pictures of the saints.
(Blessed St. James of Compostela, be merciful to us all! And
what then?) Why then he, the boy, had been very much
frightened and wished he had not come, but the little dwarf
spirit had seen him and jumped into the tree after him, climbing—oh! so fast! And he had tried to climb higher and had
slipped and fallen to the ground. (Oh, the poor, wicked, brave,
bad boy!)

Then the wizard had come and picked him up and spoken
strange words to him and all the pain had gone away from the
places where he had bumped himself (Marvellous! marvellous!) and he had carried him into the house. And inside, it
was like the streets of Heaven, all gold and glittering. And the
familiar spirits had sat beside the fire, nine in number, and the
music had stopped playing. But the wizard's servant had

brought him marvellous fruits in a silver dish, like fruits of Paradise, very sweet and delicious, and he had eaten them, and drunk a strange, rich drink from a goblet covered with red and blue jewels. Oh, yes—and there had been a tall crucifix on the wall, big, big, with a lamp burning before it and a strange sweet perfume like the smell in church on Easter Day.

(A crucifix? That was strange. Perhaps the magician was not so wicked, after all. And what next?)

Next, the wizard's servant had told him not to be afraid, and had asked his name and his age and whether he could repeat his Paternoster. So he had said that prayer and the Ave Maria and part of the Credo, but the Credo was long and he had forgotten what came after *"ascendit in coelum."* So the wizard had prompted him and they had finished saying it together. And the wizard had pronounced the sacred names and words without flinching and in the right order, so far as he could tell. And then the servant had asked further about himself and his family, and he had told about the death of the black goat and about his sister's lover, who had left her because she had not so much money as the merchant's daughter. Then the wizard and his servant had spoken together and laughed, and the servant had said: "My master gives this message to your sister: that where there is no love there is no wealth, but he that is bold shall have gold for the asking." And with that, the wizard had put forth his hand into the air and taken from it—out of the empty air, yes, truly—one, two, three, four, five pieces of money and given them to him. And he was afraid to take them till he had made the sign of the cross upon them, and then, as they did not vanish or turn into fiery serpents, he had taken them, and here they were!

So the gold pieces were examined and admired in fear and trembling, and then, by grandfather's advice, placed under the feet of the image of Our Lady, after a sprinkling with Holy Water for their better purification. And on the next morning, as they were still there, they were shown to the priest, who arrived, tardy and flustered upon his last night's summons, and by him pronounced to be good Spanish coin, whereof one piece being devoted to the Church to put all right with Heaven, the rest might be put to secular uses without peril to the soul. After which, the good padre made his hasty way to the cottage, and returned, after an hour, filled with good reports of the wizard.

"For, my children," said he, "this is no evil sorcerer, but a Christian man, speaking the language of the Faith. He and I have conversed together with edification. Moreover, he keeps very good wine and is altogether a very worthy person. Nor did I perceive any familiar spirits or flaming apparitions; but it is true that there is a crucifix and also a very handsome Testament with pictures in gold and colour. *Benedicite*, my children. This is a good and learned man."

And away he went back to his presbytery; and that winter the chapel of Our Lady had a new altar-cloth.

After that, each night saw a little group of people clustered at a safe distance to hear the music which poured out from the wizard's windows, and from time to time a few bold spirits would creep up close enough to peer through the chinks of the shutters and glimpse the marvels within.

The wizard had been in residence about a month, and sat one night after his evening meal in conversation with his servant. The black hood was pushed back from his head, disclosing a sleek poll of fair hair, and a pair of rather humorous grey eyes, with a cynical droop of the lids. A glass of Cockburn 1908 stood on the table at his elbow and from the arm of his chair a red-and-green parrot gazed unwinkingly at the fire.

"Time is getting on, Juan," said the magician. "This business is very good fun and all that—but is there anything doing with the old lady?"

"I think so, my lord. I have dropped a word or two here and there of marvellous cures and miracles. I think she will come. Perhaps even tonight."

"Thank goodness! I want to get the thing over before Wetherall comes back, or we may find ourselves in Queer Street. It will take some weeks, you know, before we are ready to move, even if the scheme works at all. Damn it, what's that?"

Juan rose and went into the inner room, to return in a minute carrying the lemur.

"Micky had been playing with your hair-brushes," he said indulgently, "Naughty one, be quiet! Are you ready for a little practice, my lord?"

"Oh, rather, yes! I'm getting quite a dab at this job. If all else fails, I shall try for an engagement with Maskelyne."

Juan laughed, showing his white teeth. He brought out a set of billiard-balls, coins, and other conjuring apparatus, palming and multiplying them negligently as he went. The other took them from him, and the lesson proceeded.

"Hush!" said the wizard, retrieving a ball which had tiresomely slipped from his fingers in the very act of vanishing. "There's somebody coming up the path."

He pulled his robe about his face and slipped silently into the inner room. Juan grinned, removed the decanter and glasses and extinguished the lamp. In the firelight the great eyes of the lemur gleamed strongly as it hung on the back of the high chair. Juan pulled a large folio from the shelf, lit a scented pastille in a curiously shaped copper vase, and pulled forward a heavy iron cauldron which stood on the hearth. As he piled the logs about it, there came a knock. He opened the door, the lemur running at his heels.

"Whom do you seek, mother?" he asked, in Basque.

"Is the Wise One at home?"

"His body is at home, mother; his spirit holds converse with the unseen. Enter. What would you with us?"

"I have come, as I said—ah, Mary! Is that a spirit?"

"God made spirits and bodies also. Enter and fear not."

The old woman came tremblingly forward.

"Hast thou spoken with him of what I told thee?"

"I have. I have shown him the sickness of thy mistress— her husband's sufferings—all."

"What said he?"

"Nothing; he read in his book."

"Think you he can heal her?"

"I do not know; the enchantment is a strong one; but my master is mighty for good."

"Will he see me?"

"I will ask him. Remain here, and beware thou show no fear, whatever befall."

"I will be courageous," said the old woman, fingering her beads.

Juan withdrew. There was a nerve-shattering interval. The lemur had climbed up to the back of the chair again and swung, teeth-chattering, among the leaping shadows. The parrot cocked his head and spoke a few gruff words from his corner. An aromatic steam began to rise from the cauldron. Then, slowly into the red light, three, four, seven white shapes came stealthily and sat down in a circle about the hearth. Then, a faint music, that seemed to roll in from leagues away. The flame flickered and dropped. There was a tall cabinet against the wall, with gold figures on it that seemed to move with the moving firelight.

Then, out of the darkness, a strange voice chanted in an unearthly tongue that sobbed and thundered.

Martha's knees gave under her. She sank down. The seven white cats rose and stretched themselves, and came sidling slowly about her. She looked up and saw the wizard standing before her, a book in one hand and a silver wand in the other. The upper part of his face was hidden, but she saw his pale lips move and presently he spoke, in a deep, husky tone that vibrated solemnly in the dim room:

"ὦ πέπον, εἰ μὲν γὰρ πόλεμον περ ὶ τόνδε φυγόντε,
αἰεὶ δὴ μέλλοιμεν ἀγήρω τ' ἀθανάτω τε
ἔσσεσθ', οὔτε κεν αὐτὸς ἐνὶ πρώτοισι μαχοίμην,
οὔτε κε σὲ στέλλοιμι μάχην ἐς κυδιάνειραν . . ."

The great syllables went rolling on. Then the wizard paused and added, in a kinder tone:

"Great stuff, this Homer. 'It goes so thunderingly as though it conjured devils.' What do I do next?"

The servant had come back, and now whispered in Martha's ear.

"Speak now," said he. "The master is willing to help you."

Thus encouraged, Martha stammered out her request. She had come to ask the Wise Man to help her mistress, who lay under an enchantment. She had brought an offering—the best she could find, for she had not liked to take anything of her master's during his absence. But here were a silver penny, an oat-cake, and a bottle of wine, very much at the wizard's service, if such small matters could please him.

The wizard, setting aside his book, gravely accepted the silver penny, turned it magically into six gold pieces, and laid the offering on the table. Over the oat-cake and the wine he showed a little hesitation, but at length, murmuring:

"Ergo omnis longo solvit se Teucria luctu"

(a line notorious for its grave spondaic cadence), he metamorphosed the one into a pair of pigeons and the other into a curious little crystal tree in a metal pot, and set them beside the coins. Martha's eyes nearly started from her head, but Juan whispered encouragingly:

"The good intention gives value to the gift. The master is pleased. Hush!"

The music ceased on a loud chord. The wizard, speaking now with greater assurance, delivered himself with fair accuracy of a page or so from Homer's Catalogue of the Ships, and, drawing from the folds of his robe his long white hand laden with antique rings, produced from mid-air a small casket of shining metal, which he proffered to the suppliant.

"The master says," prompted the servant, "that you shall take this casket, and give to your lady of the wafers which it contains, one at every meal. When all have been consumed, seek this place again. And remember to say three Aves and two Paters morning and evening for the intention of the lady's health. Thus, by faith and diligence, the cure may be accomplished."

Martha received the casket with trembling hands.

"Tendebantque manus ripae ulterioris amore," said the wizard, with emphasis. *"Poluphloisboio thalasses. Ne plus ultra. Valete. Plaudite."*

He stalked away into the darkness, and the audience was over.

"It is working, then?" said the wizard to Juan.

The time was five weeks later, and five more consignments of enchanted wafers had been ceremoniously dispatched to the grim house on the mountain.

"It is working," agreed Juan. "The intelligence is returning, the body is becoming livelier, and the hair is growing again."

"Thank the Lord! It was a shot in the dark, Juan, and even now I can hardly believe that anyone in the world could think of such a devilish trick. When does Wetherall return?"

"In three weeks' time."

"Then we had better fix our grand finale for today fortnight. See that the mules are ready, and go down to the town and get a message off to the yacht."

"Yes, my lord."

"That will give you a week to get clear with the menagerie and the baggage. And—I say, how about Martha? Is it dangerous to leave her behind, do you think?"

"I will try to persuade her to come back with us."

"Do. I should hate anything unpleasant to happen to her. The man's a criminal lunatic. Oh, Lord! I'll be glad when this is over. I want to get into a proper suit of clothes again. What Bunter would say if he saw this—"

The wizard laughed, lit a cigar, and turned on the gramophone.

The last act was duly staged a fortnight later.

It had taken some trouble to persuade Martha of the necessity of bringing her mistress to the wizard's house.

Indeed, that supernatural personage had been obliged to make an alarming display of wrath and declaim two whole choruses from Euripides before gaining his point. The final touch was put to the terrors of the evening by a demonstration of the ghastly effects of a sodium flame—which lends a very corpse-like aspect to the human countenance, particularly in a lonely cottage on a dark night, and accompanied by incantations and the *Danse Macabre* of Saint-Saëns.

Eventually the wizard was placated by a promise, and Martha departed, bearing with her a charm, engrossed upon parchment, which her mistress was to read and thereafter hang about her neck in a white silk bag.

Considered as a magical formula, the document was perhaps a little unimpressive in its language, but its meaning was such as a child could understand. It was in English, and ran:

> You have been ill and in trouble, but your friends are ready to cure you and help you. Don't be afraid, but do whatever Martha tells you, and you will soon be quite well and happy again.

"And even if she can't understand it," said the wizard to his man, "it can't possibly do any harm."

The events of that terrible night have become legend in the village. They tell by the fireside with bated breath how Martha brought the strange, foreign lady to the wizard's house, that she might be finally and for ever freed from the power of the Evil One. It was a dark night and a stormy one, with the wind howling terribly through the mountains.

The lady had become much better and brighter through the wizard's magic—though this, perhaps, was only a fresh glamour and delusion—and she had followed Martha like a little child on that strange and secret journey. They had crept out very quietly to elude the vigilance of old Tomaso, who had strict orders from the doctor never to let the lady stir one step from the house. As for that, Tomaso swore that he had

been cast into an enchanted sleep—but who knows? There
may have been no more to it than over-much wine. Martha
was a cunning woman, and, some said, little better than a
witch herself.

Be that as it might, Martha and the lady had come to the
cottage, and there the wizard had spoken many things in a
strange tongue, and the lady had spoken likewise. Yes—she
who for so long had only grunted like a beast, had talked with
the wizard and answered him. Then the wizard had drawn
strange signs upon the floor round about the lady and himself.
And when the lamp was extinguished, the signs glowed
awfully, with a pale light of their own. The wizard also drew a
circle about Martha herself, and warned her to keep inside it.
Presently they heard a rushing noise, like great wings beating,
and all the familiars leaped about, and the little white man
with the black face ran up the curtain and swung from the
pole. Then a voice cried out: "He comes! He comes!" and the
wizard opened the door of the tall cabinet with gold images
upon it, that stood in the centre of the circle, and he and the
lady stepped inside it and shut the doors after them.

The rushing sound grew louder and the familiar spirits
screamed and chattered—and then, all of a sudden, there was
a thunder-clap and a great flash of light and the cabinet was
shivered into pieces and fell down. And lo and behold! the
wizard and the lady had vanished clean away and were never
more seen or heard of.

This was Martha's story, told the next day to her neighbours. How she had escaped from the terrible house she could
not remember. But when, some time after, a group of villagers
summoned up courage to visit the place again, they found it
bare and empty. Lady, wizard, servant, familiars, furniture,
bags, and baggage—all were gone, leaving not a trace behind
them, except a few mysterious lines and figures traced on the
floor of the cottage.

This was a wonder indeed. More awful still was the disappearance of Martha herself, which took place three nights
afterwards.

Next day, the American doctor returned, to find an empty hearth and a legend.

"Yacht ahoy!"

Langley peered anxiously over the rail of the *Abracadabra* as the boat loomed out of the blackness. When the first passenger came aboard, he ran hastily to greet him.

"Is it all right, Wimsey?"

"Absolutely all right. She's a bit bewildered, of course — but you needn't be afraid. She's like a child, but she's getting better every day. Bear up, old man — there's nothing to shock you about her."

Langley moved hesitatingly forward as a muffled female figure was hoisted gently on board.

"Speak to her," said Wimsey. "She may or may not recognize you. I can't say."

Langley summoned up his courage. "Good evening, Mrs. Wetherall," he said, and held out his hand.

The woman pushed the cloak from her face. Her blue eyes gazed shyly at him in the lamplight — then a smile broke out upon her lips.

"Why, I know you — of course I know you. You're Mr. Langley. I'm so glad to see you."

She clasped his hand in hers.

"Well, Langley," said Lord Peter, as he manipulated the syphon, "a more abominable crime it has never been my fortune to discover. My religious beliefs are a little ill-defined, but I hope something really beastly happens to Wetherall in the next world. Say when!

"You know, there were one or two very queer points about that story you told me. They gave me a line on the thing from the start.

"To begin with, there was this extraordinary kind of decay or imbecility settlin' in on a girl in her twenties — so conveniently, too, just after you'd been hangin' round the Wetherall home and showin' perhaps a trifle too much sensibility, don't

you see? And then there was this tale of the conditions clearin'
up regularly once a year or so—not like any ordinary brain-
trouble. Looked as if it was being controlled by somebody.

"Then there was the fact that Mrs. Wetherall had been
under her husband's medical eye from the beginning, with no
family or friends who knew anything about her to keep a
check on the fellow. Then there was the determined isolation
of her in a place where no doctor could see her and where,
even if she had a lucid interval, there wasn't a soul who could
understand or be understood by her. Queer, too, that it should
be a part of the world where you, with your interests, might
reasonably be expected to turn up some day and be treated to
a sight of what she had turned into. Then there were Wetherall's well-known researches, and the fact that he kept in touch
with a chemist in London.

"All that gave me a theory, but I had to test it before I
could be sure I was right. Wetherall was going to America,
and that gave me a chance; but of course he left strict orders
that nobody should get into or out of his house during his
absence. I had, somehow, to establish an authority greater
than his over old Martha, who is a faithful soul, God bless her!
Hence, exit Lord Peter Wimsey and enter the magician. The
treatment was tried and proved successful—hence the elope-
ment and the rescue.

"Well, now, listen—and don't go off the deep end. It's all
over now. Alice Wetherall is one of those unfortunate people
who suffer from congenital thyroid deficiency. You know the
thyroid gland in your throat—the one that stokes the engine
and keeps the old brain going. In some people the thing
doesn't work properly, and they turn out cretinous imbeciles.
Their bodies don't grow and their minds don't work. But feed
'em the stuff, and they come absolutely all right—cheery and
handsome and intelligent and lively as crickets. Only, don't
you see, you have to *keep* feeding it to 'em, otherwise they just
go back to an imbecile condition.

"Wetherall found this girl when he was a bright young
student just learning about the thyroid. Twenty years ago,

very few experiments had been made in this kind of treatment, but he was a bit of a pioneer. He gets hold of the kid, works a miraculous cure, and, bein' naturally bucked with himself, adopts her, gets her educated, likes the look of her, and finally marries her. You understand, don't you, that there's nothing fundamentally unsound about those thyroid deficients. Keep 'em going on the little daily dose, and they're normal in every way, fit to live an ordinary life and have ordinary healthy children.

"Nobody, naturally, knew anything about this thyroid business except the girl herself and her husband. All goes well till *you* come along. Then Wetherall gets jealous—"

"He had no cause."

Wimsey shrugged his shoulders.

"Possibly, my lad, the lady displayed a preference—we needn't go into that. Anyhow, Wetherall did get jealous and saw a perfectly marvellous revenge in his power. He carried his wife off to the Pyrenees, isolated her from all help, and then simply sat back and starved her of her thyroid extract. No doubt he told her what he was going to do, and why. It would please him to hear her desperate appeals—to let her feel herself slipping back day by day, hour by hour, into something less than a beast—"

"Oh, God!"

"As you say. Of course, after a time, a few months, she would cease to know what was happening to her. He would still have the satisfaction of watching her—seeing her skin thicken, her body coarsen, her hair fall out, her eyes grow vacant, her speech die away into mere animal noises, her brain go to mush, her habits—"

"Stop it, Wimsey."

"Well, you saw it all yourself. But that wouldn't be enough for him. So, every so often, he would feed her the thyroid again and bring her back sufficiently to realize her own degradation—"

"If only I had the brute here!"

"Just as well you haven't. Well then, one day—by a stroke

of luck—Mr. Langley, the amorous Mr. Langley, actually turns up. What a triumph to let him see—"

Langley stopped him again.

"Right-ho! but it was ingenious, wasn't it? So simple. The more I think of it, the more it fascinates me. But it was just that extra refinement of cruelty that defeated him. Because, when you told me the story, I couldn't help recognizing the symptoms of thyroid deficiency, and I thought, 'Just supposing'—so I hunted up the chemist whose name you saw on the parcel, and, after unwinding a lot of red tape, got him to admit that he had several times sent Wetherall consignments of thyroid extract. So then I was almost sure, don't you see.

"I got a doctor's advice and a supply of gland extract, hired a tame Spanish conjurer and some performing cats and things, and barged off complete with disguise and a trick cabinet devised by the ingenious Mr. Devant. I'm a bit of a conjurer myself, and between us we didn't do so badly. The local superstitions helped, of course, and so did the gramophone records. Schubert's 'Unfinished' is first class for producing an atmosphere of gloom and mystery, so are luminous paint and the remnants of a classical education."

"Look here, Wimsey, will she get all right again?"

"Right as ninepence, and I imagine that any American court would give her a divorce on the grounds of persistent cruelty. After that—it's up to you!"

Lord Peter's friends greeted his reappearance in London with mild surprise.

"And what have *you* been doing with yourself?" demanded the Hon. Freddy Arbuthnot.

"Eloping with another man's wife," replied his lordship. "But only," he hastened to add, "in a purely Pickwickian sense. Nothing in it for yours truly. Oh, well! Let's toddle round to the Holborn Empire, and see what George Robey can do for us."

THE QUEEN'S SQUARE

You Jack o' Di'monds, you Jack o' Di'monds," said Mark Sambourne, shaking a reproachful head, "I know you of old." He rummaged beneath the white satin of his costume, panelled with gigantic oblongs and spotted to represent a set of dominoes. "Hang this fancy rig! Where the blazes has the fellow put my pockets? You rob my pocket, yes, you rob-a my pocket, you rob my pocket of silver and go-ho-hold. How much do you make it?" He extracted a fountain-pen and a cheque-book.

"Five-seventeen-six," said Lord Peter Wimsey. "That's right, isn't it, partner?" His huge blue-and-scarlet sleeves rustled as he turned to Lady Hermione Creethorpe, who, in her Queen of Clubs costume, looked a very redoubtable virgin, as, indeed, she was.

"Quite right," said the old lady, "and I consider that very cheap."

"We haven't been playing long," said Wimsey apologetically.

"It would have been more, Auntie," observed Mrs. Wrayburn, "if you hadn't been greedy. You shouldn't have doubled those four spades of mine."

Lady Hermione snorted, and Wimsey hastily cut in:

"It's a pity we've got to stop, but Deverill will never forgive us if we're not there to dance Sir Roger. He feels strongly about it. What's the time? Twenty past one. Sir Roger is timed to start sharp at half past. I supposed we'd better tootle back to the ballroom."

"I suppose we had," agreed Mrs. Wrayburn. She stood up, displaying her dress, boldly patterned with the red and black points of a backgammon board. "It's very good of you," she added, as Lady Hermione's voluminous skirts swept through the hall ahead of them, "to chuck your dancing to give Auntie her bridge. She does so hate to miss it."

"Not at all," replied Wimsey. "It's a pleasure. And in any case I was jolly glad of a rest. These costumes are dashed hot for dancing in."

"You make a splendid Jack of Diamonds, though. Such a good idea of Lady Deverill's, to make everybody come as a game. It cuts out all those wearisome pierrots and columbines." They skirted the south-west angle of the ballroom and emerged into the south corridor, lit by a great hanging lantern in four lurid colours. Under the arcading they paused and stood watching the floor, where Sir Charles Deverill's guests were fox-trotting to a lively tune discoursed by the band in the musicians' gallery at the far end. "Hullo, Giles!" added Mrs. Wrayburn, "you look hot."

"I am hot," said Giles Pomfret. "I wish to goodness I hadn't been so clever about this infernal costume. It's a beautiful billiard-table, but I can't sit down in it." He mopped his heated brow, crowned with an elegant green lamp-shade. "The only rest I can get is to hitch my behind on a radiator, and as they're all in full blast, it's not very cooling. Thank goodness, I can always make these damned sandwich boards an excuse to get out of dancing." He propped himself against the nearest column looking martyred

"Nina Hartford comes off best," said Mrs. Wrayburn. "Water-polo—so sensible—just a bathing-dress and a ball; though I must say it would look better on a less *Restoration* figure. You playing-cards are much the prettiest, and I think the

PLAN OF THE BALLROOM

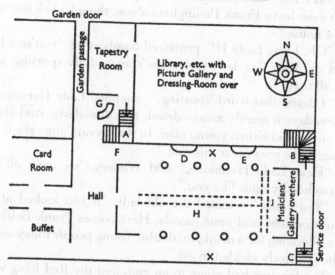

A, Stair to Dressing-room and Gallery; B, Stair to Gallery; C, Stair to Musicians' Gallery only; D, Settee where Joan Carstairs sat; E, Settee where Jim Playfair sat; F, Where Waits stood; G, Where Ephraim Dodd sat; H, Guests' "Sir Roger"; J, Servants' "Sir Roger"; XX, Hanging Lanterns; O O O O, Arcading.

chess-pieces run you close. There goes Gerda Bellingham, dancing with her husband—isn't she *too* marvellous in that red wig? And the bustle and everything—my dear, so attractive. I'm glad they didn't make themselves too Lewis Carroll; Charmian Grayle is the sweetest White Queen—where is she, by the way?"

"I don't like that young woman," said Lady Hermione; "she's fast."

"Dear lady!"

"I've no doubt you think me old-fashioned. Well, I'm glad I am. I say she's fast, and, what's more, heartless. I was watching her before supper, and I'm sorry for Tony Lee. She's been flirting as hard as she can go with Harry Vibart—not to give it a worse name—and she's got Jim Playfair on a string, too. She can't even leave Frank Bellingham alone, though she's staying in his house."

"Oh, I say, Lady H!" protested Sambourne, "you're a bit hard on Miss Grayle. I mean, she's an awfully sporting kid and all that."

"I detest that word 'sporting,'" snapped Lady Hermione. "Nowadays it merely means drunk and disorderly. And she's not such a kid either, young man. In three years' time she'll be a hag, if she goes on at this rate."

"Dear Lady Hermione," said Wimsey, "we can't all be untouched by time, like you."

"You could," retorted the old lady, "if you looked after your stomachs and your morals. Here comes Frank Bellingham—looking for a drink, no doubt. Young people today seem to be positively pickled in gin."

The fox-trot had come to an end, and the Red King was threading his way towards them through a group of applauding couples.

"Hullo, Bellingham!" said Wimsey. "Your crown's crooked. Allow me." He set wig and head-dress to rights with skilful fingers. "Not that I blame you. What crown is safe in these Bolshevik days?"

"Thanks," said Bellingham. "I say, I want a drink."

"What did I tell you?" said Lady Hermione.

"Buzz along, then, old man," said Wimsey. "You've got four minutes. Mind you turn up in time for Sir Roger."

"Right you are. Oh, I'm dancing it with Gerda, by the way. If you see her, you might tell her where I've gone to."

"We will. Lady Hermione, you're honouring me, of course?"

"Nonsense! You're not expecting me to dance at my age? The Old Maid ought to be a wallflower."

"Nothing of the sort. If only I'd had the luck to be born earlier, you and I should have appeared side by side, as Matrimony. Of course you're going to dance it with me—unless you mean to throw me over for one of these youngsters."

"I've no use for youngsters," said Lady Hermione. "No guts. Spindle-shanks." She darted a swift glance at Wimsey's scarlet hose. "You at least have some suggestion of calves. I can stand up with you without blushing for you."

Wimsey bowed his scarlet cap and curled wig in deep reverence over the gnarled knuckles extended to him.

"You make me the happiest of men. We'll show them all how to do it. Right hand, left hand, both hands across, back to back, round you go and up the middle. There's Deverill going down to tell the band to begin. Punctual old bird, isn't he? Just two minutes to go . . . What's the matter, Miss Carstairs? Lost your partner?"

"Yes—have you seen Tony Lee anywhere?"

"The White King? Not a sign. Nor the White Queen either. I expect they're together somewhere."

"Probably. Poor old Jimmie Playfair is sitting patiently in the north corridor, looking like Casabianca."

"You'd better go along and console him," said Wimsey, laughing.

Joan Carstairs made a face and disappeared in the direction of the buffet, just as Sir Charles Deverill, giver of the party, bustled up to Wimsey and his companions, resplendent in a Chinese costume patterned with red and green dragons, bamboos, circles, and characters, and carrying on his shoulder a stuffed bird with an enormous tail.

"Now, now," he exclaimed, "come along, come along, come along! All ready for Sir Roger. Got your partner, Wimsey? Ah, yes, Lady Hermione—splendid. You must come and stand next to your dear mother and me, Wimsey. Don't be late, don't be late. We want to dance it right through. The waits will begin at two o'clock—I hope they will arrive in good time. Dear me, dear me! Why aren't the servants in yet? I told Watson—I must go and speak to him."

He darted away, and Wimsey, laughing, led his partner up to the top of the room, where his mother, the Dowager Duchess of Denver, stood waiting, magnificent as the Queen of Spades.

"Ah! here you are," said the Duchess placidly. "Dear Sir Charles—he was getting quite flustered. Such a man for punctuality—he ought to have been a Royalty. A delightful party, Hermione, isn't it? Sir Roger and the waits—quite medieval—and a Yule-log in the hall, with the steam-radiators and everything—so oppressive!"

"Tumty, tumty, tiddledy, tumty, tumty, tiddledy," sang Lord Peter, as the band broke into the old tune. "I do adore this music. Foot it featly here and there—oh! there's Gerda Bellingham. Just a moment! Mrs. Bellingham—hi! your royal spouse awaits your Red Majesty's pleasure in the buffet. Do hurry him up. He's only got half a minute."

The Red Queen smiled at him, her pale face and black eyes startlingly brilliant beneath her scarlet wig and crown.

"I'll bring him up to scratch all right," she said, and passed on, laughing.

"So she will," said the Dowager. "You'll see that young man in the Cabinet before very long. Such a handsome couple on a public platform, and very sound, I'm told, about pigs, and that's so important, the British breakfast-table being what it is."

Sir Charles Deverill, looking a trifle heated, came hurrying back and took his place at the head of the double line of guests, which now extended three-quarters of the way down the ballroom. At the lower end, just in front of the Musicians' Gallery, the staff had filed in, to form a second Sir Roger, at right angles to the main set. The clock chimed the half-hour. Sir Charles, craning an anxious neck, counted the dancers.

"Eighteen couples. We're two couples short. How vexatious! Who are missing?"

"The Bellinghams?" said Wimsey. "No, they're here. It's the White King and Queen, Badminton and Diabolo."

"There's Badminton!" cried Mrs. Wrayburn, signalling frantically across the room. "Jim! Jim! Bother! He's gone back again. He's waiting for Charmian Grayle."

"Well, we can't wait any longer," said Sir Charles peevishly. "Duchess, will you lead off?"

The Dowager obediently threw her black velvet train over her arm and skipped away down the centre, displaying an uncommonly neat pair of scarlet ankles. The two lines of dancers, breaking into the hop-and-skip step of the country dance, jigged sympathetically. Below them, the cross lines of black and white and livery coats followed their example with respect. Sir Charles Deverill, dancing solemnly down after the Duchess, joined hands with Nina Hartford from the far end of the line. Tumty, tumty, tiddledy, tumty, tumty, tiddledy . . . the first couple turned outward and led the dancers down. Wimsey, catching the hand of Lady Hermione, stooped with her beneath the arch and came triumphantly up to the top of the room, in a magnificent rustle of silk and satin. "My love," sighed Wimsey, "was clad in the black velvet, and I myself in cramoisie." The old lady, well pleased, rapped him over the knuckles with her gilt sceptre. Hands clapped merrily.

"Down we go again," said Wimsey, and the Queen of Clubs and Emperor of the great Mahjongg dynasty twirled and capered in the centre. The Queen of Spades danced up to meet her Jack of Diamonds. "Bézique," said Wimsey; "double Bézique," as he gave both his hands to the Dowager. Tumty, tumty, tiddledy. He again gave his hand to the Queen of Clubs and led her down. Under their lifted arms the other seventeen couples passed. Then Lady Deverill and her partner followed them down — then five more couples.

"We're working nicely to time," said Sir Charles, with his eye on the clock. "I worked it out at two minutes per couple. Ah! here's one of the missing pairs." He waved an agitated arm. "Come into the centre — come along — in here."

A man whose head was decorated with a huge shuttle-cock, and Joan Carstairs, dressed as a Diabolo, had emerged from the north corridor. Sir Charles, like a fussy rooster with two frightened hens, guided and pushed them into place between two couples who had not yet done their "hands across," and heaved a sigh of relief. It would have worried him to see them miss their turn. The clock chimed a quarter to two.

"I say, Playfair, have you seen Charmian Grayle or Tony

Lee anywhere about?" asked Giles Pomfret of the Badminton costume. "Sir Charles is quite upset because we aren't complete."

"Not a sign of 'em. I was supposed to be dancing this with Charmian, but she vanished upstairs and hasn't come down again. Then Joan came barging along looking for Tony, and we thought we'd better see it through together."

"Here are the waits coming in," broke in Joan Carstairs. "Aren't they sweet? Too-too-truly-rural!"

Between the columns on the north side of the ballroom the waits could be seen filing into place in the corridor, under the command of the Vicar. Sir Roger jigged on his exhausting way. Hands across. Down the centre and up again. Giles Pomfret, groaning, scrambled in his sandwich boards beneath the lengthening arch of hands for the fifteenth time. Tumty, tiddledy. The nineteenth couple wove their way through the dance. Once again, Sir Charles and the Dowager Duchess, both as fresh as paint, stood at the top of the room. The clapping was loudly renewed; the orchestra fell silent; the guests broke up into groups; the servants arranged themselves in a neat line at the lower end of the room; the clock struck two; and the Vicar, receiving a signal from Sir Charles, held his tuning-fork to his ear and gave forth a sonorous A. The waits burst shrilly into the opening bars of "Good King Wenceslas."

It was just as the night was growing darker and the wind blowing stronger that a figure came thrusting its way through the ranks of the singers, and hurried across to where Sir Charles stood; Tony Lee, with his face as white as his costume.

"Charmian . . . in the tapestry room . . . dead . . . strangled."

Superintendent Johnson sat in the library, taking down the evidence of the haggard revellers, who were ushered in upon him one by one. First, Tony Lee, his haunted eyes like dark hollows in a mask of grey paper.

"Miss Grayle had promised to dance with me the last dance before Sir Roger; it was a fox-trot. I waited for her in the passage under the Musicians' Gallery. She never came. I did not search for her. I did not see her dancing with anyone else. When the dance was nearly over, I went out into the garden, by way of the service door under the musicians' stair. I stayed in the garden till Sir Roger de Coverley was over—"

"Was anybody with you, sir?"

"No, nobody."

"You stayed alone in the garden from—yes, from 1:20 past 2 o'clock. Rather disagreeable, was it not, sir, with the snow on the ground?" The Superintendent glanced keenly from Tony's stained and sodden white shoes to his strained face.

"I didn't notice. The room was hot—I wanted air. I saw the waits arrive at about 1:40—I dare say they saw me. I came in a little after 2 o'clock—"

"By the service door again, sir?"

"No; by the garden door on the other side of the house, at the end of the passage which runs along beside the tapestry room. I heard singing going on in the ballroom and saw two men sitting in the little recess at the foot of the staircase on the left-hand side of the passage. I think one of them was the gardener. I went into the tapestry room—"

"With any particular purpose in mind, sir?"

"No—except that I wasn't keen on rejoining the party. I wanted to be quiet." He paused; the Superintendent said nothing. "Then I went into the tapestry room. The light was out. I switched it on and saw—Miss Grayle. She was lying close against the radiator. I thought she had fainted. I went over to her and found she was—dead. I only waited long enough to be sure, and then I went into the ballroom and gave the alarm."

"Thank you, sir. Now, may I ask, what were your relations with Miss Grayle?"

"I-I admired her very much."

"Engaged to her, sir?"

"No, not exactly."

"No quarrel—misunderstanding—anything of that sort?"

"Oh, no!"

Superintendent Johnson looked at him again, and again said nothing, but his experienced mind informed him:

"He's lying."

Aloud he only thanked and dismissed Tony. The White King stumbled drearily out, and the Red King took his place.

"Miss Grayle," said Frank Bellingham, "is a friend of my wife and myself; she was staying at our house. Mr. Lee is also our guest. We all came in one party. I believe there was some kind of understanding between Miss Grayle and Mr. Lee—no actual engagement. She was a very bright, lively, popular girl. I have known her for about six years, and my wife has known her since our marriage. I know of no one who could have borne a grudge against Miss Grayle. I danced with her the last dance but two—it was a waltz. After that came a fox-trot and then Sir Roger. She left me at the end of the waltz; I think she said she was going upstairs to tidy. I think she went out by the door at the upper end of the ballroom. I never saw her again. The ladies' dressing-room is on the second floor, next door to the picture-gallery. You reach it by the staircase that goes up from the garden-passage. You have to pass the door of the tapestry room to get there. The only other way to the dressing-room is by the stair at the east end of the ballroom, which goes up to the picture-gallery. You would then have to pass through the picture-gallery to get to the dressing-room. I know the house well; my wife and I have often stayed here."

Next came Lady Hermione, whose evidence, delivered at great length, amounted to this:

"Charmian Grayle was a minx and no loss to anybody. I am not surprised that someone has strangled her. Women like that ought to be strangled. I would cheerfully have strangled her myself. She has been making Tony Lee's life a burden to him for the last six weeks. I saw her flirting with Mr. Vibart tonight on purpose to make Mr. Lee jealous. She made eyes at Mr. Bellingham and Mr. Playfair. She made eyes at everybody. I should think at least half a dozen people had very good reason to wish her dead."

Mr. Vibart, who arrived dressed in a gaudy Polo costume,

and still ludicrously clutching a hobby-horse, said that he had danced several times that evening with Miss Grayle. She was a damn sportin' girl, rattlin' good fun. Well, a bit hot, perhaps, but, dash it all, the poor kid was dead. He might have kissed her once or twice, perhaps, but no harm in that. Well, perhaps poor old Lee did take it a bit hard. Miss Grayle liked pulling Tony's leg. He himself had liked Miss Grayle and was dashed cut-up about the whole beastly business.

Mrs. Bellingham confirmed her husband's evidence. Miss Grayle had been their guest, and they were all on the very best of terms. She felt sure that Mr. Lee and Miss Grayle had been very fond of one another. She had not seen Miss Grayle during the last three dances, but had attached no importance to that. If she had thought about it at all, she would have supposed Miss Grayle was sitting out with somebody. She herself had not been up to the dressing-room since about midnight, and had not seen Miss Grayle go upstairs. She had first missed Miss Grayle when they all stood up for Sir Roger.

Mrs. Wrayburn mentioned that she had seen Miss Carstairs in the ballroom looking for Mr. Lee, just as Sir Charles Deverill went down to speak to the band. Miss Carstairs had then mentioned that Mr. Playfair was in the north corridor, waiting for Miss Grayle. She could say for certain that the time was then 1:28. She had seen Mr. Playfair himself at 1:30. He had looked in from the corridor and gone out again. The whole party had then been standing up together, except Miss Grayle, Miss Carstairs, Mr. Lee, and Mr. Playfair. She knew that, because Sir Charles had counted the couples.

Then came Jim Playfair, with a most valuable piece of evidence.

"Miss Grayle was engaged to me for Sir Roger de Coverley. I went to wait for her in the north corridor as soon as the previous dance was over. That was at 1:25. I sat on the settee in the eastern half of the corridor. I saw Sir Charles go down to speak to the band. Almost immediately afterwards, I saw Miss Grayle come out of the passage, under the Musicians' Gallery and go up the stairs at the end of the corridor. I called out: 'Hurry up! they're just going to begin.' I do not think she heard me; she did not reply. I am quite sure I saw her. The staircase has open banisters. There is no light in that corner except from the swinging lantern in the corridor, but that is very powerful. I could not be mistaken in the costume. I waited for Miss Grayle till the dance was half over; then I gave it up and joined forces with Miss Carstairs, who had also mislaid her partner."

The maid in attendance on the dressing-room was next examined. She and the gardener were the only two servants who had not danced Sir Roger. She had not quitted the dressing-room at any time since supper, except that she might have gone as far as the door. Miss Grayle had certainly not entered the dressing-room during the last hour of the dance.

The Vicar, much worried and distressed, said that his party had arrived by the garden door at 1:40. He had noticed a man in a white costume smoking a cigarette in the garden. The waits had removed their outer clothing in the garden passage and then gone out to take up their position in the north corridor. Nobody had passed them till Mr. Lee had come in with his sad news.

Mr. Ephraim Dodd, the sexton, made an important addition to this evidence. This aged gentleman was, as he confessed, no singer, but was accustomed to go round with the waits to carry the lantern and collecting box. He had taken a seat in the garden passage "to rest me pore feet." He had seen the gentleman come in from the garden "all in white with a crown on 'is 'ead." The choir were then singing "Bring me flesh and bring me wine." The gentleman had looked about a bit, "made a face, like," and gone into the room at the foot of the stairs. He hadn't been absent "more nor a minute," when he "come out faster than he gone in," and had rushed immediately into the ballroom.

In addition to all this, there was, of course, the evidence of Dr. Pattison. He was a guest at the dance, and had hastened to view the body of Miss Grayle as soon as the alarm was given.

He was of opinion that she had been brutally strangled by someone standing in front of her. She was a tall, strong girl, and he thought it would have needed a man's strength to overpower her. When he saw her at five minutes past two he concluded that she must have been killed within the last hour, but not within the last five minutes or so. The body was still quite warm, but, since it had fallen close to the hot radiator, they could not rely very much upon that indication.

Superintendent Johnson rubbed a thoughtful ear and turned to Lord Peter Wimsey, who had been able to confirm much of the previous evidence and, in particular, the exact times at which various incidents had occurred. The Superintendent knew Wimsey well, and made no bones about taking him into his confidence.

"You see how it stands, my lord. If the poor young lady was killed when Dr. Pattison says, it narrows it down a good bit. She was last seen dancing with Mr. Bellingham at—call it 1:20. At 2 o'clock she was dead. That gives us forty minutes. But if we're to believe Mr. Playfair, it narrows it down still further. He says he saw her alive just after Sir Charles went down to speak to the band, which you put at 1:28. That means that there's only five people who could possibly have done it, because all the rest were in the ballroom after that, dancing Sir Roger. There's the maid in the dressing-room; between you and me, sir, I think we can leave her out. She's a little slip of a thing, and it's not clear what motive she could have had. Besides, I've known her from a child, and she isn't the sort to do it. Then there's the gardener; I haven't seen him yet, but there again, he's a man I know well, and I'd as soon suspect myself. Well now, there's this Mr. Tony Lee, Miss Carstairs, and Mr. Playfair himself. The girl's the least probable, for physical reasons, and besides, strangling isn't a woman's crime—not as a rule. But Mr. Lee—that's a queer story, if you like. What was he doing all that time out in the garden by himself?"

"It sounds to me," said Wimsey, "as if Miss Grayle had given him the push and he had gone into the garden to eat worms."

"Exactly, my lord; and that's where his motive might come in."

"So it might," said Wimsey, "but look here. There's a couple of inches of snow on the ground. If you can confirm the time at which he went out, you ought to be able to see, from his tracks, whether he came in again before Ephraim Dodd saw him. Also, where he went in the interval and whether he was alone."

"That's a good idea, my lord. I'll send my sergeant to make inquiries."

"Then there's Mr. Bellingham. Suppose he killed her after the end of his waltz with her. Did anyone see him in the interval between that and the fox-trot?"

"Quite, my lord. I've thought of that. But you see where *that* leads. It means that Mr. Playfair must have been in a conspiracy with him to do it. And from all we hear, that doesn't seem likely."

"No more it does. In fact, I happen to know that Mr. Bellingham and Mr. Playfair were not on the best of terms. You can wash that out."

"I think so, my lord. And that brings us to Mr. Playfair. It's him we're relying on for the time. We haven't found anyone who saw Miss Grayle during the dance before his—that was the fox-trot. What was to prevent him doing it then? Wait a bit. What does he say himself? Says he danced the fox-trot with the Duchess of Denver." The Superintendent's face fell, and he hunted through his notes again. "She confirms that. Says she was with him during the interval and danced the whole dance with him. Well, my lord, I suppose we can take Her Grace's word for it."

"I think you can," said Wimsey, smiling. "I've known my mother practically since my birth, and have always found her very reliable."

"Yes, my lord. Well, that brings us to the end of the fox-trot. After that, Miss Carstairs saw Mr. Playfair waiting in the north corridor. She says she noticed him several times during the interval and spoke to him. And Mrs. Wrayburn saw him there at 1:30 or thereabouts. Then at 1:45 he and Miss Carstairs came and joined the company. Now, is there anyone who can check all these points? That's the next thing we've got to see to."

Within a very few minutes, abundant confirmation was forthcoming. Mervyn Bunter, Lord Peter's personal man, said that he had been helping to take refreshments along to the buffet. Throughout the interval between the waltz and the fox-trot, Mr. Lee had been standing by the service door beneath the musicians' stair, and half-way through the fox-trot he had been seen to go out into the garden by way of the servants' hall. The police-sergeant had examined the tracks in the snow and found that Mr. Lee had not been joined by any other person, and that there was only the one set of his footprints, leaving the house by the servants' hall and returning by the garden door near the tapestry room. Several persons were also found who had seen Mr. Bellingham in the interval between the waltz and the fox-trot, and who were able to say that he had danced the fox-trot through with Mrs. Bellingham. Joan Carstairs had also been seen continuously throughout the waltz and the fox-trot, and during the following interval and the beginning of Sir Roger. Moreover, the servants who had danced at the lower end of the room were positive that from 1:29 to 1:45 Mr. Playfair had sat continuously on the settee in the north corridor, except for the few seconds during which he had glanced into the ballroom. They were also certain that during that time no one had gone up the staircase at the lower end of the corridor, while Mr. Dodd was equally positive that, after 1:40, nobody except Mr. Lee had entered the garden passage or the tapestry room.

Finally, the circle was closed by William Hoggarty, the gardener. He asserted with the most obvious sincerity that from 1:30 to 1:40 he had been stationed in the garden passage to receive the waits and marshal them to their places. During that time, no one had come down the stair from the picture-gallery or entered the tapestry room. From 1:40 onwards, he had sat beside Mr. Dodd in the passage and nobody had passed him except Mr. Lee.

These points being settled, there was no further reason to doubt Jim Playfair's evidence, since his partners were able to prove his whereabouts during the waltz, the fox-trot, and the intervening interval. At 1:28 or just after, he had seen Charmian Grayle alive. At 2:20 she had been found dead in the tapestry room. During that interval, no one had been seen to enter the room, and every person had been accounted for.

At 6 o'clock, the exhausted guests had been allowed to go to their rooms, accommodation being provided in the house for those who, like the Bellinghams, had come from a distance, since the Superintendent had announced his intention of interrogating them all afresh later in the day.

This new inquiry produced no result. Lord Peter Wimsey did not take part in it. He and Bunter (who was an expert photographer) occupied themselves in photographing the ballroom and adjacent rooms and corridors from every imaginable point of view, for, as Lord Peter said, "You never know what may turn out to be relevant." Late in the afternoon they retired together to the cellar, where with dishes, chemicals, and safe-light hastily procured from the local chemist, they proceeded to develop the plates.

"That's the lot, my lord," observed Bunter at length, sloshing the final plate in the water and tipping it into the hypo. "You can switch the light on now, my lord."

Wimsey did so, blinking in the sudden white glare.

"A very hefty bit of work," said he. "Hullo! What's that plateful of blood you've got there?"

"That's the red backing they put on these plates, my lord, to obviate halation. You may have observed me washing it off before inserting the plate in the developing-dish. Halation, my lord, is a phenomenon —"

Wimsey was not attending.

"But why didn't I notice it before?" he demanded. "That stuff looked to me exactly like clear water."

"So it would, my lord, in the red safe-light. The appearance of whiteness is produced," added Bunter sententiously, "by the reflection of *all* the available light. When all the available light is red, red and white are, naturally, indistinguishable. Similarly, in a green light—"

"Good God!" said Wimsey. "Wait a moment, Bunter, I must think this out . . . Here! damn those plates—let them be. I want you upstairs."

He led the way at a canter to the ballroom, dark now, with the windows in the south corridor already curtained and only the dimness of the December evening filtering through the high windows of the clerestory above the arcading. He first turned on the three great chandeliers in the ballroom itself. Owing to the heavy oak panelling that rose to the roof at both ends and all four angles of the room, these threw no light at all upon the staircase at the lower end of the north corridor. Next, he turned on the light in the four-sided hanging lantern, which hung in the north corridor above and between the two settees. A vivid shaft of green light immediately flooded the lower half of the corridor and the staircase; the upper half was bathed in strong amber, while the remaining sides of the lantern showed red towards the ballroom and blue towards the corridor wall.

Wimsey shook his head.

"Not much room for error there. Unless—I know! Run, Bunter, and ask Miss Carstairs and Mr. Playfair to come here a moment."

While Bunter was gone, Wimsey borrowed a step-ladder from the kitchen and carefully examined the fixing of the lantern. It was a temporary affair, the lantern being supported by a hook screwed into a beam and lit by means of a flex run from the socket of a permanent fixture at a little distance.

"Now, you two," said Wimsey, when the two guests arrived, "I want to make a little experiment. Will you sit down on this settee, Playfair, as you did last night. And you, Miss Carstairs—I picked you out to help because you're wearing a white dress. Will you go up the stairs at the end of the corridor as Miss Grayle did last night. I want to know whether it looks the same to Playfair as it did then — bar all the other people, of course."

He watched them as they carried out this manoeuvre. Jim Playfair looked puzzled.

"It doesn't seem quite the same, somehow. I don't know what the difference is, but there is a difference."

Joan, returning, agreed with him.

"I was sitting on that other settee part of the time," she said, "and it looks different to me. I think it's darker."

"Lighter," said Jim.

"Good!" said Wimsey. "That's what I wanted you to say. Now, Bunter, swing that lantern through a quarter-turn to the left."

The moment this was done, Joan gave a little cry.

"That's it! That's it! The blue light! I remember thinking how frosty-faced those poor waits looked as they came in."

"And you, Playfair?"

"That's right," said Jim, satisfied. "The light was red last night. *I* remember thinking how warm and cosy it looked."

Wimsey laughed.

"We're on to it, Bunter. What's the chessboard rule? *The Queen stands on a square of her own colour.* Find the maid who looked after the dressing-room, and ask her whether Mrs. Bellingham was there last night between the fox-trot and Sir Roger."

In five minutes Bunter was back with his report.

"The maid says, my lord, that Mrs. Bellingham did not come into the dressing-room at that time. But she saw her come out of the picture-gallery and run downstairs towards the tapestry room just as the band struck up Sir Roger."

"And that," said Wimsey, "was at 1:29."

"Mrs. Bellingham?" said Jim. "But you said you saw her yourself in the ballroom before 1:30. She couldn't have had time to commit the murder."

"No, she couldn't," said Wimsey. "But Charmian Grayle was dead long before that. It was the Red Queen, not the

White, you saw upon the staircase. Find out why Mrs. Bellingham lied about her movements, and then we shall know the truth."

"A very sad affair, my lord," said Superintendent Johnson, some hours later. "Mr. Bellingham came across with it like a gentleman as soon as we told him we had evidence against his wife. It appears that Miss Grayle knew certain facts about him which would have been very damaging to his political career. She'd been getting money out of him for years. Earlier in the evening she surprised him by making fresh demands. During the last waltz they had together, they went into the tapestry room and a quarrel took place. He lost his temper and laid hands on her. He says he never meant to hurt her seriously, but she started to scream and he took hold of her throat to silence her and—sort of accidentally—throttled her. When he found what he'd done, he left her there and came away, feeling, as he says, all of a daze. He had the next dance with his wife. He told her what had happened, and then discovered that he'd left the little sceptre affair he was carrying in the room with the body. Mrs. Bellingham—she's a brave woman—undertook to fetch it back. She slipped through the dark passage under the Musicians' Gallery—which was empty—and up the stair to the picture-gallery. She did not hear Mr. Playfair speak to her. She ran through the gallery and down the other stair, secured the sceptre, and hid it under her own dress. Later, she heard from Mr. Playfair about what he saw, and realized that in the red light he had mistaken her for the White Queen. In the early hours of this morning, she slipped downstairs and managed to get the lantern shifted round. Of course, she's an accessory after the fact, but she's the kind of wife a man would like to have. I hope they let her off light."

"Amen!" said Lord Peter Wimsey.

THE NECKLACE OF PEARLS

Sir Septimus Shale was accustomed to assert his authority once in the year and once only. He allowed his young and fashionable wife to fill his house with diagrammatic furniture made of steel; to collect advanced artists and anti-grammatical poets; to believe in cocktails and relativity and to dress as extravagantly as she pleased; but he did insist on an old-fashioned Christmas. He was a simple-hearted man, who really liked plum-pudding and cracker mottoes, and he could not get it out of his head that other people, "at bottom," enjoyed these things also. At Christmas, therefore, he firmly retired to his country house in Essex, called in the servants to hang holly and mistletoe upon the cubist electric fittings; loaded the steel sideboard with delicacies from Fortnum & Mason; hung up stockings at the heads of the polished walnut bedsteads; and even, on this occasion only, had the electric radiators removed from the modernist grates and installed wood fires and a Yule log. He then gathered his family and friends about him, filled them with as much Dickensian good fare as he could persuade them to swallow, and, after their Christmas dinner, set them down to play "Charades" and "Clumps" and "Animal, Vegetable, and Mineral" in the drawing-room, concluding these diversions by "Hide-and-Seek" in the dark all over the house. Because Sir Septimus was a very rich man, his guests fell in with this invariable programme, and if they were bored, they did not tell him so.

Another charming and traditional custom which he followed was that of presenting to his daughter Margharita a pearl on each successive birthday—this anniversary happening to coincide with Christmas Eve. The pearls now numbered twenty, and the collection was beginning to enjoy a certain celebrity, and had been photographed in the Society papers. Though not sensationally large—each one being about the size of a marrow-fat pea—the pearls were of very great value. They were of exquisite colour and perfect shape and matched to a hair's-weight. On this particular Christmas Eve, the presentation of the twenty-first pearl had been the occasion of a very special ceremony. There was a dance and there were speeches. On the Christmas night following, the more restricted family party took place, with the turkey and the Victorian games. There were eleven guests, in addition to Sir Septimus and Lady Shale and their daughter, nearly all related or connected to them in some way: John Shale, a brother with his wife and their son and daughter Henry and Betty; Betty's fiancé, Oswald Truegood, a young man with parliamentary ambitions; George Comphrey, a cousin of Lady Shale's, aged about thirty and known as a man about town; Lavinia Prescott, asked on George's account; Joyce Trivett, asked on Henry Shale's account; Richard and Beryl Dennison, distant relations of Lady Shale, who lived a gay and expensive life in town on nobody precisely knew what resources; and Lord Peter Wimsey, asked, in a touching spirit of unreasonable hope, on Margharita's account. There were also, of course, William Norgate, secretary to Sir Septimus, and Miss Tomkins, secretary to Lady Shale, who had to be there because, without their calm efficiency, the Christmas arrangements could not have been carried through.

Dinner was over—a seemingly endless succession of soup, fish, turkey, roast beef, plum-pudding, mince-pies, crystallized fruit, nuts, and five kinds of wine, presided over by Sir Septimus, all smiles, by Lady Shale, all mocking deprecation, and by Margharita, pretty and bored, with the necklace of twenty-one pearls gleaming softly on her slender throat. Gorged and dyspeptic and longing only for the horizontal position, the company had been shepherded into the drawing-room and set to play "Musical Chairs" (Miss Tomkins at the piano), "Hunt the Slipper" (slipper provided by Miss Tomkins), and "Dumb Crambo" (costumes by Miss Tomkins and Mr. William Norgate). The back drawing-room (for Sir Septimus clung to these old-fashioned names) provided an admirable dressing-room, being screened by folding doors from the large drawing-room in which the audience sat on aluminum chairs, scrabbling uneasy toes on a floor of black glass under the tremendous illumination of electricity reflected from a brass ceiling.

It was William Norgate who, after taking the temperature of the meeting, suggested to Lady Shale that they should play at something less athletic. Lady Shale agreed and, as usual, suggested bridge. Sir Septimus, as usual, blew the suggestion aside.

"Bridge? Nonsense! Nonsense! Play bridge every day of your lives. This is Christmas time. Something we can all play together. How about 'Animal, Vegetable, and Mineral'?"

This intellectual pastime was a favourite with Sir Septimus; he was rather good at putting pregnant questions. After a brief discussion, it became evident that this game was an inevitable part of the programme. The party settled down to it, Sir Septimus undertaking to "go out" first and set the thing going.

Presently they had guessed among other things Miss Tomkins's mother's photograph, a gramophone record of "I want to be happy" (much scientific research into the exact composition of records, settled by William Norgate out of the

Encyclopaedia Britannica), the smallest stickleback in the stream at the bottom of the garden, the new planet Pluto, the scarf worn by Mrs. Dennison (very confusing, because it was not silk, which would be animal, or artificial silk, which would be vegetable, but made of spun glass — mineral, a very clever choice of subject), and had failed to guess the Prime Minister's wireless speech — which was voted not fair, since nobody could decide whether it was animal by nature or a kind of gas. It was decided that they should do one more word and then go on to "Hide-and-Seek." Oswald Truegood had retired into the back room and shut the door behind him while the party discussed the next subject of examination, when suddenly Sir Septimus broke in on the argument by calling to his daughter:

"Hullo, Margy! What have you done with your necklace?"

"I took it off, Dad, because I thought it might get broken in 'Dumb Crambo.' It's over here on this table. No, it isn't. Did you take it, mother?"

"No, I didn't. If I'd seen it, I should have. You are a careless child."

"I believe you've got it yourself, Dad. You're teasing."

Sir Septimus denied the accusation with some energy. Everybody got up and began to hunt about. There were not many places in that bare and polished room where a necklace could be hidden. After ten minutes' fruitless investigation, Richard Dennison, who had been seated next to the table where the pearls had been placed, began to look rather uncomfortable.

"Awkward, you know," he remarked to Wimsey.

At this moment, Oswald Truegood put his head through the folding-doors and asked whether they hadn't settled on something by now, because he was getting the fidgets.

This directed the attention of the searchers to the inner room. Margharita must have been mistaken. She had taken it in there, and it had got mixed up with the dressing-up clothes somehow. The room was ransacked. Everything was lifted up and shaken. The thing began to look serious. After half an hour of desperate energy it became apparent that the pearls were nowhere to be found.

"They must be somewhere in these two rooms, you know," said Wimsey. "The back drawing-room has no door and nobody could have gone out of the front drawing-room without being seen. Unless the windows—"

No. The windows were all guarded on the outside by heavy shutters which it needed two footmen to take down and replace. The pearls had not gone out that way. In fact, the mere suggestion that they had left the drawing-room at all was disagreeable. Because—because—

It was William Norgate, efficient as ever, who coldly and boldly faced the issue.

"I think, Sir Septimus, it would be a relief to the minds of everybody present if we could all be searched."

Sir Septimus was horrified, but the guests, having found a leader, backed up Norgate. The door was locked, and the search was conducted—the ladies in the inner room and the men in the outer.

Nothing resulted from it except some very interesting information about the belongings habitually carried about by the average man and woman. It was natural that Lord Peter Wimsey should possess a pair of forceps, a pocket lens, and a small folding foot-rule—was he not a Sherlock Holmes in high life? But that Oswald Truegood should have two liver-pills in a screw of paper and Henry Shale a pocket edition of *The Odes of Horace* was unexpected. Why did John Shale distend the pockets of his dress-suit with a stump of red sealing-wax, an ugly little mascot, and a five-shilling piece? George Comphrey had a pair of folding scissors, and three wrapped lumps of sugar, of the sort served in restaurants and dining-cars—evidence of a not uncommon form of kleptomania; but that the tidy and exact Norgate should burden himself with a reel of white cotton, three separate lengths of string, and twelve safety-pins on a card seemed really remarkable till one remembered that he had superintended all the Christmas decorations. Richard Dennison, amid some confusion and laughter, was found to cherish a lady's garter, a powder-compact, and half a potato; the last-named, he said, was a prophylactic against rheumatism (to which he was subject), while the other objects belonged to his wife. On the ladies' side, the more striking exhibits were a little book on palmistry, three invisible hair-pins, and a baby's photograph (Miss Tomkins); a Chinese trick cigarette-case with a secret compartment (Beryl Dennison); a *very* private letter and an outfit for mending stocking-ladders (Lavinia Prescott); and a pair of eyebrow tweezers and a small packet of white powder, said to be for headaches (Betty Shale). An agitating moment followed the production from Joyce Trivett's handbag of a small string of pearls—but it was promptly remembered that these had come out of one of the crackers at dinnertime, and they were, in fact, synthetic. In short, the search was unproductive of anything beyond a general shamefacedness and the discomfort always produced by undressing and re-dressing in a hurry at the wrong time of the day.

It was then that somebody, very grudgingly and haltingly, mentioned the horrid word "Police." Sir Septimus, naturally, was appalled by the idea. It was disgusting. He would not allow it. The pearls must be somewhere. They must search the rooms again. Could not Lord Peter Wimsey, with his experience of—er—mysterious happenings, do something to assist them?

"Eh?" said his lordship. "Oh, by Jove, yes—by all means, certainly. That is to say, provided nobody supposes—eh, what? I mean to say, you don't know that I'm not a suspicious character, do you, what?"

Lady Shale interposed with authority.

"We don't think *anybody* ought to be suspected," she said, "but, if we did, we'd know it couldn't be you. You know *far* too much about crimes to want to commit one."

"All right," said Wimsey. "But after the way the place has been gone over—" He shrugged his shoulders.

"Yes, I'm afraid you won't be able to find any footprints," said Margharita. "But we may have overlooked something." Wimsey nodded.

"I'll try. Do you all mind sitting down on your chairs in the outer room and staying there. All except one of you—I'd better have a witness to anything I do or find. Sir Septimus— you'd be the best person, I think."

He shepherded them to their places and began a slow circuit of the two rooms, exploring every surface, gazing up to the polished brazen ceiling, and crawling on hands and knees in the approved fashion across the black and shining desert of the floors. Sir Septimus followed, staring when Wimsey stared, bending with his hands upon his knees when Wimsey crawled, and puffing at intervals with astonishment and chagrin. Their progress rather resembled that of a man taking out a very inquisitive puppy for a very leisurely constitutional. Fortunately, Lady Shale's taste in furnishing made investigation easier; there were scarcely any nooks or corners where anything could be concealed.

They reached the inner drawing-room, and here the dressing-up clothes were again minutely examined, but without result. Finally, Wimsey lay down flat on his stomach to squint under a steel cabinet which was one of the very few pieces of furniture which possessed short legs. Something about it seemed to catch his attention. He rolled up his sleeve and plunged his arm into the cavity, kicked convulsively in the effort to reach farther than was humanly possible, pulled out from his pocket and extended his folding foot-rule, fished with it under the cabinet, and eventually succeeded in extracting what he sought.

It was a very minute object—in fact, a pin. Not an ordinary pin, but one resembling those used by entomologists to impale extremely small moths on the setting-board. It was about three-quarters of an inch in length, as fine as a very fine needle, with a sharp point and a particularly small head.

"Bless my soul!" said Sir Septimus. "What's that?"

"Does anybody here happen to collect moths or beetles or

anything?" asked Wimsey, squatting on his haunches and examining the pin.

"I'm pretty sure they don't," replied Sir Septimus. "I'll ask them."

"Don't do that." Wimsey bent his head and stared at the floor, from which his own face stared meditatively back at him. "I see," said Wimsey presently. "That's how it was done. All right, Sir Septimus. I know where the pearls are, but I don't know who took them. Perhaps it would be as well—for everybody's satisfaction—just to find out. In the meantime they are perfectly safe. Don't tell anyone that we've found this pin or that we've discovered anything. Send all these people to bed. Lock the drawing-room door and keep the key, and we'll get our man—or woman—by breakfast-time."

"God bless my soul," said Sir Septimus, very much puzzled.

Lord Peter Wimsey kept careful watch that night upon the drawing-room door. Nobody, however, came near it. Either the thief suspected a trap or he felt confident that any time would do to recover the pearls. Wimsey, however, did not feel that he was wasting his time. He was making a list of people who had been left alone in the back drawing-room during the playing of "Animal, Vegetable, and Mineral." The list ran as follows:

> Sir Septimus Shale
> Lavinia Prescott
> William Norgate
> Joyce Trivett and Henry Shale (together, because they had claimed to be incapable of guessing anything unaided)
> Mrs. Dennison
> Betty Shale
> George Comphrey
> Richard Dennison
> Miss Tomkins
> Oswald Truegood

He also made out a list of the persons to whom pearls might be useful or desirable. Unfortunately, this list agreed in almost all respects with the first (always excepting Sir Septimus) and so was not very helpful. The two secretaries had both come well recommended, but that was exactly what they would have done had they come with ulterior designs; the Dennisons were notorious livers from hand to mouth; Betty Shale carried mysterious white powders in her handbag, and was known to be in with a rather rapid set in town; Henry was a harmless dilettante, but Joyce Trivett could twist him round her little finger and was what Jane Austen liked to call "expensive and dissipated"; Comphrey speculated; Oswald Truegood was rather frequently present at Epsom and Newmarket—the search for motives was only too fatally easy.

When the second housemaid and the under-footman appeared in the passage with household implements, Wimsey abandoned his vigil, but he was down early to breakfast. Sir Septimus with his wife and daughter were down before him, and a certain air of tension made itself felt. Wimsey, standing on the hearth before the fire, made conversation about the weather and politics.

The party assembled gradually, but, as though by common consent, nothing was said about pearls until after breakfast, when Oswald Truegood took the bull by the horns.

"Well now!" said he. "How's the detective getting along? Got your man, Wimsey?"

"Not yet," said Wimsey easily.

Sir Septimus, looking at Wimsey as though for his cue, cleared his throat and dashed into speech.

"All very tiresome," he said, "all very unpleasant. Hr'rm. Nothing for it but the police, I'm afraid. Just at Christmas, too. Hr'rm. Spoilt the party. Can't stand seeing all this stuff about the place." He waved his hand towards the festoons of evergreens and coloured paper that adorned the walls. "Take it all down, eh, what? No heart in it. Hr'rm. Burn the lot."

"What a pity, when we worked so hard over it," said Joyce.

"Oh, leave it, Uncle," said Henry Shale. "You're bothering too much about the pearls. They're sure to turn up."

"Shall I ring for James?" suggested William Norgate.

"No," interrupted Comphrey, "let's do it ourselves. It'll give us something to do and take our minds off our troubles."

"That's right," said Sir Septimus. "Start right away. Hate the sight of it."

He savagely hauled a great branch of holly down from the mantelpiece and flung it, crackling, into the fire.

"That's the stuff," said Richard Dennison. "Make a good old blaze!" He leapt up from the table and snatched the mistletoe from the chandelier. "Here goes! One more kiss for somebody before it's too late."

"Isn't it unlucky to take it down before the New Year?" suggested Miss Tomkins.

"Unlucky be hanged. We'll have it all down. Off the stairs and out of the drawing-room too. Somebody go and collect it."

"Isn't the drawing-room locked?" asked Oswald.

"No. Lord Peter says the pearls aren't there, wherever else they are, so it's unlocked. That's right, isn't it, Wimsey?"

"Quite right. The pearls were taken out of these rooms. I can't tell yet how, but I'm positive of it. In fact, I'll pledge my reputation that wherever they are, they're not up there."

"Oh, well," said Comphrey, "in that case, have at it! Come along, Lavinia—you and Dennison do the drawing-room and I'll do the back room. We'll have a race."

"But if the police are coming in," said Dennison, "oughtn't everything to be left just as it is?"

"Damn the police!" shouted Sir Septimus. "They don't want evergreens."

Oswald and Margharita were already pulling the holly and ivy from the staircase, amid peals of laughter. The party dispersed. Wimsey went quietly upstairs and into the drawing-room, where the work of demolition was taking place at a great rate, George having bet the other two ten shillings to a tanner that they would not finish their part of the job before he finished his.

"You mustn't help," said Lavinia, laughing to Wimsey. "It wouldn't be fair."

Wimsey said nothing, but waited till the room was clear. Then he followed them down again to the hall, where the fire was sending up a great roaring and spluttering, suggestive of Guy Fawkes' night. He whispered to Sir Septimus, who went forward and touched George Comphrey on the shoulder.

"Lord Peter wants to say something to you, my boy," he said.

Comphrey started and went with him a little reluctantly, as it seemed. He was not looking very well.

"Mr. Comphrey," said Wimsey, "I fancy these are some of your property." He held out the palm of his hand, in which rested twenty-two fine, small-headed pins.

"Ingenious," said Wimsey, "but something less ingenious would have served his turn better. It was very unlucky, Sir Septimus, that you should have mentioned the pearls when you did. Of course, he hoped that the loss wouldn't be discovered till we'd chucked guessing games and taken to 'Hide-and-Seek.' Then the pearls might have been anywhere in the house, we shouldn't have locked the drawing-room door, and he could have recovered them at his leisure. He had had this possibility in his mind when he came here, obviously, and that was why he brought the pins, and Miss Shale's taking off the necklace to play 'Dumb Crambo' gave him his opportunity.

"He had spent Christmas here before, and knew perfectly well that 'Animal, Vegetable, and Mineral' would form part of the entertainment. He had only to gather up the necklace from the table when it came to his turn to retire, and he knew he could count on at least five minutes by himself while we were all arguing about the choice of a word. He had only to snip the pearls from the string with his pocket-scissors, burn the string in the grate, and fasten the pearls to the mistletoe with the fine pins. The mistletoe was hung on the chandelier, pretty high—it's a lofty room—but he could easily reach it by standing on the glass table, which wouldn't show footmarks, and it was almost certain that nobody would think of examining the mistletoe for extra berries. I shouldn't have thought of it myself if I hadn't found that pin which he had dropped. That gave me the idea that the pearls had been separated and the rest was easy. I took the pearls off the mistletoe last night—the clasp was there, too, pinned among the holly-leaves. Here they are. Comphrey must have got a nasty shock this morning. I knew he was our man when he suggested that the guests should tackle the decorations themselves and that he should do the back drawing-room—but I wish I had seen his face when he came to the mistletoe and found the pearls gone."

"And you worked it all out when you found the pin?" said Sir Septimus.

"Yes; I knew then where the pearls had gone to."

"But you never even looked at the mistletoe."

"I saw it reflected in the black glass floor, and it struck me then how much the mistletoe berries looked like pearls."

IN THE TEETH OF
THE EVIDENCE

Well, old son," said Mr. Lamplough, "and what can we do for you to-day?"

"Oh, some of your whizz-bang business, I suppose," said Lord Peter Wimsey, seating himself resentfully in the green velvet torture-chair and making a face in the direction of the drill. "Jolly old left-hand upper grinder come to bits on me. I was only eating an omelette, too. Can't understand why they always pick these moments. If I'd been cracking nuts or chewing peppermint jumbles I could understand it."

"Yes?" said Mr. Lamplough, soothingly. He drew an electric bulb, complete with mirror, as though by magic out of a kind of Maskelyne-and-Devant contraption on Lord Peter's left; a trail of flex followed it, issuing apparently from the bowels of the earth. "Any pain?"

"No *pain*," said Wimsey, irritably, "unless you count a sharp edge fit to saw your tongue off. Point is, why should it go pop like that? I wasn't doing anything to it."

"No?" said Mr. Lamplough, his manner hovering between the professional and the friendly, for he was an old Winchester man and a member of one of Wimsey's clubs, and had frequently met him on the cricket-field in the days of their youth.

"Well, if you'll stop talking half a moment, we'll have a look at it. Ah!"

"Don't say, 'Ah!' like that, as if you'd found pyorrhoea and necrosis of the jaw and were gloating over it, you damned old ghoul. Just carve it out and stop it up and be hanged to you. And, by the way, what have you been up to? Why should I meet an inspector of police on your doorstep? You needn't pretend he came to have his bridgework attended to, because I saw his sergeant waiting for him outside."

"Well, it was rather curious," said Mr. Lamplough, dexterously gagging his friend with one hand and dabbing cotton-wool into the offending cavity with the other. "I suppose I oughtn't to tell you, but if I don't, you'll get it all out of your friends at Scotland Yard. They wanted to see my predecessor's books. Possibly you noticed that bit in the papers about a dental man being found dead in a blazing garage on Wimbledon Common?"

"Yonk—ugh?" said Lord Peter Wimsey.

"Last night," said Mr. Lamplough. "Pooped off about nine pipemma, and it took them three hours to put it out. One of those wooden garages—and the big job was to keep the blaze away from the house. Fortunately it's at the end of the row, with nobody at home. Apparently this man Prendergast was all alone there—just going off for a holiday or something—and he contrived to set himself and his car and his garage alight last night and was burnt to death. In fact, when they found him, he was so badly charred that they couldn't be sure it was he. So, being sticklers for routine, they had a look at his teeth."

"Oh, yes?" said Wimsey, watching Mr. Lamplough fitting a new drill into its socket. "Didn't anybody have a go at putting the fire out?"

"Oh, yes—but as it was a wooden shed, full of petrol, it simply went up like a bonfire. Just a little bit over this way, please. That's splendid." Gr-r-r, whizz, gr-r-r. "As a matter of fact, they seem to think it might just possibly be suicide. The man's married, with three children, and immured and all that sort of thing." Whizz, gr-r-r, buzz, gr-r-r, whizz. "His family's down at Worthing, staying with his mother-in-law or something. Tell me if I hurt you." Gr-r-r. "And I don't suppose he was doing any too well. Still, of course, he may easily have had an accident when filling up. I gather he was starting off that night to join them."

"A—ow—oo—oo—uh—ihi—ih?" inquired Wimsey naturally enough.

"How do I come into it?" said Mr. Lamplough, who, from long experience was expert in the interpretation of mumblings. "Well, only because the chap whose practice I took over here did this fellow Prendergast's dental work for him." Whizz. "He died, but left his books behind him for my guidance, in case any of his old patients should feel inclined to trust me." Gr-r-r, whizz. "I'm sorry. Did you feel that? As a matter of fact, some of them actually do. I suppose it's an instinct to trundle round to the same old place when you're in pain, like the dying elephants. Will you rinse, please?"

"I see," said Wimsey, when he had finished washing out chips of himself and exploring his ravaged molar with his tongue. "How odd it is that these cavities always seem so large. I feel as if I could put my head into this one. Still, I suppose you know what you're about. And are Prendergast's teeth all right?"

"Haven't had time to hunt through the ledger yet, but I've said I'll go down to have a look at them as soon as I've finished with you. It's my lunch-time anyway, and my two o'clock patient isn't coming, thank goodness. She usually brings five spoilt children, and they all want to sit round and watch, and play with the apparatus. One of them got loose last time and tried to electrocute itself on the X-ray plant next door. And she thinks that children should be done at half-price. A little wider if you can manage it." Gr-r-r. "Yes, that's very nice. Now we can dress that and put in a temporary. Rinse, please."

"Yes," said Wimsey, "and for goodness' sake make it firm

and not too much of your foul oil of cloves. I don't want bits to come out in the middle of dinner. You can't imagine the nastiness of caviar flavoured with cloves."

"No?" said Mr. Lamplough. "You may find this a little cold." Squirt, swish. "Rinse, please. You may notice it when the dressing goes in. Oh, you did notice it? Good. That shows that the nerve's all right. Only a little longer now. There! Yes, you may get down now. Another rinse? Certainly. When would you like to come in again?"

"Don't be silly, old horse," said Wimsey. "I am coming out to Wimbledon with you straight away. You'll get there twice as fast if I drive you. I've never had a corpse-in-blazing-garage before, and I want to learn."

There is nothing really attractive about corpses in blazing garages. Even Wimsey's war experience did not quite reconcile him to the object that lay on the mortuary slab in the police station. Charred out of all resemblance to humanity, it turned even the police surgeon pale, while Mr. Lamplough was so overcome that he had to lay down the books he had brought with him and retire into the open to recover himself. Meanwhile Wimsey, having put himself on terms of mutual confidence and esteem with the police officials, thoughtfully turned over the little pile of blackened odds and ends that represented the contents of Mr. Prendergast's pockets. There was nothing remarkable about them. The leather note-case still held the remains of a thickish wad of notes—doubtless cash in hand for the holiday at Worthing. The handsome gold watch (obviously a presentation) had stopped at seven minutes past nine. Wimsey remarked on its good state of preservation. Sheltered between the left arm and the body—that seemed to be the explanation.

"Looks as though the first sudden blaze had regularly overcome him," said the police Inspector. "He evidently made no attempt to get out. He'd simply fallen forward over the wheel, with his head on the dashboard. That's why the face is so disfigured. I'll show you the remains of the car presently if you're interested, my lord. If the other gentleman's feeling better we may as well take the body first."

Taking the body was a long and unpleasant job. Mr. Lamplough, nerving himself with an effort and producing a pair of forceps and a probe, went gingerly over the jaws—reduced almost to their bony structure by the furnace heat to which they had been exposed—while the police surgeon checked entries in the ledger. Mr. Prendergast had a dental history extending back over ten years in the ledger, and had already had two or three fillings done before that time. These had been noted at the time when he first came to Mr. Lamplough's predecessor.

At the end of a long examination, the surgeon looked up from the notes he had been making.

"Well, now," he said, "let's check that again. Allowing for renewal of old work, I think we've got a pretty accurate picture of the present state of his mouth. There ought to be nine fillings in all. Small amalgam filling in right lower back wisdom tooth; big amalgam ditto in right lower back molar; amalgam fillings in right upper first and second bicuspids at point of contact; right upper incisor crowned—that all right?"

"I expect so," said Mr. Lamplough, "except that the right upper incisor seems to be missing altogether, but possibly the crown came loose and fell out." He probed delicately. "The jaw is very brittle—I can't make anything of the canal—but there's nothing against it."

"We may find the crown in the garage," suggested the Inspector.

"Fused porcelain filling in left upper canine," went on the surgeon; "amalgam fillings in left upper first bicuspid and lower second bicuspid and left lower thirteen-year-old molar. That seems to be all. No teeth missing and no artificials. How old was this man, Inspector?"

"About forty-five, Doc."

"My age. I only wish I had as good a set of teeth," said the surgeon. Mr. Lamplough agreed with him.

"Then I take it, this is Mr. Prendergast all right," said the Inspector.

"Not a doubt of it, I should say," replied Mr. Lamplough; "though I should like to find that missing crown."

"We'd better go round to the house, then," said the Inspector. "Well, yes, thank you, my lord, I shouldn't mind a lift in that. Some car. Well, the only point now is, whether it was accident or suicide. Round to the right, my lord, and then second on the left—I'll tell you as we go."

"A bit out of the way for a dental man," observed Mr. Lamplough, as they emerged upon some scattered houses near the Common.

The Inspector made a grimace.

"I thought the same, sir, but it appears Mrs. Prendergast persuaded him to come here. So good for the children. Not so good for the practice, though. If you ask me, I should say Mrs. P. was the biggest argument we have for suicide. Here we are."

The last sentence was scarcely necessary. There was a little crowd about the gate of a small detached villa at the end of a row of similar houses. From a pile of dismal debris in the garden a smell of burning still rose, disgustingly. The Inspector pushed through the gate with his companions, pursued by the comments of the bystanders.

"That's the Inspector . . . that's Dr. Maggs . . . that'll be another doctor, him with the little bag . . . who's the bloke in the eye-glass? . . . Looks a proper nobleman, don't he, Florrie? . . . Why he'll be the insurance bloke . . . Coo! Look at his grand car . . . that's where the money goes. . . . That's a Rolls, that is . . . no, silly, it's a Daimler. . . . Ow, well, it's all advertisement these days."

Wimsey giggled indecorously all the way up the garden path. The sight of the skeleton car amid the sodden and fire-blackened remains of the garage sobered him. Two police constables, crouched over the ruin with a sieve, stood up and saluted.

"How are you getting on, Jenkins?"

"Haven't got anything very much yet, sir, bar an ivory

cigarette-holder. This gentleman"—indicating a stout, bald man in spectacles, who was squatting among the damaged coach-work—"is Mr. Tolley, from the motorworks, come with a note from the Superintendent, sir."

"Ah, yes. Can you give any opinion about this, Mr. Tolley? Dr. Maggs you know. Mr. Lamplough, Lord Peter Wimsey. By the way, Jenkins, Mr. Lamplough has been going into the corpse's dentistry, and he's looking for a lost tooth. You might see if you can find it. Now, Mr. Tolley?"

"Can't see much doubt about how it happened," said Mr. Tolley, picking his teeth thoughtfully. "Regular death-traps, these little saloons, when anything goes wrong unexpectedly. There's a front tank, you see, and it looks as though there might have been a bit of a leak behind the dash, somewhere. Possibly the seam of the tank had got strained a bit, or the union had come loose. It's loose now, as a matter of fact, but that's not unusual after a fire, Rouse case or no Rouse case. You can get quite a lot of slow dripping from a damaged tank or pipe, and there seems to have been a coconut mat round the controls, which would prevent you from noticing. There'd be a smell, of course, but these little garages do often get to smell of petrol, and he kept several cans of the stuff here. More than the legal amount—but *that's* not unusual either. Looks to me as though he'd filled up his tank—there are two empty tins near the bonnet, with the caps loose—got in, shut the door, started up the car, perhaps, and then lit a cigarette. Then, if there were any petrol fumes about from a leak, the whole show would go up in his face—whoosh!"

"How was the ignition?"

"Off. He may never have switched it on, but it's quite likely he switched it off again when the flames went up. Silly thing to do, but lots of people *do* do it. The proper thing, of course, is to switch off the petrol and leave the engine running so as to empty the carburettor, but you don't always think straight when you're being burnt alive. Or he may have meant to turn off the petrol and been overcome before he could manage it. The tank's over here to the left, you see."

"On the other hand," said Wimsey, "he may have committed suicide and faked the accident."

"Nasty way of committing suicide."

"Suppose he'd taken poison first."

"He'd have had to stay alive long enough to fire the car."

"That's true. Suppose he'd shot himself—would the flash from the—no, that's silly—you'd have found the weapon in the case. Or a hypodermic? Same objection. Prussic acid might have done it—I mean, he might just have had time to take a tablet and then fire the car. Prussic acid's pretty quick, but it isn't absolutely instantaneous."

"I'll have a look for it, anyway," said Dr. Maggs.

They were interrupted by the constable.

"Excuse me, sir, but I think we've found the tooth. Mr. Lamplough says this is it."

Between his pudgy finger and thumb he held up a small, bony object, from which a small stalk of metal still protruded.

"That's a right upper incisor crown all right by the look of it," said Mr. Lamplough. "I suppose the cement gave way with the heat. Some cements are sensitive to heat, some, on the other hand, to damp. Well, that settles it, doesn't it?"

"Yes—well, we shall have to break it to the widow. Not that she can be in very much doubt, I imagine."

Mrs. Prendergast—a very much made-up lady with a face set in lines of habitual peevishness—received the news with a burst of loud sobs. She informed them, when she was sufficiently recovered, that Arthur had always been careless about petrol, that he smoked too much, that she had often warned him about the danger of small saloons, that she had told him he ought to get a bigger car, that the one he had was not really large enough for her and the whole family, that he *would* drive at night, though she had always said it was dangerous, and that if he'd listened to her, it would never have happened.

"Poor Arthur was not a good driver. Only last week, when he was taking us down to Worthing, he drove the car right up on a bank in trying to pass a lorry, and frightened us all dreadfully."

"Ah!" said the Inspector. "No doubt that's how the tank got strained." Very cautiously he inquired whether Mr. Prendergast could have had any reason for taking his own life. The widow was indignant. It was true that the practice had been declining of late, but Arthur would never have been so wicked as to do such a thing. Why, only three months ago, he had taken out a life-insurance for £500 and he'd never have invalidated it by committing suicide within the term stipulated by the policy. Inconsiderate of her as Arthur was, and whatever injuries he had done her as a wife, he wouldn't rob his innocent children.

The Inspector pricked up his ears at the word "injuries." What injuries?

Oh, well, of course, she'd known all the time that Arthur was carrying on with that Mrs. Fielding. You couldn't deceive her with all this stuff about teeth needing continual attention. And it was all very well to say that Mrs. Fielding's house was better run than her own. *That* wasn't surprising—a rich widow with no children and no responsibilities, of course she could afford to have everything nice. You couldn't expect a busy wife to do miracles on such a small housekeeping allowance. If Arthur had wanted things different, he should have been more generous, and it was easy enough for Mrs. Fielding to attract men, dressed up like a fashion-plate and no better than she should be. She'd told Arthur that if it didn't stop she'd divorce him. And since then he'd taken to spending all his evenings in Town, and what was he doing there—

The Inspector stemmed the torrent by asking for Mrs. Fielding's address.

"I'm sure I don't know," said Mrs. Prendergast. "She did live at Number 57, but she went abroad after I made it clear I wasn't going to stand any more of it. It's very nice to be some people, with plenty of money to spend. I've never been abroad since our honeymoon, and that was only to Boulogne."

At the end of this conversation, the Inspector sought Dr. Maggs and begged him to be thorough in his search for prussic acid.

The remaining testimony was that of Gladys, the general servant. She had left Mr. Prendergast's house the day before at 6 o'clock. She was to have taken a week's holiday while the Prendergasts were at Worthing. She had thought that Mr. Prendergast had seemed worried and nervous the last few days, but that had not surprised her, because she knew he disliked staying with his wife's people. She (Gladys) had finished her work and put out a cold supper and then gone home with her employer's permission. He had a patient—a gentleman from Australia, or some such a place, who wanted his teeth attended to in a hurry before going off on his travels again. Mr. Prendergast had explained that he would be working late, and would shut up the house himself, and she need not wait. Further inquiry showed that Mr. Prendergast had "scarcely touched" his supper, being, presumably, in a hurry to get off. Apparently, then, the patient had been the last person to see Mr. Prendergast alive.

The dentist's appointment-book was next examined. The patient figured there as "Mr. Williams 5:30," and the address-book placed Mr. Williams at a small hotel in Bloomsbury. The manager of the hotel said that Mr. Williams had stayed there for a week. He had given no address except "Adelaide," and had mentioned that he was revisiting the old country for the first time after twenty years and had no friends in London. Unfortunately, he could not be interviewed. At about half-past ten the previous night, a messenger had called, bringing his car, to pay his bill and remove his luggage. No address had been left for forwarding letters. It was not a district messenger, but a man in a slouch hat and heavy dark overcoat. The night-porter had not seen his face very clearly, as only one light was on in the hall. He had told them to hurry up, as Mr. Williams wanted to catch the boat-train from Waterloo. Inquiry at the booking-office showed that a Mr. Williams had actually travelled on that train, being booked to Paris. The ticket had been taken that same night. So Mr. Williams had disappeared into the blue, and even if they could trace him, it seemed unlikely that he could throw much light on Mr. Prendergast's state of mind immediately previous to the disaster. It seemed a little odd, at first, that Mr. Williams, from Adelaide, staying in Bloomsbury, should have travelled to Wimbledon to get his teeth attended to, but the simple explanation was the likeliest: namely, that the friendless Williams had struck up an acquaintance with Prendergast in a café or some such place, and that a casual mention of his dental necessities had led to a project of mutual profit and assistance.

After which, nothing seemed to be left but for the coroner to bring in a verdict of Death by Misadventure and for the widow to send in her claim to the Insurance Company, when Dr. Maggs upset the whole scheme of things by announcing that he had discovered traces of a large injection of hyoscine in the body, and what about it? The Inspector, on hearing this, observed callously that he was not surprised. If ever a man had an excuse for suicide, he thought it was Mrs. Prendergast's husband. He thought that it would be desirable to make a careful search among the scorched laurels surrounding what had been Mr. Prendergast's garage. Lord Peter Wimsey agreed, but committed himself to the prophecy that the syringe would not be found.

Lord Peter Wimsey was entirely wrong. The syringe was found next day, in a position suggesting that it had been thrown out of the window of the garage after use. Traces of the poison were discovered to be present in it. "It's a slow-working drug," observed Dr. Maggs. "No doubt he jabbed himself, threw the syringe away, hoping it would never be looked for, and then, before he lost consciousness, climbed into the car and set light to it. A clumsy way of doing it."

"A damned ingenious way of doing it," said Wimsey. "I don't believe in that syringe, somehow." He rang up his dentist. "Lamplough, old horse," he said, "I wish you'd do something for me. I wish you'd go over those teeth again. No—not my teeth; Prendergast's."

"Oh, blow it!" said Mr. Lamplough, uneasily.

"No, but I wish you would," said his lordship.

The body was still unburied. Mr. Lamplough, grumbling

very much, went down to Wimbledon with Wimsey, and again
went through his distasteful task. This time he started on the
left side.

"Lower thirteen-year-old molar and second bicuspid filled
amalgam. The fire's got at those a bit, but they're all right.
First upper bicuspid—bicuspids are stupid sort of teeth—
always the first to go. That filling looks to have been rather
carelessly put in—not what I should call good work; it seems
to extend over the next tooth—possibly the fire did that. Left
upper canine, cast porcelain filling on anterior face—"

"Half a jiff," said Wimsey, "Maggs's note says 'fused
porcelain.' Is it the same thing?"

"No. Different process. Well, I suppose it's fused porcelain—difficult to see. I should have said it was cast, myself, but
that's as may be."

"Let's verify it in the ledger. I wish Maggs had put the
dates in—goodness knows how far I shall have to hunt back,
and I don't understand this chap's writing or his dashed
abbreviations."

"You won't have to go back very far if it's cast. The stuff
only came in about 1928, from America. There was quite a
rage for it then, but for some reason it didn't take on extraordinarily well over here. But some men use it."

"Oh, then it isn't cast," said Wimsey. "There's nothing here
about canines, back to '28. Let's make sure; '27, '26, '25, '24,
'23. Here you are. Canine, something or other."

"That's it," said Lamplough, coming to look over his shoulder. "Fused porcelain. I must be wrong, then. Easily see by
taking it out. The grain's different, and so is the way it's put in."

"How, different?"

"Well," said Mr. Lamplough, "one's a cast, you see."

"And the other's fused. I did grasp that much. Well, go
ahead and take it out."

"Can't very well; not here."

"Then take it home and do it there. Don't you see, Lamplough, how important it is? If it is cast porcelain, or whatever
you call it, it *can't* have been done in '23. And if it was removed

later, then another dentist must have done it. And he may have done other things—and in that case, those things ought to be there, and they're not. Don't you *see?*"

"I see you're getting rather *agitato*," said Mr. Lamplough; "all I can say is, I refuse to have this thing taken along to my surgery. Corpses aren't popular in Harley Street."

In the end, the body was removed, by permission, to the dental department of the local hospital. Here Mr. Lamplough, assisted by the staff dental expert, Dr. Maggs, and the police, delicately extracted the filling from the canine.

"If that," said he triumphantly, "is not cast porcelain I will extract all my own teeth without an anæsthetic and swallow them. What do you say, Benton?"

The hospital dentist agreed with him. Mr. Lamplough, who had suddenly developed an eager interest in the problem, nodded, and inserted a careful probe between the upper right bicuspids, with their adjacent fillings.

"Come and look at this, Benton. Allowing for the action of the fire and all this muck, wouldn't you have said this was a very recent filling? There, at the point of contact. Might have been done yesterday. And—here—wait a minute. Where's the lower jaw gone to? Get that fitted up. Give me a bit of carbon. Look at the tremendous bite there ought to be here, with that big molar coming down on to it. That filling's miles too high for the job. Wimsey—when was this bottom right-hand back molar filled?"

"Two years ago," said Wimsey.

"That's impossible," said the two dentists together, and Mr. Benton added:

"If you clean away the mess, you'll see it's a new filling. Never been bitten on, I should say. Look here, Mr. Lamplough, there's something odd here."

"Odd? I should say there was. I never thought about it when I was checking it up yesterday, but look at this old cavity in the lateral here. Why didn't he have that filled when all this other work was done? Now it's cleaned out you can see it plainly. Have you got a long probe? It's quite deep and must

have given him jip. I say, Inspector, I want to have some of
these fillings out. Do you mind?"

"Go ahead," said the Inspector, "we've got plenty of
witnesses."

With Mr. Benton supporting the grisly patient and Mr.
Lamplough manipulating the drill, the filling of one of the
molars was speedily drilled out, and Mr. Lamplough said:
"Oh, gosh!"—which, as Lord Peter remarked, just showed
you what a dentist meant when he said "Ah!"

"Try the bicuspids," suggested Mr. Benton.

"Or this thirteen-year-old," chimed in his colleague.

"Hold hard, gentlemen," protested the Inspector, "don't
spoil the specimen altogether."

Mr. Lamplough drilled away without heeding him.
Another filling came out, and Mr. Lamplough said "Gosh!"
again.

"It's all right," said Wimsey, grinning, "you can get out
your warrant, Inspector."

"What's that, my lord?"

"Murder," said Wimsey.

"Why?" said the Inspector. "Do these gentlemen mean
that Mr. Prendergast got a new dentist who poisoned his teeth
for him?"

"No," said Mr. Lamplough; "at least, not what you mean
by poisoning. But I've never seen such work in my life. Why,
in two places the man hasn't even troubled to clear out the
decay at all. He's just enlarged the cavity and stopped it up
again anyhow. Why this chap didn't get thundering abscesses
I don't know."

"Perhaps," said Wimsey, "the stoppings were put in too
recently. Hullo! what now?"

"This one's all right. No decay here. Doesn't look as if
there ever had been, either. But one can't tell about that."

"I dare say there never was. Get your warrant out,
Inspector."

"For the murder of Mr. Prendergast? And against
whom?"

"No. Against Arthur Prendergast for the murder of one Mr. Williams, and, incidentally, for arson and attempted fraud. And against Mrs. Fielding too, if you like, for conspiracy. Though you mayn't be able to prove that part of it."

It turned out, when they found Mr. Prendergast in Rouen, that he had thought out the scheme well in advance. The one thing he had had to wait for had been to find a patient of his own height and build, with a good set of teeth and few home ties. When the unhappy Williams had fallen into his clutches, he had few preparations to make. Mrs. Prendergast had to be packed off to Worthing—a journey she was ready enough to take at any time—and the maid given a holiday. Then the necessary dental accessories had to be prepared and the victim invited out to tea at Wimbledon. Then the murder—a stunning blow from behind, followed by an injection. Then, the slow and horrid process of faking the teeth to correspond with Mr. Prendergast's own. Next, the exchange of clothes and the body carried down and placed in the car. The hypodermic put where it might be overlooked on a casual inspection and yet might plausibly be found if the presence of the drug should be discovered; ready, in the one case, to support a verdict of Accident and, in the second, of Suicide. Then the car soaked in petrol, the union loosened, the cans left about. The garage door and window left open, to lend colour to the story and provide a draught, and, finally, light set to the car by means of a train of petrol laid through the garage door. Then, flight to the station through the winter darkness and so by underground to London. The risk of being recognised on the underground was small, in Williams's hat and clothes and with a scarf wound about the lower part of the face. The next step was to pick up Williams's luggage and take the boat-train to join the wealthy and enamoured Mrs. Fielding in France. After which, Williams and Mrs. Williams could have returned to England, or not, as they pleased.

"Quite a student of criminology," remarked Wimsey, at the conclusion of this little adventure. "He'd studied Rouse and Furnace all right, and profited by their mistakes. Pity he overlooked that matter of the cast porcelain. Makes a quicker job, does it, Lamplough? Well, more haste, less speed. I do wonder, though, at what point of the proceedings Williams actually died."

"Shut up," said Mr. Lamplough, "and, by the way, I've still got to finish that filling for you."

ABSOLUTELY ELSEWHERE

Lord Peter Wimsey sat with Chief-Inspector Parker, of the C.I.D., and Inspector Henley, of the Baldock police, in the library at "The Lilacs."

"So you see," said Parker, "that all the obvious suspects were elsewhere at the time."

"What do you mean by 'elsewhere'?" demanded Wimsey, peevishly. Parker had hauled him down to Wapley, on the Great North Road, without his breakfast, and his temper had suffered. "Do you mean that they couldn't have reached the scene of the murder without travelling at over 186,000 miles a second? Because, if you don't mean, that, they weren't absolutely elsewhere. They were only relatively and apparently elsewhere."

"For heaven's sake, don't go all Eddington. Humanly speaking, they were elsewhere, and if we're going to nail one of them we shall have to do it without going into their Fitzgerald contractions and coefficients of spherical curvature. I think, Inspector, we had better have them in one by one, so that I can hear all their stories again. You can check them up if they depart from their original statements at any point. Let's take the butler first."

The Inspector put his head out into the hall and said: "Hamworthy."

The butler was a man of middle age, whose spherical curvature was certainly worthy of consideration. His large face was pale and puffy, and he looked unwell. However, he embarked on his story without hesitation.

"I have been in the late Mr. Grimbold's service for twenty years, gentlemen, and have always found him a good master. He was a strict gentleman, but very just. I know he was considered very hard in business matters, but I suppose he had to be that. He was a bachelor, but he brought up his two nephews, Mr. Harcourt and Mr. Neville, and was very good to them. In his private life I should call him a kind and considerate man. His profession? Yes, I suppose you would call him a money-lender.

"About the events of last night, sir, yes. I shut up the house at 7:30 as usual. Everything was done exactly to time, sir, — Mr. Grimbold was very regular in his habits. I locked all the windows on the ground floor, as was customary during the winter months. I am quite sure I didn't miss anything out. They all have burglar-proof bolts and I should have noticed if they had been out of order. I also locked and bolted the front door and put up the chain."

"How about the conservatory door?"

"That, sir, is a Yale lock. I tried it, and saw that it was shut. No, I didn't fasten the catch. It was always left that way, sir, in case Mr. Grimbold had business which kept him in town late, so that he could get in without disturbing the household."

"But he had no business in town last night?"

"No, sir, but it was always left that way. Nobody could get in without the key, and Mr. Grimbold had that on his ring."

"Is there no other key in existence?"

"I believe" — the butler coughed — "I believe, sir, though I do not know, that there is *one*, sir, — in the possession of — of a lady, sir, who is at present in Paris."

"I see. Mr. Grimbold was about sixty years old, I believe. Just so. What is the name of this lady?"

"Mrs. Winter, sir. She lives at Wapley, but since her husband died last month, sir, I understand she has been residing abroad."

"I see. Better make a note of that, Inspector. Now, how about the upper rooms and the back door?"

"The upper-room windows were all fastened in the same way, sir, except Mr. Grimbold's bedroom and the cook's room and mine, sir; but they couldn't be reached without a ladder, and the ladder is locked up in the tool-shed."

"That's all right," put in Inspector Henley. "We went into that last night. The shed was locked and, what's more, there were unbroken cobwebs between the ladder and the wall."

"I went through all the rooms at half-past seven, sir, and there was nothing out of order."

"You may take it from me," said the Inspector, again, "that there was no interference with any of the locks. Carry on, Hamworthy."

"Yes, sir. While I was seeing to the house, Mr. Grimbold came down into the library for his glass of sherry. At 7:45 the soup was served and I called Mr. Grimbold to dinner. He sat at the end of the table as usual, facing the serving-hatch."

"With his back to the library door," said Parker, making a mark on a rough plan of the room, which lay before him. "Was that door shut?"

"Oh, yes, sir. All the doors and windows were shut."

"It looks a dashed draughty room," said Wimsey. "Two doors and a serving-hatch and two French windows."

"Yes, my lord; but they are all very well-fitting, and the curtains were drawn."

His lordship moved across to the connecting door and opened it.

"Yes," he said; "good and heavy and moves in sinister silence. I like these thick carpets, but the pattern's a bit fierce." He shut the door noiselessly and returned to his seat.

"Mr. Grimbold would take about five minutes over his soup, sir. When he had done, I removed it and put on the fish. I did not have to leave the room; everything comes through the serving-hatch. The wine—that is, the Chablis—was already on the table. That course was only a small portion of turbot, and would take Mr. Grimbold about five minutes again. I removed that, and put on the roast pheasant. I was just about to serve Mr. Grimbold with the vegetables, when the telephone-bell rang. Mr. Grimbold said: 'You'd better see who it is. I'll help myself.' It was not the cook's business, of course, to answer the telephone."

"Are there no other servants?"

"Only the woman who comes in to clean during the day, sir. I went out to the instrument, shutting the door behind me."

"Was that this telephone or the one in the hall?"

"The one in the hall, sir. I always used that one, unless I happened to be actually in the library at the time. The call was from Mr. Neville Grimbold in town, sir. He and Mr. Harcourt have a flat in Jermyn Street. Mr. Neville spoke, and I recognised his voice. He said: 'Is that you, Hamworthy? Wait a moment. Mr. Harcourt wants you.' He put the receiver down and then Mr. Harcourt came on. He said: 'Hamworthy, I want to run down to-night to see my uncle, if he's at home.' I said: 'Yes, sir, I'll tell him.' The young gentlemen often come down for a night or two, sir. We keep their bedrooms ready for them. Mr. Harcourt said he would be starting at once and expected to get down by about half-past nine. While he was speaking I heard the big grandfather-clock up in their flat chime the quarters and strike eight, and immediately after, our own hall-clock struck, and then I heard the Exchange say 'Three minutes.' So the call must have come through at three minutes to eight, sir."

"Then there's no doubt about the time. That's a comfort. What next, Hamworthy?"

"Mr. Harcourt asked for another call and said: 'Mr. Neville has got something to say,' and then Mr. Neville came back to the 'phone. He said he was going up to Scotland shortly, and wanted me to send up a country suit and some stockings and shirts that he had left down here. He wanted the suit sent to the cleaner's first, and there were various other instructions, so that he asked for another three minutes. That would be at 8:30, sir, yes. And about a minute after that, while he was still speaking, the front-door bell rang. I couldn't very well leave the 'phone, so the caller had to wait, and at five past eight he rang the bell again. I was just going to ask Mr. Neville to excuse me, when I saw Cook come out of the kitchen and go through the hall to the front door. Mr. Neville asked me to repeat his instructions, and then the Exchange interrupted us again, so he rang off, and when I turned round I saw Cook just closing the library door. I went to meet her, and she said: 'Here's that Mr. Payne again, wanting Mr. Grimbold. I've put him in the library, but I don't like the looks of him.' So I said: 'All right; I'll fix him,' and Cook went back to the kitchen."

"One moment," said Parker. "Who's Mr. Payne?"

"He's one of Mr. Grimbold's clients, sir. He lives about five minutes away, across the fields, and he's been here before, making trouble. I think he owes Mr. Grimbold money, sir, and wanted more time to pay."

"He's here, waiting in the hall," added Henley.

"Oh?" said Wimsey. "The unshaven party with the scowl and the ash-plant, and the blood-stained coat?"

"That's him, my lord," said the butler. "Well, sir," — he turned to Parker again — "I started to go along to the library, when it come over me sudden-like that I'd never taken in the claret — Mr. Grimbold would be getting very annoyed. So I went back to my pantry — you see where that is, sir, — and fetched it from where it was warming before the fire. I had a little hunt then for the salver, sir, till I found I had put down my evening paper on top of it, but I wasn't more than a minute, sir, before I got back into the dining-room. And then, sir" — the butler's voice faltered — "then I saw Mr. Grimbold fallen forward on the table, sir, all across his plate, like. I thought he must have been took ill, and I hurried up to him and found — I found he was dead, sir, with a dreadful wound in his back."

"No weapon anywhere?"

"Not that I could see, sir. There was a terrible lot of blood.

It made me feel shockingly faint, sir, and for a minute I didn't hardly know what to do. As soon as I could think of anything, I rushed over to the serving-hatch and called Cook. She came hurrying in and let out an awful scream when she saw the master. Then I remembered Mr. Payne and opened the library door. He was standing there, and he began at once, asking how long he'd have to wait. So I said: 'Here's an awful thing! Mr. Grimbold has been murdered!' and he pushed past me into the dining-room, and the first thing he said was: 'How about those windows?' He pulled back the curtain of the one nearest the library, and there was the window standing open. 'This is the way he went,' he said, and started to rush out. I said, 'No, you don't'—thinking he meant to get away, and I hung on to him. He called me a lot of names, and then he said: 'Look here, my man, be reasonable. The fellow's getting away all this time. We must have a look for him.' So I said, 'Not without I go with you.' And he said, 'All right.' So I told Cook not to touch anything but to ring up the police, and Mr. Payne and I went out after I'd fetched my torch from the pantry."

"Did Payne go with you to fetch it?"

"Yes, sir. Well, him and me went out and we searched about in the garden, but we couldn't see any footprints or anything, because it's an asphalt path all round the house and down to the gate. And we couldn't see any weapon, either. So then he said: 'We'd better go back and get the car and search the roads,' but I said: 'No, he'll be away by then,' because it's only a quarter of a mile from our gate to the Great North Road, and it would take us five or ten minutes before we could start. So Mr. Payne said: 'Perhaps you're right,' and came back to the house with me. Well, then, sir, the constable came from Wapley, and after a bit, the Inspector here and Dr. Crofts from Baldock, and they made a search and asked a lot of questions, which I answered to the best of my ability, and I can't tell you no more, sir."

"Did you notice," asked Parker, "whether Mr. Payne had any stains of blood about him?"

"No, sir,—I can't say that he had. When I first saw him, he was standing in here, right under the light, and I think I should have seen it if there was anything, sir. I can't say fairer than that."

"Of course you've searched this room, Inspector, for bloodstains or a weapon or for anything such as gloves or a cloth, or anything that might have been used to protect the murderer from bloodstains?"

"Yes, Mr. Parker. We searched very carefully."

"Could anybody have come downstairs while you were in the dining-room with Mr. Grimbold?"

"Well, sir, I suppose they might. But they'd have to have got into the house before half-past seven, sir, and hidden themselves somewhere. Still, there's no doubt it might have happened that way. They couldn't come down by the back stairs, of course, because they'd have had to pass the kitchen, and Cook would have heard them, the passage being flagged, sir, but the front stairs—well, I don't know hardly what to say about that."

"That's how the man got in, depend upon it," said Parker. "Don't look so distressed, Hamworthy. You can't be expected to search all the cupboards in the house every evening for concealed criminals. Now I think I had better see the two nephews. I suppose they and their uncle got on together all right?"

"Oh, yes, sir. Never had a word of any sort. It's been a great blow to them, sir. They were terribly upset when Mr. Grimbold was ill in the summer—"

"He was ill, was he?"

"Yes, sir, with his heart, last July. He took a very bad turn, sir, and we had to send for Mr. Neville. But he pulled round wonderfully, sir,—only he never seemed to be quite such a cheerful gentleman afterwards. I think it made him feel he wasn't getting younger, sir. But I'm sure nobody ever thought he'd be cut off like this."

"How is his money left?" asked Parker.

"Well, sir, that I don't know. I believe it would be divided between the two gentlemen, sir—not but what they have plenty of their own. But Mr. Harcourt would be able to tell you, sir. He's the executor."

"Very well, we'll ask him. Are the brothers on good terms?"

"Oh, yes, indeed, sir. Most devoted. Mr. Neville would do anything for Mr. Harcourt—and Mr. Harcourt for him, I'm sure. A very pleasant pair of gentlemen, sir. You couldn't have nicer."

"Thanks, Hamworthy. That will do for the moment, unless anybody else has anything to ask?"

"How much of the pheasant was eaten, Hamworthy?"

"Well, my lord, not a great deal of it—I mean, nothing like all of what Mr. Grimbold had on his plate. But he'd ate some of it. It might have taken three or four minutes or so to eat what he had done, my lord, judging by what I helped him to."

"There was nothing to suggest that he had been interrupted, for example, by somebody coming to the windows, or of his having got up to let the person in?"

"Nothing at all, my lord, that I could see."

"The chair was pushed in close to the table when I saw him," put in the Inspector, "and his napkin was on his knees and the knife and fork lying just under his hands, as though he had dropped them when the blow came. I understand that the body was not disturbed."

"No, sir. I never moved it—except, of course, to make sure that he was dead. But I never felt any doubt of that, sir, when I saw that dreadful wound in his back. I just lifted his head and let it fall forward again, same as before."

"All right, then, Hamworthy. Ask Mr. Harcourt to come in."

Mr. Harcourt Grimbold was a brisk-looking man of about thirty-five. He explained that he was a stockbroker and his brother Neville an official in the Ministry of Public Health, and that they had been brought up by their uncle from the ages of eleven and ten respectively. He was aware that his uncle had had many business enemies, but for his own part he had received nothing from him but kindness.

"I'm afraid I can't tell you much about this terrible business, as I didn't get here till 9:45 last night, when, of course, it was all over."

"That was a little later than you hoped to be here?"

"Just a little. My tail-lamp went out between Welwyn Garden City and Welwyn, and I was stopped by a bobby. I went to a garage in Welwyn, where they found that the lead had come loose. They put it right, and that delayed me for a few minutes more."

"It's about forty miles from here to London?"

"Just over. In the ordinary way, at that time of night, I should reckon an hour and a quarter from door to door. I'm not a speed merchant."

"Did you drive yourself?"

"Yes. I have a chauffeur, but I don't always bring him down here with me."

"When did you leave London?"

"About 8:20, I should think. Neville went round to the garage and fetched the car as soon as he'd finished telephoning, while I put my toothbrush and so on in my bag."

"You didn't hear about the death of your uncle before you left?"

"No. They didn't think of ringing me up, I gather, till after I had started. The police tried to get Neville later on, but he'd gone round to the club, or something. I 'phoned him myself after I got here, and he came down this morning."

"Well, now, Mr. Grimbold, can you tell us anything about your late uncle's affairs?"

"You mean his will? Who profits, and that kind of thing? Well, I do, for one, and Neville, for another. And Mrs.—have you heard of a Mrs. Winter?"

"Something, yes."

"Well, she does, for a third. And then, of course, old Hamworthy gets a nice little nest-egg, and the cook gets something, and there is a legacy of £500 to the clerk at my uncle's London office. But the bulk of it goes to us and to Mrs. Winter. I know what you're going to ask—how much is it? I haven't the

faintest idea, but I know it must be something pretty considerable. The old man never let on to a soul how much he really
was worth, and we never bothered about it. I'm turning over
a good bit, and Neville's salary is a heavy burden on a long-
suffering public, so we only had a mild, academic kind of
interest in the question."

"Do you suppose Hamworthy knew he was down for a
legacy?"

"Oh, yes—there was no secret about that. He was to get
£100 and a life-interest in £200 a year, provided, of course, he
was still in my uncle's service when he—my uncle, I mean—
died."

"And he wasn't under notice, or anything?"

"N-no. No. Not more than usual. My uncle gave every-
body notice about once a month, to keep them up to the mark.
But it never came to anything. He was like the Queen of
Hearts in *Alice*—he never executed nobody, you know."

"I see. We'd better ask Hamworthy about that, though.
Now, this Mrs. Winter. Do you know anything about her?"

"Oh, yes. She's a nice woman. Of course, she was Uncle
William's mistress for donkey's years, but her husband was
practically potty with drink, and you could scarcely blame her.
I wired her this morning and here's her reply, just come."

He handed Parker a telegram, despatched from Paris,
which read: "Terribly shocked and grieved. Returning immediately. Love and sympathy. Lucy."

"You are on friendly terms with her, then?"

"Good Lord, yes. Why not? We were always damned sorry
for her. Uncle William would have taken her away with him
somewhere, only she wouldn't leave Winter. In fact, I think they
had practically settled that they were to get married now that
Winter has had the grace to peg out. She's only about thirty-
eight, and it's time she had some sort of show in life, poor thing."

"So, in spite of the money, she hadn't really very much to
gain by your uncle's death?"

"Not a thing. Unless, of course, she wanted to marry
somebody younger, and was afraid of losing the cash. But I

believe she was honestly fond of the old boy. Anyhow, she couldn't have done the murder, because she's in Paris."

"H'm!" said Parker. "I suppose she is. We'd better make sure, though. I'll ring through to the Yard and have her looked out for at the ports. Is this 'phone through to the Exchange?"

"Yes," said the Inspector. "It doesn't have to go through the hall 'phone; they're connected in parallel."

"All right. Well, I don't think we need trouble you further, at the moment, Mr. Grimbold. I'll put my call through, and after that we'll send for the next witness. . . . Give me White-hall 1212, please. . . . I suppose the time of Mr. Harcourt's call from town has been checked, Inspector?"

"Yes, Mr. Parker. It was put in at 7:57 and renewed at 8 o'clock and 8:03. Quite an expensive little item. And we've also checked up on the constable who spoke to him about his lights and the garage that put them right for him. He got into Welwyn at 9:05 and left again about 9:15. The number of the car is right, too."

"Well, he's out of it in any case, but it's just as well to check all we can. . . . Hullo, is that Scotland Yard? Put me through to Chief-Inspector Hardy. Chief-Inspector Parker speaking."

As soon as he had finished with his call, Parker sent for Neville Grimbold. He was rather like his brother, only a little slimmer and a little more suave in speech, as befitted a Civil Servant. He had nothing to add, except to confirm his brother's story and to explain that he had gone to a cinema from 8:20 to about 10 o'clock, and then on to his club, so that he had heard nothing about the tragedy till later in the evening.

The cook was the next witness. She had a great deal to say, but nothing very convincing to tell. She had not happened to see Hamworthy go to the pantry for the claret; oth-erwise she confirmed his story. She scouted the idea that somebody had been concealed in one of the upper rooms, because the daily woman, Mrs. Crabbe, had been in the house till nearly dinner-time, putting camphor-bags in all the wardrobes; and, anyhow, she had no doubt but what "that Payne" had stabbed Mr. Grimbold—"a nasty, murdering beast." After which, it only remained to interview the murderous Mr. Payne.

Mr. Payne was almost aggressively frank. He had been treated very harshly by Mr. Grimbold. What with exorbitant usury and accumulated interest added to the principal, he had already paid back about five times the original loan, and now Mr. Grimbold had refused him any more time to pay, and had announced his intention of foreclosing on the security, namely, Mr. Payne's house and land. It was all the more brutal because Mr. Payne had every prospect of being able to pay off the entire debt in six months' time, owing to some sort of interest or share in something or other which was confidently expected to turn up trumps. In his opinion, old Grimbold had refused to renew on purpose, so as to prevent him from paying—what *he* wanted was the property. Grimbold's death was the saving of the situation, because it would postpone settlement till after the confidently-expected trumps had turned up. Mr. Payne would have murdered old Grimbold with pleasure, but he hadn't done so, and in any case he wasn't the sort of man to stab anybody in the back, though, if the money-lender had been a younger man, he, Payne, would have been happy to break all his bones for him. There it was, and they could take it or leave it. If that old fool, Hamworthy, hadn't got in his way, he'd have laid hands on the murderer all right—if Hamworthy was a fool which he doubted. Blood? Yes, there was blood on his coat. He had got that in struggling with Hamworthy at the window. Hamworthy's hands had been all over blood when he made his appearance in the library. No doubt he had got it from the corpse. He, Payne, had taken care not to change his clothes, because, if he had done so, somebody would have tried to make out that he was hiding something. Actually, he had not been home, or asked to go home, since the murder. Mr. Payne added that he objected strongly to the atti-

tude taken up by the local police, who had treated him with
undisguised hostility. To which Inspector Henley replied that
Mr. Payne was quite mistaken.

"Mr. Payne," said Lord Peter, "will you tell me one thing?
When you heard the commotion in the dining-room, and the
cook screaming, and so on, why didn't you go in at once to
find out what was the matter?"

"Why?" retorted Mr. Payne. "Because I never heard anything of the sort, that's why. The first thing I knew about it
was seeing the butler-fellow standing there in the doorway,
waving his bloody hands about and gibbering."

"Ah!" said Wimsey. "I thought it was a good, solid door.
Shall we ask the lady to go in and scream for us now, with the
dining-room window open?"

The Inspector departed on this errand, while the rest of
the company waited anxiously to count the screams. Nothing
happened, however, till Henley put his head in and asked,
what about it?

"Nothing," said Parker.

"It's a well-built house," said Wimsey. "I suppose any
sound coming through the window would be muffled by the
conservatory. Well, Mr. Payne, if you didn't hear the screams
it's not surprising that you didn't hear the murderer. Are those
all your witnesses, Charles? Because I've got to get back to
London to see a man about a dog. But I'll leave you two sug-
gestions with my blessing. One is, that you should look for a
car, which was parked within a quarter of a mile of this house
last night, between 7:30 and 8:15; the second is, that you
should all come and sit in the dining-room to-night, with the
doors and windows shut, and watch the French windows. I'll
give Mr. Parker a ring about eight. Oh, and you might lend me
the key of the conservatory door. I've got a theory about it."

The Chief Inspector handed over the key, and his lordship
departed.

The party assembled in the dining-room was in no very
companionable mood. In fact, all the conversation was sup-

plied by the police, who kept up a chatty exchange of fishing reminiscences, while Mr. Payne glowered, the two Grimbolds smoked cigarette after cigarette, and the cook and the butler balanced themselves nervously on the extreme edges of their chairs. It was a relief when the telephone-bell rang.

Parker glanced at his watch as he got up to answer it. "Seven-fifty-seven," he observed, and saw the butler pass his handkerchief over his twitching lips. "Keep your eye on the windows." He went out into the hall.

"Hullo!" he said.

"Is that Chief-Inspector Parker?" asked a voice he knew well. "This is Lord Peter Wimsey's man speaking from his lordship's rooms in London. Would you hold the line a moment? His lordship wishes to speak to you."

Parker heard the receiver set down and lifted again. Then Wimsey's voice came through: "Hullo, old man? Have you found that car yet?"

"We've heard of *a* car," replied the Chief Inspector cautiously, "at a Road-House on the Great North Road, about five minutes' walk from the house."

"Was the number A B J 28?"

"Yes. How did you know?"

"I thought it might be. It was hired from a London garage at five o'clock yesterday afternoon and brought back just before ten. Have you traced Mrs. Winter?"

"Yes, I think so. She landed from the Calais boat this evening. So apparently she's O.K."

"I thought she might be. Now, listen. Do you know that Harcourt Grimbold's affairs are in a bit of a mess? He nearly had a crisis last July, but somebody came to his rescue—possibly Uncle, don't you think? All rather fishy, my informant saith. And I'm told, very confidentially, that he's got badly caught over the Biggars-Whitlow crash. But of course he'll have no difficulty in raising money now, on the strength of Uncle's will. But I imagine the July business gave Uncle William a jolt. I expect—"

He was interrupted by a little burst of tinkling music, followed by the eight silvery strokes of a bell.

"Hear that? Recognise it? That's the big French clock in my sitting-room. . . . What? All right, Exchange, give me another three minutes. Bunter wants to speak to you again."

The receiver rattled, and the servant's suave voice took up the tale.

"His lordship asks me to ask you, sir, to ring off at once and go straight into the dining-room."

Parker obeyed. As he entered the room, he got an instantaneous impression of six people, sitting as he had left them, in an expectant semi-circle, their eyes strained towards the French windows. Then the library door opened noiselessly and Lord Peter Wimsey walked in.

"Good God!" exclaimed Parker, involuntarily. "How did you get here?" The six heads jerked round suddenly.

"On the back of the light waves," said Wimsey, smoothing back his hair. "I have travelled eighty miles to be with you, at 186,000 miles a second."

"It was rather obvious, really," said Wimsey, when they had secured Harcourt Grimbold (who fought desperately) and his brother Neville (who collapsed and had to be revived with brandy). "It had to be those two; they were so very much elsewhere—almost absolutely elsewhere. The murder could only have been committed between 7:57 and 8:06, and there had to be a reason for that prolonged 'phone-call about something that Harcourt could very well have explained when he came. And the murderer had to be in the library before 7:57, or he would have been seen in the hall—unless Grimbold had let him in by the French window, which didn't appear likely.

"Here's how it was worked. Harcourt set off from Town in a hired car about six o'clock, driving himself. He parked the car at the Road-House, giving some explanation. I suppose he wasn't known there?"

"No; it's quite a new place; only opened last month."

"Ah! Then he walked the last quarter-mile on foot, arriving here at 7:45. It was dark, and he probably wore goloshes, so as not to make a noise coming up the path. He let himself into the conservatory with a duplicate key."

"How did he get that?"

"Pinched Uncle William's key off his ring last July, when the old boy was ill. It was probably the shock of hearing that his dear nephew was in trouble that caused the illness. Harcourt was here at the time—you remember it was only Neville that had to be 'sent for'—and I suppose Uncle paid up then, on conditions. But I doubt if he'd have done as much again— especially as he was thinking of getting married. And I expect, too, Harcourt thought that Uncle might easily alter his will after marriage. He might even have founded a family, and what would poor Harcourt do then, poor thing? From every point of view, it was better that Uncle should depart this life. So the duplicate key was cut and the plot thought out, and Brother Neville, who would 'do anything for Mr. Harcourt,' was roped in to help. I'm inclined to think that Harcourt must have done something rather worse than merely lose money, and Neville may have troubles of his own. But where was I?"

"Coming in at the conservatory door."

"Oh, yes—that's the way I came to-night. He'd take cover in the garden and would know when Uncle William went into the dining-room, because he'd see the library light go out. Remember, he knew the household. He came in, in the dark, locking the outer door after him, and waited by the telephone till Neville's call came through from London. When the bell stopped ringing, he lifted the receiver in the library. As soon as Neville had spoken his little piece, Harcourt chipped in. Nobody could hear him through these sound-proof doors, and Hamworthy couldn't possibly tell that his voice wasn't coming from London. In fact, it *was* coming from London, because, as the 'phones are connected in parallel, it could only come by way of the Exchange. At eight o'clock, the grandfather clock in Jermyn Street struck—further proof that the London line was open. The minute Harcourt heard that, he called on Neville to speak again, and hung up under cover of the rattle

of Neville's receiver. Then Neville detained Hamworthy with
a lot of rot about a suit, while Harcourt walked into the
dining-room, stabbed his uncle and departed by the window.
He had five good minutes in which to hurry back to his
car and drive off—and Hamworthy and Payne actually gave
him a few minutes more by suspecting and hampering one
another."

"Why didn't he go back through the library and conservatory?"

"He hoped everybody would think that the murderer had
come in by the window. In the meantime, Neville left London
at 8:20 in Harcourt's car, carefully drawing the attention of a
policeman and a garage man to the licence number as he
passed through Welwyn. At an appointed place outside Welwyn he met Harcourt, primed him with his little story about
tail-lights, and changed cars with him. Neville returned to
town with the hired 'bus; Harcourt came back here with his
own car. But I'm afraid you'll have a little difficulty in finding
the weapon and the duplicate key and Harcourt's bloodstained gloves and coat. Neville probably took them back, and
they may be anywhere. There's a good, big river in London."

STRIDING FOLLY

$\mathcal{S}$hall I expect you next
Wednesday for our game as usual?" asked Mr. Mellilow.

"Of course, of course," replied Mr. Creech. "Very glad
there's no ill feeling, Mellilow. Next Wednesday as usual.
Unless . . ." His heavy face darkened for a moment, as though
at some disagreeable recollection. "There may be a man coming to see me. If I'm not here by nine, don't expect me. In that
case, I'll come on Thursday."

Mr. Mellilow let his visitor out through the French window and watched him across the lawn to the wicket-gate leading to the Hall grounds. It was a clear October night, with a
gibbous moon going down the sky. Mr. Mellilow slipped on
his goloshes (for he was careful of his health and the grass was
wet) and himself went down past the sundial and the fish-
pond and through the sunk garden till he came to the fence
that bounded his tiny freehold on the southern side. He leaned
his arms on the rail and gazed across the little valley at the
tumbling river and the wide slope beyond, which was
crowned, at a mile's distance, by the ridiculous stone tower
known as the Folly. The valley, the slope, and the tower all
belonged to Striding Hall. They lay there, peaceful and lovely

in the moonlight, as though nothing could ever disturb their fantastic solitude. But Mr. Mellilow knew better.

He had bought the cottage to end his days in, thinking that here was a corner of England the same yesterday, today, and for ever. It was strange that he, a chess player, should not have been able to see three moves ahead. The first move had been the death of the old squire. The second had been the purchase by Creech of the whole Striding property. Even then, he had not been able to see why a rich business man — unmarried and with no rural interests — should have come to live in a post so remote. True, there were three considerable towns at a few miles' distance, but the village itself was on the road to nowhere. Fool! He had forgotten the Grid! It had come, like a great, ugly chessrook swooping from an unconsidered corner, marching over the country, straddling four, six, eight parishes at a time, planting hideous pylons to mark its progress, and squatting now at Mr. Mellilow's very door.

For Creech had just calmly announced that he was selling the valley to the Electrical Company; and there would be a huge power-plant on the river and workmen's bungalows on the slope, and then Development — which, to Mr. Mellilow, was another name for the devil. It was ironical that Mr. Mellilow, alone in the village, had received Creech with kindness, excusing his vulgar humour and insensitive manners, because he thought Creech was lonely and believed him to be well-meaning, and because he was glad to have a neighbour who could give him a weekly game of chess.

Mr. Mellilow came in sorrowful, and restored his goloshes to their usual resting-place on the verandah by the French window. He put the chessmen away and the cat out and locked up the cottage — for he lived quite alone, with a woman coming in by the day. Then he went up to bed with his mind full of the Folly, and presently he fell asleep and dreamed.

He was standing in a landscape whose style seemed very familiar to him. There was a wide plain, intersected with hedgerows, and crossed in the middle distance by a river, over which was a small stone bridge. Enormous blue-black thunder-clouds hung heavy overheard, and the air had the electric stillness of something stretched to snapping-point. Far off, beyond the river, a livid streak of sunlight pierced the clouds and lit up with theatrical brilliance a tall, solitary tower. The scene had a curious unreality, as though of painted canvas. It was a picture, and he had an odd conviction that he recognized the handling and could put a name to the artist. " 'Smooth and tight,' " were the words that occurred to him. And then, " 'It's bound to break before long.' " And then, " 'I ought not to have come out without my goloshes.' "

It was important, it was imperative that he should get to the bridge. But the faster he walked, the greater the distance grew, and without his goloshes the going was very difficult. Sometimes he was bogged to the knee, sometimes he floundered on steep banks of shifting shale; and the air was not merely oppressive—it was *hot* like the inside of an oven. He was running now, with the breath labouring in his throat, and when he looked up he was astonished to see how close he was to the tower. The bridge was fantastically small, dwindled to a pinpoint on the horizon, but the tower fronted him just across the river, and close on his right was a dark wood, which had not been there before.

Something flickered on the wood's edge, out and in again, shy and swift as a rabbit; and now the wood was between him and the bridge and the tower behind it, still glowing in that unnatural streak of sunlight. He was at the river's brink, but the bridge was nowhere to be seen—and the tower, the tower was moving. It had crossed the river. It had taken the wood in one gigantic leap. It was no more than fifty yards off, immensely high, shining, and painted. Even as he ran, dodging and twisting, it took another field in its stride, and when he turned to flee it was there before him. It was a double tower— twin towers—a tower and its mirror image, advancing with a swift and awful stealth from either side to crush him. He was pinned now between them, panting. He saw their smooth, yellow sides tapering up to heaven, and about their feet went a monstrous stir, like the quiver of a crouching cat.

Then the low sky burst like a sluice and through the drench of the rain he leapt at a doorway in the foot of the tower before him and found himself climbing the familiar stair of Striding Folly. "My goloshes will be here," he said, with a passionate sense of relief. The lightning stabbed suddenly through a loop-hole and he saw a black crow lying dead upon the stairs. Then thunder . . . like the rolling of drums.

The daily woman was hammering upon the door. "You *have* slept in," she said, "and no mistake."

Mr. Mellilow, finishing his supper on the following Wednesday, rather hoped that Mr. Creech would not come. He had thought a good deal during the week about the electric power scheme, and the more he thought about it, the less he liked it. He had discovered another thing which had increased his dislike. Sir Henry Hunter, who owned a good deal of land on the other side of the market town, had, it appeared, offered the company a site more suitable than Striding in every way on extremely favourable terms. The choice of Striding seemed inexplicable, unless on the supposition that Creech had bribed the surveyor. Sir Henry voiced his suspicions without any mincing of words. He admitted, however, that he could prove nothing.

"But he's crooked," he said. "I have heard things about him in Town. Other things. Ugly rumours."

Mr. Mellilow suggested that the deal might not, after all, go through.

"You're an optimist," said Sir Henry. "Nothing stops a fellow like Creech. Except death. He's a man with enemies. . . ." He broke off, adding darkly: "Let's hope he breaks his damned neck one of these days—and the sooner the better."

Mr. Mellilow was uncomfortable. He did not like to hear about crooked transactions. Business men, he supposed, were like that; but if they were, he would rather not play games with them. It spoilt things, somehow. Better, perhaps, not to think too much about it. He took up the newspaper, determined to occupy his mind, while waiting for Creech, with that day's chess problem. White to play and mate in three.

He had just become pleasantly absorbed when a knock came at the front door. Creech? As early as eight o'clock? Surely not. And in any case, he would have come by the lawn and the French window. But who else would visit the cottage of an evening? Rather disconcerted, he rose to let the visitor in. But the man who stood on the threshold was a stranger.

"Mr. Mellilow?"

"Yes, my name is Mellilow. What can I do for you?"

(A motorist, he supposed, enquiring his way or wanting to borrow something.)

"Ah! that is good. I have come to play chess with you."

"To play chess?" repeated Mr. Mellilow, astonished.

"Yes; I am a commercial traveller. My car has broken down in the village. I have to stay at the inn, and I ask the good Potts if there is anyone who can give me a game of chess to pass the evening. He tells me Mr. Mellilow lives here and plays well. Indeed, I recognize the name. Have I not read *Mellilow on Pawn-Play*? It is yours, no?"

Rather flattered, Mr. Mellilow admitted the authorship of this little work.

"So. I congratulate you. And you will do me the favour to play with me, hey? Unless I intrude, or you have company."

"No," said Mr. Mellilow. "I am more or less expecting a friend, but he won't turn up till nine and perhaps he won't come at all."

"If he come, I go," said the stranger. "It is very good of you." He had somehow oozed his way into the house without any direct invitation and was removing his hat and overcoat. He was a big man with a short, thick, curly beard and tinted spectacles, and he spoke in a deep voice with a slight foreign accent. "My name," he added, "is Moses. I represent Messrs. Cohen and Gold of Farringdon Street, the manufacturers of electrical fittings."

He grinned widely, and Mr. Mellilow's heart contracted. Such haste seemed almost indecent. Before the site was even taken! He felt an unreasonable resentment against this harmless Jew. Then he rebuked himself. It was not the man's fault.

"Come in," he said, with more cordiality in his voice than he really felt, "I shall be very glad to give you a game."

"I am very grateful," said Mr. Moses, squeezing his great bulk through into the sitting-room. "Ha! You are working out the *Record*'s three-mover. It is elegant but not profound. You will not take long to break his back. You permit that I disturb?"

Mr. Mellilow nodded, and the stranger began to arrange the board for play.

"You have hurt your hand?" enquired Mr. Mellilow.

"It is nothing," replied Mr. Moses, turning back the glove he wore and displaying a quantity of sticking-plaster. "I break my knuckles trying to start the dam' car. She kick me. Bah! A trifle. I wear a glove to protect him. So, we begin?"

"Won't you have something to drink first?"

"No, no, thank you very much. I have refreshed myself already at the inn. Too many drinks are not good. But do not let that prevent you."

Mr. Mellilow helped himself to a modest whisky and soda and sat down to the board. He won the draw and took the white pieces, playing his king's pawn to king's fourth.

"So!" said Mr. Moses, as the next few moves and countermoves followed their prescribed course, "the *giuoco piano*, hey? Nothing spectacular. We try the strength. When we know what we have each to meet, then the surprises will begin."

The first game proceeded cautiously. Whoever Mr. Moses might be, he was a sound and intelligent player, not easily stampeded into indiscretions. Twice Mr. Mellilow baited a delicate trap; twice, with a broad smile, Mr. Moses stepped daintily out between the closing jaws. The third trap was set more carefully. Gradually, and fighting every step of the way, black was forced behind his last defences. Yet another five minutes, and Mr. Mellilow said gently: "Check"; adding, "and mate in four." Mr. Moses nodded. "That was good." He glanced at the clock. "One hour. You give me my revenge, hey? Now we know one another. Now we shall see."

Mr. Mellilow agreed. Ten minutes past nine. Creech would

not come now. The pieces were set up again. This time, Mr.
Moses took white, opening with the difficult and dangerous
Steinitz gambit. Within a few minutes Mr. Mellilow realized
that, up till now, his opponent had been playing with him in a
double sense. He experienced that eager and palpitating excitement which attends the process of biting off more than one can
chew. By half-past nine, he was definitely on the defensive; at a
quarter to ten, he thought he spied a way out; five minutes later,
Mr. Moses said, suddenly, "It grows late: we must begin to push
a little," and thrust forward a knight, leaving his queen *en prise*.

Mr. Mellilow took prompt advantage of the oversight —
and became aware, too late, that he was menaced by the
advance of a white rook.

Stupid! How had he come to overlook that? There was an
answer, of course . . . but he wished the little room were not so
hot and that the stranger's eyes were not so inscrutable behind
the tinted glasses. If he could manœuvre his king out of harm's
way for the moment and force his pawn through, he had still a
chance. The rook moved in upon him as he twisted and
dodged; it came swooping and striding over the board, four,
six, eight squares at a time; and now the second white rook
had darted out from its corner; they were closing in upon
him—a double castle, twin castles, a castle and its mirror
image: O God! It was his dream of striding towers, smooth
and yellow and painted. Mr. Mellilow wiped his forehead.

"Check!" said Mr. Moses. And again, "Check!" And then,
"Checkmate!"

Mr. Mellilow pulled himself together. This would never
do. His heart was thumping as though he had been running a
race. It was ridiculous to be so much overwrought by a game
of chess; and if there was one kind of man in the world that he
despised, it was a bad loser. The stranger was uttering some
polite commonplace—he could not tell what—and replacing
the pieces in their box.

"I must go now," said Mr. Moses. "I thank you very much
for the pleasure you have so kindly given me. . . . Pardon me,
you are a little unwell?"

"No, no," said Mr. Mellilow. "It is the heat of the fire and the lamp. I have enjoyed our games very much. Won't you take anything before you go?"

"No, I thank you. I must be back before the good Potts locks me out. Again, my hearty thanks."

He grasped Mr. Mellilow's hand in his gloved grip and passed out quickly into the hall. In another moment he had seized hat and coat and was gone. His footsteps died away along the cobbled path.

Mr. Mellilow returned to the sitting-room. A curious episode; he could scarcely believe that it had really happened. There lay the empty board, the pieces in their box, the *Record* on the old oak chest with a solitary tumbler beside it; he might have dozed off and dreamed the whole thing, for all the trace the stranger's visit had left. Certainly the room was very hot. He threw the French window open. A lop-sided moon had risen, chequering the valley and the slope beyond with patches of black and white. High up, and distant, the Folly made a pale streak upon the sky. Mr. Mellilow thought he would walk down to the bridge to clear his head. He groped in the accustomed corner for his goloshes. They were not there. "Where on earth has that woman put them?" muttered Mr. Mellilow. And he answered himself, irrationally but with complete conviction, "My goloshes are up at the Folly."

His feet seemed to move of their own accord. He was through the garden now, walking quickly down the field to the little wooden foot-bridge. His goloshes were at the Folly. It was imperative that he should fetch them back; the smallest delay would be fatal. "This is ridiculous," thought Mr. Mellilow to himself. "It is that foolish dream running in my head. Mrs. Gibbs must have taken them away to clean them, but while I am here, I may as well go on; the walk will do me good."

The power of the dream was so strong upon him that he was almost surprised to find the bridge in its accustomed place. He put his hand on the rail and was comforted by the roughness of the untrimmed bark. Half a mile uphill now to the Folly. Its smooth sides shone in the moonlight, and he turned suddenly, expecting to see the double image striding the fields behind him. Nothing so sensational was to be seen, however. He breasted the slope with renewed courage. Now he stood close beneath the tower—and with a little shock he saw that the door at its base stood open.

He stepped inside, and immediately the darkness was all about him like a blanket. He felt with his foot for the stair and groped his way up between the newel and the wall. Now in gloom, not in the gleam of a loophole, the spiral seemed to turn endlessly. Then, as his head rose into the pale glimmer of the fourth window, he saw a shapeless blackness sprawled upon the stair. With a sudden dreadful certainty that *this* was what he had come to see, he mounted further and stooped over it. Creech was lying there, dead. Close beside the body lay a pair of goloshes. As Mr. Mellilow moved to pick them up, something rolled beneath his foot. It was a white chessrook.

The police-surgeon said that Creech had been dead since about nine o'clock. It was proved that at eight-fifty he had set out towards the wicket-gate to play chess with Mr. Mellilow. And in the morning light the prints of Mr. Mellilow's goloshes were clear, leading down the gravelled path on the far side of the lawn, past the sundial and the fish-pond, and through the sunk garden and so over the muddy field and the foot-bridge, and up the slope to the Folly. Deep footprints they were, and close together, such as a man might make who carried a monstrous burden. A good mile to the Folly and half of it uphill. The doctor looked inquiringly at Mr. Mellilow's spare form.

"Oh, yes," said Mr. Mellilow. "I could have carried him. It's a matter of knack, not strength. You see—" he blushed faintly, "I'm not really a gentleman. My father was a miller and I spent my whole boyhood carrying sacks. Only I was always fond of my books, and so I managed to educate myself and earn a little money. It would be silly to pretend I couldn't have carried Creech. But I didn't do it, of course."

"It's unfortunate," said the superintendent, "that we can't

find no trace of this man Moses." His voice was the most unpleasant Mr. Mellilow had ever heard—a sceptical voice with an edge like a saw. "He never come down to the Feathers, that's a certainty. Potts never set eyes on him, let alone sent him up here with a tale about chess. Nor nobody saw no car neither. An odd gentleman this Mr. Moses seem to have been. No footmarks to the front door? Well, it's cobbles, so you wouldn't expect none. That his glass of whisky by any chance, sir? ... Oh? he wouldn't have a drink, wouldn't he? Ah! And you played two games of chess in this very room? Ah! very absorbing pursoot, so I'm told. You didn't hear poor Mr. Creech come up the garden?"

"The window was shut," said Mr. Mellilow, "and the curtains drawn. And Mr. Creech always walked straight over the grass from the wicket-gate."

"H'm!" said the superintendent. "So he comes, or somebody comes, right up on to the verandah and sneaks a pair of goloshes; and you and this Mr. Moses are so occupied you don't hear nothing."

"Come, superintendent," said the Chief Constable, who was sitting on Mr. Mellilow's oak chest and looked rather uncomfortable. "I don't think that's impossible. The man might have worn tennis-shoes or something. How about finger-prints on the chessmen?"

"He wore a glove on his right hand," said Mr. Mellilow unhappily. "I remember that he didn't use his left hand at all — not even when taking a piece."

"A very remarkable gentleman," said the superintendent again. "No finger-prints, no footprints, no drinks, no eyes visible, no features to speak of, pops in and out without leaving no trace—a kind of vanishing gentleman." Mr. Mellilow made a helpless gesture. "These the chessmen you was using?" Mr. Mellilow nodded, and the superintendent turned the box upside-down upon the board, carefully extending a vast enclosing paw to keep the pieces from rolling away. "Let's see. Two big 'uns with spikes. Four chaps with split-open 'eads.

Four 'orses. Two black 'uns—what d'you call these? Rooks, eh? Look more like churches to me. One white church—rook if you like. What's gone with the other one? Or don't these rook-affairs go in pairs like the rest?"

"They must be both there," said Mr. Mellilow. "He was using two white rooks in the end-game. He mated me with them—I remember. . . ."

He remembered only too well. The dream and the double castle moving to crush him. He watched the superintendent feeling in his pocket and suddenly knew the name of the terror that had flickered in and out of the black wood.

The superintendent set down the white rook that had lain by the corpse at the Folly. Colour, height, and weight matched with the rook on the board.

"Staunton men," said the Chief Constable, "all of a pattern."

But the superintendent, with his back to the French window, was watching Mr. Mellilow's grey face.

"He must have put it in his pocket," said Mr. Mellilow. "He cleared the pieces away at the end of the game."

"But he couldn't have taken it up to Striding Folly," said the superintendent, "nor he couldn't have done the murder, by your own account."

"Is it possible that you carried it up to the Folly yourself," asked the Chief Constable, "and dropped it there when you found the body?"

"The gentleman has said that he saw this man Moses put it away," said the superintendent.

They were watching him now, all of them. Mr. Mellilow clasped his head in his hands. His forehead was drenched. "Something must break soon," he thought.

Like a thunderclap there came a blow on the window; the superintendent leapt nearly out of his skin.

"Lord, my lord!" he complained, opening the window and letting a gust of fresh air into the room, "how you startled me!"

Mr. Mellilow gasped. Who was this? His brain wasn't

working properly. That friend of the Chief Constable's, of course, who had disappeared somehow during the conversation. Like the bridge in his dream. Disappeared. Gone out of the picture.

"Absorbin' game, detectin'," said the Chief Constable's friend. "Very much like chess. People come creepin' right up on to the verandah and you never even notice them. In broad daylight, too. Tell me, Mr. Mellilow—what made you go up last night to the Folly?"

Mr. Mellilow hesitated. This was the point in his story that he had made no attempt to explain. Mr. Moses had sounded unlikely enough; a dream about goloshes would sound more unlikely still.

"Come now," said the Chief Constable's friend, polishing his monocle on his handkerchief and replacing it with an exaggerated lifting of the eyebrows. "What was it? Woman, woman, lovely woman? Meet me by moonlight and all that kind of thing?"

"Certainly not," said Mr. Mellilow indignantly. "I wanted a breath of fresh—" He stopped, uncertainly. There was something in the other man's childish-foolish face that urged him to speak the reckless truth. "I had a dream," he said.

The superintendent shuffled his feet, and the Chief Constable crossed one leg awkwardly over the other.

"Warned of God in a dream," said the man with the monocle, unexpectedly. "What did you dream of?" He followed Mr. Mellilow's glance at the board. "Chess?"

"Of two moving castles," said Mr. Mellilow, "and the dead body of a black crow."

"A pretty piece of used and inverted symbolism," said the other. "The dead body of a black crow becomes a dead man with a white rook."

"But that came afterwards," said the Chief Constable.

"So did the end-game with the two rooks," said Mr. Mellilow.

"Our friend's memory works both ways," said the man

with the monocle, "like the White Queen's. She, by the way, could believe as many as six impossible things before breakfast. So can I. Pharaoh, tell your dream."

"Time's getting on, Wimsey," said the Chief Constable.

"Let time pass," retorted the other, "for, as a great chess-player observed, it helps more than reasoning."

"What player was that?" demanded Mr. Mellilow.

"A lady," said Lord Peter Wimsey, "who played with living men and mated kings, popes, and emperors."

"Oh," said Mr. Mellilow. "Well—" He told his tale from the beginning, making no secret of his grudge against Creech and his nightmare fancy of the striding electric pylons. "I think," he said, "that was what gave me the dream." And he went on to his story of the goloshes, the bridge, the moving towers, and death on the stairs at the Folly.

"A damned lucky dream for you," said Wimsey. "But I see now why they chose you. Look! It is all clear as daylight. If you had had no dream—if the murderer had been able to come back later and replace your goloshes—if someone else had found the body in the morning with the chess-rook beside it and your tracks leading back and home again, that might have been mate in one move. There are two men to look for, superintendent. One of them belongs to Creech's household, for he knew that Creech came every Wednesday through the wicket-gate to play chess with you; and he knew that Creech's chessmen and yours were twin sets. The other was a stranger—probably the man whom Creech half-expected to call upon him. One lay in wait for Creech and strangled him near the wicket-gate as he arrived; fetched your goloshes from the vernadah, and carried the body down to the Folly. And the other came here in disguise to hold you in play and give you an alibi that no one could believe. The one man is strong in his hands and strong in the back—a sturdy, stocky man with feet no bigger than yours. The other is a big man, with noticeable eyes and probably clean-shaven, and he plays brilliant chess.

Look among Creech's enemies for those two men and ask them where they were between eight o'clock and ten-thirty last night."

"Why didn't the strangler bring back the goloshes?" asked the Chief Constable.

"Ah!" said Wimsey; "that was where the plan went wrong. I think he waited up at the Folly to see the light go out in the cottage. He thought it would be too great a risk to come up twice on to the verandah while Mr. Mellilow was there."

"Do you mean," asked Mr. Mellilow, "that he was there, in the Folly, watching me, when I was groping up those black stairs?"

"He may have been," said Wimsey. "But probably, when he saw you coming up the slope, he knew that things had gone wrong and fled away in the opposite direction, to the high road that runs behind the Folly. Mr. Moses, of course, went, as he came, by the road that passes Mr. Mellilow's door, removing his disguise in the nearest convenient place."

"That's all very well, my lord," said the superintendent, "but where's the proof of it?"

"Everywhere," said Wimsey. "Go and look at the tracks again. There's one set going outwards in goloshes, deep and short, made when the body was carried down. One made later, in walking shoes, which is Mr. Mellilow's track going outwards towards the Folly. And the third is Mr. Mellilow again, coming back, the track of a man running very fast. Two out and only one in. Where is the man who went out and never came back?"

"Yes," said the superintendent doggedly. "But suppose Mr. Mellilow made that second lot of tracks himself to put us off the scent, like? I'm not saying he did, mind you, but why couldn't he have?"

"Because," said Wimsey, "he had no time. The in-and-out tracks left by the shoes were made *after* the body was carried down. There is no other bridge for three miles on either side, and the river runs waist-deep. It can't be forded; so it must be crossed by the bridge. But at half-past ten Mr. Mellilow was in the Feathers, on *this* side of the river, ringing up the police. It couldn't be done, Super, unless he had wings. The bridge is there to prove it; for the bridge was crossed three times only."

"The bridge," said Mr. Mellilow, with a great sigh. "I knew in my dream there was something important about that. I knew I was safe if only I could get to the bridge."

THE HAUNTED POLICEMAN

Good God!" said his lordship.
"Did I do that?"

"All the evidence points that way," replied his wife.

"Then I can only say that I never knew so convincing a
body of evidence produce such an inadequate result."

The nurse appeared to take this reflection personally. She
said in a tone of rebuke:

"He's a *beautiful* boy."

"H'm," said Peter. He adjusted his eyeglass more carefully.
"Well, you're the expert witness. Hand him over."

The nurse did so with a dubious air. She was relieved to
see that this disconcerting parent handled the child compe-
tently; as, in a man who was an experienced uncle, was not,
after all, so very surprising. Lord Peter sat down gingerly on
the edge of the bed.

"Do you feel it's up to standard?" he inquired with some
anxiety. "Of course, *your* workmanship's always sound — but
you never know with these collaborate efforts."

"I think it'll do," said Harriet drowsily.

"Good." He turned abruptly to the nurse. "All right; we'll
keep it. Take it and put it away, and tell 'em to invoice it to me.
It's a very interesting addition to you, Harriet; but it would

have been a hell of a rotten substitute." His voice wavered a little, for the last twenty-four hours had been very trying ones, and he had had the fright of his life.

The doctor, who had been doing something in the other room entered in time to catch the last words.

"There was never any likelihood of that, you goop," he said, cheerfully. "Now, you've seen all there is to be seen, and you'd better run away and play." He led his charge firmly to the door. "Go to bed," he advised him in kindly accents; "you look all in."

"I'm all right," said Peter. "I haven't been doing anything. And look here —" he stabbed a belligerent finger in the direction of the adjoining room, "tell those nurses of yours, if I want to pick my son up, I'll pick him up. If his mother wants to kiss him, she can damn well kiss him. I'll have none of your infernal hygiene in *my* house."

"Very well," said the doctor, "just as you like. Anything for a quiet life. I rather believe in a few healthy germs myself. Builds up resistance. No, thanks, I won't have a drink. I've got to go on to another one, and an alcoholic breath impairs confidence."

"Another one?" said Peter, aghast.

"One of my hospital mothers. You're not the only fish in the sea by a long chalk. One born every minute."

"God! What a hell of a world." They passed down the great curved stair. In the hall a sleepy footman clung, yawning, to his post of duty.

"All right, William," said Peter. "Buzz off now; I'll lock up." He let the doctor out. "Good night—and thanks very much, old man. I'm sorry I swore at you."

"They mostly do," replied the doctor philosophically. "Well, bung-ho, Flim. I'll look in again later, just to earn my fee, but I shan't be wanted. You've married into a good tough family, and I congratulate you."

The car, spluttering and protesting a little after its long wait in the cold, drove off, leaving Peter alone on the doorstep. Now that it was all over and he could go to bed, he felt extraordinarily wakeful. He would have liked to go to a party.

He leaned back against the wrought-iron railings and lit a cigarette, staring vaguely into the lamp-lit dusk of the Square. It was thus that he saw the policeman.

The blue-uniformed figure came up from the direction of South Audley Street. He, too, was smoking, and he walked, not with the firm tramp of a constable on his beat, but with the hesitating step of a man who has lost his bearings. When he came in sight, he had pushed back his helmet and was rubbing his head in a puzzled manner. Official habit made him look sharply at the bare-headed gentleman in evening dress, abandoned on a doorstep at three in the morning, but since the gentleman appeared to be sober and bore no signs of being about to commit a felony, he averted his gaze and prepared to pass on.

" 'Morning, Officer," said the gentleman, as he came abreast with him.

" 'Morning, sir," said the policeman.

"You're off duty early," pursued Peter, who wanted somebody to talk to. "Come in and have a drink."

This offer reawakened all the official suspicion.

"Not just now, sir, thank you," replied the policeman guardedly.

"Yes, now. That's the point." Peter tossed away his cigarette-end. It described a fiery arc in the air and shot out a little train of sparks as it struck the pavement. "I've got a son."

"Oh, ah!" said the policeman, relieved by this innocent confidence. "Your first, eh?"

"And last, if I know anything about it."

"That's what my brother says, every time," said the policeman. "Never no more, he says. He's got eleven. Well, sir, good luck to it. I see how you're situated, and thank you kindly, but after what the Sergeant said I dunno as I better. Though if I was to die this moment, not a drop 'as passed me lips since me supper beer."

Peter put his head on one side and considered this.

"The Sergeant said you were drunk?"

"He did, sir."

"And you were not?"

"No, sir. I saw everything just the same as I told him, though what's become of it now is more than I can say. But drunk I was not, sir, no more than you are yourself."

"Then," said Peter, "as Mr. Joseph Surface remarked to Lady Teazle, what is troubling you is the consciousness of your own innocence. He insinuated that you have looked on the wine when it was red—you'd better come in and make it so. You'll feel better."

The policeman hesitated.

"Well, sir, I dunno. Fact is, I've had a bit of a shock."

"So've I," said Peter. "Come in for God's sake and keep me company."

"Well, sir—" said the policeman again. He mounted the steps slowly.

The logs in the hall chimney were glowing a deep red through their ashes. Peter raked them apart, so that the young flame shot up between them. "Sit down," he said; "I'll be back in a moment."

The policeman sat down, removed his helmet, and stared about him, trying to remember who occupied the big house at the corner of the Square. The engraved coat of arms upon the great silver bowl on the chimney-piece told him nothing, even though it was repeated in colour upon the backs of two tapestried chairs: three white mice skipping upon a black ground. Peter, returning quietly from the shadows beneath the stair, caught him as he traced the outlines with a thick finger.

"A student of heraldry?" he said. "Seventeenth-century work and not very graceful. You're new to this beat, aren't you? My name's Wimsey."

He put down a tray on the table.

"If you'd rather have beer or whisky, say so. These bottles are only a concession to my mood."

The policeman eyed the long necks and bulging silver-wrapped corks with curiosity. "Champagne?" he said. "Never tasted it, sir. But I'd like to try the stuff."

"You'll find it thin," said Peter, "but if you drink enough of it, you'll tell me the story of your life." The cork popped, and the wine frothed out into the wide glasses.

"Well!" said the policeman. "Here's to your good lady, sir, and the new young gentleman. Long life and all the best. A bit in the nature of cider, ain't it, sir?"

"Just a trifle. Give me your opinion after the third glass, if you can put up with it so long. And thanks for your good wishes. You a married man?"

"Not yet, sir. Hoping to be when I get promotion. If only the Sergeant—but that's neither here nor there. You been married long, sir, if I may ask?"

"Just over a year."

"Ah! and do you find it comfortable, sir?"

Peter laughed.

"I've spent the last twenty-four hours wondering why, when I'd had the blazing luck to get on to a perfectly good thing, I should be fool enough to risk the whole show on a damned silly experiment."

The policeman nodded sympathetically.

"I see what you mean, sir. Seems to me, life's like that. If you don't take risks, you get nowhere. If you do, they may go wrong, and then where are you? And 'alf the time, when things happen, they happen first, before you can even think about 'em."

"Quite right," said Peter, and filled the glasses again. He found the policeman soothing. True to his class and training, he turned naturally in moments of emotion to the company of the common man. Indeed, when the recent domestic crisis had threatened to destroy his nerve, he had headed for the butler's pantry with the swift instinct of the homing pigeon. There, they had treated him with great humanity, and allowed him to clean the silver.

With a mind oddly clarified by champagne and lack of sleep, he watched the constable's reaction to Pol Roger 1926. The first glass had produced a philosophy of life; the second produced a name—Alfred Burt—and further hints of some mysterious grievance against the Station Sergeant; the third glass, as prophesied, produced the story.

"You were right, sir" (said the policeman) "when you spotted I was new to the beat. I only come on it at the beginning of the week, and that accounts for me not being acquainted with you, sir, nor with most of the residents about here. Jessop, now, he knows everybody, and so did Pinker—but he's been took off to another division. You'd remember Pinker—big chap, make two o' me, with a sandy moustache. Yes, I thought you would.

"Well, sir, as I was saying, me knowing the district in a general way, but not, so to speak, like the palm o' me 'and, might account for me making a bit of a fool of myself, but it don't account for me seeing what I did see. See it I did, and not drunk nor nothing like it. And as for making a mistake in the number, well, that might happen to anybody. All the same, sir, thirteen was the number I see, plain as the nose on your face."

"You can't put it stronger than that," said Peter, whose nose was of a kind difficult to overlook.

"You know Merriman's End, sir?"

"I think I do. Isn't it a long cul-de-sac running somewhere at the back of South Audley Street, with a row of houses on one side and a high wall on the other?"

"That's right, sir. Tall, narrow houses they are, all alike, with deep porches and pillars to them."

"Yes. Like an escape from the worst square in Pimlico. Horrible. Fortunately, I believe the street was never finished, or we should have had another row of the monstrosities on the opposite side. This house is pure eighteenth century. How does it strike you?"

P.C. Burt contemplated the wide hall—the Adam fireplace and panelling with their graceful shallow mouldings, the pedimented doorways, the high roundheaded window lighting hall and gallery, the noble proportions of the stair. He sought for a phrase.

"It's a gentleman's house," he pronounced at length.

"Room to breathe, if you see what I mean. Seems like you couldn't act vulgar in it." He shook his head. "Mind you, I wouldn't call it cosy. It ain't the place I'd choose to sit down to a kipper in me shirt-sleeves. But it's got class. I never thought about it before, but now you mention it I see what's wrong with them other houses in Merriman's End. They're sort of squeezed-like. I been into more'n one o' them to-night, and that's what they are: they're squeezed. But I was going to tell you about that.

"Just upon midnight it was" (pursued the policeman) "when I turns into Merriman's End in the ordinary course of my dooties. I'd got pretty near down towards the far end, when I see a fellow lurking about in a suspicious way under the wall. There's back gates there, you know, sir, leading into some gardens, and this chap was hanging about inside one of the gateways. A rough-looking fellow, in a baggy old coat—might a-been a tramp off the Embankment. I turned my light on him—that street's not very well lit, and it's a dark night—but I couldn't see much of his face, because he had on a ragged old hat and a big scarf round his neck. I thought he was up to no good, and I was just about to ask him what he was doing there, when I hear a most awful yell come out o' one o' them houses opposite. Ghastly it was, sir. 'Help!' it said. 'Murder! Help!,' fit to freeze your marrow."

"Man's voice or woman's?"

"Man's, sir, I think. More of a roaring kind of yell, if you take my meaning. I says, 'Hullo! What's up there? Which house is it?' The chap says nothing, but he points, and him and me runs across together. Just as we gets to the house there's a noise like as if someone was being strangled just inside, and a thump, as it might be something falling against the door."

"Good God!" said Peter.

"I gives a shout and rings the bell. 'Hoy!' I says. 'What's up here?' and then I knocks on the door. There's no answer, so I rings and knocks again. Then the chap who was with me, he pushed open the letter-flap and squints through it."

"Was there a light in the house?"

"It was all dark, sir, except the fan-light over the door. That was lit up bright, and when I looks up, I see the number of the house — Number 13, painted plain as you like on the transom. Well, this chap peers in, and all of a sudden he gives a kind of gurgle and falls back. 'Here!' I says, 'what's amiss? Let me have a look.' So I puts me eye to the flap and I looks in."

P.C. Burt paused and drew a long breath. Peter cut the wire of the second bottle.

"Now, sir," said the policeman, "believe me or believe me not, I was as sober at that moment as I am now. I can tell you everything I see in that house, same as if it was wrote up there on that wall. Not as it was a great lot, because the flap wasn't all that wide, but by squinnying a bit, I could make shift to see right across the hall and a piece on both sides and part way up the stairs. And here's what I see, and you take notice of every word, on account of what came after."

He took another gulp of the Pol Roger to loosen his tongue and continued:

"There was the floor of the hall. I could see that very plain. All black and white squares it was, like marble, and it stretched back a good long way. About half-way along, on the left, was the staircase, with a red carpet, and the figure of a white naked woman at the foot, carrying a big pot full of blue and yellow flowers. In the wall next the stairs there was an open door, and a room all lit up. I could just see the end of a table, with a lot of glass and silver on it. Between that door and the front door there was a big black cabinet, shiny, with gold figures painted on it, like them things they had at the Exhibition. Right at the back of the hall there was a place like a conservatory, but I couldn't see what was in it, only it looked very gay. There was a door on the right, and that was open, too. A very pretty drawing-room, by what I could see of it, with pale blue paper and pictures on the walls. There were pictures in the hall, too, and a table on the right with a copper bowl, like as it might be for visitors' cards to be put in. Now, I see all that, sir, and I put it to you, if it hadn't a-been there, how could I describe it so plain?"

"I have known people describe what wasn't there," said Peter thoughtfully, "but it was seldom anything of that kind. Rats, cats, and snakes I have heard of, and occasionally naked female figures; but delirious lacquer cabinets and hall-tables are new to me."

"As you say, sir," agreed the policeman, "and I see you believe me so far. But here's something else, what you mayn't find quite so easy. There was a man laying in that hall, sir, as sure as I sit here, and he was dead. He was a big man and clean-shaven, and he wore evening dress. Somebody had stuck a knife into his throat. I could see the handle of it—it looked like a carving-knife, and the blood had run out, all shiny, over the marble squares."

The policeman looked at Peter, passed his handkerchief over his forehead, and finished the fourth glass of champagne.

"His head was up against the end of the hall-table," he went on, "and his feet must have been up against the door, but I couldn't see anything quite close to me, because of the letter-box. You understand, sir, I was looking through the wire cage of the box, and there was something inside—letters, I suppose—that cut off my view downwards. But I see all the rest—in front and a bit of both sides; and it must have been regularly burnt in upon me brain, as they say, for I don't suppose I was looking more than a quarter of a minute or so. Then all the lights went out at once, same as if somebody had turned off the main switch. So I looks round, and I don't mind telling you I felt a bit queer. And *when* I looks round, lo and behold! My bloke in the muffler had hopped it."

"The devil he had," said Peter.

"Hopped it," repeated the policeman, "and there I was. And just there, sir, is where I made my big mistake, for I thought he couldn't a-got far, and I started off up the street after him. But I couldn't see him, and I couldn't see nobody. All the houses was dark, and it come over me what a sight of funny things may go on, and nobody take a mite o' notice. The way I'd shouted and banged on the door, you'd a-thought it'd a-brought out every soul in the street, not to mention that awful yelling. But there—you may have noticed it yourself, sir. A man may leave his ground-floor windows open, or have his chimney a-fire, and you may make noise enough to wake the dead, trying to draw his attention, and nobody give no heed. He's fast asleep, and the neighbours say, 'Blast that row, but it's no business of mine,' and stick their 'eads under the bed-clothes."

"Yes," said Peter. "London's like that."

"That's right, sir. A village is different. You can't pick up a pin there without somebody coming up to ask where you got it from—but London keeps itself to itself. . . . Well, something'll have to be done, I thinks to myself, and I blows me whistle. They heard that all right. Windows started to go up all along the street. That's London, too."

Peter nodded. "London will sleep through the last trump. Puddley-in-the-Rut and Doddering-in-the-Dumps will look down their noses and put on virtuous airs. But God, who is never surprised, will say to his angel, 'Whistle 'em up, Michael, whistle 'em up; East and West will rise from the dead at the sound of the policeman's whistle.' "

"Quite so, sir," said P.C. Burt; and wondered for the first time whether there might not be something in this champagne stuff after all. He waited for a moment and then resumed:

"Well, it so happened that just when I sounded my whis-tle, Withers—that's the man on the other beat—was in Audley Square, coming to meet me. You know, sir, we has times for meeting one another, arranged different-like every night; and twelve o'clock in the Square was our rendy-voos to-night. So up he comes in, you might say, no time at all, and finds me there, with everyone a-hollering at me from the windows to know what was up. Well, naturally I didn't want the whole bunch of 'em running out into the street and our man getting away in the crowd, so I just tells 'em there's nothing, only a bit of an accident farther along. And then I see Withers and glad enough I was. We stands there at the top o' the street, and I tells him there's a dead man laying in the hall at Number 13, and it looks to me like murder. 'Number 13?' he says, 'you can't mean Number 13. There ain't no Number 13 in Merriman's End, you fathead; it's all even numbers.' And so it is, sir, for the houses on the other side were never built, so there's no odd numbers at all, barrin' Number 1, as is the big house on the corner.

"Well, that give me a bit of a jolt. I wasn't so much put out at not having remembered about the numbers, for as I tell you, I never was on the beat before this week. No; but I knew I'd seen that there number writ up plain as pie on the fan-light, and I didn't see how I could have been mistaken. But when Withers heard the rest of the story, he thought maybe I'd misread it for Number 12. It couldn't be 18, for there's only sixteen houses in the road; nor it couldn't be 16 neither, for I knew it wasn't the end house. But we thought it might be 12 or 10; so away we goes to look.

"We didn't have no difficulty about getting in at Number 12. There was a very pleasant old gentleman came down in his dressing-gown, asking what the disturbance was, and could he be of use. I apologized for disturbing him, and said I was afraid there'd been an accident in one of the houses, and had he heard anything. Of course, the minute he opened the door I could see it wasn't Number 12 we wanted; there was only a little hall with polished boards, and the walls plain panelled— all very bare and neat—and no black cabinet nor naked woman nor nothing. The old gentleman said, yes, his son had heard somebody shouting and knocking a few minutes earlier. He'd got up and put his head out of the window, but couldn't see nothing, but they both thought from the sound it was Number 14 forgotten his latchkey again. So we thanked him very much and went on to Number 14.

"We had a bit of a job to get Number 14 downstairs. A fiery sort of gentleman he was, something in the military way I thought, but he turned out to be a retired Indian civil servant. A dark gentleman, with a big voice, and his servant was dark, too—some sort of a nigger. The gentleman wanted to know what the blazes all this row was about, and why a decent citizen wasn't allowed to get his proper sleep. He supposed that young fool at Number 12 was drunk again. Withers had to speak a bit sharp to him; but at last the nigger came down and let us in. Well, we had to apologize once more. The hall was not a bit like—the staircase was on the wrong side, for one thing, and though there was a statue at the foot of it, it was some kind of a heathen idol with a lot of heads and arms, and the walls were covered with all sorts of brass stuff and native goods—you know the kind of thing. There was a black and white linoleum on the floor, and that was about all there was to it. The servant had a soft sort of way with him I didn't half like. He said he slept at the back and had heard nothing till his master rang for him. Then the gentleman came to the top of the stairs and shouted out it was no use disturbing him; the noise came from Number 12 as usual, and if that young man didn't stop his blanky Bohemian goings-on, he'd have the law on his father. I asked if he'd seen anything, and he said, no, he hadn't. Of course, sir, me and that other chap was inside the porch, and you can't see anything what goes on inside those porches from the other houses, because they're filled in at the sides with coloured glass—all the lot of them."

Lord Peter Wimsey looked at the policeman and then looked at the bottle, as though estimating the alcoholic contents of each. With deliberation, he filled both glasses again.

"Well, sir," said P.C. Burt, after refreshing himself, "by this time Withers was looking at me in rather an odd-fashioned manner. However, he said nothing, and we went back to Number 10, where there was two maiden ladies and a hall full of stuffed birds and wallpaper like a florists' catalogue. The one who slept in the front was deaf as a post, and the one who slept at the back hadn't heard nothing. But we got hold of their maids, and the cook said she'd heard the voice calling 'Help!' and thought it was in Number 12, and she'd hid her head in the pillow and said her prayers. The housemaid was a sensible girl. She'd looked out when she'd heard me knocking. She couldn't see anything at first, owing to us being in the porch, but she thought something must be going on, so, not wishing to catch cold, she went back to put on her bedroom slippers. When she got back to the window she was just in time to see a man running up the road. He went very quick and very silent, as if he had goloshes on, and she could see the ends of his muffler flying out behind him. She saw him run out of the street and turn to the right, and then she heard me coming along after him. Unfortunately, her eye being on the man, she didn't notice which porch I came out of. Well, that showed I wasn't inventing the whole story at any rate, because there was my bloke in the muffler. The girl didn't recognize him at all, but that wasn't surprising, because she'd only just entered the old ladies' service. Besides, it wasn't likely the man had anything to do with it, because he was outside with me when the yelling started. My belief is he was the sort as doesn't care to have his pockets examined too close, and the minute my back was turned he thought he'd be better and more comfortable elsewhere.

"Now there ain't no need" (continued the policeman) "for me to trouble you, sir, with all them houses what we went into. We made inquiries at the whole lot, from Number 2 to Number 16, and there wasn't one of them had a hall in any ways conformable to what that chap and I saw through the letter-box. Nor there wasn't a soul in 'em could give us any help more than what we'd had already. You see, sir, though it took me a bit o' time telling, it all went very quick. There was the yells; they didn't last beyond a few seconds or so, and before they was finished, we was across the road and inside the porch. Then there was me shouting and knocking; but I hadn't been long at that afore the chap with me looks through the box. Then I had my look inside, for fifteen seconds it might be, and while I'm doing that, my chap's away up the street. Then I runs after him, and then I blows me whistle. The whole thing might take a minute, or a minute and a half maybe. Not more.

"Well, sir; by the time we'd been into every house in Merriman's End, I was feeling a bit queer again, I can tell you, and Withers, he was looking queerer. He says to me, 'Burt,' he says, 'is this your idea of a joke? Because if so, the 'Olborn

Empire's where you ought to be, not the police force.' So I tells him over again, most solemn, what I see — 'and,' I says, 'if only we could lay hands on that chap in the muffler, he could tell you he seen it, too. And what's more,' I says, 'do you think I'd risk me job, playing a silly trick like that?' He says, 'Well, it beats me,' he says. 'If I didn't know you was a sober kind of chap, I'd say you was seein' things.' 'Things?' I says to him, 'I see that there corpse a-layin' there with the knife in his neck, and that was enough for me. 'Orrible, he looked, and the blood all over the floor.' 'Well,' he says, 'maybe he wasn't dead after all, and they've cleared him out of the way.' 'And cleared the house away, too, I suppose,' I said to him. So Withers says, in an odd sort o' voice, 'You're sure about the house? You wasn't letting your imagination run away with you over naked females and such?' That was a nice thing to say. I said, 'No, I wasn't. There's been some monkey business going on in this street and I'm going to get to the bottom of it, if we has to comb-out London for that chap in the muffler.' 'Yes,' says Withers, nasty-like, 'it's a pity he cleared off so sudden.' 'Well,' I says, 'you can't say I imagined *him*, anyhow, because that there girl saw him, and a mercy she did,' I said, 'or you'd be saying next I ought to be in Colney Hatch.' 'Well,' he says, 'I dunno what you think you're going to do about it. You better ring up the station and ask for instructions.'

"Which I did. And Sergeant Jones, he came down himself, and he listens attentive-like to what we both has to say, and then he walks along the street, slow-like, from end to end. And then he comes back and says to me, 'Now, Burt,' he says, 'just you describe that hall to me again, careful.' Which I does, same as I described it to you, sir. And he says, 'You're sure there was the room on the left of the stairs with the glass and silver on the table; and the room on the right with the pictures in it?' And I says, 'Yes, Sergeant, I'm quite sure of that.' And Withers says, 'Ah!' in a kind of got-you-now voice, if you take my meaning. And the Sergeant says, 'Now, Burt,' he says, 'pull yourself together and take a look at these here houses.

Don't you see they're all single-fronted? There ain't one on
'em has rooms *both* sides o' the front hall. Look at the windows, you fool,' he says."

Lord Peter poured out the last of the champagne.

"I don't mind telling you, sir" (went on the policeman),
"that I was fair knocked silly. To think of me never noticing
that! Withers had noticed it all right, and that's what made
him think I was drunk or barmy. But I stuck to what I'd seen.
I said, there must be two of them houses knocked into one,
somewhere; but that didn't work, because we'd been into all of
them, and there wasn't no such thing—not without there was
one o' them concealed doors like you read about in crook stories. 'Well, anyhow,' I says to the Sergeant, 'the yells was real
all right, because other people heard 'em. Just you ask, and
they'll tell you.' So the Sergeant says, 'Well, Burt, I'll give you
every chance.' So he knocked up Number 12 again—not
wishing to annoy Number 14 any more than he was already—
and this time the son comes down. An agreeable gentleman he
was, too; not a bit put out. He says, Oh, yes, he'd heard the
yells and his father'd heard them too. 'Number 14,' he says,
'that's where the trouble is. A very odd bloke, is Number 14,
and I shouldn't be surprised if he beats that unfortunate servant of his. The Englishman abroad, you know! The outposts
of Empire and all that kind of thing. They're rough and
ready—and then the curry in them parts is bad for the liver.'
So I was for inquiring at Number 14 again; but the Sergeant,
he loses patience and says, 'You know quite well,' he says, 'it
ain't Number 14, and in my opinion, Burt, you're either dotty
or drunk. You best go home straight away,' he says, 'and sober
up, and I'll see you again when you can give a better account
of yourself.' So I argues a bit, but it ain't no use, and away he
goes, and Withers goes back to his beat. And I walks up and
down a bit till Jessop comes to take over, and then I comes
away, and that's when I sees you, sir.

"But I ain't drunk, sir—at least, I wasn't then, though
there do seem to be a kind of a swimming in me head at this
moment. Maybe that stuff's stronger than it tastes. But I

wasn't drunk then, and I'm pretty sure I'm not dotty. I'm haunted, sir, that's what it is—haunted. It might be there was someone killed in one of them houses a many years ago, and that's what I see to-night. Perhaps they changed the numbering of the street on account of it—I've heard tell of such things—and when the same night comes round the house goes back to what it was before. But there I am, with a black mark against me, and it ain't a fair trick for no ghost to go getting a plain man into trouble. And I'm sure, sir, you'll agree with me."

The policeman's narrative had lasted some time, and the hands of the grandfather clock stood at a quarter to five. Peter Wimsey gazed benevolently at his companion, for whom he was beginning to feel a positive affection. He was, if anything, slightly more drunk than the policeman, for he had missed tea and had no appetite for his dinner; but the wine had not clouded his wits; it had only increased excitability and postponed sleep. He said:

"When you looked through the letter-box, could you see any part of the ceiling, or the lights?"

"No, sir; on account, you see, of the flap. I could see right and left and straight forward; but not upwards, and none of the near part of the floor."

"When you looked at the house from outside, there was no light except through the fan-light. But when you looked through the flap, all the rooms were lit, right and left and at the back?"

"That's so, sir."

"Are there back doors to the houses?"

"Yes, sir. Coming out of Merriman's End, you turn to the right, and there's an opening a little way along which takes you to the back doors."

"You seem to have a very distinct visual memory. I wonder if your other kinds of memory are as good. Can you tell me, for instance, whether any of the houses you went into had any particular smell? Especially 10, 12, and 14?"

"Smell, sir?" The policeman closed his eyes to stimulate recollection. "Why, yes, sir. Number 10, where the two ladies

live, that had a sort of an old-fashioned smell. I can't put me
tongue to it. Not lavender—but something as ladies keeps in
bowls and such—rose-leaves and what not. Pot-pourri, that's
the stuff. Pot-pourri. And Number 12—well, no, there was
nothing particular there, except I remember thinking they
must keep pretty good servants, though we didn't see anybody
except the family. All that floor and panelling was polished
beautiful—you could see your face in it. Beeswax and turpentine, I says to meself. And elbow-grease. What you'd call a
clean house with a good, clean smell. But Number 14—that
was different. I didn't like the smell of that. Stuffy, like as if
the nigger had been burning some o' that there incense to his
idols, maybe. I never could abide niggers."

"Ah!" said Peter. "What you say is very suggestive." He
placed his finger-tips together and shot his last question
over them:

"Ever been inside the National Gallery?"

"No, sir," said the policeman, astonished. "I can't say as I
ever was."

"That's London again," said Peter. "We're the last people
in the world to know anything of our great metropolitan insti-
tutions. Now, what is the best way to tackle this bunch of
toughs, I wonder? It's a little early for a call. Still, there's nothing like doing one's good deed before breakfast, and the
sooner you're set right with the Sergeant, the better. Let me
see. Yes—I think that may do it. Costume pieces are not as a
rule in my line, but my routine has been so much upset
already, one way and another, that an irregularity more or less
will hardly matter. Wait there for me while I have a bath and
change. I may be a little time; but it would hardly be decent to
get there before six."

The bath had been an attractive thought, but was perhaps
ill advised, for a curious languor stole over him with the touch
of the hot water. The champagne was losing its effervescence.
It was with an effort that he dragged himself out and reawakened himself with a cold shower. The matter of dress required
a little thought. A pair of grey flannel trousers was easily

found, and though they were rather too well creased for the part he meant to play, he thought that with luck they would probably pass unnoticed. The shirt was a difficulty. His collection of shirts was a notable one, but they were mostly of an inconspicuous and gentlemanly sort. He hesitated for some time over a white shirt with an open sports collar, but decided at length upon a blue one, bought as an experiment and held to be not quite successful. A red tie, if he had possessed such a thing, would have been convincing. After some consideration, he remembered that he had seen his wife in a rather wide Liberty tie, whose prevailing colour was orange. That, he felt, would do if he could find it. On her it had looked rather well; on him, it would be completely abominable. He went through into the next room; it was queer to find it empty. A peculiar sensation came over him. Here *he* was, rifling his wife's drawers, and there *she* was, spirited out of reach at the top of the house with a couple of nurses and an entirely new baby, which might turn into goodness knew what.

He sat down before the glass and stared at himself. He felt as though he ought to have changed somehow in the night; but he only looked unshaven and, he thought, a trifle intoxicated. Both were quite good things to look at the moment, though hardly suitable for the father of a family. He pulled out all the drawers in the dressing-table; they emitted vaguely familiar smells of face-powder and handkerchief sachet. He tried the big built-in wardrobe: frocks, costumes, and trays full of underwear, which made him feel sentimental. At last he struck a promising vein of gloves and stockings. The next tray held ties, the orange of the desired Liberty creation gleaming in a friendly way among them. He put it on, and observed with pleasure that the effect was Bohemian beyond description. He wandered out again, leaving all the drawers open behind him as though a burglar had passed through the room. An ancient tweed jacket of his own, of a very countrified pattern, suitable only for fishing in Scotland, was next unearthed, together with a pair of brown canvas shoes. He secured his trousers by a belt, searched for and found an old soft-brimmed felt hat of no recognizable colour, and, after removing a few trout-flies from the hat-band and tucking his shirt-sleeves well up inside the coat-sleeve, decided that he would do. As an after-thought, he returned to his wife's room and selected a wide woollen scarf in a shade of greenish blue. Thus equipped, he came downstairs again, to find P.C. Burt fast asleep, with his mouth open and snoring.

Peter was hurt. Here he was, sacrificing himself in the interests of this stupid policeman, and the man hadn't the common decency to appreciate it. However, there was no point in waking him yet. He yawned horribly and sat down.

It was the footman who wakened the sleepers at half-past six. If he was surprised to see his master, very strangely attired, slumbering in the hall in the company of a large policeman, he was too well trained to admit the fact even to himself. He merely removed the tray. The faint clink of glass roused Peter, who slept like a cat at all times.

"Hullo, William," he said. "Have I overslept myself? What's the time?"

"Five and twenty to seven, my lord."

"Just about right." He remembered that the footman slept on the top floor. "All quiet on the Western Front, William?"

"Not altogether quiet, my lord." William permitted himself a slight smile. "The young master was lively about five. But all satisfactory, I gather from Nurse Jenkyn."

"Nurse Jenkyn? Is that the young one? Don't let yourself be run away with, William. I say, just give P.C. Burt a light prod in the ribs, would you? He and I have business together."

In Merriman's End the activities of the morning were beginning. The milkman came jingling out of the cul-de-sac; lights were twinkling in upper rooms; hands were withdrawing curtains; in front of Number 10 the housemaid was already scrubbing the steps. Peter posted his policeman at the top of the street.

"I don't want to make my first appearance with official

accompaniment," he said. "Come along when I beckon. What, by the way, is the name of the agreeable gentleman in Number 12? I think he may be of some assistance to us."

"Mr. O'Halloran, sir."

The policeman looked at Peter expectantly. He seemed to have abandoned all initiative and to place implicit confidence in this hospitable and eccentric gentleman. Peter slouched down the street with his hands in his trousers pocket, and his shabby hat pulled rakishly over his eyes. At Number 12 he paused and examined the windows. Those on the ground floor were open; the house was awake. He marched up the steps, took a brief glance through the flap of the letter-box, and rang the bell. A maid in a neat blue dress and white cap and apron opened the door.

"Good morning," said Peter, slightly raising the shabby hat; "is Mr. O'Halloran in?" He gave the *r* a soft continental roll. "Not the old gentleman. I mean young Mr. O'Halloran?"

"He's in," said the maid doubtfully, "but he isn't up yet."

"Oh!" said Peter. "Well, it is a little early for a visit. But I desire to see him urgently. I am—there is a little trouble where I live. Could you entreat him—would you be so kind? I have walked all the way," he added, pathetically, and with perfect truth.

"Have you, sir?" said the maid. She added kindly, "You do look tired, sir, and that's a fact."

"It is nothing," said Peter. "It is only that I forgot to have any dinner. But if I can see Mr. O'Halloran it will be all right."

"You'd better come in, sir," said the maid. "I'll see if I can wake him." She conducted the exhausted stranger in and offered him a chair. "What name shall I say, sir?"

"Petrovinsky," said his lordship, hardily. As he had rather expected, neither the unusual name nor the unusual clothes of this unusually early visitor seemed to cause very much surprise. The maid left him in the tidy little panelled hall and went upstairs without so much as a glance at the umbrella-stand.

Left to himself, Peter sat still noticing that the hall was remarkably bare of furniture, and was lit by a single electric pendant almost immediately inside the front door. The letter-box was the usual wire-cage, the bottom of which had been carefully lined with brown paper. From the back of the house came a smell of frying bacon.

Presently there was the sound of somebody running downstairs. A young man appeared in a dressing-gown. He called out as he came: "Is that you, Stefan? Your name came up as Mr. Whiskey. Has Marfa run away again, or—What the hell? Who the devil are you, sir?"

"Wimsey," said Peter, mildly, "not Whisky; Wimsey, the policeman's friend. I just looked in to congratulate you on a mastery of the art of false perspective which I thought had perished with the ingenious Van Hoogstraaten, or at least with Grace and Lambelet."

"Oh!" said the young man. He had a pleasant counte-nance, with humorous eyes and ears pointed like a faun's. He laughed a little ruefully. "I suppose my beautiful murder is out. It was too good to last. Those bobbies! I hope to God they gave Number 14 a bad night. May I ask how you came to be involved in the matter?"

"I," said Peter, "am the kind of person in whom distressed constables confide—I cannot imagine why. And when I had the picture of that sturdy blue-clad figure, led so persuasively by a Bohemian stranger and invited to peer through a hole, I was irresistibly transported in mind to the National Gallery. Many a time have I squinted sideways through those holes into the little black box, and admired that Dutch interior of many vistas painted so convincingly on the four flat sides of the box. How right you were to preserve your eloquent silence! Your Irish tongue would have given you away. The servants, I gather, were purposely kept out of sight."

"Tell me," said Mr. O'Halloran, seating himself sideways upon the hall-table, "do you know by heart the occupation of every resident in this quarter of London? I do not paint under my own name."

"No," said Peter. "Like the good Dr. Watson, the constable could observe, though he could not reason from his observation; it was the smell of turpentine that betrayed you. I gather that at the time of his first call the apparatus was not very far off."

"It was folded together and lying under the stairs," replied the painter. "It has since been removed to the studio. My father had only just had time to get it out of the way and hitch down the 'Number 13' from the fan-light before the police reinforcements arrived. He had not even time to put back this table I am sitting on; a brief search would have discovered it in the dining-room. My father is a remarkable sportsman; I cannot too highly recommend the presence of mind he displayed while I was hareing round the houses and leaving him to hold the fort. It would have been so simple and so unenterprising to explain; but my father, being an Irishman, enjoys treading on the coat-tails of authority."

"I should like to meet your father. The only thing I do not thoroughly understand is the reason of this elaborate plot. Were you by any chance executing a burglary round the corner, and keeping the police in play while you did it?"

"I never thought of that," said the young man, with regret in his voice. "No. The bobby was not the predestined victim. He happened to be present at a full-dress rehearsal, and the joke was too good to be lost. The fact is, my uncle is Sir Lucius Preston, the R.A."

"Ah!" said Peter, "the light begins to break."

"My own style of draughtsmanship," pursued Mr. O'Halloran, "is modern. My uncle has on several occasions informed me that I draw like that only because I do not know how to draw. The idea was that he should be invited to dinner tomorrow and regaled with a story of the mysterious 'Number 13,' said to appear from time to time in this street and to be haunted by strange noises. Having thus detained him till close upon midnight, I should have set out to see him to the top of the street. As we went along, the cries would have broken out. I should have led him back —"

"Nothing," said Peter, "could be clearer. After the preliminary shock he would have been forced to confess that your draughtsmanship was a triumph of academic accuracy."

"I hope," said Mr. O'Halloran, "the performance may still go forward as originally intended." He looked with some anxiety at Peter, who replied:

"I hope so, indeed. I also hope that your uncle's heart is a strong one. But may I, in the meantime, signal to my unfortunate policeman and relieve his mind? He is in danger of losing his promotion, through a suspicion that he was drunk on duty."

"Good God!" said Mr. O'Halloran. "No—I don't want that to happen. Fetch him in."

The difficulty was to make P.C. Burt recognize in the daylight what he had seen by night through the letter-flap. Of the framework of painted canvas, with its forms and figures oddly foreshortened and distorted, he could make little. Only when the thing was set up and lighted in the curtained studio was he at length reluctantly convinced.

"It's wonderful," he said. "It's like Maskelyne and Devant. I wish the Sergeant could a-seen it."

"Lure him down here to-morrow night," said Mr. O'Halloran. "Let him come as my uncle's bodyguard. You—" he turned to Peter—"you seem to have a way with policemen. Can't you inveigle the fellow along? Your impersonation of starving and disconsolate Bloomsbury is fully as convincing as mine. How about it?"

"I don't know," said Peter. "The costume gives me pain. Besides, is it kind to a p.b. policeman? I give you the R.A., but when it comes to the guardians of the law—damn it all! I'm a family man, and I must have *some* sense of responsibility."

TALBOYS

Father!"

"Yes, my son."

"You know those peaches of Mr. Puffett's, the whacking great big ones you said I wasn't to take?"

"Well?"

"Well, I've tooken them."

Lord Peter Wimsey rolled over on his back and stared at his offspring in consternation. His wife laid down her sewing.

"Oh, Bredon, how naughty! Poor Mr. Puffett was going to exhibit them at the Flower Show."

"Well, Mummy, I didn't mean to. It was a dare."

Having offered this explanation for what it was worth, Master Bredon Wimsey again turned candid eyes upon his father, who groaned and sat up.

"And *must* you come and tell me about it? I hope, Bredon, you are not developing into a prig."

"Well, Father, Mr. Puffett saw me. An' he's coming up to have a word with you when he's put on a clean collar."

"Oh, I see," said his lordship, relieved. "And you thought you'd better come and get it over before my temper became further inflamed by hearing his version of the matter?"

"Yes, please, sir."

"That is rational, at any rate. Very well, Bredon. Go up into my bedroom and prepare for execution. You will find the cane behind the dressing-table."

"Yes, Father. You won't be long, will you, sir?"

"I shall allow precisely the right time for apprehension and remorse. Off with you!"

The culprit vanished hastily in the direction of the house; the executioner heaved himself to his feet and followed at a leisurely pace, rolling up his sleeves as he went with a certain grimness.

"My dear!" exclaimed Miss Quirk. She gazed in horror through her spectacles at Harriet, who had placidly returned to her patchwork. "Surely, *surely* you don't allow him to cane that mite of a child."

"Allow?" said Harriet, amused. "That's hardly the right word, is it?"

"But Harriet, dear, he oughtn't to do it. You don't realise how dangerous it is. He may ruin the boy's character for life. One must reason with these little people, not break their spirit by brutality. When you inflict pain and humiliation on a child like that, you make him feel helpless and inferior, and all that suppressed resentment will break out later in the most extraordinary and shocking ways."

"Oh, I don't think he resents it," said Harriet. "He's devoted to his father."

"Well, if he is," retorted Miss Quirk, "it must be a sort of masochism, and it ought to be stopped—I mean, it ought to be led gently in some other direction. It's unnatural. How could anyone feel a *healthy* devotion for a person who beats him?"

"I can't think; but it often seems to happen. Peter's mother used to lay into him with a slipper, and they've always been the best of friends."

"If I had a child belonging to me," said Miss Quirk, "I would never permit anybody to lay a hand on him. All my little nephews and nieces have been brought up on enlightened modern lines. They never even hear the word 'don't.' Now, you see what happens. Just *because* your boy was told *not* to pick the peaches, he picked them. If he hadn't been forbidden to do it, he wouldn't have been disobedient."

"No," said Harriet, "I suppose that's quite true. He would have picked the peaches just the same, but it wouldn't have been disobedience."

"Exactly," cried Miss Quirk, triumphantly. "You see — you manufacture a crime and then punish the poor child for it. Besides if it hadn't been for the prohibition, he'd have left the fruit alone."

"You don't know Bredon. He never leaves anything alone."

"Of course not," said Miss Quirk, "and he never will, so long as you surround him with prohibitions. His meddling with what doesn't belong to him is just an act of defiance."

"He's not defiant very often," said Harriet, "but of course it's very difficult to refuse a dare from a big boy like George Waggett. I expect it was George; it usually is."

"No doubt," observed Miss Quirk, "the village children are all brought up in an atmosphere of faultfinding and defiance. That kind of thing is contagious. Democratic principles are all very well, but I should scarcely have thought it wise to expose your little boy to contamination."

"Would you forbid him to play with George Waggett?" Miss Quirk was not to be caught.

"I should never *forbid* anything. I should endeavour to suggest some more suitable companion. Bredon could be encouraged to look after his little brother; that would give him a useful outlet for his energies and allow him to feel himself important."

"Oh, but he's really good with Roger," said Harriet, equably. She looked up, to see chastiser and chastised emerging from the house, hand in hand. "They seem to be quite good friends. Bredon was rather uplifted when he was promoted to a cane; he thinks it dignified and grown-up. . . . Well, ruffian, how many did you get?"

"Three," said Master Bredon confidentially. "Awful hard ones. One for being naughty, an' one for being young ass enough to be caught, and one for making a 'fernal nuisance of myself on a hot day."

"Oh, dear," said Miss Quirk, appalled by the immorality of all this. "And are you sorry for having taken poor Mr. Puffett's peaches, so that he can't get a prize at the Show?"

Bredon looked at her in astonishment.

"We've done all that," he said, with a touch of indignation. His father thought it well to intervene.

"It's a rule in this household," he announced, "that once we've been whacked, nothing more can be said. The topic is withdrawn from circulation."

"Oh," said Miss Quirk. She still felt that something ought to be done to compensate the victim of brutality and relieve his repressions. "Well, as you're a good boy, would you like to come and sit on my knee?"

"No, thank you," said Bredon. Training, or natural politeness, prompted him to amplify the refusal. "Thank you very much all the same."

"A more tactless suggestion," said Peter, "I never heard." He dropped into a deck-chair, picked up his son and heir by the waist-belt and slung him face downwards across his knees. "You'll have to eat your tea on all fours, like Nebuchadnezzar."

"Who was Nebuchadnezzar?"

"Nebuchadnezzar, the King of the Jews—" began Peter. His version of that monarch's iniquities was interrupted by the appearance, from behind the house, of a stout figure, unsuitably clad for the season in sweater, corduroy trousers, and bowler hat. "The curse is come upon me, cried the Lady of Shalott."

"Who was the Lady of Shalott?"

"I'll tell you at bedtime. Here is Mr. Puffett, breathing out threatenings and slaughter. We must now stand up and face the music. " 'Afternoon, Puffett."

" 'Arternoon, me lord and me lady," said Mr. Puffett. He removed his bowler and mopped his streaming brow. "And miss," he added, with a vague gesture in Miss Quirk's direction. "I made bold, me lord, to come round—"

"That," said Peter, "was very kind of you. Otherwise, of course, we should have come to see you and say we were sorry. We were overcome by a sudden irresistible impulse, attributable, we think, to the beauty of the fruit and the exciting nature of the enterprise. We hope very much that we have left enough for the Flower Show, and we will be careful not to do it again. We should like to mention that a measure of justice has already been done, in the shape of three of the juiciest, but if there is anything further coming to us, we shall try to receive it in a becoming spirit of penitence."

"Well, there!" said Mr. Puffett. "If I didn't say to Jinny, 'Jinny,' I says, 'I 'ope the young gentleman doesn't tell 'is lordship. He'll be main angry,' I says, 'and I wouldn't wonder if 'e didn't wallop 'im.' 'Oh, Dad,' she says, 'run up quick, never mind your Sunday coat, and tell 'is lordship as 'e didn't take only two peaches and there's plenty left,' she says. So I comes as quick as I can, only I 'ad ter wash, what with doin' out the pigsties, and jest to put on a clean collar; but not bein' as young as I was, and gettin' stout-like, I don't get up the 'ill as quick as I might. There wasn't no call to thrash the young gentleman, me lord, me 'avin' caught 'im afore much 'arm was done. Boys will be boys—and I'll lay what you like it was some of them other young devils put 'im up to it, begging your pardon, me lady."

"Well, Bredon," said his father, "it's very kind of Mr. Puffett to take that view of it. Suppose you go with him up to the house and ask Bunter to draw him a glass of beer. And on the way, you may say whatever your good feeling may suggest."

He waited till the oddly-assorted couple were half-way across the lawn, and then called, "Puffett?"

"Me lord?" said Mr. Puffett, returning alone.

"Was there really much damage done?"

"No, me lord. Only two peaches, like I said. I jest popped out from be'ind the potting-shed in time, and 'e was off like one o'clock."

"Thank heaven! From what he said, I was afraid he had wolfed the lot. And, look here, Puffett. Don't ask him who put him up to it. I shouldn't imagine he'd tell, but he might fancy he was a bit of a hero for refusing."

"I get you," said Mr. Puffett. " 'E's a proper 'igh-sperrited young gentleman, ain't 'e?" He winked, and went ponderously to rejoin his penitent robber.

The episode was considered closed; and everybody (except Miss Quirk) was surprised when Mr. Puffett arrived next morning at breakfast-time and announced without preliminary:

"Beg pardon, me lord, but all my peaches 'as bin took in the night, and I'd be glad to know 'oo done it."

"All your peaches taken, Puffett?"

"Every blessed one of 'em, me lord, practically speakin'. And the Flower Show termorrer."

"Coo!" said Master Bredon. He looked up from his plate, and found Miss Quirk's eye fixed upon him.

"That's a dirty trick," said his lordship. "Have you any idea who it was? Or would you like me to come and look into the matter for you?"

Mr. Puffett turned his bowler hat slowly over between his large hands.

"Not wishin' yer lordship ter put yerself out," he said slowly. "But it jest crossed me mind as summun at the 'ouse might be able ter throw light, as it were, upon the subjick."

"I shouldn't think so," said Peter, "but it's easy to ask. Harriet, do you by any chance know anything about the disappearance of Puffett's peaches?"

Harriet shook her head.

"Not a thing. Roger, dear, please eat your egg not quite so splashily. You've given yourself a moustache like Mr. Billing's."

"Can you give us any help, Bredon?"

"No."

"No, what?"

"No, sir. Please, Mummy, may I get down?"

"Just a minute, darling. You haven't folded up your napkin."

"Oh, sorry."

"Miss Quirk?"

Miss Quirk was so much aghast at hearing this flat denial that she had remained staring at the eldest Master Wimsey, and started on hearing herself addressed.

"Do *I* know anything? Well!" She hesitated. "Now, Bredon, am I to tell Daddy? Wouldn't you rather do it yourself?" Bredon shot a quick look at his father, but made no answer. That was only to be expected. Beat a child, and you make him a liar and a coward. "Come now," said Miss Quirk, coaxingly, "it would be *ever* so much nicer and better and braver to own up, don't you think? It'll make Mummy and Daddy very very sad if you leave it to *me* to tell them."

"To tell us what?" inquired Harriet.

"My dear Harriet," said Miss Quirk, annoyed by this foolish question, "if I tell you *what*, then I've told you, haven't I? And I'm quite *sure* Bredon would much rather tell you himself."

"Bredon," said his father, "have you any idea what Miss Quirk thinks you ought to tell us? Because, if so, you could tell us and we could get on."

"No, sir. I don't know anything about Mr. Puffett's peaches. May I get down *now*, Mummy, please?"

"Oh, Bredon!" cried Miss Quirk, reproachfully. "When I saw you, you know, with my own eyes! Ever so early—at five o'clock this morning. Now, won't you say what you were doing?"

"Oh, that!" said Bredon and blushed. Mr. Puffett scratched his head.

"What were you doing?" asked Harriet gently. "Not anything naughty, darling, were you? Or is it a secret?"

Bredon nodded. "Yes, it's a secret. Something we were doing." He sighed. "I don't think it's naughty, Mum."

"I expect it is, though," said Peter in a resigned tone. "Your secrets so often are. Quite unintentionally, no doubt, but they do have a tendency that way. Be warned in time, Bredon, and undo it, or stop doing it, before I discover it. I understand it had nothing to do with Mr. Puffett's peaches?"

"Oh, no, Father. Please, Mummy, may I—?"

"Yes, dear, you may get down. But you must ask Miss Quirk to excuse you."

"Please, Miss Quirk, will you excuse me?"

"Yes, certainly," said Miss Quirk in a mournful tone. Bredon scrambled down hastily, said, "I'm *very* sorry about your peaches, Mr. Puffett," and made his escape.

"I am sorry to have to say it," said Miss Quirk, "but I think, Mr. Puffett, you will find your peaches in the woodshed. I woke up early this morning, and I saw Bredon and another little boy crossing the yard, carrying something between them in a bucket. I waved at them from the window, and they hurried off to the woodshed in what I *can* only call a furtive kind of way."

"Well, Puffett," said his lordship, "I'm sorry about this. Shall I come up and take a look at the place? Or do you wish to search the woodshed? I am quite sure you will not find your peaches there, though I should hesitate to say what else you might not find."

"I'd be grateful," replied Mr. Puffett, "to 'ave yer advice, me lord, if so be as you could spare the time. What beats me, it's a wide bed, and yet there ain't no footprints, in a manner of speaking, except as it might be young master's, there. Which, footprints bein' in a manner your lordship's walk in life, I made bold to come. But, Master Bredon 'avin' said it weren't him, I reckon them marks'll be wot 'e left yesterday, though 'ow a man or boy either could cross that there bed of damp earth and not leave no sign of 'imself, unless 'e wos a bird, is more than I can make out, nor Jinny neither."

Mr. Tom Puffett was proud of his walled garden. He had built the wall himself (for he was a builder by trade), and it was a handsome brick structure, ten feet high, and topped on all four sides with a noble parapet of broken bottle-glass. The garden lay on the opposite side of the road from the little house where its owner lived with his daughter and son-in-law, and possessed a solid wooden gate, locked at night with a padlock. On either side of it were flourishing orchards; at the back ran a deeply rutted land, still muddy—for the summer, up to the last few days, had been a wet one.

"That there gate," said Mr. Puffett, "was locked last night at nine o'clock as ever is, an' it was still locked when I came in at seven this mornin'; so 'ooever done it 'ad to climb this yer wall."

"So I see," replied Lord Peter. "My demon child is of tender years; still, I admit that he is capable of almost anything, when suitably inspired and assisted. But I don't think he would have done it after yesterday's little incident, and I am positive that if he had done it, he'd have said so."

"Reckon you're right," agreed Mr. Puffett, unlocking the door, "though when I was a nipper like 'im, if I'd 'ad that old woman a-jorin' at me, I'd a-said anythink."

"So'd I," said Peter. "She's a friend of my sister-in-law's, said to need a country holiday. I feel we shall all shortly need a town holiday. Your plums seem to be doing well. H'm. A pebble path isn't the best medium for showing footprints."

"That it's not," admitted Mr. Puffett. He led the way between the neat flower and vegetable beds to the far end of the garden. Here at the foot of the wall was a border about nine feet wide, the middle section of which was empty except for some rows of late-sown peas. At the back, trained against the wall, stood the peach-tree, on which one great, solitary fruit glowed rosily among the dark leafage. Across the bed ran a double line of small footprints.

"Did you hoe this bed over after my son's visit yesterday?"

"No, my lord."

"Then he hasn't been here since. Those are his marks all right—I ought to know; I see enough of them on my own flower-beds." Peter's mouth twitched a little. "Look! He came very softly, trying most honourably not to tread on the peas. He pinched a peach and bolted it where he stood. I enquire, with a parent's natural anxiety, whether he ejected the stone, and observe, with relief, that he did. He moved on, he took a second peach, you popped out from the potting-shed, he started like a guilty thing and ran off in a hurry—this time, I am sorry to see, trampling on the peas. I hope he deposited the second peach-stone somewhere. Well, Puffett, you're right; there are no other footprints. Could the thief have put down a plank and walked on that, I wonder?"

"There's no planks here," said Mr. Puffett, "except the little 'un I uses meself for bedding-out. That's three feet long or thereabouts. Would yer like ter look at it, me lord?"

"No good. A little reflection shows that one cannot cross a nine-foot bed on a three-foot plank without shifting the plank, and that one cannot at the same time stand on the plank and shift it. You're sure there's only one? Yes? Then that's washed out."

"Could 'e a-brought one with 'im?"

"The orchard walls are high and hard to climb, even without the additional encumbrance of a nine-foot plank. Besides, I'm almost sure no plank has been used. I think, if it had, the edges would have left some mark. No, Puffett, nobody crossed this bed. By the way, doesn't it strike you as odd that the thief should have left just one big peach behind? It's pretty conspicuous. Was that done merely to point the joke? Or—wait a minute, what's that?"

Something had caught his eye at the back of the box border, some dozen feet to the right of where they were standing. He picked it up. It was a peach; firm and red and not quite ripe. He stood weighing it thoughtfully in his hand.

"Having picked the peach, he found it wasn't ripe and chucked it away in a temper. Is that likely, Puffett, do you think? And unless I am mistaken, there are quite a number of green leaves scattered about the foot of the tree. How often, when one picks a peach, does one break off the leaves as well?"

He looked expectantly at Mr. Puffett, who returned no answer.

"I think," went on Peter, "we will go and have a look in the lane."

Immediately behind the wall ran a rough grass verge. Mr. Puffett, leading the way to this, was peremptorily waved back and was thereafter treated to a fine exposition of detective work in the traditional manner; his lordship, extended on his stomach, thrusting his long nose and long fingers delicately through each successive tuft of grass, Mr. Puffett himself, stopping with legs well apart and hands on knees, peering anxiously at him from the edge of the lane. Presently the sleuth sat up on his heels and said:

"Here you are, Puffett. There were two men. They came up the lane from the direction of the village, wearing hobnailed boots and carrying a ladder between them. They set up the ladder *here;* the grass, you see, is still a little bent, and there are two deepish dents in the soil. One man climbed to the top and took the peaches, while the other, I think, stood at the foot to keep guard and receive the fruit in a bag or basket or something. This isn't a case of larking youngsters, Puffett; from the length of the strides they were grown men. What enemies have you made in your harmless career? Or who are your chief rivals in the peach class?"

"Well, there," said Mr. Puffett, slowly. "There's the Vicar shows peaches, and Dr. Jellyband from Great Pagford, and Jack Baker—he's the policeman, you know, came when Joe Sellon went off to Canada. And there's old Critch; him and me had a dispute about a chimbley. And Maggs the blacksmith—'e didn't 'arf like it w'en I wiped 'is eye last year with me vegetable marrers. Oh, and Waggett the butcher, 'e shows peaches. But I dunno as any o' them 'ud do me a turn like this 'ere. But see 'ere, me lord, 'ow did they *get* peaches? They couldn't reach 'em from the top of the ladder, nor yet off the wall, let alone sitting on them there bottles. The top o' the tree's five foot below the top o' the wall."

"That's simple," said Peter. "Think of the broken leaves and the peach in the box border, and consider how *you* would have done it. By the way, if you want proof that the robbing was done from this side, get a ladder and look over. I'll lay you anything you like, you'll find that the one peach that was left is hidden by the leaves from anybody looking *down* on it, though it's clearly enough seen from the garden. No, there's no difficulty about how it was done; the difficulty is to put one's hand on the culprits. Unfortunately, there's no footprint clear enough to show the complete pattern of the hob-nails."

He considered a moment, while Mr. Puffett watched him with the air of one confidently expecting a good conjuring trick.

"One could make a house to house visitation," went on his lordship, "and ask questions, or search. But it's surprising how things disappear, and how people dry up when asked direct questions. Children especially. Look here, Puffett, I'm not at all sure my prodigal son mightn't be able to throw some light on this, after all. But leave me to conduct the examination; it may need delicate handling."

There is one drawback about retreating to a really small place in the country and leaving behind you the stately public-ity of town life in a house with ten servants. When you have tucked in yourselves, and your three children, and your indis-pensable man and your equally indispensable and devoted maid, both time and space become rather fully occupied. You may, by taking your husband into your own room and accom-modating the two elder boys in his dressing-room, squeeze in an extra person who, like Miss Quirk, has been wished upon you; but it is scarcely possible to run after her all day to see that she is not getting into mischief. This is more particularly the case if you are a novelist by profession, and if, moreover, your idea of a happy holiday is to dispose as completely and briskly as possible of children, book, servants, and visitor, so as to snatch all the available moments for playing the fool with a congenial, but admittedly distracting, husband. Harriet Wimsey, writing for dear life in the sitting-room, kept one eye on her paper and the other on Master Paul Wimsey, who was disembowelling his old stuffed rabbit in the window-seat. Her ears were open for a yell from young Roger, whose rough-and-tumble with the puppy on the lawn might at any moment end in disaster. Her consciousness was occupied with her plot, her subconsciousness with the fact that she was three months behind on her contract. If she gave an occasional vague thought to her first-born, it was only to wonder whether he was hindering Bunter at his work, or merely concocting, in his own quiet way, some more than usually hideous shock for his parents. Himself was the last person he ever damaged; he was a child with a singular talent for falling on his feet. She had no attention to spare for Miss Quirk.

Miss Quirk had tried the woodshed, but it was empty, and among its contents she could find nothing more suspicious than a hatchet, a saw, a rabbit-hutch, a piece of old carpet, and a wet ring among the sawdust. She was not surprised that the evidence had been removed; Bredon had been extraordinarily anxious to leave the breakfast-table, and his parents had shut their eyes and let him go. Nor had Peter troubled to examine the premises; he had walked straight out of the house with that man Puffett, who naturally could not insist upon a search. Both Peter and Harriet were obviously burking enquiry; they did not want to admit the consequences of their wickedly mistaken system of training.

"Mummy! Come out an' play wiv' me an' Bom-bom!"

"Presently, darling. I've only got a little bit to finish."

"When's presently, Mummy?"

"Very soon. In about ten minutes."

"What's ten minutes, Mummy?"

Harriet laid down her pen. As a conscientious parent, she could not let this opportunity pass. Four years old was said to be too early, but children differed and you never knew.

"Look, darling. Here's the clock. When this long hand gets to *that*, that'll be ten minutes."

"When *this* gets to *that?*"

"Yes, darling. Sit quiet just for a little bit and look after it and tell me when it gets there."

An interval. Miss Quirk had by this time searched the garage, the greenhouse, and the shed that housed the electric plant.

"It isn't moving, Mummy."

"Yes, it is, really, only it goes very, *very* slowly. You'll have to keep a very sharp eye on it."

Miss Quirk had reached the back parts of the house itself. She entered by the back door and passed through the scullery into a passage containing, among other things, the door of the boot-hole. In this retreat, she discovered a small village maiden, cleaning a pair of very youthful boots.

"Have you seen—?" began Miss Quirk. Then her eye fell on the boots. "Are those Master Bredon's boots?"

"Yes, miss," said the girl, with the startled look peculiar to young servants when suddenly questioned by strangers.

"They're very dirty," said Miss Quirk. She remembered that Bredon had worn clean sandals when he came in to breakfast. "Give those to me for a moment," said Miss Quirk.

The small maid looked round with a gasp for advice and assistance, but both Bunter and the maid seemed to be occupied elsewhere, and one could not refuse a request from a lady staying in the house. Miss Quirk took charge of the boots. "I'll bring them back presently," she said, with a nod, and passed on. Fresh, damp earth on Bredon's boots, and something secret brought home in a pail—it scarcely needed a Peter Wimsey to put two and two together. But Peter Wimsey was refusing to detect in the right place. Miss Quirk would show him.

Miss Quirk went on along the passage and came to a door. As she approached it, it opened and Bredon's face, very dirty, appeared round the edge. At sight of her, it popped in again like a bolting rabbit.

"Ah!" said Miss Quirk. She pushed the door briskly. But even a child of six, if he can reach it and is determined, can make proper use of a bolt.

"Roger, darling, no! Shaking won't make it go any faster. It'll only give the poor clock tummyache. Oh, look, what a dreadful mess Paul's made with his rabbit. Help him pick up the bits, dear, and then you'll see, the ten minutes will be up."

Peter, returning from Mr. Puffett's garden, found his wife and two-thirds of his family rolling vigorously about the lawn with Bom-bom. Being invited to roll, he rolled, but with only half his attention.

"It's a curious thing," he observed plaintively, "that though my family makes a great deal of noise and always seems to be on top of me" (this was, at the moment, a fact), "I never can lay hands on the bit of it I want at the moment. Where is the pest, Bredon?"

"I haven't dared to ask."

Peter rose up, with his youngest son clinging, leech-like, to his shoulder, and went in search of Bunter, who knew everything without asking.

"Master Bredon, my lord, is engaged at present in altercation with Miss Quirk through the furnace-room door."

"Good God, Bunter! Which of them is inside?"

"Master Bredon, my lord."

"I breathe again. I feared we might have to effect a rescue. Catch hold of this incubus, will you, and hand him back to her ladyship."

All Miss Quirk's coaxing had been impotent to lure Bredon out of the furnace-room. At Peter's voice she turned quickly.

"Oh, Peter! Do get the child to come out. He's got those peaches in there, and I'm sure he'll make himself ill."

Lord Peter raised his already sufficiently surprised eyebrows.

"If your expert efforts fail," said he, "will my brutal threats have any effect, do you suppose? Besides, even if he *were* eating peaches, ought we, in this peremptory way, to suppress that natural expression of his personality? And whatever makes you imagine that we keep peaches in the furnace-room?"

"I know he's got them there," said Miss Quirk. "And I don't blame the child. If you beat a boy for stealing, he'll steal again. Besides, look at these boots he went out in this morning—all covered with damp mould."

Lord Peter took the boots and examined them with interest.

"Elementary, my dear Watson. But allow me to suggest that some training is necessary, even for the work of a practical domestic detective. This mould is not the same colour as the mould in Puffett's garden, and in fact is not garden mould at all. Further, if you take the trouble to look at the flower-beds, you will see that they are not wet enough to leave as much mud as this on a pair of boots. Thirdly, I can do all the detective work required in this family. And fourthly, you might realise that it is rather discourteous of you to insist that my son is a liar."

"Very well," said Miss Quirk, a little red in the face. "Fetch him out of there, and you'll see."

"But why should I fetch him out, and implant a horrible frustration-complex around the furnace-room?"

"As you like," said Miss Quirk. "It's no business of mine."

"True," said Peter. He watched her stride angrily away, and said:

"Bredon! You can come out. She's gone."

There was the sound of the sliding of iron, and his son slithered out like an eel, pulling the door carefully to behind him.

"You're not very clean, are you?" said his father, dispassionately. "It looks to me as though the furnace-room needed dusting. I'm not very clean myself, if it comes to that. I've been crawling in the lane behind Mr. Puffett's garden, trying to find out who stole his peaches."

"*She* says *I* did."

"I'll tell you a secret, Bredon. Grown-up people don't always know everything, though they try to pretend they do. That is called 'prestige,' and is responsible for most of the wars that devastate the continent of Europe."

"I think," said Bredon, who was accustomed to his father's meaningless outbursts of speech, "she's silly."

"So do I; but don't say I said so."

"And rude."

"*And* rude. I, on the other hand, am silly, but seldom rude. Your mother is neither rude nor silly."

"Which am I?"

"You are an egotistical extravert of the most irrepressible type. Why do you wear boots when you go mud-larking? It's much less trouble to clean your feet than your boots."

"There's thistles and nettles."

"True, O King! Yes, I know the place now. Down by the stream, at the far end of the paddock. . . . Is that the Secret you've got in the furnace-room?"

Bredon nodded, his mouth obstinately shut.

"Can't you let me in on it?"

Bredon shook his head.

"No, I don't think so," he explained candidly. "You see, you might feel you ought to stop it."

"That's awkward. It's so often my duty to stop things. Miss Quirk thinks I oughtn't ever to stop anything, but I don't feel I can go quite as far as that. I wonder what the devil you've been up to. We've had newts and frogs and sticklebacks, and tadpoles are out of season. I hope it isn't adders, Bredon, or you'll swell up and turn purple. I can stand for most livestock, but not adders."

" 'Tisn't *adders*," replied his son, with dawning hope. "Only very nearly. An' I don't know what it lives on. I say, if you will let me keep it, d'you mind coming in quick, 'cos I 'spect it's creeped out of the bucket."

"In that case," said his lordship, "I think we'd better conduct a search of the premises instantly. My nerves are fairly good; but if it were to go up the flue and come out in the kitchen —"

He followed his offspring hastily into the furnace-room.

"I wish," said Harriet, a little irritably, for she strongly disliked being lectured about her duties and being thus prevented from attending to them, "you wouldn't always talk about 'a' child, as if all children were alike. Even my three are all quite different."

"Mothers always think their own children are different," said Miss Quirk. "But the fundamental principles of child-psychology are the same in all. I have studied the subject. Take this question of punishment. When you punish a child—"

"*Which* child?"

"Any child—you harm the delicate mechanism of its reaction to life. Some become hardened, some become cowed, but in either case you set up a feeling of inferiority."

"It's not so simple. Don't take any child—take mine. If you reason with Bredon, he gets obstinate. He knows perfectly well when he's been naughty, and sometimes he prefers to be naughty and take the consequences. Roger's another matter. I don't think we shall ever whip Roger because he's sensitive and easily frightened and rather likes having his feelings appealed to. But he's already beginning to feel a little inferior to Bredon, because he isn't allowed to be whipped. I suppose we shall have to persuade him that whipping is part of the eldest son's prerogative. Which will be all right provided we don't have to whip Paul."

There were so many dreadful errors in this speech that Miss Quirk scarcely knew where to begin.

"I think it's such a mistake to let the younger ones fancy that there is anything superior in being the eldest. My little nephews and nieces—"

"Yes," said Harriet. "But one's got to prepare people for life, hasn't one? The day is bound to come when they realise that all Peter's real property is entailed."

Miss Quirk said she so much preferred the French custom of dividing all property equally. "It's *so* much better for the children."

"Yes; but it's very bad for the property."

"But Peter wouldn't put his property before his children!" Harriet smiled.

"My dear Miss Quirk! Peter's fifty-two, and he's reverting to type."

Peter at that moment was not looking or behaving like fifty-two, but he was rapidly reverting to a much more ancient and early type than the English landed gentleman. He had, with some difficulty, retrieved the serpent from the ash-hole, and now sat on a heap of clinker, watching it as it squirmed at the bottom of the bucket.

"Golly, what a whopper!" he said, reverently. "How did you catch him, old man?"

"Well we went to get minnows, and he came swimming along, and Joey Maggs caught him in his net. And he wanted to kill him along of biting, but I said he couldn' bite, 'cos you told us the difference between snakes. And Joe bet me I wouldn't let him bite me, an' I said I didn' mind and he said, Is it a dare? an' I said, Yes, if I can have him afterwards, so I let him bite me, only of course he didn' bite an' George helped me bring him back in the bucket."

"So Joey Maggs caught him in his net, did he?"

"Yes, but I knew he wasn't an adder. And please, sir, will you give me a net, 'cos Joe's got a lovely big one, only he was awfully late this morning and we thought he wasn't coming, and he said somebody had hidden his net."

"Did he? That's very interesting."

"Yes. May I have a net, please?"

"You may."

"Oh, thank you, Father. May I keep him, please, and what does he live on?"

"Beetles, I think." Peter plunged his hand into the bucket, and the snake wound itself about his wrist and slithered along his arm. "Come on, Cuthbert. You remind me of when I was at my prep. school, and we put one the dead spit of you into—" He caught himself up, too late.

"Where, Father?"

"Well, there was a master we all hated, and we put a snake in his bed. It's rather frequently done. In fact, I believe it's what grass-snakes are for."

"Is it very naughty to put snakes in people you don't like's beds?"

"Yes. Exceedingly naughty. No nice boy would ever think of doing such a thing. . . . I say, *Bredon*—"

● ● ● ●

Harriet Wimsey sometimes found her eldest son disconcerting. "You know, Peter, he's a most unconvincing-looking child. *I* know he's yours, because there is nobody else's he could be. And the colour's more or less right. But where on earth did he get that square, stolid appearance, and that incredible snub nose?"

But at that instant, in the furnace-room, over the body of the writhing Cuthbert, square-face and hatchet-face stared at one another and grew into an awful, impish likeness.

"Oh, Father!"

"I don't know what your mother will say. We shall get into most frightful trouble. You'd better leave it to me. Cut along now, and ask Bunter if he's got such a thing as a strong flour-bag and a stout piece of string, because you'll never make Cuthbert stay in this bucket. And for God's sake, don't go about looking like Guy Fawkes and Gunpowder Treason. When you've brought the bag, go and wash yourself. I want you to run down with a note to Mr. Puffett's."

Mr. Puffett made his final appearance just after dinner, explaining that he had not been able to come earlier, "along of a job out Lopsley way." He was both grateful and astonished.

"To think of it being old Billy Maggs and that brother of his, and all along o' them perishin' old vegetable marrers. You wouldn't think a chap cud 'arbour a grievance that way, would yer? 'Tain't even as though 'e wor a-showin' peaches of his own. It beats me. Said 'e did it for a joke. 'Joke?' I says to 'im. 'I'd like to 'ear wot the magistrate ud say to that there kinder joke.' 'Owsumdever, I got me peaches back, and the Show bein' termorrer, mebbe they won't 'ave took no 'arm. Good thing 'im and they boys 'adn't 'ave ate the lot."

The household congratulated Mr. Puffett on this happy termination to the incident. Mr. Puffett chuckled.

"Ter think o' Billy Maggs an' that good-fer-nothin' brother of 'is a-standin' on that there ladder a-fishin' for any peaches with young Joey's stickle-back net. A proper silly sight they'd a-bin if anybody'd come that way. 'Think yerselves clever,' I says to Bill. 'W'y, 'is lordship didn't only cast one eye over the place afore 'e says, "W'y Puffett," 'e says, " 'ere's Billy Maggs an' that there brother of 'is been a-wallerin' all over your wall like a 'erd of elephants." ' Ah! An' a proper fool 'e looked. 'Course, I see now it couldn't only a-been a net, knockin' the leaves about that way. But that there unripe 'un got away from 'im all right. 'Bill,' I says, 'you'll never make no fisherman, lettin' 'em get away from you like that.' Pulled 'is leg proper, I did. But see 'ere, me lord, 'ow did yer come ter know it was Billy Maggs's Joey's net? 'E ain't the only one."

"A little judicious inquiry in the proper quarter," replied his lordship. "Billy Maggs's Joe gave the show away, unbeknownst. But see here, Puffett, don't blame Joe. He knew nothing about it, nor did my boy. Only from something Joe said to Bredon I put two and two together."

"Ah!" said Mr. Puffett, "an' that reminds me. I've got more peaches back nor I wants for the Show, so I made bold to bring 'arf-a-dozen round for Master Bredon. I don't mind tellin' you, I did think for about 'arf a minute it might a-bin 'im. Only 'arf a minute, mind you—but knowin' wot boys is, I did jest think it might be."

"It's very kind of you," said Harriet. "Bredon's in bed now, but we'll give them to him in the morning. He'll enjoy them so much and be so pleased to know you've quite forgiven him for those other two."

"Oh, *them!*" replied Mr. Puffett. "Don't you say nothing more about them. Jest a bit o' fun, that wos. Well, good-night all, and many thanks to your lordship. Coo!" said Mr. Puffett, as Peter escorted him to the door, "ter think o' Billy Maggs and that there spindle-shanked brother of 'is a-fishin' for peaches with a kid's net a-top o' my wall. I didden 'arf make 'em all laugh round at the Crown."

Miss Quirk had said nothing. Peter slipped upstairs by the back way, through Harriet's bedroom into his own. In the big four-poster, one boy was asleep, but the other sat up at his cautious approach.

"Have you done the deed, Mr. Scatterblood?"

"No, Cap'en Teach, but your orders shall be carried out in one twirl of a marlin spike. In the meantime, the bold Mr. Puffett has recovered his lost treasure and has haled the criminals up before him and had them hanged at the yard-arm after a drum-head court-martial. He has sent you a share of the loot."

"Oh, good egg! What did *she* say?"

"Nothing. Mind you, Bredon, if she apologises, we'll have to call Cuthbert off. A guest is a guest, so long as she behaves like a gentleman."

"Yes, I see. Oh, I do hope she won't apologise!"

"That's a very immoral thing to hope. If you bounce like that, you'll wake your brother."

"Father! Do you think she'll fall down in a fit an' foam at the mouth?"

"I sincerely hope not. As it is, I'm taking my life in my hands. If I perish in the attempt, remember I was true to the Jolly Roger. Good-night, Cap'en Teach."

"Good-night, Mr. Scatterblood. I *do* love you."

Lord Peter Wimsey embraced his son, assumed the personality of Mr. Scatterblood and crept softly down the back way to the furnace-room. Cuthbert, safe in his bag, was drowsing upon a hot-water bottle, and made no demonstration as he was borne upstairs.

Miss Quirk did not apologise, and the subject of peaches was not mentioned again. But she may have sensed a certain constraint in the atmosphere, for she rose rather earlier than usual, saying she was tired and thought she would go to bed.

"Peter," said Harriet, when they were alone; "what *are* you and Bredon up to? You have both been so unnaturally quiet since lunch. You must be in some sort of mischief."

"To a Teach or a Scatterblood," said Peter with dignity, "there is no such word as mischief. We call it piracy on the high seas."

"I knew it," replied Harriet, resignedly. "If I'd realised the disastrous effect sons would have on your character, I'd never have trusted you with any. Oh, dear! I'm thankful that woman's gone to bed; she's *so* in the way."

"Isn't she? I think she must have picked up her infant psychology from the woman's page in the *Morning Star*. Harriet, absolve me now from all my sins of the future, so that I may enjoy them without remorse."

His wife was not unmoved by this appeal, only observing after an interval, "There's something deplorably frivolous about making love to one's wife after seven years of marriage. Is it my lord's pleasure to come to bed?"

"It is your lord's very great pleasure."

My lord, who in the uncanonical process of obtaining absolution without confession or penitence, had almost lost sight of the sin, was recalled to himself by his wife's exclamation as they passed through the outer bedroom.

"Peter! Where is Bredon?"

He was saved from having to reply by a succession of long and blood-curdling shrieks, followed by a confused outcry.

"Heavens!" said Harriet. "Something's happened to Paul!" She shot through her own room on to the Privy Stair, which, by a subsidiary flight, communicated with the back bedrooms. Peter followed more slowly.

On the landing stood Miss Quirk in her nightgown. She had Bredon's head tucked under her arm, and was smacking him with impressive though ill-directed energy. She continued to shriek as she smacked. Bredon, accustomed to a more scientific discipline, was taking the situation stolidly, but the nursemaid, with her head thrust out of an adjacent door, was crying, "Lor', whatever is it?" Bunter, clattering down from the attic in his pyjamas with a long pair of fire-tongs in his hand, pulled up short in observing his master and mistress, and, with some dim recollection of his military service, brought his weapon to the present.

Peter seized Miss Quirk by the arm and extricated his son's head from chancery.

"Dear me!" he said. "I thought you objected to corporal chastisement."

Miss Quirk was in no mood for ethical discussion.

"That horrible boy!" she said, panting. "He put a snake in my bed. A disgusting, slimy snake. A snake!"

"Another erroneous inference," said Peter. "I put it there myself."

"You? *You* put a snake in my bed?"

"But I knew all about it," put in Bredon, anxious that the honour and blame should be equitably distributed. "It was all his idea, but it was my snake."

His father rounded upon him. "I didn't tell *you* to come wandering out of your bed."

"No, sir; but you didn't tell me not to."

"Well," said Peter, with a certain grimness, "you got what you came for." He rubbed his son's rump in a comforting manner.

"Huh!" said Bredon. "*She* can't whack for toffee."

"May I ask," demanded Miss Quirk with trembling dignity, "*why* I should have been subjected to this abominable outrage?"

"I fancy," said Peter, "I must have been suffering from ingrowing resentment. It's better to let these impulses have their natural outlet, don't you agree? Repression is always so dangerous. Bunter, find Master Bredon's snake for him and return it carefully to the furnace-room. It answers to the name of Cuthbert."

MONTAGUE EGG STORIES

THE POISONED DOW '08

Good morning, miss," said Mr. Montague Egg, removing his smart trilby with something of a flourish as the front door opened. "Here I am again, you see. Not forgotten me, have you? That's right, because I couldn't forget a young lady like you, not in a hundred years. How's his lordship to-day? Think he'd be willing to see me for a minute or two?"

He smiled pleasantly, bearing in mind Maxim Number Ten of the *Salesman's Handbook*, "The goodwill of the maid is nine-tenths of the trade."

The parlourmaid, however, seemed nervous and embarrassed.

"I don't—oh, yes—come in, please. His lordship—that is to say—I'm afraid—"

Mr. Egg stepped in promptly, sample case in hand, and, to his great surprise, found himself confronted by a policeman, who, in somewhat gruff tones, demanded his name and business.

"Travelling representative of Plummet & Rose, Wines and Spirits, Piccadilly," said Mr. Egg, with the air of one who has nothing to conceal. "Here's my card. What's up, sergeant?"

"Plummet & Rose?" said the policeman. "Ah, well, just sit

down a moment, will you? The inspector'll want to have a word with you, I shouldn't wonder."

More and more astonished, Mr. Egg obediently took a seat, and in a few minutes' time found himself ushered into a small sitting-room which was occupied by a uniformed police inspector and another policeman with a note-book.

"Ah!" said the inspector. "Take a seat, will you, Mr.—ha, hum—Egg. Perhaps you can give us a little light on this affair. Do you know anything about a case of port wine that was sold to Lord Borrodale last spring?"

"Certainly I do," replied Mr. Egg, "if you mean the Dow '08. I made the sale myself. Six dozen at 192s. a dozen. Ordered from me, personally, March 3rd. Dispatched from our head office March 8th. Receipt acknowledged March 10th, with cheque in settlement. All in order our end. Nothing wrong with it, I hope? We've had no complaint. In fact, I've just called to ask his lordship how he liked it and to ask if he'd care to place a further order."

"I see," said the inspector. "You just happened to call to-day in the course of your usual round? No special reason?"

Mr. Egg, now convinced that something was very wrong indeed, replied by placing his order-book and road schedule at the inspector's disposal.

"Yes," said the inspector, when he had glanced through them. "That seems to be all right. Well, now, Mr. Egg, I'm sorry to say that Lord Borrodale was found dead in his study this morning under circumstances strongly suggestive of his having taken poison. And what's more, it looks very much as if the poison had been administered to him in a glass of this port wine of yours."

"You don't say!" said Mr. Egg incredulously. "I'm very sorry to hear that. It won't do us any good, either. Not but what the wine was wholesome enough when we sent it out. Naturally, it wouldn't pay us to go putting anything funny into our wines; I needn't tell you that. But it's not the sort of publicity we care for. What makes you think it was the port, anyway?"

For answer, the inspector pushed over to him a glass decanter which stood upon the table.

"See what you think yourself. It's all right—we've tested it for finger-prints already. Here's a glass if you want one, but I shouldn't advise you to swallow anything—not unless you're fed up with life."

Mr. Egg took a cautious sniff at the decanter and frowned. He poured out a thimbleful of the wine, sniffed and frowned again. Then he took an experimental drop upon his tongue, and immediately expectorated, with the utmost possible delicacy, into a convenient flower-pot.

"Oh, dear, oh, dear," said Mr. Montague Egg. His rosy face was puckered with distress. "Tastes to me as though the old gentleman had been dropping his cigar-ends into it."

The inspector exchanged a glance with the policeman.

"You're not far out," he said. "The doctor hasn't quite finished his post-mortem, but he says it looks to him like nicotine poisoning. Now, here's the problem. Lord Borrodale was accustomed to drink a couple of glasses of port in his study every night after dinner. Last night the wine was taken in to him as usual at 9 o'clock. It was a new bottle, and Craven—that's the butler—brought it straight up from the cellar in a basket arrangement—"

"A cradle," interjected Mr. Egg.

"—a cradle, if that's what you call it. James the footman followed him, carrying the decanter and a wineglass on a tray. Lord Borrodale inspected the bottle, which still bore the original seal, and then Craven drew the cork and decanted the wine in full view of Lord Borrodale and the footman. Then both servants left the room and retired to the kitchen quarters, and as they went, they heard Lord Borrodale lock the study door after them."

"What did he do that for?"

"It seems he usually did. He was writing his memoirs—he was a famous judge, you know—and as some of the papers he was using were highly confidential, he preferred to make himself safe against sudden intruders. At 11 o'clock, when the household went to bed, James noticed that the light was still on in the study. In the morning it was discovered that Lord Borrodale had not been to bed. The study door was still locked and, when it was broken open, they found him lying dead on the floor. It looked as though he had been taken ill, had tried to reach the bell, and had collapsed on the way. The doctor says he must have died at about 10 o'clock."

"Suicide?" suggested Mr. Egg.

"Well, there are difficulties about that. The position of the body, for one thing. Also, we've carefully searched the room and found no traces of any bottle or anything that he could have kept the poison in. Besides, he seems to have enjoyed his life. He had no financial or domestic worries, and in spite of his advanced age his health was excellent. Why should he commit suicide?"

"But if he didn't," objected Mr. Egg, "how was it he didn't notice the bad taste and smell of the wine?"

"Well, he seems to have been smoking a pretty powerful cigar at the time," said the inspector (Mr. Egg shook a reproachful head), "and I'm told he was suffering from a slight cold, so that his taste and smell may not have been in full working order. There are no finger-prints on the decanter or the glass except his own and those of the butler and the footman—though, of course, that wouldn't prevent anybody dropping poison into either of them, if only the door hadn't been locked. The windows were both fastened on the inside, too, with burglar-proof catches."

"How about the decanter?" asked Mr. Egg, jealous for the reputation of his firm. "Was it clean when it came in?"

"Yes, it was. James washed it out immediately before it went into the study; the cook swears she saw him do it. He used water from the tap and then swilled it round with a drop of brandy."

"Quite right," said Mr. Egg approvingly.

"And there's nothing wrong with the brandy, either, for Craven took a glass of it himself afterwards—to settle his palpitations, so he says." The inspector sniffed meaningly. "The glass was wiped out by James when he put it on the tray, and then the whole thing was carried along to the study. Nothing was put down or left for a moment between leaving the pantry and entering the study, but Craven recollects that as he was crossing the hall Miss Waynfleet stopped him and spoke to him for a moment about some arrangements for the following day."

"Miss Waynfleet? That's the niece, isn't it? I saw her on my last visit. A very charming young lady."

"Lord Borrodale's heiress," remarked the inspector meaningly.

"A very *nice* young lady," said Mr. Egg, with emphasis. "And I understand you to say that Craven was carrying only the cradle, not the decanter or the glass."

"That's so."

"Well, then, I don't see that she could have put anything into what James was carrying." Mr. Egg paused. "The seal on the cork, now—you say Lord Borrodale saw it?"

"Yes, and so did Craven and James. You can see it for yourself, if you like—what's left of it."

The inspector produced an ash-tray, which held a few fragments of dark blue sealing-wax, together with a small quantity of cigar-ash. Mr. Egg inspected them carefully.

"That's our wax and our seal, all right," he pronounced. "The top of the cork has been sliced off cleanly with a sharp knife and the mark's intact. 'Plummet & Rose. Dow 1908.' Nothing wrong with that. How about the strainer?"

"Washed out that same afternoon in boiling water by the kitchenmaid. Wiped immediately before using by James, who brought it in on the tray with the decanter and the glass. Taken out with the bottle and washed again at once, unfortunately—otherwise, of course, it might have told us something about when the nicotine got into the port wine."

"Well," said Mr. Egg obstinately, "it didn't get in at our place, that's a certainty. What's more, I don't believe it ever was in the bottle at all. How could it be? Where *is* the bottle, by the way?"

"It's just been packed up to go to the analyst, I think," said the inspector, "but as you're here, you'd better have a look at it. Podgers, let's have that bottle again. There are no finger-prints on it except Craven's, by the way, so it doesn't look as if it had been tampered with."

The policeman produced a brown paper parcel, from which he extracted a port-bottle, its mouth plugged with a clean cork. Some of the original dust of the cellar still clung to it, mingled with finger-print powder. Mr. Egg removed the cork and took a long, strong sniff at the contents. Then his face changed.

"Where did you get this bottle from?" he demanded sharply.

"From Craven. Naturally, it was one of the first things we asked to see. He took us along to the cellar and pointed it out."

"Was it standing by itself or with a lot of other bottles?"

"It was standing on the cellar floor at the end of a row of empties, all belonging to the same bin; he explained that he put them on the floor in the order in which they were used, till the time came for them to be collected and taken away."

Mr. Egg thoughtfully tilted the bottle; a few drops of thick red liquid, turbid with disturbed crust, escaped into his wine-glass. He smelt them again and tasted them. His snub nose looked pugnacious.

"Well?" asked the inspector.

"No nicotine there, at all events," said Mr. Egg, "unless my nose deceives me, which, you will understand, inspector, isn't likely, my nose being my livelihood, so to speak. No. You'll have to send it to be analysed of course; I quite understand that, but I'd be ready to bet quite a little bit of money you'll find that bottle innocent. And that, I needn't tell you, will be a great relief to our minds. And I'm sure, speaking for myself, I very much appreciate the kind way you've put the matter before me."

"That's all right; your expert knowledge is of value. We can probably now exclude the bottle straight away and con-centrate on the decanter."

"Just so," replied Mr. Egg. "Ye-es. Do you happen to know how many of the six dozen bottles had been used?"

"No, but Craven can tell us, if you really want to know."

"Just for my own satisfaction," said Mr. Egg. "Just to be sure that this *is* the right bottle, you know. I shouldn't like to feel I might have misled you in any way."

The inspector rang the bell, and the butler promptly appeared—an elderly man of intensely respectable appearance.

"Craven," said the inspector, "this is Mr. Egg of Plummet & Rose's."

"I am already acquainted with Mr. Egg."

"Quite. He is naturally interested in the history of the port wine. He would like to know—what is it, exactly, Mr. Egg?"

"This bottle," said Monty, rapping it lightly with his finger-nail, "it's the one you opened last night?"

"Yes, sir."

"Sure of that?"

"Yes, sir."

"How many dozen have you got left?"

"I couldn't say off-hand, sir, without the cellarbook."

"And that's in the cellar, eh? I'd like to have a look at your cellars—I'm told they're very fine. All in apple-pie order, I'm sure. Right temperature and all that?"

"Undoubtedly, sir."

"We'll all go and look at the cellar," suggested the inspector, who in spite of his expressed confidence seemed to have doubts about leaving Mr. Egg alone with the butler.

Craven bowed and led the way, pausing only to fetch the keys from his pantry.

"This nicotine, now," prattled Mr. Egg, as they proceeded down a long corridor, "is it very deadly? I mean, would you require a great quantity of it to poison a person?"

"I understand from the doctor," replied the inspector, "that a few drops of the pure extract, or whatever they call it, would produce death in anything from twenty minutes to seven or eight hours."

"Dear, dear!" said Mr. Egg. "And how much of the port had the poor old gentleman taken? The full two glasses?"

"Yes, sir; to judge by the decanter, he had. Lord Borrodale had the habit of drinking his port straight off. He did not sip it, sir."

Mr. Egg was distressed.

"Not the right thing at all," he said mournfully. "No, no. Smell, sip, and savour to bring out the flavour—that's the rule for wine, you know. Is there such a thing as a pond or stream in the garden, Mr. Craven?"

"No, sir," said the butler, a little surprised.

"Ah! I was just wondering. Somebody must have brought the nicotine along in something or other, you know. What would they do afterwards with the little bottle or whatever it was?"

"Easy enough to throw it in among the bushes or bury it, surely," said Craven. "There's six acres of garden, not counting the meadow or the courtyard. Or there are the water-butts, of course, and the well."

"How stupid of me," confessed Mr. Egg. "I never thought of that. Ah! this is the cellar, is it? Splendid—a real slap-up outfit, I call this. Nice, even temperature, too. Same summer and winter, eh? Well away from the house-furnace?"

"Oh, yes, indeed, sir. That's the other side of the house. Be careful of the last step, gentlemen; it's a little broken away. Here is where the Dow '08 stood, sir. No. 17 bin—one, two, three and a half dozen remaining, sir."

Mr. Egg nodded and, holding his electric torch close to the protruding necks of the bottles, made a careful examination of the seals.

"Yes," he said, "here they are. Three and a half dozen, as you say. Sad to think that the throat they should have gone down lies, as you might say, closed up by Death. I often think, as I make my rounds, what a pity it is we don't all grow mellower and softer in our old age, same as this wine. A fine old gentleman, Lord Borrodale, or so I'm told, but something of a tough nut, if that's not disrespectful."

"He was hard, sir," agreed the butler, "but just. A very just master."

"Quite," said Mr. Egg. "And these, I take it, are the empties. Twelve, twenty-four, twenty-nine—and one is thirty—and three and a half dozen is forty-two—seventy-two—six dozen—that's O.K. by me." He lifted the empty bottles one by one. "They say dead men tell no tales, but they talk to little Monty Egg all right. This one, for instance. If this ever held Plummet & Rose's Dow '08 you can take Monty Egg and scramble him. Wrong smell, wrong crust, and that splash of white-wash was never put on by our cellar-man. Very easy to mix up one empty bottle with another. Twelve, twenty-four, twenty-eight and one is twenty-nine. I wonder what's become of the thirtieth bottle."

"I'm sure I never took one away," said the butler.

"The pantry keys—on a nail inside the door—very accessible," said Monty.

"Just a moment," interrupted the inspector. "Do you say that that bottle doesn't belong to the same bunch of port wine?"

"No, it doesn't—but no doubt Lord Borrodale sometimes went in for a change of vintage." Mr. Egg inverted the bottle and shook it sharply. "Quite dry. Curious. Had a dead spider at the bottom of it. You'd be surprised how long a spider can exist without food. Curious that this empty bottle, which comes in the middle of the row, should be drier than the one at the beginning of the row, and should contain a dead spider. We see a deal of curious things in our calling, inspector—we're encouraged to notice things, as you might say. 'The salesman with the open eye sees commissions mount up high.' You might call this bottle a curious thing. And here's another. That other bottle, the one you said was opened last night, Craven—how did you come to make a mistake like that? If my nose is to be trusted, not to mention my palate, that bottle's been open a week at least."

"Has it indeed, sir? I'm sure it's the one as I put here at the end of this row. Somebody must have been and changed it."

"But—" said the inspector. He stopped in mid-speech, as though struck by a sudden thought. "I think you'd better let me have those cellar keys of yours, Craven, and we'll get this cellar properly examined. That'll do for the moment. If you'll just step upstairs with me, Mr. Egg, I'd like a word with you."

"Always happy to oblige," said Monty agreeably. They returned to the upper air.

"I don't know if you realise, Mr. Egg," observed the inspector, "the bearing, or, as I might say, the inference of what you said just now. Supposing you're right about this bottle not being the right one, somebody's changed it on purpose, and the right one's missing. And, what's more, the person that changed the bottle left no finger-prints behind him—or her."

"I see what you mean," said Mr. Egg, who had indeed drawn this inference some time ago, "and what's more, it looks as if the poison had been in the bottle after all, doesn't it? And that—you're going to say—is a serious look-out for Plummet & Rose, seeing there's no doubt our seal was on the bottle when it was brought into Lord Borrodale's room. I don't deny it, inspector. It's useless to bluster and say 'No, no,' when it's perfectly clear that the facts are so. That's a very useful motto for a man that wants to get on in our line of business."

"Well, Mr. Egg," said the inspector, laughing, "what will you say to the next inference? Since nobody but you had any interest in changing that bottle over, it looks as though I ought to clap the handcuffs on you."

"Now, that's a disagreeable sort of an inference," protested Mr. Egg, "and I hope you won't follow it up. I shouldn't like anything of that sort to happen, and my employers wouldn't fancy it either. Don't you think that, before we do anything we might have cause to regret, it would be a good idea to have a look in the furnace-room?"

"Why the furnace-room?"

"Because," said Mr. Egg, "it's the place that Craven particularly didn't mention when we were asking him where anybody might have put a thing he wanted to get rid of."

The inspector appeared to be struck by this line of reasoning. He enlisted the aid of a couple of constables, and very soon the ashes of the furnace that supplied the central heating were being assiduously raked over. The first find was a thick mass of semi-molten glass, which looked as though it might once have been part of a wine bottle.

"Looks as though you might be right," said the inspector, "but I don't see how we're to prove anything. We're not likely to get any nicotine out of this."

"I suppose not," agreed Mr. Egg sadly. "But"—his face brightened—"how about this?"

From the sieve in which the constable was sifting the ashes he picked out a thin piece of warped and twisted metal, to which a lump of charred bone still clung.

"What on earth's that?"

"It doesn't look like much, but I think it might once have been a corkscrew," suggested Mr. Egg mildly. "There's something homely and familiar about it. And, if you'll look here, I think you'll see that the metal part of it is hollow. And I shouldn't be surprised if the thick bone handle was hollow, too. It's very badly charred, of course, but if you were to split it open, and if you were to find a hollow inside it, and possibly a little melted rubber—well, that might explain a lot."

The inspector smacked his thigh.

"By Jove, Mr. Egg!" he exclaimed, "I believe I see what you're getting at. You mean that if this corkscrew had been made hollow, and contained a rubber reservoir, inside, like a fountain-pen, filled with poison, the poison might be made to flow down the hollow shaft by pressure on some sort of plunger arrangement."

"That's it," said Mr. Egg. "It would have to be screwed into the cork very carefully, of course, so as not to damage the tube, and it would have to be made long enough to project beyond the bottom of the cork, but still, it might be done. What's more, it has been done, or why should there be this little hole in the metal, about a quarter of an inch from the tip?

Ordinary corkscrews never have holes in them—not in my experience, and I've been, as you might say, brought up on corkscrews."

"But who, in that case—?"

"Well, the man who drew the cork, don't you think? The man whose finger-prints were on the bottle."

"Craven? But where's his motive?"

"I don't know," said Mr. Egg, "but Lord Borrodale was a judge, and a hard judge too. If you were to have Craven's finger-prints sent up to Scotland Yard, they might recognise them. I don't know. It's possible, isn't it? Or maybe Miss Waynfleet might know something about him. Or he might just possibly be mentioned in Lord Borrodale's memoirs that he was writing."

The inspector lost no time in following up this suggestion. Neither Scotland Yard nor Miss Waynfleet had anything to say against the butler, who had been two years in his situation and had always been quite satisfactory, but a reference to the records of Lord Borrodale's judicial career showed that, a good many years before, he had inflicted a savage sentence of penal servitude on a young man called Craven, who was by trade a skilled metal-worker and had apparently been involved in a fraud upon his employer. A little further investigation showed that this young man had been released from prison six months previously.

"Craven's son, of course," said the inspector. "And he had the manual skill to make the corkscrew in exact imitation of the one ordinarily used in the household. Wonder where they got the nicotine from? Well, we shall soon be able to check that up. I believe it's not difficult to obtain it for use in the garden. I'm very much obliged to you for your expert assistance, Mr. Egg. It would have taken us a long time to get to the rights and wrongs of those bottles. I suppose, when you found that Craven had given you the wrong one, you began to suspect him?"

"Oh, no," said Mr. Egg, with modest pride, "I knew it was Craven the minute he came into the room."

"No, did you? You're a regular Sherlock, aren't you? But why?"

"He called me 'sir,'" explained Mr. Egg, coughing delicately. "Last time I called he addressed me as 'young fellow' and told me that tradesmen must go round to the back door. A bad error of policy. 'Whether you're wrong or whether you're right, it's always better to be polite,' as it says in the *Salesman's Handbook*."

SLEUTHS ON THE SCENT

The commercial room at the Pig and Pewter presented to Mr. Montague Egg the aspect of a dim cavern in which some primæval inhabitant had been cooking his mammoth-meat over a fire of damp seaweed. In other words, it was ill lit, cold, smoky, and permeated with an odour of stale food.

"Oh dear, oh dear!" muttered Mr. Egg. He poked at the sullen coals, releasing a volume of pea-coloured smoke which made him cough.

Mr. Egg rang the bell.

"Oh, if you please, sir," said the maid who answered the summons, "I'm sure I'm very sorry, but it's always this way when the wind's in the east, sir, and we've tried ever so many sorts of cowls and chimney-pots, you'd be surprised. The man was here to-day a-working in it, which is why the fire wasn't lit till just now, sir, but they don't seem able to do nothink with it. But there's a beautiful fire in the bar-parlour, sir, if you cared to step along. There's a very pleasant party in there, sir. I'm sure you would be comfortable. There's another commercial gentleman like yourself, sir, and old Mr. Faggott and Sergeant Jukes over from Drabblesford. Oh, and there's two parties of motorists, but they're all quite nice and quiet, sir."

"That'll suit me all right," said Mr. Egg amiably. But he made a mental note, nevertheless, that he would warn his fellow-commercials against the Pig and Pewter at Mugbury, for an inn is judged by its commercial room. Moreover, the dinner had been bad, with a badness not to be explained by his own rather late arrival.

In the bar-parlour, however, things were better. At one side of the cheerful hearth sat old Mr. Faggott, an aged countryman, beneath whose scanty white beard dangled a long, scarlet comforter. In his hand was a tankard of ale. Opposite to him, also with a tankard, was a large man, obviously a policeman in mufti. At a table in front of the fireplace sat an alert-looking, darkish, youngish man whom Mr. Egg instantly identified as the commercial gentleman by the stout leather bag at his side. He was drinking sherry. A young man and a girl in motor-cycling kit were whispering together at another table, over a whisky-and-polly and a glass of port. Another man, with his hat and burberry on, was ordering Guinness at the little serving-hatch which communicated with the bar, while, in a far corner, an indeterminate male figure sat silent and half concealed by a slouch hat and a newspaper. Mr. Egg saluted the company with respect and observed that it was a nasty night.

The commercial gentleman uttered an emphatic agreement. "I ought to have got on to Drabblesford to-night," he added, "but with this frost and drizzle and frost again the roads are in such a state, I think I'd better stay where I am."

"Same here," said Mr. Egg, approaching the hatch. "Half of mild-and-bitter, please. Cold, too, isn't it?"

"Very cold," said the policeman.

"Ar," said old Mr. Faggott.

"Foul," said the man in the burberry, returning from the hatch and seating himself near the commercial gentleman. "I've reason to know it. Skidded into a telegraph-pole two miles out. You should see my bumpers. Well! I suppose it's only to be expected this time of year."

"Ar!" said old Mr. Faggott. There was a pause.

"Well," said Mr. Egg, politely raising his tankard, "here's luck!"

The company acknowledged the courtesy in a suitable manner, and another pause followed. It was broken by the traveller.

"Acquainted with this part of the country, sir?"

"Why, no," said Monty Egg. "It's not my usual beat. Bastable covers it as a rule—Henry Bastable—perhaps you know him? He and I travel for Plummet & Rose, Wines and Spirits."

"Tall, red-haired fellow?"

"That's him. Laid up with rheumatic fever, poor chap, so I'm taking over temporarily. My name's Egg—Montague Egg."

"Oh, yes, I think I've heard of you from Taylor of Harrogate Bros. Redwood is my name. Fragonard & Co., perfumes and toilet accessories."

Mr. Egg bowed and inquired, in a discreet and general way, how Mr. Redwood was finding things.

"Not too bad. Of course, money's a bit tight; that's only to be expected. But, considering everything, not too bad. I've got a line here, by the way, which is doing pretty well and may give *you* something to think about." He bent over, unstrapped his bag and produced a tall flask, its glass stopper neatly secured with a twist of fine string. "Tell me what you think of that." He removed the string and handed the sample to Monty.

"Parma violet?" said that gentleman, with a glance at the label. "The young lady should be the best judge of this. Allow me, miss. Sweets to the sweet," he added gallantly. "You'll excuse me, I'm sure."

The girl giggled.

"Go on, Gert," said her companion. "Never refuse a good offer." He removed the stopper and sniffed heartily at the perfume. "This is high-class stuff, this is. Put a drop on your handkerchief. Here—I'll do it for you!"

"Oh! it's lovely!" said the girl. "Refined, I call it. Get along, Arthur, do! Leave my handkerchief alone—what they'll all think of you! I'm sure this gentleman won't mind you having a drop for yourself if you want it."

Arthur favoured the company with a large wink, and sprinkled his handkerchief liberally. Monty rescued the flask and passed it to the man in the burberry.

"Excuse me, sir," said Mr. Redwood, "but if I might point it out, it's not everybody knows the right way to test perfume. Just dab a little on the hand, wait while the liquid evaporates, and then raise the hand to the nostrils."

"Like this?" said the man in the burberry, dexterously hitching the stopper out with his little finger, pouring a drop of perfume into his left palm, and re-stoppering the bottle, all in one movement. "Yes, I see what you mean."

"That's very interesting," said Monty, much impressed and following the example set him. "Same as when you put old brandy in a thin glass and cradle it in the hollow of the palm to bring out the aroma. The warmth of the hand makes the ethers expand. I'm very glad to know from you, Mr. Redwood, what is the correct method with perfumes. Ready to learn means ready to earn — that's Monty Egg, every time. A very fine perfume indeed. Would you like to try it, sir?"

He offered the bottle first to the aged countryman (who shook his head, remarking acidly that he "couldn't abide smells and sich nastiness") and then to the policeman, who, disdaining refinements, took a strong sniff at the bottle and pronounced the scent "good, but a bit powerful for his liking."

"Well, well, tastes differ," said Monty. He glanced round, and, observing the silent man in the far corner, approached him confidently with a request for his opinion.

"What the devil's the matter with *you*?" growled this person, emerging reluctantly from behind his barricade of newspaper, and displaying a bristling and bellicose fair moustache and a pair of sulky blue eyes. "There seems to be no peace in this bar. Scent? Can't abide the stuff." He snatched the perfume impatiently from Mr. Egg's hand, sniffed, and thrust the stopper back with such blind and fumbling haste that it missed the neck of the flask altogether and rolled away under the table. "Well, it's scent. What else do you want me to say about it? I'm not going to buy it, if that's what you're after."

"Certainly not, sir," said Mr. Redwood, hurt, and hastening to retrieve his scattered property. "Wonder what's bitten him," he continued, in a confidential undertone. "Nasty glitter in his eye. Hands all of a tremble. Better look out for him, sergeant. We don't want murder done. Well, anyhow, madam and gentlemen, what should you say if I was to tell you that we're able to retail that large bottle, as it stands—retail it, mind you—at three shillings and sixpence?"

"Three-and-six?" said Mr. Egg, surprised. "Why, I should have thought that wouldn't so much as pay the duty on the spirit."

"Nor it would," triumphed Mr. Redwood, "if it was spirit. But it isn't, and that's the whole point. It's a trade secret and I can't say more, but if you were to be asked whether that was or was not the finest Parma violet, equal to the most expensive marks, I don't mind betting you'd never know the difference."

"No, indeed," said Mr. Egg. "Wonderful, I call it. Pity they can't discover something similar to help the wine and spirit business, though I needn't say it wouldn't altogether do, or what would the Chancellor of the Exchequer have to say about it? Talking of that, what are you drinking? And you, miss? I hope you'll allow me, gentlemen. Same again all round, please."

The landlord hastened to fulfil the order and, as he passed through the bar-parlour, switched on the wireless, which instantly responded with the 9 o'clock time-signal, followed clearly by the voice of the announcer:

"This is the National programme from London. Before I read the weather report, here is a police message. In connection with the murder of Alice Steward, at Nottingham, we are asked by the Commissioner of Police to broadcast the following. The police are anxious to get in touch with a young man named Gerald Beeton, who is known to have visited the deceased on the afternoon preceding her death. This man is aged thirty-five, medium height, medium build, fair hair, small moustache, grey or blue eyes, full face, fresh colour. When last seen was wearing a grey lounge suit, soft grey hat, and fawn overcoat, and is thought to be now travelling the country in a Morris car, number unknown. Will this man, or anyone able to throw light on his whereabouts, please communicate at once with the Superintendent of Police, Nottingham, or with any police-station? Here is the weather report. A deep depression ...."

"Oh, switch it off, George," urged Mr. Redwood. "We don't want to hear about depressions."

"That's right," agreed the landlord, switching off. "What gets me is these police descriptions. How'd they think any-one's going to recognise a man from the sort of stuff they give you? Medium this and medium the other, and ordinary face and fair complexion and a soft hat—might be anybody."

"So it might," said Monty. "It might be me."

"Well, that's true, it might," said Mr. Redwood. "Or it might be this gentleman."

"That's a fact," admitted the man in the burberry. "Or it might be fifty men out of every hundred."

"Yes, or"—Monty jerked his head cautiously towards the newspaper in the corner—"him!"

"Well, so you say," said Redwood, "but nobody else has seen him to look at. Unless it's George."

"I wouldn't care to swear to him," said the landlord, with a smile. "He come straight in here and ordered a drink and paid for it without so much as looking at me, but from what I did see of him the description would fit him as well as anybody. And what's more, he's got a Morris car—it's in the garage now."

"That's nothing against him," said Monty. "So've I."

"And I," said the man in the burberry.

"And I," chimed in Redwood. "Encourage home indus-tries, I say. But it's no help to identifying a man. Beg your par-don, sergeant, and all that, but why don't the police make it a bit easier for the public?"

"Why," said the sergeant, "because they 'as to rely on the damnfool description given to them by the public. That's why."

"One up to you," said Redwood pleasantly. "Tell me, ser-geant, all this stuff about wanting to interview the fellow is all eyewash, isn't it? I mean, what they really want to do is arrest him."

"That ain't for me to say," replied the sergeant ponderously. "You must use your own judgement about that. What they're asking for is an interview, him being known to have been one of the last people to see her before she was done in. If he's sensible, he'll turn up. If he don't answer to the summons—well, you can think what you like."

"Who is he, anyway?" asked Monty.

"Now you want to know something. Ain't you seen the evening papers?"

"No; I've been on the road since five o'clock."

"Well, it's like this here. This old lady, Miss Alice Steward, lived all alone with a maid in a little 'ouse on the outskirts of Nottingham. Yesterday afternoon was the maid's afternoon out, and just as she was stepping out of the door, a bloke drives up in a Morris—or so *she* says, though you can't trust these girls, and if you ask me, it may just as well have been an Austin or Wolseley, or anything else, for that matter. He asks to see Miss Steward and the girl shows him into the sitting-room, and as she does so she hears the old girl say, 'Why, Gerald!'—like that. Well, she goes off to the pictures and leaves 'em to it, and when she gets back at 10 o'clock, she finds the old lady lying with 'er 'ead bashed in."

Mr. Redwood leaned across and nudged Mr. Egg. The stranger in the far corner had ceased to read his paper, and was peering stealthily round the edge of it.

"That's brought *him* to life, anyway," muttered Mr. Redwood. "Well, sergeant, but how did the girl know the fellow's surname and who he was?"

"Why," replied the sergeant, "she remembered once 'earing the old lady speak of a man called Gerald Beeton—a good many years ago, or so she said, and she couldn't tell us much about it. Only she remembered the name, because it was the same as the one on her cookery-book."

"Was that at Lewes?" demanded the young man called Arthur suddenly.

"Might have been," admitted the sergeant, glancing rather sharply at him. "The old lady came from Lewes. Why?"

"I remember, when I was a kid at school, hearing my mother mention an old Miss Steward at Lewes, who was very rich and had adopted a young fellow out of a chemist's shop. I think he ran away, and turned out badly, or something. Anyway, the old lady left the town. She was supposed to be very rich and to keep all her money in a tin box, or something. My mother's cousin knew an old girl who was Miss Steward's housekeeper—but I dare say it was all rot. Anyhow, that was about six or seven years ago, and I believe my mother's cousin is dead now and the housekeeper too. My mother," went on the young man called Arthur, anticipating the next question, "died two years ago."

"That's very interesting, all the same," said Mr. Egg encouragingly. "You ought to tell the police about it."

"Well, I have, haven't I?" said Arthur, with a grin, indicating the sergeant. "Though I expect they know it already. Or do I have to go to the police-station?"

"For the present purpose," replied the sergeant, "I am a police-station. But you might give me your name and address."

The young man gave his name as Arthur Bunce, with an address in London. At this point the girl Gertrude was struck with an idea.

"But what about the tin box? D'you think he killed her to get it?"

"There's been nothing in the papers about the tin box," put in the man in the burberry.

"They don't let everything get into the papers," said the sergeant.

"It doesn't seem to be in the paper our disagreeable friend is reading," murmured Mr. Redwood, and as he spoke, that person rose from his seat and came over to the serving-hatch, ostensibly to order more beer, but with the evident intention of overhearing more of the conversation.

"I wonder if they'll catch the fellow," pursued Redwood

thoughtfully. "They—by Jove! yes, that explains it—they must be keeping a pretty sharp look-out. I wondered why they held me up outside Wintonbury to examine my driving-licence. I suppose they're checking all the Morrises on the roads. Some job."

"All the Morrises in this district, anyway," said Monty. "They held me up just outside Thugford."

"Oho!" cried Arthur Bunce, "that looks as though they've got a line on the fellow. Now, sergeant, come across with it. What do you know about this, eh?"

"I can't tell you anything about that," replied Sergeant Jukes, in a stately manner. The disagreeable man moved away from the serving-hatch, and at the same moment the sergeant rose and walked over to a distant table to knock out his pipe, rather unnecessarily, into a flower-pot. He remained there, refilling the pipe from his pouch, his bulky form towering between the Disagreeable Man and the door.

"They'll never catch him," said the Disagreeable Man, suddenly and unexpectedly. "They'll never catch him. And do you know why? I'll tell you. Not because he's too clever for them, but because he's too stupid. It's all too ordinary. I don't suppose it was this man Beeton at all. Don't you read your papers? Didn't you see that the old lady's sitting-room was on the ground floor, and that the dining-room window was found open at the top? It would be the easiest thing in the world for a man to slip in through the dining-room—Miss Steward was rather deaf—and catch her unawares and bash her on the head. There's only crazy paving between the garden gate and the windows, and there was a black frost yesterday night, so he'd leave no footmarks on the carpet. That's the difficult sort of murder to trace—no subtlety, no apparent motive. Look at the Reading murder, look at—"

"Hold hard a minute, sir," interrupted the sergeant. "How do you know there was crazy paving? *That's* not in the papers, as far as I know."

The Disagreeable Man stopped short in the full tide of his eloquence, and appeared disconcerted.

"I've seen the place, as a matter of fact," he said with some reluctance. "Went there this morning to look at it—for private reasons, which I needn't trouble you with."

"That's a funny thing to do, sir."

"It may be, but it's no business of yours."

"Oh, no, sir, of course not," said the sergeant. "We all of us has our little 'obbies, and crazy paving may be yours. Landscape gardener, sir?"

"Not exactly."

"A journalist, perhaps?" suggested Mr. Redwood.

"That's nearer," said the other. "Looking at my three fountain-pens, eh? Quite the amateur detective."

"The gentleman can't be a journalist," said Mr. Egg. "You will pardon me, sir, but a journalist couldn't help but take an interest in Mr. Redwood's synthetic alcohol or whatever it is. I fancy I might put a name to your profession if I was called upon to do so. Every man carries the marks of his trade, though it's not always as conspicuous as Mr. Redwood's sample case or mine. Take books, for instance. I always know an academic gentleman by the way he opens a book. It's in his blood, as you might say. Or take bottles. I handle them one way—it's my trade. A doctor or a chemist handles them another way. This scent-bottle, for example. If you or I was to take the stopper out of this bottle, how would we do it? How would you do it, Mr. Redwood?"

"Me?" said Mr. Redwood. "Why, dash it all! On the word 'one' I'd apply the thumb and two fingers of the right hand *to* the stopper and on the word 'two' I would elevate them briskly, retaining a firm grip on the bottle with the left hand in case of accident. What would you do?" He turned to the man in the burberry.

"Same as you," said that gentleman, suiting the action to the word. "I don't see any difficulty about that. There's only one way I know of to take out stoppers, and that's to take 'em out. What d'you expect me to do? Whistle 'em out?"

"But this gentleman's quite right, all the same," put in the Disagreeable Man. "You do it that way because you aren't accustomed to measuring and pouring with one hand while the other's occupied. But a doctor or a chemist pulls the stopper out with his little finger, like this, and lifts the bottle in the same hand, holding the measuring-glass in his left—so—and when he—"

"Hi! Beeton!" cried Mr. Egg in a shrill voice, "look out!"

The flask slipped from the hand of the Disagreeable Man and crashed on the table's edge as the man in the burberry started to his feet. An overpowering odour of violets filled the room. The sergeant darted forward—there was a brief but violent struggle. The girl screamed. The landlord rushed in from the bar, and a crowd of men surged in after him and blocked the doorway.

"There," said the sergeant, emerging a little breathless from the mix-up, "you best come quiet. Wait a minute! Gotter charge you. Gerald Beeton, I arrest you for the murder of Alice Steward—stand still, can't you?—and I warns you as anything you say may be taken down and used in evidence at your trial. Thank you, sir. If you'll give me a 'and with him to the door, I've got a pal waiting just up the road, with a police car."

In a few minutes' time Sergeant Jukes returned, struggling into his overcoat. His amateur helpers accompanied him, their faces bright, as of those who have done their good deed for the day.

"That was a very neat dodge of yours, sir," said the sergeant, addressing Mr. Egg, who was administering a stiff pick-me-up to the young lady, while Mr. Redwood and the landlord together sought to remove the drench of Parma violet from the carpet. "Whew! Smells a bit strong, don't it? Regular barber's shop. We had the office he was expected this way, and I had an idea that one of you gentlemen might be the man, but I didn't know which. Mr. Bunce here saying that Beeton had been a chemist was a big help; and you, sir, I must say you touched him off proper."

"Not at all," said Mr. Egg. "I noticed the way he took that stopper out the first time—it showed he had been trained to laboratory work. That might have been an accident, of course. But afterwards, when he pretended he didn't know the right way to do it, I thought it was time to see if he'd answer to his name."

"Good wheeze," said the Disagreeable Man agreeably. "Mind if I use it some time?"

"Ah!" said Sergeant Jukes. "You gave me a bit of a turn, sir, with that crazy paving. Whatever did you—"

"Professional curiosity," said the other, with a grin. "I write detective stories. But our friend Mr. Egg is a better hand at the real thing."

"No, no," said Monty. "We all helped. The hardest problem's easy of solution when each one makes his little contribution. Isn't that so, Mr. Faggott?"

The aged countryman had risen to his feet.

"Place fair stinks o' that dratted stuff," he said disapprovingly. "I can't abide such nastiness." He hobbled out and shut the door.

MURDER IN THE MORNING

Half a mile along the main road to Ditchley, and then turn off to the left at the sign-post," said the Traveller in Mangles; "but I think you'll be wasting your time."

"Oh, well," said Mr. Montague Egg cheerfully, "I'll have a shot at the old bird. As the *Salesman's Handbook* says: 'Don't let the smallest chance slip by; you never know until you try.' After all, he's supposed to be rich, isn't he?"

"Mattresses stuffed with gold sovereigns, or so the neighbours say," acknowledged the Traveller in Mangles with a grin. "But they'd say anything."

"Thought you said there weren't any neighbours."

"No more they are. Manner of speaking. Well, good luck to it!"

Mr. Egg acknowledged the courtesy with a wave of his smart trilby, and let his clutch in with quiet determination.

The main road was thronged with the usual traffic of a Saturday morning in June—worthy holiday-makers bound for Melbury Woods or for the seashore about Beachampton—but as soon as he turned into the little narrow lane by the sign-post which said "Hatchford Mill 2 Miles," he was plunged into a profound solitude and silence, broken only by the scurry of an occasional rabbit from the hedgerow and the chug of his own Morris. Whatever else the mysterious Mr. Pinchbeck might be, he certainly was a solitary soul, and when, about a mile and a half down the lane, Monty caught sight of the tiny cottage, set far back in the middle of a neglected-looking field, he began to think that the Traveller in Mangles had been right. Rich though he might be, Mr. Pinchbeck was probably not a very likely customer for the wines and spirits supplied by Messrs. Plummet & Rose of Piccadilly. But, remembering Maxim Five of the *Salesman's Handbook*, "If you're a salesman worth the name at all, you can sell razors to a billiard-ball," Mr. Egg stopped his car at the entrance to the field, lifted the sagging gate and dragged it open, creaking in every rotten rail, and drove forward over the rough track, scarred with the ruts left by wet-weather traffic.

The cottage door was shut. Monty beat a cheerful tattoo upon its blistered surface, and was not very much surprised to get no answer. He knocked again, and then, unwilling to abandon his quest now he had come so far, walked round to the back. Here again he got no answer. Was Mr. Pinchbeck out? It was said that he never went out. Being by nature persistent and inquisitive, Mr. Egg stepped up to the window and looked in. What he saw made him whistle softly. He returned to the back door, pushed it open and entered.

When you arrive at a person's house with no intention beyond selling him a case of whisky or a dozen or so of port, it is disconcerting to find him stretched on his own kitchen floor, with his head battered to pulp. Mr. Egg had served two years on the Western Front, but he did not like what he saw. He put the table-cloth over it. Then, being a methodical sort of person, he looked at his watch, which marked 10:25. After a minute's pause for consideration, he made a rapid tour of the premises, then set off, driving as fast as he could, to fetch the police.

The inquest upon Mr. Humphrey Pinchbeck took place the following day, and resulted in a verdict of wilful murder against some person or persons unknown. During the next fortnight, Mr. Montague Egg, with some uneasiness, watched the newspapers. The police were following up a clue. A man was requested to communicate with the police. The man was described—a striking-looking person with a red beard and a check suit, driving a sports car with the registered number WOE 1313. The man was found. The man was charged, and Mr. Montague Egg, three hundred miles away, was informed, to his disgust, that he would be required to give evidence before the magistrates at Beachampton.

The accused, who gave his name as Theodore Barton, age forty-two, profession poet (at which Monty stared very hard, never having seen a poet at such close quarters), was a tall, powerfully built man, dressed in flamboyant tweeds, and having a certain air of rather disreputable magnificence about him. One would expect, thought Monty, to find him hanging about bars in the East Central district of London. His eyes were bold, and the upper part of his face handsome in its way; the mouth was hidden by the abundance of his tawny beard. He appeared to be perfectly at his ease, and was represented by a solicitor.

Montague Egg was called at an early stage to give evidence of the finding of the body. He mentioned that the time was 10:25 A.M. on Saturday, June 18th, and that the body was still quite warm when he saw it. The front door was locked; the back door shut, but not locked. The kitchen was greatly disordered, as though there had been a violent struggle, and a blood-stained poker lay beside the dead man. He had made a rapid search before sending for the police. In a bedroom upstairs he had seen a heavy iron box standing open and empty, with the keys hanging from the lock. There was no other person in the cottage, nor yet concealed about the little yard, but there were marks as though a large car had recently stood in a shed at the back of the house. In the sitting-room were the remains of breakfast for two persons. He (Mr. Egg) had passed down the lane from the high-road in his car, and had met nobody at all on the way. He had spent perhaps five

or ten minutes in searching the place, and had then driven
back by the way he came.

At this point Detective-Inspector Ramage explained that
the lane leading to the cottage ran on for half a mile or so to
pass Hatchford Mill, and then bent back to enter the main
Beachampton road again at a point three miles nearer Ditchley.

The next witness was a baker named Bowles. He gave evidence that he had called at the cottage with his van at 10:15, to
deliver two loaves of bread. He had gone to the back door,
which had been opened by Mr. Pinchbeck in person. The old
gentleman had appeared to be in perfect health, but a little
flurried and irritable. He had not seen any other person in the
kitchen, but had an impression that before he knocked he had
heard two men's voices talking loudly and excitedly. The lad
who had accompanied Bowles on his round confirmed this,
adding that he fancied he had seen the outline of a man move
across the kitchen window.

Mrs. Chapman, from Hatchford Mill, then came forward
to say that she was accustomed to go in every weekday to Mr.
Pinchbeck's cottage to do a bit of cleaning. She arrived at 7:30
and left at 9 o'clock. On Saturday 18th she had come as usual,
to find that a visitor had arrived unexpectedly the night
before. She identified the accused, Theodore Barton, as that
visitor. He had apparently slept on the couch in the sitting-
room, and was departing again that morning. She saw his car
in the shed; it was a little sports one, and she had particularly
noticed the number, WOE 1313, thinking that there was an
unlucky number and no mistake. The interior of the shed was
not visible from the back door. She had set breakfast for the
two of them. The milkman and the postman had called before
she left, and the grocer's van must have come soon after, for it
was down at the Mill by 9:30. Nobody else ever called at the
cottage, so far as she knew. Mr. Pinchbeck was a vegetarian
and grew his own garden-stuff. She had never known him
have a visitor before. She had heard nothing in the nature of
"words" between Mr. Pinchbeck and the accused, but had

thought the old man was not in the best of spirits. "He seemed a bit put out, like."

Then came another witness from the Mill, who had heard a car with a powerful engine drive very rapidly past the Mill a little before half-past ten. He had run out to look, fast cars being a rarity in the lane, but had seen nothing, on account of the trees which bordered the road at the corner just beyond the Mill.

At this point the police put in a statement made by the accused on his arrest. He said that he was the nephew of the deceased, and frankly admitted that he had spent the night at the cottage. Deceased had seemed pleased to see him, as they had not met for some time. On hearing that his nephew was "rather hard up," deceased had remonstrated with him about following so ill paid a profession as poetry, but had kindly offered him a small loan, which he, the accused, had gratefully accepted. Mr. Pinchbeck had then opened the box in his bedroom and brought out a number of banknotes, of which he had handed over "ten fivers," accompanying the gift by a little sermon on hard work and thrift. This had happened at about 9:45 or a little earlier—at any rate, after Mrs. Chapman was safely off the premises. The box had appeared to be full of banknotes and securities, and Mr. Pinchbeck had expressed distrust both of Mrs. Chapman and of the tradesmen in general. (Here Mrs. Chapman voiced an indignant protest, and had to be soothed by the Bench.) The statement went on to say that the accused had had no sort of quarrel with his uncle, and had left the cottage at, he thought, 10 o'clock or thereabouts, and driven on through Ditchley and Frogthorpe to Beachampton. There he had left his car with a friend, to whom it belonged, and had hired a motorboat and gone over to spend a fortnight in Brittany. Here he had heard nothing about his uncle's death till the arrival of Detective-Inspector Ramage had informed him of the suspicion against him. He had, of course, hastened back immediately to establish his innocence.

The police theory was that, as soon as the last tradesman

had left the house, Barton had killed the old man, taken his keys, stolen the money, and escaped, supposing that the body would not be found till Mrs. Chapman arrived on the Monday morning.

While Theodore Barton's solicitor was extracting from Inspector Ramage the admission that the only money found on the accused at the time of his arrest was six Bank of England five-pound notes and a few shillings' worth of French money, Mr. Egg became aware that somebody was breathing very hard and excitedly down the back of his neck, and, on turning round, found himself face to face with an elderly woman, whose rather prominent eyes seemed ready to pop out of her head with agitation.

"Oh!" said the woman, bouncing in her seat. "Oh, dear!"

"I beg your pardon," said Mr. Egg, ever courteous. "Am I in your way, or anything?"

"Oh! oh, thank you! Oh, do tell me what I ought to do. There's something I ought to tell them. Poor man. He isn't guilty at all. I *know* he isn't. Oh, please do tell me what I ought to do. Do I have to go to the police? Oh, dear, oh, dear! I thought—I didn't know—I've never been in a place like this before! Oh, I know they'll bring him in guilty. Please, *please* stop them!"

"They can't bring him in guilty in this court," said Monty soothingly. "They can send him up for trial—"

"Oh, but they mustn't! He didn't do it. He wasn't there. Oh, please do something about it."

She appeared so earnest that Mr. Egg, slightly clearing his throat and settling his tie, rose boldly to his feet and exclaimed in stentorian accents: "Your worship!"

The Bench stared. The solicitor stared. The accused stared. Everybody stared.

"There is a lady here," said Monty, feeling that he must go through with it, "who tells me she has important evidence to give on behalf of the accused."

The staring eyes became focused upon the lady, who

instantly started up, dropping her handbag, and crying: "Oh, dear! I'm so sorry! I'm afraid I ought to have gone to the police."

The solicitor, in whose face surprise, annoyance, and anticipation struggled curiously together, at once came forward. The lady was extricated and short whispered consultation followed, after which the solicitor said:

"Your worship, my client's instructions were to reserve his defence, but, since the lady, whom I have never seen until this moment, has so generously come forward with her statement, which appears to be a complete answer to the charge, perhaps your worship would prefer to hear her at this stage."

After a little discussion, the Bench decided that they would like to hear the evidence, if the accused was agreeable. Accordingly, the lady was put in the box, and sworn, in the name of Millicent Adela Queek.

"I am a spinster, and employed as art mistress at Woodbury High School for Girls. Saturday 18th was a holiday, of course, and I thought I would have a little picnic, all by my lonesome, in Melbury Woods. I started off in my own little car just about 9:30. It would take me about half an hour to get to Ditchley—I never drive very fast, and there was a lot of traffic on the road—most dangerous. When I got to Ditchley, I turned to the right, along the main road to Beachampton. After a little time I began to wonder whether I had put in quite enough petrol. My gauge isn't very reliable, you know, so I thought I'd better stop and make *quite* certain. So I pulled up at a roadside garage. I don't know *exactly* where it was, but it was quite a little way beyond Ditchley—between that and Helpington. It was one of those *dreadfully* ugly places, made of corrugated iron painted bright red. I don't think they should allow them to put up things like that. I asked the man there—a most obliging young man—to fill my tank, and while I was there I saw this gentleman—yes, I mean Mr. Barton, the accused—drive up in his car. He was coming from the Ditchley direction and driving rather fast. He pulled up on the left-hand side of the road. The garage is on the right, but I saw him very distinctly. I couldn't mistake him — his beard, you know, and the clothes he was wearing — so distinctive. It was the same suit he is wearing now. Besides, I noticed the number of his car. Such a curious one, is it not? WOE 1313. Yes. Well, he opened the bonnet and did something to his plugs, I think, and then he drove on."

"What time was this?"

"I was just going to tell you. When I came to look at my watch I found it had stopped. Most vexatious. I think it was due to the vibration of the steering-wheel. But I looked up at the garage clock — there was one just over the door — and it said 10:20. So I set my watch by that. Then I went on to Melbury Woods and had my little picnic. So fortunate, wasn't it? that I looked at the clock then. Because my watch stopped again later on. But I do *know* that it was 10:20 when this gentleman stopped at the garage, so I don't see how he could have been doing a murder at that poor man's cottage between 10:15 and 10:25, because it must be well over twenty miles away — more, I should think."

Miss Queek ended her statement with a little gasp, and looked round triumphantly.

Detective-Inspector Ramage's face was a study. Miss Queek went on to explain why she had not come forward earlier with her story.

"When I read the description in the papers I thought it *must* be the same car I had seen, because of the number — but of course I couldn't be sure it was the same man, could I? Descriptions are *so* misleading. And naturally I didn't want to be mixed up with a police case. The school, you know — parents don't like it. But I thought, if I came and saw this gentleman for myself, then I should be quite certain. And Miss Wagstaffe — our head-mistress — so kindly gave me leave to come, though to-day is very inconvenient, being my busiest afternoon. But I said it might be a matter of life and death, and so it is, isn't it?"

The magistrate thanked Miss Queek for her public-spirited intervention, and then, at the urgent request of both parties, adjourned the court for further inquiry into the new evidence.

Since it was extremely important that Miss Queek should identify the garage in question as soon as possible, it was arranged that she should set out at once in search of it, accompanied by Inspector Ramage and his sergeant, Mr. Barton's solicitor going with them to see fair play for his client. A slight difficulty arose, however. It appeared that the police car was not quite big enough to take the whole party comfortably, and Mr. Montague Egg, climbing into his own Morris, found himself hailed by the inspector with the request for a lift.

"By all means," said Monty; "a pleasure. Besides, you'll be able to keep your eye on me. Because, if that chap didn't do it, it looks to me as though I must be the guilty party."

"I wouldn't say that, sir," said the inspector, obviously taken aback by this bit of thought-reading.

"I couldn't blame you if you did," said Monty. He smiled, remembering his favourite motto for salesmen: "A cheerful voice and cheerful look put orders in the order-book," and buzzed merrily away in the wake of the police car along the road from Beachampton to Ditchley.

"We ought to be getting near it now," remarked Ramage when they had left Helpington behind them. "We're ten miles from Ditchley and about twenty-five from Pinchbeck's cottage. Let's see—it'll be the left-hand side of the road, going in this direction. Hullo! this looks rather like it," he added presently. "They're pulling up."

The police car had stopped before an ugly corrugated-iron structure, standing rather isolated on the near side of the road, and adorned with a miscellaneous collection of enamelled advertisement-boards and a lot of petrol pumps. Mr. Egg brought the Morris alongside.

"Is this the place, Miss Queek?"

"Well, I don't know. It was like this, and it was about here. But I can't be sure. All these dreadful little places are so much alike, but—Well, there! how stupid of me! Of course this isn't it. There's no clock. There ought to be a clock just over the door. *So* sorry to have made such a silly mistake. We must go on a little farther. It must be quite near here."

The little procession moved forward again, and five miles farther on came once more to a halt. This time there could surely be no mistake. Another hideous red corrugated garage, more boards, more petrol pumps, and a clock, whose hands pointed (correctly, as the inspector ascertained by reference to his watch) to 7:15.

"I'm sure this must be it," said Miss Queek. "Yes—I recognise the man," she added, as the garage proprietor came out to see what was wanted.

The proprietor, when questioned, was not able to swear with any certainty to having filled Miss Queek's tank on June 18th. He had filled so many tanks before and since. But in the matter of the clock he was definite. It kept, and always had kept, perfect time, and it had never stopped or been out of order since it was first installed. If his clock had pointed to 10:20, then 10:20 was the time, and he would testify as much in any court in the kingdom. He could not remember having seen the car with the registered number WOE 1313, but there was no reason why he should, since it had not come in for attention. Motorists who wanted to do a spot of inspection often pulled up near his garage, in case they should find some trouble that needed expert assistance, but such incidents were so usual that he would pay no heed to them, especially on a busy morning.

Miss Queek, however, felt quite certain. She recognised the man, the garage, and the clock. As a further precaution, the party went on as far as Ditchley, but, though the roadside was peppered the whole way with garages, there was no other exactly corresponding to the description. Either they were the wrong colour, or built of the wrong materials, or they had no clock.

"Well," said the inspector, rather ruefully, "unless we can prove collusion (which doesn't seem likely, seeing the kind of woman she is), that washes that out. That garage where she saw Barton is eighteen miles from Pinchbeck's cottage, and since we know the old man was alive at 10:15, Barton can't have killed him—not unless he was averaging 200 miles an hour or so, which can't be done yet awhile. Well, we've got to start all over again."

"It looks a bit awkward for me," said Monty pleasantly.

"I don't know about that. There's the voices that baker fellow heard in the kitchen. I know that couldn't have been you, because I've checked up your times." Mr. Ramage grinned. "Perhaps the rest of the money may turn up somewhere. It's all in the day's work. We'd better be getting back again."

Monty drove the first eighteen miles in thoughtful silence. They had just passed the garage with the clock (at which the inspector shook a mortified fist in passing), when Mr. Egg uttered an exclamation and pulled up.

"Hullo!" said the inspector.

"I've got an idea," said Monty. He pulled out a pocket-diary and consulted it. "Yes—I thought so. I've discovered a coincidence. Let's check up on it. Do you mind? 'Don't trust to luck, but be exact and verify the smallest fact.' " He replaced the diary and drove on, overhauling the police car. In process of time they came to the garage which had first attracted their attention—the one which conformed to specification, except in the particular that it displayed no clock. Here he stopped, and the police car, following in their tracks, stopped also.

The proprietor emerged expectantly, and the first thing that struck one about him was his resemblance to the man they had interviewed at the other garage. Monty commented politely on the fact.

"Quite right," said the man. "He's my brother."

"Your garages are alike, too," said Monty.

"Bought off the same firm," said the man. "Supplied in parts. Mass-production. Readily erected overnight by any handy man."

"That's the stuff," said Mr. Egg approvingly. "Standardisation means immense saving in labour, time, expense. You haven't got a clock, though."

"Not yet. I've got one on order."

"Never had one?"

"Never."

"Ever seen this lady before?"

The man looked Miss Queek carefully over from head to foot.

"Yes, I fancy I have. Came in one morning for petrol, didn't you, miss? Saturday fortnight or thereabouts. I've a good memory for faces."

"What time would that be?"

"Ten to eleven, or a few minutes after. I remember I was just boiling up a kettle for my elevenses. I generally take a cup of tea about then."

"Ten-fifty," said the inspector eagerly. "And this is—" he made a rapid calculation—"just on twenty-two miles from the cottage. Say half an hour from the time of the murder. Forty-four miles an hour—he could do that on his head in a fast sports car."

"Yes, but—" interrupted the solicitor.

"Just a minute," said Monty. "Didn't you," he went on, addressing the proprietor, "once have one of those clock-faces with movable hands to show lighting-up time?"

"Yes, I did. I've still got it, as a matter of fact. It used to hang over the door. But I took it down last Sunday. People found it rather a nuisance; they were always mistaking it for a real clock."

"And lighting-up time on June 18th," said Monty softly, "was 10:20, according to my diary."

"Well there," said Inspector Ramage, smiting his thigh. "Now, that's really clever of you, Mr. Egg."

"A brain-wave, a brain-wave," admitted Monty. " 'The salesman who will use his brains will spare himself a world of pains'—or so the *Handbook* says."

ONE TOO MANY

When Simon Grant, the Napoleon of Consolidated Nitro-Phosphates and Heaven knows how many affiliated companies, vanished off the face of the earth one rainy November night, it would have been, in any case, only natural that his family and friends should be disturbed, and that there should be a slight flurry on the Stock Exchange. But when, in the course of the next few days, it became painfully evident that Consolidated Nitro-Phosphates had been consolidated in nothing but the name—that they were, in fact, not even ripe for liquidation, but had (so to speak) already passed that point and evaporated into thin air, such assets as they possessed having mysteriously disappeared at the same time as Simon Grant—then the hue-and-cry went out with a noise that shook three continents and, incidentally, jogged Mr. Montague Egg for an hour or so out of his blameless routine.

Not that Mr. Egg had any money in Nitro-Phosphates, or could claim any sort of acquaintance with the missing financier. His connection with the case was entirely fortuitous, the by-product of a savage budgetary announcement by the Chancellor of the Exchequer, which threatened to have alarming results for the wine and spirits trade. Mr. Egg, travelling representative of Messrs. Plummet & Rose of Piccadilly, had reached Birmingham in his wanderings, when he was urgently summoned back to town by his employers for a special conference upon policy, and thus—though he did not know it at the time—he enjoyed the distinction of travelling by the very train from which Simon Grant so suddenly and unaccountably vanished.

The facts in the case of Simon Grant were disconcertingly simple. At this time the L.M.S. Railway were running a night express from Birmingham to London which, leaving Birmingham at 9:50, stopped only at Coventry and Rugby before running into Euston at 12:10. Mr. Grant had attended a dinner given in his honour by certain prominent business men in Coventry, and after dinner had had the unblushing effrontery to make a speech about the Prosperity of British Business. After this, he had hastened away to take the Birmingham express as far as Rugby, where he was engaged to stay the night with that pillar of financial rectitude, Lord Buddlethorp. He was seen into a first-class carriage at 9:57 by two eminently respectable Coventry magnates, who had remained chatting with him till the train started. There was one other person in his carriage—no less a man, in fact, than Sir Hicklebury Bowles, the well-known sporting baronet. In the course of conversation, he had mentioned to Sir Hicklebury (whom he knew slightly) that he was travelling alone, his secretary having succumbed to an attack of influenza. About half way between Coventry and Rugby, Mr. Grant had gone out into the corridor, muttering something about the heat. He had never been seen again.

At first, a very sinister light had been thrown on the incident by the fact that a door in the corridor, a little way up the train, had been found swinging open at Rugby, and the subsequent discovery of Mr. Grant's hat and overcoat a few miles farther up the line had led everybody to fear the worst. Careful examination, however, failed to produce either Simon Grant's corpse or any evidence of any heavy body having fallen from the train. In a pocket of the overcoat was a first-class ticket from Coventry to Rugby, and it seemed clear that, without this, he could not have passed the barrier at Rugby. Moreover, Lord Buddlethorp had sent his car with a chauffeur and a footman to meet the train at Rugby. The chauffeur had stood at the barrier and the footman had paraded the platform in search of the financier. Both knew him very well by sight, and between them they asserted positively that he had never left the train. Nobody had arrived at the barrier ticketless, or with the wrong ticket, and a check-up of the tickets issued for Rugby at Birmingham and Coventry revealed no discrepancy.

There remained two possibilities, both tempting and plausible. The Birmingham-London express reached Rugby at 10:24, departing again at 10:28. But, swift and impressive as it was, it was not the only, or the most important, pebble on the station beach, for over against it upon the down line was the Irish Mail, snorting and blowing in its three-minute halt before it roared away northwards at 10:25. If the express had been on time, Simon Grant might have slipped across and boarded it, and been at Holyhead by 2:25 to catch the steamer, and be in Dublin by 6:35, and Heaven only knew where a few hours after. As for the confident assertion of Lord Buddlethorp's footman, a trifling disguise—easily assumed in a lavatory or an empty compartment—would be amply sufficient to deceive him. To Chief Inspector Peacock, in charge of the investigations, the possibility appeared highly probable. It had also the advantage that the passengers crossing by the mailboat could be readily reckoned up and accounted for.

The question of tickets now became matter for inquiry. It was not likely that Simon Grant would have tried to secure them during his hasty one-minute dash for the Mail. Either he had taken them beforehand, or some accomplice had met him at Rugby and handed them over. Chief Inspector Peacock was elated when he discovered that tickets covering the train-and-steamer route from Rugby to Dublin had actually been purchased for the night in question from the L.M.S. agents in London in the absurd and incredible name of Solomon Grundy. Mr. Peacock was well acquainted with the feeble cunning which prompts people, when adopting an alias, to cling to their own initials. The underlying motive is, no doubt, a dread lest those same initials, inscribed on a watch, cigarette-case, or what-not, should arouse suspicion, but the tendency is so well known that the choice of initials arouses in itself the very suspicion it is intended to allay. Mr. Peacock's hopes rose very high indeed when he discovered, in addition, that Solomon Grundy (Great Heavens, what a name!) had gone out of his way to give a fictitious and, indeed, non-existent address to the man at the ticket-office. And then, just when the prospect seemed at its brightest, the whole theory received its death-blow. Not only had no Mr. Solomon Grundy travelled by the mailboat that night or any night—not only had his ticket never been presented or even cancelled—but it turned out to be impossible that Mr. Simon Grant should have boarded the Irish Mail at all. For some tedious and infuriating reason connected with an overheated axle-box, the Birmingham-London express, on that night of all nights, had steamed into Rugby three minutes behind time and two minutes after the departure of the Mail. If this had been Simon Grant's plan of escape, something had undoubtedly gone wrong with it.

And, that being so, Chief Inspector Peacock came back to the old question: What had become of Simon Grant?

Talking it over with his colleagues, the Chief Inspector came eventually to the conclusion that Grant had, in fact, intended to take the Irish Mail, leaving the open door and the scattered garments behind him by way of confusing the trail for the police. What, then, would he do, when he found the Mail already gone? He could only leave the station and take another train. He had not left the station by the barrier, and careful enquiry convinced Mr. Peacock that it would have been extremely difficult for him to make his way out along the line unobserved, or hang about the railway premises till the following morning. An unfortunate suicide had taken place only the previous week, which had made the railwaymen particularly observant of stray passengers who might attempt to wander on to the permanent way; and, in addition, there happened to be two gangs of platelayers working with flares at points strategically placed for observation. So that Peacock, while not altogether dismissing this part of the investigation, turned it over as routine work to his subordinates, and bent his mind to consider a second main possibility that had already occurred to him before he had been led away by speculations on the Irish Mail.

This was, that Simon Grant had never left the express at all, but had gone straight through to Euston. London has great advantages as a hiding-place—and what better thing could Grant have done, when his first scheme failed him, than return to the express and continue his journey? His watch would have warned him, before he reached Rugby, that the Mail had probably left; a hasty inquiry and a quick dash to the booking-office, and he would be ready to continue his journey.

The only drawback was that when the Chief Inspector questioned the officials in the booking-office he was met by the positive statement that no ticket of any kind had been issued that night later than 10:15. Nor yet had any passenger arrived at Euston minus a ticket. And the possibility of an accomplice on the platform had now to be dismissed, since the original plan of escape had not involved an accomplice, and it was not reasonable to suppose that one had been provided beforehand for such an emergency.

But, argued the Chief Inspector, the emergency might have been foreseen and a ticket purchased in advance. And if so, it was going to be extremely difficult to prove, since the number of tickets issued would correspond with the number of passengers. He set in train, however, an exhaustive investigation into the question of the tickets issued in London, Birmingham, Coventry, and Rugby during the few weeks previous to the disappearance, thinking that he might easily light upon a return half which had come to hand very much subsequent to the date of issue, and that this might suggest a line of enquiry. In addition, he sent out a broadcast appeal, and this is where his line of enquiry impinged upon the orbit of Mr. Montague Egg.

To the Chief Commissioner of Police. — DEAR SIR,

wrote Mr. Egg in his neat commercial hand,

understanding as per the daily Press and the B.B.C.
that you desire to receive communications from all persons travelling by the 9:50 P.M. Birmingham-London
express on the 4th ult., I beg to inform you that I travelled by same (3rd class) from Coventry to Euston
on the date mentioned and that I am entirely at your
disposal for all enquiries. Being attached to the firm
of Plummet & Rose, wine and spirit merchants, Piccadilly, as travelling representative, my permanent
address will not find me at present, but I beg to enclose
list of hotels where I shall be staying in the immediate
future and remain, dear sir, yours faithfully.

In consequence of this letter, Mr. Egg was one evening
mysteriously called out of the commercial room at the Cat and
Fiddle in Oldham to speak with a Mr. Peacock.

"Pleased, I'm sure," said Mr. Egg, prepared for anything
from a colossal order for wine and spirits to a forgotten
acquaintance with a bad-luck story. "Monty-on-the-spot,
that's me. What can I do for you, sir?"

Chief Inspector Peacock appeared to want every conceivable detail of information about Mr. Egg, his affairs, and, in
particular, his late journey to town. Monty disposed capably
of the preliminaries and mentioned that he had arrived at the
station with plenty of time to spare, and so had contrived to
get a seat as soon as the train came in.

"And I was glad I did," he added. "I like to be comfortable,
you know, and the train was rather crowded."

"I know it was crowded," said Mr. Peacock, with a groan.
"And well I may, when I tell you that we have had to get in
touch with every single person on that train, and interview as
many of them as we could get hold of personally."

"Some job," said Mr. Egg, with the respect of one expert

interviewer to another. "Do you mean you've got in touch with them all?"

"Every blessed one," said Mr. Peacock, "including several officious nuisances who weren't there at all, but hoped for a spot of notoriety."

"Talking of spots," said Monty, "what will you take?"

Mr. Peacock thanked him, and accepted a small whisky-and-soda. "Can you remember at all what part of the train you were in?"

"Certainly," said Mr. Egg promptly. "Third-class smoker, middle of the coach, middle of the train. Safest, you know, in case of accidents. Corner seat, corridor side, facing engine. Immediately opposite me, picture of York Minster, being visited by two ladies and a gentleman, in costumes of 1904 or thereabouts. Noticed it particularly, because everything else about the train was up to date. Thought it a pity."

"Hum," said Mr. Peacock. "Do you remember who else was in the compartment at Coventry?"

Monty screwed up his eyes as though to squeeze recollection out through his eyelids.

"Next me, stout, red, bald man, very sleepy, in tweeds. Been having one or two. He'd come from Birmingham. Next him, lanky young chap with pimples and a very bad bowler. Got in after me and tripped over my feet. Looked like a clerk. And a young sailor in the corner seat—there when I arrived. Talked all the time to the fellow in the corner opposite, who looked like some sort of a parson—collar round the wrong way, clerical hat, walrus moustache, dark spectacles, puffy cheeks, and a tell-me-my-good-man way of talking. Next him—oh! yes, a fellow smoking a pipe of horrible scented sort of tobacco—might have been a small tradesman, but I didn't see much of him, because he was reading a paper most of the time. Then there was a nice, inoffensive, gentlemanly old bird who needed a haircut. He had pince-nez—very crooked—and never took his eyes off a learned-looking book. And opposite me there was a chap with a big brown beard in a yellow inverness cloak—foreign-looking—with a big, soft felt hat. He came from Birmingham, and so did the parson, but the other two on that side got in after I did."

The Chief Inspector smiled as he turned over the pages of a formidable bunch of documents. "You're an admirable witness, Mr. Egg. Your account tallies perfectly with those of your seven fellow-travellers, but it's the only one of the eight that's complete. You are obviously observant."

"My job," said Monty complacently.

"Of course. You may be interested to know that the gentlemanly old bird with the long hair was Professor Amblefoot of London University, the great authority of the Higher Calculus, and that he described you as a fair-haired, well-mannered young man."

"Much obliged to him, I'm sure," said Mr. Egg.

"The foreigner is Dr. Schleicher of Kew—resident there three years—the sailor and the parson we know all about—the drunk chap is O.K. too—we had his wife along, very voluble—the tradesman is a well-known Coventry resident, something to do with the Church Council of St. Michael's, and the pimply lad is one of Messrs. Morrison's clerks. They're all square. And they all went through to town, didn't they? Nobody left at Rugby?"

"Nobody," said Mr. Egg.

"Pity," said the Chief Inspector. "The truth is, Mr. Egg, that we can't hear of any person in the train who hasn't come forward and given an account of himself, and the number of people who have come forward precisely corresponds with the number of tickets collected at the barriers at Euston. You didn't observe any person continually hanging about the corridor, I suppose?"

"Not permanently," said Monty. "The chap with the beard got up and prowled a bit from time to time, I remember—seemed restless. I thought he perhaps didn't feel very well. But he'd only be absent a few minutes at a time. He seemed to be a nervous, unpleasant sort of chap—chewed his nails, you know, and muttered in German, but he—"

"Chewed his nails?"

"Yes. Very unpleasant, I must say. 'Well-kept hands that please the sight seize the trade and hold it tight, but bitten nails and grubby claws well may give the buyer pause.' So the *Salesman's Handbook* says"—and Monty smirked gently at his own finger-tips. "This person's hands were—definitely not gentlemanly. Bitten to the quick."

"But that's really extraordinary," said Peacock. "Dr. Schleicher's hands are particularly well kept. I interviewed him myself yesterday. Surely he can't suddenly have abandoned the habit of nail-biting? People don't—not like that. And why should he? Was there anything else you noticed about the man opposite you?"

"I don't think so. Yes. Stop a moment. He smoked cigars at a most extraordinary rate. I remember his going out into the corridor with one smoked down to about an inch and coming back, five minutes afterwards, with a new one smoked half way through. Full-sized Coronas too—good ones; and I know quite a bit about cigars."

Peacock stared and then smote his hand lightly upon the table.

"I've got it!" he said. "I remember where I met a set of badly chewed-up nails lately. By Jove! Yes, but how could he . . ."

Monty waited for enlightenment.

"Simon Grant's secretary. He was supposed to be in town all that day and evening, having 'flu—but how do I know that he was? But, even so, what good could he do by being in the train in disguise? And what could Dr. Schleicher have to do with it? It's Simon Grant we want—and Schleicher isn't Grant—at least"—the Chief Inspector paused and went on more dubiously—"I don't see how he could be. They know him well in the district, though he's said to be away from home a good deal, and he's got a wife—"

"Oh, has he?" said Mr. Egg, with a meaning emphasis.

"A double life, you mean?" said the Chief Inspector.

"*And* a double wife," said Mr. Egg. "You will pardon my asking a delicate question, but—er—are you certain you would spot a false beard at once, if you weren't altogether expecting it?"

"In a good light, I probably should, but by the light of the doctor's reading-lamp—But what's the game, Mr. Egg? If Schleicher is Grant, who was the man you saw in the train—the man with the bitten finger-nails? Grant doesn't bite his nails, I know that—he's rather particular about his appearance, so I'm told, though I've never met him myself."

"Well," said Mr. Egg, "since you ask me, why shouldn't the other man in the train be all three of them?"

"All three of which?"

"Grant and Schleicher and the secretary."

"I don't quite get you."

"Well, I mean—supposing Grant is Schleicher, with a nice ready-made personality all handy for him to step into, built up, as you may say, over the last three years, with money salted away in the name of Schleicher—well, I mean, there he is, as you might say, waiting to slip over to the Continent as soon as the fuss has died down—complete with unofficial lady."

"But the secretary?"

"The secretary was the man in the train, made up as Grant made up as Schleicher. I mean, speaking as a fool, I thought he might be."

"But where was Schleicher—I mean, Grant?"

"He was the man in the train, too. I mean, he may have been."

"Do you mean there were two of them?"

"Yes—at least, that's how I see it. You're the best judge, and I shouldn't like to put myself forward. But they'd be playing Box and Cox. Secretary gets in at Birmingham as Schleicher. Grant gets in at Coventry as Grant. Between Coventry and Rugby Grant changes to Schleicher in a wash-place or somewhere, and hangs about the platform and corridor till the train starts with him in it. He retires presently into a wash-place again. At a prearranged moment, secretary gets up, walks along the corridor and retires elsewhere, while Grant comes out and takes his place. Presently Grant walks down the corridor and secretary comes back to the compartment. They're never both visible at the same time, except for the two or three minutes while Grant is re-entering the train at Rugby, while honest witnesses like me are ready to come forward and swear that Schleicher got in at Birmingham, sat tight in his seat at Coventry and Rugby, and went straight through to Euston—as he did. I can't say I noticed any difference between the two Schleichers, except in the matter of the cigar. But they were very hairy and muffled up."

The Chief Inspector turned this over in his mind.

"Which of them was Schleicher when they got out at Euston?"

"Grant, surely. The secretary would remove his disguise at the last moment and emerge as himself, taking the thousand-to-one chance of somebody recognising him."

Peacock swore softly. "If that's what he did," he exclaimed, "we've got him on toast. Wait a moment, though. I *knew* there was a snag. If that's what they did, there ought to have been an extra third-class ticket at Euston. They can't both have travelled on one ticket."

"Why not?" said Mr. Egg. "I have often—at least, I don't exactly mean that, but I have from time to time laid a wager with an acquaintance that I would travel on his ticket, and got away with it."

"Perhaps," said Chief Inspector Peacock, "you would oblige me, sir, by outlining your method."

"Oh, certainly," said Mr. Egg. " 'Speak the truth with cheerful ease if you would both convince and please'— Monty's favourite motto. If I had been Mr. Grant's secretary, I'd have taken a return ticket from Birmingham to London, and when the outward half had been inspected for the last time at Rugby, I'd pretend to put it in my pocket. But I wouldn't really. I'd shove it down at the edge of my seat and go for my stroll along the corridor. Then when Grant took my place—recognising the right seat by an attaché-case, or something of that sort left on it—he'd retrieve the ticket and retain it. At the end of the journey, I'd slip off my beard and spectacles and so on, stick them in my overcoat pocket and fold the conspicuous overcoat inside-out and carry it on my arm. Then I'd wait to see Grant get out, and follow him up to the barrier, keeping a little way behind. He'd go through, giving up his ticket, and I'd follow along with a bunch of other people, making a little bustle and confusion in the gateway. The ticket-collector would stop me and say: 'I haven't got your ticket, sir.' I'd be indignant, and say: 'Oh, yes, you have.' He'd say: 'I don't think so, sir.' Then I'd protest, and he'd probably ask me to stand aside a minute while he dealt with the other passengers. Then I'd say: 'See here, my man, I'm quite sure I gave up my ticket. Look! Here's the return half, number so-and-so. Just look through your bunch and see if you haven't got the companion half.' He looks and he finds it, and says: 'I beg your pardon, sir; you're quite right. Here it is.' I say: 'Don't mention it,' and go through. And even if he suspects me, he can't prove anything, and the other fellow is well out of the way by that time."

"I see," said the Chief Inspector. "How often did you say you had indulged in this little game?"

"Well, never twice at the same station. It doesn't do to repeat one's effects too often."

"I think I'd better interview Schleicher and his secretary again," said Peacock pensively. "And the ticket-collector. I suppose we were meant to think that Grant had skipped to the Irish Mail. I admit we should have thought so but for the accident that the Mail left before the London train came in. However, it takes a clever criminal to beat our organisation. By the way, Mr. Egg, I hope you will not make a habit—"

"Talking of bad habits," said Monty happily, "what about another spot?"

MURDER AT PENTECOST

Buzz off, Flathers," said the
young man in flannels. "We're thrilled by your news, but we
don't want your religious opinions. And, for the Lord's sake,
stop talking about 'undergrads,' like a ruddy commercial traveller. Hop it!"

The person addressed, a pimply youth in a commoner's
gown, bleated a little, but withdrew from the table, intimidated.

"Appalling little tick," commented the young man in flan-
nels to his companion. "He's on my staircase, too. Thank
Heaven, I move out next term. I suppose it's true about the
Master? Poor old blighter—I'm quite sorry I cut his lecture.
Have some more coffee?"

"No, thanks, Radcott. I must be pushing off in a minute.
It's getting too near lunch-time."

Mr. Montague Egg, seated at the next small table, had
pricked up his ears. He now turned, with an apologetic cough,
to the young man called Radcott.

"Excuse me, sir," he said, with some diffidence. "I didn't
intend to overhear what you gentlemen were saying, but
might I ask a question?" Emboldened by Radcott's expression, which, though surprised, was frank and friendly, he went

on: "I happen to be a commercial traveller—Egg is my name, Montague Egg, representing Plummet & Rose, Wines and Spirits, Piccadilly. Might I ask what is wrong with saying 'undergrads'? Is the expression offensive in any way?"

Mr. Radcott blushed a fiery red to the roots of his flaxen hair.

"I'm frightfully sorry," he said ingenuously, and suddenly looking extremely young. "Damn stupid thing of me to say. Beastly brick."

"Don't mention it, I'm sure," said Monty.

"Didn't mean anything personal. Only, that chap Flathers gets my goat. He ought to know that nobody says 'undergrads' except townees and journalists and people outside the university."

"What ought we to say? 'Undergraduates'?"

"'Undergraduates' is correct."

"I'm very much obliged," said Monty. "Always willing to learn. It's easy to make a mistake in a thing like that, and, of course, it prejudices the customer against one. The *Salesman's Handbook* doesn't give any guidance about it; I shall have to make a memo for myself. Let me see. How would this do? 'To call an Oxford gent an—'"

"I think I should say 'Oxford man'—it's the more technical form of expression."

"Oh, yes. 'To call an Oxford man an undergrad proclaims you an outsider and a cad.' That's very easy to remember."

"You seem to have a turn for this kind of thing," said Radcott, amused.

"Well, I think perhaps I have," admitted Monty, with a touch of pride. "Would the same thing apply at Cambridge?"

"Certainly," replied Radcott's companion. "And you might add that 'To call the university the 'varsity is out of date, if not precisely narsity.' I apologise for the rhyme. 'Varsity has somehow a flavour of the 'nineties."

"So has the port I'm recommending," said Mr. Egg brightly. "Still, one's sales-talk must be up to date, naturally;

and smart, though not vulgar. In the wine and spirit trade we make refinement our aim. I am really much obliged to you, gentlemen, for your help. This is my first visit to Oxford. Could you tell me where to find Pentecost College? I have a letter of introduction to a gentleman there."

"Pentecost?" said Radcott. "I don't think I'd start there, if I were you."

"No?" said Mr. Egg, suspecting some obscure point of university etiquette. "Why not?"

"Because," replied Radcott surprisingly, "I understand from the regrettable Flathers that some public benefactor has just murdered the Master, and in the circumstances I doubt whether the Bursar will be able to give proper attention to the merits of rival vintages."

"Murdered the Master?" echoed Mr. Egg.

"Socked him one — literally, I am told, with a brickbat enclosed in a Woolworth sock — as he was returning to his house from delivering his too-well-known lecture on Plato's use of the Enclitics. The whole school of *Literæ Humaniores* will naturally be under suspicion, but, personally, I believe Flathers did it himself. You may have heard him informing us that judgement overtakes the evil-doer, and inviting us to a meeting for prayer and repentance in the South Lecture-Room. Such men are dangerous."

"Was the Master of Pentecost an evil-doer?"

"He has written several learned works disproving the existence of Providence, and I must say that I, in common with the whole Pentecostal community, have always looked on him as one of Nature's worst mistakes. Still, to slay him more or less on his own doorstep seems to me to be in poor taste. It will upset the examination candidates, who face their ordeal next week. And it will mean cancelling the Commem. Ball. Besides, the police have been called in, and are certain to annoy the Senior Common Room by walking on the grass in the quad. However, what's done can't be undone. Let us pass to a pleasanter subject. I understand that you have some port to dispose of. I, on the other hand, have recently suffered bereavement at the hands of a bunch of rowing hearties, who invaded my rooms the other night and poured my last dozen of Cockburn '04 down their leathery and undiscriminating throttles. If you care to stroll round with me to Pentecost, Mr. Egg, bringing your literature with you, we might be able to do business."

Mr. Egg expressed himself as delighted to accept Radcott's invitation, and was soon trotting along the Cornmarket at his conductor's athletic heels. At the corner of Broad Street the second undergraduate left them, while they turned on, past Balliol and Trinity, asleep in the June sunshine, and presently reached the main entrance of Pentecost.

Just as they did so, a small, elderly man, wearing a light overcoat and carrying an M.A. gown over his arm, came ambling short-sightedly across the street from the direction of the Bodleian Library. A passing car just missed whirling him into eternity, as Radcott stretched out a long arm and raked him into safety on the pavement.

"Look out, Mr. Temple," said Radcott. "We shall be having *you* murdered next."

"Murdered?" queried Mr. Temple, blinking. "Oh, you refer to the motor-car. But I saw it coming. I saw it quite distinctly. Yes, yes. But why 'next'? Has anybody else been murdered?"

"Only the Master of Pentecost," said Radcott, pinching Mr. Egg's arm.

"The Master? Dr. Greeby? You don't say so! Murdered? Dear me! Poor Greeby! This will upset my whole day's work." His pale-blue eyes shifted, and a curious, wavering look came into them. "Justice is slow but sure. Yes, yes. The sword of the Lord and of Gideon. But the blood—that is always so disconcerting, is it not? And yet, I washed my hands, you know." He stretched out both hands and looked at them in a puzzled way. "Ah, yes—poor Greeby has paid the price of his sins. Excuse my running away from you—I have urgent business at the police-station."

"If," said Mr. Radcott, again pinching Monty's arm, "you

want to give yourself up for the murder, Mr. Temple, you had better come along with us. The police are bound to be about the place somewhere."

"Oh, yes, of course, so they are. Yes. Very thoughtful of you. That will save me a great deal of time, and I have an important chapter to finish. A beautiful day, is it not, Mr. — I fear I do not know your name. Or do I? I am growing sadly forgetful."

Radcott mentioned his name, and the oddly assorted trio turned together towards the main entrance to the college. The great gate was shut; at the postern stood the porter, and at his side a massive figure in blue, who demanded their names.

Radcott, having been duly identified by the porter, produced Monty and his credentials.

"And this," he went on, "is, of course, Mr. Temple. You know him. He is looking for your Superintendent."

"Right you are, sir," replied the policeman. "You'll find him in the cloisters. . . . At his old game, I suppose?" he added, as the small figure of Mr. Temple shuffled away across the sun-baked expanse of the quad.

"Oh, yes," said Radcott. "He was on to it like a shot. Must be quite exciting for the old bird to have a murder so near home. Where was his last?"

"Lincoln, sir; last Tuesday. Young fellow shot his young woman in the Cathedral. Mr. Temple was down at the station the next day, just before lunch, explaining that he'd done it because the poor girl was the Scarlet Woman."

"Mr. Temple," said Radcott, "has a mission in life. He is the sword of the Lord and of Gideon. Every time a murder is committed in this country, Mr. Temple lays claim to it. It is true that his body can always be shown to have been quietly in bed or at the Bodleian while the dirty work was afoot, but to an idealistic philosopher that need present no difficulty. But what *is* all this about the Master, actually?"

"Well, sir, you know that little entry between the cloisters and the Master's residence? At twenty minutes past ten this morning, Dr. Greeby was found lying dead there, with his lecture-notes scattered all round him and a brickbat in a woollen sock lying beside his head. He'd been lecturing in a room in the Main Quadrangle at nine o'clock, and was, as far as we can tell, the last to leave the lecture-room. A party of American ladies and gentlemen passed through the cloisters a little after 10 o'clock, and they have been found, and say there was nobody about there then, so far as they could see — but, of course, sir, the murderer might have been hanging about the entry, because, naturally, they wouldn't go that way but through Boniface Passage to the Inner Quad and the chapel. One of the young gentlemen says he saw the Master cross the Main Quad on his way to the cloisters at 10:50, so he'd reach the entry in about two minutes after that. The Regius Professor of Morphology came along at 10:20, and found the body, and when the doctor arrived, five minutes later, he said Dr. Greeby must have been dead about a quarter of an hour. So that puts it somewhere round about 10:10, you see, sir."

"When did these Americans leave the chapel?"

"Ah, there you are, sir!" replied the constable. He seemed very ready to talk, thought Mr. Egg, and deduced, rightly, that Mr. Radcott was well and favourably known to the Oxford branch of the Force. "If that there party had come back through the cloisters, they might have been able to tell us something. But they didn't. They went on through the Inner Quad into the garden, and the verger didn't leave the chapel, on account of a lady who had just arrived and wanted to look at the carving on the reredos."

"And did the lady also come through the cloisters?"

"She did, sir, and she's the person we want to find, because it seems as though she must have passed through the cloisters very close to the time of the murder. She came into the chapel just on 10:15, because the verger recollected of the clock chiming a few minutes after she came in and her mentioning how sweet the notes was. You see the lady come in, didn't you, Mr. Dabbs?"

"I saw *a* lady," replied the porter, "but then I see a lot of ladies one way and another. This one came across from the Bodleian round about 10 o'clock. Elderly lady, she was, dressed kind of old-fashioned, with her skirts round her heels and one of them hats like a rook's nest and a bit of elastic round the back. Looked like she might be a female don—leastways, the way female dons used to look. And she had the twitches—you know—jerked her head a bit. You get hundreds like 'em. They goes to sit in the cloisters and listen to the fountain and the little birds. But as to noticing a corpse or a murderer, it's my belief they wouldn't know such a thing if they saw it. I didn't see the lady again, so she must have gone out through the garden."

"Very likely," said Radcott. "May Mr. Egg and I go in through the cloisters, officer? Because it's the only way to my rooms, unless we go round by St. Scholastica's Gate."

"All the other gates are locked, sir. You go on and speak to the Super; he'll let you through. You'll find him in the cloisters with Professor Staines and Dr. Moyle."

"Bodley's Librarian? What's he got to do with it?"

"They think he may know the lady, sir, if she's a Bodley reader."

"Oh, I see. Come along, Mr. Egg."

Radcott led the way across the Main Quadrangle and through a dark little passage at one corner, into the cool shade of the cloisters. Framed by the arcades of ancient stone, the green lawn drowsed tranquilly in the noonday heat. There was no sound but the echo of their own footsteps, the plash and tinkle of the little fountain and the subdued chirping of chaffinches, as they paced the alternate sunshine and shadow of the pavement. About midway along the north side of the cloisters they came upon another dim little covered passageway, at the entrance to which a police-sergeant was kneeling, examining the ground with the aid of an electric torch.

"Hullo, sergeant!" said Radcott. "Doing the Sherlock Holmes stunt? Show us the bloodstained footprints."

"No blood, sir, unfortunately. Might make our job easier if there were. And no footprints neither. The poor gentleman was sandbagged, and we think the murderer must have climbed up here to do it, for the deceased was a tall gentleman and he was hit right on the top of the head, sir." The sergeant indicated a little niche, like a blocked-up window, about four feet from the ground. "Looks as if he'd waited up here, sir, for Dr. Greeby to go by."

"He must have been well acquainted with his victim's habits," suggested Mr. Egg.

"Not a bit of it," retorted Radcott. "He'd only to look at the lecture-list to know the time and place. This passage leads to the Master's House and the Fellows' Garden and nowhere else, and it's the way Dr. Greeby would naturally go after his lecture, unless he was lecturing elsewhere, which he wasn't. Fairly able-bodied, your murderer, sergeant, to get up here. At least—I don't know."

Before the policeman could stop him, he had placed one hand on the side of the niche and a foot on a projecting band of masonry below it, and swung himself up.

"Hi, sir! Come down, please. The Super won't like that."

"Why? Oh, gosh! Finger-prints, I suppose. I forgot. Never mind; you can take mine if you want them, for comparison. Give you practice. Anyhow, a baby in arms could get up here. Come on, Mr. Egg; we'd better beat it before I'm arrested for obstruction."

But at this moment Radcott was hailed by a worried-looking don, who came through the passage from the far side, accompanied by three or four other people.

"Oh, Mr. Radcott! One moment, Superintendent, this gentleman will be able to tell you what you want to know; he was at Dr. Greeby's lecture. That is so, is it not, Mr. Radcott?"

"Well, no, not exactly, sir," replied Radcott, with some embarrassment. "I should have been, but, by a regrettable accident, I cut—that is to say, I was on the river, sir, and didn't get back in time."

"Very vexatious," said Professor Staines, while the Superintendent merely observed:

"Any witness to your being on the river, sir?"

"None," replied Radcott. "I was alone in a canoe, up a
backwater—earnestly studying Aristotle. But I really didn't
murder the Master. His lectures were—if I may say so—dull,
but not to that point exasperating."

"That is a very impudent observation, Mr. Radcott," said
the Professor severely, "and in execrable taste."

The Superintendent, murmuring something about routine, took down in a note-book the alleged times of Mr. Radcott's departure and return, and then said:

"I don't think I need detain any of you gentlemen further.
If we want to see you again, Mr. Temple, we will let you
know."

"Certainly, certainly. I shall just have a sandwich at the
café and return to the Bodleian. As for the lady, I can only
repeat that she sat at my table from about half-past nine till
just before ten, and returned again at ten-thirty. Very restless
and disturbing. I do wish, Dr. Moyle, that some arrangement
could be made to give me that table to myself, or that I could
be given a place apart in the library. Ladies are always restless
and disturbing. She was still there when I left, but I very much
hope she has now gone for good. You are sure you don't want
to lock me up now? I am quite at your service."

"Not just yet, sir. You will hear from us presently."

"Thank you, thank you. I should like to finish my chapter.
For the present, then, I will wish you good-day."

The little bent figure wandered away, and the Superintendent touched his head significantly.

"Poor gentleman! Quite harmless, of course. I needn't ask
you, Dr. Moyle, where *he* was at the time?"

"Oh, he was in his usual corner of Duke Humphrey's
Library. He admits it, you see, when he is asked. In any case, I
know definitely that he was there this morning, because he
took out a Phi book, and of course had to apply personally to
me for it. He asked for it at 9:30 and returned it at 12:15. As

regards the lady, I think I have seen her before. One of the older school of learned ladies, I fancy. If she is an outside reader, I must have her name and address somewhere, but she may, of course, be a member of the University. I fear I could not undertake to know them all by sight. But I will inquire. It is, in fact, quite possible that she is still in the library, and, if not, Franklin may know when she went and who she is. I will look into the matter immediately. I need not say, Professor, how deeply I deplore this lamentable affair. Poor dear Greeby! Such a loss to classical scholarship!"

At this point, Radcott gently drew Mr. Egg away. A few yards farther down the cloisters, they turned into another and rather wider passage, which brought them out into the Inner Quadrangle, one side of which was occupied by the chapel. Mounting three dark flights of stone steps on the opposite side, they reached Radcott's rooms, where the undergraduate thrust his new acquaintance into an armchair, and, producing some bottles of beer from beneath the window-seat, besought him to make himself at home.

"Well," he observed presently, "you've had a fairly lively introduction to Oxford life—one murder and one madman. Poor old Temple. Quite one of our prize exhibits. Used to be a Fellow here, donkey's years ago. There was some fuss, and he disappeared for a time. Then he turned up again, ten years since, perfectly potty; took lodgings in Holywell, and has haunted the Bodder and the police-station alternately ever since. Fine Greek scholar he is, too. Quite reasonable, except on the one point. I hope old Moyle finds his mysterious lady, though it's nonsense to pretend that they keep tabs on all the people who use the library. You've only got to walk in firmly, as if the place belonged to you, and, if you're challenged, say in a loud, injured tone that you've been a reader for years. If you borrow a gown, they won't even challenge you."

"Is that so, really?" said Mr. Egg.

"Prove it, if you like. Take my gown, toddle across to the Bodder, march straight in past the showcases and through the little wicket marked 'Readers Only,' into Duke

Humphrey's Library; do what you like, short of stealing the books or setting fire to the place—and if anybody says anything to you, I'll order six dozen of anything you like. That's fair, isn't it?"

Mr. Egg accepted this offer with alacrity, and in a few moments, arrayed in a scholar's gown, was climbing the stair that leads to England's most famous library. With a slight tremor, he pushed open the swinging glass door and plunged into the hallowed atmosphere of mouldering leather that distinguishes such temples of learning.

Just inside, he came upon Dr. Moyle in conversation with the door-keeper. Mr. Egg, bending nonchalantly to examine an illegible manuscript in a showcase, had little difficulty in hearing what they said, since, like all official attendants upon reading-rooms, they took no trouble to lower their voices.

"I know the lady, Dr. Moyle. That is to say, she has been here several times lately. She usually wears an M.A. gown. I saw her here this morning, but I didn't notice when she left. I don't think I ever heard her name, but seeing that she was a senior member of the University—"

Mr. Egg waited to hear no more. An idea was burgeoning in his mind. He walked away, courageously pushed open the Readers' Wicket, and stalked down the solemn mediæval length of Duke Humphrey's Library. In the remotest and darkest bay, he observed Mr. Temple, who, having apparently had his sandwich and forgotten about the murder, sat alone, writing busily, amid a pile of repellent volumes, with a large attaché-case full of papers open before him.

Leaning over the table, Mr. Egg addressed him in an urgent whisper:

"Excuse me, sir. The police Superintendent asked me to say that they think they have found the lady, and would be glad if you would kindly step down at once and identify her."

"The lady?" Mr. Temple looked up vaguely. "Oh, yes—the lady. To be sure. Immediately? That is not very convenient. Is it so very urgent?"

"They said particularly to lose no time, sir," said Mr. Egg.

Mr. Temple muttered something, rose, seemed to hesitate whether to clear up his papers or not, and finally shovelled them all into the bulging attaché-case, which he locked upon them.

"Let me carry this for you, sir," said Monty, seizing it promptly and shepherding Mr. Temple briskly out. "They're still in the cloisters, I think, but the Super said, would you kindly wait a few moments for him in the porter's lodge. Here we are."

He handed Mr. Temple and his attaché-case over to the care of the porter, who looked a little surprised at seeing Mr. Egg in academic dress, but, on hearing the Superintendent's name, said nothing. Mr. Egg hastened through quad and cloisters and mounted Mr. Radcott's staircase at a run.

"Excuse me, sir," he demanded breathlessly of that young gentleman, "but what is a Phi book?"

"A Phi book," replied Radcott, in some surprise, "is a book deemed by Bodley's Librarian to be of an indelicate nature, and catalogued accordingly, by some dead-and-gone humourist, under the Greek letter *phi*. Why the question?"

"Well," said Mr. Egg, "it just occurred to me how simple it would be for anybody to walk into the Bodleian, disguise himself in a retired corner—say in Duke Humphrey's Library—walk out, commit a murder, return, change back to his own clothes, and walk out. Nobody would stop a person from coming in again, if he—or she—had previously been seen to go out—especially if the disguise had been used in the library before. Just a change of clothes and an M.A. gown would be enough."

"What in the world are you getting at?"

"This lady, who was in the cloisters at the time of the murder. Mr. Temple says she was sitting at his table. But isn't it funny that Mr. Temple should have drawn special attention to himself by asking for a Phi book, to-day of all days? If he was once a Fellow of this college, he'd know which way Dr. Greeby would go after his lecture; and he may have had a grudge against him on account of that old trouble, whatever it was. He'd know about the niche in the wall, too. And he's got an attaché-case with him that might easily hold a lady's hat and a skirt long enough to hide his trousers. And why is he wearing a topcoat on such a hot day, if not to conceal the upper portion of his garments? Not that it's any business of mine—but—well, I just took the liberty of asking myself. And I've got him out there, with his case, and the porter keeping an eye on him."

Thus Mr. Egg, rather breathlessly. Radcott gaped at him.

"Temple? My dear man, you're as potty as he is. Why, he's always confessing—he confessed to this—you can't possibly suppose—"

"I dare say I'm wrong," said Mr. Egg. "But isn't there a fable about the man who cried 'Wolf!' so often that nobody would believe him when the wolf really came? There's a motto in the *Salesman's Handbook* that I always admire very much. It says: 'Discretion plays a major part in making up the salesman's art, for truths that no one can believe are calculated to deceive.' I think that's rather subtle, don't you?"

MAHER-SHALAL-HASHBAZ

No Londoner can ever resist the attraction of a street crowd. Mr. Montague Egg, driving up Kingsway, and observing a group of people staring into the branches of one of the slender plane-trees which embellish that thoroughfare, drew up to see what all the excitement was about.

"Poor puss!" cried the bystanders, snapping encouraging fingers. "Poor pussy, then! Kitty, kitty, kitty, come on!"

"Look, baby, look at the pretty pussy!"

"Fetch her a bit of cat's-meat."

"She'll come down when she's tired of it."

"Chuck a stone at her!"

"Now then, what's all this about?"

The slender, shabby child who stood so forlornly holding the empty basket appealed to the policeman.

"Oh, do please send these people away! How *can* he come down, with everybody shouting at him? He's frightened, poor darling."

From among the swaying branches a pair of amber eyes gleamed wrathfully down. The policeman scratched his head.

"Bit of a job, ain't it, missie? However did he come to get up there?"

"The fastening came undone, and he jumped out of the basket just as we were getting off the 'bus. Oh, please do something!"

Mr. Montague Egg, casting his eye over the crowd, perceived on its outskirts a window-cleaner with his ladders upon a truck. He hailed him.

"Fetch that ladder along, sonnie, and we'll soon get him down, if you'll allow me to try, miss. If we leave him to himself, he'll probably stick up there for ages. 'It's hard to reassure, persuade, or charm the customer who once has felt alarm.' Carefully, now. That's the ticket."

"Oh, thank you so much! Oh, do be gentle with him. He does so hate being handled."

"That's all right, miss; don't you worry. Always the gentleman, that's Monty Egg. Kind about the house and clean with children. Up she goes!"

And Mr. Egg, clapping his smart trilby upon his head and uttering crooning noises, ascended into the leafage. A loud explosion of spitting sounds and a small shower of twigs floated down to the spectators, and presently Mr. Egg followed, rather awkwardly, clutching a reluctant bunch of ginger fur. The girl held out the basket, the four furiously kicking legs were somehow bundled in, a tradesman's lad produced a piece of string, the lid was secured, the window-cleaner was rewarded and removed his ladder, and the crowd dispersed. Mr. Egg, winding his pocket-handkerchief about a lacerated wrist, picked the scattered leaves out of his collar and straightened his tie.

"Oh, he's scratched you dreadfully!" lamented the girl, her blue eyes large and tragic.

"Not at all," replied Mr. Egg. "Very happy to have been of assistance, I am sure. Can I have the pleasure of driving you anywhere? It'll be pleasanter for him than a 'bus, and if we pull up the windows he can't jump out, even if he does get the basket open again."

The girl protested, but Mr. Egg firmly bustled her into his little saloon and inquired where she wanted to go.

"It's this address," said the girl, pulling a newspaper cutting out of her worn handbag. "Somewhere in Soho, isn't it?"

Mr. Egg, with some surprise, read the advertisement:

WANTED: hard-working, capable CAT (either sex), keep down mice in pleasant villa residence and be companion to middle-aged couple. Ten shillings and good home to suitable applicant. Apply personally to Mr. John Doe, La Cigale Bienheureuse, Frith St., W., on Tuesday between 11 and 1 o'clock.

"That's a funny set-out," said Mr. Egg, frowning.

"Oh! do you think there's anything wrong with it? Is it just a joke?"

"Well," said Mr. Egg, "I can't quite see why anybody wants to pay ten bob for an ordinary cat, can you? I mean, they usually come gratis and f.o.b. from somebody who doesn't like drowning kittens. And I don't quite believe in Mr. John Doe; he sounds like what they call a legal fiction."

"Oh, dear!" cried the girl, with tears in the blue eyes. "I did so hope it would be all right. You see, we're so dreadfully hard up, with father out of work, and Maggie—that's my stepmother—says she won't keep Maher-shalal-hashbaz any longer, because he scratches the table-legs and eats as much as a Christian, bless him!—though he doesn't really—only a little milk and a bit of cat's-meat, and he's a beautiful mouser, only there aren't many mice where we live—and I thought, if I could get him a good home—and ten shillings for some new boots for Dad, he needs them so badly—"

"Oh, well, cheer up," said Mr. Egg. "Perhaps they're willing to pay for a full-grown, certified mouser. Or—tell you what—it may be one of these cinema stunts. We'll go and see, anyhow; only I think you'd better let me come with you and interview Mr. Doe. I'm quite respectable," he added hastily. "Here's my card. Montague Egg, travelling representative of Plummet & Rose, Wines and Spirits, Piccadilly. Interviewing customers is my long suit. 'The salesman's job is to get the trade—don't leave the house till the deal is made'—that's Monty's motto."

"My name's Jean Maitland, and Dad's in the commercial line himself—at least, he was till he got bronchitis last winter, and now he isn't strong enough to go on the road."

"Bad luck!" said Monty sympathetically, as he turned down High Holborn. He liked this child of sixteen or so, and registered a vow that "something should be done about it."

It seemed as though there were other people who thought ten shillings good payment for a cat. The pavement before the grubby little Soho restaurant was thick with cat-owners, some carrying baskets, some clutching their animals in their arms. The air resounded with the mournful cries of the prisoners.

"Some competition," said Monty. "Well, anyhow, the post doesn't seem to be filled yet. Hang on to me, and we'll try what we can do."

They waited for some time. It seemed that the applicants were being passed out through a back entrance, for, though many went in, some returned. Eventually they secured a place in the queue going up a dingy staircase, and, after a further eternity, found themselves facing a dark and discouraging door. Presently this was opened by a stout and pursy-faced man, with very sharp little eyes, who said briskly: "Next, please!" and they walked in.

"Mr. John Doe?" said Monty.

"Yes. Brought your cat? Oh, the young lady's cat. I see. Sit down, please. Name and address, miss?"

The girl gave an address south of the Thames, and the man made a note of it, "in case," he explained, "the chosen candidate should prove unsuitable, and I might want to write to you again. Now, let us see the cat."

The basket was opened, and a ginger head emerged resentfully.

"Oh, yes. Fine specimen. Poor pussy, then. He doesn't seem very friendly."

"He's frightened by the journey, but he's a darling when he once knows you, and a splendid mouser. And so clean."

"That's important. Must have him clean. And he must work for his living, you know."

"Oh, he will. He can tackle rats or anything. We call him Maher-shalal-hashbaz, because he 'makes haste to the spoil.' But he answers to Mash, don't you, darling?"

"I see. Well, he seems to be in good condition. No fleas? No diseases? My wife is very particular."

"Oh, no. He's a splendid healthy cat. Fleas, indeed!"

"No offence, but I must be particular, because we shall make a great pet of him. I don't care much for his colour. Ten shillings is a high price to pay for a ginger one. I don't know whether—"

"Come, come," said Monty. "Nothing was said in your advertisement about colour. This lady has come a long way to bring you the cat, and you can't expect her to take less than she's offered. You'll never get a better cat than this; everyone knows that the ginger ones are the best mousers—they've got more go in them. And look at his handsome white shirt-front. It *shows* you how beautifully clean he is. And think of the advantage—you can *see* him—you and your good lady won't go tripping over him in a dark corner, same as you do with these black and tabby ones. As a matter of fact, we ought to charge extra for such a handsome colour as this. They're much rarer and more high-class than the ordinary cat."

"There's something in that," admitted Mr. Doe. "Well, look here, Miss Maitland. Suppose you bring Maher—what you said—out to our place this evening, and if my wife likes him we will keep him. Here's the address. And you must come at six precisely, please, as we shall be going out later."

Monty looked at the address, which was at the northern extremity of the Edgware-Morden Tube.

"It's a very long way to come on the chance," he said resolutely. "You will have to pay Miss Maitland's expenses."

"Oh, certainly," said Mr. Doe. "That's only fair. Here is half a crown. You can return me the change this evening. Very well, thank you. Your cat will have a really happy home if he comes to us. Put him back in his basket now. The other way out, please. Mind the step. *Good* morning."

Mr. Egg and his new friend, stumbling down an excessively confined and stuffy back staircase into a malodorous by-street, looked at one another.

"He seemed rather an abrupt sort of person," said Miss Maitland. "I do *hope* he'll be kind to Maher-shalal-hashbaz. You were *marvellous* about the gingeriness—I thought he was going to be stuffy about that. My angel Mash! how *anybody* could object to his beautiful colour!"

"Um!" said Mr. Egg. "Well, Mr. Doe may be O.K., but I shall believe in his ten shillings when I see it. And, in any case, you're not going to his house alone. I shall call for you in the car at five o'clock."

"But, Mr. Egg—I can't allow you! Besides, you've taken half a crown off him for my fare."

"That's only business," said Mr. Egg. "Five o'clock sharp I shall be there."

"Well, come at four, and let us give you a cup of tea, anyway. That's the least we can do."

"Pleased, I'm sure," said Mr. Egg.

The house occupied by Mr. John Doe was a new detached villa standing solitary at the extreme end of a new and unmade suburban road. It was Mrs. Doe who answered the bell—a small, frightened-looking woman with watery eyes and a nervous habit of plucking at her pale lips with her fingers. Maher-shalal-hashbaz was released from his basket in the sitting-room, where Mr. Doe was reclining in an armchair, reading the evening paper. The cat sniffed suspiciously at him, but softened to Mrs. Doe's timid advances so far as to allow his ears to be tickled.

"Well, my dear," said Mr. Doe, "will he do? You don't object to the colour, eh?"

"Oh, no. He's a beautiful cat. I like him very much."

"Right. Then we'll take him. Here you are, Miss Maitland. Ten shillings. Please sign this receipt. Thanks. Never mind about the change from the half-crown. There you are, my dear; you've got your cat, and I hope we shall see no more of those mice. Now"—he glanced at his watch—"I'm afraid you must say good-bye to your pet quickly, Miss Maitland; we've got to get off. He'll be quite safe with us."

Monty strolled out with gentlemanly reticence into the hall while the last words were said. It was, no doubt, the same gentlemanly feeling which led him to move away from the sitting-room door towards the back part of the house; but he had only waited a very few minutes when Jean Maitland came out, sniffing valiantly into a small handkerchief, and followed by Mrs. Doe.

"You're fond of your cat, aren't you, my dear? I do hope you don't feel too—"

"There, there, Flossie," said her husband, appearing suddenly at her shoulders, "Miss Maitland knows he'll be well looked after." He showed them out, and shut the door quickly upon them.

"If you *don't* feel happy about it," said Mr. Egg uneasily, "we'll have him back in two twos."

"No, it's all right," said Jean. "If you don't mind, let's get in at once and drive away—rather fast."

As they lurched over the uneven road, Mr. Egg saw a lad coming down it. In one hand he carried a basket. He was whistling loudly.

"Look!" said Monty. "One of our hated rivals. We've got in ahead of him, anyhow. 'The salesman first upon the field gets the bargain signed and sealed.' Damn it!" he added to himself, as he pressed down the accelerator, "I *hope* it's O.K. I wonder."

Although Mr. Egg had worked energetically to get Maher-shalal-hashbaz settled in the world, he was not easy in his mind. The matter preyed upon his spirits to such an extent that, finding himself back in London on the following Saturday week, he made an expedition south of the Thames to make inquiries. And when the Maitlands' door was opened by

Jean, there by her side, arching his back and brandishing his tail, was Maher-shalal-hashbaz.

"Yes," said the girl, "he found his way back, the clever darling! Just a week ago to-day—and he was dreadfully thin and draggled—how he did it, I can't think. But we simply couldn't send him away again, could we, Maggie?"

"No," said Mrs. Maitland. "I don't like the cat, and never did, but there! I suppose even cats have their feelings. But it's an awkward thing about the money."

"Yes," said Jean. "You see, when he got back and we decided to keep him, I wrote to Mr. Doe and explained, and sent him a postal order for the ten shillings. And this morning the letter came back from the Post Office, marked 'Not Known.' So we don't know what to do about it."

"I never did believe in Mr. John Doe," said Monty. "If you ask me, Miss Maitland, he was no good, and I shouldn't bother any more about him."

But the girl was not satisfied, and presently the obliging Mr. Egg found himself driving out northwards in search of the mysterious Mr. Doe, carrying the postal order with him.

The door of the villa was opened by a neatly dressed, elderly woman whom he had never seen before. Mr. Egg inquired for Mr. John Doe.

"He doesn't live here. Never heard of him."

Monty explained that he wanted the gentleman who had purchased the cat.

"Cat?" said the woman. Her face changed. "Step inside, will you? George!" she called to somebody inside the house, "here's a gentleman called about a cat. Perhaps you'd like to—" The rest of the sentence was whispered into the ear of a man who emerged from the sitting-room, and who appeared to be, and was in fact, her husband.

George looked Mr. Egg carefully up and down. "I don't know nobody here called Doe," said he; "but if it's the late tenant you're wanting, they've left. Packed and went off in a hurry the day after the old gentleman was buried. I'm the caretaker for the landlord. And if you've missed a cat, maybe you'd like to come and have a look out here."

He led the way through the house and out at the back door into the garden. In the middle of one of the flowerbeds was a large hole, like an irregularly shaped and shallow grave. A spade stood upright in the mould. And laid in two lugubrious rows upon the lawn were the corpses of some very dead cats. At a hasty estimate, Mr. Egg reckoned that there must be close on fifty of them.

"If any of these is yours," said George, "you're welcome to it. But they ain't in what you might call good condition."

"Good Lord!" said Mr. Egg, appalled, and thought with pleasure of Maher-shalal-hashbaz, tail erect, welcoming him on the Maitlands' threshold. "Come back and tell me about this. It's—it's unbelievable!"

It turned out that the name of the late tenants had been Proctor. The family consisted of an old Mr. Proctor, an invalid, to whom the house belonged, and his married nephew and the nephew's wife.

"They didn't have no servant sleeping in. Old Mrs. Crabbe used to do for them, coming in daily, and she always told me that the old gentleman couldn't abide cats. They made him ill like—I've known folks like that afore. And, of course, they had to be careful, him being so frail and his heart so bad he might have popped off any minute. What it seemed to us when I found all them cats buried, like, was as how maybe young Proctor had killed them to prevent the old gentleman seeing 'em and getting a shock. But the queer thing is that all them cats looks to have been killed about the same time, and not so long ago, neither."

Mr. Egg remembered the advertisement, and the false name, and the applicants passed out by a different door, so that none of them could possibly tell how many cats had been bought and paid for. And he remembered also the careful injunction to bring the cat at 6 o'clock precisely, and the whistling lad with the basket who had appeared on the scene about a quarter of an hour after them. He remembered another thing—a faint miauling noise that had struck upon his ear as he stood in the hall while Jean was saying good-bye to Maher-shalal-hashbaz, and the worried look on Mrs. Proctor's face when she had asked if Jean was fond of her pet. It looked as though Mr. Proctor junior had been collecting cats for some rather sinister purpose. Collecting them from every quarter of London. From quarters as far apart as possible—or why so much care to take down names and addresses?

"What did the old gentleman die of?" he asked.

"Well," said Mrs. George, "it was just heart-failure, or so the doctor said. Last Tuesday week he passed away in the night, poor soul, and Mrs. Crabbe that laid him out said he had a dreadful look of horror on his poor face, but the doctor said that wasn't anything out of the way, not with his disease. But what the doctor didn't see, being too busy to come round, was them terrible scratches on his face and arms. Must have regular clawed himself in his agony—oh, dear, oh, dear! But there! Anybody knew as he might go off at any time like the blowing out of a candle."

"I know that, Sally," said her husband. "But what about them scratches on the bedroom door? Don't tell me he did that, too. Or, if he did, why didn't somebody hear him and come along to help him? It's all very well for Mr. Timbs— that's the landlord—to say as tramps must have got into the house after the Proctors left, and put us in here to look after the place, but why should tramps go for to do a useless bit of damage like that?"

"A 'eartless lot, them Proctors, that's what I say," said Mrs. George. "A-snoring away, most likely, and leaving their uncle to die by himself. And wasn't the lawyer upset about it, neither! Coming along in the morning to make the old gentleman's will, and him passed away so sudden. And seeing they came in for all his money after all, you'd think they might have given him a better funeral. Mean, I call it—not a flower, hardly—only one half-guinea wreath—and no oak—only elm and a shabby lot of handles. Such trash! You'd think they'd be ashamed."

Mr. Egg was silent. He was not a man of strong imagination, but he saw a very horrible picture in his mind. He saw an old, sick man asleep, and hands that quietly opened the bedroom door, and dragged in, one after the other, sacks that moved and squirmed and mewed. He saw the sacks left open on the floor, and the door being softly shut and locked on the outside. And then, in the dim glow of the night-light, he saw shadowy shapes that leapt and flitted about the room—black and tabby and ginger—up and down, prowling on noiseless feet, thudding on velvet paws from tables and chairs. And then, plump up on the bed—a great ginger cat with amber eyes—and the sleeper waking with a cry—and after that a nightmare of terror and disgust behind the locked and remorseless door. A very old, sick man, stumbling and gasping for breath, striking out at the shadowy horrors that pursued and fled him—and the last tearing pain at the heart when merciful death overtook him. Then, nothing but a mewing of cats and a scratching at the door, and outside, the listener, with his ear bent to the keyhole.

Mr. Egg passed his handkerchief over his forehead; he did not like his thoughts. But he had to go on, and see the murderer sliding through the door in the early morning—hurrying to collect his innocent accomplices before Mrs. Crabbe should come—knowing that it must be done quickly and the corpse made decent—and that when people came to the house there must be no mysterious miaulings to surprise them. To set the cats free would not be enough—they might hang about the house. No; the water-butt and then the grave in the garden. But Maher-shalal-hashbaz—noble Maher-shalal-hashbaz had fought for his life. He was not going to be drowned in any water-butts. He had kicked himself loose ("and I hope," thought Mr. Egg, "he scratched him all to blazes"), and he had toiled his way home across London. If only Maher-shalal-hashbaz could tell what he knew! But Monty Egg knew something, and he could tell.

"And I *will* tell, what's more," said Monty Egg to himself, as he wrote down the name and address of Mr. Proctor's solicitor. He supposed it must be murder to terrify an old man to death; he was not sure, but he meant to find out. He cast about in his mind for a consoling motto from the *Salesman's Handbook*, but, for the first time in his life, could find nothing that really fitted the case.

"I seem to have stepped regularly out of my line," he thought sadly; "but still, as a citizen —"

And then he smiled, recollecting the first and last aphorism in his favourite book:

> *To serve the Public is the aim*
> *Of every salesman worth the name.*

A SHOT AT GOAL

A workman put in his head at the door of the Saloon Bar.

"Is Mr. Robbins here?"

The stout gentleman who was discussing football with Mr. Montague Egg turned at the sound of his name.

"Yes? Oh, it's Warren. What is it, Warren?"

"A note, sir. Handed in at the Mills just after you left. As it was marked 'Urgent' I thought I'd best bring it down. I'd have took it up to the house, sir, only they told me in the town as you'd stepped in to the Eagle."

"Thanks," said Mr. Robbins. "Urgent only to the sender, I expect, as usual." He tore open the envelope and glanced at the message, and his face changed. "Who brought this?"

"I couldn't say, sir. It was pushed in through the letter-flap in the gate."

"Ah, very good. Thank you, Warren."

The workman withdrew, and Mr. Robbins said, after a moment's thought:

"If Mr. Edgar should look in, Bowles, will you tell him I've changed my mind and gone back to the Mill, and I'll be glad if he'd come and see me there, before he goes up to the house."

"Right you are, sir."

"I'll take a few sandwiches with me. There's a bit of work I want to put in, and it may keep me."

Mr. Bowles obligingly put up the sandwiches into a parcel, and Mr. Robbins departed, with a brief "Good night, all."

"That's the general manager up at the Mills," observed Mr. Bowles. "Been here five years now. Takes a great interest in the town. He's a member of the Football Committee."

"So I gathered," said Mr. Egg.

"I see you're keen on the game," went on the landlord.

"In a business capacity," replied Mr. Egg, "I'm keen on whatever the gentleman I'm talking to is keen on. As it says in the *Salesman's Handbook*, 'The haberdasher gets the golfer's trade by talking, not of buttons, but of Braid.' Isn't that right, sir?"

He appealed to a quiet, dark man in plus-fours.

"Very smart," said the latter, smiling. "And apt," he added, with a glance at his own golf clubs leaning against the counter. Mr. Egg permitted himself a modest smirk.

"Well," said Mr. Bowles, "from a business point of view, you're dead right. In a place like this you've got to keep on the right side of them you live by. And so I told Hughie Searle only yesterday."

Mr. Egg nodded. The Twiddleton Mills were a very small factory, reproducing only a limited output of the superior homespuns known as Twiddleton Tweeds; but Twiddleton was a very small town, and the Mills formed the axis about which its life revolved.

"Who's Hughie Searle?" demanded Mr. Egg.

"Best goal the Twiddleton Trojans ever had," replied Mr. Bowles. "Born and bred in the town, too. But he got across Mr. Robbins over that business about young Fletcher, and he's been dropped out of the team. I don't say it's fair, but you can't blame the committee. They're all business men and they've got to eat out of Robbins's hand, as you might say. And I told Hughie, Bill Fletcher might be a friend of his, but there's two sides to every question, and when it comes to language and threats to a gentleman in Mr. Robbins's position, you can't hardly expect him to pass it over."

"No," said Mr. Charteris, the quiet man, suddenly, "unless you take the view that footballers should be picked on their form as players, and not for personal considerations."

"Ah!" said Mr. Bowles, "but that's what Vicar would call a counsel of perfection. People talk a lot about the team spirit and let the best side win, but if you was to sit in this bar and listen to what goes on, it's all spite and jealousy, or else it's how to scrape up enough money to entice away some other team's center-forward, or it's complaints about favoritism or wrong decisions, or something that leaves a nasty taste in the mouth. The game's not what it was when I was a lad. Too much commercialism, and enough back-biting to stock an old maid's tea-party."

"What happened to Bill Fletcher, by the way?" asked the quiet man.

"Chucked up his job and left the town," said the landlord. "I think he's gone to live with his father at Wickersby. They're still using that invention of his, whatever it was, up at the Mills, and they do say it saves them a lot of money, and he wasn't rightly done by. But Mr. Entwistle told me Fletcher hadn't a leg to stand on, according to the terms of the contract, and being a solicitor, he should know."

"The way of an inventor is hard in this country," said the quiet man.

"Very likely, sir," agreed Mr. Bowles. "I never had no turn that way myself, and perhaps it's just as well. Ah! Good evening, Mr. Edgar. Your dad was in here a few minutes back and left a message as he'd changed his mind and gone back to the Mills and he'd be obliged if you'd go and see him up there right away."

"Oh, did he?" said the young man who had just come in. He was a tall, loose-limbed, loose-lipped youngster, somewhat showily dressed, and appeared to have been drinking rather more than was good for him. "Give us a double whisky,

Bowles, and look here, if anybody asks you, I didn't come in here, and I never got the Governor's message. See?"

"Very good, Mr. Edgar," said the landlord, with a surreptitious wink at Monty. He eyed Edgar Robbins thoughtfully, as though gauging his capacity, seemed to decide that he could just take a double whisky without overflowing, and fulfilled the order. Edgar put the drink down in a gulp, glanced at the clock, which marked twenty minutes to eight, muttered something, and banged his way out of the bar, nearly colliding in the doorway with another young man, who scowled angrily at his retreating back.

"Did you see that?" said the newcomer. "I'd like to teach that young —— manners. Him and his —— old father are a pair, the dirty —— !"

"Now then, Hughie!" protested Mr. Bowles. An elderly man, who had been reading his paper by the fire, got up and went out with a look of disgust. "I can't allow that sort of language in my bar. You've driven that gentleman away, and him a stranger to the town. A nice idea he'll get of Twiddleton. And in front of Mr. Charteris, too. I'm surprised."

"Sorry, Mr. Charteris. Sorry, Mr. Bowles. But I've had about enough of Robbinses. The old man's got his knife into me, all right. Dropping me for that fool Benson, against the Swallows! I don't mind standing aside for a better man—but Benson! Him keep goal—keeping chickens is all he's fit for. It's a damned insult. And young Edgar charging into me like a clumsy great goat and never saying so much as 'Pardon,' the insolent lout."

"Steady," said Mr. Bowles. " 'Tisn't the first time you've stood up to a charge, Hughie. Young Edgar's had one over the eight. And he's a bit put out. His dad left a message he was going up to the Mills and wanted to see him there, and Mr. Edgar wasn't having any. Told me to say he hadn't been in and didn't get the message. Spot of trouble there, I wouldn't wonder. Maybe the old gentleman's on to some of the ways he spends the money."

"Time, too," said Hughie. "Half of old-an'-mild, Mr. Bowles, if you please. Young Edgar's too much of a gentleman to work at the Mills, but he's not too grand to take the cash and spend it on skirts. Be damned to the lot of them! I haven't finished with old Robbins yet."

"The less you have to do with Mr. Robbins the better," said Mr. Bowles, severely. "You'll let that temper of yours get the better of you once too often, and say something you'll be sorry for. What's the time? Quarter to. Your chop'll be just about ready now, Mr. Egg, if you'll kindly step through to the parlor."

"I must be getting along, too," said Charteris. He picked up his clubs, bestowed a pleasant farewell upon the company, and went out, leaving Hughie Searle alone before the bar, his dark eyes glowering, and his bullet head humped sulkily between his broad, square shoulders.

At half-past eight, Mr. Egg, having consumed his chop and chips, strolled back into the bar. Hughie Searle had gone, but the room had filled up and Mr. Bowles, assisted now by a barman, was doing a brisk trade. The Eagle was the only hotel of genuine importance in the little town, and all Twiddletonians of any standing passed through its hospitable door most evenings in the week. Mr. Egg had not been working that district of late, but he rediscovered several patrons and acquaintances who remembered him from six years back and were glad to see him. He was deep in conversation with Mr. Harcourt, the bank manager, when the door was hastily flung open and a man rushed in breathlessly, his eyes starting out of his head.

"Help! Murder! I want the police!"

Every head turned; every mug and glass hung suspended; Mr. Bowles, grasping the handle of the beer-engine, let half a pint of bitter overflow the pot and go frothing down the pipe.

"Why, Ted, what's up?"

The man staggered to the settle and dropped down, panting. Eager faces bent over him.

"Anything wrong up at the Mills?"

"Mr. Robbins—lying in his office—with his 'ead bashed in—all of a mask of blood. Get the police! It's murder!"

"Old Mr. Robbins!"

"Yes, the boss. A dretful sight it was."

"But 'oo done it?"

"Think I stopped to see? I come off, fast as me legs could carry me."

"Didn't you ring up the police?"

"Wot? And 'ave 'im come up behind and dot me one? Not me! There might be a gang of 'em 'anging round the place."

"Well, *you're* a fine night-watchman," said Mr. Bowles, "I don't think. Racing down here that-a-way and the murderer may be escaping all this while. Didn't think to lock the gate after you, I suppose? 'Course you didn't. Now, you pull yourself together and take a couple of the lads and go straight on back to the Mills, and I'll ring up Inspector Weybridge. That's right, George. You give 'im a brandy and try and make a man of 'im."

"I'll run him up to the Mills," suggested Mr. Egg, to whom a murder or a mystery was very nearly as satisfying as an order for 12 dozen ports at 190s. the dozen. "My car's just out in the yard. I can start her up in two seconds."

"That's fine," said the landlord. "And I don't mind if I come myself. George, reach me my big stick, in case we meet anything, and ring up the police-station and tell the Missus I've gone out for a bit and can she come and 'elp in the bar. Now then, Ted my lad. Up you come! Mr. Robbins murdered! That's a nice thing to 'appen."

Mr. Egg, by this time, had got his car started. Mr. Bowles climbed in beside him and Ted was accommodated in the back seat, between the banker and a young farmer, who had added themselves to the party.

A run of half a mile brought them to the Twiddleton Mills. The big gates were locked, but the small side-gate stood wide open.

"Look at that!" said Mr. Bowles. "Whoever it was, he'll

have took hisself off by now, if he's any sense. Ted Baggitt ain't got no 'ead, and never 'ad, since I knew him.'"

They crossed a yard and came to the door leading to the offices, which also stood wide open. A light was burning in a room on the right, and through a third open door they looked into the manager's room. Slumped in his swivel chair, his head and arms sprawled over the desk, lay what had been Mr. Robbins. One side of his skull had been ferociously battered in, and the sight was horrid enough to subdue the exuberance even of Mr. Bowles. The wretched Ted sank down on a chair by the wall and began to whimper.

"He's dead, all right," said Monty. "Best not touch anything, but it can't hurt if I—eh?"

He extracted a clean handkerchief from his pocket and laid it over the dead man's head; after which it was clean no longer.

"I don't see no weapon," said Mr. Bowles, gazing vaguely first at the fireplace and then at the desk, which was strewn with scattered papers.

"There's a big brass paper-weight missing," said Mr. Harcourt. "It used to stand just here, by the blotting-pad. I've seen it scores of times."

Monty nodded. "The man will have been sitting here, in this chair at the side of the desk. They'll have talked a bit, and then he'll have jumped up, snatching the paper-weight, and caught Mr. Robbins on the head just as he was getting to his feet. The blow was struck from in front, as you'll have noticed."

"That looks," said the banker, "as though the murder was not premeditated."

"That's a fact," replied Monty. He peered gingerly at the dead man. "There's a bit of torn paper here in his left hand; perhaps that'll tell us something. No, no, Mr. Bowles. Excuse me. Best leave everything just as it is till the police come. That sounds like them now."

The noise of footsteps crossing the yard bore out his

remark. A small group of men came in at the door, and Mr. Egg found himself looking, for the second time that evening, into the face of the quiet man in plus-fours.

"We meet again, Mr. Egg," said Mr. Charteris. "I'm the Chief Constable, and these are Dr. Small and Inspector Weybridge. This is a bad business. See what you can tell us about it, Doctor. Now, where's the man who found the body? What's your name? Ted Baggitt? Very well, Baggitt, what do you know about this?"

"Nothing at all, sir—only the finding of him. I come on duty, sir, when the man on the gate goes off at half-past seven. Mr. Robbins had left the Mills when I came on, but about a quarter to eight, back he comes again. He lets himself in with his own key and meets me just outside the door. 'I've come up to do a bit o' private work,' he says, 'and Mr. Edgar may come along later, but don't you bother,' he says, 'I'll let him in myself.' So I leaves him in this here office and goes off to get me bit o' supper ready. My little room's down in the other building."

"And did Mr. Edgar come?"

"Yes, sir. Leastways, the outer bell rang about 8 o'clock, but I didn't take no notice, seeing what Mr. Robbins said. I didn't hear nothing more, sir, nor see nobody, till I'd 'ad me supper and come out this way to start me first round just about 9 o'clock. Then I see this 'ere door open, and I looks in, and there's poor Mr. Robbins a-laying dead. So I says, 'O Gawd!' I says to myself, 'we'll all be murdered.' And I takes to me 'eels."

"You never actually saw Mr. Edgar?"

"No, sir." The man's face looked troubled. "No, sir—I never see 'im. You don't think it could have been 'im, sir? That would be an awful thing, to be sure."

"Mr. Edgar?" cried Mr. Bowles, in horror. "But you was there yourself, sir, when he said he wasn't coming to the Mills."

"Yes," said the Chief Constable. "Of course, he might have wanted us to think just that. It would be a very bold way to stage an alibi, but it's possible. Still, at present we've no proof that he did come. Well, Doctor, what about it?"

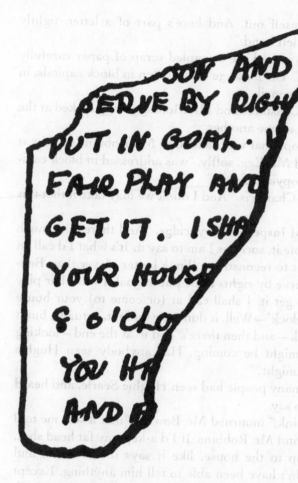

SON AND SERVE BY RIGH
PUT IN GOAL.
FAIR PLAY AND
GET IT. I SHA
YOUR HOUSE
8 o'CLO
YOU HA
AND A

"Dead about an hour to an hour and a half," replied Dr. Small. "Struck with a heavy instrument with sharp edges. A paper-weight, did you say, Mr. Harcourt? Yes, it might well be something like that."

"What's that?" asked Charteris. And when the banker had explained:

"I see. Weybridge, tell them to have a look round for the weapon. It may have been thrown away somewhere. Be careful of any possible finger-prints. Anything else, Doctor?"

"His keys are in his pocket, so the murderer didn't use

them to let himself out. And here's part of a letter, tightly clenched in his left hand."

The doctor spread the crumpled scrap of paper carefully out on the desk. The message was written in block capitals, in purple copying-pencil.

The Chief Constable and Mr. Montague Egg looked at the paper and then at one another.

"The envelope that was handed to Mr. Robbins tonight at the Eagle," said Mr. Egg, softly, "was addressed in block capitals in purple copying-pencil."

"Yes," said Charteris. "And I think we may take it that this is it."

"H'm!" said Inspector Weybridge. "And there ain't much doubt who wrote it, sorry as I am to say it. It's what I'd call an easy dockiment to reconstruct. 'I'm a better player than Benson, and I deserve by rights to be put in goal. I want fair play and I mean to get it. I shall call at (or come to) your house tonight at 8 o'clock'—Well, it don't say tonight, actually, but it do say 8 o'clock—and then there's 'and if' at the end—looking like a threat might be coming. Has anybody seen Hughie Searle about tonight?"

Only too many people had seen Hughie Searle, and heard what he had to say.

"And to think," mourned Mr. Bowles, "that it was me told him where to find Mr. Robbins. If I'd a-kept my fat head shut, he'd a-gone up to the house, like it says in the letter, and nobody wouldn't have been able to tell him anything. Except Mr. Edgar. Gosh!" added the landlord, "of course—that's why Mr. Robbins changed his mind and came up here, and left a message to Mr. Edgar to come, thinking he might be a protection in case Hughie guessed where he'd gone and follered him up."

"That's about the size of it," agreed Weybridge. "The point is was it Hughie who came, or was it Mr. Edgar?"

"The time would fit either of 'em," said Mr. Bowles, "for they left the Eagle within five minutes of one another, or it might be ten. If Hughie had his bicycle, he could a-got here by eight, easy. He didn't stay in the bar more nor a minute or so after you went into the parlor, Mr. Egg."

"Well," said the Chief Constable, "we must find out if anybody saw either of them in the town at 8 o'clock or thereabouts. Let's work it out. Suppose it was Mr. Edgar. His father is expecting him and lets him in. They come in here, and Mr. Robbins takes out this letter and shows it to him. Then Mr. Edgar suddenly loses his temper and strikes out, killing his father, either accidentally or of set purpose. Then what does he do? He takes the trouble to tear away as much of this letter as he can, including the signature, if there was one—on purpose to keep all the suspicion to himself. That's either very stupid or very honest of him. Then, instead of taking the keys and making his escape that way, he runs and hides somewhere, till Baggitt is fool enough to open the gate and leave the way clear for him."

"It looks more to me," said the Inspector, "as if the man that wrote that letter did the murder."

"Meaning Searle. Very well. In that case, Mr. Robbins let him in, thinking it was Mr. Edgar. Once in, he couldn't very well be turned out by a man double his age and half his strength, and Baggitt was some way away, so Mr. Robbins makes the best of a bad job and takes him into the office. They discuss this little matter of goal-keeping; Mr. Robbins says something that gets Searle's goat, and it all happens the same way as before, except that it's more natural that Searle should destroy the letter, if he wrote it, and that he shouldn't wait to look for the keys, since he wouldn't know as well as Mr. Edgar where the old man kept them."

"I can't believe, if you'll excuse me," said Mr. Bowles, "that Hughie would go to do such a thing for such a reason. It's true he's got a hot temper, and uses language—but to take a brass paper-weight to an elderly gentleman! That don't seem like Hughie."

"You'll pardon my putting my oar in," said Mr. Egg, "but even the humblest suggestion may be of use. 'When it's a question of stamps to lick, the office-boy knows most of the trick,' as it says in the *Handbook*. I wouldn't be too sure that young Searle wrote that letter. What's his job in life?"

"He's a motor-mechanic down at Hobson's garage."

"Ever been in a drawing office or advertising business? Anything of an artist, or skilled letterer? That sort of thing?"

"Nothing of that sort," replied Mr. Bowles firmly.

"I only ask," said Monty, "because this letter was written by somebody who's been accustomed to write in capitals as quick and easy as you or I would write an ordinary hand. See how the letters are joined together, and how free the movement of the pencil is. It's rough, but it's clear, and it comes natural to the writer, that's the point. It's not the printing script they teach you in the schools. And it isn't done laboriously, by way of disguise. It's the script of somebody accustomed to roughing out headlines."

"I see what you mean," said Charteris. "That's smart."

"About this man Fletcher, who had a grievance," pursued Monty. "He's gone to live with his father. What's his father's profession?"

"I believe he's head-compositor at a small jobbing printer's," said Mr. Bowles.

"Just the man," said Monty. "And that word 'son' might very well be 'son' and not 'Benson,' mightn't it?"

"So it might," said the Chief Constable. "But if you mean to suggest that the murderer was this man Fletcher, or his father, how did he know where to find Mr. Robbins? Nobody knew he was coming up to the Mills except you and me and Bowles, and Mr. Edgar Robbins and Hughie."

"One other person, sir," replied Monty. "The elderly party who was sitting in the bar with his newspaper — the man who was a stranger to you, Mr. Bowles. He went out just after he had heard that Mr. Robbins would be up at the Mills, and that Mr. Edgar would *not* be there to protect him."

"By Jove, you're right!" Charteris thought this over for a moment. "But all this about playing in goal —"

"Ah!" said Monty, "if you bar 'guage' which they always spell 'guage,' that word is the biggest stumbling-block a printer can have. Trips him up every time. It's a disease with 'em. 'You've acted like a thief by my son, and deserve by right to be put in gaol.' Don't you think that sounds more natural? Personally," added Mr. Egg. "I take the soft option and write it JAIL—it mayn't look so classy, but it's safer."

DIRT CHEAP

Mr. Montague Egg was
startled out of his beauty sleep by the ugly noise next door.

"Wah! wah! wah!" in a series of crescendo roars. Then
followed a long, choking gurgle.

The Griffin at Cuttlesbury was an old-fashioned and ill-
kept hotel. Neither Mr. Egg nor his fellow-commercials would
have dreamed of patronizing it in ordinary circumstances. But
the Green Man had been put temporarily out of commission
by a disastrous fire; and that was how Mr. Egg, after an ill-
cooked and indigestible dinner, came to be lying in a lumpy
bed in this fusty, dusty bedroom, without electric light or even
a bedside candle and matches, so slovenly was the service.

As full consciousness slowly returned to him, Mr. Egg
took stock of the situation. There were, he knew, only three
bedrooms in this isolated corridor; his own, in the middle; on
the left, No. 8, containing old Waters, of Messrs. Brotherhood, Ltd., the soft-drinks-and-confectionery firm; on the
right, No. 10, allotted to that stout man who traveled in jewelry, whose name was Pringle, and who had stuffed himself up
that evening with dubious mackerel and underdone pork, to
the admiration of all beholders. Close behind the head of
Monty's bed, the rich and rhythmical snoring of old Waters

shook the thin partition like the vibration of a passing lorry. It must be Pringle who was making the uproar; mackerel and pork were the most probable explanation.

The bellowing had ceased; only a few faint grunts were now to be heard. He didn't know Pringle, and hadn't liked the look of him very much. But perhaps the man was really ill. It would be only decent to go and find out.

He swung his legs reluctantly over the side of the bed and thrust his feet into his slippers. Without troubling to search for matches and light the gloomy gas-jet with the broken mantle at the far end of the room, he felt his way to the door, unlocked it, and stepped out into the corridor. At the far end, another gas-jet burned dimly on the bypass, throwing a misleading jumble of light and shadow on the two creaking steps that separated the corridor from the main landing.

In No. 8, old Waters snored on undisturbed. Monty turned to his right and knocked at the door of No. 10.

"Who's there?" demanded a stifled voice.

"Me — Egg," said Monty. He turned the handle as he spoke, but the door was locked. "Are you all right? I heard you call out."

"Sorry." The bed creaked as though the speaker were levering himself up to a sitting position. "Nightmare. Sorry I disturbed you."

"Don't mention it," said Mr. Egg, pleased to have his diagnosis confirmed. "Sure there's nothing I can do?"

"No, thanks, quite all right." Mr. Pringle seemed to have buried his head in the blankets again.

"Good night, then," said Monty.

"G'night."

Mr. Egg slipped back to his own room. The snores in No. 8 were increasing in vehemence, and, as he shut and relocked his door, ended suddenly in a ferocious snort. All was quiet. Monty wondered what time it was, but while he was feeling in his coat-pocket for his matches, a clock began to strike with a sweet, vibrating, mellow tone that seemed to come from a considerable distance. He counted twelve strokes. It was earlier than he thought. Being tired, he had gone up to bed at half-past ten and had heard Waters pass his door only a few minutes after. There was now no sound of movement in the hotel. In the main street below, a car passed. The snoring in No. 8 began again.

Mr. Egg returned to his uncomfortable mattress and once more disposed his plump body to slumber. He hated being roused from his first deep, delicious unconsciousness. Confound Waters! Drowsily counting the snores, he began to doze.

Click! a door in the passage had opened. Then came stealthy footsteps, interrupted by a creak and a stumble. Somebody had tripped up the two badly-lighted steps on the way to the landing. Listening to the steady rumbling of Waters, Monty decided, with a certain grim satisfaction, that the mackerel and pork had finally proved too much for Mr. Pringle.

Then, quite suddenly, he fell fast asleep.

At six o'clock, he was awakened again by a clatter in the corridor and a banging on the door of No. 8. Waters, confound him, catching an early train. The chambermaid was giggling next door. One of the boys, was old Waters, but Mr. Egg wished he would keep his gallantries for a more appropriate time of day. Stump, stump past the door; creak, trip, curse—Waters falling up the two steps on his way to the bathroom. Blessed interval of peace. Trip, creak, curse, stump, stump, crash—Waters returning from his bath and banging his bedroom door. Bang, rustle, thump—Waters dressing and strapping his bags. Stump, stump, creak, trip, curse—thank heaven! that was the last of Waters.

Monty stretched out his hand for his watch, whose face was now dimly visible in the morning light that filtered through the dingy curtains. Two minutes to seven—a good half-hour before he need get up. Presently, the four quarters and the hour from the town clock, and, closely following them, the sweet, vibrating musical tones of a clock in the distance. Then silence, punctuated only by the faraway comings and goings of the hotel staff. Mr. Egg dropped off again.

At twenty minutes past seven the corridor rang with piercing and reiterated screams.

Monty leapt up. This time, something really was the matter. He ran to the door, dragging on his dressing-gown as he went. Three or four people came hurrying down the steps from the landing.

The chambermaid stood at the door of No. 10. She had dropped the can she was carrying, and a stream of water was soaking over the carpet. Her face was green, her soiled cap was thrust awry, and she was shrieking with the shrill, automatic regularity of violent hysteria.

Inside, on the bed, sprawled the gross body of Mr. Pringle. His face was swollen, and there were ugly purple marks on his thick neck. Blood had run from his nose and mouth and stained the pillows. His clothes were huddled on a chair, his suit-case stood open on the floor, his false teeth grinned from the tooth-glass on the wash-stand, but his traveler's bag with its samples of jewelry was nowhere to be seen. Mr. Pringle lay robbed and murdered.

With a dreadful feeling of reproach, Mr. Egg realized that he must actually have heard the murder committed — actually spoken with the murderer. He explained all this to Inspector Monk.

"I couldn't say whether the voice sounded like his. I had scarcely spoken to him. He didn't sit at my table at dinner, and we only exchanged a few words later on in the bar-parlor. The voice was muffled — it might easily have been the voice of a man who has just woken up and was speaking from half under the blankets and without his false teeth. I don't suppose I should recognize the voice again."

"That's very natural, Mr. Egg; don't distress yourself. Now, about this Mr. Waters, who left by the early train. You say you heard him snoring all the time?"

"Yes — both before and after. I know him; he's a highly respectable man."

"Quite. Well, we shall have to get into touch with him some time, I suppose, but obviously, if he slept right through it he won't be able to tell us anything. I think we must take it that the person you spoke to was the murderer. You say you can fix the time?"

"Yes." Monty described again how he had heard the clock strike twelve. "And by the way," he added, "I can't, of course, produce any alibi for myself, but my employers, Messrs. Plummet & Rose, Wines & Spirits, Piccadilly, would speak for me as to character."

"We'll look into that, Mr. Egg. Don't you worry," said Inspector Monk, imperturbably. "Let me see, haven't I heard your name before? Ever meet a friend of mine called Ramage?"

"Inspector Ramage of Ditchley? Why, yes. There was a little problem about a garage clock."

"That's right. He said you were a smart chap."

"Much obliged to him, I'm sure."

"So for the moment we'll accept your evidence and see where that gets us. Now, this clock here. Was it accurate, do you suppose?"

"Well, I heard it strike again this morning, and it was right then by my watch. At least," said Monty, as some obscure doubt fluttered uneasily into the back of his mind and fluttered elusively away again, "I *think* it was the same clock. It had the same note—deep and quick and what you might call humming. Rather a pretty strike."

"H'm," said the Inspector. "We'd better check that up. May have been wrong last night and right again this morning. We'll take a turn round the house and see if we can identify it. Ruggles, make Mr. Bates understand that nobody must leave the place, and tell him we'll be as quick as we can. Now, Mr. Egg."

There were only six striking clocks in the Griffin. The grandfather on the stairs was promptly eliminated; his voice was thin and high and quavering, like the voice of the very old gentleman that he was. The garage clock, too, had quite the wrong kind of strike, while the clock in the coffee-room and the ugly bronze monster in the drawing-room were both inaudible from Monty's room, and the clock in the bar was a cuckoo clock. But when they came to the kitchen, just beneath Monty's bedroom, Monty said at once:

"That looks like it."

It was an old American eight-day wall-clock, in a rose-wood veneer case, with a painted dial and the picture of a bee-hive on its glass door.

"I know the kind," said Monty, "it strikes on a coiled spring and gives just that sort of rich, humming tone, like a church bell, but much quicker."

The Inspector opened the clock and peered inside.

"Quite right," he said. "Now let's check him up. Twenty minutes to nine. Correct. Now, you go upstairs and I'll push the hands on to nine o'clock, and you tell us if that's what you heard."

In his bedroom, with the door shut, Monty listened again to that deep, quick, vibratory note. He hurried downstairs.

"It's exactly like it, as far as I can tell."

"Good. Then, if the clock hasn't been tampered with, we've got our time settled."

It proved unexpectedly easy to show that the clock had been right at midnight. The cook had set it by the Town Hall clock, just before going to bed at eleven. She had then locked the kitchen door and taken away the key, as she always did. "Otherwise that there Boots would be down at all hours, sneaking food from the larder." And the Boots—an unwholesome-looking lad of sixteen—had reluctantly confirmed this statement by admitting that he had tried the kitchen door half an hour later and found it securely fastened. There was no other access to the kitchen, except by the back door and windows—all bolted on the inside.

"Very well," said the Inspector. "Now we can look into all these people's alibis. And in the meantime, Ruggles, you'd better have a good hunt for Pringle's sample case. We know he took it to bed with him," he added, turning to Monty, whom he seemed disposed to confide in, "because the barman saw him. And it can't have been taken out of the hotel before the body was discovered, because all the outside doors were

locked and the keys removed—we've verified that—and
nobody went out after they were opened except your friend
Waters, and on your showing, he's not the murderer. Unless,
of course, he's an accomplice."

"Not Waters," said Mr. Egg stoutly. "Honest as the day, is
old Waters. Won't even wangle his expense-sheet. 'Account
with rigid honesty for £ and *s* and even *d*.' Waters's pet passage
from the *Salesman's Handbook*."

"Very good," replied the Inspector, "but where's that
case?"

The management and staff of the Griffin being all examined and satisfactorily accounted for, Inspector Monk turned
his attention to the guests. After the memorable dinner of
mackerel and pork, Mr. Egg, Mr. Waters, and two other commercial gentlemen named Loveday and Turnbull had played
bridge till half-past ten, when Mr. Egg and Mr. Waters had
retired. The other two had then gone down to the bar until it
closed at eleven, after which they had gone up to Mr. Loveday's room on the other side of the house. Here they had chatted till half-past twelve and had then separated. At one
o'clock, Mr. Loveday had gone in to borrow a dose of fruit
salts from Mr. Turnbull, who traveled in that commodity.
They thus provided alibis for one another, and there seemed to
be no reason to disbelieve them.

Then came an elderly lady called Mrs. Flack, who was
obviously incapable of strangling a large man single-handed.
Her room was on the main landing, and she slept undisturbed
till about half-past twelve, when somebody came past her door
and turned on the water in the bathroom. At a little before
one, this inconsiderate person had returned to his room. Otherwise she had heard nothing.

The only other guest, besides Waters and Pringle himself,
was a person who had arrived with Mr. Pringle in the latter's
car and said that he was a "photographic agent," answering to
the name of Alistair Cobb. Inspector Monk did not like the
look of him, but he was important, having spent a good part of
the evening with the murdered man.

"Get it out of your heads," said Mr. Cobb, sleeking his hair, "that I know anything much about Pringle. Never set eyes on him till seven o'clock last night. I'd missed the 'bus (literally, I mean) from Tadworthy—you know it, little one-horse place about four miles out—and there wasn't another till nine. So I was starting out to leg it with my suit-case when Pringle came by and offered me a lift. Said he often gave people lifts. Companionable chap. Didn't like driving alone."

Mr. Egg (who was present at the interview, a privilege no doubt attributable to Inspector Ramage's favorable opinion of him) shuddered at this rash behavior on the part of a traveler in jewelry, and was disagreeably reminded of the late Mr. Rouse, of burning-car celebrity.

"He was a decent old geezer," went on Mr. Cobb, reminiscently. "Quite a gay old lad. He brought me along here—"

"You had business in Cuttlesbury?"

"Sure thing. Photographs, you know. Enlarge Dad and Mother's wedding-group free. With gilt frame, twenty-five shillings. Dirt Cheap. You know the game?"

"I do," replied the Inspector, with an emphasis that made it clear that he thought the game a very doubtful one.

"Just so," said Mr. Cobb with a wink. "Well, we had dinner—and a dashed bad dinner too. Then we had a bit of a yarn in the bar-parlor. Bates and the barman saw us there. Then Bates went off to play billiards with some young fellow who dropped in, and we sat on till just about eleven. Then Pringle barged off—said he wasn't feeling the thing, and I'm not surprised. That mackerel—"

"Never mind the mackerel now," said Monk. "The barman says you and Pringle had a final drink at five to eleven, and then Pringle went off to bed, taking his bag with him. Did you go straight to the billiards-room at that point?"

"Yes, right away. We played—"

"Just a minute. Bates says you made a 'phone call first."

"So I did. At least, I went up first and found Bates and the other chap just finishing their game. So I said I'd make my call and then take Bates on. You can check the call for the time. I made it to the Bull at Tadworthy. I'd left a pair of gloves in the bar. A man answered me and said he'd found them and would send them on."

The Inspector made a note.

"And how long did you play billiards?"

"Till round about a quarter-past twelve. Then Bates said he'd had enough, as he had to get up early, so we drank the drinks I'd won off him and I pushed up to bed."

The Inspector nodded. This confirmed the landlord's evidence.

"My room's on the main landing," went on Mr. Cobb. "No, not the side near the corridor where the disturbance was—the other side. But I went across and had a bath; the bathroom's near the steps that go down to the corridor. It would be about ten to one when I got back. All quiet then on the Western Front."

"What did you and Pringle talk about downstairs?"

"Oh, this and that," replied Mr. Cobb easily. "We got swapping yarns and so on. Pringle had a hot one or two, and yours truly kept his end up. Have a fag, Inspector?"

"No, thanks. Did Pringle happen to mention—Yes, Ruggles, what is it? Excuse me one moment, gentlemen."

He stepped to the door for a word with the sergeant, returning in a minute or two with a card in his hand.

"I suppose your photographic supplies don't include this kind of thing, Mr. Cobb?"

Mr. Cobb blew out a long cloud of smoke with a whistling noise.

"No," said he, "no-ho! Where d'you get this pretty thing from?"

"Ever seen it before?"

Mr. Cobb hesitated. "Well, since you ask me, yes. The late lamented Pringle showed it me last night. Wouldn't have said anything if you hadn't asked me. Speak no ill of the dead and so on. But he *was* a bit up and coming, was Pringle."

"Sure it was the same one?"

"Looks like it. Same pretty lady—same pretty pose, any-how."

"Where did he carry it?" asked the Inspector, taking the photograph back and attaching it to his notes with a paper-clip—but not before Mr. Egg had snatched a glimpse of it and been suitably shocked.

"In his breast-pocket," replied Mr. Cobb, after a moment's thought.

"I see. Pringle told you what his job was, I suppose. Did he happen to say anything about taking precautions against thieves, or anything of that sort?"

"He did mention that he had valuable stuff in his bag and always locked his bedroom door," returned Mr. Cobb, with an air of great frankness. "Not that I asked him. No affair of mine what he did."

"Quite so. Well, Mr. Cobb, I don't think I need trouble you further at present, but I'd be obliged if you'd stay in the hotel till I've seen you again. Sorry to inconvenience you."

"Not at all," said the obliging Mr. Cobb. "It's all the same to me." He sauntered out, smiling pleasantly.

"Pah!" said Inspector Monk. "There's a nasty piece of work for you. Cheap dirt. And a liar, too. You saw that photo? (And how anybody can print such filth beats me.) Well, that hadn't been carried round in a breast-pocket. Edges quite sharp. Fresh out of its envelope, from the look of it. Don't mind betting you'd find the rest of the series in that fellow's suit-case. But naturally he won't admit it—it's a punishable offense to sell them."

"Where was this one found?"

"Under Pringle's bed. If Cobb hadn't got an alibi—and I'm pretty sure Bates is telling the truth, and as a matter of fact, the cook's window looks on to the billiards-room win-dow, and she saw them playing there until 12:15. Unless they're all in it together, which isn't likely. And still no sign of Pringle's bag. But we can't get over the evidence of that clock. You're sure it struck twelve?"

"Absolutely. I couldn't mistake one or two strokes for twelve."

"No, of course not." The Inspector drummed on the table and stared into vacancy. Monty took this for a dismissal. He went back into his own bedroom. The bed had not yet been made nor the slops emptied, the slatternly routine of the Griffin having been reduced to complete chaos by the catastrophe. He threw himself into a broken-springed armchair, lit a cigarette, and meditated.

He had been brooding for ten minutes or so when he heard the town clock chime the quarters and strike eleven. Mechanically he waited, expecting to hear the answering melodious strike of the kitchen clock, but nothing came. Then he remembered that Monk had set the hands twenty minutes forward that morning, so that it must have struck some time since. And then he bounded to his feet with a loud exclamation.

"Heavens! What a fool I am! This morning at seven the town clock struck first, and the kitchen clock immediately after. *But last night I never heard the town clock strike at all.* The kitchen clock *must* have been altered somehow or other. Unless—unless—unless, by gosh! I wonder if that could be it. Yes. Yes, it's possible. *Just before that clock struck twelve, Waters stopped snoring.*"

He ran from the room and plunged hastily into No. 8. Like his own room, it was in disorder. Like his own room, it did not appear to have been dusted for weeks. And on the night-table by Waters's bed, which stood close against the thin partition between the two rooms, there was a mark in the dust, as though some object measuring about three inches by three and a half had stood there during the night.

Mr. Egg darted out of the room and along the corridor. He fell up the two ill-lighted steps with a curse, turned the corner, and burst into the bathroom. Its window looked out upon a narrow side-street, communicating at one end with the main road and at the other with a lane that ran between warehouses. Rushing downstairs, Mr. Egg caught Inspector Monk just emerging from the coffee-room.

"Hold Cobb!" panted Mr. Egg. "I believe I've bust his alibi. Where's Waters gone to? I want to put a call through to him. Quick!"

"Waters said he was catching a train to Sawcaster," said Monk, rather astonished.

"Then," said Monty, calling upon his professional knowledge, "he'll put up at the Ring o' Bells, and he'll visit Hunter's, Merriman's, and Hackett & Brown's. We'll get him at one place or the other."

After a hectic half-hour at the telephone, he ran his quarry to earth at one of Sawcaster's leading confectionery establishments.

"Waters," gasped Monty urgently, "I want you to answer some questions, old man, and you can ask me why afterwards. Never mind how silly they sound. Do you carry a travelling-clock? You do? What's it like? Old-fashioned repeater? Yes? About three inches square—squarish? Yes? Stood on your bedtable last night? Does it strike on a coiled spring? It does? Thank heaven for that! Deep, quick, soft note like a church bell? Yes, yes, yes! Now, old boy, think hard. Did you wake up last night and strike that repeater? You did? You're sure? Good man! At what time? It struck twelve? What time does that mean? *Any time between twelve and one o'clock?* Then, for God's sake, Waters, take the next train back to Cuttlesbury, because your dashed clock has nearly made you and me accomplices in a murder. Yes, MURDER. . . . Hold on a moment, Inspector Monk wants to speak to you."

"Well," said the Inspector, as he replaced the receiver, "your evidence might have landed us in a nice pickle, mightn't it? It's a good job you had that brain-wave. *Now* we'll go through Mr. Dirty Cobb's luggage and see if he's got any more juicy photos. I suppose he took 'em along to show Pringle."

"That's it. I couldn't understand how the murderer got into the room. Naturally Pringle would lock his door. But of course he'd left it open for Cobb, who'd promised to slip along later and show him something to make his hair curl—'on the strict q.t.' and all that. It must have given Cobb a shock when

Pringle yelled and I knocked at the door. But he was all there, I will say that for him. He's probably a first-class salesman in his own rotten line. 'Don't let a sudden question rout you, but always keep your wits about you,' as it says in the *Handbook*."

"But look here," said the Inspector, "what did he do with Pringle's bag?"

"Dropped it out of the bathroom window to the accomplice he had summoned by 'phone from Tadworthy. Why, dash it all!" cried Monty, wiping his forehead, "I heard the car go by, just after that confounded clock struck twelve."

BITTER ALMONDS

Dash it!" exclaimed Mr. Montague Egg, "there's another perfectly good customer gone west."

He frowned at his morning paper, which informed him that an inquest would be held that day on the body of Mr. Bernard Whipley, a wealthy and rather eccentric old gentleman, to whom the firm of Plummet & Rose had from time to time sold a considerable quantity of their choice vintage wines, fine old matured spirits, and liqueurs.

Monty had more than once been invited by Mr. Whipley to sample his own goods, sitting in the pleasant study at Cedar Lawn—a bottle of ancient port, carried up carefully from the cellar by Mr. Whipley himself, or a liqueur brandy, brought out from the tall mahogany cabinet that stood in the alcove.

Mr. Whipley never allowed anybody but himself to handle anything alcoholic. You never, he said, could trust servants, and he had no fancy for being robbed, or finding the cook with her head under the kitchen dresser.

So Mr. Egg frowned and sighed, and then frowned still more, on seeing that Mr. Whipley had been discovered dead, apparently from prussic acid poisoning, after drinking an after-dinner glass of crème de menthe.

It is not agreeable when customers suddenly die poisoned after partaking of the drinks one has supplied to them, and it is not good for business.

Mr. Egg glanced at his watch. The town where he was at that moment reading the paper was only fifteen miles distant from the late Mr. Whipley's place of residence. Monty decided that it might be just as well to run over and attend the inquest. He was, at any rate, in a position to offer testimony as to the harmless nature of crème de menthe as supplied by Messrs. Plummet & Rose.

Accordingly he drove over there as soon as he had finished his breakfast, and by sending in his card to the coroner, secured for himself a convenient seat in the crowded little schoolroom where the inquest was being held.

The first witness was the housekeeper, Mrs. Minchin, a stout, elderly person of almost exaggerated respectability. She said she had been over twenty years in Mr. Whipley's service. He was nearly eighty years old, but very active and healthy, except that he had to be careful of his heart, as was only to be expected.

She had always found him an excellent employer. He had been, perhaps, a little close about financial matters and had kept a very sharp eye on the housekeeping, but personally she was not afraid of such, being as careful of his interests as she would be of her own. She had kept house for him ever since his wife's death.

"He was quite in his usual health on Monday evening," Mrs. Minchin went on. "Mr. Raymond Whipley had telephoned in the afternoon to say he would be down for dinner—"

"That is Mr. Whipley's son?"

"Yes—his only child." Here Mrs. Minchin glanced across at a thin, sallow, young-old man, seated near Mr. Egg on the bench reserved for witnesses, and sniffed rather meaningly. "Mr. and Mrs. Cedric were staying in the house. Mr. Cedric Whipley is Mr. Whipley's nephew. He had no other relations."

Mr. Egg identified Mr. and Mrs. Cedric Whipley as the

fashionably dressed young man and woman in black who sat on the other side of Mr. Raymond. The witness proceeded.

"Mr. Raymond arrived in his car at half-past six, and went in at once to see his father in the study. He came out again when the dressing gong rang for dinner, at a quarter past seven. He passed me in the hall, and I thought he looked rather upset. As Mr. Whipley didn't come out, I went in to him. He was sitting at his writing table, reading something that looked to me like a legal paper.

"I said, 'Excuse me, Mr. Whipley, sir, but did you hear the gong?' He was sometimes a little hard of hearing, though wonderfully keen in all his faculties, considering his age. He looked up and said, 'All right, Mrs. Minchin,' and went back to what he was doing. I said to myself, 'Mr. Raymond's been putting him out again.' At half-past—"

"One moment. What had you in your mind about Mr. Raymond?"

"Well, nothing much, only Mr. Whipley didn't always approve of Mr. Raymond's goings-on, and they sometimes had words about it. Mr. Whipley disliked Mr. Raymond's business.

"At half-past seven," continued the witness, "Mr. Whipley went upstairs to dress, and he seemed all right then, only his step was tired and heavy. I was waiting in the hall, in case he needed any assistance, and as he passed me he asked me to telephone to Mr. Whitehead to ask him to come over the next morning—Mr. Whitehead the lawyer. He did not say what it was for. I did as he asked me, and when Mr. Whipley came down again, about ten minutes to eight, I told him Mr. Whitehead had had the message, and would be with him at ten the next day."

"Did anybody else hear you say that?"

"Yes. Mr. Raymond and Mr. and Mrs. Cedric were in the hall, having their cocktails. They must all have heard me. Dinner was served at eight—"

"Were you present at dinner?"

"No. I have my meals in my own room. Dinner was over

about a quarter to nine, and the parlor-maid took coffee into the drawing-room for Mr. and Mrs. Cedric, and into the study for Mr. Whipley and Mr. Raymond. I was alone in my room till 9 o'clock, when Mr. and Mrs. Cedric came in to have a little chat. We were all together till just before half-past nine, when we heard the study door slam violently, and a few minutes later, Mr. Raymond came in, looking very queer. He had his hat and coat on.

"Mr. Cedric said: 'Hullo, Ray!' He took no notice, and said to me, 'I shan't be staying the night, after all, Mrs. Minchin. I'm going back to Town at once.' I said, 'Very good, Mr. Raymond. Does Mr. Whipley know of your change of plans?' He laughed in a funny way, and said: 'Oh, yes. He knows all about it.' He went out again and Mr. Cedric followed him and, I think, said something like, 'Don't lose your hair, old man.' Mrs. Cedric said to me, she was afraid Mr. Raymond might have had a quarrel with the old gentleman.

"About ten minutes later, I heard the two young gentlemen coming downstairs, and went out to see that Mr. Raymond had left nothing behind him, as he was apt to be forgetful. He was just going out of the front door with Mr. Cedric. I ran after him with his scarf, which he had left on the hall-stand. He drove away in his car very quickly and I came back into the house with Mr. Cedric.

"As we passed the study door, Mr. Cedric said, 'I wonder whether my uncle —' and then he stopped, and said, 'No, better let him alone till tomorrow.' We went back to my room, where Mrs. Cedric was waiting for us. She said, 'What's the matter, Cedric?' and he answered, 'Uncle Henry's found out about Ella. I told Ray he'd better be careful.' She said, 'Oh, dear!' and after that we changed the conversation.

"Mr. and Mrs. Cedric sat with me till about eleven-thirty, when they left me to go up to bed. I put my room in order and then came out to make my usual round of the house. When I put out the light in the hall, I noticed that the light was still on in Mr. Whipley's study. It was unusual for him to be up so late, so I went to see if he had fallen asleep over a book.

"I got no answer when I knocked, so I went in, and there he was, lying back in his chair, dead. There were two empty coffee-cups and two empty liqueur glasses on the table and a half-empty flask of crème de menthe. I called Mr. Cedric at once, and he told me to leave everything exactly as it was, and to telephone to Dr. Baker."

The next witness was the parlor-maid, who had waited at table. She said that nothing unusual had happened during the dinner, except that Mr. Whipley and his son both seemed rather silent and preoccupied.

At the end of the meal, Mr. Raymond had said, "Look here, father, we can't leave it like this." Mr. Whipley had said, "If you have changed your mind you had better tell me at once," and had ordered coffee to be sent into the study. Mr. Raymond said, "I can't change my mind, but if you would only listen—" Mr. Whipley did not reply.

On going into the study with the coffee and the liqueur glasses, the parlor-maid saw Mr. Raymond seated at the table. Mr. Whipley was standing at the cabinet, with his back turned to his son, apparently getting out the liqueurs.

He said to Mr. Raymond, "What will you have?" Mr. Raymond replied, "Crème de menthe." Mr. Whipley said, "You would—that's a woman's drink." The parlor-maid then went out and did not see either gentleman again.

Mr. Egg smiled to himself as he listened. He could hear old Mr. Whipley saying it.

Then he composed his chubby face to a more serious expression, as the coroner proceeded to call Mr. Cedric Whipley.

Mr. Cedric corroborated the housekeeper's story. He said he was aged thirty-six, and was a junior partner in the publishing firm of Freeman & Toplady. He was acquainted with the circumstance of Mr. Whipley's quarrel with his son. Mr. Whipley had, in fact, asked him and his wife to the house in order that he might discuss the situation with them. The trouble had to do with Raymond's engagement to a certain lady.

Mr. Whipley had talked rather impulsively about altering his will, but he (Cedric) had urged him to think the matter over calmly. He had accompanied Raymond upstairs on the night of the tragedy and had understood from him that Mr. Whipley had threatened to cut his son off with the proverbial shilling. He had told Raymond to take things easy and the old man would "simmer down." Raymond had taken his interference in bad part.

After Raymond's departure he had thought it better to leave the old man to himself. On leaving Mrs. Minchin's room with his wife, he had gone straight upstairs without entering the study. He thought it would be about a quarter of an hour after that, that he had come down in answer to Mrs. Minchin's call, to find his uncle dead.

He had bent over the body to examine it, and had then thought he detected a faint smell of almonds about the lips. He had smelt the liquor glasses, but without touching them and, fancying that one of them also smelt of almonds, had instructed Mrs. Minchin to leave everything exactly as it was. He had then formed the impression that his uncle might have committed suicide.

There was a rustle in the little court when Mr. Raymond Whipley took his place at the coroner's table. He was a lean, effeminate, and rather unwholesome-looking person of anything between thirty and forty years of age.

He said that he was "a photographic artist" by profession. He had a studio in Bond Street. His "expressionist studies" of well-known men and women had gained considerable notice in the West End. His father had not approved of his activities. He had old-fashioned prejudices.

"I understand," said the coroner, "that prussic acid is frequently used in photography."

Mr. Raymond Whipley smiled winningly at this ominous question.

"Cyanide of potassium," he said. "Oh, dear, yes. Quite frequently."

"You are acquainted with its use for photography?"

"Oh, yes. I don't use it often. But I have some by me, if that's what you want to know."

"Thank you. Now can you tell me about this alleged difference of opinion with your father?"

"Yes. He found out that I was engaged to marry a lady connected with the stage. I don't know who told him. Probably my cousin Cedric. He'll deny it, of course, but I expect it was jolly old Cedric. My father sent for me and really cut up quite rough about it. Full of diehard prejudices, you know. We had quite a little rumpus before dinner. After dinner, I asked to see him again—thought I could talk him round. But he was really very offensive. I couldn't stand it. It upset me. So I barged off back to Town."

"Did he say anything about sending for Mr. Whitehead?"

"Oh, yes. Said if I married Ella, he'd cut me out of his will. Quite the stern parent and all that. I said, cut away, then."

"Did he say in whose favor he thought of making his new will?"

"No, he didn't say. I expect Cedric would have come in for something. He's the only other relation, of course."

"Will you describe very carefully what happened in the study after dinner?"

"We went in, and I sat down at the table near the fire. My father went to the cabinet where he keeps his spirits and liqueurs and asked me what I would have. I said I would have a crème de menthe, and he sneered at me in his usual pleasant way. He fetched out the flask and told me to help myself, when the girl brought in the glasses. I did so. I had coffee and crème de menthe. He did not drink anything while I was there. He was rather excited and walked up and down, threatening me with this and that.

"After a bit I said, 'Your coffee's getting cold, father.' Then he told me to go to hell, and I said, 'Right you are.' He added a very disagreeable remark about my fiancée. I am afraid I then lost my temper and used some—shall we say, unfilial expression. I went out and banged the door. When I left him he was standing up behind the table, facing me.

"I went to tell Mrs. Minchin that I was going back to Town. Cedric started to butt in, but I told him I knew who it was I had to thank for all this trouble, and if he wanted the old man's money he was welcome to it. That's all I know about it."

"If your father drank nothing while you were with him, how do you explain the fact that both the liqueur glasses and both the coffee-cups had been used?"

"I suppose he used his after I had gone. He certainly did not drink anything before I went."

"And he was alive when you left the study?"

"Very much so."

Mr. Whitehead, the lawyer, explained the terms of the deceased man's will. It left an income of two thousand a year to Cedric Whipley, with reversion to Raymond, who was the residuary legatee.

"Did deceased ever express any intention of altering his will?"

"He did. On the day before his death he said that he was very much dissatisfied with his son's conduct, and that unless he could get him to see reason, he would cut him off with an annuity of a thousand a year, and leave the rest of the estate to Mr. Cedric Whipley. He disliked Mr. Raymond's fiancée and said he would not have that woman's children coming in for his money. I tried to dissuade him, but I think he supposed that when the lady heard of his intentions she would break off the engagement. When Mrs. Minchin rang me up on the night in question I was convinced in my own mind that he intended to execute a new will."

"But since he had no time to do so, the will in favor of Mr. Raymond Whipley will now stand?"

"That is so."

Inspector Brown of the County Police then gave evidence about finger-prints. He said that one coffee-cup and one liqueur glass bore the finger-prints of Mr. Raymond Whipley, and the other cup and the glass which held the poison, those of

Mr. Whipley, senior. There were no other prints, except, of course, those of the parlor-maid, on the cups or glasses, while the flask of crème de menthe bore those of both father and son.

Bearing in mind the possibility of suicide, the police had made a careful search of the room for any bottle or phial which might have contained the poison. They had found nothing, either in the cabinet or elsewhere. They had, indeed, collected from the back of the fireplace the half-burnt fragment of a lead-foil capsule, which bore the letters ". . . . AU . . . tier & Cie," stamped round the edge.

From its size, however, it was clear that this capsule had covered the stopper of a half-liter bottle, and it seemed highly improbable that an intending suicide would purchase prussic acid by the half-liter, nor was there any newly opened bottle to which the capsule appeared to belong.

At this point a horrible thought began to emerge from Mr. Egg's inner consciousness—a dim recollection of something he had once read in a book. He lost the remainder of Inspector Brown's evidence, which was purely formal, and only began to take notice again when, after the cook and housemaid had proved that they had been together the whole evening, the doctor was called to give the medical evidence.

He said that deceased had undoubtedly died of prussic acid poisoning. Only a very small amount of the cyanide had been found in the stomach, but even a small dose would be fatal to a man of his age and natural frailty. Prussic acid was one of the most rapidly fatal of all known poisons, producing unconsciousness and death within a very few minutes after being swallowed.

"When did you first see the body, doctor?"

"I arrived at the house at five minutes to twelve. Mr. Whipley had been dead at least two hours, and probably a little more."

"He could not possibly have died within, say, half an hour of your arrival?"

"Not possibly. I place the death round about half-past nine and certainly not later than ten-thirty."

The analyst's report was next produced. The contents of

the flask of crème de menthe and the coffee dregs in both cups
had been examined and found to be perfectly harmless. Both
liqueur glasses contained a few drops of crème de menthe, and
in one—that which bore the finger-prints of old Mr. Whipley—there was a distinct trace of hydrocyanic acid.

Even before the coroner began his summing up it was
plain that things looked very black for Raymond Whipley.
There was the motive, the fact that he alone had easy access to
the deadly cyanide, and the time of death, coinciding almost
exactly with that of his hasty and agitated flight from the
house.

Suicide seemed to be excluded; the other members of the
household could prove each other's alibis; there was no suggestion that any stranger had entered the house from outside.
The jury brought in the inevitable verdict of murder against
Raymond Whipley.

Mr. Egg rapidly made his way out of court. Two things
were troubling him—Mrs. Minchin's evidence and that half-
remembered warning that he had read in a book. He went
down to the village post-office and sent a telegram to his
employers. Then he turned his steps to the local inn, ordered a
high tea, and ate it slowly, with his thoughts elsewhere. He
had an idea that this case was going to be bad for business.

In about an hour's time, the reply to his telegram was
handed to him. It ran: "June 14, 1893. Freeman and
Toplady, 1931," and was signed by the senior partner of
Plummet & Rose.

Mr. Egg's round and cheerful face became overcast by a
cloud of perplexity and distress. He shut himself into the landlord's private room alone and put through an expensive trunk
call to Town. Emerging, less perplexed but still gloomy, he got
into his car and set off in search of the coroner.

That official welcomed him cheerfully. He was a hearty
and rubicund man with a shrewd eye and a brisk manner.
Inspector Brown and the chief constable were with him when
Monty was shown in.

"Well, Mr. Egg," said the coroner, "I'm sure you're happy

to be assured that this unfortunate case conveys no imputation against the purity of the goods supplied by your firm."

"That's just what I've taken the liberty of coming to you about," said Monty. "Business is business, but, on the other hand, facts are facts, and our people are ready to face them. I've been on the 'phone to Mr. Plummet, and he authorized me to put the thing before you.

"If I didn't," added Mr. Egg, candidly, "somebody else might, and that would make matters worse. Don't wait for unpleasant disclosures to burst. If the truth must be told, see that *you* tell it first. Monty's maxim—from the *Salesman's Handbook*. Remarkable book, full of common-sense. Talking of common-sense, a spot of that commodity wouldn't have hurt our young friend, would it?"

"Meaning Raymond Whipley?" said the coroner. "That young man is a pathological case, if you ask me."

"You're right there, sir," agreed the Inspector. "I've seen a sight of foolish crooks, but he licks the lot. Barmy, I'd call him. Quarrelling with his dad, doing him in and running away in that suspicious manner—why didn't he put up an electric sign to say 'I done it'? But as you say, I don't think he's quite all there."

"Well, that may be," said Monty, "but over and above that, there's old Mr. Whipley. You see, gentlemen, I know all my customers. It's my job, as you may say, to have all their fancies by heart. No good offering an 1847 Oleroso to a gentleman that likes his sherry light and dry, or tantalizing a customer that's under orders to stick to hock with bargains in vintage port.

"Now, what I'd like you to tell me is, how did the late Mr. Whipley come to be drinking crème de menthe at all? He only kept it by him for ladies; it was a flavor he couldn't do with in any shape or form. You heard what he said about it to Mr. Raymond."

"That's a point," said the chief constable. "I may say it had already occurred to us. But he must have taken the poison in something."

"Well, I only say, bear that in mind—that, and the foolishness of the murder, if it was done the way the jury brought it in. But now about this lead-foil capsule. I can tell you something about that. I didn't intrude myself at the inquest, because I hadn't got the facts, but I've got them now and here they are. You know, gentlemen, it stands to reason, if a capsule was taken off a bottle that day in the study, there must have been a bottle belonging to it. And where is it? It's got to be somewhere. A bottle's a bottle, when all's said and done.

"Now, gentlemen, Mr. Whipley dealt with my employers, Plummet & Rose, for over fifty years. It's an old-established firm. And that capsule was put out by a firm of French shippers who went into liquidation in 1900; Prelatier & Cie was their name, and we were their agents in this country. Now, that capsule came off a bottle of Noyeau sent out by them — you can see the last two letters of the word on the stamp — and we delivered a bottle of Prelatier's Noyeau to Mr. Whipley, with some other samples of liqueur, on June 14, 1893."

"Noyeau?" said the coroner, with interest.

"I see that means something to you, doctor," said Mr. Egg.

"It does, indeed," said the coroner. "Noyeau is a liqueur flavored with oil of bitter almonds, or peach-stones — correct me if I'm wrong, Mr. Egg — and contains, therefore, a small proportion of hydrocyanic acid."

"That's it," said Monty. "Of course, in the ordinary way, there isn't enough of it to hurt anybody in a single glassful, or even two. But if you let a bottle stand long enough, the oil will rise to the top, and the first glass out of an old bottle of Noyeau has been known to cause death. I know that, because I read it in a book called *Foods and Poisons*, published a few years ago by Freeman & Toplady."

"Cedric Whipley's firm," said the inspector.

"Exactly so," said Monty.

"What, precisely, are you suggesting, Mr. Egg?" inquired the chief constable.

"Not murder, sir," said Monty. "No, not that — though I suppose it might have come to that, in a way. I'm suggesting that after Mr. Raymond had left the study, the old gentleman got fidgety and restless, the way one does when one's been through a bit of an upset. I think he started to drink up his cold coffee, and then wanted a spot of liqueur to take with it.

"He goes to the cabinet—doesn't seem to fancy anything, roots about, and comes upon this old bottle of Noyeau that's been standing unopened for the last forty years. He takes it out, removes the capsule and throws it into the fire, and draws a cork with his corkscrew, as I've seen him do many a time. Then he pours off the first glass, not thinking about the danger, drinks it off as he's sitting in his chair and dies without hardly having time to call out."

"That's very ingenious," said the chief constable. "But what became of the bottle and the corkscrew? And how do you account for the crème de menthe in the glass?"

"Ah!" said Monty, "there you are. Somebody saw to that, and it wasn't Mr. Raymond, because it would have been all to his advantage to leave things as they were. But suppose, round about half-past eleven, when Mrs. Minchin was tidying her room and the other servants were in bed, another party had gone into the study and seen Mr. Whipley lying dead, with the bottle of Noyeau beside him, and had guessed what had happened.

"Supposing this party had then put the corkscrew back into the cupboard, tipped a few drops of crème de menthe from Mr. Raymond's glass into the dead gentleman's, and carried the Noyeau bottle away to be disposed of at leisure. What would it look like then?"

"But how could the party do that, without leaving prints on Mr. Raymond's glass?"

"That's easy," said Monty. "He'd only to lift the glass by taking the stem between the roots of his fingers. So. All you'd find would be a faint smudge at the base of the bowl."

"And the motive?" demanded the chief constable.

"Well, gentlemen, that's not for me to say. But if Mr. Raymond was to be hanged for murdering his father, I fancy his father's money would go to the next of kin—to that gentleman who published the book that tells you all about Noyeau.

"It's very unfortunate," said Mr. Egg, "that my firm should have supplied the goods in question, but there you are. If accidents happen and you are to blame, take steps to avoid repetition of same. Not that we should admit any responsibility, far from it, the nature of the commodity being what it is. But we might perhaps insert a warning in our forthcoming Catalogue.

"And à propos, gentlemen, let me make a note to send you our *New Centenary History of the House of Plummet & Rose*. It will be a very refined production, got up regardless, and worthy of a position on any library shelf."

FALSE WEIGHT

"**H**ullo!" said Mr. Montague Egg.

He knew the Royal Oak, at Pondering Parva, and it was not, in a general way, a place he would have chosen to stop at. It did but little business, its food was bad, its landlord surly, and it offered few opportunities to an enterprising traveler in high-class wines and spirits. But to find it at half-past eight in the morning the center of an interested crowd, with a police car and an ambulance drawn up before the door, was a challenge to any man's curiosity. Mr. Egg took his foot from the accelerator, and eased the car to a standstill.

"What's up here?" he asked a bystander.

"Somebody killed. . . . Old Rudd's cut 'is missus's throat. . . . No, he ain't—George done it. . . . That ain't right, neither, it was thieves and they've gone off with the till . . . George, he come down and found the blood running all over the floor. . . . Hear that? that's Liz Rudd a-hollerin' . . . she got highsterics. . . . Thought you said 'e'd cut 'er throat. . . . No, I didn't, Jim said that, he don't know nothin'. I tell you 'tis George. . . . Ah! here's the Inspector a-comin' out; now we'll hear summat. . . ."

Mr. Egg was already out of the car and approaching the

bar entrance. A uniformed Inspector of police met him on the doorstep.

"Now then, you can't come in here. Who are you, and what do you want?"

"My name's Montague Egg—traveling for Plummet & Rose, Wines and Spirits, Piccadilly. I've come to see Mr. Rudd."

"Well, you can't see him now, so you'd better buzz off. Wait a minute. You say you're a commercial traveler. This your regular district?"

Mr. Egg replied that it was.

"Then you might be able to give us some information. Come in, will you?"

"Wait while I fetch my bag," said Monty. He was interested, but not to the point of forgetting that a traveler's first duty is to his samples and credentials. He fetched the heavy case from the car and carried it into the inn to the accompaniment of cries from the crowd: "That's the photographer, see his camera?" Setting it down inside the door, he looked round the bar of the Royal Oak. At a table near the window sat a police-constable, writing in a notebook. A large, pug-faced man, whom Monty recognized as Rudd, the landlord, was leaning back against the bar in his shirt-sleeves. He was unshaven, and looked as though he had dressed hurriedly. A tousle-headed young fellow, with immense muscles and no forehead to speak of, stood scowling beside him. From a room somewhere at the back came a noise of feminine shrieking and sobbing. That was all, except that a door on the right, labeled "Bar-parlor," stood open, and through it could be seen the back of a man in an overcoat, who was bending over something on the floor.

The Inspector took Mr. Egg's papers, looked them through, and returned them.

"You're on the road early," he said.

"Yes," said Monty. "I meant to get through to Pettiford last night, but the fog held me up at Madgebury. I'm making up for lost time. I slept at the Old Bell—they can tell you all about me there."

"Ah!" said the Inspector, with a glance at the constable. "Well, now, Mr. Egg. I believe all you commercial gentlemen know each other pretty well, as a rule. We'd like to see if you can identify this man in here."

"I'll try," said Monty, "though of course I don't know every traveler on the road. But surely his name will be on his papers."

"That's just it," replied the Inspector. "His papers must have been in his sample case, and that's gone. He's got some letters on him, but they don't—well, we'll go into that later on. This way, please."

He marched into the room on the right. Monty followed him. The stooping man stood up.

"No doubt about this, Birch," he observed. "Head battered in. Dead eight to ten hours. Couldn't possibly have done it himself, or by accident. Weapon probably that bottle over there. Better try it for finger-prints. Anything else you want to know? Because, if not, I'll be getting back to my breakfast. I'll leave word with the coroner as I go, if you like."

"Thanks, doctor. Eight to ten hours, eh? That fits Rudd's story all right. Now, Mr. Egg, come and have a look at this, will you?"

The doctor stepped aside, and Monty saw the dead body of a man. He was a small man, dressed in a neat blue serge suit. His hair was sleek and black, and he wore a small toothbrush moustache. The blood from an open wound on the temple had run down and caked on his smooth cheek. He appeared to be about thirty-five or forty years of age.

"Oh, yes, I know him," said Monty. "I know him quite well, as a matter of fact. His name is Wagstaffe, and he travels—traveled—for Applebaum & Moss, the big cheap jewelers."

"Oh *did* he?" said Inspector Birch, with emphasis. "That case of his would contain jewelry then, I suppose."

"Yes—and watches, and that sort of thing."

"Humph!" said the Inspector. "And can you tell me why

he should be carrying letters about in his pocket addressed to a number of other people? Here's one — Joseph Smith, Esq. Here's another — Mr. William Brown. And here's a very touching one — Harry Thorne, Esq. Hot stuff, that one is."

"Do you need any telling, Inspector?" inquired Mr. Egg, softly.

"I don't know that I do, if it comes to that. Ah! you commercial gentlemen are all alike, aren't you? A wife in every port of call, eh?"

"Not me, Inspector. No wedding-bells for Monty Egg. But I'm afraid it's true about poor Wagstaffe. Well, he seems to have got what was coming to him, doesn't he?"

"You're right. He put up a bit of a struggle, though, from the looks of it." Inspector Birch glanced round the bar-parlor. It was a small room, and every piece of furniture in it seemed to have suffered violence. A small round table before the fireplace had been knocked over, and a broken whisky-bottle had distributed its contents in an odorous stream across the linoleum. Chairs had been pushed back and over-turned, the glass front of a what-not was starred as though by a blow from a threshing foot, and a grandfather clock, standing near the fireplace, had been canted over sideways, so that only the edge of the mantelpiece kept it from falling. Mr. Egg's eyes wandered to the clock-face, and the Inspector's followed them. The hands stood at ten minutes past eleven.

"Yes," said Mr. Birch. "And unless he's a liar, we know pretty well when this happened and who did it. Do you know anything about a commercial called Slater?"

"I've heard of an Archibald Slater," said Monty. "Travels in lingerie."

"That's the man. Is he in a good way of business? Good screw, I mean? Comfortable, and all that?"

"I should think so. He works for a good firm." Monty named it. "But I don't know him personally. He used to work Yorkshire and Lancashire, I believe. He's taken over old Cripps's district."

"You can't say if he'd be likely to murder another chap and pinch his samples?"

Monty protested. The last thing any commercial would be likely to do. There was a freemasonry of the road.

"Hum!" said the Inspector. "Now, listen here. We'll get Rudd's story again, and have it taken down."

The landlord's account was clear enough. The first traveler—now identified as Wagstaffe—had arrived at 7:30. He had meant, he said, to push on to Pettiford, but the fog was too thick. He had ordered dinner, and had afterwards gone in to sit in the bar-parlor, which was empty. The Royal Oak did very little high-class hotel business, and there was nobody in that night except some laborers in the four-ale bar. At half-past nine, Slater had turned up, also alleging the fog as the reason for breaking his journey. He had already dined, and presently joined Wagstaffe in the bar-parlor. On entering, he had been heard to say to Wagstaffe "in a nasty sort of voice," "Oh, it's you, is it?" After that, the door had been shut, but presently Wagstaffe had knocked upon the hatch between the parlor and the bar and asked for a bottle of Scotch. At half-past ten, the bar being closed and the glasses washed up, Rudd had gone in and found the two men talking beside the fire. They both seemed flushed and angry. Rudd said that he and his wife and the barman were going to bed, as they had to get up early. Would the guests please put out the light when they came upstairs?

Here the landlord broke off to explain that there were no bedrooms over the bar-parlor—only a large, empty room running over the whole front of the house and used for meetings of parish societies, and so forth. The sleeping accommodation all ran out at the back, and you could not hear, from the bedrooms, anything that went on in the ground-floor part. He then went on:

"It would be about twenty past eleven when I heard someone come up and knock at our bedroom door. I got out of bed and opened it, and there was Slater. He looked very queer and upset. He said that the weather had cleared and he'd made up his mind to push on to Pettiford. It seemed funny to me, but I looked out of the window and saw that the fog had gone and there was a sharp frost and moonlight. I said he'd have to pay for his room, and he didn't make no bones about that. I put on a dressing-gown and went with him down the back stairs into the office. That's behind the bar. I made out his bill and he paid it, and then I let him out the back way into the garage. He took his bags with him—"

"How many bags?"

"Two."

"Did he bring two with him when he came?"

"Couldn't say, I'm sure. I never see them to notice. He planked all his stuff down in the bar-parlor when he come, and when I come out of the office with his change he was standing ready with them in the passage, with his hat and coat on. I didn't go out into the yard with him, because it was bitter cold, and I weren't none too pleased to be fetched out of my bed; but I heard the car drive out a few minutes later. Then I went back to bed again, and I noticed through the office window that the light was still on in the bar-parlor, so that the door must have been open. See what I mean? There's the back door of the parlor leading into the office, and when that's open, you can see the light from the yard, through the office window. So I thinks, that other fellow's still sitting up—I'll charge him extra for burning all that light. And I goes to bed."

"You didn't go in and see that he was still there."

"No, I didn't," said Mr. Rudd. "It was too perishing cold to be hanging about. I went to bed and to sleep."

"That's a pity. Did you go to sleep at once?"

"Yes, I click."

"You didn't hear Wagstaffe come upstairs at all?"

"I didn't hear a thing. But Mrs. Rudd was awake till midnight, and he hadn't come up then. And it stands to reason he never come up at all, don't it?"

"It looks that way," agreed the Inspector cautiously. "And how about George?"

The barman confirmed Rudd's story, and added a little to it. He said that he had gone into the bar-parlor between 9:30 and 10 o'clock and had interrupted the two men in what looked like a violent quarrel. Slater had been saying, "You little rat— I've a good mind to break every bone in your body." He thought they were both drunk. He had said nothing to them, but made up the fire and gone away. He had heard no more quarreling. After Rudd had gone up at 10:30, he had looked in again, and they were then talking quietly and appeared to be reading some letters. He had then gone to bed, and been wakened by the sound of footsteps and the departure of the car.

"And after that?" asked Inspector Birch.

George's eyes were lowered sullenly.

"Mr. Rudd came upstairs again."

"Yes?"

"Well, that's all. I went to sleep."

"You didn't hear anybody else moving about?"

"No. I went to sleep, I tell you."

"What time did Mr. Rudd come up?"

"Dunno. I didn't trouble to look."

"Did you hear twelve strike?"

"I didn't hear nothing. I was asleep."

"How many bags did this man Slater bring with him?"

"Only one."

"You're sure of that?"

"Well, I think so."

"And the other man—Wagstaffe—did he have a bag?"

"Yes, he had a bag. Took it into the parlor with him."

"Did these men sign the register?"

"Slater did when he arrived," said the landlord. "Wagstaffe didn't. I meant to remind him in the morning."

"Then Slater wasn't premeditating anything when he arrived," said Birch. "Looks like it was a casual meeting. All right, Rudd. I'll see your wife later. Now carry on, and don't go shooting your mouth off too much. We've got the number of Slater's car," he added, to nobody in particular. "If he's really gone to Pettiford, they'll pull him in."

"Just so," said Monty. "I suppose," he added, tentatively, "that clock's telling the truth?"

"Thinking he might have been put back, eh?" said the Inspector. "Like in that play they've got on in town?"

"Well," admitted Monty, "it seems funny, the way the criminal carefully knocked grandpa over, just as if he was going out of his way to provide evidence against himself. It doesn't seem natural. Praise with discretion; purchasers are quick to distrust those who lay it on too thick, as it says in the *Salesman's Handbook*."

"We'll soon see," said the Inspector, advancing upon the clock. "Wait a bit, though; we'd better try the case for finger-prints."

The arrival of a photographer and an apparatus for bringing up and recording finger-prints led to the discovery of so many signs of handling, both on the clock and on the bottle, as to prove that the use of dusters and furniture polish must have been abandoned for a very long time at the Royal Oak. Eventually the photographs were taken, and the Inspector and a constable lifted the clock back into place. It appeared to have suffered no great shock, but only to have stopped when the pendulum came up against the side of the case, for on being righted and started it ticked away merrily. Mr. Birch lifted a thick forefinger to the minute-hand; then he checked himself.

"No," he said, "we'll leave grandpa to himself. If there's been any jiggery-pokery, there might be something to be found on the hands, though they're a bit narrow to carry a print. But you never know. I suppose he'll run all right for an hour or two."

"Oh, yes," said Mr. Egg, opening the case and peering in. "The weights are rather near the bottom, especially one of them, but I should say he had another twelve hours or so in him. What's to-day? Saturday? They probably wind him on Sunday morning."

"Probably," agreed the Inspector. "Well, thank you, Mr. Egg. I don't think we need detain you any longer."

"No objection to me having a spot of ale in the bar, I suppose," suggested Monty, "it'll be open in half an hour or so, and I didn't have much breakfast."

"I didn't have any," said Inspector Birch, wistfully.

From this point, the procedure was obvious. The Inspector was just finishing a large mound of bacon and eggs when a commotion at the door announced the arrival of a police-sergeant with the absconding Mr. Slater. The latter was a large, angry-looking man who, as soon as he entered the room, began to protest violently.

"Cut that out, my lad," said Mr. Birch. "How many bags did you find with him, Sergeant?"

"Only one, sir—his own."

"I tell you," said Slater, "I know nothing about all this. I left Wagstaffe here in the bar-parlor at twenty past eleven or thereabouts, and he was all right then—only drunk. I drove away at half-past, or it might be a quarter to twelve. I brought one bag and I took one bag, and here it is, and anybody who says anything else is telling a lie. If I'd been doing a murder, do you think I'd have gone straight off to Pettiford and sat eating my breakfast in the Four Bells, waiting for you to catch me?"

"You might and you mightn't," said Mr. Birch. "Did you know this man Wagstaffe?"

The angry eyes shifted uneasily.

"I'd met him," said Slater.

"They say you were quarreling with him."

"Well—he was drunk, and made himself unpleasant. That's one reason why I pushed off."

"I see." The Inspector glanced through the correspondence taken from the dead man's pocket.

"Your name's Archibald, isn't it? Have you got a sister Edith? . . . No, you don't!"

Slater had made a quick grab at the letter in Birch's hand.

"Well," he admitted sulkily, "I don't mind telling you that that swine Wagstaffe was a dirty scoundrel. Thorne's the name we knew him by, and my sister's his wife—or thought she was, till it turned out he was married to somebody else under another name, the skunk. They got married while I was away up North, and I knew nothing about it till I came into this district, and he's been careful to keep out of my way—till last night. Not that there was anything I could do to him, except try and get maintenance for the kid, and in the end he said he'd pay. I—look here, Inspector, I quite realize that this looks bad, but—"

"Hi!" exclaimed Monty. "Don't forget the clock. It's just going to strike."

"Yes," said the Inspector. "Ten past eleven that clock marked when it was knocked over in the struggle. You were out of here by twenty past. If it strikes one now, we'll know it's been put back—if it strikes twelve, then it's telling the truth, and you're for it."

The case stood open. As the first stroke of the hammer fell, they watched, fascinated while the striking weight moved slowly down from where it hung, three or four inches below the other.

The clock struck twelve.

"That's something, anyway," said Mr. Birch, grimly.

"It's not true!" cried Slater wildly. Then he added, more soberly, "The man might have been killed after I left, but still before midnight, and the hands put back three quarters of an hour."

And while the Inspector hesitated:

"Half a minute," said Monty. "If you'll excuse me, Inspector, I've just thought of something. Twelve o'clock is the longest run that weight ever does, and it's only dropped something under half an inch. Now, how does it come to hang so far below the driving weight? You see what I mean? During the long hours from six to twelve, the striking weight gets ahead of the driving weight and hangs below it, but during the short hours, the driving weight catches up on it, so that—in my experience, anyhow—there's never more than half an inch or so between them in an eight-day clock, and they finish up level. Now, how did this fellow here get all this long start on his chum?"

"Wound up carelessly," suggested the Inspector.

"Either that," said Monty, "or the clock's been *put on eleven hours*. That's the only way to put back a striking clock, unless you have the sense to take the striking weight off altogether, which most people haven't the wits to think of."

"Whew!" said Mr. Birch. "Now, who'd know about that, I wonder? Who winds this clock? We'd better ask Rudd."

"I wouldn't ask him, if you'll forgive me putting myself forward," said Mr. Egg, thoughtfully.

"Oh!" said Mr. Birch. "I see." He pulled at his moustache. "Wait a minute. I've got it."

He plunged out, and presently returned with a boy of about fourteen.

"Sonnie," said he, "who winds up the grandfather clock?"

"Dad does, every Sunday morning."

"Did you see him do it last Sunday?"

"Oh, yes."

"Can you remember if he wound the two weights up to the same height—or were they apart, like this?"

"He always winds them up tight—fourteen winds—that's two turns for every day—and when the weight's wound up, it goes bump."

The Inspector nodded.

"That's all—run away. Mr. Egg, it looks as if you'd got hold of something right enough. Here, Sergeant!"

The sergeant gave him an understanding wink and went out. Half an hour elapsed, marked only by the almost imperceptible descent of the driving weight and the solemn ticking of the clock. Then the sergeant came in again, with a bag in his hand.

"Quite right, sir—under a heap of sacking in the hen-house. It must be either Rudd or the barman, George."

"They must both be in it," said the Inspector. "But which of them did the job, damned if I know. We'll have to wait for those finger-prints."

"Why not ask them for the key of the clock?" put in Mr. Egg.

"What for?"

"Just an idea of mine."

"All right. Send Rudd in. Rudd, we want the key of this clock."

"Oh, do you?" said the landlord. "Well, I haven't got it, see? I don't know where it's gone, and you can put that in your pipe and smoke it. A nice job this is, in a respectable house."

"All right," said the Inspector, "we'll ask George. Where's this clock-key, George?"

The barman passed a hand across his dry mouth. "It's in that there pot on the chimbley-piece," he said.

"It's not there," said the Inspector, peering into the pot.

"No," said Monty. "And how did Rudd know it wasn't there, if he wasn't hunting for it last night to wind that weight back to the right place, after he'd put the clock eleven hours forward? No wonder the place is turned upside-down."

The landlord turned a dirty green color, and George broke out into a whimper.

"Please, sir, I never knew nothing about it till it was all over. I didn't have no hand in it."

"Put the bracelets on 'em both, Sergeant," said Inspector Birch. "And you, Slater, remember your evidence will be wanted. Much obliged to you, Mr. Egg. But it's a funny thing where that key can have gone to."

"Better ask young Hopeful," said Mr. Egg. "It's surprising how a little thing like that will trip a man up. As the *Salesman's Handbook* says: Attend to details and you'll make your sale — a little weight will often turn the scale."

THE PROFESSOR'S MANUSCRIPT

"S ee here, Monty," said Mr. Hopgood (traveling representative for Messrs. Brotherhood, Ltd.) to Mr. Egg (traveling representative for Messrs. Plummet & Rose); "while you're here, why don't you have a go at old Professor Pindar? I should say he was just about in your line."

Mr. Egg brought his mind back—a little unwillingly— from the headlines in his morning paper ("SCREEN STAR'S MARRIAGE ROMANCE PLANE DASH"—"CONTINENT COMB-OUT FOR MISSING FINANCIER"—"COUNTRY-HOUSE MYSTERY BLAZE ARSON SUSPICIONS"—"BUDGET INCOME-TAX REMISSION POSSIBILITY"), and inquired who Professor Pindar might be when he was at home.

"He's a funny old bird that's come and settled down at Wellingtonia House," replied Mr. Hopgood. "You know, where the Fennels used to live. Bought the place last January and moved in about a month ago. Writes books, or something. I went along yesterday to see if there was anything doing in our way. Heard he was a retired sort of old party. Thought he might be good for a case of Sparkling Pompayne or something else in the soft drinks line. Quite rude to me, he was. Called it 'gut-rot,' and spilled a piece of poetry about 'windy waters.'

Shouldn't have expected such strong expressions from a brainy-looking old gent like him. Apologized for taking up his time, of course, and said to myself, 'Here's where young Monty gets in with his matured spirits and fine old fruity.' Thought I'd give you the tip, that's all—but suit yourself, of course."

Mr. Egg thanked Mr. Hopgood, and agreed that Professor Pindar sounded like a useful prospect.

"One gets to see him all right, then?" he asked.

"Yes—only you have to state your business," said Mr. Hopgood. "Housekeeper's a bit of a dragon. No good trying on the old tale of being sent round by his dear friend Mr. So-and-so, because, for one thing, he's got no friends round here and, for another, they know that one."

"In that case—" began Mr. Egg; but Mr. Hopgood did not appear to notice that he had said anything odd, and he felt it was hardly worthwhile to start an argument, especially as the morning was getting on, and he had not yet read about the film-star's marriage dash or the country-house arson suspicions. He turned his attention to these, discovered that the romance was the lady's fifth marriage and that the fire was thought to be yet another ramification of the insurance ramp, went on to ascertain that the person detained the day before in Constantinople was not, after all, the absconding head of Mammoth Industries, Ltd., and that the hope of sixpence off the income-tax was little more than the *Daily Trumpet* correspondent's dream of wish-fulfilment, and then embarked upon a juicy leader-page article headed "CAN COMMERCIAL TRAVELERS BE CHRISTIANS?—by One of Them," which interested him, not so much because he had any doubts about commercial morality as because he fancied he knew who the author was.

Before very long, however, his own commercial conscience (which was sensitive) reminded him that he was wasting his employer's time, and he went out to inquire into a complaint received from the landlord of the Ring of Bells that the last case of Plummet & Rose's Superior Old Tawny (full body, fine masculine flavor) was not up to sample, owing to alleged faulty corking.

Having disposed of this little unpleasantness, and traced the trouble to the fact that the landlord had thoughtlessly run the main pipe of a new heating installation behind the racks housing the Superior Old Tawny, Mr. Egg asked to be directed to Wellingtonia House.

"It's about five miles out of the town," said the landlord. "Take the road to Great Windings, turn off to the left by the tower they call Grabb's Folly, and then it's down the lane on the right past the old water-mill. Biggish place with a high brick wall right down in the hollow. Damp, in my opinion. Shouldn't care to live there myself. All right if you like peace and quietness, but I prefer to see a bit of life myself. So does the missus. But this old chap ain't married, so I suppose it's all right for him. Lives there alone with a housekeeper and a handyman and about fifty million tons of books. I was sorry to hear he'd taken the house. What we want there is a family with a bit of money, to bring some trade into the town."

"Not a rich man, then?" asked Mr. Egg, mentally substituting a cheaper line for the Cockburn 1896 (a grand ancient wine thirty-five years in bottle) with which he had hoped to tempt the Professor.

"He may have," replied the landlord; "must have, I suppose, since he's bought the place freehold. But what's the odds if he don't spend it? Never goes anywhere. No entertaining. Bit of a crank, by what they tell me."

"Butcher's meat?" inquired Mr. Egg.

"Oh, yes," said the landlord, "and only the best cuts. But what's one old gentleman's steak and chop when you come to think of it? That don't make a lot of difference in the week's turn-over."

However, the thought of the steak and chops comforted Mr. Egg as he drove by Grabb's Folly and the old water-mill and turned down the little, winding lane between high hedgerows starred with dog-violets and the lesser celandine. Grilled meat and wine went together almost as certainly as nut-cutlets and home-made lemonade.

The door of Wellingtonia House was opened by a middle-aged woman in an apron, at sight of whom Mr. Egg instantly dismissed the manner he used for domestic servants and substituted the one reserved for persons "out of the top drawer," as he phrased it. A pre-War gentlewoman in a post-War job, he decided. He produced his card and stated his business frankly.

"Well," said the housekeeper. She looked Mr. Egg searchingly up and down. "Professor Pindar is a very busy man, but he may like to see you. He is very particular about his wines — especially vintage port."

"Vintage port, madam," replied Mr. Egg, "is a speciality with us."

"*Real* vintage port?" asked the housekeeper, smiling.

Mr. Egg was hurt, though he tried not to show it. He mentioned a few of Messrs. Plummet & Rose's choicer shipments, and produced a list.

"Come in," said the housekeeper. "I'll take the list to Professor Pindar. He may like to see you himself, though I can't promise. He is very hard at work upon his book, and he can't possibly spare very much time."

"Certainly not, madam," said Mr. Egg, stepping in and wiping his boots carefully. They were perfectly clean, but the ritual was part of his regular routine, as laid down by the *Salesman's Handbook*. ("Be clean and courteous; raise your hat, And wipe your boots upon the mat: Such proofs of gentlemanly feeling Are to the ladies most appealing.") "In my opinion," he added, as he followed his conductress through a handsome hall and down a long and thickly-carpeted passage, "more sales are lost through being too persistent than through not being persistent enough. There's a little verse, madam, that I try to bear in mind: 'Don't stay too long; the customer has other things to do than sitting in the parlour and listening to you; And if, through your loquacity, she lets the dinner burn, She will not soon forget it, and it does you a bad turn.' I will just show the Professor my list, and if he is not interested, I will promise to go away at once."

The housekeeper laughed. "You are more reasonable than

most of them," she said, and showed him into a large and lofty room, lined from floor to ceiling with bookshelves. "Wait here a minute, and I will see what Professor Pindar says."

She was gone for some time, and Mr. Egg, being left to contemplate, with awe and some astonishment, the array of learning all about him, became restless, and even a little reckless. He walked about the library, trying to ascertain from the titles of the books what Professor Pindar was professor of. His interests, however, appeared to be catholic, for the books dealt with many subjects. One of them, a stout, calf-bound octavo in a long row of calf-bound octavos, attracted Mr. Egg's attention. It was an eighteenth-century treatise on Brewing and Distilling, and he extended a cautious finger to hook it from the shelf. It was, however, too tightly wedged between a bound collection of Pamphlets and a play by Ben Jonson to come out easily, and he abandoned the attempt. Curiosity made him next tiptoe over to the formidable great desk strewn with manuscripts. This gave more information. In the center, near the typewriter, lay a pile of neatly-typed sheets, embellished with footnotes and a good many passages of what looked to Mr. Egg like Greek, though it might, of course, have been Russian or Arabic, or any other language with a queer alphabet. The half-finished page upon the blotter broke off abruptly with the words: "This was the opinion of St. Augustine, though Clement of Alexandria expressly declares—" Here the sentence ended, as though the writer had paused to consult his authority. The open folio on the table was, however, neither St. Augustine nor Clement of Alexandria, but Origen. Close beside it stood a metal strong-box with a combination-lock, which Mr. Egg judged to contain some rare manuscript or other.

The sound of a hand upon the door-handle caused him to start guiltily away from the table, and when the door opened he had whisked round with his back to the desk and was staring abstractedly at a shelf crammed with immense tomes, ranging from Aristotle's works to a Jacobean Life of Queen Elizabeth.

Professor Pindar was a very bent and tottery old gentleman, and the hairiest person Mr. Egg had ever set eyes upon. His beard began at his cheekbones and draped his chest as far as the penultimate waistcoat-button. Over a pair of very sharp gray eyes, heavy gray eyebrows hung like a pent-house. He wore a black skull-cap, from beneath which more gray hair flowed so as to conceal his collar. He wore a rather shabby black velvet jacket, gray trousers, which had forgotten the last time they had ever seen a trousers-press, and a pair of carpet slippers, over which gray woolen socks wreathed themselves in folds. His face (what could be seen of it) was thin, and he spoke with a curious whistle and click due to an extremely ill-fitting set of dentures.

"Hso you are the young man from the wine-merchant's, hish, click," said the Professor. "Hsit down. Click." He waved his hand to a chair some little distance away, and himself shuffled to the desk and seated himself. "You brought me a list—where have I—ah! yesh! click! here it is, hish. Let me hsee." He fumbled about himself and produced a pair of steel spectacles. "Hish! yesh! Very interesting. What made you think of calling on me, click, hey? Hish."

Mr. Egg said that he had been advised to call by Messrs. Brotherhood's representative.

"I thought, sir," he said ingenuously, "that if you disapproved so much of soft drinks, you might appreciate something more, shall we say, full-bodied."

"You did, did you?" said the Professor. "Very shrewd of you. Click! Hsmart of you, hish. Got some good hish stuff here." He waved the list. "Don't believe in highclassh wine-merchants touting for customers shthough. Infra dig. Hey?"

Mr. Egg explained that the pressure of competition had driven Messrs. Plummet & Rose to this undoubtedly rather modern expedient. "But of course, sir," he added, "we exercise our discretion. I should not dream of showing a gentleman like yourself the list we issue to licensed houses."

"Humph!" said Professor Pindar. "Well—" He entered upon a discussion of the wine-list, showing himself remarkably knowledgeable for an aged scholar whose interests were centered upon the Fathers of the Church. He was, he said, thinking of laying down a small cellar, though he should have to get some new racks installed, since the former owners had allowed that part of the establishment to fall into decay.

Mr. Egg ventured a mild witticism about "rack and ruin," and booked a useful little order for some Warre, Dow & Cockburn ports, together with a few dozen selected burgundies, to be delivered in a month's time, when the cellar accommodation should be ready for them.

"You are thinking of settling permanently in this part of the country, sir?" he ventured, as he rose (mindful of instructions) to take his leave.

"Yes. Why not, hey?" snapped the Professor.

"Very glad to hear it, sir," said Monty. "Always very glad to hear of a good customer, you know."

"Yes, of coursh," replied Professor Pindar. "Naturally. I exshpect to be here until I have finished my book, at any rate. May take years, click! *Hishtory of the Early Chrishtian Chursh*, hish, click." Here his teeth seemed to take so alarming a leap from his jaws that Mr. Egg made an instinctive dive forward to catch them, and wondered why the Professor should have hit on a subject and title so impossible of pronunciation.

"But that means nothing to *you*, I take it, hey?" concluded the Professor, opening the door.

"Nothing, I'm sorry to say, sir," said Mr. Egg, who knew where to draw the line between the pretence of interest and the confession of ignorance. "Like the Swan of Avon, if I may put it that way, I have small Latin and less Greek, and that's the only resemblance between me and him, I'm afraid."

The Professor laughed, perilously, and followed up this exercise with a terrific click.

"Mrs. Tabbitt!" he called, "show this gentleman out."

The housekeeper reappeared and took charge of Mr. Egg, who departed, full of polite thanks for esteemed favors.

"Well," thought Montague Egg, "that's a puzzler, that is. All the same, it's no business of mine, and I don't want to make a mistake. I wonder who I could ask. Wait a minute. Mr. Griffiths—he's the man. He'd know in a moment."

It so happened that he was due to return to Town that day. He attended to his business and then, as soon as he was free, went round to call upon a very good customer and friend of his, who was the senior partner in the extremely respectable publishing firm of Griffiths & Seabright. Mr. Griffiths listened to his story with considerable interest.

"Pindar?" said he. "Never heard of him. Early Fathers of the Church, eh? Well, Dr. Abcock is the man for that. We'll ring him up. Hullo! is that Dr. Abcock? Sorry to bother you, but have you ever heard of a Professor Pindar who writes your kind of stuff? You haven't . . . I don't know. Wait a moment."

He took down various stout volumes and consulted them.

"He doesn't seem to hold any English or Scotch professorship," he observed, presently. "Of course, it might be foreign or American—did he speak with any sort of accent, Egg?— No?—Well, that proves nothing, of course. Anybody can get a professorship from those odd American universities. Well, never mind, Doctor, don't bother. Yes, a book. I rather wanted to get the thing vetted. I'll let you know again later."

He turned to Monty.

"Nothing very definite there," he said, "but I'll tell you what I'll do. I'll call on this man—or perhaps it will be better to write. I'll say I've heard about the work and would like to make an offer for it. That might produce something. You're a bit of a terror, aren't you, Egg? Have a spot of one of your own wares before you go."

It was some time before Mr. Egg heard again from Mr. Griffiths. Then a letter was forwarded to him in York, whither his travels had taken him.

DEAR EGG,

I wrote to your Professor, and with a good bit of trouble extracted an answer and a typescript. Now, there's no doubt at all about the MS. It's first-class of its kind. Rather unorthodox, in some ways, but stuffed as full of scholarship as an egg (sorry) is of meat. But his letter was what I should call evasive. He doesn't say where he got his professorship. Possibly he bestowed the title on himself, honoris causa. But the book is so darned good that I'm going to make a stiff push to get it for G. & S. I'm writing to ask the mysterious Professor for an appointment and will send you a line if I get it.

The next communication reached Mr. Egg in Lincoln.

DEAR EGG,

Curiouser and curiouser. Professor Pindar absolutely refuses to see me or to discuss his book with me, though he is ready to consider an offer. Abcock is getting excited about it, and has written to ask for further information on several controversial points in the MS. We cannot understand how a man of such remarkable learning and ability should have remained all this time unknown to the experts in his particular subject. I think our best chance is to get hold of old Dr. Wilverton. He knows all about everything and everybody, only he is so very eccentric that it is rather difficult to get anything out of him. But you can be sure of one thing—the man who wrote that book is a bona fide scholar, so your doubts must have been ill-founded. But I'm immensely grateful to you for putting me on to Professor Pindar, whoever he is. The work will make a big noise in the little world of learning.

Mr. Egg had returned to London before he heard from Mr. Griffiths again. Then he was rung up and requested, in rather excited tones, to come round and meet the great and eccentric Dr. Lovell Wilverton at Mr. Griffiths's house. When he got there he found the publisher and Dr. Abcock seated by the fire, while a strange little man in a check suit and steel spectacles ramped irritably up and down the room.

"It's no use," spluttered Dr. Wilverton, "it's no use to tell me. I know. I say I *know*. The views expressed—the style—the—everything points the same way. Besides, I tell you, I've seen that passage on Clement of Alexandria before. Poor Donne! He was a most brilliant scholar—*the* most brilliant scholar who ever passed through my hands. I went to see him once, at the horrible little hut on the Essex Marshes that he retired to after the—the collapse, you know—and he showed me the stuff then. Mistaken? Of course I'm not mistaken. I'm never mistaken. Couldn't be. I've often wondered since where that manuscript went to. If only I'd been in England at the time I should have secured it. Sold with the rest of his things, for junk, I suppose, to pay the rent."

"Just a moment, Wilverton," said Dr. Abcock, soothingly. "You're going too fast for us. You say, this *History of the Early Christian Church* was written by a young man called Roger Donne, a pupil of yours, who unfortunately took to drink and went to live in very great poverty in a hut on the Essex Marshes. Now it turns up, in typescript, which you say Donne wouldn't have used, masquerading as the work of an old person calling himself Professor Pindar, of Wellingtonia House, in Somerset. Are you suggesting that Pindar stole the manuscript or bought it from Donne? Or that he is Donne in disguise?"

"Of course he isn't Donne," said Dr. Wilverton, angrily. "I told you, didn't I? Donne's dead. He died last year when I was in Syria. I suppose this old impostor bought the manuscript at the sale."

Mr. Egg smote his thigh with his palm.

"Why, of course, sir," he said. "The deed-box I saw on the table. That would have the original manuscript in it, and this old professor-man just copied it out on his own typewriter."

"But what for?" asked Mr. Griffiths. "It's a remarkable book, but it's not a thing one would get a lot of money out of."

"No," agreed Monty, "but it would be an awfully good

proof that the Professor really was what he pretended to be. Suppose the police made investigations—there was the Professor, and there was the book, and any expert they showed it to (unless they had the luck to hit on Dr. Lovell Wilverton, of course) would recognize it for the work of a really learned gentleman."

"Police?" said Dr. Abcock, sharply. "Why the police? Who do you suppose this Pindar really is?"

Mr. Egg extracted a newspaper cutting from his pocket.

"Him, sir," he said. "Greenholt, the missing financier who absconded with all the remaining assets of Mammoth Industries, Ltd., just a week before Professor Pindar came and settled at Wellingtonia House. Here's his description: sixty years old, grey eyes, false teeth. Why, a bunch of hair and a bad set of dentures, a velvet coat and skull-cap, and there you are. There's your Professor Pindar. I did think the hair was just a bit overdone. And that Mrs. Tabbitt was a lady, all right, and here's a photo of Mrs. Greenholt. Take away the make-up and scrag her hair back in a bun, and they're as like as two peas."

"Great heavens!" exclaimed Mr. Griffiths. "And they've been combing Europe for the fellow. Egg, I shouldn't wonder if you're right. Give me the 'phone. We'll get on to Scotland Yard. Hullo! Give me Whitehall 1212."

"You seem to be something of a detective, Mr. Egg," said Dr. Lovell Wilverton, later in the evening, when word had come through of the arrest of Robert Greenholt at Wellingtonia House. "Do you mind telling me what first put this idea into your head?"

"Well, sir," replied Mr. Egg, modestly, "I'm not a brainy man, but in my line one learns to size a party up pretty quickly. The first thing that seemed odd was that this Professor wouldn't see my friend, Hopgood, of Brotherhood, Ltd., till he knew where he came from, and then, when he did see him, told him he couldn't stick soft drinks. Now, you know, sir, as a rule, a busy gentleman won't see a commercial at all if he's not interested in the goods. It's one of our big difficulties.

It looked as though the Professor wanted to be seen, in his character as a professor, by anybody and everybody, provided that it wasn't anybody who knew too much about books and so on. Then there was the butcher. He supplied steaks and chops to the household, which looked like a gentleman with good teeth; but when I got there, I found a hairy old boy whose dental plate was so wonky he could hardly have chewed scrambled eggs with it. But the thing that really bothered me was the books in that library. I'm no reader, unless it's a crook yarn or something of that kind, but I visit a good many learned gentlemen, and I've now and again cast my eye on their shelves, always liking to improve myself. Now, there were three things in that library that weren't like the library of any gentlemen that uses his books. First, the books were all mixed up, with different subjects alongside one another, instead of all the same subject together. Then, the books were too neat, all big books in one place and all small ones in another. And then they were too snug in the shelves. No gentleman that likes books or needs to consult them quickly keeps them as tight as that—they won't come out when you want them and besides, it breaks the bindings. That's true, I know, because I asked a friend of mine in the second-hand book business. So you see," said Mr. Egg, persuasively, "Greek or no Greek, I couldn't believe that gentleman ever read any of his books. I expect he just bought up somebody's library—or you can have 'em delivered by the yard; it's often done by rich gentlemen who get their libraries done by furnishing firms."

"Bless my soul," said Dr. Lovell Wilverton, "is Saul also among the Prophets? You seem to be an observant man, Mr. Egg."

"I try to be," replied Mr. Egg. "Never miss a chance of learning for that word spells '£' plus 'earning.'—You'll find that in the *Salesman's Handbook*. Very neat, sir, don't you think?"

OTHER STORIES

THE MAN WHO KNEW HOW

For perhaps the twentieth time since the train had left Carlisle, Pender glanced up from *Murder at the Manse* and caught the eye of the man opposite.

He frowned a little. It was irritating to be watched so closely, and always with that faint, sardonic smile. It was still more irritating to allow oneself to be so much disturbed by the smile and the scrutiny. Pender wrenched himself back to his book with a determination to concentrate upon the problem of the minister murdered in the library. But the story was of the academic kind that crowds all its exciting incidents in the first chapter, and proceeds thereafter by a long series of deductions to a scientific solution in the last. The thin thread of interest, spun precariously upon the wheel of Pender's reasoning brain, had been snapped. Twice he had to turn back to verify points that he had missed in reading. Then he became aware that his eyes had followed three closely argued pages without conveying anything whatever to his intelligence. He was not thinking about the murdered minister at all—he was becoming more and more actively conscious of the other man's face. A queer face, Pender thought.

There was nothing especially remarkable about the features in themselves; it was their expression that daunted Pender. It was a secret face, the face of one who knew a great deal to other people's disadvantage. The mouth was a little crooked and tightly tucked in at the corners, as though savouring a hidden amusement. The eyes, behind a pair of rimless pince-nez, glittered curiously; but that was possibly due to the light reflected in the glasses. Pender wondered what the man's profession might be. He was dressed in a dark lounge suit, a raincoat and a shabby soft hat; his age was perhaps about forty.

Pender coughed unnecessarily and settled back into his corner, raising the detective story high before his face, barrier-fashion. This was worse than useless. He gained the impression that the man saw through the manœuvre and was secretly entertained by it. He wanted to fidget, but felt obscurely that his doing so would in some way constitute a victory for the other man. In his self-consciousness he held himself so rigid that attention to his book became a sheer physical impossibility.

There was no stop now before Rugby, and it was unlikely that any passenger would enter from the corridor to break up this disagreeable *solitude à deux*. But something must be done. The silence had lasted so long that any remark, however trivial, would—so Pender felt—burst upon the tense atmosphere with the unnatural clatter of an alarm clock. One could, of course, go out into the corridor and not return, but that would be an acknowledgment of defeat. Pender lowered *Murder at the Manse* and caught the man's eye again.

"Getting tired of it?" asked the man.

"Night journeys are always a bit tedious," replied Pender, half relieved and half reluctant. "Would you like a book?"

He took *The Paper-Clip Clue* from his attaché-case and held it out hopefully. The other man glanced at the title and shook his head.

"Thanks very much," he said, "but I never read detective stories. They're so—inadequate, don't you think so?"

"They are rather lacking in characterization and human interest, certainly," said Pender, "but on a railway journey—"

"I don't mean that," said the other man. "I am not concerned with humanity. But all these murderers are so incompetent—they bore me."

"Oh, I don't know," replied Pender. "At any rate they are usually a good deal more imaginative and ingenious than murderers in real life."

"Than the murderers who are found out in real life, yes," admitted the other man.

"Even some of those did pretty well before they got pinched," objected Pender. "Crippen, for instance; he need never have been caught if he hadn't lost his head and run off to America. George Joseph Smith did away with at least two brides quite successfully before fate and the *News of the World* intervened."

"Yes," said the other man, "but look at the clumsiness of it all; the elaboration, the lies, the paraphernalia. Absolutely unnecessary."

"Oh come!" said Pender. "You can't expect committing a murder and getting away with it to be as simple as shelling peas."

"Ah!" said the other man. "You think that, do you?"

Pender waited for him to elaborate this remark, but nothing came of it. The man leaned back and smiled in his secret way at the roof of the carriage; he appeared to think the conversation not worth going on with. Pender, taking up his book again, found himself attracted by his companion's hands. They were white and surprisingly long in the fingers. He watched them gently tapping upon their owner's knee—then resolutely turned a page—then put the book down once more and said:

"Well, if it's so easy, how would *you* set about committing a murder?"

"I?" repeated the man. The light on his glasses made his eyes quite blank to Pender, but his voice sounded gently amused. "That's different; *I* should not have to think twice about it."

"Why not?"

"Because I happen to know how to do it."

"Do you indeed?" muttered Pender, rebelliously.

"Oh, yes; there's nothing in it."

"How can you be sure? You haven't tried, I suppose?"

"It isn't a case of trying," said the man. "There's nothing tentative about my method. That's just the beauty of it."

"It's easy to say that," retorted Pender, "but what *is* this wonderful method?"

"You can't expect me to tell you that, can you?" said the other man, bringing his eyes back to rest on Pender's. "It might not be safe. You look harmless enough, but who could look more harmless than Crippen? Nobody is fit to be trusted with *absolute* control over other people's lives."

"Bosh!" exclaimed Pender. "I shouldn't think of murdering anybody."

"Oh, yes, you would," said the other man, "if you really believed it was safe. So would anybody. Why are all these tremendous artificial barriers built up around murder by the Church and the law? Just because it's everybody's crime, and just as natural as breathing."

"But that's ridiculous!" cried Pender, warmly.

"You think so, do you? That's what most people would say. But I wouldn't trust 'em. Not with sulphate of thanatol to be bought for twopence at any chemist's."

"Sulphate of what?" asked Pender sharply.

"Ah! you think I'm giving something away. Well, it's a mixture of that and one or two other things—all equally ordinary and cheap. For ninepence you could make up enough to poison the entire Cabinet—and even you would hardly call that a crime, would you? But of course one wouldn't polish the whole lot off at once; it might look funny if they all died simultaneously in their baths."

"Why in their baths?"

"That's the way it would take them. It's the action of the hot water that brings on the effect of the stuff, you see. Any time from a few hours to a few days after administration. It's quite a simple chemical reaction and it couldn't possibly be detected by analysis. It would just look like heart failure."

Pender eyed him uneasily. He did not like the smile; it was not only derisive, it was smug, it was almost—gloating—triumphant! He could not quite put a name to it.

"You know," pursued the man, thoughtfully pulling a pipe from his pocket and beginning to fill it, "it is very odd how often one seems to read of people being found dead in their baths. It must be a very common accident. Quite temptingly so. After all, there is a fascination about murder. The thing grows upon one—that is, I imagine it would, you know."

"Very likely," said Pender.

"Look at Palmer. Look at Gesina Gottfried. Look at Armstrong. No, I wouldn't trust anybody with that formula—not even a virtuous young man like yourself."

The long white fingers tamped the tobacco firmly into the bowl and struck a match.

"But how about you?" said Pender, irritated. (Nobody cares to be called a virtuous young man.) "If nobody is fit to be trusted—"

"I'm not, eh?" replied the man. "Well, that's true, but it's past praying for now, isn't it? I know the thing and I can't unknow it again. It's unfortunate, but there it is. At any rate you have the comfort of knowing that nothing disagreeable is likely to happen to *me*. Dear me! Rugby already. I get out here. I have a little bit of business to do at Rugby."

He rose and shook himself, buttoned his raincoat about him, and pulled the shabby hat more firmly down above his enigmatic glasses. The train slowed down and stopped. With a brief good-night and a crooked smile the man stepped on to the platform. Pender watched him stride quickly away into the drizzle beyond the radius of the gaslight.

"Dotty or something," said Pender, oddly relieved. "Thank goodness, I seem to be going to have the carriage to myself."

He returned to *Murder at the Manse*, but his attention still kept wandering.

"What was the name of that stuff the fellow talked about?"

For the life of him he could not remember.

It was on the following afternoon that Pender saw the news-item. He had bought the *Standard* to read at lunch, and the word "Bath" caught his eye; otherwise he would probably have missed the paragraph altogether, for it was only a short one.

Wealthy Manufacturer Dies in Bath
Wife's Tragic Discovery

A distressing discovery was made early this morning by Mrs. John Brittlesea, wife of the well-known head of Brittlesea's Engineering Works at Rugby. Finding that her husband, whom she had seen alive and well less than an hour previously, did not come down in time for his breakfast, she searched for him in the bathroom, where, on the door being broken down, the engineer was found lying dead in his bath, life having been extinct, according to the medical men, for half an hour. The cause of the death is pronounced to be heart failure. The deceased manufacturer . . .

"That's an odd coincidence," said Pender. "At Rugby. I should think my unknown friend would be interested — if he is still there, doing his bit of business. I wonder what his business is, by the way."

It is a very curious thing how, when once your attention is attracted to any particular set of circumstances, that set of circumstances seems to haunt you. You get appendicitis: immediately the newspapers are filled with paragraphs about statesmen suffering from appendicitis and victims dying of it; you learn that all your acquaintances have had it, or know friends who have had it, and either died of it, or recovered from it with more surprising and spectacular rapidity than yourself; you cannot open a popular magazine without seeing its cure mentioned as one of the triumphs of modern surgery, or dip into a scientific treatise without coming across a comparison of the vermiform appendix in men and monkeys. Probably these references to appendicitis are equally frequent at all times, but you only notice them when your mind is attuned to the subject. At any rate, it was in this way that Pender accounted to himself for the extraordinary frequency with which people seemed to die in their baths at this period.

The thing pursued him at every turn. Always the same sequence of events: the hot bath, the discovery of the corpse, the inquest; always the same medical opinion: heart failure following immersion in too-hot water. It began to seem to Pender that it was scarcely safe to enter a hot bath at all. He took to making his own bath cooler and cooler every day, until it almost ceased to be enjoyable.

He skimmed his paper each morning for headlines about baths before settling down to read the news; and was at once relieved and vaguely disappointed if a week passed without a hot-bath tragedy.

One of the sudden deaths that occurred in this way was that of a young and beautiful woman whose husband, an analytical chemist, had tried without success to divorce her a few months previously. The coroner displayed a tendency to suspect foul play, and put the husband through a severe cross-examination. There seemed, however, to be no getting behind the doctor's evidence. Pender, brooding fancifully over the improbable possible, wished, as he did every day of the week, that he could remember the name of that drug the man in the train had mentioned.

Then came the excitement in Pender's own neighbourhood. An old Mr. Skimmings, who lived alone with a housekeeper in a street just round the corner, was found dead in his bathroom. His heart had never been strong. The housekeeper told the milkman that she had always expected something of the sort to happen, for the old gentleman would always take his bath so hot. Pender went to the inquest.

The housekeeper gave her evidence. Mr. Skimmings had been the kindest of employers, and she was heartbroken at losing him. No, she had not been aware that Mr. Skimmings had left her a large sum of money, but it was just like his goodness of heart. The verdict was Death by Misadventure.

Pender, that evening, went out for his usual stroll with the dog. Some feeling of curiosity moved him to go round past the late Mr. Skimmings's house. As he loitered by, glancing up at the blank windows, the garden-gate opened and a man came out. In the light of a street lamp, Pender recognised him at once.

"Hullo!" he said.

"Oh, it's you, is it?" said the man. "Viewing the site of the tragedy, eh? What do *you* think about it all?"

"Oh, nothing very much," said Pender. "I didn't know him. Odd, our meeting again like this."

"Yes, isn't it? You live near here, I suppose."

"Yes," said Pender; and then wished he hadn't. "Do you live in these parts too?"

"Me?" said the man. "Oh, no. I was only here on a little matter of business."

"Last time we met," said Pender, "you had business at Rugby." They had fallen into step together, and were walking slowly down to the turning Pender had to take in order to reach his house.

"So I had," agreed the other man. "My business takes me all over the country. I never know where I may be wanted next."

"It was while you were at Rugby that old Brittlesea was found dead in his bath, wasn't it?" remarked Pender carelessly.

"Yes. Funny thing, coincidence." The man glanced up at him sideways through his glittering glasses. "Left all his money to his wife, didn't he? She's a rich woman now. Good-looking girl — a lot younger than he was."

They were passing Pender's gate. "Come in and have a drink," said Pender, and again immediately regretted the impulse.

The man accepted, and they went into Pender's bachelor study.

"Remarkable lot of these bath-deaths there have been lately, haven't there?" observed Pender carelessly, as he splashed soda into the tumblers.

"You think it's remarkable?" said the man, with his usual irritating trick of querying everything that was said to him. "Well, I don't know. Perhaps it is. But it's always a fairly common accident."

"I suppose I've been taking more notice on account of that conversation we had in the train." Pender laughed, a little self-consciously. "It just makes me wonder—you know how one does—whether anybody else had happened to hit on that drug you mentioned—what was its name?"

The man ignored the question.

"Oh, I shouldn't think so," he said. "I fancy I'm the only person who knows about that. I only stumbled on the thing by accident myself when I was looking for something else. I don't imagine it could have been discovered simultaneously in so many parts of the country. But all these verdicts just show, don't they, what a safe way it would be of getting rid of a person."

"You're a chemist, then?" asked Pender, catching at the one phrase which seemed to promise information.

"Oh, I'm a bit of everything. Sort of general utility-man. I do a good bit of studying on my own, too. You've got one or two interesting books here, I see."

Pender was flattered. For a man in his position—he had been in a bank until he came into that little bit of money—he felt that he had improved his mind to some purpose, and he knew that his collection of modern first editions would be worth money some day. He went over to the glass-fronted bookcase and pulled out a volume or two to show his visitor.

The man displayed intelligence, and presently joined him in front of the shelves.

"These, I take it, represent your personal tastes?" He took

down a volume of Henry James and glanced at the flyleaf. "That your name? E. Pender?"

Pender admitted that it was. "You have the advantage of me," he added.

"Oh! I am one of the great Smith clan," said the other with a laugh, "and work for my bread. You seem to be very nicely fixed here."

Pender explained about the clerkship and the legacy.

"Very nice, isn't it?" said Smith. "Not married? No. You're one of the lucky ones. Not likely to be needing any sulphate of . . . any useful drugs in the near future. And you never will, if you stick to what you've got and keep off women and speculation."

He smiled up sideways at Pender. Now that his hat was off, Pender saw that he had a quantity of closely curled grey hair, which made him look older than he had appeared in the railway carriage.

"No, I shan't be coming to you for assistance yet awhile," said Pender, laughing. "Besides, how should I find you if I wanted you?"

"You wouldn't have to," said Smith. "*I* should find *you*. There's never any difficulty about that." He grinned, oddly. "Well, I'd better be getting on. Thank you for your hospitality. I don't expect we shall meet again—but we may, of course. Things work out so queerly, don't they?"

When he had gone, Pender returned to his own armchair. He took up his glass of whisky, which stood there nearly full.

"Funny!" he said to himself. "I don't remember pouring that out. I suppose I got interested and did it mechanically." He emptied his glass slowly, thinking about Smith.

What in the world was Smith doing at Skimmings's house?

An odd business altogether. If Skimmings's housekeeper had known about that money . . . But she had not known, and if she had, how could she have found out about Smith and his sulphate of . . . the word had been on the tip of his tongue then.

"You would not need to find me. *I* should find *you*." What had the man meant by that? But this was ridiculous. Smith was not the devil, presumably. But if he really had this secret—if he liked to put a price upon it—nonsense.

"Business at Rugby—a little bit of business at Skimmings's house." Oh, absurd!

"Nobody is fit to be trusted. *Absolute* power over another man's life . . . it grows on you."

Lunacy! And, if there was anything in it, the man was mad to tell Pender about it. If Pender chose to speak he could get the fellow hanged. The very existence of Pender would be dangerous.

That whisky!

More and more, thinking it over, Pender became persuaded that he had never poured it out. Smith must have done it while his back was turned. Why that sudden display of interest in the bookshelves? It had had no connection with anything that had gone before. Now Pender came to think of it, it had been a very stiff whisky. Was it imagination, or had there been something about the flavour of it?

A cold sweat broke out on Pender's forehead.

A quarter of an hour later, after a powerful dose of mustard and water, Pender was downstairs again, very cold and shivering, huddling over the fire. He had had a narrow escape—if he had escaped. He did not know how the stuff worked, but he would not take a hot bath again for some days. One never knew.

Whether the mustard and water had done the trick in time, or whether the hot bath was an essential part of the treatment, Pender's life was saved for the time being. But he was still uneasy. He kept the front door on the chain and warned his servant to let no strangers into the house.

He ordered two more morning papers and the *News of the World* on Sundays, and kept a careful watch upon their columns. Deaths in baths became an obsession with him. He neglected his first editions and took to attending inquests.

Three weeks later he found himself at Lincoln. A man had died of heart failure in a Turkish bath — a fat man, of sedentary habits. The jury added a rider to their verdict of Misadventure, to the effect that the management should exercise a stricter supervision over the bathers and should never permit them to be left unattended in the hot room.

As Pender emerged from the hall he saw ahead of him a shabby hat that seemed familiar. He plunged after it, and caught Mr. Smith about to step into a taxi.

"Smith," he cried, gasping a little. He clutched him fiercely by the shoulder.

"What, you again?" said Smith. "Taking notes of the case, eh? *Can I do anything for you?*"

"You devil!" said Pender. "You're mixed up in this! You tried to kill me the other day."

"Did I? Why should I do that?"

"You'll swing for this," shouted Pender menacingly.

A policeman pushed his way through the gathering crowd.

"Here!" said he, "what's all this about?"

Smith touched his forehead significantly.

"It's all right, officer," said he. "The gentleman seems to think I'm here for no good. Here's my card. The coroner knows me. But he attacked me. You'd better keep an eye on him."

"That's right," said a bystander.

"This man tried to kill me," said Pender.

The policeman nodded.

"Don't you worry about that, sir," he said. "You think better of it. The 'eat in there has upset you a bit. All right, *all* right."

"But I want to charge him," said Pender.

"I wouldn't do that if I was you," said the policeman.

"I tell you," said Pender, "that this man Smith has been trying to poison me. He's a murderer. He's poisoned scores of people."

The policeman winked at Smith.

"Best be off, sir," he said. "I'll settle this. Now, my lad" —

he held Pender firmly by the arms — "just you keep cool and take it quiet. That gentleman's name ain't Smith nor nothing like it. You've got a bit mixed up like."

"Well, what is his name?" demanded Pender.

"Never you mind," replied the constable. "You leave him alone, or you'll be getting yourself into trouble."

The taxi had driven away. Pender glanced round at the circle of amused faces and gave in.

"All right, officer," he said. "I won't give you any trouble. I'll come round with you to the police-station and tell you about it."

"What do you think o' that one?" asked the inspector of the sergeant when Pender had stumbled out of the station.

"Up the pole an' 'alf-way round the flag, if you ask me," replied his subordinate. "Got one o' them ideez fix what they talk about."

"H'm!" replied the inspector. "Well, we've got his name and address. Better make a note of 'em. He might turn up again. Poisoning people so as they die in their baths, eh? That's a pretty good 'un. Wonderful how these barmy ones thinks it all out, isn't it?"

The spring that year was a bad one — cold and foggy. It was March when Pender went down to an inquest at Deptford, but a thick blanket of mist was hanging over the river as though it were November. The cold ate into your bones. As he sat in the dingy little court, peering through the yellow twilight of gas and fog, he could scarcely see the witnesses as they came to the table. Everybody in the place seemed to be coughing. Pender was coughing too. His bones ached, and he felt as though he were about due for a bout of influenza.

Straining his eyes, he thought he recognised a face on the other side of the room, but the smarting fog which penetrated every crack stung and blinded him. He felt in his overcoat pocket, and his hand closed comfortably on something thick and heavy. Ever since that day in Lincoln he had gone about armed for protection. Not a revolver—he was no hand with firearms. A sandbag was much better. He had bought one from an old man wheeling a barrow. It was meant for keeping out draughts from the door—a good, old-fashioned affair.

The inevitable verdict was returned. The spectators began to push their way out. Pender had to hurry now, not to lose sight of his man. He elbowed his way along, muttering apologies. At the door he almost touched the man, but a stout woman intervened. He plunged past her, and she gave a little squeak of indignation. The man in front turned his head, and the light over the door glinted on his glasses.

Pender pulled his hat over his eyes and followed. His shoes had crêpe rubber soles and made no sound on the sticking pavement. The man went on, jogging quietly up one street and down another, and never looking back. The fog was so thick that Pender was forced to keep within a few yards of him. Where was he going? Into the lighted streets? Home by 'bus or tram? No. He turned off to the left, down a narrow street.

The fog was thicker here. Pender could no longer see his quarry, but he heard the footsteps going on before him at the same even pace. It seemed to him that they were two alone in the world—pursued and pursuer, slayer and avenger. The street began to slope more rapidly. They must be coming out somewhere near the river.

Suddenly the dim shapes of the houses fell away on either side. There was an open space, with a lamp vaguely visible in the middle. The footsteps paused. Pender, silently hurrying after, saw the man standing close beneath the lamp, apparently consulting something in a note-book.

Four steps, and Pender was upon him. He drew the sandbag from his pocket. The man looked up.

"I've got you this time," said Pender, and struck with all his force.

Pender had been quite right. He did get influenza. It was a week before he was out and about again. The weather had changed, and the air was fresh and sweet. In spite of the weakness left by the malady he felt as though a heavy weight had been lifted from his shoulders. He tottered down to a favourite bookshop of his in the Strand, and picked up a D. H. Lawrence "first" at a price which he knew to be a bargain. Encouraged by this, he turned into a small chop-house, chiefly frequented by Fleet Street men, and ordered a grilled cutlet and a half-tankard of bitter.

Two journalists were seated at the next table.

"Going to poor old Buckley's funeral?" asked one.

"Yes," said the other. "Poor devil! Fancy his getting sloshed on the head like that. He must have been on his way down to interview the widow of that fellow who died in a bath. It's a rough district. Probably one of Jimmy the Card's crowd had it in for him. He was a great crime-reporter—they won't get another like Bill Buckley in a hurry."

"He was a decent sort, too. Great old sport. No end of a leg-puller. Remember his great stunt about sulphate of thanatol?"

Pender started. *That* was the word that had eluded him for so many months. A curious dizziness came over him and he took a pull at the tankard to steady himself.

". . . looking at you as sober as a judge," the journalist was saying. "He used to work off that wheeze on poor boobs in railway carriages to see how they'd take it. Would you believe that one chap actually offered him—"

"Hullo!" interrupted his friend. "That bloke over there has fainted. I thought he was looking a bit white."

THE FOUNTAIN PLAYS

Yes," said Mr. Spiller, in a satisfied tone, "I must say I like a bit of ornamental water. Gives a finish to the place."

"The Versailles touch," agreed Ronald Proudfoot.

Mr. Spiller glanced sharply at him, as though suspecting sarcasm, but his lean face expressed nothing whatever. Mr. Spiller was never quite at his ease in the company of his daughter's fiancé, though he was proud of the girl's achievement. With all his (to Mr. Spiller) unamiable qualities, Ronald Proudfoot was a perfect gentleman, and Betty was completely wrapped up in him.

"The only thing it wants," continued Mr. Spiller, "to *my* mind, that is, is Opening Up. To make a Vista, so to say. You don't get the Effect with these bushes on all four sides."

"Oh, I don't know, Mr. Spiller," objected Mrs. Digby in her mild voice. "Don't you think it makes rather a fascinating surprise? You come along the path, never dreaming there's anything behind those lilacs, and then you turn the corner and come suddenly upon it. I'm sure, when you brought me down to see it this afternoon, it quite took my breath away."

"There's that, of course," admitted Mr. Spiller. It occurred to him, not for the first time, that there was something very

attractive about Mrs. Digby's silvery personality. She had distinction, too. A widow and widower of the sensible time of life,
with a bit of money on both sides, might do worse than settle
down comfortably in a pleasant house with half an acre of garden and a bit of ornamental water.

"And it's so pretty and secluded," went on Mrs. Digby,
"with these glorious rhododendrons. Look how pretty they
are, all sprayed with the water—like fairy jewels—and the
rustic seat against those dark cypresses at the back. Really
Italian. And the scent of the lilac is so marvellous!"

Mr. Spiller knew that the cypresses were, in fact, yews,
but he did not correct her. A little ignorance was becoming in
a woman. He glanced from the cotoneasters at one side of the
fountain to the rhododendrons on the other, their rainbow
flower-trusses sparkling with diamond drops.

"I wasn't thinking of touching the rhododendrons or the
cotoneasters," he said. "I only thought of cutting through that
great hedge of lilac, so as to make a Vista from the house. But
the ladies must always have the last word, mustn't they—er—
Ronald?" (He never could bring out Proudfoot's Christian
name naturally.) "If you like it as it is, Mrs. Digby, that settles
it. The lilacs shall stay."

"It's too flattering of you," said Mrs. Digby, "but you
mustn't think of altering your plans for me. I haven't any right
to interfere with your beautiful garden."

"Indeed you have," said Mr. Spiller. "I defer to your taste
entirely. You have spoken for the lilacs, and henceforward
they are sacred."

"I shall be afraid to give an opinion on anything, after
that," said Mrs. Digby, shaking her head. "But whatever you
decide to do, I'm sure it will be lovely. It was a marvellous idea
to think of putting the fountain there. It makes all the difference to the garden."

Mr. Spiller thought she was quite right. And indeed,
though the fountain was rather flattered by the name of "ornamental water," consisting as it did of a marble basin set in the
centre of a pool about four feet square, it made a brave show,

with its plume of dancing water, fifteen feet high, towering over the smaller shrubs and almost overtopping the tall lilacs. And its cooling splash and tinkle soothed the ear on this pleasant day of early summer.

"Costs a bit to run, doesn't it?" demanded Mr. Gooch. He had been silent up till now, and Mrs. Digby felt that his remark betrayed a rather sordid outlook on life. Indeed, from the first moment of meeting Mr. Gooch, she had pronounced him decidedly common, and wondered that he should be on such intimate terms with her host.

"No, no," replied Mr. Spiller. "No, it's not expensive. You see, it uses the same water over and over again. Most ingenious. The fountains in Trafalgar Square work on the same principle, I believe. Of course, I had to pay a bit to have it put in, but I think it's worth the money."

"Yes, indeed," said Mrs. Digby.

"I always said you were a warm man, Spiller," said Mr. Gooch, with his vulgar laugh. "Wish I was in your shoes. A snug spot, that's what I call this place. Snug."

"I'm not a millionaire," answered Mr. Spiller, rather shortly. "But things might be worse in these times. Of course," he added, more cheerfully, "one has to be careful. I turn the fountain off at night, for instance, to save leakage and waste."

"I'll swear you do, you damned old miser," said Mr. Gooch, offensively.

Mr. Spiller was saved replying by the sounding of a gong in the distance.

"Ah! there's dinner," he announced, with a certain relief in his tone. The party wound their way out between the lilacs, and paced gently up the long crazy pavement, past the herbaceous borders and the two long beds of raw little ticketed roses, to the glorified villa which Mr. Spiller had christened "The Pleasaunce."

It seemed to Mrs. Digby that there was a slightly strained atmosphere about dinner, though Betty, pretty as a picture and very much in love with Ronald Proudfoot, made a perfectly charming little hostess. The jarring note was sounded by

Mr. Gooch. He ate too noisily, drank far too freely, got on Proudfoot's nerves, and behaved to Mr. Spiller with a kind of veiled insolence which was embarrassing and disagreeable to listen to. She wondered again where he had come from, and why Mr. Spiller put up with him. She knew little about him, except that from time to time he turned up on a visit to "The Pleasaunce," usually staying there about a month and being, apparently, well supplied with cash. She had an idea that he was some kind of commission agent, though she could not recall any distinct statement on this point. Mr. Spiller had settled down in the village about three years previously, and she had always liked him. Though not, in any sense of the word, a cultivated man, he was kind, generous, and unassuming, and his devotion to Betty had something very lovable about it. Mr. Gooch had started coming about a year later. Mrs. Digby said to herself that if ever she was in a position to lay down the law at "The Pleasaunce"—and she had begun to think matters were tending that way—her influence would be directed to getting rid of Mr. Gooch.

"How about a spot of bridge?" suggested Ronald Proudfoot, when coffee had been served. It was nice, reflected Mrs. Digby, to have coffee brought in by the manservant. Masters was really a very well-trained butler, though he did combine the office with that of chauffeur. One would be comfortable at "The Pleasaunce." From the dining-room window she could see the neat garage housing the Wolseley saloon on the ground floor, with a room for the chauffeur above it, and topped off by a handsome gilded weather-vane a-glitter in the last rays of the sun. A good cook, a smart parlourmaid, and everything done exactly as one could wish—if she were to marry Mr. Spiller she would be able, for the first time in her life, to afford a personal maid as well. There would be plenty of room in the house, and of course, when Betty was married—

Betty, she thought, was not over-pleased that Ronald had suggested bridge. Bridge is not a game that lends itself to the expression of tender feeling, and it would perhaps have looked better if Ronald had enticed Betty out to sit in the lilac-scented dusk under the yew-hedge by the fountain. Mrs. Digby was sometimes afraid that Betty was the more in love of the two. But if Ronald wanted anything he had to have it, of course, and personally, Mrs. Digby enjoyed nothing better than a quiet rubber. Besides, the arrangement had the advantage that it got rid of Mr. Gooch. "Don't play bridge," Mr. Gooch was wont to say. "Never had time to learn. We didn't play bridge where I was brought up." He repeated the remark now, and followed it up with a contemptuous snort directed at Mr. Spiller.

"Never too late to begin," said the latter pacifically.

"Not me!" retorted Mr. Gooch. "I'm going to have a turn in the garden. Where's that fellow Masters? Tell him to take the whisky and soda down to the fountain. The decanter, mind—one drink's no good to yours truly." He plunged a thick hand into the box of Coronas on the side-table, took out a handful of cigars, and passed out through the French window of the library on to the terrace. Mr. Spiller rang the bell and gave the order without comment, and presently they saw Masters pad down the long crazy path between the rose-beds and the herbaceous borders, bearing the whisky and soda on a tray.

The other four played on till 10:30, when, a rubber coming to an end, Mrs. Digby rose and said it was time she went home. Her host gallantly offered to accompany her. "These two young people can look after themselves for a moment," he added, with a conspiratorial smile.

"The young can look after themselves better than the old, these days." She laughed a little shyly, and raised no objection when Mr. Spiller drew her hand into his arm as they walked the couple of hundred yards to her cottage. She hesitated a moment whether to ask him in, but decided that a sweet decorum suited her style best. She stretched out a soft, beringed hand to him over the top of the little white gate. His pressure lingered—he would have kissed the hand, so insidious was the scent of the red and white hawthorns in her trim garden, but before he had summoned up courage, she had withdrawn it from his clasp and was gone.

Mr. Spiller, opening his own front door in an agreeable dream, encountered Masters.

"Where is everybody, Masters?"

"Mr. Proudfoot left five or ten minutes since, sir, and Miss Elizabeth has retired."

"Oh!" Mr. Spiller was a little startled. The new generation, he thought sadly, did not make love like the old. He hoped there was nothing wrong. Another irritating thought presented itself.

"Has Mr. Gooch come in?"

"I could not say, sir. Shall I go and see?"

"No, never mind." If Gooch had been sozzling himself up with whisky since dinner-time, it was just as well Masters should keep away from him. You never knew. Masters was one of these soft-spoken beggars, but he might take advantage. Better not to trust servants, anyhow.

"You can cut along to bed. I'll lock up."

"Very good, sir."

"Oh, by the way, is the fountain turned off?"

"Yes, sir. I turned it off myself, sir, at half-past ten, seeing that you were engaged, sir."

"Quite right. Good-night, Masters."

"Good-night, sir."

He heard the man go out by the back and cross the paved court to the garage. Thoughtfully he bolted both entrances, and returned to the library. The whisky decanter was not in its usual place—no doubt it was still with Gooch in the garden—but he mixed himself a small brandy and soda, and drank it. He supposed he must now face the tiresome business of getting Gooch up to bed. Then, suddenly, he realised that the encounter would take place here and not in the garden. Gooch was coming in through the French window. He was drunk, but not, Mr. Spiller observed with relief, incapably so.

"Well?" said Gooch.

"Well?" retorted Mr. Spiller.

"Had a good time with the accommodating widow, eh? Enjoyed yourself? Lucky old hound, aren't you? Fallen soft in your old age, eh?"

"There, that'll do," said Mr. Spiller.

"Oh, will it? That's good. That's rich. That'll do, eh? Think I'm Masters, talking to me like that?" Mr. Gooch gave a thick chuckle. "Well, I'm not Masters, I'm master here. Get that into your head. I'm master and you damn well know it."

"All right," replied Mr. Spiller meekly, "but buzz off to bed now, there's a good fellow. It's getting late and I'm tired."

"You'll be tireder before I've done with you." Mr. Gooch thrust both hands into his pockets and stood—a bulky and threatening figure—swaying rather dangerously. "I'm short of cash," he added. "Had a bad week—cleaned me out. Time you stumped up a bit more."

"Nonsense," said Mr. Spiller, with some spirit. "I pay you your allowance as we agreed, and let you come and stay here whenever you like, and that's all you get from me."

"Oh, is it? Getting a bit above yourself, aren't you, Number Bleeding 4132?"

"Hush!" said Mr. Spiller, glancing hastily round as though the furniture had ears and tongues.

"Hush! hush!" repeated Mr. Gooch mockingly. "You're in a good position to dictate terms, aren't you, 4132? Hush! The servants might hear! Betty might hear! Betty's young man might hear. Hah! Betty's young man—he'd be particularly pleased to know her father was an escaped jail-bird, wouldn't he? Liable at any moment to be hauled back to work out his ten years' hard for forgery? And when I think," added Mr. Gooch, "that a man like me, that was only in for a short stretch and worked it out good and proper, is dependent on the charity—ha, ha!—of my dear friend 4132, while he's rolling in wealth—"

"I'm not rolling in wealth, Sam," said Mr. Spiller, "and you know darn well I'm not. But I don't want any trouble. I'll do what I can, if you'll promise faithfully this time that you won't ask for any more of these big sums, because my income won't stand it."

"Oh, I'll promise that all right," agreed Mr. Gooch cheerfully. "You give me five thousand down —"

Mr. Spiller uttered a strangled exclamation.

"Five thousand? How do you suppose I'm to lay hands on five thousand all at once? Don't be an idiot, Sam. I'll give you a cheque for five hundred —"

"Five thousand," insisted Mr. Gooch, "or up goes the monkey."

"But I haven't got it," objected Mr. Spiller.

"Then you'd bloody well better find it," returned Mr. Gooch.

"How do you expect me to find all that?"

"That's your look-out. You oughtn't to be so damned extravagant. Spending good money, that you ought to be giving *me*, on fountains and stuff. Now, it's no good kicking, Mr. Respectable 4132 — I'm the man on top and you're for it, my lad, if you don't look after me properly. See?"

Mr. Spiller saw only too clearly. He saw, as he had seen indeed for some time, that his friend Gooch had him by the short hairs. He expostulated again feebly, and Gooch replied with a laugh and an offensive reference to Mrs. Digby.

Mr. Spiller did not realise that he had struck very hard. He hardly realised that he had struck at all. He thought he had aimed a blow, and that Gooch had dodged it and tripped over the leg of the occasional table. But he was not very clear in his mind, except on one point. Gooch was dead.

He had not fainted; he was not stunned. He was dead. He must have caught the brass curb of the fender as he fell. There was no blood, but Mr. Spiller, exploring the inert head with anxious fingers, found a spot above the temple where the bone yielded to pressure like a cracked eggshell. The noise of the fall had been thunderous. Kneeling on the library floor, Mr. Spiller waited for the inevitable cry and footsteps from upstairs.

Nothing happened. He remembered—with difficulty, for his mind seemed to be working slowly and stiffly—that above the library there was only the long drawing-room, and over that the spare-room and bathrooms. No inhabited bedroom looked out on that side of the house.

A slow, grinding, grating noise startled him. He whisked round hastily. The old-fashioned grandfather clock, wheezing as the hammer rose into action, struck eleven. He wiped the sweat from his forehead, got up, and poured himself out another, and a stiffer, brandy.

The drink did him good. It seemed to take the brake off his mind, and the wheels spun energetically. An extraordinary clarity took the place of his previous confusion.

He had murdered Gooch. He had not exactly intended to do so, but he had done it. It had not felt to him like murder, but there was not the slightest doubt what the police would think about it. And once he was in the hands of the police— Mr. Spiller shuddered. They would almost certainly want to take his finger-prints, and would be surprised to recognise a bunch of old friends.

Masters had heard him say that he would wait up for Gooch. Masters knew that everybody else had gone to bed. Masters would undoubtedly guess something. But stop!

Could Masters prove that he himself had gone to bed? Yes, probably he could. Somebody would have heard him cross the court and seen the light go up over the garage. One could not hope to throw suspicion on Masters—besides, the man hardly deserved that. But the mere idea had started Mr. Spiller's brain on a new and attractive line of thought.

What he really wanted was an alibi. If he could only confuse the police as to the time at which Gooch had died. If Gooch could be made to seem alive after he was dead . . . somehow . . .

He cast his thoughts back over stories he had read on holiday, dealing with this very matter. You dressed up as the dead man and impersonated him. You telephoned in his name. In the hearing of the butler, you spoke to the dead as though he

were alive. You made a gramophone record of his voice and
played it. You hid the body, and thereafter sent a forged letter
from some distant place —

He paused for a moment. Forgery — but he did not want to
start that old game over again. And all these things were too
elaborate, or else impracticable at that time of night.

And then it came to him suddenly that he was a fool.
Gooch must not be made to live later, but to die earlier. He
should die before 10:30, at the time when Mr. Spiller, under
the eyes of three observers, had been playing bridge.

So far, the idea was sound and even, in its broad outline,
obvious. But now one had to come down to detail. How could
he establish the time? Was there anything that had happened
at 10:30?

He helped himself to another drink, and then, quite suddenly, as though lit by a floodlight, he saw his whole plan,
picked out vividly complete, with every join and angle clear-cut.

He glanced at his watch; the hands stood at twenty minutes past eleven. He had the night before him.

He fetched an electric torch from the hall and stepped
boldly out of the French window. Close beside it, against the
wall of the house, were two taps, one ending in a nozzle for the
garden hose, the other controlling the fountain at the bottom
of the garden. This latter he turned on, and then, without troubling to muffle his footsteps, followed the crazy-paved path
down to the lilac hedge, and round by the bed of cotoneasters.
The sky, despite the beauty of the early evening, had now
turned very dark, and he could scarcely see the tall column of
pale water above the dark shrubbery, but he heard its comforting splash and ripple, and as he stepped upon the surrounding grass, he felt the blown spray upon his face. The
beam of the torch showed him the garden seat beneath the
yews, and the tray, as he had expected, standing upon it.
The whisky decanter was about half full. He emptied the
greater part of its contents into the basin, wrapping the neck
of the decanter in his handkerchief, so as to leave no finger-
prints. Then, returning to the other side of the lilacs, he satis-

fied himself that the spray of the fountain was invisible from house or garden.

The next part of the performance he did not care about. It was risky; it might be heard; in fact, he wanted it to be heard if necessary—but it was a risk. He licked his dry lips and called the dead man by name:

"Gooch! Gooch!"

No answer, except the splash of the fountain, sounding to his anxious ear abnormally loud in the stillness. He glanced round, almost as though he expected the corpse to stalk awfully out upon him from the darkness, its head hanging and its dark mouth dropping open to show the pale gleam of its dentures. Then, pulling himself together, he walked briskly back up the path and, when he reached the house again, listened. There was no movement, no sound but the ticking of the clocks. He shut the library door gently. From now on there must be no noise.

There was a pair of goloshes in the cloak-room near the pantry. He put them on and slipped like a shadow through the French window again: then round the house into the courtyard. He glanced up at the garage; there was no light in the upper story and he breathed a sigh of relief, for Masters was apt sometimes to be wakeful. Groping his way to an outhouse, he switched the torch on. His wife had been an invalid for some years before her death, and he had brought her wheeled chair with him to "The Pleasaunce," having a dim, sentimental reluctance to sell the thing. He was thankful for that, now; thankful, too, that he had purchased it from a good maker and that it ran so lightly and silently on its pneumatic tyres. He found the bicycle pump and blew the tyres up hard and, for further precaution, administered a drop of oil here and there. Then, with infinite precaution, he wheeled the chair round to the library window. How fortunate that he had put down stone flags and crazy paving everywhere, so that no wheel-tracks could show.

The job of getting the body through the window and into the chair took it out of him. Gooch had been a heavy man, and he himself was not in good training. But it was done at last. Resisting the impulse to run, he pushed his burden gently and steadily along the narrow strip of paving. He could not see very well, and he was afraid to flash his torch too often. A slip off the path into the herbaceous border would be fatal; he set his teeth and kept his gaze fixed steadily ahead of him. He felt as though, if he looked back at the house, he would see the upper windows thronged with staring white faces. The impulse to turn his head was almost irresistible, but he determined that he would not turn it.

At length he was round the edge of the lilacs and hidden from the house. The sweat was running down his face and the most ticklish part of his task was still to do. If he broke his heart in the effort, he must carry the body over the plot of lawn. No wheel-marks or heel-marks or signs of dragging must be left for the police to see. He braced himself for the effort.

It was done. The corpse of Gooch lay there by the fountain, the bruise upon the temple carefully adjusted upon the sharp stone edge of the pool, one hand dragging in the water, the limbs disposed as naturally as possible, to look as though the man had stumbled and fallen. Over it, from head to foot, the water of the fountain sprayed, swaying and bending in the night wind. Mr. Spiller looked upon his work and saw that it was good. The journey back with the lightened chair was easy. When he had returned the vehicle to the outhouse and passed for the last time through the library window, he felt as though the burden of years had been rolled from his back.

His back! He had remembered to take off his dinner-jacket while stooping in the spray of the fountain, and only his shirt was drenched. That he could dispose of in the linen-basket, but the seat of his trousers gave him some uneasiness. He mopped at himself as best he could with his handkerchief. Then he made his calculations. If he left the fountain to play for an hour or so it would, he thought, produce the desired effect. Controlling his devouring impatience, he sat down and mixed himself a final brandy.

At 1 o'clock he rose, turned off the fountain, shut the

library window with no more and no less than the usual noise and force, and went with firm footsteps up to bed.

Inspector Frampton was, to Mr. Spiller's delight, a highly intelligent officer. He picked up the clues thrown to him with the eagerness of a trained terrier. The dead man was last seen alive by Masters after dinner—8:30—just so. After which, the rest of the party had played bridge together till 10:30. Mr. Spiller had then gone out with Mrs. Digby. Just after he left, Masters had turned off the fountain. Mr. Proudfoot had left at 10:40 and Miss Spiller and the maids had then retired. Mr. Spiller had come in again at 10:45 or 10:50, and inquired for Mr. Gooch. After this, Masters had gone across to the garage, leaving Mr. Spiller to lock up. Later on, Mr. Spiller had gone down the garden to look for Mr. Gooch. He had gone no farther than the lilac hedge, and there calling to him and getting no answer, had concluded that his guest had already come in and gone to bed. The housemaid fancied she had heard him calling Mr. Gooch. She placed this episode at about half-past eleven—certainly not later. Mr. Spiller had subsequently sat up reading in the library till 1 o'clock, when he had shut the window and gone to bed also.

The body, when found by the gardener at 6:30 A.M., was still wet with the spray from the fountain, which had also soaked the grass beneath it. Since the fountain had been turned off at 10:30, this meant that Gooch must have lain there for an appreciable period before that. In view of the large quantity of whisky that he had drunk, it seemed probable that he had had a heart-attack, or had drunkenly stumbled, and, in falling, had struck his head on the edge of the pool. All these considerations fixed the time of death at from 9:30 to 10 o'clock—an opinion with which the doctor though declining to commit himself within an hour or so, concurred, and the coroner entered a verdict of accidental death.

Only the man who has been for years the helpless victim of blackmail could fully enter into Mr. Spiller's feelings.

Compunction played no part in them—the relief was far too great. To be rid of the daily irritation of Gooch's presence, of his insatiable demands for money, of the perpetual menace of his drunken malice—these boons were well worth a murder. And, Mr. Spiller insisted to himself, as he sat musing on the rustic seat by the fountain, it had not really been murder. He determined to call on Mrs. Digby that afternoon. He could ask her to marry him now without haunting fear for the future. The scent of the lilac was intoxicating.

"Excuse me, sir," said Masters.

Mr. Spiller, withdrawing his meditative gaze from the spouting water, looked inquiringly at the manservant, who stood in a respectful attitude beside him.

"If it is convenient to you, sir, I should wish to have my bedroom changed. I should wish to sleep indoors."

"Oh?" said Mr. Spiller. "Why that, Masters?"

"I am subject to be a light sleeper, sir, ever since the war, and I find the creaking of the weather-vane very disturbing."

"It creaks, does it?"

"Yes, sir. On the night that Mr. Gooch sustained his unfortunate accident, sir, the wind changed at a quarter past eleven. The creaking woke me out of my first sleep, sir, and disturbed me very much."

A coldness gripped Mr. Spiller at the pit of the stomach. The servant's eyes, in that moment, reminded him curiously of Gooch. He had never noticed any resemblance before.

"It's a curious thing, sir, if I may say so, that, with the wind shifting as it did at 11:15, Mr. Gooch's body should have become sprayed by the fountain. Up till 11:15, the spray was falling on the other side, sir. The appearance presented was as though the body had been placed in position subsequently to 11:15, sir, and the fountain turned on again."

"Very strange," said Mr. Spiller. On the other side of the lilac hedge, he heard the voices of Betty and Ronald Proudfoot, chattering as they paced to and fro between the herbaceous borders. They seemed to be happy together. The whole house seemed happier, now that Gooch was gone.

"Very strange indeed, sir. I may add that, after hearing the inspector's observations, I took the precaution to dry your dress-trousers in the linen-cupboard in the bathroom."

"Oh, yes," said Mr. Spiller.

"I shall not, of course, mention the change of wind to the authorities, sir, and now that the inquest is over, it is not likely to occur to anybody, unless their attention should be drawn to it. I think, sir, all things being taken into consideration, you might find it worth your while to retain me permanently in your service at—shall we say double my present wage to begin with?"

Mr. Spiller opened his mouth to say, "Go to Hell," but his voice failed him. He bowed his head.

"I am much obliged to you, sir," said Masters, and withdrew on silent feet.

Mr. Spiller looked at the fountain, with its tall water wavering and bending in the wind.

"Ingenious," he muttered automatically, "and it really costs nothing to run. It uses the same water over and over again."

THE MILK-BOTTLES

Mr. Hector Puncheon, of the *Morning Star*, concluded his interview with the gentleman who had won the £5,000 Football Crossword and walked rapidly away along the street. Not so rapidly, however, that he failed to note a pair of pint bottles, filled with milk, standing at the head of some area-steps. Having a deductive turn of mind, he half-consciously summed up to himself the various possibilities suggested by this phenomenon: a new baby; a houseful of young children; a houseful of cats; a weekend absence from home.

Hector was still young and enthusiastic enough to look for a "story" in almost anything. There might be one in milk-bottles. Tragedies in lonely houses, first brought to light by accumulated milk-bottles. Queer, solitary spinsters living in shuttered gloom. The Sauchiehall Street murder, and old James Fleming taking in the milk while the servant's corpse lay in the back room. What the milkman knows. Something might be made of it: why not?

He mulled the matter over in his mind, went back to the office, and, having turned in his Crossword story, sat down to spin out a breezy half-column about milk-bottles.

The Editor of the Literary Page, who always had more

material than he could use, glanced at it, sniffed at it, endorsed it in blue pencil, and sent it down to the Home Page Editor. The latter skimmed through it carelessly and tossed it into a basket labelled "Waiting," where it remained for three months. Hector Puncheon, who had never had very much hope of it, forgot it and carried on with his usual duties.

One day in August, however, the lady who usually did the little Special Article for the Home Page was struck down by a motor-bus and taken to hospital, leaving her "copy" unwritten. The Home Page Editor, at a loss for 400 words, tossed out the contents of "Waiting" on his desk, picked out Hector Puncheon's article at random and pushed it to the Sub-editor, saying, "Cut this down and shove it in."

The Sub-editor looked rapidly through it, struck out the first and last paragraphs, removed Hector's more literary passages, ran three sentences into one, gratuitously introducing two syntactical errors in the process, re-cast the story from the third person into the first, headed it "By a Milk-Roundsman," and sent it down to the printers. In this form it appeared the next morning, and Hector Puncheon, not recognizing his mutilated offspring, muttered bitterly that somebody had pinched his idea.

Two days later, the Editor of the *Morning Star* received a letter:

DEAR SIR,
Being interested to read a piece by a milk-roundsman in your paper would wish to state that there is something queer on my round and would be pleased to give any information. I as not been to the police as they do not pay attention to a working man and do not pay for same but sir I see as you printed an article by a milk-roundsman and your great paper would be fair to one as earns his living. Sir there are five milk bottles starting last Sunday morning and a couple as not been seen since. Hoping this finds you as it leaves me,
Yours respectfully,
J. HIGGINS.

In any other month of the year, Mr. Higgins's letter would probably have received no attention, but in August all news is good news. The Editor passed the letter to the News Editor, who rang a bell and sent for a subordinate, who rang a bell for another subordinate, who consulted the files of the paper. Thus, by devious methods, the matter was referred back to Hector Puncheon, who was sent to look for Mr. Higgins and get his story at the price of a few shillings if it seemed promising.

Mr. Higgins had a milk round in and about the Clerkenwell Road. He welcomed Hector Puncheon, and gladly undertook to show him for a consideration the mysterious milk-bottles. He accordingly conducted him to an obscure street and there plunged into a dark entrance beside a greengrocer's shop. They made their way up a dark and rickety staircase, smelling of cats. At the top was a gloomy little door, with a dirty visiting-card tacked on to it which bore the name: "Hugh Wilbraham." On the threshold stood five half-pint bottles filled with milk. Hector thought he had never seen anything so utterly desolate.

There was a window on the landing, through which he could see a wide vista of roofs and chimneys, scorching in the hot sun. The window was not open and apparently not made to open. Up the narrow staircase—well, the sour and fetid air seemed to press upward intolerably, like the fumes from a gas-stove.

"Who is this man, Wilbraham?" demanded Hector, trying to control his disgust at the place.

"I dunno," said the milkman. "They been living here three months. Milk-bill paid regular every Saturday by the young woman. Shabby-looking lot, but speak decent. Come down in the world, if you ask me."

"Just the two of them?"

"Yes."

"When did you see them last?"

"Saturday morning, when she paid up. Been crying, she had. What I want to know is, have they 'opped it? Because if so, what about this week's milk?"

"I see," said Hector.

"I'm responsible, in a manner of speaking," said Mr. Higgins, "but the parties having paid regular and my orders being to deliver milk, I'd like to know what I ought to do about it—see?"

"Don't the neighbors know anything about it?" suggested Hector.

"Not a lot, they don't," said Mr. Higgins, "but there ain't no furniture gone out, and that's something. You better have a word with Mrs. Bowles."

Mrs. Bowles lived on the floor below and took in washing. She did not know much about the Wilbrahams, she explained, punctuating her remarks with thumps of the iron. Kept themselves to themselves. Thought they were too good for the likes of her, she supposed, though she had always kept herself respectable, which was more than you could say of some. They had taken the top room unfurnished, beginning of last June. She had seen their furniture go up. Nothing to write home about, it wasn't. Now Mrs. Bowles's double-bedstead, that was good, it was—real brass, and as good a feather-bed as you could wish to see. The Wilbrahams hadn't so much as a decent chair or table. Rubbishing stuff. No class—not worth a couple of pounds, the whole lot of it. She thought the young man did writing or something of that, because he had once complained that the noise made by the young Bowleses disturbed his work. If he was so high and mighty, why did he come to live here? About thirty, he might be, with a nasty, sulky, spiteful look about him. She'd heard Mrs. Wilbraham—if she *was* Mrs. Wilbraham—crying time and time again, and him going on at her ever so.

When, asked Hector, had she seen them last?

Mrs. Bowles straightened her lean back, put her iron down to the fire, and took off another, which she held close to her perspiring cheek. The close room swam in heat.

"Well now," she said, " 'er—I can't call to mind *when* I seen 'er last. Saturday dinner-time 'e came in and run upstairs and I 'ears them talking 'ammer and tongs. An' Saturday evening I meets 'im coming downstairs with a suitcase. 'Bout six o'clock that 'ud be—jest as I was coming in from taking Mrs. Jepson's washing 'ome. Funny in 'is manner 'e was, too, and in an awful 'urry. Nearly knocked me down, 'e did, and not so much as said 'Pardon.' That's the last time I seen 'im, and he ain't been back, nor 'er either, or I'd 'ave 'eard them over me ceiling. Cruel it was, the way 'e useter tramp up and down at nights when we was trying to get to sleep, and then to complain of my boys on top of it!"

"Then you don't know when Mrs. Wilbraham left?"

"I do not, but gone they is, and if you ask me, they don't intend to come back. I says to young 'Iggins, if you go on leaving the milk there, I says, that's your look-out. I dare say if their sticks was to be sold up it 'ud pay a week's milk, I says, but that's about all if you ask me."

Hector thanked Mrs. Bowles, adding a small present of money, and made his way down to the floor below. This was inhabited by an aged man who seemed to have seen better days. He shook his head at Hector's inquiry.

"No, sir," he said, "I'm afraid I couldn't tell you anything. It seems strange to me, sometimes, to think how lost a man may be in this great wilderness of London. That's what Charles Dickens called it and, by heavens, sir, he was right. If I was to die tomorrow, and my health is not what it was, who could be the wiser? I buy my own little bits of food and such, you see and pick up a bit of a living where I can with fetching taxis and such. It's hard to think I used to have a nice little shop of my own. I was well-respected, sir, where I came from, but if I was to go out now, there's nobody would miss me."

"The rent-collector, perhaps?" said Hector.

"Well, yes, to be sure. But if he came once or twice and found I was out, he wouldn't press me for a week or two. He isn't a hard man, and he knows I pay when I can. After two or three weeks he might make inquiries. Oh, yes. He'd make inquiries, to be sure. And the gas-company, when they came to empty the slot-meter, but that mightn't be for a long time."

"I suppose not," said Hector, rather struck. He had not realized the casualness of life in London.

"Then you really know nothing about these Wilbrahams?"

"Very little, sir. Not since I took it upon me to speak to the young man about the way he treated his wife."

"Oh?" said Hector.

"A young man shouldn't speak harsh to a woman," said the old man, "for she has a lot to put up with at the best of times. And men are thoughtless. I know that—oh, yes, I know that. And she was fond of him, you could see that by her face. But they were in difficulties, I think, and often when a man doesn't know which way to turn to make ends meet, he's apt to speak sharp and quick, not meaning to hurt."

"When did this happen?"

"About a month ago. Not here. In St. Pancras Churchyard—that's where they were sitting. It's a pleasant place on a summer's day, with the grass and the children playing about. 'It's a pity you ever married me, isn't it?' he said, with an ugly look on his face. It upset her, poor thing. They didn't know it was me sitting next them till I spoke to him."

"And what did he say?"

"Told me to mind my own business. And I dare say he was right, too. It's a mistake to interfere between married people, but I was sorry for her."

Hector nodded.

"You didn't see anything of them last Saturday?"

"No, sir, but then I was out all day."

The greengrocer on the ground floor knew nothing. He had occasionally sold a few vegetables to Mrs. Wilbraham, but he did not live on the premises and had no information about the movements of the couple. After a little more research, which led to nothing, Hector gave the matter up. It did not seem to him that there was much in it—however, he had expended some time and a few shillings on the business and must have something to show for it. Accordingly, he concocted a brief paragraph:

FIVE MYSTERY MILK-BOTTLES

What has become of Mr. and Mrs. Hugh Wilbraham of 14B Buttercup Road, Clerkenwell? The fact that the milk had not been taken in for five days attracted the attention of Mr. J. Higgins, a roundsman, who had read the article "Milk-Bottle Mysteries" published in our Home Page on Tuesday. Mr. Wilbraham, who is said to be a literary man, was seen to leave the house with a suitcase last Saturday; neither he nor his wife, with whom he is alleged to be on bad terms, has been seen since.

The News-Editor, who happened to want half a dozen lines to fill up the foot of a column, handed this to the Sub-editor, who dexterously boiled the first two sentences into one, altered the heading to "MYSTERY 5 MILK-BOTTLES" and sent it to press.

On Friday evening, the *Evening Wire*, which had obviously been doing a little investigation of its own, came out with an expanded version of the story, occupying half a column on the news-page.

MILK-BOTTLE MYSTERY

WILD-EYED MAN WITH SUITCASE
TAXI-DRIVER'S STORY

Six unopened milk-bottles outside the door of a room in a tenement house in Clerkenwell, present today a mystery which has several disquieting features. The room, which was taken three months ago by a man, said to be a novelist, and his wife, giving the names of Mr. and Mrs. Hugh Wilbraham, is situated on the top floor of No. 14B Buttercup Road, and has remained locked for six days, while nothing has been seen of the tenants since last Saturday night, when Wilbraham was seen by Mrs. Bowles, the resident on the floor below, leaving the house in a suspicious manner with a suitcase.

A taxi-driver named Hodges, remembers that on Saturday night about 6 o'clock his taxi was standing outside the adjacent public-house, the Star & Crown, when he was hailed by a man, carrying a suitcase, and corresponding to the description of Wilbraham. The man's eyes had a wild appearance, and he seemed to be under the influence of drink or violent excitement. He directed Hodges to drive him as fast as possible to Liverpool Street Station, and seemed urgently anxious to catch the train.

It is alleged by the other residents in the house that Mr. and Mrs. Wilbraham were frequently seen and heard quarrelling and that the man had been heard to say it was a pity they had ever got married. The woman was last seen, crying bitterly, when the milkman called on Saturday morning.

A strange and sinister feature of the case is the gradual spread of a heavy and unpleasant odor proceeding from behind the locked door. It is understood that the police have been communicated with.

The News-Editor of the *Morning Star* sent for Hector Puncheon.

"Here, this is your story, isn't it?" he said. "The *Wire* seems to have got ahead of you. Go round and get on to it."

Hector Puncheon, trudging through the sultry squalor of the August evening, felt a strong repugnance to plunging into the dark entry and up those sickly stairs. Dusty newspapers blew about his feet as he passed the greengrocer's stall. Round the entry, half a dozen loiterers were gathered.

" 'Orrible, it is," said Mrs. Bowles, "wuss than when they took up the old cat from under the boards what the gas-fitter's men 'ad nailed down. I 'ad to come out to get a breath of air."

"Why don't the police do something, that's what I'd like to know?" asked a slatternly girl with a made-up face.

" 'As to get a warrant, dear, afore they can break in. Damaging property, that's what it is, and the landlord —"

"Well, 'e ought to do something 'imself. Wot 'e ever want to let to such as them for —"

"It's easy to talk. One person's money is as good as another's."

"All very well, but you could see by that fellow's face 'e was up to no good."

"Well, wot I say is, I'm sorry for 'er."

Hector pushed his way through them and boldly tackled the climb to the top floor. The air, stewed and thickened in the dark chimney of the staircase, caught him by the throat. It grew worse as he ascended.

The smell was perceptible on the first floor, mingled with the familiar odors of cats and cabbage. On the second floor it was stronger; on the top floor it was overpowering. The six bottles of milk stood, sour and dusty, outside the locked door. There was a letter-slit, Hector noticed. Lifting it, he tried to peer through. At once the stench seemed to pour out at him, nauseating, unbearable. He retreated, feeling sick. He was not sure whether it was his own head that was buzzing. No—it was not. A couple of fat black flies had come heavily through the slit. They clung to the woodwork, and crawled with satiated slowness over the blistered paint.

"Fit to turn you up, ain't it?" said a voice behind him. A man had followed him up.

"It's ghastly," said Hector.

Suddenly the squalid place seemed to heave about him. He turned and ran hurriedly down the stairs out into the street. To his horror he found a great fly, somnolently clinging to his collar.

Hector went home. He had had enough of the place. But early the next morning he remembered his duty to his newspaper. Come what might, he must get that story. He returned to Buttercup Road.

Andrews of the *Wire* was already there. He grinned when he saw Puncheon.

"Come to be in at the death?" said he.

Hector nodded, and lit a cigarette.

"Copper's just coming along," said Andrews.

The narrow passage was packed with people. Presently

two stout official forms in blue came shouldering their way through.

" 'Ere," said the foremost, "wot's all this about? Pass along there, pass along."

"Press," said Hector and Andrews in unison.

"Oh, *all* right," said the policeman. "Now then, missus, let's get along up. We've got the warrant. Where is it? Third floor. Right you are."

The procession tramped heavily up. On the top floor stood Mr. J. Higgins, with the seventh milk-bottle in his hand.

The policemen gave a huge concerted sniff.

"Somethink in there all right," said the larger of the two. " 'Ere, missus, take them kids along out o' the way. No place for them."

He strode to the door and beat upon it, summoning that which lay behind it to open in the name of the law.

There was no answer. How could there be any answer?

"Gimme that crow-bar."

The policeman set the bar to the lock and heaved. There was a crack. He heaved again. The lock shuddered and gave. As the door swung slowly back, a huge crowd of flies rose, zooming, from something close behind it.

In a pleasant hotel coffee-room at Clacton, a young man smiled at his wife over the breakfast table.

"Better than Buttercup Road, eh, Helen?" he said.

"It's marvellous. Oh, Hugh! I think I should have gone cracked in that ghastly place. Isn't it luck? Isn't it luck your getting that cheque? Just in time."

"Yes, just in time. I was about at the last gasp, old girl. Afraid I was a bit. I was a fool to get so hysterical. My nerves were all to pieces."

"I know, dear. It doesn't matter a bit. I was a fool to get so hysterical. It was a wonderful idea just to come away and get out of it all. Do you know, when you brought the news, and I could run out and buy new clothes—oh, Hugh! it was heavenly. That was the most marvellous bit. And when I was sitting at Liverpool Street waiting for you to come, I had to keep pinching the parcels to be sure it wasn't all a dream."

"Yes, I know. I didn't know if I was on my head or my heels, either. I nearly missed the train as it was—I had just to stay and finish up that last chapter."

"I know. But you did catch it."

"I did. But—I've never told you. I clean forgot about stopping the milk, as you told me."

"Blow the milk. We needn't count pennies now."

"Hear, hear!"

The young man opened his paper. Then his face suddenly became convulsed.

"My God! Look at this!"

The girl stared at the headlines.

"Oh, *Hugh!* How *awful!* That horrible Mrs. Bowles! And that silly old Nosey-Parker from downstairs! Wild-eyed man with a suspicious appearance—good gracious, Hugh! We'll never dare to go back. But, I say, dear, what's all this about a smell?"

"Smell?"

The young man slowly flushed a deep crimson.

"Hugh!" said his wife. "You *don't* mean to say you left that haddock on the table!"

DILEMMA

I have no idea who started the imbecile discussion. I think it must have been Timpany. At any rate, it is just the futile and irritating sort of topic that Timpany *would* start at the end of a long day's fishing. By the time I had settled with the landlord about a boat for the next morning and had come back to the smoking-room, they were hard at it, and had got to the problem about the Chinaman.

You know that one. If you could get a million pounds, without any evil consequences to yourself, by merely pressing a button which would electrocute a single unknown Chinaman ten thousand miles away—would you press the button? Everybody seemed to have an opinion on the point, except the sallow-faced Stranger who was not of our party.

He was modestly hidden behind a book, and I was rather sorry for him, hemmed in as he was in a corner by Timpany and his friend Popper, who are the world's champion talkers. The Colonel said Woof! of course he'd press the button. Too many damned Chinamen in the world anyway—too many damned people altogether.

And I said most people would do a lot for a million pounds.

And the Padre said (as of course he had to) that nothing could justify taking the life of a fellow-creature. And Timpany said, Think of the good one could do with a million pounds, and old Popper said it all depended on the character of the Chinaman—he might have lived to be another Confucius—and from that the talk drifted to still sillier problems, such as, if you had the choice between rescuing a diseased tramp or the Codex Sinaiticus, which would you save?

Timpany said that it was all very well to say that no decent man would hesitate for a moment (I was the silly ass who had committed myself to this sentiment). Didn't we remember that something very like that had happened once, and the awful fuss there was about it? He meant, he said, that old affair of the Davenant-Smith manuscripts.

The Padre remembered Davenant-Smith was the man who lost his life in Bunga-Bunga, researching into the cause and treatment of sleeping sickness. He was a martyr to science, if ever there was one.

Timpany agreed and went on to describe how Davenant-Smith's papers, containing all his valuable results, were sent home to his widow. There was a whole trunkful of them, not yet sorted or classified or even read. Mrs. Davenant-Smith had got hold of a bright young medico to prepare them for publication. And that night a fire broke out in her house.

I remembered then and exclaimed, "Oh yes; a drunken butler and a paraffin lamp, wasn't it?"

Timpany nodded. It had all happened in the middle of the night—a thatch and timber house, no water, and the local fire-brigade ten miles off. To cut a long story short, the young medico had had to choose between saving the papers or the sodden old fool of a butler. He'd chucked the papers out first, and when he went back for the butler, the roof fell in and he couldn't get through to him.

I heard the Padre murmur "Terrible!" and noticed that though the Stranger in the corner pretended to turn over a page of his book, he kept his melancholy dark eyes fixed on Timpany.

"All this came out at the inquest," Timpany went on. "The medico got a pretty stiff grueling. He explained that he believed the manuscripts to be of immense value to humanity, whereas he knew no particular good of the butler.

"He was severely reprimanded by the coroner, and but for the fact that the fire had started in the butler's bedroom, he might have found himself in a very unpleasant position. As it was, the jury decided that the butler was probably dead of suffocation before the alarm was given.

"But it broke the medico, of course. Nobody would think of calling in a doctor who took realistic views about human life, and thought a few thousand sick niggers in the bush more important than a butler in the hand. What happened to the poor devil I don't know. I believe he changed his name and went abroad. Anyway, somebody else did the work on the manuscripts, which form as you probably know, the basis for our whole modern practice with regard to sleeping sickness. I suppose the Davenant-Smith treatment must have saved innumerable lives. Now, Padre, was that young medico a martyr or a murderer?"

"God knows," said the Padre. "But I think, in his place, I should have tried to rescue the butler."

"Woof!" said the Colonel. "Damned awkward. Drunken old ruffian's no loss. Too many of 'em about—no good to anybody. But all the same, damned unpleasant thing, letting a man burn to death."

"Sleeping sickness is pretty unpleasant, too," observed the Stranger. "I've seen a lot of it."

"And what is your own opinion, sir?" inquired the Padre.

"The young doctor was a fool," said the Stranger, with bitter emphasis. "He should have known that the world is run by sentimentalists. He deserved everything he got."

Old Popper turned and considered the Stranger with a slow and thoughtful eye.

"The terms of that problem were comparatively simple," he observed. "The papers were undoubtedly valuable and the butler undoubtedly worthless. Now *I* could tell you of a problem that really *was* a problem. The thing actually happened to *me*—years ago, many years ago. And even now—especially now—it gives me the jim-jams to think about it."

The Colonel grunted, and Timpany said:

"Go on, Popper; tell us the story."

"I don't know that I can," said Popper. "I've tried not to dwell upon it. I've never mentioned it from that day to this. I don't think—"

"Perhaps if you told us now," said the Padre, "it might relieve your mind."

"I rather doubt it," said Popper. "Of course, I know I can count upon your sympathy. But perhaps that's the worst part of it."

We made suitable noises, and the Stranger said, rather primly, but with a queer kind of eagerness:

"I should very much like to hear your experience."

Old Popper looked at him again. Then he rang the bell and ordered a double whisky.

"Very well," he said, when he had put it down, "I'll tell you. I won't mention names, but you may possibly remember the case. It happened when I was quite a youngster, and was working as a clerk in a solicitor's office. We were instructed for the defense of a certain man—a commercial traveller—who was accused of murdering a girl. The evidence against him looked pretty formidable, but we were convinced, from his manner, that he was innocent, and we were, naturally, extremely keen to get him off. It would be a feather in our caps, and besides—well, as I say, we believed he was an innocent man.

"The case came up before the magistrate, and things didn't look any too good for our client. The defense was an alibi, but unfortunately he could bring no evidence at all to prove it. His story was that after having a row with the girl (which he admitted) he had left her in a country lane—where she was afterwards found dead, you understand—and had driven away without noticing where he was going.

"He said he remembered going into some pub or other and

getting exceedingly drunk and then driving on and on till he came to a wood, where he got out and went to sleep for a bit. He said he thought he must have woken up again about three o'clock in the morning, when it was still dark.

"He had no idea where he was, but after going through a lot of side-roads and small villages which he couldn't put a name to, he had fetched up, round about six o'clock, in a town which we will call Workingham. He had spoken to nobody after leaving the pub earlier in the evening, and the only other bit of help he could give us was that he thought he had lost a pair of woollen gloves at some time during his wanderings.

"The police theory, of course, was that after leaving the pub, he had gone back and strangled the girl and had then driven straight through to Workingham. The murder hadn't taken place till after midnight, if one could trust the medical evidence, but there was plenty of time for him to do the job and get to Workingham by six. The case went up for trial, and we didn't feel any too happy about it, though there was something about the man that made us believe he was telling the truth.

"Well, two days after the first hearing, we got a letter from a man living in a village about twenty miles from Workingham, who said he had some information for us, and I was sent up to interview him. He turned out to be a shifty-looking person of the laboring class, and after a good deal of argument and a ten-bob note had passed between us, he more or less admitted that he got his living by poaching. His story was that on the night of the murder, he had been setting snares in a wood near his village. He said that he had visited one particular snare just after 10 o'clock and again at one in the morning. He had seen no man and no car, but on his second visit to the snare, he had found a pair of woollen gloves lying close beside it. He had taken the gloves home and said nothing about them to anybody, but after reading the report of the magistrate's inquiry, he had thought it his duty to communicate with us. He also made it pretty obvious that he expected a reward for his testimony.

"He showed me the gloves, which corresponded fairly closely to the description given by our client. Not that that proved very much, because they had been described in court and might have been purchased for the occasion. Still, there they were, and if they did belong to our client, and he had left them in a wood near Workingham before one A.M., he couldn't possibly have been doing a murder at midnight eighty miles away. It did seem as though we might be able to get them identified, either by somebody who knew our man or through the manufacturer. I took down a statement from the poacher and set off home, carrying the gloves in my handbag.

"I had no car in those early days, and had to return by rail—a nasty cross-country journey in a ramshackle local train with no corridor. It was a dark November night, with a thick fog, and everything running late.

"I don't remember the crash. We found out afterwards that the London express had somehow over-run the signals and rammed us from behind just before we cleared the points. All I knew was that something hit me with a noise like Doomsday, and that, after what seemed an endless age, I was crawling out from under a pile of wreckage, with blood running into my mouth from a bad cut on my head. I had been snoozing with my feet up on the seat, otherwise I should have been cut clean in two, for when I did get clear, I could see that the three rear coaches of the local had been telescoped. The engine of the express had turned over and set fire to the wreckage, and the place was an inferno. The dead and injured were sprawled about everywhere, and the survivors were working like navvies to extricate the unfortunate devils who were trapped in the blazing coaches. The groaning and screaming were simply ghastly. Booh!! I won't dwell on that, if you don't mind. You might touch the bell, Timpany. George, bring me another whisky. Same as before.

"As soon as I got my wits about me," continued Popper, "I remembered the gloves in my handbag. *I must get them out*, I thought. I couldn't find anyone to help me, and the flames were already licking up the side of the coach. Where the bag had got to I had no idea, but somewhere underneath all that mass of twisted iron and broken woodwork was the evidence that might save our client's life.

"I was just starting in to hunt for it, when I felt a clutch on my arm. It was a woman.

" 'My baby,' she said. 'My little boy! In there!'

"She pointed to the compartment next to mine. The fire was just beginning to take hold, and when I peered in I could see the child in the light of the flames. It was lying on the underside of the overturned coach, pinned in by some timbers which had saved it from being crushed to death, but I didn't see how we were going to shift all that stuff before the fire got to it. The woman was shaking me in a kind of frenzy. 'Be quick!' she said. 'Be quick! It's too heavy—I can't lift it. Be quick!' Well, there was only one thing to do. I had another shot at getting help, but everybody seemed to have their hands full already. I clambered through the window and clawed about in the wreckage till I could reach down and satisfy myself that the boy was still alive.

"All the time I was doing it, you know, I could smell and hear the fire crackling and crunching the bones of my own compartment—eating up my bag and my papers and the gloves and everything. Each minute spent in saving the child was a nail in my client's coffin. And—do remember this—I felt certain that the man was absolutely innocent.

"And yet, you see, it was a pretty slender chance. The gloves might not be his, and even if they were, the evidence might not save him. Or, take it the other way. Even without the gloves, the jury might believe his story.

"And there was no doubt about the baby. There it was, alive and howling. And its mother was working frantically beside me, tugging at blazing planks and cutting herself on broken window glass, and calling out to the child all the time. What could I do? Though, you know, I had serious doubts whether we shouldn't lose both the child and the evidence.

"Well, anyhow, just when I was giving up hope, two men came along to lend a hand and we managed to lift the wreckage free and get the boy out. It was touch and go. His frock was alight already.

"And by that time my own compartment was nothing but a roaring furnace. There was nothing left. Not a thing. When we hunted through the red-hot ashes in the morning, all we could find was the brass lock of my handbag.

"We did our best, of course. We got the poacher to court, but he didn't stand up very well under cross-examination. And the whole thing was so vague. You can't identify a pair of gloves from a description, and we failed absolutely to find anybody who had seen the car near the wood that night. Perhaps, after all, there never was a car.

"Rightly or wrongly, we lost the case. Of course, we might have lost it anyway. The man may even have been guilty — I hope he was. But I can see his face now, as it looked when I told my story. I can see the foreman giving his verdict, with his eyes everywhere but on the prisoner."

Popper stopped speaking, and put his hands over his face.

"Was the fellow hanged?" asked the Colonel.

"Yes," said Popper in a stifled tone, "yes, he was hanged."

"And what," inquired the Padre, "became of the baby?"

Popper lowered his hands in a hopeless gesture.

"He was hanged too. Last year. For the murder of two little girls. It was a pretty revolting case."

There was a long silence. Popper finished his drink and stood up.

"But you couldn't have foreseen that," ventured the Padre at length.

"No," said Popper, "I couldn't have foreseen it. And I know you will say that I did the right thing."

The Stranger got up in his turn and laid his hand on Popper's shoulder. "These things cannot be helped," he said. "I am the man who saved the Davenant-Smith manuscripts and I have my nightmares too."

"Ah! but you've paid your debt," said Popper quickly. "I've never had to pay, you see."

"Yes," said the other man thoughtfully, "I've paid, and

time has justified me. One does what one can. What happens afterwards is no business of ours."

But as he followed Popper out of the room, he held his head erect and moved with a new assurance.

"That is a very dreadful story," said the Padre.

"Very," said I, "and there are some rather odd points about it. Did commercial travellers dash about in motorcars when Popper was a youngster? And why didn't he take that evidence straight to the police?"

Timpany chuckled.

"Of course," he said, "Popper attended the inquest on Davenant-Smith's butler. He must have spotted that doctor bloke the minute he set eyes on him. Popper's the kindest-hearted old bluffer going, but you mustn't believe a word of those stories of his. He was in great form tonight, was old Popper."

AN ARROW O'ER THE HOUSE

The fact is, Miss Robbins," said Mr. Humphrey Podd, "that we don't go the right way about it. We are too meek, too humdrum. We write—that is, I write—a story that is a hair-raiser, a flesh-creeper, a blood-curdler, calculated to make stony-eyed gorgons howl in their haunted slumbers. And what do we do with it?"

Miss Robbins, withdrawing from the typewriter the final sheet of *The Time Will Come!* by Humphrey Podd, fastened it to the rest of the chapter with a paper clip and gazed timidly at her employer.

"We send it to a publisher," she hazarded.

"Yes," repeated Mr. Podd, bitterly, "we send it to a publisher. How? Tied up in brown paper, with a servile covering note, begging to submit it for his consideration. Does he consider it? Does he even read it? No! He keeps it in a dusty basket for six months and then sends it back with hypocritical thanks and compliments."

Miss Robbins glanced involuntarily toward a drawer, in which, as she too well knew, lay entombed the still-born corpses of *Murder Marriage*, *The Deadly Elephant*, and *The Needle of Nemesis*, battered with travel and melancholy with neglect. Tears came into her eyes, for, though Heaven had denied her brains, she was as devoted to her work as any typist can be, and cherished, moreover, a secret and passionate attachment to Mr. Podd.

"Do you think a personal call—?" she began.

"That's no good," said Mr. Podd. "The beasts are never in. Or if they are, they are always in conference with somebody of importance, ha ha! No. What we want to do is to take a leaf out of the advertiser's book—create a demand—rouse expectation. The 'Watch This Space' stunt, and all that sort of thing. We must plan a campaign."

"Oh, *yes*, Mr. Podd?"

"We must be up to date, dynamic, soul-shattering," pursued the author. He swept back the lock of fair hair which was trained to tumble into his eyes at impressive moments, and assumed the air of a Napoleon. "Whom shall we select as our objective? Not Sloop—he is too well-fed. Nothing could make that swill-fatted carcase quiver. Nor Gribble and Tape, because they are both dead and you cannot hope to stagger a bone-headed Board of Directors. Horace Pincock is vulnerable, but I would rather starve in a garret than become a Horace Pincock author." (Not that there was any chance of Mr. Podd's starving, for he had an ample allowance from his widowed mother, but the expression sounded well.) "Nor Mutters and Stalk—I've met Algernon Mutters and he reminded me of a lop-eared rabbit. John Paragon is out of the question—his own advertising is pitiable, and he wouldn't appreciate us. I think we will concentrate on Milton Ramp. For a publisher he is intelligent and go-ahead, and my friends tell me he is highly strung. Go and get me a broad pen, a bottle of scarlet ink, and some of that revolting bright green paper you buy from the sixpenny bazaar."

"Oh, *yes*, Mr. Podd," breathed Miss Robbins.

The campaign against Mr. Milton Ramp opened that day with an emerald missive marked "Private and Confidential." Inside the paper bore only the words: THE TIME WILL COME! executed in scarlet letters an inch high. Miss Robbins posted this at the West Central Post Office.

"They must all be posted from different places," said Mr. Podd, "for fear of discovery."

The second message (posted in Shaftesbury Avenue) had no wording; it consisted merely of an immense scarlet arrow with a venomous-looking barb. The third (posted in Fleet Street) showed the arrow again, together with the mysterious caption: "Time has an arrow—see Eddington—its mark is ruin and desolation." The fourth drove home this ambiguous remark with a quotation from Mr. Podd's latest work: "Ruin may seem far distant, but—THE TIME WILL COME!" At this point the weekend intervened and Mr. Podd rested on his oars. He spent Sunday morning in picking out choice bits from his novel. The story lent itself to this, being concerned with the activities of an indignant gentleman wrongfully condemned to penal servitude by the machinations of a company promoter, and devoting his remaining years to a long-drawn-out series of threats and revenges. On Sunday night, Mr. Podd posted the next letter with his own hand. It was an excerpt from Chapter IV, where the hero, in a great scene, defies his oppressor, and ran:

Guilty as you are, you cannot escape forever.
Truth shall prevail. THE TIME WILL COME!

On Monday he was assailed by the thought that Mr. Ramp might take the whole thing as a joke. This worried him. He made researches into the life-history of a more celebrated author, and wrote:

You laugh now—but THE TIME WILL COME
when you *will* hear me!—see Disraeli.

This pleased him until the moment when he found Miss Robbins throwing a letter into the wastepaper basket.

"Only an advertising circular, Mr. Podd," explained Miss Robbins.

"Woman!" cried Mr. Podd, "you alarm me! How if the hippopotamus-skinned Ramp has protected himself with a bulwark of women like you? Perhaps he has never even seen our well-thought-out nerve-shatterers! Damnable thought. But stay! Did not that idea also occur to the injured Rupert Pentecost?"

"Oh, yes, Mr. Podd. In Chapter XV. I'll look it up for you."

"A quotation to suit every situation," said Mr. Podd. "Ah! thank you, Miss Robbins. Yes. 'Remember the woman whose life you laid waste! If you persist in your obduracy, the warnings will go to your private address.' That will do nicely. Pass me the red ink. Post this in Hampstead on your way home and find out where the unspeakable Ramp has his detested lair."

The task was not a hard one, for Mr. Ramp's lair was quite openly entered in the telephone directory, and the next letter was posted (from a pillar-box in Piccadilly) to that address:

Nemesis sits on the ruined hearth. THE TIME WILL COME!

This was embellished by a clock-face, in which arrow-shaped hands pointed to half-past eleven.

"We will move the time five minutes on every day," said Mr. Podd. "In another week's time the fellow ought to be twittering. We'll show him what advertising means. Talking about its paying to advertise, oughtn't we to make some suggestion about advance royalties? Five hundred would be mild for a book of this quality, but these fellows are all hard-fisted misers. Let us say £250 to start with."

"There's nothing about that in the book," said Miss Robbins.

"No, not in the book," agreed Mr. Podd, "because Jeremy Vanbrugh is supposed to be a sympathetic character—I didn't want to turn him into a blackmailer. The public can get fond of a mere murderer and doesn't mind if the detective lets him off at the end, but a blackmailing murderer *must* be hanged. It's one of the rules."

"But," said Miss Robbins, "mightn't Mr. Ramp think we were blackmailers if we asked for money?"

"That's different," replied Mr. Podd, rather irritably. "We are only asking for our due reward. He'll think so when he sees the book. Let's see: 'A first payment of £250'—no, hang it! that sounds like hire-purchase. Wait a minute. 'I only ask for £250—now—but THE TIME WILL COME when you will pay me more'—no—'pay up in full'—that's crisper. We'll push this round to both addresses."

He wrote the letters and dictated a chapter of a new book. "It will be wanted quickly when the first one gets going," he observed. "We shall hardly be able to turn them out fast enough. It will be a great strain, no doubt."

"Oh, but you have so many wonderful ideas, Mr. Podd. And I don't mind working extra."

"Thank you, Miss Robbins," said Mr. Podd, condescendingly. "You are a good girl. I don't know what I should do without you." He tossed back the Napoleon lock. "Have you got your notebook? Take down this. *The Corpse in the Sewer.* Chapter I. The Smell in the Scullery. 'Anne,' said Mrs. Fletcher to the cook, 'have you been throwing cabbage-water down the sink?' 'No, ma'am,' replied the girl, pertly, 'I should hope I know better than that—' That gives the right domestic touch for the opening, I think."

"Oh, *yes,* Mr. Podd."

Mr. Podd was lunching with a literary friend named Gamble. He did not very much like Gamble, who was one of those people who are quite spoilt by a trifling success. Gamble's novel *Waste of Shame* had, for some reason, achieved a sort of fluky popularity, and the incense had gone to his head. He was frequently seen at publishers' parties, had made a witty speech before Royalty at a literary dinner, and now made a foolish pretence of possessing inside knowledge of everyone in the publishing world. One could not afford not to know Gamble, but he was very trying to his friends. Humphrey Podd looked forward to the day when he would be able to patronize Gamble in his turn.

"Look!" said Gamble, "there's Ramp just come in. That

fellow's cracking up. Got the willies. You can see it in his face."

Mr. Podd gazed at the publisher—a thin, dark, fretted face and a pair of nervous hands that picked unceasingly at a roll of bread.

"Why?" asked Mr. Podd. "He's all right, isn't he? His stuff sells, doesn't it?"

"Oh, there's nothing wrong with the *business*," said Gamble. "You're all right, there, if you're thinking of placing anything with him. No—it's something quite different. Don't let this go any further, but I shouldn't be surprised if there was an explosion in that quarter before long."

"Explosion?" repeated Mr. Podd.

"Well, yes—but I oughtn't to say anything. I just happen to know, that's all. One gets to hear these things somehow."

Mr. Podd was annoyed. He would have liked to hear more, but he was determined not to encourage Gamble.

"Oh, well," he said, "as long as the firm's all right, that's the main thing. Chap's private life is none of my business."

"Private—ah! there you are," said Gamble, darkly. "From what I hear, it won't stay private very long. If some of the letters come into court—whew!"

"Letters?" asked Mr. Podd, suddenly interested.

"Hell!" said Gamble. "I oughtn't to have said anything about that. It was told me in confidence. Forget it, will you, old boy?"

"Oh, certainly," said Humphrey Podd, annoyed with himself and with Gamble.

"He's beginning to sit up and take notice," announced Mr. Podd to Miss Robbins. And he repeated Mr. Gamble's conversation.

"Oh, Mr. *Podd!*" exclaimed Miss Robbins. She fiddled nervously with her typewriter ribbon. "Mr. Podd!" she burst out, uncontrollably, "you don't suppose he—I mean, you never know, do you? And he might be angry."

"He'll forget it, once he sees the book," said Mr. Podd.

"Yes, but—just imagine! I mean, he might have really done something. Perhaps he's getting frightened—I mean—you'll think I'm awfully silly."

"Not at all, Miss Robbins," said Humphrey Podd.

"Well, I mean—suppose there's a dark secret in his past life—"

"That would be an idea," cried Mr. Podd, excitedly. "Wait a minute—wait a minute! Miss Robbins, you've given me the plot for a new book. Here! take this down. Title: *A Bow at a Venture*. No, dash it! I've an idea that's been used before. I've got it: *An Arrow o'er the House*. Quotation from *Hamlet:* 'That I have shot my arrow o'er the house and hurt my brother.' Plot begins. Somebody—call him Jones—writes threatening letters to—say, Robinson. Jones means it for a joke, but Robinson is frightened to death because, unknown to Jones, he really has—call it, murdered somebody. Make it a woman—female victims always go down well. Robinson commits suicide and Jones is prosecuted for blackmail and murder. I'm not sure if frightening a man to death would be brought in murder, but I expect it would. Blackmail is a felony, and if you accidentally kill somebody while you're engaged in felony, the killing is murder, so it might come in that way. I say, this idea of mine is going to be good. Wash out *The Corpse in the Sewer*—I never thought a lot of that. We'll get going straight away on this one. Jones thinks he has covered his tracks, but the police—no, not the police—they're baffled, of course. The detective. Let's see; I think we'd better use Major Hawke again for this one. He's my best detective, and if readers get keen on him in *The Time Will Come* they'll want to hear about him again—Hawke gets on the scene of the letters. It's difficult, because of course they've all been posted in different places, but—"

Miss Robbins, her pencil staggering over the paper as she struggled to follow Humphrey Podd's disjointed speech, gave a little gasp.

"Hawke traces the paper, of course—where purchased, and so on. And the ink. Oh, yes—and we can have a thumbprint on one of the envelopes. Not Jones's—his *fiancée's* I think, who has posted the letters for him. She—yes, she's a good character, but hopelessly under the influence of Jones. We'll think that out. Better marry her off to somebody nicer in the end. Not Major Hawke—somebody else. We'll invent a decent chap for her. There'll be a good scene when she is frantically burning the evidence while the police hammer at the door. We must make her overlook something of course, or Jones would never get detected—never mind, I can think that out later. Court scene—that'll be good—"

"Oh, Mr. Podd! But does poor Jones get hanged? I mean, it seems very hard lines on him, when he only meant it for a joke."

"That's where the irony comes in," said Mr. Podd, ruthlessly. "Still, I see what you mean. The public will want him saved. All right—we'll stack that. We'll make him a bad character—one of those men who trample over women's hearts and laugh at their sufferings. He gets away with all his real crimes and then—here's your irony—does himself in over this one harmless joke on a man he quite likes. Make a note, 'Jones laughs once too often.' Must get a better name than Jones. Lester is a good name. Everybody calls him 'Laughing Lester.' Fair, curly hair—put that down—but his eyes are set a little too close together. I say, this is shaping splendidly."

"And about the letter to Mr. Ramp," suggested Miss Robbins, with some hesitation, when the main lines of *An Arrow o'er the House* had been successfully laid down. "Perhaps you'd rather I didn't post it?"

"Not post it?" said Mr. Podd, amazed. "Why, it's a beauty. 'THE TIME WILL COME—and it is later than you think.' Post it, of course. Ramp's got to be roused."

Miss Robbins obediently posted the letter—with gloves on.

It was not till the arrow-headed hands on Mr. Podd's clock-face had reached 11:45, and the message had taken the form, "To-morrow, and to-morrow, and to-morrow," that it occurred to him to test the victim's reaction personally. The idea came to him at 11:45 precisely, in the middle of Piccadilly Circus. With a hoarse chuckle, which caused a passing messenger-boy to turn round and stare at him in amazement, he plunged headlong down the subway and into a public call-box in the rotunda. Here he obtained the number of Mr. Ramp's office.

The female voice that answered said that Mr. Ramp was engaged, and inquired the name of the caller. Mr. Podd was prepared for this, and said that the matter was strictly private and very urgent. Further, that he would not feel justified in giving his name to anybody but Mr. Ramp. The girl seemed less surprised and less obdurate than Mr. Podd might have expected. She put him through. A sharp, worried voice said: "Yes? yes? yes? Who's that?"

Mr. Podd lowered his naturally rather high tones to an impressive croak.

"THE TIME WILL COME," he said. There was a pause.

"*What* did you say?" demanded the sharp voice, irritably.

"THE TIME WILL COME," repeated Mr. Podd. Then, prompted by a sudden inspiration, he added: "*Shall we send the proofs to the Public Prosecutor?*"

There was another pause. Then the voice said: "I don't know what you are talking about. Who is it speaking, please?"

Mr. Podd laughed fiendishly, and rang off.

"And why not?" said Mr. Podd to Miss Robbins. "People are always sending advance proofs to Prime Ministers and literary critics. The Public Prosecutor's opinion ought to be as good as anybody's. Make a note of it."

Two days passed. The daily missive now bore only the ominous word: "TO-MORROW." Mr. Podd dictated three chapters of *An Arrow o'er the House* right off the reel and went out to tea with a friend, leaving Miss Robbins to pack up the top copy of *The Time Will Come* and dispatch it, per post, to Mr. Milton Ramp.

It was a raw and foggy day. Cold, too—Miss Robbins

stoked up the stove in Humphrey Podd's studio, for her fingers were numb with note-taking. As she stepped out into the Square, with the manuscript under her arm, she shivered, and pulled her fur more closely about her neck.

On her way to the post-office she had to pass the newsvendor at the corner of the Square. The scarlet lettering on the placards he held made a splash of brightness in the gloom and caught Miss Robbins's eye. With a sudden leap of the heart she read the words: LONDON PUBLISHER SHOT.

The manuscript slipped from her grasp. She picked it up, fumbled hurriedly in her bag for a penny, and bought a copy of the *Evening Banner*. She opened it, standing by the Square railings. A heavy splash of soot-laden water dripped from an overhanging tree upon the crown of her hat. At first she could not find what she was looking for. Eventually she discovered a few smudged lines in the Stop Press column.

> Mr. Milton Ramp, the well-known publisher, was found shot dead in his office to-day when his secretary returned from lunch. A discharged revolver lay on the floor beside him. Mr. Ramp is said to have been worried of late by domestic troubles, and by the receipt of anonymous letters. The police are making investigations.

The manuscript under Miss Robbins's arm seemed to have grown to colossal size. She looked up, and caught the eye of the newsvendor. It was an unnaturally bright eye, like a hawk's. It made her think of the chapter in *Murder Marriage* where Major Hawke had disguised himself as a newsvendor in order to watch a suspected house. She hurried back to the studio. As she bolted up the front steps, she glanced nervously back. Through the fog, she made out a dim and bulky shape advancing along the other side of the Square. It wore a helmet and a water-proof cape.

Humphrey Podd's studio flat was on the top floor. Miss Robbins took the three flights at a run, dashed to cover, and locked the door after her. Peeping out from behind the window-curtain, she saw the policeman speaking to the news-vendor.

"Thank goodness," thought Miss Robbins, "I hadn't posted the manuscript." She tore off the brown paper and gaspingly extracted the covering letter that bore Humphrey Podd's name and address. The top sheet of the manuscript followed it into the fire. Then she sat trembling. But not for long. There was the carbon copy. There were her shorthand notes. There was the story itself, which bore the unmistakable marks of Humphrey Podd's authorship. With a sick presentiment of disaster, Miss Robbins remembered that Major Hawke—that inspired detective—figured, not only in *The Time Will Come*, but also in *Murder Marriage*, which had been submitted to Mr. Milton Ramp only three months ago. Mr. Podd had said that publishers never read his manuscripts—but could one count on that? Some secretary, some hired reader, might have glanced at it, and nobody who had ever encountered Major Hawke could possibly forget him and his eccentricities.

Miss Robbins looked out of the window again. The policeman was advancing with his stately tread along the near side of the Square, and glancing up at the windows. He approached the house. He stopped. With a terrified squeak, Miss Robbins rushed to the roaring stove and crammed the manuscript in—top copy—carbon—notebook—pulling the chapters hurriedly apart to make the mass of paper burn faster. What else was there? The plotbook—that must go too. Her hand shook as she wrenched the pages out. And—oh, she had nearly forgotten the most damning evidence of all—the green paper. Mr. Podd had said that detectives could always trace the purchase of paper. She fed it desperately to the leaping flame, flinging the pen and the bottle of red ink after it for good measure, and piling fresh coal and coke on top of it.

She was still bending, hot and flushed, over the stove, when she heard footsteps coming up the stair. She dashed to the typewriter and began to pound nervously at the keys. A hand shook the door-handle.

"Hell!" said the voice of Humphrey Podd. Then came the noise of a key entering the lock. "Damn the girl—she's still out."

Mr. Podd walked in.

"You're here!" he said, astonished. "What the devil are you doing with the door locked? Look here, here's a dashed nuisance! That ass, Ramp, has gone and blown his brains out, if he ever had any, and all our advance publicity has been wasted. We'll have to start all over again."

"Oh, Mr. Podd!" cried Miss Robbins. "I'm so thankful you're here. When I saw the policeman I was afraid he'd catch you, and I didn't know where you were, to warn you—"

"No wonder Ramp looked white about the gills," pursued Mr. Podd, unheeding. "His wife's been carrying on with some man or other. Ramp got wind of it through some anonymous letters from a discharged servant, and there was a frightful bust-up last night and his wife's bolted. And now the fool's gone and shot himself. I got hold of that infuriating chap, Gamble, and wrung the whole thing out of him. He might have told me earlier, blast him! It's no good sending anything there now. I hope you didn't post that manuscript. If you did, we must get it back and try it on Sloop—What on earth's the matter with you, Miss Robbins?"

"Oh, Mr. Podd!" cried Miss Robbins. "We can't—we—I thought—oh, Mr. Podd, I've burnt the manuscripts!"

Police-constable E 999 withdrew his wistful gaze from the lighted area. Somebody in the basement was stewing tripe, and the smell came up comfortingly. He hoped there would be something equally good waiting for him at home. As he ambled along the pavement, he heard a crash and tinkle of glass, and a typewriter came hurtling out of an upper window, just missing his helmet.

"Hullo!" said P.C. E 999.

A loud shriek followed. Then a shrill female voice cried, "Help! help! murder!"

"Gor lumme!" said the constable. "They *would* go and start something just when I was getting away to my supper."

He climbed the steps and knocked thunderously upon the door.

SCRAWNS

The gate, on whose peeled and faded surface the name SCRAWNS was just legible in the dim light, fell to with a clap that shook the rotten gatepost and scattered a shower of drops from the drenched laurels. Susan Tabbit set down the heavy suitcase which had made her arm ache, and peered through the drizzle towards the little house.

It was a curious, lopsided, hunch-shouldered building, seeming not so much to preside over its patch of wintry garden as to be eavesdropping behind its own hedges. Against a streak of watery light in the west, its chimney-stacks—one at either end—suggested pricked ears, intensely aware; the more so, that its face was blind.

Susan shivered a little, and thought regretfully of the cheerful bus that she had left at the bottom of the hill. The conductor had seemed just as much surprised as the station porter had been when she mentioned her destination. He had opened his mouth as though about to make some comment, but had thought better of it. She wished she had had the courage to ask him what sort of place she was coming to. Scrawns. It was a queer name; she had thought so when she had first seen it on Mrs. Wispell's notepaper. Susan Tabbit, care of Mrs. Wispell, Scrawns, Roman Way, Dedcaster.

Her married sister had pursed up her lips when Susan gave her the address, reading it aloud with an air of disapproval. "What's she like, this Mrs. Wispell of Scrawns?" Susan had to confess that she did not know; she had taken the situation without an interview.

Now the house faced her, aloof, indifferent, but on the watch. No house should look so. She had been a fool to come; but it had been so evident that her sister was anxious to get her out of the house. There was no room for her, with all her brother-in-law's family coming. And she was short of money. She had thought it might be pleasant at Scrawns. Houseparlourmaid, to work with married couple; that had sounded all right. Three in family; that was all right, too. In her last job there had been only herself and eight in family; she had looked forward to a light place and a lively kitchen.

"And what am I thinking about?" said Susan, picking up the suitcase. "The family'll be out, as like as not, at a party or something of that. There'll be a light in the kitchen all right, I'll be bound."

She plodded over the sodden gravel, between two squares of lawn, flanked by empty beds and backed by a huddle of shrubbery; then turned along a path to the right, following the front of the house with its blank unwelcoming windows. The sidewalk was as dark as the front. She made out the outline of a French window, opening upon the path and, to her right, a wide herbaceous border, where tin labels, attached to canes, flapped forlornly. Beyond this there seemed to be a lawn, but the tall trees which surrounded it on all three sides drowned it in blackness and made its shape and extent a mystery. The path led on, through a half-open door that creaked as she pushed it back, and she found herself in a small, paved courtyard, across which the light streamed in a narrow beam from a small, lighted window.

She tried to look in at this window, but a net curtain veiled its lower half. She could only see the ceiling, low, with black rafters, from one of which there hung a paraffin lamp. Passing the window she found a door and knocked.

With the first fall of the old-fashioned iron knocker, a dog began to bark, loudly, incessantly, and furiously. She waited, her heart hammering, but nobody came. After a little, she summoned up resolution to knock afresh. This time she thought she could distinguish, through the clamor, a movement within. The barking ceased, she heard a key turn and bolts withdrawn, and the door opened.

The light within came from a doorway on the left, and outlined against it, she was only aware of an enormous bulk and a dim triangle of whiteness, blocking her entrance to the house.

"Who is it?"

The voice was unlike any she had ever heard; curiously harsh and husky and sexless, like the voice of something strangled.

"My name's Tabbit—Susan Tabbit."

"Oh, you're the new girl!" There was a pause, as though the speaker were trying, in the uncertain dusk, to sum her up and reckon out her possibilities.

"Come in."

The looming bulk retreated, and Susan again lifted her suitcase and carried it inside.

"Mrs. Wispell got my letter, saying I was coming?"

"Yes; she got it. But one can't be too careful. It's a lonely place. You can leave your bag for Jarrock. This way."

Susan stepped into the kitchen. It was a low room, not very large but appearing larger than it was because of the shadows thrown into the far corners by the wide shade of the hanging lamp. There was a good fire, which Susan was glad to see, and over the mantelpiece an array of polished copper pans winked reassuringly. Behind her she again heard the jarring of shot bolts and turned key. Then her jailer—why did that word leap uncalled into her mind?—came back and stepped for the first time into the light.

As before, her first overwhelming impression was of enormous height and size. The flat, white, wide face, the billowing breasts, the enormous girth of white-aproned haunch seemed to fill the room and swim above her. Then she forgot everything else in the shock of realizing that the huge woman was cross-eyed.

It was no mere cast; not even an ordinary squint. The left eye was swivelled so horribly far inward that half the iris was invisible, giving to that side of the face a look of blind and cunning malignity. The other eye was bright and dark and small, and fixed itself acutely on Susan's face.

"I'm Mrs. Jarrock," said the woman in her odd, hoarse voice.

It was incredible to Susan that any man who was not blind and deaf should have married a woman so hideously disfigured and with such a raven croak. She said: "How do you do?" and extended a reluctant hand, which Mrs. Jarrock's vast palm engulfed in a grasp unexpectedly hard and masculine.

"You'll like a cup of tea before you change," said Mrs. Jarrock. "You can wait at table, I suppose?"

"Oh, yes, I'm used to that."

"Then you'd better begin tonight. Jarrock's got his hands full with Mr. Alistair. It's one of his bad days. We was both upstairs, that's why you had to wait." She again glanced sharply at the girl, and the swivel eye rolled unpleasantly and uncontrollably in its socket. She turned and bent to lift the kettle from the range, and Susan could not rid herself of the notion that the left eye was still squinting at her from its ambush behind the cook's flat nose.

"Is it a good place?" asked Susan.

"It's all right," said Mrs. Jarrock, "for them as isn't nervous. *She* don't trouble herself much, but that's only to be expected, as things are, and *he's* quiet enough if you don't cross him. Mr. Alistair won't trouble you, that's Jarrock's job. There's your tea. Help yourself to milk and sugar. I wonder if Jarrock—"

She broke off short; set down the teapot and stood with her large head cocked sideways, as though listening to something going on above. Then she moved hastily across the kitchen, with a lightness of step surprising in so unwieldy a woman, and disappeared into the darkness of the passage.

Susan, listening anxiously, thought she could hear a sound like moaning and a movement of feet across the raftered ceiling. In a few minutes, Mrs. Jarrock came back, took the kettle from the fire, and handed it out to some unseen person in the passage. A prolonged whispering followed, after which Mrs. Jarrock again returned and, without offering any comment, began to make buttered toast.

Susan ate without relish. She had been hungry when she left the bus, but the atmosphere of the house disconcerted her. She had just refused a second slice of toast when she became aware that a man had entered the kitchen.

He was a tall man and powerfully built, but he stood in the doorway as though suspicious or intimidated; she realized that he had probably been standing there for some time before she observed him. Mrs. Jarrock, seeing Susan's head turn and remain arrested, looked round also.

"Oh, there you are, Jarrock. Come and take your tea."

The man moved then, skirting the wall with a curious, crablike movement, and so coming by reluctant degrees to the opposite side of the fire, where he stood, his head averted, shooting a glance at Susan from the corner of his eye.

"This here's Susan," said Mrs. Jarrock. "It's to be hoped she'll settle down and be comfortable with us. I'll be glad to have her to help with the work, as *you* know, with one thing and another."

"We'll do our betht to make things eathy for her," said the man. He lisped oddly and, though he held out his hand, he still kept his head half averted, like a cat that refuses to take notice. He retreated into an armchair, drawn rather far back from the hearth, and sat gazing into the fire. The dog which had barked when Susan knocked had followed him into the room, and now came over and sniffed at the girl's legs, uttering a menacing growl.

"Be quiet, Crippen," said the man. "Friends."

The dog, a large brindled bull-terrier, was apparently not reassured. He continued to growl, till Jarrock, hauling him back by the collar, gave him a smart cuff on the head and

ordered him under the table, where he went, sullenly. In bending to beat the dog, Jarrock for the first time turned his full
face upon Susan, and she saw, with horror, that the left side of
it, from the cheekbone downwards, could scarcely be called a
face, for it was seamed and puckered by a horrible scar, which
had dragged the mouth upwards into the appearance of a
ghastly grin, while the lefthand side of the jaw seemed shapeless and boneless, a mere bag of wrinkled flesh.

"Is everybody in this house maimed and abnormal?" she
thought, desperately. As though in answer to her thoughts,
Mrs. Jarrock spoke to her husband.

"Has he settled down now?"

"Oh, he's quiet enough," replied the man, lisping through
his shattered teeth. "He'll do all right." He retired again to his
corner and began sucking in his buttered toast, making awkward sounds.

"If you've finished your tea," said Mrs. Jarrock, "I'd better show you your room. Have you taken Susan's bag up, Jarrock?"

The man nodded without speaking, and Susan, in some
trepidation, followed the huge woman, who had lit a candle in
a brass candlestick.

"You'll find the stairs awkward at first," said the hoarse
voice, "and you'll have to mind your head in these passages.
Built in the year one, this place was, and by a crazy builder at
that, if you ask me."

She glided noiselessly along a narrow corridor and out
into a square flagged hall, where a small oil-lamp, heavily
shaded, seemed to make darkness deeper; then mounted a
flight of black oak stairs with twisted banisters of polished oak
and shining oak treads, in which the candlelight was reflected
on wavering yellow pools.

"There's only the one staircase," said Mrs. Jarrock.
"Unhandy, I calls it, but you'll have to do your best. You'll
have to wait till he's shut himself up of a morning before you
bring down the slops; he don't like to see pails about. This
here's their bedroom and that's the spare and this is Mr. Alis-

tair's room. Jarrock sleeps in with him, of course, in case —"
She stopped at the door, listening; then led the way up a narrow attic staircase.

"You're in here. It's small, but you're by yourself. And I'm
next door to you."

The candle threw their shadows, gigantically distorted,
upon the sloping ceiling, and Susan thought, fantastically: "If I
stay here, I shall grow the wrong shape, too."

"And the big attic's the master's place. You don't have
nothing to do with that. Much as your place or ours is worth
to poke your nose round the door. He keeps it locked, anyway." The cook laughed, a hoarse, throaty chuckle. "Queer
things he keeps in there, I must say. I've seen 'em —when he
brings 'em downstairs, that is. He's a funny one, is Mr. Wispell. Well, you'd better get changed into your black, then I'll
take you to the mistress."

Susan dressed hurriedly before the little, heart-shaped
mirror with its old, greenish glass that seemed to absorb more
of the candlelight than it reflected. She pulled aside the check
window-curtain and looked out. It was almost night, but she
contrived to make out that the attic looked over the garden at
the side of the house. Beneath her lay the herbaceous border,
and beyond that, the tall trees stood up like a wall. The room
itself was comfortably furnished, though, as Mrs. Jarrock had
said, extremely small and twisted into a curious shape by the
slanting flue of the great chimney, which ran up on the left-
hand side and made a great elbow beside the bedhead. There
was a minute fireplace cut into the chimney, but it had an
unused look. Probably, thought Susan, it would smoke.

At the head of the stairs she hesitated, candle in hand. She
was divided between a dread of solitude and a dread of what
she was to meet below. She tiptoed down the attic stair and
emerged upon the landing. As she did so, she saw the back of
Jarrock flitting down the lower flight, and noticed that he had
left the door of "Mr. Alistair's" room open behind him. Urged
by a curiosity powerful enough to overcome her uneasiness,
she crept to the door and peeped in.

Facing her was an old-fashioned tester bed with dull green hangings; a shaded reading-lamp burned beside it on a small table. The man on the bed lay flat on his back with closed eyes; his face was yellow and transparent as wax, with pinched, sharp nostrils; one hand, thin as a claw, lay passive upon the green counterpane; the other was hidden in the shadows of the curtains. Certainly, if Jarrock had been speaking of Mr. Alistair, he was right; this man was quiet enough now.

"Poor gentleman," whispered Susan, "he's passed away." And while the words were still on her lips a great bellow of laughter burst forth from somewhere on the floor below. It was monstrous, gargantuan, fantastic; it was an outrage upon the silent house. Susan started back, and the snuffer, jerking from the candlestick, leaped into the air and went ringing and rolling down the oak staircase to land with a brazen clang on the flags below.

Somewhere a door burst open and a loud voice, with a hint of that preposterous mirth still lurking in its depths, bawled out:

"What's that? What the devil's that? Jarrock! Did you make that filthy noise?"

"I beg your pardon, sir," said Susan, advancing in some alarm to the stairhead. "It was my fault, sir. I shook the candlestick and the snuffer fell down. I am very sorry, sir."

"You?" said the man. "Who the devil are you? Come down and let's have a look at you. Oh!" as Susan's black dress and muslin apron came into his view at the turn of the stair, "the new housemaid, hey! That's a pretty way to announce yourself. A damned good beginning! Don't you do it again, that's all. I won't have noise, d'you understand? All the noise in this house is made by me. That's my prerogative, if you know what the word means. Hey? Do you understand?"

"Yes, sir. I won't let it happen again, sir."

"That's right. And look here. If you've made a dent in those boards, d'you know what I'll do? Hey? I'll have the insides out of you, d'you hear?" He jerked back his big, bearded head, and his great guffaw seemed to shake the old house like a gust of wind. "Come on, girl, I won't eat you this time. Let's see your face. Your legs are all right, anyway. I won't have a housemaid with thick legs. Come in here and be vetted. Sidonia, here's the new girl, chucking the furniture all over the place the minute she's in the house. Did you hear it? Did you ever hear anything like it? Hey? Ha, ha!"

He pushed Susan in front of him into a sitting-room furnished in deep orange and rich blues and greens like a peacock's tail, and with white walls that caught and flung back the yellow lamplight. The windows were closely shuttered and barred.

On a couch drawn up near the fire a girl was lying. She had a little, white, heart-shaped face, framed and almost drowned in a mass of heavy red hair, and on her long fingers were several old and heavy rings. At her husband's boisterous entry she rose rather awkwardly and uncertainly.

"Walter, dear, don't shout so. My head aches, and you'll frighten the poor girl. So you're Susan. How are you? I hope you had a good journey. Are Mr. and Mrs. Jarrock looking after you?"

"Yes, thank you, madam."

"Oh! then that's all right." She looked a little helplessly at her husband, and then back to Susan. "I hope you'll be a good girl, Susan."

"I shall try to give satisfaction, madam."

"Yes, yes, I'm sure you will." She laughed, on a high, silver note like a bird's call. "Mrs. Jarrock will put you in the way of things. I hope you'll be happy and stay with us." Her pretty, aimless laughter tinkled out again.

"I hope Susan won't disappear like the last one," said Mr. Wispell. Susan caught a quick glance darted at him by his wife, but before she could decide whether it was one of fear or of warning, they were interrupted. A bell pealed sharply with a jangling of wires, and in the silence that followed the two Wispells stared uneasily at each other.

"What the devil's that?" said Mr. Wispell. "I only hope to heaven —"

Jarrock came in. He held a telegram in his hand. Wispell snatched it from him and tore it open. With an exclamation of distaste and alarm he handed it to his wife, who uttered a sharp cry.

"Walter, we can't! She mustn't. Can't we stop her?"

"Don't be a fool, Sidonia. How can we stop her?"

"Yes, Walter. But don't you understand? She'll expect to find Helen here."

"Oh, Lord!" said Mr. Wispell.

Susan went early to bed. Dinner had been a strained and melancholy meal. Mrs. Wispell talked embarrassed nothings at intervals; Mr. Wispell seemed sunk in a savage gloom, from which he only roused himself to bark at Susan for more potatoes or another slice of bread. Nor were things much better in the kitchen, for it seemed that a visitor was expected.

"Motoring down from York," muttered Mrs. Jarrock. "Goodness knows when they'll get here. But that's her all over. No consideration, and never had. I'm sorry for the mistress, that's all."

Jarrock's distorted mouth twisted into a still more ghastly semblance of a grin.

"Rich folks must have their way," he said. "Four years ago it was the same thing. A minute's notice and woe betide if everything's not right. But we'll be ready for her, oh! we'll be ready for her, you'll see." He chuckled gently to himself.

Mrs. Jarrock gave a curious, sly smile. "You'll have to help me with spare room, Susan," she said.

Later, coming down into the scullery to fill a hot-water bottle, Susan found the Jarrocks in close confabulation beside the sink.

"And see you make no noise about it," the cook was saying. "These girls have long tongues, and I wouldn't trust—"

She turned and saw Susan.

"If you've finished," she said, taking the bottle from her, "you'd best be off to bed. You've had a long journey."

The words were softly spoken, but they had an undertone

of command. Susan took up her candlestick from the kitchen. As she passed the scullery on her way upstairs, she heard the Jarrocks whispering together and noticed, just inside the back door, two spades standing, with an empty sack beside them. They had not been there before, and she wondered idly what Jarrock could be wanting with them.

She fell asleep quickly, for she was tired; but an hour or two later she woke with a start and a feeling that people were talking in the room. The rain had ceased, for through the window she could see a star shining, and the attic was lit by the diffused greyness of moonlight. Nobody was there, but the voices were no dream. She could hear their low rumble, close beside her head. She sat up and lit her candle; then slipped out of bed and crept across to the door.

The landing was empty; from the room next her own she could hear the deep and regular snoring of the cook. She came back and stood for a moment, puzzled. In the middle of the room she could hear nothing, but as she returned to the bed, she heard the voices again, smothered, as though the speakers were at the bottom of a well. Stooping, she put her ear to the empty fireplace. At once the voices became more distinct, and she realized that the great chimney was acting as a speaking-tube from the room below. Mr. Wispell was talking. ". . . better be getting on with it . . . here at any time . . ."

"The ground's soft enough." That was Jarrock speaking. She lost a few words, and then:

". . . bury her four feet deep, because of the rose-trees."

There came a silence. Then came the muffled echo of Mr. Wispell's great laugh; it rumbled with a goblin sound in the hollow chimney.

Susan crouched by the fireplace, feeling herself grow rigid with cold. The voices dropped to a subdued murmur. Then she heard a door shut and there was complete silence. She stretched her cramped limbs and stood a moment listening. Then, with fumbling haste she began to drag on her clothes. She must get out of this horrible house.

Suddenly a soft step sounded on the gravel beneath her window; it was followed by the chink of iron. Then a man's voice said: "Here, between Betty Uprichard and Evelyn Thornton." There followed the thick sound of a spade driven into heavy soil.

Susan stole to the window and looked out. Down below, in the moonlight, Mr. Wispell and Jarrock were digging, fast and feverishly, flinging up the soil about a shallow trench. A rose-tree was lifted and laid to one side, and as she watched them, the trench deepened and widened to a sinister shape.

She huddled on the last of her clothing, pulled on her coat and hat, sought for and found the handbag that held her money and set the door gently ajar. There was no sound but the deep snoring from the next-door room.

She picked up her suitcase, which she had not unpacked before tumbling into bed. She hesitated a moment; then, as swiftly and silently as she could, she tiptoed across the landing and down the steep stair. The words of Mr. Wispell came back to her with sudden sinister import. "I hope she won't disappear like the last one." Had the last one, also, seen that which she was not meant to see, and scuttled on trembling feet down the stair with its twisted black banisters? Or had she disappeared still more strangely, to lie forever four feet deep under the rose-trees? The old boards creaked beneath her weight; on the lower landing the door of Mr. Alistair's room stood ajar, and a faint light came from within it. Was he to be the tenant of the grave in the garden? Or was it meant for her, or for the visitor who was expected that night?

Her flickering candle-flame showed her the front door chained and bolted. With a caution and control inspired by sheer terror, she pulled back the complaining bolts, lowered the chain with her hand, so that it should not jangle against the door, and turned the heavy key. The garden lay still and sodden under the moonlight. Drawing the door very gently to behind her, she stood on the threshold, free. She took a deep breath and slipped down the path as silently as a shadow.

A few yards down the hill road she came to a clump of thick bushes. Inside this she thrust the suitcase. Then, relieved of its weight, she ran.

At four o'clock the next morning a young policeman was repeating a curious tale to the police-sergeant at Dedcaster.

"The young woman is pretty badly frightened," he said, "but she tells her story straight enough. Do you think we ought to look into it?"

"Sounds queerish," said the sergeant. "Maybe you'd better go and have a look. Wait a minute, I'll come with you myself. They're odd people, those Wispells. Man's an artist, isn't he? Loose-living gentry they are, as often as not. Get the car out, Blaycock; you can drive us."

"What the devil is all this?" demanded Mr. Wispell. He stood upright in the light of the police lantern, leaning upon his spade, and wiped the sweat from his forehead with an earthy hand. "Is that our girl you've got with you? What's wrong with her? Hey? Thief, hey? If you've been bagging the silver, you young besom, it'll be the worse for you."

"This young woman's come to us with a queer tale, Mr. Wispell," said the sergeant. "I'd like to know what you're a-digging of here for."

Mr. Wispell laughed. "Of here for? What should I be digging of here for? Can't I dig in my own garden without your damned interference?"

"Now, that won't work, Mr. Wispell. That's a grave, that is. People don't dig graves in their gardens in the middle of the night for fun. I want that there grave opened. What've you got inside it? Now, be careful."

"There's nobody inside it at the moment," said Mr. Wispell, "and I should be obliged if you'd make rather less noise. My wife's in a delicate state of health, and my brother-in-law, who is an invalid with an injured spine, has had a very bad turn. We've had to keep him under morphia and we've only just got him off into a natural sleep. And now you come bellowing round —"

"What's that there in that sack?" interrupted the young policeman. As they all pressed forward to look, he found Susan beside him, and reassured her with a friendly pat on the arm.

"That?" Mr. Wispell laughed again. "That's Helen. Don't damage her, I implore you—if my aunt—"

The sergeant had bent down and slit open the sacking with a pen-knife. Soiled and stained, the pale face of a woman glimmered up at him. There was earth in her eyelids.

"Marble!" said the sergeant. "Well, I'll be hanged!"

There was the sound of a car stopping at the gate.

"Heaven almighty!" ejaculated Mr. Wispell. "We're done for! Get this into the house quickly, Jarrock."

"Wait a bit, sir. What I want to know—"

Steps sounded on the gravel. Mr. Wispell flung his hands to heaven. "Too late!" he groaned.

An elderly lady, very tall and upright, was coming round the side of the house.

"What on earth are you up to out here, Walter?" she demanded, in a piercing voice. "Policemen? A nice welcome for your aunt, I must say. And what—*what* is my wedding-present doing in the garden?" she added, as her eye fell on the naked marble figure.

"Oh, Lor'!" said Mr. Wispell. He flung down the spade and stalked away into the house.

"I'm afraid," said Mrs. Wispell, "you will have to take your month's money and go, Susan. Mr. Wispell is very much annoyed. You see, it was such a hideous statue, he wouldn't have it in the house, and nobody would buy it, and besides, Mrs. Glassover might turn up at any time, so we buried it and when she wired, of course we had to dig it up. But I'm afraid Mrs. Glassover will never forgive Walter, and she's sure to alter her will and—well, he's very angry, and really I don't know how you could be so silly."

"I'm sure I'm very sorry, madam. I was a bit nervous, somehow—"

"Maybe," said Mrs. Jarrock in her hoarse voice, "the poor girl was upset-like, by Jarrock. I did ought to have explained about him and poor Mr. Alistair getting blown up in the war and you being so kind to us—but there! Being used to his poor face myself I didn't think, somehow—and what with being all upset and one thing and another . . ."

The voice of Mr. Wispell came booming down the staircase. "Has that fool of a girl cleared off?"

The young policeman took Susan by the arm. He had pleasant brown eyes and curly hair, and his voice was friendly.

"Seems to me, miss," he said, "Scrawns ain't no place for you. You'd better come along of us and eat your dinner with mother and me."

NEBUCHADNEZZAR

You have played "Nebuchad-
nezzar," of course—unless you are so ingenuous as never to
have heard of any game but Yo-yo, or whatever the latest fad
may be. "Nebuchadnezzar" is so old-fashioned that only the
sophisticated play it. It came back with charades, of which, of
course, it is only a variation. It is called "Nebuchadnezzar," I
suppose, because you could not easily find a more impossible
name with which to play it.

You choose a name—and unless your audience is very
patient, it had better be a short one—of some well-known
character. Say, Job. Then you act in dumb show a character
beginning with J, then one beginning with O, then one beginning with B. Then you act Job, and the spectators guess that
Job is what you mean, and applaud kindly. That is all. Light-
hearted people, with imagination, can get a lot of fun out of it.

Bob Lester was having a birthday party—his mother and
sister and about twenty intimate friends squashed into the little flat at Hammersmith. Everybody was either a writer or a
painter or an actor of sorts, or did something or the other quite
entertaining for a living, and they were fairly well accustomed
to amusing themselves with singsongs and games. They could
fool wittily and behave like children, and get merry on invisi-

ble quantities of claretcup, and they were all rather clever and
all knew each other extremely well. Cyril Markham felt
slightly out of it, though they were all exceedingly nice to him
and tried to cheer him up. It was nearly six months since Jane
had died, and though they all sympathized terribly with him
for her loss (they had all loved Jane), he felt that he and they
were, and ever would be, strangers and aliens to one another.
Dear Jane. They had found it hard to forgive him for marrying her and taking her away to Cornwall. It was terrible that
she should have died—only two years later—of gastroenteri-
tis. Jane would have entered into all their jokes. She would
have played absurd games with them and given an exquisite
personal grace to the absurdest. Markham could never do
that. He felt stiff, awkward, cruelly self-conscious. When Bob
suggested "Nebuchadnezzar," he courteously asked Markham
to make one of his team of actors. Too kind; too kind.
Markham said he preferred to look on, and Bob, sighing with
relief, went on to pick up a side of trusted veterans.

The two front rooms of the flat had been thrown into one
by the opening of the folding doors. Though it was November,
the night was strangely close, and one of the three tall bal-
conied windows overlooking the river had been thrown open.
Across the smoke-filled room and over the heads of the guests,
Markham could see the lights of the Surrey side dance in the
river like tall Japanese lanterns. The smaller of the two rooms
formed a stage for the players, and across the dividing doorway a pair of thick purple curtains had been hung. Outside, in
the passage, the players scuffled backwards and forwards
amid laughter. Waiting for the game to begin, Markham
stared at the curtains. They were familiar. They were surely
the curtains from his own Cornish cottage. Jane had hung
them across the living room to screen off the dining part from
the lounge part. How odd that Bob should have got them here.
No, it wasn't. Bob had given Jane her curtains for a wedding
present, and this must be another pair. They were old ones, he
knew. Damask of that quality wasn't made today.

Bob drew back the curtains, thrust out a dishevelled head,

announced: "The Nebuchadnezzar has four letters," and disappeared again. In the distance was heard a vigorous bumping, and a voice called out, "There's a clothesline in the
kitchen!" Somebody standing near the door of the room
switched off the lights, and the damask curtains were drawn
aside for the acting of the first letter.

A Japanese screen at the back of the stage, above which
appeared the head of Lavinia Forbes, elegantly attired in a silk
scarf, bound round the forehead with a cricket-belt, caused
Mrs. Lester, always precipitate, to exclaim, "Romeo and
Juliet — balcony scene!" Everybody said "Hush," and the supposed Juliet, producing from behind the screen a mirror and
lipstick, proceeded to make up her face in a very lavish manner. In the middle of this, her attention appeared to be distracted by something in the distance. She leaned over the
screen and pointed eagerly in the direction of the landing,
whence, indeed, some remarkable noises were proceeding. To
her, amid frenzied applause, entered, on hands and knees, the
twins, Peter and Paul Barnaby, got up regardless of expense
in fur coats worn with the hair outside, and champing furiously upon the clothesline. Attached to them by stout luggage-
straps was a basket-chair, which, after ominous hesitation and
creaking between the doorposts, was propelled vigorously
into the room by unseen hands, so that the charioteer — very
gorgeous in scarlet dressing-gown, striped sash and military
sabre, with a large gravy-strainer inverted upon his head —
was nearly shot on to the backs of his steeds, and was heard to
mutter an indignant "Steady on!" through his forest of crêpe
beard. The lady, from behind the screen, appeared to
harangue the driver, who replied with a vulgar and regrettable
gesture. A further brief exchange of pantomime led to the
appearance of two stout parties in bathrobes and turbans, who
proceeded to hoist the lady bodily over the screen. Somebody
said, "Look out!", the screen rocked and was hastily held up
by one of the horses, and the victim was deposited on the floor
with a thud, and promptly died with a considerable amount of
twitching and gasping. The charioteer cracked his umbrella

across the backs of his horses and was drawn round the room and off again in a masterly manner. A loud barking from the wings heralded the arrival of three savage doormats, who, after snuffling a good deal over the corpse, started to devour it in large gulps as the curtain fell.

This spirited presentation was loudly cheered, and offered little difficulty to the spectators.

"Jezebel, of course," said Tony Withers.

"Or Jehu," said Miss Holroyd.

"I do hope Lavvie wasn't hurt," said Mrs. Lester. "She came down an awful bump."

"Well, the first letter's J, anyhow," said Patricia Martin. "I liked the furious driving."

"Bob looked simply marvellous," added Bice Taylor, who was sitting just behind Mrs. Lester. Then, turning to Markham:

"But one does so miss darling Jane. She loved acting and dressing-up, didn't she? She was the gayest wee bit of a thing."

Markham nodded. Yes, Jane had always been an actress. And her gaiety had been somehow proof against the solitude of their cottage and his own morose temper. She always would sing as she went about the house, and it had got so terribly on his nerves that he had snarled at her. He had always wondered what she found to sing about. Until, of course, he had found those letters, and then he had known.

He wished he had not come to this party. He was out of place here, and Tom Deering knew it and was sneering at him. He could see Tom's dark, sardonic face in the far corner against the door. He must be remembering things too, the sleek devil. Well he, Markham, had put a spoke in Deering's wheel anyhow, that was one comfort.

In spite of the open window, the room was stifling. What did they need with that enormous fire? The blood was pumping violently through his brain—he felt as though the top of his head would lift off. There were far too many people for the place. And they made so much noise. Something fearfully elaborate must be in preparation, to judge by the long wait and the running of feet on the landing. This was a tedious game.

The lights clicked off once more, and a voice announced "Second letter," as the curtains drew apart.

The apparition of Betty Sander in an exiguous pair of pale pink cami-bockers, with her hair down her back, embracing the deeply-embarrassed George P. Brewster in a tight-fitting gent's union suit, was hailed with happy laughter.

"The bedroom scene!" exclaimed Mrs. Lester, prematurely as usual. After an affecting exchange of endearments, the couple separated, George retiring to the far side of the piano to dig industriously with the coal-scoop, while Betty seated herself on the sofa and combed her hair with her fingers. Presently there advanced through the door the crimson face of Peter Barnaby, worming along at ground-level, with energetically working tongue. Behind it trailed an endless length of green tablecloth, whose slow, humping progress proclaimed the presence within it of yet another human engine — probably the second Barnaby twin. This procession advanced to the sofa and rubbed itself against Betty's leg — then reared itself up rather awkwardly in its mufflings and jerked its head at the aspidistra on the occasional table. Betty registered horror and refusal, but presently yielded and took from amid the leaves of the aspidistra a large apple, which she proceeded to eat with expressions of enjoyment, while the combined Barnabys retired behind the sofa. At this moment, George, wiping the honest sweat from his brow, returned from his labours, with the coal-scoop over his shoulder. On seeing what Betty was about, he dropped the scoop and flung his arms to heaven. After some solicitation, however, he accepted his share of the feast, carefully polishing the apple first on his union suit. After this, he appeared to be suddenly struck by the indelicacy of the union suit and, moreover, proceeded to point the finger of scorn and reprimand at the cami-bockers. Betty, dissolved in tears, pushed to the aspidistra, tore off two large leaves ("Oh, the poor plant!" cried Mrs. Lester), and attached them severally, with string, about the waists of

George and herself. Then, from behind the Japanese screen appeared the awful presence of Bob, in the scarlet dressing-gown and a bright blue tablecloth, and wearing a large saucepan-lid tied to the back of his head. An immense beard of cotton-wool added majesty to his countenance. The delinquents fell flat on their faces, and the curtains were flung to amid rejoicings.

"Now, was that Adam and Eve?" demanded Miss Holroyd.

"I think it was Eve," said somebody. "Then the whole word might be Jehu."

"But we've had Jehu."

"No, we haven't, that was Jezebel."

"But they can't be giving us Jehu and Jezebel again."

"JE, JA, JE, JA . . ."

The lights were on again now. Queer, how white and unnatural all their faces looked. Like masks. Markham's fingers pulled at his collar. Jezebel, Adam—Wanton woman, deluded man. J, A, Jane. So long as the whoredoms of thy mother Jezebel and her witchcrafts are so many. If Deering had known that those letters had been found, would he be smiling like that? He did know. That was why he was smiling that dark smile. He knew, and he had put Bob up to this. Let the galled jade wince. Jade; J, A, Jade. J, A, Jane. Jade, Jane, Jezebel. The dogs shall eat Jezebel in the portion of Jezreel. Dogs. Dogging his footsteps. The Hound of Heaven with a saucepan-lid on his head. Jehovah. JAH. J, A, Jane . . .

The lights went out.

They had draped a sheet over some chairs to form a little tent. At the door sat Bob, in the dressing-gown and the white beard, but without the saucepan-lid. Paul Barnaby, wearing a handkerchief over his head and a short tunic with a sash round the waist, presented him with a frugal meal of two dried figs on a plate. In front of the tent stood a tin bath full of water and surrounded with aspidistras.

A noise of mingled instruments heralded the approach of George, in an Oriental costume of surpassing magnificence and a headdress made of a gilt wastepaper basket. Attended by a train of Oriental followers, he approached Bob, and indicated, with gestures of distress, some livid patches of flour on his face and arms. Bob examined him carefully, clapped him cordially on the shoulder and indicated the tin bath, going through a pantomime of washing. George seemed to be overcome with indignation and contempt. He kicked the bath scornfully and spat vulgarly into the aspidistras. Then, shaking his fist at Bob, he stalked away in high dudgeon in the direction of the piano.

"Hi!" shouted Tony Withers, "where's your chariot, old man?"

"Shut up!" returned George, disconcerted, "we can't do that horse business over again."

Lavinia, modestly attired in a kind of yashmak, now took the stage. Kneeling at George's feet, she gently expostulated with him. The other Oriental followers joined their petitions to hers and presently his frown relaxed. Returning to the tin bath, and being solemnly supplied with a piece of soap and a loofah, he scrubbed the flour from his face. On observing the effect in a shaving-mirror, he was transported with joy, prostrated himself before Bob, and offered him a handsome collection of cushion-covers and drawing-room ornaments. These being refused, he went away rejoicing, followed, surreptitiously, by Paul Barnaby. Bob appeared gratified by this result, and was just sitting down to read the *Evening News* in his tent when he observed Paul slinking back through the door with an armful of cushion-covers. Overcome with righteous anger he rose to his feet and, dexterously drawing from behind the newspaper a bag of flour, flung it over Paul's face, thus closing the episode.

Markham vaguely heard the applause, but his eyes were fixed on the purple curtains. He knew them so well. They were heavy and swung into thick, rich folds. Jane had adored those curtains. He had always said they were dark and gloomy, but she would hear nothing against them. Nowadays people lived so publicly, behind thin casement cloth and stuff like that; but that old-fashioned damask was made for concealment. Curtains like those kept their secrets forever.

Bice Taylor spoke almost in his ear.

"I don't believe it's either Naaman or Elisha. I think it's Abigail, don't you? The little maid, you know. Not so obvious. It might be J, E, A, something. Jean somebody, or the French Jean."

J for Jezebel, A for Adam, N for Naaman the leper. J, A, N, Jane, Janitor, January. This was November. Jane died in June.

"What nonsense—Abigail was somebody quite different. It's Gehazi, of course."

"Gehazi? My dear child—there's no name in four letters beginning JEG or JAG."

"Yes, there is. There's JAGO."

"Who's Jago?"

"I don't know. Somebody wrote a book called *John Jago's Ghost*. I do know that."

"It isn't a book. It's a short story by Wilkie Collins."

"Oh! is it? I only remember the title."

"But who was Jago, anyway?"

"I don't know, except that he had a ghost. And what was the point of bringing Gehazi in if it isn't Gehazi?"

"Oh, that's just to make it more difficult."

Gehazi—Naaman—He went out from before him a leper as white as snow. One felt like a leper among all these people who hated one. Leper. See the leopard-dog-thing something at his side, a leer and a lie in every eye. It was so queer that nobody would look at him. They looked round and over him at each other. That was because he was a leper—but they need never know that unless he told them. He had never noticed the pattern on the curtains before, but now the strong light showed it up—damask, damascened like a sword, damn the lot of them. How hot it was, and what a stupid oaf Bob Lester looked, playing childish games. But it was really horrible, the way these people pretended not to know that it was J, A, N, Jane. They did know, really, all the time and were wondering how long he would stick it. Let them wonder! All the same, he must think out what to do when it came to the complete word. J, A, N. Of course, if the last letter wasn't E . . . but it was bound to be E. Well, it would be a relief in a way, because then he would know that they knew.

The fourth scene was, for a change, medieval and brief. Betty in white robes, her long hair loosed, oared on the spare-room mattress across the parquet to where Arthur's Court stood grouped by the piano. Bob, simply but effectively armed in corrugated cardboard, weeping fat tears out of a sponge.

"Well, *that's* obvious," said Mrs. Lester. "The Lady of Shallott. Now, dear me, what can the word be?"

"Oh, *dear* Mrs. Lester. Not Shallott. It's Lancelot and Thingummy."

"Oh, Lancelot, is it?"

"Or, of course, Thingummy."

"Especially Thingummy," said Deering.

"Have you guessed it, Tom?"

"Yes, of course. Haven't you?"

"Well, I *think* so, but I'm not absolutely certain."

"You mustn't say until the end."

"No, all right."

Oh, yes, thought Markham. Deering would have guessed it, of course. Lancelot and Elaine. Elaine the lovable. Jane, Elaine. J, A, N, E, Jane. But it was all wrong, because Elaine was pure and faithful and died of love. Died. That was the point. Elaine was dead. Jane was dead. Jane, Elaine as Jane had lain.

He fixed his eyes on the damask curtains. There was one point where they did not quite meet, and the light from the stage showed through. Somebody called "Are you ready?" and turned off the switch on the side of the spectators. Markham could not see them any longer, but he could hear them breathing and rustling about him, packed close like wolves, pressing in upon him. The point of light still shone between the curtains. It grew larger, and glowed more intensely, yet as though from an enormous distance.

Then, very slowly this time, and in absolute silence, the curtains parted. The whole word at last.

They had done a wonderful piece of staging this time. He recognized every object, though the blaze of the electric globe had been somehow subdued. There was the bed and the dressing-table and the wardrobe with its tall glass door, and the low casement on the right. It was hot, and the scent of the syringa—philadelphus, the books said, but Jane called it syringa—came billowing in from the garden in thick puffs. The girl on the bed was asleep. Her face was hidden, turned to the wall. Dying people always turned to the wall. Too bad to have to die in June, with the scent of the syringa coming in through the window and the nightingale singing so loudly. Did they do that with a bird-whistle, or was it a gramophone record?

Somebody was moving in the shadows. He had opened the door very gently. There was a glass of lemonade on the table by the bed. It chinked against the bottle as he picked it up, but the girl did not move. He walked right forward till he stood directly beneath the light. His head was bent down as he shot the white powder into the glass and stirred it with a spoon. He went back to the bedside, walking like Agag, delicately. A,G,A,G, Adam and Gehazi. Jezebel, Adam, Naaman, Elaine, J, A, N, E. He touched the girl on the shoulder and she stirred a little. He put one arm behind her shoulders and held the glass to her lips. It clinked again as he set it down empty. Then he kissed her. He went out, shutting the door.

He had never known such silence. He could not even hear the wolfpack breathing. He was alone in the room with the girl who lay on the bed. And now she was moving. The sheet slipped from her shoulders to her breast, from her breast to her waist. She was rising to her knees, lifting herself up to face him over the footboard of the bed—gold hair, sweat-streaked forehead, eyes dark with fear and pain, black hollow of the mouth, and the glittering line of white teeth in the fallen jaw.

JANE!

Had he cried out, or had they? The room was full of light and noise, but his voice rose above it.

"Jane, Jezebel! I killed her. I poisoned her. Jane, jade, Jezebel. The doctor never knew, but she knew, and he knew, and now you all know. Get out! damn you! curse you! Let me go!"

Chairs were falling, people were shouting, clutching at him. He smashed a fist into a silly, gaping face. He was on the balcony. He was fighting for the balustrade. The lights on the Surrey side were like tall Japanese lanterns. He was over. The black water leapt to meet him. Cataracts, roaring.

It had all happened so quickly that the actors knew nothing about it. As Tom Deering pulled off his coat to dive after Markham and Mrs. Lester rushed to telephone the river police, George's voice announced "The Whole Word," and the curtains were flung open to display the tent of JAEL.

THE INSPIRATION OF MR. BUDD

£500 REWARD

THE "EVENING MESSENGER," ever anxious to further the ends of justice, has decided to offer the above reward to any person who shall give information leading to the arrest of the man, William Strickland, alias Bolton, who is wanted by the police in connection with the murder of the late Emma Strickland at 59 Acacia Crescent, Manchester.

DESCRIPTION OF THE WANTED MAN.

The following is the official description of William Strickland: Age 43; height 6 ft. 1 or 2 in.; complexion rather dark; hair silver-grey and abundant, may dye same; full grey moustache and beard, may now be clean-shaven; eyes light grey, rather close-set; hawk nose; teeth strong and white, displays them somewhat prominently when laughing, left upper eyetooth stopped with gold; left thumbnail disfigured by a recent blow.

Speaks in rather loud voice; quick, decisive manner. Good address.

May be dressed in a grey or dark blue lounge suit, with stand-up collar (size 15) and soft felt hat.

Absconded 5th inst., and may have left, or will endeavor to leave, the country.

Mr. Budd read the description through carefully once again and sighed. It was in the highest degree unlikely that William Strickland should choose his small and unsuccessful saloon, out of all the barbers' shops in London, for a haircut or a shave, still less for "dyeing same"; even if he was in London, which Mr. Budd saw no reason to suppose.

Three weeks had gone by since the murder, and the odds were a hundred to one that William Strickland had already left a country too eager with its offer of free hospitality. Nevertheless, Mr. Budd committed the description, as well as he could, to memory. It was a chance — just as the Great Crossword Tournament had been a chance, just as the Ninth Rainbow Ballot had been a chance, and the Bunko Poster Ballot, and the Monster Treasure Hunt organized by the *Evening Clarion*. Any headline with money in it could attract Mr. Budd's fascinated eye in these lean days, whether it offered a choice between fifty thousand pounds down and ten pounds a week for life, or merely a modest hundred or so.

It may seem strange, in an age of shingling and bingling, Mr. Budd should look enviously at Complete Lists of Prizewinners. Had not the hairdresser across the way, who only last year had eked out his mean ninepences with the yet meaner profits on cheap cigarettes and comic papers, lately bought out the greengrocer next door, and engaged a staff of exquisitely coiffed assistants to adorn his new "Ladies' Hairdressing Department" with its purple and orange curtains, its two rows of gleaming marble basins, and an apparatus like a Victorian chandelier for permanent waving?

Had he not installed a large electric sign surrounded by a scarlet border that ran round and round perpetually, like a kitten chasing its own cometary tail? Was it not his sandwichman even now patrolling the pavement with a luminous announcement of Treatment and Prices? And was there not at this moment an endless stream of young ladies hastening into those heavily-perfumed parlors in the desperate hope of somehow getting a shampoo and a wave "squeezed in" before closing-time?

If the reception clerk shook a regretful head, they did not think of crossing the road to Mr. Budd's dimly-lighted window. They made an appointment for days ahead and waited patiently, anxiously fingering the bristly growth at the back of the neck and the straggly bits behind the ears that so soon got out of hand.

Day after day Mr. Budd watched them flit in and out of the rival establishment, willing, praying even, in a vague, ill-directed manner, that some of them would come over to him; but they never did.

And yet Mr. Budd knew himself to be the finer artist. He had seen shingles turned out from over the way that he would never have countenanced, let alone charged three shillings and sixpence for. Shingles with an ugly hard line at the nape, shingles which were a slander on the shape of a good head or brutally emphasized the weak points of an ugly one; hurried, conscienceless shingles, botched work, handed over on a crowded afternoon to a girl who had only served a three years' apprenticeship and to whom the final mysteries of "tapering" were a sealed book.

And then there was the "tinting"—his own pet subject, which he had studied *con amore*—if only those too-sprightly matrons would come to him! He would gently dissuade them from that dreadful mahogany dye that made them look like metallic Robots—he would warn them against that widely advertised preparation which was so incalculable in its effects; he would use the cunning skill which long experience had matured in him—tint them with the infinitely delicate art which conceals itself.

Yet nobody came to Mr. Budd but the navvies and the young loungers and the men who plied their trade beneath the naphtha-flares in Wilton Street.

And why could not Mr. Budd also have burst out into marble and electricity and swum to fortune on the rising tide?

The reason is very distressing, and, as it fortunately has no bearing on the story, shall be told with merciful brevity.

Mr. Budd had a younger brother, Richard, whom he had promised his mother to look after. In happier days Mr. Budd had owned a flourishing business in their native town of Northampton, and Richard had been a bank clerk. Richard had got into bad ways (poor Mr. Budd blamed himself dreadfully for this). There had been a sad affair with a girl, and a horrid series of affairs with bookmakers, and then Richard had tried to mend bad with worse by taking money from the bank. You need to be very much more skillful than Richard to juggle successfully with bank ledgers.

The bank manager was a hard man of the old school: he prosecuted. Mr. Budd paid the bank and the bookmakers, and saw the girl through her trouble while Richard was in prison, and paid for their fares to Australia when he came out, and gave them something to start life on.

But it took all the profits of the hairdressing business, and he couldn't face all the people in Northampton any more, who had known him all his life. So he had run to vast London, the refuge of all who shrink from the eyes of their neighbors, and bought this little shop in Pimlico, which had done fairly well, until the new fashion which did so much for other hairdressing businesses killed it for lack of capital.

That is why Mr. Budd's eye was so painfully fascinated by headlines with money in them.

He put the newspaper down, and as he did so, caught sight of his own reflection in the glass and smiled, for he was not without a sense of humor. He did not look quite the man to catch a brutal murderer single-handed. He was well on in the middle forties — a trifle paunchy, with fluffy pale hair, getting a trifle thin on top (partly hereditary, partly worry, that was), five feet six at most, and softhanded, as a hairdresser must be.

Even razor in hand, he would hardly be a match for

William Strickland, height six feet one or two, who had so ferociously battered his old aunt to death, so butcherly hacked her limb from limb, so horribly disposed of her remains in the copper. Shaking his head dubiously, Mr. Budd advanced to the door, to cast a forlorn eye at the busy establishment over the way, and nearly ran into a bulky customer who dived in rather precipitately.

"I beg your pardon, sir," murmured Mr. Budd, fearful of alienating ninepence; "just stepping out for a breath of fresh air, sir. Shave, sir?"

The large man tore off his overcoat without waiting for Mr. Budd's obsequious hands.

"Are you prepared to die?" he demanded abruptly.

The question chimed in so alarmingly with Mr. Budd's thoughts about murder that for a moment it quite threw him off his professional balance.

"I beg your pardon, sir," he stammered, and in the same moment decided that the man must be a preacher of some kind. He looked rather like it, with his odd, light eyes, his bush of fiery hair, and short, jutting chin-beard. Perhaps he even wanted a subscription. That would be hard, when Mr. Budd had already set him down as ninepence, or, with tip, possibly even a shilling.

"Do you do dyeing?" said the man impatiently.

"Oh!" said Mr. Budd, relieved, "yes, sir, certainly, sir."

A stroke of luck, this. Dyeing meant quite a big sum—his mind soared to seven-and-sixpence.

"Good," said the man, sitting down and allowing Mr. Budd to put an apron about his neck. (He was safely gathered in now—he could hardly dart away down the street with a couple of yards of white cotton flapping from his shoulders.)

"Fact is," said the man, "my young lady doesn't like red hair. She says it's conspicuous. The other young ladies in her firm make jokes about it. So, as she's a good bit younger than I am, you see, I like to oblige her, and I was thinking perhaps it could be changed into something quieter, what? Dark brown, now—that's the color she has a fancy to. What do *you* say?"

It occurred to Mr. Budd that the young ladies might consider this abrupt change of coat even funnier than the original color, but in the interests of business he agreed that dark brown would be very becoming and a great deal less noticeable than red. Besides, very likely there was no young lady. A woman, he knew, will say frankly that she wants differed colored hair for a change, or just to try, or because she fancies it would suit her, but if a man is going to do a silly thing he prefers, if possible, to shuffle the responsibility on to someone else.

"Very well, then," said the customer, "go ahead. And I'm afraid the beard will have to go. My young lady doesn't like beards."

"A great many young ladies don't, sir," said Mr. Budd. "They're not so fashionable nowadays as they used to be. It's very fortunate that you can stand a clean shave very well, sir. You have just the chin for it."

"Do you think so?" said the man, examining himself a little anxiously. "I'm glad to hear it."

"Will you have the moustache off as well, sir?"

"Well, no—no, I think I'll stick to that as long as I'm allowed to, what?" He laughed loudly, and Mr. Budd approvingly noted well-kept teeth and a gold stopping. The customer was obviously ready to spend money on his personal appearance.

In fancy, Mr. Budd saw this well-off and gentlemanly customer advising all his friends to visit "his man"— "wonderful fellow—wonderful—round at the back of Victoria Station— you'd never find it by yourself—only a little place, but he knows what he's about—I'll write it down for you." It was imperative that there should be no fiasco. Hair-dyes were awkward things—there had been a case in the paper lately.

"I see you have been using a tint before, sir," said Mr. Budd with respect. "Could you tell me—?"

"Eh?" said the man. "Oh, yes—well, fact is, as I said, my fiancée's a good bit younger than I am. As I expect you can see I began to go grey early—my father was just the same—all our family—so I had it touched up—streaky bits restored, you see. But she doesn't take to the color, so I thought, if I have to dye it at all, why not a color she *does* fancy while we're about it, what?"

It is a common jest among the unthinking that hair-dressers are garrulous. This is their wisdom. The hairdresser hears many secrets and very many lies. In his discretion he occupies his unruly tongue with the weather and the political situation, lest, restless with inaction, it plunge unbridled into a mad career of inconvenient candor.

Lightly holding forth upon the caprices of the feminine mind, Mr. Budd subjected his customer's locks to the scrutiny of trained eye and fingers. Never—never in the process of nature could hair of that texture and quality have been red. It was naturally black hair, prematurely turned, as some black hair will turn, to a silvery gray. However, that was none of his business. He elicited the information he really needed—the name of the dye formerly used, and noted that he would have to be careful. Some dyes do not mix kindly with other dyes.

Chatting pleasantly, Mr. Budd lathered his customer, removed the offending beard, and executed a vigorous shampoo, preliminary to the dyeing process. As he wielded the roaring drier, he reviewed Wimbledon, the Silk-tax and the Summer Time Bill—at that moment threatened with sudden strangulation—and passed naturally on to the Manchester murder.

"The police seem to have given it up as a bad job," said the man.

"Perhaps the reward will liven things up a bit," said Mr. Budd, the thought being naturally uppermost in his mind.

"Oh, there's a reward, is there? I hadn't seen that."

"It's in tonight's paper, sir. Maybe you'd like to have a look at it."

"Thanks, I should."

Mr. Budd left the drier to blow the fiery bush of hair at its own wild will for a moment, while he fetched the *Evening Messenger*. The stranger read the paragraph carefully and Mr. Budd, watching him in the glass, after the disquieting manner of his craft, saw him suddenly draw back his left hand, which was resting carelessly on the arm of the chair, and thrust it under the apron.

But not before Mr. Budd had seen it. Not before he had taken conscious note of the horny, misshapen thumbnail. Many people had such an ugly mark, Mr. Budd told himself hurriedly—there was his friend, Bert Webber, who had sliced the top of his thumb right off in a motorcycle chain—his nail looked very much like that.

The man glanced up, and the eyes of his reflection became fixed on Mr. Budd's face with a penetrating scrutiny—a horrid warning that the real eyes were steadfastly interrogating the reflection of Mr. Budd.

"Not but what," said Mr. Budd, "the man is safe out of the country by now, I reckon. They've put it off too late."

The man laughed.

"I reckon they have," he said. Mr. Budd wondered whether many men with smashed left thumbs showed a gold left upper eyetooth. Probably there were hundreds of people like that going about the country. Likewise with silver-grey hair ("may dye same") and aged about forty-three. Undoubtedly.

Mr. Budd folded up the drier and turned off the gas. Mechanically he took up a comb and drew it through the hair that never, never in the process of nature had been that fiery red.

There came back to him, with an accuracy which quite unnerved him, the exact number and extent of the brutal wounds inflicted upon the Manchester victim—an elderly lady, rather stout, she had been. Glaring through the door, Mr. Budd noticed that his rival over the way had closed. The streets were full of people. How easy it would be—

"Be as quick as you can, won't you?" said the man, a little impatiently, but pleasantly enough. "It's getting late. I'm afraid it will keep you overtime."

"Not at all, sir," said Mr. Budd. "It's of no consequence—not the least."

No—if he tried to bolt out the door, his terrible customer

would leap upon him, drag him back, throttle his cries, and then with one frightful blow like the one he had smashed in his aunt's skull with—

Yet surely Mr. Budd was in a position of advantage. A decided man would do it. He would be out in the street before the customer could disentangle himself from the chair. Mr. Budd began to edge round towards the door.

"What's the matter?" said the customer.

"Just stepping out to look at the time, sir," said Mr. Budd, meekly pausing. (Yet he might have done it then, if he only had the courage to make the first swift step that would give the game away.)

"It's five-and-twenty past eight," said the man, "by tonight's broadcast. I'll pay extra for the overtime."

"Not on any account," said Mr. Budd. Too late now, he couldn't make another effort. He vividly saw himself tripping on the threshold—falling—the terrible fist lifted to smash him into a pulp. Or perhaps, under the familiar white apron, the disfigured hand was actually clutching a pistol.

Mr. Budd retreated to the back of the shop, collecting his materials. If only he had been quicker—more like a detective in a book—he would have observed that thumbnail, that tooth, put two and two together, and run out to give the alarm while the man's beard was wet and soapy and his face buried in the towel. Or he could have dabbed lather in his eyes—nobody could possibly commit a murder or even run away down the street with his eyes full of soap.

Even now—Mr. Budd took down a bottle, shook his head, and put it back on the shelf—even now, was it really too late? Why could he not take a bold course? He had only to open a razor, go quietly up behind the unsuspecting man, and say in a firm, loud, convincing voice: "William Strickland, put up your hands. Your life is at my mercy. Stand up till I take your gun away. Now walk straight out to the nearest police-man." Surely, in his position, that was what Sherlock Holmes would do.

But as Mr. Budd returned with a little trayful of require-
ments, it was borne in upon him that he was not of the stuff of
which great manhunters are made. For he could not seriously
see that attempt "coming off." Because if he held the razor to
the man's throat and said: "Put up your hands," the man
would probably merely catch him by the wrists and take the
razor away. And greatly as Mr. Budd feared his customer
unarmed, he felt it would be a perfect crescendo of madness to
put a razor into his hands.

Or, supposing he said, "Put up your hands," and the man
just said, "I won't." What was he to do next? To cut his throat
then and there would be murder, even if Mr. Budd could possibly have brought himself to do such a thing. They could not
remain there, fixed in one position, till the boy came to do out
the shop in the morning.

Perhaps the policeman would notice the light on and the
door unfastened and come in? Then he would say, "I congratulate you, Mr. Budd, on having captured a very dangerous
criminal." But supposing the policeman didn't happen to
notice — and Mr. Budd would have to stand all the time, and he
would get exhausted and his attention would relax, and then —

After all, Mr. Budd wasn't called upon to arrest the man
himself. "Information leading to arrest" — those were the
words. He would be able to tell them the wanted man had
been there, that he would now have dark brown hair and
moustache and no beard. He might even shadow him when he
left — he might —

It was at this moment that the Great Inspiration came to
Mr. Budd.

As he fetched a bottle from the glass-fronted case he
remembered, with odd vividness, an old-fashioned wooden
paper-knife that had belonged to his mother. Between sprigs
of blue forget-me-not, hand-painted, it bore the inscription
"Knowledge is Power."

A strange freedom and confidence were vouchsafed to Mr.
Budd; his mind was alert; he removed the razors with an easy,

natural movement, and made nonchalant conversation as he skillfully applied the dark-brown tint.

The streets were less crowded when Mr. Budd let his customer out. He watched the tall figure cross Grosvenor Place and climb on to a 24 bus.

"But that was only his artfulness," said Mr. Budd, as he put on his hat and coat and extinguished the lights carefully, "he'll take another at Victoria, like as not, and be making tracks from Charing Cross or Waterloo."

He closed the shop door, shook it, as was his wont, to make sure that the lock had caught properly, and in his turn made his way, by means of a 24, to the top of Whitehall.

The policeman was a little condescending at first when Mr. Budd demanded to see "somebody very high up," but finding the little barber insist so earnestly that he had news of the Manchester murderer, and that there wasn't any time to lose, he consented to pass him through.

Mr. Budd was interviewed first by an important-looking inspector in uniform, who listened very politely to his story and made him repeat very carefully about the gold tooth and the thumbnail and the hair which had been black before it was gray or red and was now dark-brown.

The inspector then touched a bell, and said, "Perkins, I think Sir Andrew would like to see this gentleman at once," and he was taken to another room, where sat a very shrewd, genial gentleman in mufti, who heard him with even greater attention, and called in another inspector to listen too, and to take down a very exact description of—yes, surely the undoubted William Strickland as he now appeared.

"But there's one thing more," said Mr. Budd—"and I'm sure to goodness," he added, "I hope, sir, it is the right man, because if it isn't it'll be the ruin of me—"

He crushed his soft hat into an agitated ball as he leant across the table, breathlessly uttering the story of his great professional betrayal.

• • •

"Tzee — z-z-z — tzee — tzee — z-z — tzee — z-z — "
"Dzoo — dz-dz-dz — dzoo — dz — dzoo — dzoo — dz — "
"Tzee — z — z."

The fingers of the wireless operator on the packet *Miranda* bound for Ostend moved swiftly as they jotted down the messages of the buzzing mosquito-swarms.

One of them made him laugh.

"The Old Man'd better have this, I suppose," he said.

The Old Man scratched his head when he read and rang a little bell for the steward. The steward ran down to the little round office where the purser was counting out his money and checking it before he locked it away for the night. On receiving the Old Man's message, the purser put the money quickly into the safe, picked up the passenger list, and departed aft. There was a short consultation, and the bell was rung again — this time to summon the head steward.

"Tzee — z-z — tzeez-z-z — tzee — tzee — z — tzee."

All down the Channel, all over the North Sea, up to the Mersey Docks, out into the Atlantic soared the busy mosquito-swarms. In ship after ship the wireless operator sent his message to the captain, the captain sent for the purser, the purser sent for the head steward, and the head steward called his staff about him. Huge liners, little packets, destroyers, sumptuous private yachts — every floating thing that carried aerials — every port in England, France, Holland, Germany, Denmark, Norway, every police center that could interpret the mosquito message, heard, between laughter and excitement, the tale of Mr. Budd's betrayal. Two Boy Scouts at Croydon, practicing their Morse with a homemade valve set, decoded it laboriously into an exercise book.

"Cripes," said Jim to George, "what a joke? D'you think they'll get the beggar?"

The *Miranda* docked at Ostend at 7 A.M. A man burst hurriedly into the cabin where the wireless operator was just taking off his headphones.

"Here!" he cried; "this is to go. There's something up and

the Old Man's sent over for the police. The Consul's coming on board."

The wireless operator groaned, and switched on his valves.

"Tzee—z—tzee—" a message to the English police.

"Man on board answering to description. Ticket booked name of Watson. Has locked himself in cabin and refuses to come out. Insists on having hairdresser sent out to him. Have communicated Ostend police. Await instructions."

The Old Man with sharp words and authoritative gestures cleared a way through the excited little knot of people gathered about First Class Cabin No. 36. Several passengers had got wind of "something up." Magnificently he herded them away to the gangway with their bags and suitcases. Sternly he bade the stewards and the boy, who stood gaping with his hands full of breakfast dishes, to stand away from the door. Terribly he commanded them to hold their tongues. Four or five sailors stood watchfully at his side. In the restored silence, the passenger in No. 36 could be heard pacing up and down the narrow cabin, moving things, clattering, splashing water.

Presently came steps overhead. Somebody arrived, with a message. The Old Man nodded. Six pairs of Belgian police boots came tiptoeing down the companion. The Old Man glanced at the official paper held out to him and nodded again.

"Ready?"

"Yes."

The Old Man knocked at the door of No. 36.

"Who is it?" cried a harsh, sharp voice.

"The barber is here, sir, that you sent for."

"Ah!!" There was relief in the tone. "Send him in alone, if you please. I—I have had an accident."

"Yes, sir."

At the sound of the bolt being cautiously withdrawn, the Old Man stepped forward. The door opened a chink, and was slammed to again, but the Old Man's boot was firmly wedged against the jamb. The policemen surged forward. There was a yelp and a shot which smashed harmlessly through the window of the first-class saloon, and the passenger was brought out.

"Strike me pink!" shrieked the boy, "strike me pink if he ain't gone green in the night!"

Green!!

Not for nothing had Mr. Budd studied the intricate mutual reactions of chemical dyes. In the pride of his knowledge he had set a mark on his man, to mark him out for all the billions of this overpopulated world. Was there a port in all Christendom where a murderer might slip away, with every hair on him green as a parrot—green moustache, green eyebrows, and that thick, springing shock of hair, vivid, flaring mid-summer green?

Mr. Budd got his £500. The *Evening Messenger* published the full story of his great betrayal. He trembled, fearing this sinister fame. Surely no one would ever come to him again.

On the next morning an enormous blue limousine rolled up to his door, to the immense admiration of Wilton Street. A lady, magnificent in musquash and diamonds, swept into the saloon.

"You *are* Mr. Budd, aren't you?" she cried. "The *great* Mr. Budd? Isn't it *too* wonderful? And now, *dear* Mr. Budd, you *must* do me a favor. You must dye my hair green, *at once. Now.* I want to be able to say I'm the *very first* to be done by *you.* I'm the Duchess of Winchester, and that awful Melcaster woman is chasing me down the street—the cat!"

If you want it done, I can give you the number of Mr. Budd's parlors in Bond Street. But I understand it is a terribly expensive process.

BLOOD SACRIFICE

If things went on at this rate, John Scales would be a very rich man. Already he was a man to be envied, as any ignoramus might guess who passed the King's Theatre after 8 o'clock. Old Florrie, who had sat for so many years on the corner with her little tray of matches, could have given more than a guess, for what she didn't know about the King's was hardly worth knowing. When she had ceased to adorn its boards (thanks to a dreadful accident with a careless match and gauze draperies, that had left her with a scarred face and a withered arm) she had taken her stand near the theatre for old sake's sake, and she watched over its fortunes, still, like a mother. She knew, none better, how much money it held when it was playing to capacity, what its salary list was like, how much of its earnings went in permanent charges, and what the author's share of the box-office receipts was likely to amount to. Besides, everybody who went in or out by the stage-door came and had a word with Florrie. She shared good times and bad at the King's. She had lamented over lean days caused by slumps and talkie competition, shaken her head over perilous experiments into high-brow tragedy, waxed tearful and indignant over the disastrous period (now happily past) of the Scorer-Bitterby manage-

ment, which had ended in a scandal, rejoiced when the ener-
getic Mr. Garrick Drury, launching out into management after
his tremendous triumph in the name-part of *The Wistful Harlequin*, had taken the old house over, reconditioned it inside and
out (incidentally squeezing two more rows into the recon-
structed pit), and voiced his optimistic determination to break
the run of ill-luck: and since then she had watched its steady
soaring into prosperity on the well-tried wings of old-fashioned
adventure and romance. Mr. Garrick Drury (Somerset House
knew him as Obadiah Potts, but he was none the less good-
looking for that) was an actor-manager of the sort Florrie
understood; he followed his calling in the good old way, building his successes about his own glamorous personality, talking
no nonsense about new schools of dramatic thought, and paying only lip-service to "teamwork." He had had the luck to
embark on his managerial career at a moment when the public
had grown tired of gloomy Slav tragedies of repressed hus-
bands, and human documents about drink and diseases, and
was (in its own incoherent way) clamoring for a good, romantic story to cry about, with a romantic hero suffering torments
of self-sacrifice through two-and-three-quarter acts and getting the girl in the last ten minutes. Mr. Drury (forty-two in
the daylight, thirty-five in the lamplight, and twenty-five or
what you will in a blond wig and the spotlight) was well fitted
by nature to acquire girls in this sacrificial manner, and had
learnt the trick of so lacing nineteenth-century sentiment with
twentieth-century nonchalance that the mixture went to the
heads equally of Joan who worked in the office and Aunt
Mabel up from the country.

And since Mr. Drury, leaping nightly from his Rolls
saloon with that nervous and youthful alacrity that had been
his most engaging asset for the past twenty years, always had
time to bestow at least a smile and a friendly word on old Florrie, he affected her head and heart as much as anybody else's.
Nobody was more delighted than Florrie to know that he had
again found a winner in *Bitter Laurel* now sweeping on to its
100th performance. Night by night she saluted with a satisfied

chuckle each board as it appeared: "Pit Full," "Gallery Full," "Dress Circle Full," "Upper Circle Full," "Stalls Full," "Standing Room Only," "House Full." Set to run forever, it was, and the faces that went in by the stage door looked merry and prosperous, as Florrie liked to see them.

As for the young man who had provided the raw material out of which Mr. Drury had built up this glittering monument of success, if he wasn't pleased, thought Florrie, he ought to be. Not that, in the ordinary way, one thought much about the author of a play—unless, of course, it was Shakespeare, who was different; compared with the cast, he was of small importance and rarely seen. But Mr. Drury had one day arrived arm-in-arm with a sulky-looking and ill-dressed youth whom he had introduced to Florrie, saying in his fine generous way: "Here, John, you must know Florrie. She's our mascot—we couldn't get on without her. Florrie, this is Mr. Scales, whose new play's going to make all our fortunes." Mr. Drury was never mistaken about plays; he had the golden touch. Certainly, in the last three months, Mr. Scales, though still sulky-looking, had become much better dressed.

On this particular night—Saturday, April 15th, when *Bitter Laurel* was giving its 96th performance to a full house after a packed matinée—Mr. Scales and Mr. Drury arrived together, in evening dress and, Florrie noted with concern, rather late. Mr. Drury would have to hurry, and it was tiresome of Mr. Scales to detain him, as he did, by arguing and expostulating upon the threshold. Not that Mr. Drury seemed put out. He was smiling (his smile, one-sided and slightly elfin in quality, was famous), and at last he said, with his hand (Mr. Drury's expressive hands were renowned) affectionately upon Mr. Scales's shoulder, "Sorry, old boy, can't stop now. Curtain must go up, you know. Come round and see me after the show—I'll have those fellows there." Then he vanished, still smiling the elfin smile and waving the expressive hand: and Mr. Scales, after hesitating a moment, had turned away and came down past Florrie's corner. He seemed to be still sulky and rather preoccupied, but, looking up, caught sight of Florrie and grinned at her. There was nothing elfin about Mr. Scales's smile, but it improved his face very much.

"Well, Florrie," said Mr. Scales, "we seem to be doing pretty well, financially speaking, don't we?"

Florrie eagerly agreed. "But there," she observed, "we're getting used to that. Mr. Drury's a wonderful man. It doesn't matter what he's in, they all come to see him. Of course," she added, remembering that this might not sound very kind, "he's very clever at picking the right play."

"Oh, yes," said Mr. Scales. "The play. I suppose the play has something to do with it. Not much, but something. Have you seen the play, Florrie?"

Yes, indeed, Florrie had. Mr. Drury was so kind, he always remembered to give Florrie a pass early on in the run, even if the house was ever so full.

"What did you think of it?" inquired Mr. Scales.

"I thought it was lovely," said Florrie. "I cried ever so. When he came back with only one arm and found his fiancée gone to the bad at a cocktail party—"

"Just so," said Mr. Scales.

"And the scene on the Embankment—lovely, I thought that was, when he rolls up his old army coat and says to the bobby, 'I will rest on my laurels'—that was a beautiful curtain line you gave him there, Mr. Scales. And the way he put it over—"

"Yes, rather," said Mr. Scales. "There's nobody like Drury for putting over that kind of a line."

"And when she came back to him and he wouldn't have her any more and then Lady Sylvia took him up and fell in love with him—"

"Yes, yes," said Mr. Scales. "You found that part moving?"

"Romantic," said Florrie. "And the scene between the two girls—that was splendid. All worked-up, it made you feel. And then in the end, when he took the one he really loved after all—"

"Sure-fire, isn't it?" said Mr. Scales. "Goes straight to the heart. I'm glad you think so, Florrie. Because, of course, quite apart from anything else, it's very good box-office."

"I believe you," said Florrie. "Your first play, isn't it? You're lucky to have it taken by Mr. Drury."

"Yes," said Mr. Scales, "I owe him a lot. Everybody says so, and it must be true. There are two fat gentlemen in astrakhan coats coming along tonight to settle about the film-rights. I'm a made man, Florrie, and that's always pleasant, particularly after five or six years of living hand-to-mouth. No fun in not having enough to eat, is there?"

"That there isn't," said Florrie, who knew all about it. "I'm ever so glad your luck's turned at last, dearie."

"Thank you," said Mr. Scales. "Have something to drink the health of the play." He fumbled in his breastpocket. "Here you are. A green one and a brown one. Thirty bob. Thirty pieces of silver. Spend it on something you fancy, Florrie. It's the price of blood."

"What a thing to say!" exclaimed Florrie. "But you writing gentlemen will have a bit of a joke. And I know poor Mr. Milling, who wrote the book for *Pussycat, Pussycat* and *The Lipstick Girl*, always used to say he sweated blood over every one of 'em."

A nice young gentleman, thought Florrie, as Mr. Scales passed on, but queer and, perhaps, a little bit difficult in his temper, for them that had to live with him. He had spoken very nicely about Mr. Drury, but there had been a moment when she had fancied that he was (as they said) registering sarcasm. And she didn't quite like that joke about the thirty pieces of silver—that was New Testament, and New Testament (unlike Old) was blasphemous. It was like the difference between saying, "Oh, God!" (which nobody minded) and "Oh, Christ!" (which Florrie had never held with). Still, people said all kinds of things nowadays, and thirty bob was thirty bob; it was very kind of Mr. Scales.

Mr. John Scales, slouching along Shaftesbury Avenue and wondering how he was going to put in the next three hours or so, encountered a friend just turning out of Wardour Street. The friend was a tall, thin young man, with a shabby overcoat and a face, under a dilapidated soft hat, like a hungry hawk's. There was a girl with him.

"Hullo, Mollie!" said Scales. "Hullo, Sheridan!"

"Hullo!" said Sheridan. "Look who's here! The great man himself. London's rising dramatist. Sweet Scales of Old Drury."

"Cut it out," said Scales.

"Your show seems to be booming," went on Sheridan. "Congratulations. On the boom, I mean."

"God!" said Scales, "have you seen it? I did send you tickets."

"You did—it was kind of you to think of us amid your busy life. We saw the show. In these bargain-basement days, you've managed to sell your soul in a pretty good market."

"See here, Sheridan—it wasn't my fault. I'm just as sick as you are. Sicker. But like a fool I signed the contract without a controlling clause, and by the time Drury and his producer had finished mucking the script about—"

"He didn't sell himself," said the girl, "he was took advantage of, your worship."

"Pity," said Sheridan. "It was a good play—but he done her wrong. But," he added, glancing at Scales, "I take it you drink the champagne that she sends you. You're looking prosperous."

"Well," said Scales, "what do you expect me to do? Return the check with thanks?"

"Good Lord, no," said Sheridan. "It's all right. Nobody's grudging you your luck."

"It's something, after all," said Scales defensively, "to get one's foot in at all. One can't always look a gift horse in the mouth."

"No," said Sheridan. "Good Lord, I know that. Only I'm afraid you'll find this thing hang round your neck a bit if you want to go back to your own line. You know what the public is—it likes to get what it expects. Once you've made a name for sob-stuff, you're labelled for good—or bad."

"I know. Hell. Can't do anything about it, though. Come and have a drink."

But the others had an appointment to keep, and passed on their way. The encounter was typical. Damnation, thought Scales, savagely, turning in to the Criterion Bar, wasn't it enough to have had your decent play cut about and turned into the sort of thing that made you retch to listen to it, without your friends supposing you had acquiesced in the mutilation for the sake of making money?

He had been a little worried when he knew that George Philpotts (kindly officious George, who always knew everybody) had sent *Bitter Laurel* to Drury. The very last management he himself would have selected; but also the very last management that would be likely to take so cynical and disillusioned a play. Miraculously, however, Drury had expressed himself as "dead keen" about it. There had been an interview with Drury, and Drury, damn his expressive eyes, had—yes, one had to admit it—Drury had "put himself across" with great success. He had been flattering, he had been charming. Scales had succumbed, as night by night pit and stalls and dress circle succumbed to the gracious manner and the elfin smile. "A grand piece—grand situations," Garrick Drury had said. "Of course, here and there it will need a little tidying up in production." Scales said modestly that he expected that— he knew very little about writing for the stage—he was a novelist—he was quite ready to agree to alterations, provided, naturally, nothing was done to upset the artistic unity of the thing. Mr. Garrick Drury was pained by the suggestion. As an artist himself, he should, of course, allow nothing inartistic to be done. Scales, overcome by Drury's manner, and by a flood of technicalities about sets and lighting and costing and casting poured out upon him by the producer, who was present at the interview, signed a contract giving the author a very handsome share of the royalties, and hardly noticed that he had left the management with full power to make any "reasonable" alterations to fit the play for production.

It was only gradually in the course of rehearsal, that he

discovered what was being done to his play. It was not merely that Mr. Drury had succeeded in importing into the lines given to him, as the war-shattered hero, a succulent emotionalism which was very far from the dramatist's idea of that embittered and damaged character. So much, one had expected. But the plot had slowly disintegrated and reshaped itself into something revoltingly different. Originally, for example, the girl Judith (the one who had "gone to the bad at a cocktail party") had not spurned the one-armed soldier (Mr. Drury). Far from it. She had welcomed him and several other heroes home with indiscriminate, not to say promiscuous, enthusiasm. And the hero, instead of behaving (as Mr. Drury saw to it that he did in the acted version) in a highly sacrificial manner, had gone deliberately and cynically to the bad in his turn. Nor had "Lady Sylvia," who rescued him from the Embankment, been (as Mr. Drury's second leading lady now represented her to be) a handsome and passionate girl deeply in love with the hero, but a nauseous, rich, elderly woman with a fancy for a gigolo, whose attentions the hero (now thoroughly deteriorated as a result of war and post-war experience) accepted without shame or remorse in exchange for the luxuries of life. And finally, when Judith, thoroughly shocked and brought to her senses by these developments, had tried to recapture him, the hero (as originally depicted) had so far lost all sense of decency as to prefer—though with a bitter sense of failure and frustration—to stick to Lady Sylvia, as the line of least resistance, and had ended, on Armistice Day, by tearing away the public trophies of laurel and poppy from the Cenotaph and being ignominiously removed by the police after a drunken and furious harangue in denunciation of war. Not a pleasant play, as originally written, and certainly in shocking taste; but an honest piece of work so far as it went. But Mr. Drury had pointed out that "his" public would never stand the original Lady Sylvia or the final degradation of the hero. There must be slight alterations—nothing inartistic, of course, but alterations, to make the thing more moving, more uplifting, more, in fact, true to human nature.

Because, Mr. Drury pointed out, if there was one thing you could rely on, it was the essential decency of human nature, and its immediate response to generous sentiments. His experience, he said, had proved it to him.

Scales had not given way without a struggle. He had fought hard over every line. But there was the contract. And in the end, he had actually written the new scenes and lines himself, not because he wanted to, but because at any rate his own lines would be less intolerable than the united efforts of cast and producer to write them for themselves. So that he could not even say that he had washed his hands of the whole beastly thing. Like his own (original) hero, he had taken the line of least resistance. Mr. Drury had been exceedingly grateful to him and delighted to feel that author and management were working so well together in their common interest.

"I know how you feel," he would say, "about altering your artistic work. Any artist feels the same. But I've had twenty years' experience of the stage, and it counts, you know, it counts. You don't think I'm right—my dear boy, I should feel just the same in your place. I'm terribly grateful for all this splendid work you're putting in, and I know you won't regret it. Don't worry. All young authors come up against the same difficulty. It's just a question of experience."

Hopeless. Scales, in desperation, had enlisted the services of an agent, who pointed out that it was now too late to get the contract altered. "But," said the agent, "it's quite an honest contract, as these things go. Drury's management has always had a very good name. We shall keep an eye on these subsidiary rights for you—you can leave that to us. I know it's a nuisance having to alter things here and there, but it *is* your first play, and you're lucky to have got in with Drury. He's very shrewd about what will appeal to a West End audience. When once he's established you, you'll be in a much better position to dictate terms."

Yes, of course, thought Scales—to dictate to Drury, or to anybody else who might want that type of play. But in a worse position than ever to get anybody to look at his serious work.

And the worst of it was that the agent, as well as the actor-manager, seemed to think that his concern for his own spiritual integrity didn't count, didn't matter—that he would be quite genuinely consoled by his royalties.

At the end of the first week, Garrick Drury practically said as much. His own experience had been justified by the receipts. "When all's said and done," he remarked, "the box-office is the real test. I don't say that in a commercial spirit. I'd always be ready to put on a play I believed in—as an artist— even if I lost money by it. But when the box-office is happy, it means the public is happy. The box-office is the pulse of the public. Get that and you know you've got the heart of the audience."

He couldn't see. Nobody could see. John Scales's own friends couldn't see; they merely thought he had sold himself. And as the play settled down to run remorselessly on, like a stream of treacle, John Scales realized that there would be no end to it. It was useless to hope that the public would revolt at the insincerity of the play. They probably saw through it all right, just as the critics had done. What stood in the way of the play's deserved collapse was the glorious figure of Garrick Drury. "This broken-backed play," said the *Sunday Echo*, "is only held together by the magnificent acting of Mr. Garrick Drury." "Saccharine as it is," said the *Looker-On*, "*Bitter Laurel* provides a personal triumph for Mr. Garrick Drury." "Nothing in the play is consistent," said the *Dial*, "except the assured skill of Mr. Garrick Drury, who—" "Mr. John Scales," said the *Daily Messenger*, "has constructed his situations with great skill to display Mr. Garrick Drury in all his attitudes, and that is a sure recipe for success. We prophesy a long run for *Bitter Laurel*." A true prophecy, or so it seemed.

And there was no stopping it. If only Mr. Drury would fall ill or die or lose his looks or his voice or his popularity, the beastly play might be buried and forgotten. There were circumstances under which the rights would revert to the author. But Mr. Drury lived and flourished and charmed the public, and the run went on, and after that there were the touring

rights (controlled by Mr. Drury) and film rights (largely controlled by Mr. Drury) and probably radio rights and God only
knew what else. And all Mr. Scales could do was to pocket the
wages of sin and curse Mr. Drury, who had (so pleasantly)
ruined his work, destroyed his reputation, alienated his
friends, exposed him to the contempt of the critics, and forced
him to betray his own soul.

If there was one living man in London whom John Scales
would have liked to see removed from the face of the earth, it
was Garrick Drury, to whom (as he was daily obliged to admit
to all and sundry) he owed so much. Yet Drury was a really
charming fellow. There were times when that inexhaustible
charm got so much on the author's nerves that he could readily have slain Mr. Drury for his charm alone.

Yet, when the moment came, on that night of April
15th–16th, the thing was not premeditated. Not in any real
sense. It just happened. Or did it? That was a thing that even
John Scales could not have said for certain. He may have
felt a moral conviction, but that is not the same thing as a
legal conviction. The doctor may have had his suspicions,
but if so, they were not directed against John Scales. And
whether they were right or wrong, nobody could say that it
had made any difference; the real slayer may have been the
driver of the car, or the intervening hand of Providence,
sprinkling the tarmac with April showers. Or it may have
been Garrick Drury, so courteously and charmingly accompanying John Scales in quest of a taxi, instead of getting
straight into his own car and being whirled away in the
opposite direction.

In any case, it was nearly one in the morning of Sunday
when they got the film people off the premises, after a long
and much interrupted argument, during which Scales found
himself, as usual, agreeing to a number of things he did not
approve of but could see no way to prevent.

"My dear John," said Mr. Garrick Drury, pulling off his
dressing-gown (he always conducted business interviews in a
dressing-gown, if possible, feeling, with some truth, that its

flowing outline suited him), "my dear John, I know exactly how you feel — Walter! — but it needs experience to deal with these people, and you can trust me not to allow anything inartistic — Oh, thank you, Walter. I'm extremely sorry to have kept you so late."

Walter Hopkins was Mr. Drury's personal dresser and faithful adherent. He had not the smallest objection to being kept up all night, or all the next morning for that matter. He was passionately devoted to Mr. Drury, who always rewarded his services with a kind word and the smile. He now helped Mr. Drury into his coat and overcoat and handed him his hat with a gratified murmur. The dressing-room was still exceedingly untidy, but he could not help that; toward the end of the conversation, the negotiations had become so very delicate that even the devoted Walter had had to be dismissed to lurk in an adjacent room.

"Never mind about all this," went on Mr. Drury, indicating a litter of grease-paint, towels, glasses, siphons, ashtrays, teacups (Mr. Drury's aunts had looked in), manuscripts (two optimistic authors had been given audience), mascots (five female admirers had brought Mickey Mice), flowers (handed in at the stage-door), and assorted fanmail, strewn over the furniture. "Just stick my things together and lock up the whisky. I'll see Mr. Scales to his taxi — you're sure I can't drop you anywhere, John? Oh! and bring the flowers to the car — and I'd better look through that play of young what's his name's — Ruggles, Buggles, you know who I mean — perfectly useless, of course, but I promised dear old Fanny — chuck the rest into the cupboard — and I'll pick you up in five minutes."

The night-watchman let them out; he was an infirm and aged man with a face like a rabbit, and Scales wondered what he would do if he met with a burglar or an outbreak of fire in the course of his rounds.

"Hullo!" said Garrick Drury, "it's started to rain. But there's a rank just down the Avenue. Now look here, John, old man, don't you worry about this, because — Look out!"

It all happened in a flash. A small car, coming just a trifle too fast up the greasy street, braked to avoid a prowling cat, skidded, swung round at right angles, and mounted the pavement. The two men leapt for safety—Scales rather clumsily, tripping and sprawling in the gutter. Drury, who was on the inside, made a quick backward spring, neat as an acrobat's, just not far enough. The bumper caught him behind the knee and flung him shoulder-first through the plate-glass window of a milliner's shop.

When Scales had scrambled to his feet, the car was halfway through the window, with its driver, a girl, knocked senseless over the wheel; a policeman and two taxi-drivers were running toward them from the middle of the street; and Drury, very white and his face bleeding, was extricating himself from the splintered glass, with his left arm clutched in his right hand.

"Oh, my God!" said Drury. He staggered up against the car, and between his fingers the bright blood spurted like a fountain.

Scales, shaken and bewildered by his fall, was for the moment unable to grasp what had happened; but the policeman had his wits about him.

"Never mind the lady," he said, urgently, to the taxi-men. "This gent's cut an artery. Bleed to death if we ain't quick." His large, competent fingers grasped the actor's arm, found the right spot and put firm pressure on the severed blood-vessel. The dreadful spurting ceased. "All right, sir? Lucky you 'ad the presence of mind to ketch 'old of yourself." He eased the actor down on the running board, without relaxing his grip.

"I got an 'andkercher," suggested one of the taxi-men.

"That's right," said the policeman. " 'Itch it round 'is arm above the place and pull it as tight as you can. That'll 'elp. Nasty cut it is, right to the bone, by the looks of it."

Scales looked at the shop-window and the pavement, and shuddered. It might have been a slaughter-house.

"Thanks very much," said Drury to the policeman and

the taxi-man. He summoned up the ghost of a smile, and fainted.

"Better take him into the theater," said Scales. "The stage-door's open. Only a step or two up the passage. It's Mr. Drury, the actor," he added, to explain this suggestion. "I'll run along and tell them."

The policeman nodded. Scales hurried up the passage and met Walter just emerging from the stage-door.

"Accident!" said Scales, breathless. "Mr. Drury—cut an artery—they're bringing him here."

Walter, with a cry, flung down the flowers he was carrying and darted out. Drury was being supported up the passage by the two drivers. The policeman walked beside him still keeping a strong thumb on his arm. They brought him in, stumbling over the heaps of narcissus and daffodil; the crushed blossom smelt like funeral flowers.

"There's a couch in his dressing-room," said Scales. His mind had suddenly become abnormally clear. "It's on the ground-floor. Round here to the right and across the stage."

"Oh, dear, oh, dear!" said Walter. "Oh, Mr. Drury! He won't die—he can't die! All that dreadful blood!"

"Now, keep your 'ead," admonished the policeman. "Can't you ring up a doctor and make yourself useful?"

Walter and the night-watchman made a concerted rush for the telephone, leaving Scales to guide the party across the deserted stage, black and ghostly in the light of one dim bulb high over the proscenium arch. Their way was marked by heavy red splashes on the dusty boards. As though the very sound of those boards beneath their tread had wakened the actor's instinct, Drury opened one eye.

"What's happened to those lights?" . . . Then, with return-ing consciousness, "Oh, it's the curtain line . . . Dying, Egypt, dying . . . final appearance, eh?"

"Rot, old man," said Scales, hastily, "You're not dying yet by a long chalk."

One of the taxi-drivers—an elderly man—stumbled and

panted. "Sorry," said Drury, "to be such a weight . . . can't help you much . . . find it easier . . . take your grip further down . . ." The smile was twisted, but his wits and experience were back on the job. This was not the first or the hundredth time he had been "carried out" from the stage of the King's. His bearers took his gasping instructions and successfully negotiated the corner of the set. Scales, hovering in attendance, was unreasonably irritated. Of course, Drury was behaving beautifully. Courage, presence of mind, consideration for others—all the right theatrical gestures. Couldn't the fellow be natural, even at death's door?

Here, Scales was unjust. It was natural to Drury to be theatrical in a crisis, as it is to nine people out of ten. He was, as a matter of fact, providing the best possible justification for his own theories about human nature. They got him to the dressing-room, laid him on the couch, and were thanked.

"My wife," said Drury, ". . . in Sussex. Don't startle her . . . she's had 'flu . . . heart not strong."

"All right, all right," said Scales. He found a towel and drew some water into a bowl. Walter came running in.

"Dr. Debenham's out . . . away for the weekend. . . . Blake's telephoning another one. . . . Suppose they're all away . . . whatever shall we do? . . . They oughtn't to *let* doctors go away like this."

"We'll try the police-surgeon," said the constable. "Here, you come and 'old your thumb where I've got mine. Can't trust that there bandage. Squeeze 'ard, mind, and don't let go. And don't faint," he added sharply. He turned to the taxi-men. "You better go and see what's 'appened to the young lady. I blew me whistle, so you did oughter find the other constable there. You" (to Scales) "will 'ave to stay here—I'll be wanting your evidence about the accident."

"Yes, yes," said Scales, busy with the towel.

"My face," said Drury, putting up a restless hand. "Has it got the eye?"

"No, it's only a scalp-wound. Don't get excited."

"Sure? Better dead than disfigured. Don't want to end like Florrie. Poor old Florrie. Give her my love. . . . Cheer up, Walter. . . . Rotten curtain, isn't it? . . . Get yourself a drink. . . . You're certain the eye's all right? . . . You weren't hurt, were you, old man? . . . Hell of a nuisance for you, too. . . . Stop the run. . . ."

Scales, in the act of pouring out whisky for himself and Walter (who looked nearly as ready to collapse as his employer), started, and nearly dropped the bottle. Stop the run—yes, it would stop the run. An hour ago, he had been praying for a miracle to stop the run. And the miracle had happened. And if Drury hadn't had the wits to stop the bleeding—if he had waited only one minute more—the run would have stopped, and the film would have stopped, and the whole cursed play would have stopped dead for good and all. He swallowed down the neat spirit with a jerk, and handed the second glass to Walter. It was as though he had made the thing happen by wishing for it. By wishing a little harder—Nonsense! . . . But the doctor didn't come and, though Walter was holding on like grim death (*grim death!*) to the cut artery, the blood from the smaller vessels was soaking and seeping through the cloth and the bandages . . . there was still the chance, still the likelihood, still the *hope*. . . .

This would never do. Scales dashed out into the passage and across the stage to the night-watchman's box. The policeman was still telephoning. Drury's chauffeur, haggard and alarmed, stood, cap in hand, talking to the taxi-men. The girl, it appeared, had been taken to hospital with concussion. The divisional police-surgeon had gone to an urgent case. The nearest hospital had no surgeon free at the moment. The policeman was trying the police-surgeon belonging to the next division. Scales went back.

The next half-hour was a nightmare. The patient, hovering between consciousness and unconsciousness, was still worrying about his face, about his arm, about the play. And the red stain on the couch spread and spread. . . .

Then with a bustle, a short, stout man came in, carrying a bag. He took a look at the patient, tested his pulse, asked a few questions, shook his head, muttering something about loss of blood and loss of time and weakness. The policeman, somewhere in the background, mentioned that the ambulance had arrived.

"Nonsense," said the doctor. "Can't possibly move him. Got to deal with it here and now." With a few brisk words of commendation, he dislodged Walter from his post. He worked quickly, cutting away the sodden sleeve, applying a proper tourniquet, administering some kind of stimulant, again assuring the patient that his eye was not damaged and that he was suffering from nothing but shock and loss of blood.

"You won't take my arm off?" said Drury, suddenly visited with a new alarm. "I'm an actor—I can't—I won't—you can't do it without telling me—you—"

"No, no, no," said the doctor. "Now we've stopped the bleeding. But you must lie still, or you might start it again."

"Shall I have the use of it?" The expressive eyes searched the doctor's face. "Sorry. But a stiff arm's as bad as no arm to me. Do your best . . . or I shall never play again. . . . Except in *Bitter Laurel.* . . . John, old man . . . funny, isn't it? Funny it's this arm. . . . Have to live on your play for the rest of my days . . . the only, only play . . ."

"Good God!" cried Scales, involuntarily.

"Now, I must have this room clear," said the doctor with authority. "Officer, get these people out and send me in those ambulance men."

"Come along," said the policeman. "And I'll take your statement now, sir."

"Not me!" protested Walter Hopkins, "I can't leave Mr. Drury. I can't. Let me stay. I'll help. I'll do anything—"

"The best way you can help," said the doctor, not unkindly but with determination, "is by giving me room to work. Now, please—"

Somehow they got Walter, struggling and hysterical, into

the dressing-room across the passage. Here he sat, gathered together on the edge of a chair, starting at every sound from outside, while the constable interrogated and dismissed the two taxi-men. Then Scales found himself giving a statement, in the midst of which, the doctor put his head in to say:

"I want some of you to stand by. It may be necessary to make a blood-transfusion. We must get that arm stitched, but his pulse is very weak and I don't know how he'll stand it. I don't suppose any of you know which blood-group you belong to?"

"I'll do it!" cried Walter, eagerly. "Please, sir, let it be me! I'd give all the blood in my body for Mr. Drury. I've been with him fifteen years, doctor—"

"Now, now," said the doctor.

"I'd sacrifice my life for Mr. Drury."

"Yes, I dare say," said the doctor, with a resigned look at the constable, "but there's no question of that. Where do people get these ideas? Out of the papers, I suppose. Nobody's being asked to sacrifice any lives. We only want a pint or so of blood—trifling affair for a healthy man. It won't make the slightest difference to you—do you good, I shouldn't wonder. My dear sir, don't excite yourself so much. I know you're willing—very naturally—but if you haven't the right kind of blood you're no good to me."

"I'm very strong," said Walter, palpitating. "Never had a day's illness."

"It's nothing to do with your general health," said the doctor, a little impatiently. "It's a thing you're born with. I gather there is no relation of the patient's handy. . . . What? Wife, sister, and son in Sussex—well that's rather a long way off. I'll test the two ambulance men first, but unfortunately the patient isn't a universal recipient, so we may not get the right grouping first go-off. I'd like one or two others handy, in case. Good thing I brought everything with me. Always do in an accident case. Never know what you may need, and time's everything."

He darted out, leaving behind him an atmosphere of mystery and haste. The policeman shook his head and pocketed his note-book.

"Dunno as blood-offerings is part of my dooty," he observed. "I did oughter get back to me beat. But I'll 'ave to give that there car the once-over and see what my chum 'as to say about it. I'll look in again when I done that, and if they wants me they'll know where to find me. Now, then, what do *you* want?"

"Press," said a man at the door, succinctly. "Somebody phoned to say Mr. Drury was badly hurt. That true? Very sorry to hear it. Ah! Good evening, Mr. Scales. This is all very distressing. I wonder, can you tell me . . . ?"

Scales found himself helplessly caught up in the wheels of the Press—giving an account of the accident—saying all the right things about Drury—what Drury had done for him—what Drury had done for the play—quoting Drury's words—expatiating on Drury's courage, presence of mind and thought for others—manufacturing a halo round Drury—mentioning the strange (and to the newspaper man, gratifying) coincidence that the arm actually wounded was the arm wounded in the play—hoping that Eric Brand, the understudy, would be able to carry on till Mr. Drury was sufficiently recovered to play again—feeling his hatred for Drury rise up in him like a flood with every word he uttered—and finally insisting, with a passion and emphasis that he could not explain to himself, on his own immense personal gratitude and friendship toward Drury and his desperate anxiety to see him restored to health. He felt as though, by saying this over and over again, he might stifle something—something—some frightful thing within him that was asserting itself against his will. The reporter said that Mr. Scales had his deepest sympathy. . . .

"Mr.—ha, hum—" said the doctor, popping his head in again.

"Excuse me," said Scales, quickly. He made for the door: but Walter was there before him, agitatedly offering his life-blood by the gallon. Scales thought he could see the pressman's ears prick up like a dog's. A blood-transfusion, of course, was always jam for a headline. But the doctor made short work of the reporter.

"No time for *you*," he said brusquely, pulling Scales and Walter out and slamming the door. "Yes—I want another test. Hope one of you's the right sort. If not," he added, with a sort of grim satisfaction, "we'll try bleeding the tripe-hound. Learn him not to make a fuss." He led the way back into Drury's dressing-room where the big screen which usually shrouded the wash-stand had been pulled round to conceal the couch. A space had been cleared on the table, and a number of articles laid out upon it: bottles, pipettes, needles, a porcelain slab oddly marked and stained, and a small drum of the sort used for protecting sterilized instruments. Standing near the wash-basin, one of the ambulance men was boiling a saucepan on a gas-ring.

"Now then," said the doctor. He spoke in a low tone, perfectly clear, but calculated not to carry beyond the screen. "Don't make more noise than you can help. I'll have to do it here—no gas-ring in the other room, and I don't want to leave the patient. Never mind—it won't take a minute to make the tests. I can do you both together. Here, you—I want this slab cleaned—no, never mind, here's a clean plate; that'll do—it needn't be surgically sterile." He wiped the plate carefully with a towel and set it on the table between the two men. Scales recognized its pattern of pink roses; it had often held sandwiches while he and Drury, endlessly talking, had hammered out new dialogue for *Bitter Laurel* over a quick lunch. "You understand"—the doctor looked from one to the other and addressed himself to Walter, as though feeling that the unfortunate man might burst unless some notice was taken of him soon—"that your blood—everybody's blood—belongs to one or other of four different groups." He opened the drum and picked out a needle. "There's no necessity to go into details; the point is that, for a transfusion to be successful, the donor's blood must combine in a particular way with the patient's. Now, this will only be a prick—you'll scarcely feel it." He took Walter by the ear and jabbed the needle into the lobe. "If the donor's blood belongs to an unsuitable group, it causes agglutination of the red cells, and the operation is worse than useless." He drew off a few drops of blood into a pipette. Walter watched and listened, seeming to understand very little, but soothed by the calm, professional voice. The doctor transferred two separate droplets of diluted blood to the plate, making a little ring about each with a grease pencil. "There is one type of person"—here he captured Scales and repeated the operation upon his ear with a fresh needle and pipette—"group 4, we call them, who are universal donors; their blood suits anybody. Or, of course, if one of you belongs to the patient's own blood-group, that would do nicely. Unfortunately, he's a group 3, and that's rather rare. So far, we've been unlucky." He placed two drops of Scales's blood on the other side of the plate, drawing a pencil-mark from edge to edge to separate the two pairs of specimens, set the plate neatly between the two donors, so that each stood guard over his own property, and turned again to Walter:

"Let's see, what's your name?"

As though in answer, there was a movement behind the screen. Something fell with a crash, and the ambulance man put out a scared face, saying urgently, "Doctor!" At the same moment came Drury's voice, "Walter—tell Walter—!" trailing into silence. Walter and the doctor dived for the screen together, Scales catching Walter as he pushed past him. The second ambulance man put down what he was doing and ran to assist. There was a moment of bustle and expostulation, and the doctor said, "Come, now, give him a chance." Walter came back to his place at the table. His mouth looked as though he were going to cry.

"They won't let me see him. He asked for me."

"He mustn't exert himself, you know," said Scales, mechanically.

The patient was muttering to himself and the doctor seemed to be trying to quiet him. Scales and Walter Hopkins stood waiting helplessly, with the plate between them. Four little drops of blood—absurd, thought Scales, that they should be of so much importance, when you remembered that horrible welter in the street, on the couch. On the table stood a small wooden rack, containing ampoules. He read the labels, "Stock serum No. II," "Stock serum No. III"; the words conveyed nothing to him; he noticed, stupidly, that one of the little pink roses on the border of the plate had been smudged in the firing—that Walter's hands were trembling as he supported himself upon the table.

Then the doctor reappeared, whispering to the ambulance men, "Do try to keep him quiet." Walter looked anxiously at him. "All right, so far," said the doctor. "Now then, where were we? What did you say your name was?" He labelled the specimens on Walter's side of the plate with the initials "W. H."

"Mine's John Scales," said Scales. The doctor wrote down the initials of London's popular playwright as indifferently as though they had been those of a rate-collector and took from the rack the ampoule of Serum II. Breaking it, he added a little of the contents, first to a drop of the "J. S." blood and, next, to a drop of "W. H." blood, scribbling the figure II beside each specimen. To each of the remaining drops he added, in the same way, a little of Serum III. Blood and serum met and mingled; to Scales, all four of the little red blotches looked exactly alike. He was disappointed; he had vaguely expected something more dramatic.

"It'll take a minute or two," said the doctor, gently rocking the plate. "If the blood of either of you mixes with both sera without clumping the red corpuscles, then that donor is a universal donor, and will do. Or, if it clumps with Serum II and remains clear with Serum III, then the donor belongs to the patient's own blood-group and will do excellently for him. But if it clumps with both sera or with Serum III only, then it will do for the patient in quite another sense." He set the plate down and began to fish in his pocket.

One of the ambulance men looked round the screen again. "I can't find his pulse," he announced helplessly, "and he's looking very queer." The doctor clicked his tongue in a worried way against his teeth and vanished. There were movements, and a clinking of glass.

Scales gazed down at the plate. Was there any difference to be seen? Was one of the little blotches on Walter's side beginning to curdle and separate into grains as though someone had sprinkled it with cayenne pepper? He was not sure. On his own side of the plate, the drops looked exactly alike. Again he read the labels; again he noted the pink rose that had been smudged in the firing—the pink rose—funny about the pink rose—but what was funny about it? Certainly, one of Walter's drops was beginning to look different. A hard ring was forming about its edge, and the tiny, peppery grains were growing darker and more distinct.

"He'll do now," said the doctor, returning, "but we don't want to lose any time. Let's hope—"

He bent over the plate again. It was the drop labelled III that had the queer grainy look—was that the right way or the wrong way round? Scales could not remember. The doctor was examining the specimens closely, with the help of a pencil microscope. . . . Then he straightened his back with a small sigh of relief.

"Group 4," he announced; "we're all right now."

"Which of us?" thought Scales (though he was pretty sure of the answer). He was still obscurely puzzled by the pink rose.

"Yes," went on the doctor, "no sign of agglutination. I think we can risk that without a direct match-up against the patient's blood. It would take twenty minutes and we can't spare the time." He turned to Scales. "You're the man we want."

Walter gave an anguished cry.

"Not me?"

"Hush!" said the doctor, authoritatively. "No. I'm afraid we can't let it be you. Now, you"—he turned to Scales again—"are a universal donor; very useful person to have about. Heart quite healthy, I suppose? Feels all right. You look fit enough, and thank goodness, you're not fat. Get your coat off, will you and turn up your sleeve. Ah, yes. Nice stout-looking vein. Splendid. Now, you won't take any harm—you may feel a little faint perhaps, but you'll be as right as rain in an hour or so."

"Yes," agreed Scales. He was still looking at the plate. The smudged rose was on his right. Surely it had always been on his right. Or had it started on his left? When? Before the blood-drops had been put on? or after? How could it have altered its position? When the doctor was handling the plate? Or could Walter have caught the plate with his sleeve and swiveled it round when he made his mad rush for the screen? If so, was that before the specimens had been labelled? After, surely. No, before—*after* they were taken and *before* they were labelled. And that would mean . . .

The doctor was opening the drum again; taking out bandages, forceps, a glass flask . . .

That would mean that his own blood and Walter's had changed places before the serum was added, and if so . . .

. . . Scissors, towels, a kind of syringe . . .

If there was the slightest doubt, one ought to draw attention to it and have the specimens tested again. But perhaps either of their bloods would have done equally well; in that case, the doctor would naturally give the preference to John Scales, rather than to poor Walter, shivering there like a leaf. Clump with II, clear with III; clump with III, clear with II— he couldn't remember which way it went. . . .

"No, I'm sorry," repeated the doctor. He escorted Walter firmly to the door and came back. "Poor chap—he can't make out why his blood won't do. Hopeless, of course. Just as well give the man prussic acid at once."

. . . The pink rose . . .

"Doctor—" began Scales.

And then, suddenly, Drury's voice came from behind the screen, speaking the line that had been written to be spoken with a harsh and ugly cynicism, but giving it as he had given it now on the stage for nearly a hundred performances:

"All right, all right, don't worry—I'll rest on my laurels."

The hated, heartbreaking voice—the professional actor's voice—sweet as sugar plums—liquid and mellow like an intoxicated flute.

Damn him! thought Scales, feeling the rubber band tighten above his elbow, I hope he dies. Never to hear that damned-awful voice again. I'd give anything. I'd give . . .

He watched his arm swell and mottle red and blue under the pressure of the band. The doctor gave him an injection of something. Scales said nothing. He was thinking:

Give anything. I would give my life. I would give my blood. I have *only* to give my blood—and say nothing. The plate *was* turned around. . . . No, I don't know that. It's the doctor's business to make sure. . . . I can't speak now. . . . He'll wonder why I didn't speak before. . . . Author sacrifices blood to save benefactor. . . . Roses to right of him, roses to left of him . . . roses, roses all the way. . . . I will rest on my laurels.

The needle now—plump into the vein. His own blood flowing, rising in the glass flask . . . Somebody bringing a bowl of warm water with a faint steam rising off it . . . His life for his friend . . . right as rain in an hour or two . . . blood-brothers . . . the blood is the life . . . as well give him prussic acid at once . . . to poison a man with one's own blood . . . new idea, for a murder . . . MURDER. . . .

"Don't jerk about," said the doctor.

. . . and what a motive! . . . murder to save one's artistic soul . . . Who'd believe that? . . . and losing money by it . . . your money or your life . . . his life for his friend . . . his friend for his life . . . life or death, and not to know which one was giving . . . not *really* know . . . not know at all, *really* . . . too late now . . . absurd to say anything now . . . nobody *saw* the plate turned round . . . and who would ever imagine . . . ?

"That'll do," said the doctor. He loosened the rubber band, dabbed a pad of wool over the puncture and pulled out the needle, all, it seemed to Scales, in one movement. He plopped the flask into a little stand over the bowl of water and dressed the arm with iodine. "How do you feel? A trifle faint? Go and lie down in the other room for a minute or two."

Scales opened his mouth to speak, and was suddenly assailed by a queer, sick qualm. He plunged for the door. As he went, he saw the doctor carry the flask behind the screen.

Damn that reporter! He was still hanging round. Meat and drink to the papers, this kind of thing. Heroic sacrifice by grateful author. Good story. Better story still if the heroic author were to catch him by the arm, pour into his ear the unbelievable truth—were to say, "I hated him, I hated him, I tell you—I've poisoned him—my blood's poison—serpent's blood, dragon's blood—"

And what would the doctor say? If this really had gone wrong, would he suspect? *What could he suspect?* He hadn't seen the plate move. Nobody had. He might suspect himself of negligence, but he wouldn't be likely to shout *that* from the housetops. And he *had* been negligent—pompous, fat, chattering fool. Why didn't he mark the specimens earlier? Why didn't he match-up the blood with Drury's? Why did he need to chatter so much and explain things? Tell people how easy it was to murder a benefactor?

Scales wished he knew what was happening. Walter was hovering outside in the passage. Walter was jealous—he had looked on enviously, grudgingly, as Scales came stumbling in from the operation. If only Walter knew what Scales had been doing, he might well look . . . It occurred to Scales that he had played a shabby trick on Walter—cheated him—Walter, who had wanted so much to sacrifice his right, his true, his life-giving blood. . . .

Twenty minutes . . . nearly half an hour . . . How soon would they know whether it was all right or all wrong? "As well give him prussic acid," the doctor had said. That suggested something pretty drastic. Prussic acid was quick—you died as if struck.

Scales got up, pushed Walter and the pressman aside, and crossed the passage. In Drury's room the screen had been pushed back. Scales, peeping through the door, could see Drury's face, white and glistening with sweat. The doctor bent over the patient, holding his wrist. He looked dis-

tressed—almost alarmed. Suddenly he turned, caught sight of
Scales and came over to him. He seemed to take minutes to
cross the room.

"I'm sorry," said the doctor. "I'm very much afraid—you
did your best—we all did our best."

"No good?" Scales whispered back. His tongue and palate
were like sawdust.

"One can never be certain with these things," said the doctor. "I'm very much afraid he's going." He paused and his eyes
were faintly puzzled. "So much hemorrhage," he muttered as
though explaining the trouble to himself. "Shock—cardiac
strain—excitable"—and, in a worried voice—"he complained
almost at once of a pain in the back." He added, with more
assurance: "It's always a bit of a gamble, you see, when the
operation is left so late—and sometimes there is a particular
idiosyncrasy. I should have preferred a direct test; but it's not
satisfactory if the patient dies while you wait to make sure."

With a wry smile he turned back to the couch, and Scales
followed him. If Drury could have acted death as he was acting it now! . . . Scales could not rid himself of the notion that
he *was* acting—that the shine upon the skin was grease-paint,
and the rough, painful breathing, the stereotyped stage gasp.
If truth could be so stagy, then the stage must be disconcertingly like truth.

Something sobbed at his elbow. Walter had crept into the
room, and this time the doctor made way for him.

"Oh, Mr. Drury!" said Walter.

Drury's blue lips moved. He opened his eyes: the dilated
pupils made them look black and enormous.

"Where's Brand?"

The doctor turned interrogatively to the other two men.
"His son?"

"His understudy," whispered Scales. Walter said, "He'll
be here in a minute, Mr. Drury."

"They're waiting," said Drury. He drew a difficult breath
and spoke in his old voice:

"Brand! Fetch Brand! The curtain must go up!"

Garrick Drury's death was very "good theater."

Nobody, thought Scales, could ever know. He could never really know himself. Drury might have died, anyhow, of shock. Even if the blood had been right, he might have died. One couldn't be certain, now, that the blood hadn't been right; it might have been all imagination about the smudged pink rose. Or—one might be sure, deep in one's own mind. But nobody could prove it. Or—could the doctor? There would have to be an inquest, of course. Would they make a post-mortem? Could they prove that the blood was wrong? If so, the doctor had his ready explanation—"particular idiosyncrasy" and lack of time to make further tests. He *must* give that explanation, or accuse himself of negligence.

Because nobody could prove that the plate had been moved. Walter and the doctor had not seen it—if they had, they would have spoken. Nor could it be proved that he, Scales, had seen it—he was not even certain himself, except in the hidden chambers of the heart. And he, who lost so much by Drury's death—to suppose that he could have seen and not spoken was fantastic. There are things beyond the power even of a coroner to imagine or of a coroner's jury to believe.

SUSPICION

As the atmosphere of the railway carriage thickened with tobacco-smoke, Mr. Mummery became increasingly aware that his breakfast had not agreed with him.

There could have been nothing wrong with the breakfast itself. Brown bread, rich in vitamin-content, as advised by the *Morning Star*'s health expert; bacon fried to a delicious crispness; eggs just nicely set; coffee made as only Mrs. Sutton knew how to make it. Mrs. Sutton had been a real find, and that was something to be thankful for. For Ethel, since her nervous breakdown in the Summer, had really not been fit to wrestle with the untrained girls who had come and gone in tempestuous succession. It took very little to upset Ethel nowadays, poor child. Mr. Mummery, trying hard to ignore his growing internal discomfort, hoped he was not in for an illness. Apart from the trouble it would cause at the office, it would worry Ethel terribly, and Mr. Mummery would cheerfully have laid down his rather uninteresting little life to spare Ethel a moment's uneasiness.

He slipped a digestive tablet into his mouth — he had taken lately to carrying a few tablets about with him — and opened his paper. There did not seem to be very much news. A question had been asked in the House about Government typewriters. The Prince of Wales had smilingly opened an all-British exhibition of foot-wear. A further split had occurred in the Liberal party. The police were still looking for the woman who was supposed to have poisoned a family in Lincoln. Two girls had been trapped in a burning factory. A film-star had obtained her fourth decree nisi.

At Paragon Station, Mr. Mummery descended and took a tram. The internal discomfort was taking the form of a definite nausea. Happily he contrived to reach his office before the worst occurred. He was seated at his desk, pale but in control of himself, when his partner came breezing in.

" 'Morning, Mummery," said Mr. Brookes in his loud tones, adding inevitably, "Cold enough for you?"

"Quite," replied Mr. Mummery. "Unpleasantly raw, in fact."

"Beastly, beastly," said Mr. Brookes. "Your bulbs all in?"

"Not quite all," confessed Mr. Mummery. "As a matter of fact I haven't been feeling—"

"Pity," interrupted his partner. "Great pity. Ought to get 'em in early. Mine were in last week. My little place will be a picture in the Spring. For a town garden, that is. You're lucky, living in the country. Find it better than Hull, I expect, eh? Though we get plenty of fresh air up in the Avenues. How's the missus?"

"Thank you, she's very much better."

"Glad to hear that, very glad. Hope we shall have her about again this winter as usual. Can't do without her in the Drama Society, you know. By Jove! I shan't forget her acting last year in *Romance*. She and young Welbeck positively brought the house down, didn't they? The Welbecks were asking after her only yesterday."

"Thank you, yes. I hope she will soon be able to take up her social activities again. But the doctor says she mustn't overdo it. No worry, he says—that's the important thing. She is to go easy and not rush about or undertake too much."

"Quite right, quite right. Worry's the devil and all. I cut out worrying years ago and look at me! Fit as a fiddle, for all I shan't see fifty again. *You're* not looking altogether the thing, by the way."

"A touch of dyspepsia," said Mr. Mummery. "Nothing much. Chill on the liver, that's what I put it down to."

"That's what it is," said Mr. Brookes, seizing his opportunity. "Is life worth living? It depends on the liver. Ha, ha! Well now, well now—we must do a spot of work, I suppose. Where's that lease of Ferraby's?"

Mr. Mummery, who did not feel at his conversational best that morning, rather welcomed this suggestion, and for half an hour was allowed to proceed in peace with the duties of an estate agent. Presently, however, Mr. Brookes burst into speech again.

"By the way," he said abruptly. "I suppose your wife doesn't know of a good cook, does she?"

"Well, no," replied Mr. Mummery. "They aren't so easy to find nowadays. In fact, we've only just got suited ourselves. But why? Surely your old Cookie isn't leaving you?"

"Good Lord, no!" Mr. Brookes laughed heartily. "It would take an earthquake to shake off old Cookie. No. It's for the Philipsons. Their girl's getting married. That's the worst of girls. I said to Philipson, 'You mind what you're doing,' I said. 'Get somebody you know something about, or you may find yourself landed with this poisoning woman—what's her name—Andrews. Don't want to be sending wreaths to your funeral yet awhile,' I said. He laughed, but it's no laughing matter and so I told him. What we pay the police for I simply don't know. Nearly a month now, and they can't seem to lay hands on the woman. All they say is, they think she's hanging about the neighborhood and 'may seek situation as cook.' As cook! Now I ask you!"

"You don't think she committed suicide, then?" suggested Mr. Mummery.

"Suicide, my foot!" retorted Mr. Brookes, coarsely. "Don't you believe it, my boy. That coat found in the river was all eyewash. *They* don't commit suicide, that sort don't."

"What sort?"

"Those arsenic-maniacs. They're too damned careful of their own skins. Cunning as weasels, that's what they are. It's only to be hoped they'll manage to catch her before she tries her hand on anybody else. As I told Philipson—"

"You think Mrs. Andrews did it, then?"

"Did it? Of course she did it. It's plain as the nose on your face. Looked after her old father, and he died suddenly—left her a bit of money, too. Then she keeps house for an elderly gentleman, and *he* dies suddenly. Now there's this husband and wife—man dies and woman taken very ill, of arsenic poisoning. Cook runs away, and you ask, did she do it? I don't mind betting that when they dig up the father and the other old bird they'll find *them* bung-full of arsenic, too. Once that sort gets started, they don't stop. Grows on 'em, as you might say."

"I suppose it does," said Mr. Mummery. He picked up his paper again and studied the photograph of the missing woman. "She looks harmless enough," he remarked. "Rather a nice, motherly-looking kind of woman."

"She's got a bad mouth," pronounced Mr. Brookes. He had a theory that character showed in the mouth. "I wouldn't trust that woman an inch."

As the day went on, Mr. Mummery felt better. He was rather nervous about his lunch, choosing carefully a little boiled fish and custard pudding and being particular not to rush about immediately after the meal. To his great relief, the fish and custard remained where they were put, and he was not visited by that tiresome pain which had become almost habitual in the last fortnight. By the end of the day he became quite lighthearted. The bogey of illness and doctor's bills ceased to haunt him. He bought a bunch of bronze chrysanthemums to carry home to Ethel, and it was with a feeling of pleasant anticipation that he left the train and walked up the garden path of *Mon Abri*.

He was a little dashed by not finding his wife in the sitting-room. Still clutching the bunch of chrysanthemums he pattered down the passage and pushed open the kitchen door.

Nobody was there but the cook. She was sitting at the table with her back to him, and started up almost guiltily as he approached.

"Lor', sir," she said, "you give me quite a start. I didn't hear the front door go."

"Where is Mrs. Mummery? Not feeling bad again, is she?"

"Well, sir, she's got a bit of a headache, poor lamb. I made her lay down and took her up a nice cup 'o tea at half-past four. I think she's dozing nicely now."

"Dear, dear," said Mr. Mummery.

"It was turning out the dining-room done it, if you ask me," said Mrs. Sutton. " 'Now, don't you overdo yourself, ma'am,' I says to her, but you know how she is, sir. She gets that restless, she can't bear to be doing nothing."

"I know," said Mr. Mummery. "It's not your fault, Mrs. Sutton. I'm sure you look after us both admirably. I'll just run up and have a peep at her. I won't disturb her if she's asleep. By the way, what are we having for dinner?"

"Well, I *had* made a nice steak-and-kidney pie," said Mrs. Sutton, in accents suggesting that she would readily turn it into a pumpkin or a coach-and-four if it was not approved of.

"Oh!" said Mr. Mummery. "Pastry? Well, I—"

"You'll find it beautiful and light," protested the cook, whisking open the oven-door for Mr. Mummery to see. "And it's made with butter, sir, you having said that you found lard indigestible."

"Thank you, thank you," said Mr. Mummery. "I'm sure it will be most excellent. I haven't been feeling altogether the thing just lately, and lard does not seem to suit me nowadays."

"Well, it don't suit some people, and that's a fact," agreed Mrs. Sutton. "I shouldn't wonder if you've got a bit of a chill on the liver. I'm sure this weather is enough to upset anybody."

She bustled to the table and cleared away the picture-paper which she had been reading.

"Perhaps the mistress would like her dinner sent up to her?" she suggested.

Mr. Mummery said he would go and see, and tiptoed his way upstairs. Ethel was lying snuggled under the eider-down and looked very small and fragile in the big double bed. She stirred as he came in and smiled up at him.

"Hullo, darling!" said Mr. Mummery.

"Hullo! You back? I must have been asleep. I got tired and headachy, and Mrs. Sutton packed me off upstairs."

"You've been doing too much, sweetheart," said her husband, taking her hand in his and sitting down on the edge of the bed.

"Yes — it was naughty of me. What lovely flowers, Harold. All for me?"

"All for you, Tiddley-winks," said Mr. Mummery, tenderly. "Don't I deserve something for that?"

Mrs. Mummery smiled, and Mr. Mummery took his reward several times over.

"That's quite enough, you sentimental old thing," said Mrs. Mummery. "Run away, now, I'm going to get up."

"Much better go to bed, my precious, and let Mrs. Sutton send your dinner up," said her husband.

Ethel protested, but he was firm with her. If she didn't take care of herself, she wouldn't be allowed to go to the Drama Society meetings. And everybody was so anxious to have her back. The Welbecks had been asking after her and saying that they really couldn't get on without her.

"Did they?" said Ethel with some animation. "It's very sweet of them to want me. Well, perhaps I'll go to bed after all. And how has my old Hubby been all day?"

"Not too bad, not too bad."

"No more tummy-aches?"

"Well, just a *little* tummy-ache. But it's quite gone now. Nothing for Tiddley-winks to worry about."

Mr. Mummery experienced no more distressing symptoms the next day or the next. Following the advice of the newspaper expert, he took to drinking orange-juice, and was delighted with the results of the treatment. On Thursday, however, he was taken so ill in the night that Ethel was alarmed and insisted on sending for the doctor. The doctor felt his pulse and looked at his tongue and appeared to take the matter lightly. An inquiry into what he had been eating elicited the fact that dinner had consisted of pig's trotters, followed by a milk pudding, and that, before retiring, Mr. Mummery had consumed a large glass of orange-juice, according to his new régime.

"There's your trouble," said Dr. Griffiths cheerfully. "Orange-juice is an excellent thing, and so are trotters, but not in combination. Pigs and oranges together are extraordinarily bad for the liver. I don't know why they should be, but there's no doubt that they are. Now I'll send you round a little prescription and you stick to slops for a day or two and keep off pork. And don't you worry about him, Mrs. Mummery, he's as sound as a trout. *You're* the one we've got to look after. I don't want to see those black rings under the eyes, you know. Disturbed night, of course—yes. Taking your tonic regularly? That's right. Well, don't be alarmed about your hubby. We'll soon have him out and about again."

The prophecy was fulfilled, but not immediately. Mr. Mummery, though confining his diet to Benger's food, bread-and-milk, and beef-tea skilfully prepared by Mrs. Sutton and brought to his bedside by Ethel, remained very seedy all through Friday, and was only able to stagger rather shakily downstairs on Saturday afternoon. He had evidently suffered a "thorough upset." However, he was able to attend to a few papers which Brookes had sent down from the office for his signature, and to deal with the household books. Ethel was not a business woman, and Mr. Mummery always ran over the accounts with her. Having settled up with the butcher, the baker, the dairy, and the coal-merchant, Mr. Mummery looked up inquiringly.

"Anything more, darling?"

"Well, there's Mrs. Sutton. This is the end of her month, you know."

"So it is. Well, you're quite satisfied with her, aren't you, darling?"

"Yes, rather—aren't you? She's a good cook, and a sweet, motherly old thing, too. Don't you think it was a real brain-wave of mine, engaging her like that, on the spot?"

"I do, indeed," said Mr. Mummery.

"It was a perfect providence, her turning up like that, just after that wretched Jane had gone off without even giving notice. I was in absolute *despair*. It was a little bit of a gamble, of course, taking her without any references, but naturally, if she'd been looking after a widowed mother, you couldn't expect her to give references."

"N-no," said Mr. Mummery. At the time he had felt uneasy about the matter, though he had not liked to say much because, of course, they simply had to have somebody. And the experiment had justified itself so triumphantly in practice that one couldn't say much about it now. He had once rather tentatively suggested writing to the clergyman of Mrs. Sutton's parish, but, as Ethel had said, the clergyman wouldn't have been able to tell them anything about cooking, and cooking, after all, was the chief point.

Mr. Mummery counted out the month's money.

"And by the way, my dear," he said, "you might just mention to Mrs. Sutton that if she *must* read the morning paper before I come down, I should be obliged if she would fold it neatly afterwards."

"What an old fuss-box you are, darling," said his wife.

Mr. Mummery sighed. He could not explain that it was somehow important that the morning paper should come to him fresh and prim, like a virgin. Women did not feel these things.

On Sunday, Mr. Mummery felt very much better—quite his old self, in fact. He enjoyed the *News of the World* over break-fast in bed, reading the murders rather carefully. Mr. Mummery got quite a lot of pleasure out of murders—they gave him an agreeable thrill of vicarious adventure, for, naturally, they were matters quite remote from daily life in the outskirts of Hull.

He noticed that Brookes had been perfectly right. Mrs. Andrews's father and former employer had been "dug up" and had, indeed, proved to be "bung-full" of arsenic.

He came downstairs for dinner—roast sirloin, with the potatoes done under the meat and Yorkshire pudding of delicious lightness, and an apple tart to follow. After three days of invalid diet, it was delightful to savor the crisp fat and underdone lean. He ate moderately, but with a sensuous enjoyment. Ethel, on the other hand, seemed a little lacking in appetite, but then, she had never been a great meat-eater. She was fastidious and, besides, she was (quite unnecessarily) afraid of getting fat.

It was a fine afternoon, and at three o'clock, when he was quite certain that the roast beef was "settling" properly, it occurred to Mr. Mummery that it would be a good thing to put the rest of those bulbs in. He slipped on his old gardening coat and wandered out to the potting-shed. Here he picked up a bag of tulips and a trowel, and then, remembering that he was wearing his good trousers, decided that it would be wise to take a mat to kneel on. When had he had the mat last? He could not recollect, but he rather fancied he had put it away in the corner under the potting-shelf. Stooping down, he felt about in the dark among the flower-pots. Yes, there it was, but there was a tin of something in the way. He lifted the tin carefully out. Of course, yes—the remains of the weed-killer.

Mr. Mummery glanced at the pink label, printed in staring letters with the legend: "ARSENICAL WEED-KILLER. POISON," and observed, with a mild feeling of excitement, that it was the same brand of stuff that had been associated with Mrs. Andrews's latest victim. He was rather pleased about it. It gave him a sensation of being remotely but definitely in touch with important events. Then he noticed, with surprise and a little annoyance, that the stopper had been put in quite loosely.

"However'd I come to leave it like that?" he grunted. "Shouldn't wonder if all the goodness has gone off." He removed the stopper and squinted into the can, which appeared to be half-full. Then he rammed the thing home again, giving it a sharp thump with the handle of the trowel for better security. After that he washed his hands carefully at the scullery tap, for he did not believe in taking risks.

He was a trifle disconcerted, when he came in after planting the tulips, to find visitors in the sitting-room. He was always pleased to see Mrs. Welbeck and her son, but he would rather have had warning, so that he could have scrubbed the garden-mold out of his nails more thoroughly. Not that Mrs. Welbeck appeared to notice. She was a talkative woman and paid little attention to anything but her own conversation. Much to Mr. Mummery's annoyance, she chose to prattle about the Lincoln Poisoning Case. A most unsuitable subject for the tea-table, thought Mr. Mummery, at the best of times. His own "upset" was vivid enough in his memory to make him queasy over the discussion of medical symptoms, and besides, this kind of talk was not good for Ethel. After all, the poisoner was still supposed to be in the neighborhood. It was enough to make even a strong-nerved woman uneasy. A glance at Ethel showed him that she was looking quite white and tremulous. He must stop Mrs. Welbeck somehow, or there would be a repetition of one of the old, dreadful, hysterical scenes.

He broke into the conversation with violent abruptness.

"Those Forsyth cuttings, Mrs. Welbeck," he said. "Now is just about the time to take them. If you care to come down the garden I will get them for you."

He saw a relieved glance pass between Ethel and young Welbeck. Evidently the boy understood the situation and was chafing at his mother's tactlessness. Mrs. Welbeck, brought up all standing, gasped slightly and then veered off with obliging readiness on the new tack. She accompanied her host down the garden and chattered cheerfully about horticulture while he selected and trimmed the cuttings. She complimented Mr. Mummery on the immaculacy of his garden paths. "I simply *cannot* keep the weeds down," she said.

Mr. Mummery mentioned the weed-killer and praised its efficacy.

"That stuff!" Mrs. Welbeck started at him. Then she shuddered. "I wouldn't have it in my place for a thousand pounds," she said, with emphasis.

Mr. Mummery smiled. "Oh, we keep it well away from the house," he said. "Even if I were a careless sort of person—"

He broke off. The recollection of the loosened stopper had come to him suddenly, and it was as though, deep down in his mind, some obscure assembling of ideas had taken place. He left it at that, and went into the kitchen to fetch a newspaper to wrap up the cuttings.

Their approach to the house had evidently been seen from the sitting-room window, for when they entered, young Welbeck was already on his feet and holding Ethel's hand in the act of saying goodbye. He maneuvered his mother out of the house with tactful promptness and Mr. Mummery returned to the kitchen to clear up the newspapers he had fished out of the drawer. To clear them up and to examine them more closely. Something had struck him about them, which he wanted to verify. He turned them over very carefully, sheet by sheet. Yes—he had been right. Every portrait of Mrs. Andrews, every paragraph and line about the Lincoln Poisoning Case, had been carefully cut out.

Mr. Mummery sat down by the kitchen fire. He felt as though he needed warmth. There seemed to be a curious cold lump of something at the pit of his stomach—something that he was chary of investigating.

He tried to recall the appearance of Mrs. Andrews as shown in the newspaper photographs, but he had not a good visual memory. He remembered having remarked to Brookes that it was a "motherly" face. Then he tried counting up the time since the disappearance. Nearly a month, Brookes had said—and that was a week ago. Must be over a month now. A month. He had just paid Mrs. Sutton her month's money.

"Ethel!" was the thought that hammered at the door of his brain. At all costs, he must cope with this monstrous suspicion on his own. He must spare her any shock or anxiety. And he must be sure of his ground. To dismiss the only decent cook they had ever had out of sheer, unfounded panic would be wanton cruelty to both women. If he did it at all, it would have to be done arbitrarily, preposterously—he could not suggest horrors to Ethel. However it was done, there would be trouble. Ethel would not understand and he dared not tell her.

But if by chance there was anything in this ghastly doubt — how could he expose Ethel to the appalling danger of having the woman in the house a moment longer? He thought of the family at Lincoln — the husband dead, the wife escaped by a miracle with her life. Was not any shock, any risk, better than that?

Mr. Mummery felt suddenly very lonely and tired. His illness had taken it out of him.

Those illnesses — they had begun, when? Three weeks ago he had had the first attack. Yes, but then he had always been rather subject to gastric troubles. Bilious attacks. Not so violent, perhaps, as these last, but undoubtedly bilious attacks.

He pulled himself together and went, rather heavily, into the sitting-room. Ethel was tucked up in a corner of the chesterfield.

"Tired, darling?"

"Yes, a little."

"That woman has worn you out with talking. She oughtn't to talk so much."

"No." Her head shifted wearily in the cushions. "All about that horrible case. I don't like hearing about such things."

"Of course not. Still, when a thing like that happens in the neighborhood, people will gossip and talk. It would be a relief if they caught the woman. One doesn't like to think —"

"I don't want to think of anything so hateful. She must be a horrible creature."

"Horrible. Brookes was saying the other day —"

"I don't want to hear what he said. I don't want to hear about it at all. I want to be quiet. I want to be quiet!"

He recognized the note of rising hysteria.

"Tiddley-winks shall be quiet. Don't worry, darling. We won't talk about horrors."

No. It would not do to talk about them.

Ethel went to bed early. It was understood that on Sundays Mr. Mummery should sit up till Mrs. Sutton came in. Ethel was a little anxious about this, but he assured her that he felt quite strong enough. In body, indeed, he did; it was his mind that felt weak and confused. He had decided to make a casual remark about the mutilated newspapers — just to see what Mrs. Sutton would say.

He allowed himself the usual indulgence of a whisky-and-soda as he sat waiting. At a quarter to ten he heard the familiar click of the garden gate. Footsteps passed up the gravel — squeak, squeak, to the back-door. Then the sound of the latch, the shutting of the door, the rattle of the bolts being shot home. Then a pause. Mrs. Sutton would be taking off her hat. The moment was coming.

The step sounded in the passage. The door opened. Mrs. Sutton in her neat black dress stood on the threshold. He was aware of a reluctance to face her. Then he looked up. A plump-faced woman, her face obscured by thick horn-rimmed spectacles. Was there, perhaps, something hard about the mouth? Or was it just that she had lost most of her front teeth?

"Would you be requiring anything tonight, sir, before I go up?"

"No, thank you, Mrs. Sutton."

"I hope you are feeling better, sir." Her eager interest in his health seemed to him almost sinister, but the eyes behind the thick glasses were inscrutable.

"Quite better, thank you, Mrs. Sutton."

"Mrs. Mummery is not indisposed, is she, sir? Should I take her up a glass of hot milk or anything?"

"No, thank you, no." He spoke hurriedly, and fancied that she looked disappointed.

"Very well, sir. Good night, sir."

"Good night. Oh! by the way, Mrs. Sutton — "

"Yes, sir?"

"Oh, nothing," said Mr. Mummery, "nothing."

Next morning Mr. Mummery opened his paper eagerly. He would have been glad to learn that an arrest had been made over the weekend. But there was no news for him. The chairman of a trust company had blown out his brains, and all the headlines were occupied with tales about lost millions and ruined shareholders. Both in his own paper and in those he purchased on the way to the office, the Lincoln Poisoning Tragedy had been relegated to an obscure paragraph on a back page, which informed him that the police were still baffled.

The next few days were the most uncomfortable that Mr. Mummery had ever spent. He developed a habit of coming down early in the morning and prowling about the kitchen. This made Ethel nervous, but Mrs. Sutton offered no remark. She watched him tolerantly, even, he thought, with something like amusement. After all, it was ridiculous. What was the use of supervising the breakfast, when he had to be out of the house every day between half-past nine and six?

At the office, Brookes rallied him on the frequency with which he rang up Ethel. Mr. Mummery paid no attention. It was reassuring to hear her voice and to know that she was safe and well.

Nothing happened, and by the following Thursday he began to think that he had been a fool. He came home late that night. Brookes had persuaded him to go with him to a little bachelor dinner for a friend who was about to get married. He left the others at eleven o'clock, however, refusing to make a night of it. The household was in bed when he got back but a note from Mrs. Sutton lay on the table, informing him that there was cocoa for him in the kitchen, ready for hotting-up. He hotted it up accordingly in the little saucepan where it stood. There was just one good cupful.

He sipped it thoughtfully, standing by the kitchen stove. After the first sip, he put the cup down. Was it his fancy, or was there something queer about the taste? He sipped it again, rolling it upon his tongue. It seemed to him to have a faint tang, metallic and unpleasant. In a sudden dread he ran out to the scullery and spat the mouthful into the sink.

After this, he stood quite still for a moment or two. Then, with a curious deliberation, as though his movements had been dictated to him, he fetched an empty medicine-bottle from the pantry-shelf, rinsed it under the tap and tipped the contents of the cup carefully into it. He slipped the bottle into his coat pocket and moved on tiptoe to the back-door. The bolts were difficult to draw without noise, but he managed it at last. Still on tiptoe, he stole across the garden to the potting-shed. Stooping down, he struck a match. He knew exactly where he had left the tin of weed-killer, under the shelf behind the pots at the back. Cautiously he lifted it out. The match flared up and burnt his fingers, but before he could light another his sense of touch had told him what he wanted to know. The stopper was loose again.

Panic seized Mr. Mummery, standing there in the earthy-smelling shed, in his dress-suit and overcoat, holding the tin in one hand and the match-box in the other. He wanted very badly to run and tell somebody what he had discovered.

Instead, he replaced the tin exactly where he had found it and went back to the house. As he crossed the garden again, he noticed a light in Mrs. Sutton's bedroom window. This ter-rified him more than anything which had gone before. Was she watching him? Ethel's window was dark. If she had drunk anything deadly there would be lights everywhere, move-ments, calls for the doctor, just as when he himself had been attacked. Attacked—that was the right word, he thought.

Still with the same odd presence of mind and precision, he went in, washed out the utensils and made a second brew of cocoa, which he left standing in the saucepan. He crept quietly to his bedroom. Ethel's voice greeted him on the threshold.

"How late you are, Harold. Naughty old boy! Have a good time?"

"Not bad. You all right, darling?"

"Quite all right. Did Mrs. Sutton leave something hot for you? She said she would."

"Yes, but I wasn't thirsty."

Ethel laughed. "Oh! it was *that* sort of a party, was it?"

Mr. Mummery did not attempt any denials. He undressed and got into bed and clutched his wife to him as though defying death and hell to take her from him. Next morning he would act. He thanked God that he was not too late.

Mr. Dimthorpe, the chemist, was a great friend of Mr. Mummery's. They had often sat together in the untidy little shop on Spring Bank and exchanged views on greenfly and club-root. Mr. Mummery told his story frankly to Mr. Dimthorpe and handed over the bottle of cocoa. Mr. Dimthorpe congratulated him on his prudence and intelligence.

"I will have it ready for you by this evening," he said, "and if it's what you think it is, then we shall have a clear case on which to take action."

Mr. Mummery thanked him, and was extremely vague and inattentive at business all day. But that hardly mattered, for Mr. Brookes, who had seen the party through to a riotous end in the small hours, was in no very observant mood. At half-past four, Mr. Mummery shut up his desk decisively and announced that he was off early, he had a call to make.

Mr. Dimthorpe was ready for him.

"No doubt about it," he said. "I used Marsh's test. It's a heavy dose, no wonder you tasted it. There must be four or five grains of pure arsenic in that bottle. Look, here's the mirror. You can see it for yourself."

Mr. Mummery gazed at the little glass tube with its ominous purple-black stain.

"Will you ring up the police from here?" asked the chemist.

"No," said Mr. Mummery. "No—I want to get home. God knows what's happening there. And I've only just time to catch my train."

"All right," said Mr. Dimthorpe. "Leave it to me. I'll ring them up for you."

The local train did not go fast enough for Mr. Mummery. Ethel—poisoned—dying—dead—Ethel—poisoned dying—dead—the wheels drummed in his ears. He almost ran out of the station and along the road. A car was standing at his door. He saw it from the end of the street and broke into a gallop. It had happened already. The doctor was there. Fool, murderer that he was to have left things so late.

Then, while he was still a hundred and fifty yards off, he saw the front door open. A man came out followed by Ethel herself. The visitor got into his car and was driven away. Ethel went in again. She was safe — safe!

He could hardly control himself to hang up his hat and coat and go in looking reasonably calm. His wife had returned to the armchair by the fire and greeted him in some surprise. There were tea-things on the table.

"Back early, aren't you?"

"Yes — business was slack. Somebody been to tea?"

"Yes, young Welbeck. About the arrangements for the Drama Society." She spoke briefly but with an undertone of excitement.

A qualm came over Mr. Mummery. Would a guest be any protection? His face must have shown his feelings, for Ethel stared at him in amazement.

"What's the matter, Harold, you look so queer."

"Darling," said Mr. Mummery, "there's something I want to tell you about." He sat down and took her hand in his. "Something a little unpleasant, I'm afraid — "

"Oh, ma'am!"

The cook was in the doorway.

"I beg your pardon, sir — I didn't know you was in. Will you be taking tea or can I clear away? And oh, ma'am, there was a young man at the fishmonger's and he's just come from Grimsby and they've caught that dreadful woman — that Mrs. Andrews. Isn't it a good thing? It worritted me dreadful to think she was going about like that, but they've caught her. Taken a job as housekeeper she had to two elderly ladies and they found the wicked poison on her. Girl as spotted her will get a reward. I been keeping my eyes open for her, but it's at Grimsby she was all the time."

Mr. Mummery clutched at the arm of his chair. It had all been a mad mistake then. He wanted to shout or cry. He wanted to apologize to this foolish, pleasant, excited woman. All a mistake.

But there had been the cocoa. Mr. Dimthorpe. Marsh's test. Five grains of arsenic. Who, then—?

He glanced around at his wife, and in her eyes he saw something that he had never seen before. . . .

THE LEOPARD LADY

If the boy is in your way," said a voice in Tressider's ear, "ask at Rapallo's for Smith & Smith."

Tressider started and looked round. There was nobody near him—unless you counted the bookstall clerk, and the aged gentleman with crooked pince-nez halfway down his nose, who stood poring over a copy of *Blackwood*. Obviously, neither of these two could have uttered that sinister whisper. A yard or two away stood a porter, wearily explaining to a militant woman and a dejected little man that the 5:30 having now gone there was no other train before 9:15. All three were utter strangers to Tressider. He shook himself. It must have been his own subconscious wish that had externalized itself in this curious form. He must keep a hold on himself. Hidden wishes that took shape as audible promptings and whisperings were apt to lead to Colney Hatch—or Broadmoor.

But what in the world had suggested the names "Rapallo's" and "Smith & Smith"? Rapallo—that was a town in Italy or somewhere, he fancied. But the word had come to him as "Rapallo's" as though it were the name of a firm or person. And "Smith & Smith," too. Fantastic. Then he glanced up at the bookstall. Of course, yes— "W. H. Smith & Son"; that must have been the point from which the suggestion had started, and his repressed desires had somehow pushed their message past his censor in that preposterous sentence.

"If the boy is in your way, ask at Rapallo's for Smith & Smith."

He let his eye wander over the books and magazines spread out on the stall. Was there anything—yes, there was. A pile of little red books, of which the topmost bore the title: "How to ask for What you Want in ITALY." There was the other factor of the equation. "Italy" had been the match laid to the train, and the resulting spark had been, queerly but understandably enough, "Rapallo's."

Satisfied, he handed a shilling across the stall and asked for *The Strand Magazine*. He tucked his purchase under his arm and then, glancing at the station clock, decided that he had just time for a quick one before his train went. He turned into the buffet, pausing on the way to buy a packet of cigarettes at the kiosk, where the militant woman was already arming herself with milk-chocolate against her wait for the 9:15. He noticed, with a certain grim satisfaction, that the dejected man had made his escape, and was not altogether surprised to encounter him again in the buffet, hurriedly absorbing something yellow out of a glass.

He was some little time getting served, for there was quite a crowd about the bar. But even if he did miss his train, there was another in twenty minutes' time, and his odd experience had shaken him. The old gentleman with *Blackwood's* had drifted up to the door by the time he left, and, indeed, nearly collided with Tressider in his short-sighted progress. Tressider absently apologized for what was not his fault, and made for the barrier. Here there was again a trifling delay while he searched for his ticket, and a porter who stood beside him with some hand-luggage eventually lost patience and pushed past him with a brief, "By your leave, sir." Eventually, however, he found himself in a first-class carriage with four minutes to spare.

He threw his hat up on to the rack and himself into a corner seat, and immediately, with an automatic anxiety to banish his own thoughts, opened his magazine. As he did so, a card fluttered from between the leaves on to his knee. With an exclamation of impatience directed against the advertisers who filled the pages of magazines with insets, he picked it up, intending to throw it under the seat. A line of black capitals caught his eyes:

SMITH & SMITH

and beneath, in smaller type:

REMOVALS.

He turned the card over. It was about the size of an "At Home" card. The other side was completely blank. There was no address; no explanation. An impulse seized him. He snatched up his hat and made for the door. The train was moving as he sprang out, and he staggered as his feet touched the platform. A porter sprang to his side with a warning shout.

"Shouldn't do that, sir," said the man, reprovingly.

"All right, all right," said Tressider, "I've left something behind."

"That's dangerous, that is," said the porter. "Against regulations."

"Oh, all *right*," said Tressider, fumbling for a coin. As he handed it over, he recognized the porter as the man who had jostled him at the barrier and had stood behind him at the bookstall talking to the militant woman and the dejected man. He dismissed the man hastily, feeling unaccountably uneasy under his official eye. He ran past the barrier with a hasty word to the ticket collector who still stood there, and made his way back to the bookstall.

"*Strand Magazine*," he demanded, curtly, and then, thinking he caught an astonished expression in the eye of the clerk, he muttered:

"Dropped the other."

The clerk said nothing, but handed over the magazine and

accepted Tressider's shilling. Only when he was turning away did Tressider realize that he was still clutching the original copy of the *Strand* under his arm. Well, let the man think what he liked.

Unable to wait, he dived into the General Waiting Room and shook the new *Strand* open. Several insets flew out—one about learning new languages by gramophone, one about Insurance, one about Hire Purchase Payments. He gathered them up and tossed them aside again. Then he examined the magazine, page by page. There was no white card with the name "Smith & Smith."

He stood, trembling, in the dusty gas-light of the waiting room. Had he imagined the card? Was his brain playing tricks with him again? He could not remember what he had done with the card. He searched both magazines and all his pockets. It was not there. He must have left it in the train.

He *must* have left it in the train.

Sweat broke out upon his forehead. It was a terrible thing to go mad. If he had not seen that card—but he *had* seen it. He could see the shape and spacing of the black capitals distinctly.

After a moment or two, an idea came to him. A firm that advertised itself must have an address, perhaps a telephone number. But, of course, not necessarily in London. Those magazines went all over the world. What was the good of advertising without a name or address? Still, he would look. The words "Smith & Smith, Removals," in the London Telephone Directory would steady his nerves considerably.

He went out and sought the nearest telephone cabinet. The directory hung there on its stout chain. Only when he opened it did he realize how many hundred firms called "Smith & Smith" there might be in London. The small print made his eyes ache, but he persevered, and was at length rewarded by finding an entry: "Smith & Smith, Frntre Removrs & Haulage Cntrctrs," with an address in Greenwich.

That should have satisfied him, but it did not. He could not believe that a firm of Furniture Removers and Haulage Contractors at Greenwich would advertise, without address, in a magazine of world-wide circulation. Only firms whose name was a household word could do that kind of thing. And besides, in that second *Strand* there had been no advertisement.

Then how had that card got there? Had the bookstall clerk slipped it in? Or the militant woman who had stood beside him at the tobacco kiosk? Or the dejected man sipping whisky and soda in the buffet? Or the old gentleman who had passed him in the entrance? Or the porter who had waited behind him at the barrier? It came suddenly into his mind that all these five had been near him when he had heard the voice of his repressed wish whisper so persuasively, and so objectively:

"If the boy is in your way, ask at Rapallo's for Smith & Smith."

With a kind of greedy reluctance, he turned the pages of the Telephone Directory backwards to R.

There it was. There could be no mistake about it this time.

"Rapallo's Sandwich & Cocktail Bar," with an address in Conduit Street.

A minute later, Tressider was hailing a taxi outside the station. His wife would be expecting him, but she must wait. He had often been detained in town before.

He gave the taxi the Conduit Street address.

It was a small place, but had nothing sinister about it. Clean, white-draped tables with individual lights and a big mahogany bar, whose wide semi-circle took up nearly half the available floor-space. The door closed behind Tressider with a comfortable, chuckling click. He went up to the bar and, with an indescribable fluttering of the heart, said to the white-coated attendant:

"I was told to ask here for Messrs. Smith & Smith."

"What name, sir?" asked the man, showing neither hesitation nor surprise.

"Jones," said Tressider, uninventively.

"Maurice, have we any message for a Mr. Jones from — whom did you say, sir? Oh, yes. From Messrs. Smith & Smith?"

The second barman turned round and enveloped Tressider in a brief, searching glance.

"Oh, yes," he said. "Quite right, sir. Mr. Smith is expecting you. Will you step this way?"

He led Tressider to the back of the room, where a stoutish, middle-aged man in a dark tweed suit was seated at a table eating an American sandwich.

The stout man looked up, revealing small chubby features beneath an enormous expanse of polished and dome-like skull. He smiled pleasantly.

"You are magnificently punctual," he said, in a clear, soft voice, with a fluting quality which made it very delightful to listen to. "I hardly expected you to get here quite so soon." And then, as the barman turned away, he added:

"Pray sit down, Mr. Tressider."

"You look a little unnerved," said Mr. Smith. "Perhaps you had a rush from the station. Let me recommend one of Rapallo's special cocktails." He made a sign to the barman, who brought over two glasses filled with a curious dark-colored liqueur. "You will find it slightly bitter, but very effective. You need not be alarmed, by the way. Choose whichever glass you like and leave me the other. It is quite immaterial which."

Tressider, a little confounded by the smiling ease with which Mr. Smith read his thoughts, took one of the glasses at random. Mr. Smith immediately took the other and drank off one-half of the contents. Tressider sipped his. The liqueur was certainly bitter but not altogether unpleasant.

"It will do you good," said Mr. Smith, prosaically. "The boy, I take it, is quite well?" he went on, almost in the same breath.

"Perfectly well," said Tressider, staring.

"Of course. Your wife takes such good care of him, doesn't

she? A thoroughly good and conscientious woman, as most women are, bless their dear hearts. The child is six years old, I think?"

"Rising six."

"Just so. A long time to go yet before he attains his majority. Fifteen years—yes, a considerable time, in which very many things may happen. You yourself, for instance, will be hard on sixty—the best part of your life at an end, while his is just beginning. He is a young gentleman of great expectations, to quote the divine Dickens. And he is starting well, despite the sad handicap of losing both his parents at so early an age. A fine, healthy youngster, is he not? No measles? mumps? whooping-cough? that sort of thing?"

"Not so far," muttered Tressider.

"No. Your almost-parental care has shielded him from all the ills that youthful flesh is heir to. How wise your brother was, Mr. Tressider. Some people might have thought it foolish of him to leave Cyril in your sole guardianship, considering that there was only his little life between you and the Tressider estate. Foolish—and even inconsiderate. For, after all, it is a great responsibility, is it not? A child seems to hold its life by so frail a tenure. But your brother was a wise man, after all. Knowing your upright, virtuous wife and yourself so well, he did the best thing he could possibly have done for Cyril when he left him in your care. Eh?"

"Of course," said Tressider, thickly.

Mr. Smith finished his liqueur.

"You are not drinking," he protested.

"Look here," said Tressider, gulping down the remainder of his drink, "you seem to know a lot about me and my affairs."

"Oh, but that is common knowledge, surely. The doings of so rich and fortunate a little boy as Cyril Tressider are chronicled in every newspaper paragraph. Perhaps the newspapers do not know quite so much about Mr. Tressider, his uncle and guardian. They may not realize quite how deeply he was involved in the Megatherium catastrophe, nor how much he has lost in one way and another on the turf. Still, they know, naturally, that he is an upright English gentleman and that both he and his wife are devoted to the boy."

Tressider leaned his elbow on the table and, holding his head propped on his hand, tried to read Mr. Smith's countenance. He found it difficult, for Mr. Smith and the room and everything about him seemed to advance and recede in the oddest manner. He thought he might be in for a dose of fever.

"Children . . ." Mr. Smith's voice fluted toward him from an enormous distance. "Accidents, naturally, will sometimes happen. No one can prevent it. Childish ailments may leave distressing after effects . . . babyish habits, however judiciously checked, may lead . . . Pardon me, I fear you are not feeling altogether the thing."

"I feel damned queer," said Tressider. "I—at the station today—hallucinations—I can't understand—"

Suddenly, from the pit in which it had lurked, chained and growling, Terror leapt at him. It shook his bones and cramped his stomach. It was like a palpable enemy, suffocating and tearing him. He gripped the table. He saw Mr. Smith's huge face loom down upon him, immense, immeasurable.

"Dear, dear!" The voice boomed in his ear like a great silver bell. "You are really not well. Allow me. Just a sip of this."

He drank, and the Terror, defeated, withdrew from him. A vast peace surged over his brain. He laughed. Everything was jolly, jolly, jolly. He wanted to sing.

Mr. Smith beckoned to the barman.

"Is the car ready?" he asked.

Tressider stood by Mr. Smith's side. The car had gone, and they were alone before the tall green gates that towered into the summer twilight. Mile upon mile they had driven through town and country; mile upon mile, with the river rolling beside them and the scent of trees and water blown in upon the July breeze. They had been many hours upon the journey and yet the soft dusk was hardly deeper than when they had set out. For them, as for Joshua, sun and stars had stood still in their courses. That this was so, Tressider knew, for he was not drunk or dreaming. His senses had never been more acute, his perceptions more vivid. Every leaf upon the tall poplars that shivered above the gates was vivid to him with a particular beauty of sound, shape, and odor. The gates, which bore in great letters the name "SMITH & SMITH—REMOVALS," opened at Smith's touch. The long avenue of poplars stretched up to a squat gray house with a pillared portico.

Many times in the weeks that followed, Tressider asked himself whether he had after all dreamed that strange adventure at the House of the Poplars. From the first whisper by the station bookstall to the journey by car down to his own home in Essex, every episode had had a nightmare quality. Yet surely, no nightmare had ever been so consecutive nor so clearly memorable in waking moments. There was the room with its pale grey walls and shining floor—a luminous pool in the soft mingling of electric light and dying daylight from the high, unshuttered windows. There were the four men—Mr. Smith, of the restaurant; Mr. Smyth, with his narrow yellow face disfigured by a scar like an acid burn; Mr. Smythe, square and sullen, with short, strong hands and hairy knuckles; and Dr. Schmidt, the giggling man with the scanty red beard and steel-rimmed spectacles. And there was the girl with the slanting golden eyes like a cat's, he thought. They called her "Miss Smith," but her name should have been Melusine.

Nor could he have dreamed the conversation, which was businesslike and brief.

"It has long been evident to us," said Mr. Smith, "that society is in need of a suitable organization for the Removal of unnecessary persons. Private and amateur attempts at Removal are so frequently attended with subsequent inconvenience and even danger to the Remover, who, in addition, usually has to carry out his work with very makeshift materials. It is our pleasure and privilege to attend to all the disagreeable details of such Removals for our clients at a moderate—I may say, a merely nominal—expense. Provided our terms are strictly adhered to, we can guarantee our clients against all unpleasant repercussions, preserving, of course, inviolable secrecy as to the whole transaction."

Dr. Schmidt sniggered faintly.

"In the matter of young Cyril Tressider, for example," went on Mr. Smith, "I can conceive nothing more unnecessary than the existence of this wearisome child. He is an orphan; his only relations are Mr. and Mrs. Tressider who, however amiably disposed they may feel toward the boy, are financially embarrassed by his presence in the world. If he were to be quietly Removed, who would be the loser? Not himself, for he would be spared the sins and troubles of life on this ill-regulated planet; not his relations, for he has none but his uncle and aunt who would be better for his disappearance; not his tenants and dependants, since his good uncle would be there to take his place. I suggest, Mr. Tressider, that the small sum of one thousand pounds would be profitably spent in Removing this boy to that happy land 'far, far beyond the stars,' where he might play with the young-eyed cherubim (to quote our glorious poet), remote from the accidents of measles or stomach-ache to which, alas! all young children are so unhappily liable here below."

"A thousand?" said Tressider, and laughed, "I would give five, gladly, to be rid of the youngster."

Dr. Schmidt sniggered. "We should not like to be rapacious," he said. "No. One thousand pounds will amply repay the very trifling trouble."

"How about the risk?" said Tressider.

"We have abolished risk," replied Mr. Smith. "For us, and for our clients, the word does not exist. Tell me, the boy resides with you at your home in Essex? Yes. Is he a good little boy?"

"Decent enough kid, as far as that goes."

"No bad habits?"

"He's a bit of a liar, like lots of kids."

"How so, my friend?" asked Dr. Schmidt.

"He romances. Pretends he's had all kinds of adventures

with giants and fairies and tigers and what not. You know the kind of thing. Doesn't seem able to tell the truth. It worries his aunt a good deal."

"Ah!" Dr. Schmidt seemed to take over the interview at this point. "The good Mrs. Tressider, she does not encourage the romancing?"

"No. She does her best. Tells Cyril that he'll go to a bad place if he tells her stories. But it's wonderful how the little beggar persists. Sometimes we have to spank him. But he's damnably obstinate. There's a bad streak in the boy somewhere. Unsound. Not English, that sort of thing."

"Sad," said Dr. Schmidt, sniggering, so that the word became a long bleat. "Sa-a-d. It would be a pity if the poor little boy should miss the golden gates after all. That would distress me."

"It would be still more distressing, Schmidt, that a person with a failing of that kind should be placed in any position of importance as the owner of the Tressider estates. Honor and uprightness, coupled with a healthy lack of imagination, have made this country what it is."

"True," said Dr. Schmidt. "How beautifully you put it, my dear Smith. No doubt, Mr. Tressider, your little ward finds much scope for imaginative adventure when playing about in the deserted grounds of Crantonbury Place, situated so conveniently next door to your abode."

"You seem to know a lot," said Tressider.

"Our organization," explained Dr. Schmidt, with a wave of the hand. "It is melancholy to see these fine old country mansions thus deserted, but one man's loss is the gain of the little boy next door. I should encourage little Cyril to play in the grounds of Crantonbury Hall. His little limbs will grow strong running about among the over-grown bushes and the straggling garden-beds where the strawberry grows underneath the nettle. I quote your Shakespeare, my dear Smith. It is a calamity that the fountains should be silent and the great fish-pond run dry. The nine men's morris is filled up with mud—Shakespeare again. Nevertheless, there are still many possibilities in an old garden."

He giggled and pulled at his thin beard.

If this fantastic conversation had never taken place, how was it that Tressider could remember every word so clearly? He remembered, too, signing a paper—the "Removal Order," Smith had called it—and a check for £1,000, payable to Smith & Smith, and post-dated October 1st.

"We like to allow a margin," said Mr. Smith. "We cannot at this moment predict to a day when the Removal will be carried out. But from now to October 1st should provide ample time. If you should change your mind before the Removal has taken place, you have only to leave word to that effect at Rapallo's. But *after* the Removal, it would be too late to make any alterations. Indeed, in such a case, there might be—er—unpleasantness of a kind which I should not care to specify. But, between gentlemen, such a situation could not, naturally, arise. Are you likely to be absent from home at any time in the near future?"

Tressider shook his head.

"No? Forgive me, but I think you would be well advised to spend—let us say the month of September—abroad. Or perhaps in Scotland. There is salmon, there is trout, there is grouse, there is partridge—all agreeable creatures to kill."

Dr. Schmidt sniggered again.

"Just as you like, of course," went on Mr. Smith. "But if you and perhaps your wife also—"

"My wife wouldn't leave Cyril."

"Yourself, then. A holiday from domesticity is sometimes an excellent thing."

"I will think about it," said Tressider.

He had thought often about it. He also thought frequently about the blank counterfoil in his checkbook. That, at least, was a fact. He was thinking about it in Scotland on September 15th, as he tramped across the moors, gun on shoulder. It might be a good thing to stop that check.

"Auntie Edith!"

"Yes, Cyril."

Mrs. Tressider was a thin woman with a strong, Puritan face; a woman of narrow but fixed affections and limited outlook.

"Auntie, I've had a wonderful adventure."

Mrs. Tressider pressed her pale lips together.

"Now, Cyril. Think before hand. Don't exaggerate, dear. You look very hot and excited."

"Yes, Auntie. I met a fairy—"

"Cyril!"

"No, *really*, Auntie, I did. She lives in Crantonbury Hall—in the old grotto. A real, live fairy. And she was all dressed in gold and lovely colors like a rainbow, red and green and blue and yellow and *all* sorts of colors. And a gold crown on her head and stars in her hair. And I wasn't a bit frightened, Auntie, and she said—"

"Cyril dear—"

"Yes, Auntie, *really*. I'm not 'zaggerating. She was ever so beautiful. And she said I was a brave boy, just like Jack-and-the-Beanstalk, and I was to marry her when I grew up, and live in Fairyland. Only I'm not big enough yet. And she had lions and tigers and leopards all round her with gold collars and diamonds on them. And she took me into her fairy palace—"

"Cyril!"

"And we ate fairy fruit off gold plates and she's going to teach me the language of the birds and give me a pair of seven-league boots all for myself, so that I can go *all* over the world and be a hero."

"That's a very exciting story you've made up, darling, but of course it's only a story, isn't it?"

"No, '*tisn't* only a story. It's quite true. You see if it isn't."

"Darling, even in fun you mustn't say it's *true*. There couldn't be lions and tigers and leopards at Crantonbury Hall."

"Well . . ." the child paused. "Well, pr'aps I was 'zaggerating just a teeny, weeny bit. But there was two leopards."

"Oh, Cyril! Two leopards?"

"Yes, with golden collars and chains. And the fairy was ever so tall and beautiful, with lovely goldeny eyes just like the leopards'. She said she was the fairy of the leopards, and they were fairies too, and after we'd had the fairy feast the leopards grew wings and she got on their backs—on one of them's back, I mean—and flew *right* away over the roof."

Mrs. Tressider sighed.

"I don't think Nannie ought to tell you so many fairy tales. You know there aren't any fairies, really."

"That's all *you* know about it," said Cyril, rather rudely. "There is fairies, and I've seen one, and I'm to be the King of the Fairies when I'm bigger."

"You mustn't contradict me like that, Cyril. And it's *very naughty* to say what isn't true."

"But it *is* true, Auntie."

"You mustn't say that, darling. I've told you ever so many times that it's very nice to make up stories, but we mustn't ever forget that it's all make-believe."

"But I *did* see the fairy."

"If you say that any more, Auntie will be very cross with you—"

"But I did, I did. I *swear* I did."

"Cyril!" Mrs. Tressider was definitely shocked. "That is a very wicked word to use. You must go straight to bed without your supper, and Auntie doesn't want to see you again till you have apologized for being so rude and telling such naughty stories."

"But, Auntie—"

"That will do," said Mrs. Tressider, and rang the bell. Cyril was led away in tears.

"If you please, ma'am," said Nannie, catching Mrs. Tressider as she rose from the dinner-table, "Master Cyril don't seem very well, ma'am. He says he has a bad stomach-ache."

Cyril did seem feverish and queer when his aunt went up to him. He was flushed and feverish, and his eyes were unnaturally bright and frightened. He complained of a dreadful pain under his pajama-girdle.

"That's what happens to naughty little boys who tell stories," said Mrs. Tressider, who had old-fashioned ideas about improving the occasion. "Now Nannie will have to give you some nasty medicine."

Nannie, advancing, armed with a horrid tumblerful of greeny-gray licorice powder, had her own moral to draw.

"I expect you've been eating them nasty old crab-apples out of the old garden," she remarked. "I'm sure I've told you time and again, Master Cyril, to leave them things alone."

"I didn't eat nothing," said Cyril, " 'cept the fairy feast in the palace with the leopard lady."

"We don't want to hear about the leopard lady any more," said Mrs. Tressider. "Now, own up darling, that was all imagination and nonsense, wasn't it? He does look feverish," she added in an aside to Nannie. "Perhaps we'd better send for Dr. Simmonds. With Mr. Tressider away, one feels rather anxious. Now, Cyril, drink up your medicine and say you're sorry. . . ."

When Dr. Simmonds arrived an hour later (for he had been out when summoned) he found his patient delirious and Mrs. Tressider thoroughly alarmed. Dr. Simmonds wasted no time with licorice powder, but used the stomach pump. His face was grave.

"What has he been eating?" he asked, and shook his head at Nannie's suggestion of green apples. Mrs. Tressider, white and anxious, went into details about the child's story of the leopard lady.

"He looked feverish when he came in," she said, "but I thought he was just excited with his make-believe games."

"Imaginative children are often unable to distinguish between fact and fancy," said the doctor. "I think he very probably did eat something that he shouldn't have done; it would be all part of the game he was playing with himself."

"I made him confess in the end that he was making it all up," said Mrs. Tressider.

"H'm," said Dr. Simmonds. "Well, I don't think you'd better worry him about it any more. He's a highly-strung child and he'll need all his strength —"

"You don't mean he's in any danger, Doctor?"

"Oh, I hope not, I hope not. But children are rather kittle little cattle and something has upset him badly. Is Mr. Tressider at home?"

"Ought I to send for him?"

"It might be as well. By the way, could you let me have a clean bottle? I should like to take away some of the contents of the stomach for examination. Just to be on the safe side, you know. I don't want to alarm you — it's just that, in a case of this kind, it is as well to know what one has to deal with."

Before morning, Cyril was collapsed, blue in the face and cold, and another doctor had been called in. Tressider, when he hurriedly arrived by the midnight train, was greeted by the news that there was very little hope.

"I am afraid, Mr. Tressider, that the boy has managed to pick up something poisonous. We are having an analysis made. The symptoms are suggestive of poisoning by solanine, or some alkali of that group. Nightshade — is there any garden nightshade at Crantonbury Hall?" Thus Dr. Pratt, a specialist and expensive.

Mr. Tressider did not know, but said he thought they might go and see next day. The search-party was accordingly sent out in the morning. They discovered no nightshade, but Dr. Pratt, prowling about the weed-grown kitchen garden made a discovery.

"Look!" he said. "These old potato-plants have got potato-apples on them. The potato belongs to the genus Solanum, and the apples, and sometimes even the tubers themselves, have occasionally given rise to poisonous symptoms. If the boy had happened to pluck and eat some of these berries—"

"He did, then," said Dr. Simmonds. "See here."

He lifted a plant on which a number of short stalks still remained to show where the potato-apples had been.

"I had no idea," said Tressider, "that the things were as poisonous as that."

"They are not as a rule," said Dr. Pratt. "But here and there one finds a plant which is particularly rich in the poisonous principle, solanine. There was a classical case, in 1885 or thereabouts—"

He prosed on. Mrs. Tressider could not bear it. She left them and went upstairs to sit by Cyril's bedside.

"I want to see the lovely leopard lady," said Cyril, faintly.

"Yes, yes—she's coming, darling," said Mrs. Tressider.

"With her leopards?"

"Yes, darling. And lions and tigers."

"Because I've got to be King of the Fairies when I grow up."

"Of course you have, darling."

On the third day, Cyril died.

The expert's analysis confirmed Dr. Pratt's diagnosis. Seeds and skin of the potato-apple had been identified in the contents of the stomach. Death was from solanine poisoning, a remarkable quantity of the alkali having been present in the potato-apples. An examination of other berries taken from the same plants showed that the potatoes in question were, undoubtedly, particularly rich in solanine. Verdict: Death by misadventure. Children, said the coroner, were very apt to chew and eat strange plants and berries, and the potato-apples undoubtedly had an attractive appearance—like a little green tomato—the jury had no doubt often seen it in their own gardens. It was, however, very seldom that the effects were so tragic as in the present sad case. No blame could possibly attach to Mr. and Mrs. Tressider, who had repeatedly warned the child not to eat anything he did not know the name of, and had usually found him an obedient child in this respect.

Tressider, to whom nobody had thought to mention the story of the leopard lady, showed a becoming grief at the death of his little ward. He purchased a handsome suit of black and ordered a new saloon car. In this he went about a good deal by himself in the days that followed the inquest, driving, on one occasion, as far as Greenwich.

He had looked up the address in the telephone-book and presently found himself rolling down a quiet riverside lane. Yes—there they were, on the right, two shabby green gates across which, in faded white lettering, ran the words:

SMITH & SMITH
REMOVALS

He got out of the car and stood, hesitating a little. The autumn had come early that year, and as he stood, a yellow poplar leaf, shaken from its hold by the wind, fluttered delicately to his feet.

He pushed at the gates, which opened slowly, with a rusty creaking. There was no avenue of poplars and no squat gray house with a pillared portico. An untidy yard met his gaze. At the back was a tumble-down warehouse, and on either side of the gate a sickly poplar whispered fretfully. A ruddy-faced man, engaged in harnessing a cart-horse to an open lorry, came forward to greet him.

"Could I speak to Mr. Smith?" asked Tressider.

"It's Mr. Benton you'll be wanting," replied the man. "There ain't no Mr. Smith."

"Oh!" said Tressider. "Then which of the gentlemen is it that has a very high, bald forehead—a rather stoutish gentleman. I thought—"

"Nobody like that here," said the man. "You've made a mistake, mister. There's only Mr. Benton—he's tall, with gray 'air and specs, and Mr. Tinworth, the young gentleman, him that's a bit lame. Was you wanting a Removal by any chance?"

"No, no," said Tressider, rather hastily. "I thought I knew Mr. Smith, that's all. Has he retired lately?"

"Lord, no." The man laughed heartily. "There ain't been a Mr. Smith here, not in donkey's years. Come to think of it, they're all dead, I believe. Jim! What's happened to old Mr. Smith and his brother what used to run this show?"

A little elderly man came out of the warehouse, wiping his hands on his apron.

"Dead these ten years," he said. "What's up?"

"Gent here thought he knowed the parties."

"Well, they're dead," repeated Jim.

"Thank you," said Tressider.

He went back to the car. For the hundredth time he asked himself whether he should stop the check. The death of Cyril could only be a coincidence. It was now or never, for this was September 30th.

He vacillated, and put the matter off till next day. At ten o'clock in the morning he rang up the bank.

"A check —" he gave the number —"for £1,000, payable to Smith & Smith. Has it been cashed?"

"Yes, Mr. Tressider. Nine-thirty this morning. Hope there's nothing wrong about it."

"Nothing whatever, thanks. I just wanted to know."

Then he *had* drawn it. And somebody had cashed it.

Next day there was a letter. It was typewritten and bore no address of origin; only the printed heading SMITH & SMITH and the date, October 1.

DEAR SIR, —

With reference to your esteemed order of the 12th July for a Removal from your residence in Essex, we trust that this commission has been carried out to your satisfaction. We beg to acknowledge your obliging favor of One Thousand Pounds (£1,000) and return herewith the Order of Removal which you were good enough to hand to us. Assuring you of our best attention at all times,

Faithfully yours,
SMITH & SMITH.

The enclosure ran as follows:

I, Arthur Tressider of [here followed his address in Essex], hereby confess that I murdered my ward and nephew, Cyril Tressider, in the following manner. Knowing that the child was in the habit of playing in the garden of Crantonbury Hall, adjoining my own residence, and vacant for the last twelve months, I searched this garden carefully and discovered there a number of old potato-plants, some of them bearing potato-apples. Into these potato-apples I injected with a small syringe a powerful solution of the poisonous alkali solanine, of which a certain quantity is always present in these plants. I prepared this solution from plants of solanum which I had already secretly gathered. I had no difficulty in doing this, having paid some attention as a young man to the study of chemistry. I felt sure that the child would be tempted to eat these berries, but had he failed to do so I had various other schemes of a similar nature in reserve, on which I should have fallen back if necessary. I committed this abominable crime in order to secure the Tressider estates, entailed upon me as next heir. I now make this confession, being troubled in my conscience.

ARTHUR TRESSIDER.

OCTOBER 1, 193—

The sweat stood on Tressider's forehead.
"How did they know I had studied chemistry?"

He seemed to hear the sniggering voice of Dr. Schmidt: "Our organization —"

He burned the papers and went out without saying his customary farewell to his wife. It was not until some time later that he heard the story of the leopard lady, and he thought of Miss Smith, the girl with the yellow eyes like cat's eyes, who should have been called Melusine.

THE CYPRIAN CAT

It's extraordinarily decent of
you to come along and see me like this, Harringay. Believe me,
I do appreciate it. It isn't every busy K.C. who'd do as much
for such a hopeless sort of client. I only wish I could spin you
a more workable kind of story, but honestly, I can only tell you
exactly what I told Peabody. Of course, I can see he doesn't
believe a word of it, and I don't blame him. He thinks I ought
to be able to make up a more plausible tale than that—and I
suppose I could, but where's the use? One's almost bound to
fall down somewhere if one tries to swear to a lie. What I'm
going to tell you is the absolute truth. I fired one shot and one
shot only, and that was at the cat. It's funny that one should be
hanged for shooting at a cat.

Merridew and I were always the best of friends; school
and college and all that sort of thing. We didn't see very much
of each other after the war, because we were living at opposite
ends of the country; but we met in Town from time to time and
wrote occasionally and each of us knew that the other was
there in the background, so to speak. Two years ago, he wrote
and told me he was getting married. He was just turned forty
and the girl was fifteen years younger, and he was tremen-
dously in love. It gave me a bit of a jolt—you know how it is

when your friends marry. You feel they will never be quite the same again; and I'd got used to the idea that Merridew and I were cut out to be old bachelors. But of course I congratulated him and sent him a wedding present, and I did sincerely hope he'd be happy. He was obviously over head and ears; almost dangerously so, I thought, considering all things. Though except for the difference of age it seemed suitable enough. He told me he had met her at—of all places—a rectory garden-party down in Norfolk, and that she had actually never been out of her native village. I mean, literally—not so much as a trip to the nearest town. I'm not trying to convey that she wasn't pukka, or anything like that. Her father was some queer sort of recluse—a medievalist, or something—desperately poor. He died shortly after their marriage.

I didn't see anything of them for the first year or so. Merridew is a civil engineer, you know, and he took his wife away after the honeymoon to Liverpool, where he was doing something in connection with the harbor. It must have been a big change for her from the wilds of Norfolk. I was in Birmingham, with my nose kept pretty close to the grindstone, so we only exchanged occasional letters. His were what I can only call deliriously happy, especially at first. Later on, he seemed a little worried about his wife's health. She was restless; town life didn't suit her; he'd be glad when he could finish up his Liverpool job and get her away into the country. There wasn't any doubt about their happiness, you understand—she'd got him body and soul as they say, and as far as I could make out it was mutual. I want to make that perfectly clear.

Well, to cut a long story short, Merridew wrote to me at the beginning of last month and said he was just off to a new job—a waterworks extension scheme down in Somerset; and he asked if I could possibly cut loose and join them there for a few weeks. He wanted to have a yarn with me, and Felice was longing to make my acquaintance. They had got rooms at the village inn. It was rather a remote spot, but there was fishing and scenery and so forth, and I should be able to keep Felice company while he was working up at the dam. I was about fed up with Birmingham, what with the heat and one thing and another, and it looked pretty good to me, and I was due for a holiday anyhow, so I fixed up to go. I had a bit of business to do in Town, which I calculated would take me about a week, so I said I'd go down to Little Hexham on June 20th.

As it happened, my business in London finished itself off unexpectedly soon, and on the sixteenth I found myself absolutely free and stuck in a hotel with road-drills working just under the windows and a tar-spraying machine to make things livelier. You remember what a hot month it was—flaming June and no mistake about it. I didn't see any point in waiting, so I sent off a wire to Merridew, packed my bag, and took the train for Somerset the same evening. I couldn't get a compartment to myself, but I found a first-class smoker with only three seats occupied, and stowed myself thankfully into the fourth corner. There was a military-looking old boy, an elderly female with a lot of bags and baskets, and a girl. I thought I should have a nice, peaceful journey.

So I should have, if it hadn't been for the unfortunate way I'm built. It was quite all right at first—as a matter of fact, I think I was half asleep, and I only woke up properly at seven o'clock, when the waiter came to say that dinner was on. The other people weren't taking it, and when I came back from the restaurant car I found that the old boy had gone, and there were only the two women left. I settled down in my corner again, and gradually, as we went along, I found a horrible feeling creeping over me that there was a cat in the compartment somewhere. I'm one of those wretched people who can't stand cats. I don't mean just that I prefer dogs—I mean that the presence of a cat in the same room with me makes me feel like nothing on earth. I can't describe it, but I believe quite a lot of people are affected that way. Something to do with electricity, or so they tell me. I've read that very often the dislike is mutual, but it isn't so with me. The brutes seem to find me abominably fascinating—make a bee-line for my legs every time. It's a funny sort of complaint, and it doesn't make me at all popular with dear old ladies.

Anyway, I began to feel more and more awful and I realized that the old girl at the other end of the seat must have a cat in one of her innumerable baskets. I thought of asking her to put it out in the corridor, or calling the guard and having it removed, but I knew how silly it would sound and made up my mind to try and stick it. I couldn't say the animal was misbehaving itself or anything, and she looked a pleasant old lady; it wasn't her fault that I was a freak. I tried to distract my mind by looking at the girl.

She was worth looking at, too—very slim, and dark with one of those dead-white skins that make you think of magnolia blossom. She had the most astonishing eyes, too—I've never seen eyes quite like them; a very pale brown, almost amber, set wide apart and a little slanting, and they seemed to have a kind of luminosity of their own, if you get what I mean. I don't know if this sounds—I don't want you to think I was bowled over, or anything. As a matter of fact she held no sort of attraction for me, though I could imagine a different type of man going potty about her. She was just unusual, that was all. But however much I tried to think of other things I couldn't get rid of the uncomfortable feeling, and eventually I gave it up and went out into the corridor. I just mention this because it will help you to understand the rest of the story. If you can only realize how perfectly awful I feel when there's a cat about—even when it's shut up in a basket—you'll understand better how I came to buy the revolver.

Well, we got to Hexham Junction, which was the nearest station to Little Hexham, and there was old Merridew waiting on the platform. The girl was getting out too—but not the old lady with the cat, thank goodness—and I was just handing her traps out after her when he came galloping up and hailed us.

"Hullo!" he said, "why that's splendid! Have you introduced yourselves?" So I tumbled to it then that the girl was Mrs. Merridew, who'd been up to Town on a shopping expedition, and I explained to her about my change of plans and she said how jolly it was that I could come—the usual things. I noticed what an attractive low voice she had and how graceful her movements were, and I understood—though, mind you, I didn't share—Merridew's infatuation.

We got into his car—Mrs. Merridew sat in the back and I got up beside Merridew, and was very glad to feel the air and to get rid of the oppressive electric feeling I'd had in the train. He told me the place suited them wonderfully, and had given Felice an absolutely new lease of life, so to speak. He said he was very fit, too, but I thought myself that he looked rather fagged and nervy.

You'd have liked that inn, Harringay. The real, old-fashioned stuff, as quaint as you make 'em, and everything genuine—none of your Tottenham Court Road antiques. We'd all had our grub, and Mrs. Merridew said she was tired; so she went up to bed early and Merridew and I had a drink and went for a stroll round the village. It's a tiny hamlet quite at the other end of nowhere; lights out at ten, little thatched houses with pinched-up attic windows like furry ears—the place purred in its sleep. Merridew's working gang didn't sleep there of course—they'd run up huts for them at the dams, a mile beyond the village.

The landlord was just locking up the bar when we came in—a block of a man with an absolutely expressionless face. His wife was a thin, sandy-haired woman who looked as though she was too down-trodden to open her mouth. But I found out afterwards that was a mistake, for one evening when he'd taken one or two over the eight and showed signs of wanting to make a night of it, his wife sent him off upstairs with a gesture and a look that took the heart out of him. That first night she was sitting in the porch, and hardly glanced at us as we passed her. I always thought her an uncomfortable kind of woman, but she certainly kept her house most exquisitely neat and clean.

They'd given me a noble bedroom, close under the eaves with a long, low casement window overlooking the garden. The sheets smelt of lavender, and I was between them and asleep almost before you could count ten. I was tired, you see. But later in the night I woke up. I was too hot, so took off some of the blankets and then strolled across to the window to get a breath of air. The garden was bathed in moonshine and on the lawn I could see something twisting and turning oddly. I stared a bit before I made it out to be two cats. They didn't worry me at that distance, and I watched them for a bit before I turned in again. They were rolling over one another and jumping away again and chasing their own shadows on the grass, intent on their own mysterious business — taking themselves seriously, the way cats always do. It looked like a kind of ritual dance. Then something seemed to startle them, and they scampered away.

I went back to bed, but I couldn't get to sleep again. My nerves seemed to be all on edge. I lay watching the window and listening to a kind of soft rustling noise that seemed to be going on in the big wistaria that ran along my side of the house. And then something landed with a soft thud on the sill — a great Cyprian cat.

What did you say? Well, one of those striped gray and black cats. Tabby, that's right. In my part of the country they call them Cyprus cats, or Cyprian cats. I'd never seen such a monster. It stood with its head cocked sideways, staring into the room and rubbing its ears very softly against the upright bar of the casement.

Of course, I couldn't do with that. I shooed the brute away, and it made off without a sound. Heat or no heat, I shut and fastened the window. Far out in the shrubbery, I thought I heard a faint miauling; then silence. After that, I went straight off to sleep again and lay like a log until the girl came in to call me.

The next day, Merridew ran us up in his car to see the place where they were making the dam, and that was the first time I realized that Felice's nerviness had not been altogether cured. He showed us where they had diverted part of the river into a swift little stream that was to be used for working the dynamo of an electrical plant. There were a couple of planks laid across the stream, and he wanted to take us over to show us the engine. It wasn't extraordinarily wide or dangerous, but

Mrs. Merridew peremptorily refused to cross it, and got quite hysterical when he tried to insist. Eventually he and I went over and inspected the machinery by ourselves. When we got back she had recovered her temper and apologized for being so silly. Merridew abased himself, of course, and I began to feel a little *de trop*. She told me afterwards that she had once fallen into a river as a child, and been nearly drowned, and it had left her with a what d'ye call it—a complex about running water. And but for this one trifling episode, I never heard a single sharp word pass between them all the time I was there; nor, for a whole week, did I notice anything else to suggest a flaw in Mrs. Merridew's radiant health. Indeed, as the days wore on to midsummer and the heat grew more intense, her whole body seemed to glow with vitality. It was as though she was lit up from within.

Merridew was out all day and working very hard. I thought he was overdoing it and asked him if he was sleeping badly. He told me that, on the contrary, he fell asleep every night the moment his head touched the pillow, and—what was most unusual with him—had no dreams of any kind. I myself felt well enough, but the hot weather made me languid and disinclined for exertion. Mrs. Merridew took me out for long drives in the car. I would sit for hours, lulled into a half-slumber by the rush of warm air and the purring of the engine, and gazing at my driver, upright at the wheel, her eyes fixed unwaveringly upon the spinning road. We explored the whole of the country to the south and east of Little Hexham, and once or twice went as far north as Bath. Once I suggested that we should turn eastward over the bridge and run down into what looked like rather beautiful wooded country, but Mrs. Merridew didn't care for the idea; she said it was a bad road and that the scenery on that side was disappointing.

Altogether, I spent a pleasant week at Little Hexham, and if it had not been for the cats I should have been perfectly comfortable. Every night the garden seemed to be haunted by them—the Cyprian cat that I had seen the first night of my stay, and a little ginger one and a horrible stinking black Tom were especially tiresome, and one night there was a terrified white kitten that mewed for an hour on end under my window. I flung boots and books at my visitors till I was heartily weary, but they seemed determined to make the inn garden their rendezvous. The nuisance grew worse from night to night; on one occasion I counted fifteen of them, sitting on their hinder-ends in a circle, while the Cyprian cat danced her shadow-dance among them, working in and out like a weaver's shuttle. I had to keep my window shut, for the Cyprian cat evidently made a habit of climbing up by the wistaria. The door, too; for once when I had gone down to fetch something from the sitting room, I found her on my bed, kneading the coverlet with her paws—pr'rp, pr'rp, pr'rp— with her eyes closed in a sensuous ecstasy. I beat her off, and she spat at me as she fled into the dark passage.

I asked the landlady about her, but she replied rather curtly that they kept no cat at the inn, and it is true that I never saw any of the beasts in the daytime; but one evening about dusk I caught the landlord in one of the outhouses. He had the ginger cat on his shoulder, and was feeding her with something that looked like strips of liver. I remonstrated with him for encouraging the cats about the place and asked whether I could have a different room, explaining that the nightly caterwauling disturbed me. He half opened his slits of eyes and murmured that he would ask his wife about it; but nothing was done, and in fact I believe there was no other bedroom in the house.

And all this time the weather got hotter and heavier, working up for thunder, with the sky like brass and the earth like iron, and the air quivering over it so that it hurt your eyes to look at it.

All right, Harringay—I am trying to keep to the point. And I'm not concealing anything from you. I say that my relations with Mrs. Merridew were perfectly ordinary. Of course, I saw a good deal of her, because as I explained Merridew was out all day. We went up to the dam with him in the morning and brought the car back, and naturally we had to amuse one another as best we could till the evening. She seemed quite pleased to be in my company, and I couldn't dislike her. I can't tell you what we talked about—nothing in particular. She was not a talkative woman. She would sit or lie for hours in the sunshine, hardly speaking—only stretching out her body to the light and heat. Sometimes she would spend a whole afternoon playing with a twig or a pebble, while I sat by and smoked. Restful! No. No—I shouldn't call her a restful personality, exactly. Not to me, at any rate. In the evening she would liven up and talk a little more, but she generally went up to bed early, and left Merridew and me to yarn together in the garden.

Oh! about the revolver. Yes. I bought that in Bath, when I had been at Little Hexham exactly a week. We drove over in the morning, and while Mrs. Merridew got some things for her husband, I prowled round the second-hand shops. I had intended to get an air gun or a peashooter or something of that kind, when I saw this. You've seen it, of course. It's very tiny—what people in books describe as "little more than a toy," but quite deadly enough. The old boy who sold it to me didn't seem to know much about firearms. He'd taken it in pawn some time back, he told me, and there were ten rounds of ammunition with it. He made no bones about a license or anything—glad enough to make a sale, no doubt, without putting difficulties in a customer's way. I told him I knew how to handle it, and mentioned by way of a joke that I meant to take a pot shot or two at the cats. That seemed to wake him up a bit. He was a dried-up little fellow, with a scrawny grey beard and a stringy neck. He asked me where I was staying. I told him at Little Hexham.

"You better be careful, sir," he said. "They think a heap of their cats down there, and it's reckoned unlucky to kill them." And then he added something I couldn't quite catch, about a silver bullet. He was a doddering old fellow, and he seemed to have some sort of scruple about letting me take the parcel away, but I assured him that I was perfectly capable of looking after it and myself. I left him standing at the door of his shop, pulling at his beard and staring after me.

That night the thunder came. The sky had turned to lead before evening, but the dull heat was more oppressive than the sunshine. But the Merridews seemed to be in a state of nerves—he sulky and swearing at the weather and the flies, and she wrought up to a queer kind of vivid excitement. Thunder affects some people that way. I wasn't much better, and to make things worse I got the feeling that the house was full of cats. I couldn't see them but I knew they were there, lurking behind the cupboards and flitting noiselessly about the corridors. I could scarcely sit in the parlor and I was thankful to escape to my room. Cats or no cats I had to open the window, and I sat there with my pajama jacket unbuttoned, trying to get a breath of air. But the place was like the inside of a copper furnace. And pitch dark. I could scarcely see from my window where the bushes ended and the lawn began. But I could hear and feel the cats. There were little scrapings in the wistaria and scufflings among the leaves, and about eleven o'clock one of them started the concert with a loud and hideous wail. Then another and another joined in—I'll swear there were fifty of them. And presently I got that foul sensation of nausea, and the flesh crawled on my bones, and I knew that one of them was slinking close to me in the darkness. I looked round quickly, and there she stood, the great Cyprian; right against my shoulder, her eyes glowing like green lamps. I yelled and struck out at her, and she snarled as she leaped out and down. I heard her thump the gravel, and the yowling burst out all over the garden with renewed vehemence. And then all in a moment there was utter silence, and in the far distance there came a flickering blue flash and then another. In the first of them I saw the far garden wall, topped along all its length with cats, like a nursery frieze. When the second flash came the wall was empty.

At two o'clock the rain came. For three hours before that I had sat there, watching the lightning as it spat across the sky and exulting in the crash of the thunder. The storm seemed to carry off all the electrical disturbance in my body; I could have shouted with excitement and relief. Then the first heavy drops fell; then a steady downpour; then a deluge. It struck the iron-backed garden with a noise like steel rods falling. The smell of the ground came up intoxicatingly, and the wind rose and flung the rain in against my face. At the other end of the passage I heard a window thrown to and fastened, but I leaned out into the tumult and let the water drench my head and shoulders. The thunder still rumbled intermittently, but with less noise and farther off, and in an occasional flash I saw the white grille of falling water drawn between me and the garden.

It was after one of these thunder peals that I became aware of a knocking at my door. I opened it, and there was Merridew. He had a candle in his hand, and his face was terrified. "Felice!" he said, abruptly. "She's ill. I can't wake her. For God's sake, come and give me a hand."

I hurried down the passage after him. There were two beds in his room—a great four-poster, hung with crimson damask, and a small camp bedstead drawn up near to the window. The small bed was empty, the bedclothes tossed aside; evidently he had just risen from it. In the four-poster lay Mrs. Merridew, naked, with only a sheet upon her. She was stretched flat upon her back, her long black hair in two plaits over her shoulders. Her face was waxen and shrunk, like the face of a corpse, and her pulse, when I felt it, was so faint that at first I could scarcely feel it. Her breathing was very slow and shallow and her flesh cold. I shook her, but there was no response at all. I lifted her eyelids, and noticed how the eyeballs were turned up under the upper lid, so that only the whites were visible. The touch of my fingertip upon the sensitive ball evoked no reaction. I immediately wondered whether she took drugs.

Merridew seemed to think it necessary to make some explanation. He was babbling about the heat—she couldn't bear so much as a silk nightgown—she had suggested that he should occupy the other bed—he had slept heavily—right through the thunder. The rain blowing in on his face had aroused him. He had got up and shut the window. Then he had called to Felice to know if she was all right—he thought the storm might have frightened her. There was no answer. He had struck a light. Her condition had alarmed him—and so on.

I told him to pull himself together and to try whether, by chafing his wife's hands and feet, we could restore the circulation. I had it firmly in my mind that she was under the influence of some opiate. We set to work, rubbing and pinching and slapping her with wet towels and shouting her name in her ear. It was like handling a dead woman, except for the very slight but perfectly regular rise and fall of her bosom, on which—with a kind of surprise that there should be any flaw on its magnolia whiteness—I noticed a large brown mole, just over the heart. To my perturbed fancy it suggested a wound and a menace. We had been hard at it for some time, with the sweat pouring off us, when we became aware of something going on outside the window—a stealthy bumping and scraping against the panes. I snatched up the candle and looked out.

On the sill, the Cyprian cat sat and clawed at the casement. Her drenched fur clung limply to her body, her eyes glared into mine, her mouth was opened in protest. She scrabbled furiously at the latch, her hind claws slipping and scratching on the woodwork. I hammered on the pane and bawled at her, and she struck back at the glass as though possessed. As I cursed her and turned away she set up a long, despairing wail.

Merridew called to me to bring back the candle and leave the brute alone. I returned to the bed, but the dismal crying went on and on incessantly. I suggested to Merridew that he should wake the landlord and get hot-water bottles and some brandy from the bar and see if a messenger could not be sent for a doctor. He departed on this errand, while I went on with my massage. It seemed to me that the pulse was growing still fainter. Then I suddenly recollected that I had a small brandy flask in my bag. I ran out to fetch it, and as I did so the cat suddenly stopped its howling.

As I entered my own room the air blowing through the open window struck gratefully upon me. I found my bag in the dark and was rummaging for the flask among my shirts and socks when I heard a loud, triumphant mew, and turned round in time to see the Cyprian cat crouched for a moment on the sill, before it sprang in past me and out at the door. I found the flask and hastened back with it, just as Merridew and the landlord came running up the stairs.

We all went into the room together. As we did so, Mrs. Merridew stirred, sat up, and asked us what in the world was the matter.

I have seldom felt quite such a fool.

Next day the weather was cooler; the storm had cleared the air. What Merridew had said to his wife I do not know. None of us made any public allusion to the night's disturbance, and to all appearances Mrs. Merridew was in the best of health and spirits. Merridew took a day off from the waterworks, and we all went for a long drive and picnic together. We were on the best of terms with one another. Ask Merridew—he will tell you the same thing. He would not—he could not, surely—say otherwise. I can't believe, Harringay, I simply cannot believe that he could imagine or suspect me—I say, there was nothing to suspect. Nothing.

Yes—this is the important date—the 24th of June. I can't tell you any more details; there is nothing to tell. We came back and had dinner just as usual. All three of us were together all day, till bedtime. On my honor I had no private interview of any kind that day, either with him or with her. I was the first to go to bed, and I heard the others come upstairs about half an hour later. They were talking cheerfully.

It was a moonlight night. For once, no caterwauling came to trouble me. I didn't even bother to shut the window or the door. I put the revolver on the chair beside me before I lay down. Yes, it was loaded. I had no special object in putting it there, except that I meant to have a go at the cats if they started their games again.

I was desperately tired, and thought I should drop off to sleep at once, but I didn't. I must have been overtired, I suppose. I lay and looked at the moonlight. And then, about midnight, I heard what I had been half expecting: a stealthy scrabbling in the wistaria and a faint miauling sound.

I sat up in bed and reached for the revolver. I heard the "plop" as the big cat sprung up on to the windowledge; I saw her black and silver flanks, and the outline of her round head, pricked ears, and upright tail. I aimed and fired, and the beast let out one frightful cry and sprang down into the room.

I jumped out of bed. The crack of the shot had sounded terrific in the silent house, and somewhere I heard a distant voice call out. I pursued the cat into the passage, revolver in hand—with some idea of finishing it off, I suppose. And then, at the door of Merridew's room, I saw Mrs. Merridew. She stood with one hand on each doorpost, swaying to and fro. Then she fell down at my feet. Her bare breast was all stained with blood. And as I stood staring at her, clutching the revolver, Merridew came out and found us—like that.

Well, Harringay, that's my story, exactly as I told it to Peabody. I'm afraid it won't sound very well in Court, but what can I say? The trail of blood led from my room to hers; the cat must have run that way; I *know* it was the cat I shot. I can't offer any explanation. I don't know who shot Mrs. Merridew, or why. I can't help it if the people at the inn say they never saw the Cyprian cat; Merridew saw it that other night, and I know he wouldn't lie about it. Search the house, Harringay—that's the only thing to do. Pull the place to pieces, till you find the body of the Cyprian cat. It will have my bullet in it.

AFTERWORD

by John Curran

The year 1920 is the generally accepted dawn of the Golden Age of detective fiction. Sherlock Holmes was then still appearing in the pages of the *Strand Magazine* and the last collection of his investigations, *The Case-Book of Sherlock Holmes*, was published in 1927; G. K. Chesterton's Father Brown was still solving mysteries and saving souls. Agatha Christie and Freeman Wills Crofts published their first titles, *The Mysterious Affair at Styles* and *The Cask*, respectively, in 1920, and before the end of the decade Margery Allingham, Anthony Berkeley, John Dickson Carr, and Ellery Queen would also publish their first detective novels. This was the era in which the puzzle dominated, and fair play to the reader in the presentation of information and clues was of paramount importance. Almost simultaneously in 1929, the British detective novelist Father Ronald Knox and S. S. Van Dine, the American creator of Philo Vance, formulated their rules for the creation of detective fiction: No clue could be withheld from the reader. The detective could not pick up "a mysterious object" at the murder scene without telling the reader exactly what it was. Secret passages, poisons unknown to science, evil Chinamen, twin brothers (or even sisters), and "supernatural agencies" were all forbidden. All of the information pertinent to the only correct solution to the crime had to be given to the reader. The question of romance within the covers of a detective story was a contentious one—Van Dine ruled it out of court without discussion while Knox remained diplomatically silent on the matter. And in 1923 Dorothy L. Sayers published *Whose Body?*

Born in June 1893 in Oxford, where her father, Rev. Henry Sayers, was headmaster of Christ Church Choir School, Dorothy L. Sayers was, like her great contemporary, Agatha Christie, educated at home. At the age of sixteen, she attended Godolphin College and in 1912 went to Somerville College, Oxford, one of the first all-women colleges, from which she graduated with a First Class Honors degree in French. Her first proper job, in 1922, was as a copywriter at the advertising agency S. H. Benson, a background she was to put to good use over a decade later when she wrote *Murder Must Advertise* (1933).

In January 1924 Sayers gave birth to a baby boy, John Anthony. This event, far more shocking a century ago than can now be appreciated, remained a well-kept secret until long after Sayers's death. After an unhappy love affair, she had found solace with one Bill White who, on learning of her condition, disappeared. Nobody at Benson realized her situation —a two-month leave of absence was not questioned—and she successfully kept the baby's existence a secret while her cousin, Ivy Shrimpton, raised him. John Anthony was "good friends" with Sayers for most of his adult life, although he never lived under her roof. In April 1926 Dorothy married "Mac" Fleming, a freelance writer as well as a painter and photographer, twelve years her senior; as his health deteriorated —he had been gassed during the Great War—Dorothy became the major breadwinner.

It would seem that nothing nobler than economic necessity was the motivation behind her decision to write a book. She had some experience of professional writing—she had already published poetry, and, more surprisingly, written film scenarios—before beginning her first detective novel, *Whose*

Body? in 1921. Published two years later, it sent forth her aristocratic sleuth, Lord Peter Wimsey, to solve the mystery of an unidentified corpse, clad only in a pair of pince-nez, found in a bath. In creating this immortal character she endowed him with some of the advantages Fate had denied in her own life. Wimsey, with an enviable address in Piccadilly—note the similarity of "110A Piccadilly" to Sherlock Holmes's "221B Baker Street"—was a lord with a manservant, a wealthy bibliophile with a wine cellar, a superb musician, and a gifted linguist; later, he was a happy husband with an intelligent and strong-minded wife and, ultimately, a family. If, as is claimed, Sayers, to their joint detriment, fell in love with Wimsey, can you blame her? So confident was she of his success that she embarked on Wimsey's second investigation, *Clouds of Witness*, even before *Whose Body?* was published.

SAYERS THE DETECTIVE NOVELIST

In a 1937 essay on the genesis of *Gaudy Night* Sayers wrote: "When in a light-hearted moment I set out, fifteen years ago, to write the first 'Lord Peter' book, it was with the avowed intention of producing something 'less like a conventional detective story and more like a novel.'" Although she admitted that *Whose Body?* was "conventional to the last degree," she felt that "each successive book of mine worked gradually nearer to the sort of thing I had in view." Its immediate successor, *Clouds of Witness*, begins very much as a conventional Golden Age detective novel with a mysterious death at a secluded shooting lodge in Yorkshire. As the investigation proceeds, it transpires that many of those present night have secrets, none more so than Wimsey's brother, Gerald, Duke of Denver. The novel culminates in an unexpected revelation during the most dramatic murder trial in the genre.

Unnatural Death (1927), the title of which is not the least clever element, contains one of the most sinister characters in the entire Sayers output. And the method of the murder—the discovery of which is trickier than the identity of the villain—is chillingly plausible. In *The Unpleasantness at the*

Bellona Club (1928), that bulwark of British male society, the gentleman's club, is exposed to gentle—and sometimes not so gentle—mockery as Wimsey uncovers nefarious deeds within its walls and among its members. And the plight of returned First World War veterans is also a potent element in a plot that turns on a question of timing.

The Documents in the Case (1930) is noteworthy for a variety of reasons. It is Sayers's only non-Wimsey novel, it is her only coauthored novel, and, as the title suggests, it is told in the form of letters rather than a straight narrative. It was her collaborator, Robert Eustace, a doctor, who suggested the scientific idea at the heart of the plot. Darker in tone than the Wimsey novels—probably because of Lord Peter's absence—and with a smaller than usual cast of characters, it concerns a poisoning in a remote cottage. Although Sayers herself was disappointed with it, the novel remains a fascinating experiment.

Sayers introduced Harriet Vane in *Strong Poison* (1930) and allowed her and Wimsey to embark on a three-book courtship culminating in marriage in *Busman's Honeymoon* (1937). This is the longest—and, some would argue, the most wearisome and embarrassing—courtship in the annals of detective fiction. Detective-fiction purists contend that this type of romantic relationship—between detective and suspect—has no place in a detective story. Other sleuths have managed to meet, court, marry, and produce children without any of the soul-searching in which Peter and Harriet indulged. Ngaio Marsh's Roderick Alleyn met and married (offstage) Agatha Troy; Margery Allingham's Albert Campion and Amanda Fitton meet, marry, and produce a son—between *Sweet Danger* (1933) and *Traitor's Purse* (1941)—with much less agonizing.

Five Red Herrings (1931) is for lovers of the clue-and-alibi story. Set in Galloway, an area of Scotland well-known to Sayers from regular holidays, it has a wonderful gimmick to tantalize those readers who like to play the game alongside the detective. After a member of an artist's colony is found dead near his easel, Wimsey, without taking the reader into his confidence, notices something odd about the scene. In order to underline her adherence to fair play, Sayers inserts a paragraph in which she assures readers that they have all the information necessary to come to the same conclusion as Wimsey. And so they have.

"What would we be lookin' for?" [Sergeant Dalziel] demanded, reasonably.

(Here Lord Peter Wimsey told the Sergeant what he was to look for and why, but as the intelligent reader will readily supply these details for himself, they are omitted from this page.)

It's not a spoiler to say that a possible title for the novel, suggested by Sayers, was *There's Something Missing*.

Murder Must Advertise (1933) draws heavily on Sayers's experience at Benson as Lord Peter, working incognito, joins Pym's Publicity to investigate the death, some time earlier, of a copywriter. Apart from the ramifications of a clever plot, the reader learns more about office life in the years between the wars than could be garnered from a dozen social histories. Opinion is equally divided as to whether Sayers's best novel is *The Nine Tailors* (1934) or *Gaudy Night* (1935), and a compelling case could be made for either. The former contains yet another example of Sayers's resourcefulness at inventing imaginative murder methods—earlier, both *Unnatural Death* and *Strong Poison* had shown similar ingenuity—and settings; the background of campanology was unique in the world of detective fiction. *Gaudy Night* is a fascinating glimpse into the rarefied, pre–Second World War atmosphere of all-women education—again drawn from firsthand experience—coupled with an exploration of the vexed (even eighty years ago) question of woman's place in society, the family, and academia. This, surely, is the book that Sayers hoped would be "less like a conventional detective story and more like a novel."

But my favorite Sayers novel remains *Have His Carcase*

(1932). While on a walking-holiday to recover from the broken heart sustained before and during *Strong Poison*, Harriet Vane discovers a dead body in a pool of blood, as a result of throat-cutting, on the beach at Wilvercombe. With admirable sang-froid she searches the corpse, takes photos, collects evidence, and walks four miles to raise the alarm, after which she calls a newspaper and dictates—no mobile phones or laptops—her story. Is it any wonder that Lord Peter loves this woman? And surely these opening chapters bear out P. D. James's contention that a body found in civilized, peaceful surroundings has a much more powerful and dramatic impact than one found in a back alley. Part of the plot of *Have His Carcase* is predicated on a piece of now well-known medical lore, and the clues, all eleven of them, are not just mentioned but, in some cases, brought to the reader's attention again and again. No accusations of cheating can be levelled at the era's leading advocate of the fair-play rule. But while the detective plot is ingenious, the characters' portraits—middle-aged Mrs. Weldon and her search for love, pathetic itinerant barber Mr. Bright, as well as the doomed Paul Alexis—are masterly.

It must be admitted that Lord Peter's swan song, *Busman's Honeymoon* (1937)—which began life as a stage play the previous year—is disappointing when considered as detective fiction. Called unequivocally, by its author, "a love story with detective interruptions," it is exactly that. And the interruptions are not convincing. Raymond Chandler, in his famous—some would say infamous—essay "The Simple Art of Murder," was scathing. "This is what is vulgarly known as having God sit in your lap; a murderer who needs that much help from Providence must be in the wrong business."Although I make it a point of principle to disagree with anything, and everything, Chandler wrote about classic detective fiction, I find myself reluctantly siding with him here.

Long after you have finished reading them I guarantee that certain scenes—chilling, dramatic, hilarious, poignant—from the Lord Peter novels will stay with you. Who could forget the scene on the moors in *Clouds of Witness*, so reminiscent of *The Hound of the Baskervilles*; or the sacrosanct atmosphere of the gentleman's club, as it is contaminated by *The Unpleasantness at the Bellona Club*; or Wimsey as Harlequin in the fountain at Dian de Momerie's party in *Murder Must Advertise*; or the biblical flood at the climax of *The Nine Tailors*; or the blood-soaked interruption to Harriet's idyllic reverie in *Have His Carcase*; or the fate of the magnificent, hand-carved chess set in *Gaudy Night*; or the sinister Mrs. de Forrest trying to seduce Wimsey in her Mayfair flat in *Unnatural Death*; or Miss Climpson's stage-managed séance in *Strong Poison*; or the multi-transport, alibi-testing journey that climaxes *Five Red Herrings*?

It is slightly disillusioning to realize that after the 1939 appearance of the short-story collection *In the Teeth of the Evidence*, Sayers wrote no more crime fiction. (The 1972 collection *Striding Folly* consisted of three final short stories: "The Haunted Policeman," "Striding Folly," first published in 1939, and "Talboys," written in 1942.) Thereafter, she turned her not inconsiderable attention to religion and Dante. She wrote *The Zeal of Thy House* (1937) and *The Devil to Pay* (1939), both plays with religious themes, and, more controversially, *The Man Born to Be King*. This ground-breaking cycle of twelve plays for BBC Radio, broadcast in 1942, told the story of Christ in contemporary language. It provoked endless correspondence between the BBC and Sayers as she defended her artistic integrity. Its reception, however, was enthusiastic, and the entire enterprise was considered a triumph, both for religious broadcasting in general and for Sayers personally.

Her next focus of attention was the famous Italian writer of the Middle Ages, Dante Alighieri. In August 1944, as the sirens sounded over London during the Second World War, Sayers grabbed a book to pass the time in the air-raid shelter and discovered that it was Dante's *Inferno*. This was not her first contact with the writer, but the masterly combination of Italian poetry and religion that consumed her in that shelter inspired her to undertake a translation. The first volume, Dante's *Hell*, appeared in 1949, with *Purgatory* coming out six years later; she was still working on *Heaven* at the time of her death.

Apart from the main series characters, Sayers also created lesser, but no less memorable, minor characters. Lord Peter's manservant, Mervyn Bunter—even the name is inspired—makes an appearance in all of the novels and in some of the short stories. As imperturbable as Wodehouse's immortal Jeeves, he can offer sartorial advice and prepare a gourmet meal just as well as he can make discreet enquiries or take crime-scene photographs.

Inspector Charles Parker of Scotland Yard is that rare example of a policeman in Golden Age detective fiction not portrayed as totally dependent on the clever amateur. Intelligent, honest, and hardworking, he meets Lady Mary, Wimsey's brother, in *Clouds of Witness*. Ill-advisedly, she had been involved with the victim, and Parker, instrumental in solving the case, embarks on a romantic relationship, which continues, mainly offstage, through a few novels, eventually leading to marriage by the time of *Have His Carcase*. Solid, sensible, likeable, and very much his own man, as indeed he needs to be, he and Peter also form a close bond.

In *Unnatural Death*, where she makes her first appearance, Miss Alexandra Katherine Climpson is described by Wimsey as "my ears, my tongue and especially my nose. She asks questions which a young man could not put without a blush." Because Wimsey feels that middle-aged women and their natural curiosity and resourcefulness are wasted, he sets up a typing bureau, known as the Cattery, installs Miss Climpson at its head, and calls on its services when involved in inquiries where men might fear to tread. Miss Climpson herself carries out just such an investigation into the death of Rosanna Spearman in *Unnatural Death*, and she makes a further appearance in *Strong Poison* when she plays an important, albeit very entertaining, role in clearing up the mystery of Philip Boyes's death. Throughout her investigations on Lord Peter's behalf, she displays a resourcefulness belied by her appearance and demeanour, both of which disguise a mind with a clear-sighted outlook on her fellow men and—crucially in *Unnatural Death*—women.

Although Montague Egg, a little-known Sayers creation, appears in less than a dozen short stories, all of his investigations are neat puzzle tales, turning usually on a small but clever point. As a salesman of fine wines Egg travels the country, involving himself in crime as frequently as salesmanship. He has a saying for every occasion, culled from his salesman's handbook, and although it says nothing of his crime-solving abilities, his number-one maxim is "to serve the public is the aim of every salesman worth the name."

SHORT STORIES

Taken overall, the Lord Peter short stories are arguably less interesting than those without him. Perhaps because he needs a book-length appearance to be properly appreciated, *Lord Peter Views the Body*, the first collection, is best read at intervals; like vintage wine, the stories need to be savored rather than gulped. That said, lovers of the more abstruse crosswords should not miss "The Fascinating Problem of Uncle Meleager's Will"; "The Queen's Square," "Absolutely Elsewhere," and "The Necklace of Pearls," from later collections, are typically clever detective stories. But some of the non-Wimsey stories—"Hangman's Holiday" and "In the Teeth of the Evidence" each contain a mixture of Wimsey and non-Wimsey stories—are among Sayers's best. "Suspicion" and "The Fountain Plays" are both wonderfully clever suspense stories; the former has been filmed and dramatized for stage and radio. The whimsical "An Arrow o'er the House" and "The Milk Bottles" and the thoughtful "Dilemma" and "The Man Who Knew How" show Sayers's mastery of the crime—as distinct from detective—short story. "Blood Sacrifice," her contribution to *Six Against the Yard*, is a psychological study with dark criminal overtones. Montague Egg, whose very unobtrusiveness, like a certain Miss Marple, is his strength, is seen at his best in "Murder in the Morning" and "The Professor's Manuscript."

SAYERS AND THE DETECTION CLUB

Although the exact details of the origin of the famous Detection Club are, somewhat appropriately, shrouded in mystery, there can be little doubt that Sayers was hugely influential in its foundation. In her introduction to their first collaborative novel, *The Floating Admiral* (1931), she explains: "It is a private association of writers of detective fiction in Great Britain, existing chiefly for the purpose of eating dinners together at suitable intervals and of talking illimitable shop." As Sayers's description observes, membership was confined to writers of detective fiction, as distinct from thrillers, crime stories, or spy stories; only authors of novels with a logical process of deduction from clues honestly presented to the reader were eligible for consideration. Prospective members had to be proposed, and Sayers devised an elaborate ritual for induction into the club, involving ceremonial robes and darkness lit by candles, with Eric the Skull (filched, according to legend, from one of the teaching hospitals) lending an appropriate macabre element to the proceedings. And, most important, an oath; happily acting as mistress of ceremonies, Sayers extracted promises from prospective candidates:

> Do you promise that your detectives shall well and truly detect the crimes presented to them, using those wits which it may please you to bestow upon them and not placing reliance on, nor making use of Divine Revelation, Feminine Intuition, Mumbo-Jumbo, Jiggery-Pokery, Coincidence or the Act of God?
>
> I do.
>
> Do you solemnly swear never to conceal a vital clue from the reader?
>
> I do.
>
> Do you promise to observe a seemly moderation in the use of Gangs, Conspiracies, Death-Rays, Ghosts, Hypnotism, Trap-Doors, Chinamen, Super-

Criminals and Lunatics; and utterly and forever to forswear Mysterious Poisons unknown to Science?
I do.

As can be judged, the oath, while lighthearted in tone, was also explicit in outlawing anything in a detective story that could be considered cheating: unknown poisons, coincidence, feminine intuition, gangs, and conspiracies. All these militated against the fairness between writer and reader that was, in effect, the basis of detective fiction. Despite the fact that she had produced no fiction for the last twenty years of her life, Sayers was president of the Detection Club from 1938 (and the death of the first president, G. K. Chesterton) until her death. The presidency was subsequently accepted—on condition that she would never have to make a speech—by Agatha Christie.

In order to maintain a healthy financial position, the Club undertook to produce collaborative titles. Their first ventures were two radio plays, *Behind the Screen* (1929) and *The Scoop* (1930), followed by the novels *The Floating Admiral* (1931) and *Ask a Policeman* (1933) and a themed short-story collection, *Six Against the Yard* (1936; *Six Against Scotland Yard* in the United States). Sayers was involved in all of these ventures and would seem to have been the mastermind behind most of them. Surviving correspondence attests to the fact that it was she who coordinated the scripts for the radio plays and was the name best known to—and feared by—the BBC during the productions of each. BBC executive J. R. Ackerley referred to "the terrific vitality, bullying, and bounce of that dreadful woman Dorothy L. Sayers"; this fractious relationship was revisited some years later during production of her scripts for *The Man Born to Be King*. Each of the Detection Club ventures involved variations on the game-like qualities of Golden Age detective fiction. *The Floating Admiral* was written by thirteen writers, each contributing a chapter—and a proposed solution, although unseen by their successor—and passing it onto the

next collaborator. Exhibiting her customary thoroughness,
Sayers's proposed solution and notes ran to almost twenty
pages, half as long as her actual chapter. In *Ask a Policeman*
(1933), six writers "swapped" detectives to solve the murder
of newspaper baron Lord Comstock in Hursley Lodge. So
Sayers wrote of Anthony Berkeley's Roger Sheringham while
Berkeley took on (brilliantly, it should be noted) Lord Peter
Wimsey. *Six Against the Yard* was very different from its pre-
decessors: Six writers each devised a "perfect murder," and
Superintendent Cornish, a real-life former policeman from
Scotland Yard, examined each story to spot the flaws in each
"perfect" plan. Sayers took great offense at his criticism of her
very clever story, "Blood Sacrifice."

SAYERS AS EDITOR
At the request of Victor Gollancz, her publisher, Sayers edited
the anthology *Great Short Stories of Detection Mystery and Horror*
in 1928, and it remains to this day a model collection. Her forty-
page introduction was one of the earliest attempts to trace
the origins of the detective story and to discuss in detail the
influence that Edgar Allan Poe had had on the genre. She
analyzed five—other critics counted only three—of his short
stories and identified in them ideas and themes that continue
to dominate detective fiction to the present day. She wrote
cogently of developments since Poe's day, discussing trends
and ideas in then-current detective fiction, and presented the
stories in the anthology under specific headings: "The Police
Detective," "The Intuitive Detective," "The Scientific and
Medical Detective," and even "The Comic Detective." Although many of the writers she discussed are long forgotten,
her analysis of their plots—whether good or bad—remains a
model of literary criticism. Because it was as a literary form
that Sayers wanted detective fiction to be considered, it remained her earnest hope that "the modern detective story [will
be] compelled to achieve a higher level of writing and a more
competent delineation of character." Ironically, in view of the
Wimsey-Vane relationship that would begin two years later in

Strong Poison, Sayers complained that "some of the finest detective stories are marred by a conventional love story irrelevant to the action and perfunctorily worked in. . . . Far more blameworthy are the heroes who insist on fooling about after young women when they ought to be putting their minds on the job of detection." How often must those words have come back to haunt her.

Almost a decade later she edited the more compact, but no less impressive, *Tales of Detection* (1936), also with an erudite introduction. Although shorter than its predecessor, it was, even as the Golden Age drew to a close, no less notable in discussing the developments since the earlier collection. She sounded more confident in her assessment of the future of detective fiction and felt that, although writers could "now handle the mechanical elements of the plot," they had yet "to discover the best way of combining these with a serious artistic treatment of the psychological element, so that the intellectual and the common man can find common ground for enjoyment of the mystery novel."

SAYERS AS REVIEWER

For two years, between June 1933 and August 1935, Sayers reviewed crime fiction for the *Sunday Times*. More than 350 titles were discussed in her column, which, in turn, meant that she read, on average, three books a week, every week, throughout the period. And during those years she also published *Murder Must Advertise*, *The Nine Tailors*, and *Gaudy Night*. Although many of the titles she reviewed were by well-known authors such as Agatha Christie, Ellery Queen, R. Austin Freeman, and Georgette Heyer, it is noticeable how many of the names she discussed have completely disappeared. Through this column she is credited with boosting the career of one of the greatest names of the period between the wars, John Dickson Carr, when she gave him a rave review for *The Mad Hatter Mystery* in September 1933. She wrote: "Mr. Carr can lead us away from the small, brightly-lit stage of the ordinary detective plot into the menace of outer darkness . . .

in short, he can write. This is the most attractive mystery I have read for a long time." Her praise appeared for years on reprints—not just of *The Mad Hatter Mystery* but other Carr books as well.

On December 17, 1957, after a day of Christmas shopping in London, Dorothy L. Sayers returned home to Witham and collapsed at the foot of the stairs, where she was found the next morning. The more sensational papers could not resist a headline—DETECTIVE NOVELIST FOUND DEAD AT FOOT OF STAIRS—about a woman who had been a force in British life for almost half a century. Whether as novelist, short-story writer, essayist, editor, historian, or reviewer, Sayers was a towering figure in the development of the detective story. Her contribution to the genre, in an impressive range of capacities, was immeasurable. Although her career as a detective novelist spanned a mere fourteen years—from *Whose Body?* (1923) to *Busman's Honeymoon* (1937)—she continued until her premature death to contribute to the promotion and acceptance of the literary form with which her name is forever linked.

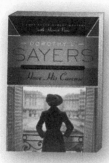